德古意特认知语言学应用丛书

COGNITIVE POETICS

GOALS, GAINS AND GAPS

认知诗学：
目标、成果和挑战

Geert Brône, Jeroen Vandaele 编

上海外语教育出版社
SHANGHAI FOREIGN LANGUAGE EDUCATION PRESS
www.sflep.com

De Gruyter Mouton

图书在版编目（CIP）数据

认知诗学：目标、成果和挑战/吉尔特·布隆纳，耶洛恩·范迪勒编.
—上海：上海外语教育出版社，2017
（德古意特认知语言学应用丛书）
ISBN 978-7-5446-5039-7

I. ①认… II. ①吉… ②耶… III. ①诗学—研究—英文 IV. ①I052

中国版本图书馆CIP数据核字（2017）第251387号

Cognitive Poetics: Goals, Gains and Gaps edited by Geert Brône, Jeroen
Vandaele
© Walter de Gruyter GmbH Berlin Boston. All rights reserved.
This work is a reprint edition of the original work from De Gruyter, *Cognitive
Poetics: Goals, Gains and Gaps* edited by Geert Brône, Jeroen Vandaele and is
only intended for sale throughout the People's Republic of China, excluding the
territories of Hong Kong, Macau and Taiwan. The work may not be translated
or copied in whole or part without the written permission of the publisher
(Walter de Gruyter GmbH, Genthiner Straße 13, 10785 Berlin, Germany).
本书由德古意特出版社授权上海外语教育出版社有限公司出版。
仅供在中华人民共和国境内（香港、澳门、台湾除外）销售。

图字：09–2017–666号

出版发行：**上海外语教育出版社**
（上海外国语大学内） 邮编：200083
电　　话：021–65425300（总机）
电子邮箱：bookinfo@sflep.com.cn
网　　址：http://www.sflep.com
责任编辑：蒋浚浚

印　　刷：上海叶大印务发展有限公司
开　　本：700×1000　1/16　印张 35.75　字数 718千字
版　　次：2018 年 5 月第 1 版　　2018 年 5 月第 1 次印刷
印　　数：1 500 册

书　　号：ISBN 978-7-5446-5039-7 / I
定　　价：110.00 元

本版图书如有印装质量问题，可向本社调换
质量服务热线：4008-213-263　电子邮箱：editorial@sflep.com

出版说明

认知语言学是语言学的一门重要分支学科，自20世纪80年代诞生以来，受到了国际和国内学界的广泛关注。近年来，外教社陆续推出了一系列相关丛书，集中体现了国际、国内的优质研究成果。其中"国际认知语言学经典论丛"收入了Ronald Langacker、Leonard Talmy、Dirk Geeraers等国际认知语言学领域顶尖学者的经典作品；"外教社认知语言学丛书·普及系列"、"外教社认知语言学丛书·应用系列"则体现了国内学界的最新研究成果。这些丛书因内容权威、见解独到受到了外语界的广泛好评。

认知语言学作为一门新兴的跨领域学科，与多种学科有密切的联系，具有很强的应用意义。因此，我们又从德古意特出版社近年来推出的相关学术图书中精选了6种，组成"德古意特认知语言学应用丛书"，引进出版。丛书反映了近十几年来认知语言学应用领域的前沿成果，集中体现了该学科的理论与实践、应用与展望，及其与人工智能、诗学、语言教学等领域的联系和互动，信息量大，时效性强，代表了国际认知语言学应用研究方面的最高水准。丛书作者汇集了Gitte Kristiansen、Francisco J. Ruiz de Mendoza Ibáñez、René Dirven等国际认知语言学界领军人物，以及欧美相关领域的优秀学者，体现了国际认知语言学应用研究方面的最强阵容。

相信丛书的引进可进一步帮助国内读者了解这一领域的研究热点和最新成果，为国内研究者带来新的启示。

Cognitive Poetics

Goals, Gains and Gaps

edited by
Geert Brône
Jeroen Vandaele

Table of contents

Part III: Stance

Part IV: Critique

Cognitive poetics.
A critical introduction

Jeroen Vandaele and Geert Brône*

1. Foundations and goals of cognitive poetics

Literary criticism produces some sort of knowledge on a discourse that is already taken to produce some sort of knowledge, to know, literature. Both discipline and object may be said to provide insights into the workings of more or less interacting minds-in-bodies-in-worlds (cf. Turner 1991: vii–viii), that is, into the actions, thoughts and feelings of characters in a fictional world, for readers in the actual world. In relatively recent times, the science-oriented paradigm called "science of the mind" or "cognitive science" has equally turned the mind into its primary object of investigation. Thus, although the sciences and the humanities tend to legitimate quite different epistemic projects, i.e. different methods and aims of knowledge, it is unstartling that cognitive science from its very start has been making overtures to literature and literary studies.

The epistemic marriage between cognitive science and literary studies has been going on for more than twenty-five years now, if we take Lakoff and Johnson's *Metaphors We Live By* (1980) as the seminal work that led to a more co-ordinated interdisciplinary collaboration.[1] Admittedly, taking the birth of Cognitive Linguistics as the crucial incentive for a cognitive poetics ignores earlier interdisciplinary efforts made by, for example, story grammarians in the 1970s (Rumelhart 1975 and 1977 for instance), but it may also be argued that story grammar's reduction of (readers' and characters') mental life – the mind as an awkward entity in a world of perceivable states of affairs and evolutions – does not live up to the cognitive

* We would like to thank Mouton de Gruyter's anonymous reviewer for invaluable comments on an earlier manuscript of this volume.

1. See e.g. Van Oort (2003: 238): "Since the publication in 1980 of George Lakoff and Mark Johnson's influential *Metaphors We Live By*, literary critics have been encouraged by the idea of a cognitive poetics – of, that is, a systematic theory of the mind in which literature is not merely peripheral but central to the understanding of human psychology".

standard adopted by both literary theorists and cognitive linguists. As the poetician Meir Sternberg observed, minimalist *quasi*-generative notions of "motive" and "agency" appear "all too shallow, instrumental, under-developed, overrationalized, beside the narrative standard, and hopeless vis-à-vis modernism's turn inward" (2003: 371). In the same vein, in Cognitive Linguistics Lakoff (1987) has forcefully argued that any "objectivist conception of mind" must, for example, rule out "perception, which can fool us; the body which has its frailties; society, which has its pressures and special interests; memories, which can fade; mental images, which can differ from person to person; and imagination – especially metaphor and metonymy – which cannot fit the objectively given world" (1987: 183).

If it is the *felt qualities* of mental life that we are addressing, the broad phenomenology of mind as opposed to mere "computation" or "process-ing" of symbols, then Cognitive Linguistics (CL) and poetics seem natu-ral allies. In terms of research focus, early cognitive linguistic investi-gations could indeed be seen as first invitations to a joint cognitive poetic project. In the early 1980's non-objectivist cognitive scholars (such as Jerome Bruner, George Lakoff, Mark Turner, Mark Johnson, Len Talmy, Gilles Fauconnier) turned towards domains that are traditionally con-sidered crucial for literary studies: metaphors, narrative, Gestalt, figure, ground, and the phenomenology of subjective meaning in general. Im-portantly, this specific branch of cognitive research started treating liter-ary figures of *speech* as routine (and nonroutine) figures of *thought* (on which, see **Freeman**, this volume).[2] Suddenly, the literary mode of think-ing seemed all around, and our minds were promoted to "literary minds", to use Turner's (1996) catch phrase; our everyday minds were claimed to structure experiences by projecting (*meta pherein*) on them small known narrative (and other) patterns.

The apparent common ground between Cognitive Linguistics and liter-ary studies did not, however, lead to a joint interdisciplinary effort from the very onset. In this sense, the seminal work by the literary cognitive scientist Mark Turner occupies a rather exceptional position. Generally

---

2. Literary scholars have not been oblivious to the broad cognitive-discursive aspect of metaphor. In the chapter "Le déclin de la rhétorique: la tropologie" of his *La métaphore vive* (1975), the French hermeneutician Paul Ricoeur explains that metaphor is not a trope on the level of the word but "une attribu-tion insolite au niveau même du discours-phrase" (63). Lively metaphors involve a cognitive operation expressed and/or set into motion by an original discursive attribution.

speaking literary scholars have been sceptical about the explanatory power of cognitive approaches. In fact, many sceptical scholars may have perfectly good reasons to temper the enthusiasm of those who do advocate a cognitive poetics. Echoing earlier complaints about Structuralism (see **Sternberg**, this volume) and semiotics (see Culler 2001), Tony Jackson diagnoses that "[d]espite regular, enthusiastic claims for radically new insights, the actual application of [cognitive] theories to [literary] texts has much too often produced interpretations that are painfully obvious" (2005: 528). If this is true and if it is a structural problem, then hermeneutics, i.e. the type of literary explanation that seeks "to discover new and better interpretations" for literary texts (Culler 1997: 61), might not directly benefit from an alliance with Cognitive Linguistics (or broader: cognitive science). Importantly though, the poststructuralist poetician Jonathan Culler has also argued that literary explanation divides attention between two projects, one hermeneutic, the other "poetic". Unlike hermeneutics, Culler contends, "[p]oetics starts with attested meanings or effects and asks how they are achieved" (1997: 61).[3] If this is true, literary hermeneutics might just wait and see, while poetics critically partakes in the cognitive literary endeavour. This is indeed the profile that Freeman envisages for cognitive poetics when she contends that the new field generally "focuses on process, not product" (2002: 43). Without overstressing the poetics-hermeneutics distinction, a cognitive poetics could try to listen to both partners, to reconcile the interests of the mind's science and of full-blown historicized literary interpretation. The Critique section and the dialogic structure of his volume, with main chapters and commentaries, want to reflect the interdisciplinary exchange of ideas between cognitively oriented, poetic and text-interpretive research.

Now, to complicate interdisciplinary matters even further, the cognitive literary interest in artful discourse has not been limited to cognitive linguists like Lakoff, Turner, Johnson, Talmy and Fauconnier. In his "field map" of "studies in literature and cognition", Alan Richardson traces "cognitive literary criticism" back to a series of books and essays published in the 1980s by Reuven Tsur, Norman Holland, Robert de Beau-

---

3. Culler's distinction between poetics and hermeneutics specifies for literary studies the otherwise well-known distinction between studying (general) laws and (specific) events. In the area of philosophy, Nelson Goodman similarly distinguishes between "criticism" and "history", observing that "history and criticism differ not in having separate subject matters or unrelated tasks but in exchanging ends for means" (1978: 38–39).

grande and others (2004: 1). "Only in the mid-1990s", Richardson explains, "with a small but steadily growing presence at professional meetings and the rapid exchange of information made possible by the World Wide Web, did an active community begin to constitute itself out of a geographically and intellectually diverse group of literary scholars interested in cognition and neuroscience". Thus, rather than a paradigm held together by common disciplinary claims, hypotheses and methodologies (2004: 2), cognitivist criticism has come to be understood as a broad "field" which shares cognitive science's "overriding interest in the active (and largely unconscious) mental processing" that makes behaviour (i.c. reading literature) understandable (2004: 1). This characterization of cognitive scientific thinking remains necessarily broad (or even vague) because it reflects the field's current state of the art, its diverse or even opposed hypotheses and methods. As a type of criticism instructed by (and instructing) cognitive science, cognitive literary criticism seems to inherit (and further contribute to) the great diversity of cognitive science.

Let us specify, in this light, that the present volume is primarily intended to promote dialogue between Cognitive Linguistics (as a special branch of cognitive science) and literary studies, although this "core dialogue" will be supplemented with approaches from other cognitive literary fields (most notably in **Tsur**, **Culpeper** and **Louwerse and Van Peer**). Thus, the collection follows up on Margaret Freeman's (2000) suggestion to study literature with the aid of cognitive linguistic insights – a study for which she has "appropriated" Tsur's term "cognitive poetics" (*dixit* Richardson 2004: 5–6) – but the volume also acknowledges more general cognitive efforts such as Semino and Culpeper (2002), Gavins and Steen (2003), Veivo et al. (2005), Toolan and Weber (2005), Dancygier (2006), Hogan and Pandit (2006), and others. In short, the majority of the studies in this volume can be said to represent a paradigm – Cognitive Linguistics – interacting with two interdisciplinary fields – poetics and cognitive science. The result, we hope, offers a general overview of some important goals, gains and gaps of cognitive poetics.

The selection of chapters for this volume reflects a combined objective. First, studies were solicited that address key issues in both Cognitive Linguistics and literary studies. Topics relevant for poeticians include the construction of (text) worlds, character(ization), narrative perspective, distancing discourse (including irony), humour, emotion, poetic imagery, and others. Most of these issues are approached by applying cognitive linguistic concepts and insights, in an attempt to explore more systematically their explanatory potential for cognitive poetics. Among the CL concepts drawn upon in this collection are embodied cognition, construal and conceptualization, viewpoint mental spaces, iconicity, metaphorical mapping and conceptual blending, construction grammar, figure/ground alignment in cognition, and other central topics in the field. Second, as already mentioned, the ensuing dialogue between cognitive and literary "partners" is also promoted through the use of short response articles included after each of the chapters, in some cases followed by a rebuttal by the authors – a system inspired by the commentary system of the journal *Behavioral and Brain Sciences*. In the responses, an expert on the topic, methodology or theory of each chapter highlights the main strengths and potential weaknesses of the presented study. By including these commentaries and rebuttals in the volume, we hope to give a flavour of the internal dynamics of cognitive poetics, and to provide a balanced (i.e. strongly interdisciplinary) account of the main goals, gains and gaps of a cognitive approach to literary studies. The discussions will often highlight similarities and incompatibilities between literary key topics (e.g. narrative perspective) and cognitive linguistic concepts (e.g. cognitive linguistic viewpoint).

2.   Gains of cognitive poetics

Even if cognitive science (including CL) and poetics constitute natural allies in many ways, an interdisciplinary collaboration is by no means a straightforward enterprise, since it is notoriously hard to provide both rigorous empirical methods and powerful interpretive concepts. Even within the respective disciplinary boundaries of cognitive science (including CL) and poetics, different positions – sometimes radically so – have emerged on the trade-off between empirical control and first-person, introspective analysis (on this trade-off, see e.g. Deacon 1997). For cognitive science in general, Richardson (2004: 2) and Hogan (2003: 30) mention the discussions on whether mental processing is a matter of symbol manipulation or of neural networks or both. In Cognitive Linguistics, some researchers plead for more empirical control (see e.g. **Geeraerts** in this volume; Gibbs 2007; Grondelaers et al. 2007), while others stress the importance of introspection for specific research questions (Rohrer 2005; Talmy 2000, 1).[4] Within literary studies, some scholars will have a metho-

---

4.   But empirical concerns may be found in unexpected places. The literary scholar Tony E. Jackson writes: "Going forward with blending theory will require, I would argue, some further specification of how it operates in the em-

dological preference for empirical journals such as *Poetics* whereas others, who favour less restrictive methods and concepts, will prefer to publish in e.g. *The Yale Journal of Criticism*. Given this tension between the "two cultures" of scholarly investigation (to use C.P. Snow's famous phrase), one of the major challenges for cognitive poetics is their reconciliation in a field that addresses *cognitive scientific* underpinnings of *subjective-cultural* reading experiences. Is a middle ground somehow conceivable between rich first-person phenomenology and rigorous third-person observation? Can we think of a field that combines cognitive insights in cognition and language structure with poetics' insights in literary meaning production?

One of the major thrusts of this volume is that some middle ground is in fact attainable if poetics joins forces with Cognitive Linguistics in strategic areas. Cognitive Linguistics, as a special branch of cognitive science, stands out as a paradigm mainly because it pays due attention to the rich phenomenology of thought and language, and is therefore compatible with the traditional project of poetics. Although CL is non-idealist, anti-Cartesian, and although many cognitive linguists strive for empirically falsifiable hypotheses and empirical control, the paradigm does not simply reduce the mental realm to deterministic predictability (Lakoff 1987). Observable facts are not its fetish; intricate theories of the mind are at its core.

Given the intermediary position of CL within the cognitive sciences, a CL-oriented cognitive poetics may be a valuable attempt to reconcile hard empiricism with soft mental life by relating literary meaning production to principles of meaning construction in fields that are easier to monitor (as **Steen** e.g. argues in this volume). It is a well-known tenet of CL (and *pace* Fodor) that the language system does not constitute a separate cognitive module (see also Deacon 1997), i.e. that apparently irreconcilable cognitive phenomena (from perception, language and reasoning on the highest level, to genre differences on the specific level of linguistic meaning construction) are guided by or built from the same set of basic-level cognitive mechanisms. Although this hypothesis is more testable in less complex language uses, the nonmodularity hypothesis for language and the principles of cognitive grounding in body and society should in principle shed light on poetic language as well.

-----

bodied mind, some further empirical understanding of perhaps how it can turn out to be a problem itself as well as a solution to a problem or of how it can conflict with other elements of our cognitive architecture" (2002: 173).

To use a paradox, then, we would say that cognitive poetics can be *indirectly empirical* in CL's phenomenologically rich but principled way. Cognitive poetics may show awareness of CL findings (and cognitive science in general) and try to attune its conceptual apparatus to current knowledge about the mind's workings. In this paradoxical indirect empiricism could be found one "reasonable necessity for bringing the concepts or methods of one discipline into working relation with the concepts or methods of another discipline", as Jackson requests (2002: 162). It would not simply be "plug[ging] [...] the vocabulary of cognitive rhetoric [...] into the interpretation" (2002: 173), it would be plugging interpretive concepts in a broader framework of the mind. While hermeneuticians may indeed prefer to focus on historicized and very specific mindsets and give full reign to subjective discourse as a preferential mode of representation, poeticians may want to combine interesting interpretations with cognitive views on the mind's role in textual interpretation. On the one hand, Culler's (2001) very similar (self)criticism of the previous wave of "semiotic poetics" – a plugging of words more than a new theory for interpretation – is an important warning. On the other hand, semiotics itself has usually not been constrained by experiment in neighbouring branches and yet its plugging into literary criticism was not void per se – because semiotics *is* an important frame – but only in (some) scholarly practice. Like for semiotics, the proof of the pudding will be in the eating (although there is no new pudding without a new recipe).

On our view, "indirect empiricism" is the recipe already chosen by Stockwell (2002) and most contributors of Gavins and Steen (2003) and Semino and Culpeper (2002).

[Cognitive poetics] suggests that readings may be explained *with reference to* general human principles of linguistic and cognitive processing, which ties the study of literature in with linguistics, psychology, and cognitive science in general (Gavins and Steen 2003: 2; italics added).

Cognitive stylistics combines the kind of explicit, rigorous and detailed linguistic analysis of literary texts that is typical of the stylistics tradition with *a systematic and theoretically informed consideration* of the cognitive structures and processes that underlie the production and reception of language (Semino and Culpeper 2002: ix; italics added).

Obviously, the idea of indirect empiricism is not free of scepticism, because it may be seen as a one-way street. "[I]t is difficult to see", Jackson writes, "how we [literary scholars, JV & GB] could legitimately disprove or revise the [cognitive] theory by using it in our usual, nonempirical-scientific interpretive practice" (2002: 177). This is indeed a danger but, again, as with literary semiotics, the proof of the pudding will have to be in the eating. The best literary-semiotic analyses (Barthes, Eco, Greimas, Culler, Lotman, Groupe Mu) *have* been very influential and insightful. Moreover, the fact that **Tsur** (this volume) – a cognitive poetician well-known for his criticism of Cognitive Linguistics – questions Stockwell's (2002) use of the concepts "figure" and "ground" along the lines of Lan-gacker's Cognitive Grammar, seems to show that "interpretive refutation" of cognitive linguistic concepts is absolutely possible. The interaction be-tween Tsur, Stockwell and Langacker helps to theorize cognition in the absence of constant empirical checks. CL is more concerned than poetics with embedding concepts and hypotheses in an empirically testable framework but it is not totally geared toward empirical control: first-per-son phenomenology also keeps pulling on CL's other arm. Literary scholars could do just that: help the "interpretive" cognitive linguists pul-ling on the phenomenological arm of CL. Literary analysis may import CL concepts, stretch their meaning if necessary, send them back home and see if they're still welcomed. Since CL has a maximalist, nonreductive view on linguistic semantics (Langacker 1987, 1988), it cannot simply ne-glect poeticians' interpretations of artful discourse. Such would be a cog-nitive poetics full of gaps, but not short of gains and possibilities.

Except for **Giora** et al. and **Louwerse and Van Peer**, who favour stricter forms of empiricism, most authors of the present volume also seem to work on the indirectly empirical basis. They explore the cognitive poetic use of concepts such as construal, mental space, distance, emotion, ico-nicity, figure and ground, etc. In doing so, they look for a balance between interpretive relevance and cognitive principledness.

3.   Outline of the volume

The chapters and responses in this volume are grouped into four sections of comparable length: Story, Figure, Stance and Critique. The Story sec-tion includes three chapters (**Semino**, **Herman**, **Culpeper**) dealing with cognitive mechanisms, discursive means and mental products related to narrativity: narrative worlds, perspective and focalization in/on narrative worlds, characterization, narrative as information gapping and (tentative) closure. The Figure section deals with the different incarnations of the concept of figure in cognitive poetics, including figure-as-gestalt (**Tsur**), figure-as-trope (i.c. metaphor; **Steen**) and figure-as-icon (**Freeman**). The juxtaposition of these different interpretations of a key concept ("figure") reminds us of the various trajectories in cognitive poetics (and the inevitable terminological confusion) but does offer food for further thought (see below). In comparison to the Story section, the essays under the Figure heading focus on figurative Gestalts that are nonnarrative, although they do allow for joint ventures with stories: metaphorical conceptualization, figure-ground reversals and iconicity do not necessarily (re)present time although they can bear on the temporality of (discourse) worlds. The third section, "Stance", joins three chapters (**Antonopoulou and Nikiforidou, Dancygier and Vandelanotte, Giora et al.**) on procedures that are meant to express or create discursive attitudes, like humour, irony or distance in general. Again, these stances can join forces at will with narrative and/or figurative resources of discursive cognition: narrators can use figure-ground reversals for humorous or distancing purposes; characters can be ironic through metaphors; "detached" poetic musings can be iconic of life via information-gapping and partial closures and, thus, be protonarrative. This will depend on how the author wanted it to work (*intentio auctoris*), on how s/he encoded it (text hermeneutics), and on how the reader can or wants to interpret it (*intentio lectoris*) in a given cultural framework. The fourth and last section of the volume, "Critique", includes two chapters (**Louwerse and Van Peer, Sternberg**) that critically assess the current state of affairs in cognitive poetics, and more specifically the incorporation of insights from Cognitive Linguistics as only one of the contributing fields in the interdisciplinary conglomerate of cognitive science. The chapters in the Critique section point at significant lacunae in cognitive poetic practice and suggest alternative research lines to be pursued – both in theory (Sternberg) and practice (Louwerse and Van Peer).

The first section, Story, opens with a chapter by **Elena Semino** on "text worlds". Semino discusses and demonstrates a range of approaches to the study of text worlds, drawing from narratology and cognitive poetics. Two texts are analysed in detail: Carol Ann Duffy's poem *Mrs Midas* and (an English translation of) the story of King Midas in Ovid's *Metamorphoses*. Duffy's poem, which was included in the collection *The World's Wife*, is a contemporary re-writing of the Midas myth, from the perspective of Midas' imaginary wife. Semino begins by applying Possible Worlds Theory to the two texts, and, following Doležel, she argues that intertextuality can involve the relationship between different text worlds, as well as the levels of wording and style. She then considers the contribution of a selection of relevant theories from cognitive research, and shows in detail how the distinctive nature of the world projected by Duffy's poem can be explained in terms of Fauconnier and Turner's Blending Theory. Semino thus combines the best of several worlds, such as the metaphysically elegant Mental Space approach – which cognitive linguists apply introspectively – and a cognitive sort of Possible Worlds Theory attuned to larger fictional texts. As Semino shows, both have advantages: "While possible-worlds theorists such as Ryan have proposed typologies of sub-worlds within fictional worlds, cognitive linguists provide detailed classifications of the kinds of linguistic expressions that act as triggers for the online construction of mental representations". On the one hand, "[p]ossible-world theorists do not [...] aim to account for how text worlds are incrementally constructed by readers or listeners during online text processing", and on the other hand, Mental Space Theory's "[c]omplex analytical machinery" creates "visual representations that often become impossibly complicated when applied to stretches of text longer than a few sentences". The chapter finishes with some reflections on future challenges in the study of text worlds. In her response to Semino's chapter, **Shweta Narayan** provides further thoughts on representational methods, on how Conceptual Blending Theory can account for the dynamic, incremental construction of story worlds and on why the specifics of text world furnishing lead to readers' emotional involvement.

Semino's chapter is followed by **David Herman**'s exploration of "cognitive approaches to narrative analysis". Herman outlines strategies for incorporating into the domain of narrative analysis research that explores the nexus of language, mind, and world. The chapter is part of an ongoing effort to foster the development of cognitive narratology, which can be defined as the study of mind-relevant dimensions of storytelling practices, wherever – and by whatever means – those practices occur. In his chapter in the present volume, Herman focuses on three key problem domains – concepts of "role" or character, theories of emotion, and approaches to narrative perspective or focalization – to sketch directions for cognitive narratological research. Drawing on work in text processing, social psychology, discourse analysis, and cognitive grammar, the chapter also examines stories presented in a variety of media, from *The Incredible Hulk* comics, to a television interview, to a tape-recorded narrative told in face-to-face interaction, to short stories from James Joyce's 1914 collection, *Dubliners*. In his section on *Dubliners* Herman shows how microlevel linguistic perspective, as described by the cognitive linguists Langacker and Talmy, can contribute to (understanding) a particular sort of narrative perspective – it may enlighten the narratological "who sees (cognizes)?" issue, what is called "focalization" in narratology (Genette 1972; Bal 1997).[5] The spatial focalization of narrative texts is partly triggered by the repertory of conceptualization devices as CL conceives it. Herman's essay is placed in a historical perspective by **Peter Stockwell**, who points at the many potential benefits of narratological research that pays attention to aesthetics, stylistic texture and narrative perspective from a general cognitive point of view.

Jonathan Culpeper's chapter outlines a cognitive poetic (or stylistic) approach to characterization, drawing from but also updating its original exposition in Culpeper (2001). It opens with some consideration of what a cognitive stylistic approach to characterization might consist of, and dispels some myths about the enterprise. The bulk of the chapter focuses on what cognitive research can do for characterization, and thus focuses on the mechanisms which readers use to form interpretations of characters. The particular issues addressed are: (1) variability in interpretation, (2) shared interpretations versus individual interpretations, (3) the interaction between and relative weighting of textual information versus prior knowledge in interpretation, (4) the role of context in interpreting characters, and (5) how particular features in the text can bias interpretation. Theoretical input is drawn from, in particular, social cognition (notably, schema theory and attribution theory), as well as text comprehension. The field of social cognition, of course, has focused on the study of "real life" people. At various points in the chapter, differences between real people and fictional characters are identified. One of the central aims of the chapter is to understand better and more precisely aspects of characterization alluded to (often dimly and intuitively) by literary critics. This includes, for example, the well-known distinction made by Forster ([1927] 1987) between "flat" and "round" characters. **Uri Margolin** summarizes Culpeper approvingly and adds some critical notes: constancy of behav-

---

5. Narrative analysis is generally not too concerned with categorizing the exact linguistic means by which a text focalizes whatever goes on in a certain fictional world. Cf. Dan Shen's view on "characterization" in narratology and stylistics: "Rimmon-Kenan, as a narratologist, is concerned with the features, effects, advantages, and disadvantages of 'direct definition' as a mode of characterization (60–61). While narratology focuses on what counts as 'direct definition' and what is its structural function, stylistics centers on what specific words are used in depicting a character, what effects are conveyed by those words as opposed to other potential choices" (2005: 388).

iour does not equal comic behaviour or caricature; rhetorical approaches (Booth, Sternberg, etc.) are absent from Culpeper's account; more generally, a model is not a theory, "since only arguments or claims can account for anything".

The second section of the volume consists, as mentioned, of three chapters that explore the different uses of the "figure" concept in cognitive poetics. Among the common cognitive uses of "figure" are, as already said, figure-as-gestalt, figure-as-trope and figure-as-icon. Perhaps provocatively, the present volume brings these uses together under one heading because they are different but not unrelated. Regarding metaphor, arguably the most central figure-as-trope (Glucksberg 2001: 3–15), Glicksohn and Goodblatt (1993) argue e.g. that it "is different from the sum (or comparison) of its parts" and that "[t]he metaphor can thus be considered a gestalt" (87). Creative or poetic metaphor is "an emergent whole" which "involves an act of perceptual restructuring" (1993: 89). Clearly, their gestalt conception of metaphor is compatible with **Tsur**'s view on poetic processing as the restructuring of figures in general (gestalts), and it strongly reminds us of cognitive linguistic concerns (emergent meaning, blending). Glicksohn and Goodblatt state for instance that "a true metaphor, for the interactionist [Max Black, JV & GB], is characterized by a 'eureka' effect, as the elements blend and the new whole is recognized" (87). Blending theorists would not disagree with this characterization of "true metaphor". In relation to figure-as-icon, finally, metaphors may be thought of as cognitive gestalts of a *higher order* than the purely perceptual icons which, according to Deacon (1997), are "default" perceptions involving neither indexical nor symbolic cognitive processes. In any event, perceptual and conceptual figures are emergent gestalts tied to the emotions, they are able to re-figure habitual patterns and they are performed in many ways and on many levels in literature. Three chapters further explore the emergence of – and the complex links between – various sorts of perceptual and conceptual gestalts (or "figures") in literature.

Margaret Freeman's chapter ties the poetic language of Dickinson to CL views on emotion and iconicity, two crucial notions of the embodiment or "grounding" hypothesis – which contends that language partly makes sense because it is tied to our bodily being-in-the-world. Affect is a crucial aspect of embodiment because it pervades percepts, concepts and agency. As Merleau-Ponty argued, and as has been confirmed by studies in neurobiology (see Gallagher 2005: 146–151), hormonal changes e.g. colour perception (sexually, for instance). In her chapter Freeman is concerned with the emotionality that impregnates conceptual structure. "One of the most challenging tasks facing Cognitive Linguistics", she writes, "is to find ways to articulate [the] connections" between "form-meaning in sound (and sight)" and feeling (sensations and emotions). Her cognitive poetic essay is therefore on the expression of feeling, on the "forms of feeling" – paradoxical as this expression may sound Forms, she argues, are never merely forms: they always carry an emotional weight. This is an idea that reminds poeticians of Bakhtin's poetic views, who famously insisted that all forms are crucially ethical, agency-related. However, whereas Bakhtin insists on the situatedness of discourse (Bakhtinian "chronotopy"), Freeman finds poetic rupture (and rapture) in the loss of parameters, in a temporary elimination (or reduction) of the self-other boundary. The form of Dickinson's poetry enacts a self-less state. The poetic rupture she accomplishes, so we learn, is both alienating – moving away from the normalizing self – and deepening contact with experience – away from the self, indeed, but toward the "non-self". To this end, Freeman returns to Susanne Langer's (and Schiller's) idea of art as *Schein* ('semblance'), a spiritual play free from all practical purposes, or "minding" as Freeman calls it. Art offers us nonconceptual and "nondiscursive" (not reality-bound) figures: the figures of "the primordial precategorial" or, as Merleau-Ponty has it, "the existing flux before objectification into objects" (quoted in Freeman). This is what Freeman terms poetic iconicity. Dickinson's poem shows "by iconic presentation" that "careless use of language can be harmful", not just by "blending the ideas of writing and disease to create a metaphor of a word as infection, but also by making this metaphor iconically represent ourselves as readers reading Dickinson's text and as a result inhaling the semblance of 'Despair.'"

Gerard Steen's contribution on poetic metaphor has a different agenda. Steen is less interested in the emotional effect of Tennyson's poem *Now Sleeps the Crimson Petal* than in applying to it a general method of metaphor analysis. As is well-known, metaphor has two senses: (1) "metaphor as a form of linguistic expression and communication" and "metaphor as a form of conceptual representation and symbolization" (Glucksberg 2001: 4). Now Steen's procedure aims to go from linguistic expression to conceptual representation in five steps. First he identifies in Tennyson's poem the metaphor-related words. These may be metaphorically used or they may be used more literally but still indicate a metaphor. Next, if necessary, he completes the explicit discourse elements with possibly implicit conceptual elements in order to build clause-like structures, i.e. two (sets of) propositions which evoke a comparison between their respective elements. The propositions are then arranged as an analogy and values for these propositions are inferred (if they are not already stated by the discourse). He argues that the inference of target domain values is constrained by the specific discourse, whereas source domain values are usually determined by more general considerations of meaning and knowledge. In a final step, further inferences are drawn from the completed analogy. If it is true that these final inferences are hard to constrain (predict) via parameters, at least we see in this descriptive model *where* metaphorical creativity is situated. Steen admits that readers may not go through all the motions all the time; that the fourth and fifth steps – the inferential ones – may even retroactively motivate how the apparently mechanistic step two (propositionalization) is carried out; and that he ignores if related correspondences in complex meaning networks are carried out (in step five) as a series of separate mental actions or as "an integrated scenario".

In his commentary on Freeman (and on Steen, see below), **Ming-Yu Tseng** points out that it is indeed very useful to reinterpret the form-meaning pairings of language as form-feeling pairings, and he goes on to observe that iconic pairings – pairings in which form mimes meaning – occur as "a mish-mash, a cocktail, a peppering of linguistic devices interacting and contributing to the overall effect". In literature and elsewhere, he writes, "iconicity is best seen as 'accumulative homology.'" These devices are traces of drama which inject life in words. From a reader's viewpoint, Haiman's (1999) "sublimation trajectory" in text production thus becomes a "dramatization trajectory", a grounding of the words in performance, a certain iconic relationship between words and the drama which they re-enact. Tseng also comments on Steen. He believes that Steen's chapter has didactic value and that Freeman's and Steen's essays together "shed light on the depth of cognitive poetics".

With **Reuven Tsur** we return to the emotion of form. His chapter zooms in on the gestaltist "figure-ground phenomenon", which refers to the characteristic organization of perception into a figure that "stands out" against an undifferentiated background. What is figural at any one moment depends on patterns of sensory stimulation and on the momentary interests of the perceiver. Figure-ground relationship is shown to be an important element of the way we organize reality in our awareness, including works of art. Poets may reverse our habitual figure-ground organizations of extralinguistic reality so as to achieve poetic effects. This flexibility (despite habit) has counterparts in music and the visual arts. Tsur's chapter observes how in Escher's drawings the same shapes may become figure and ground respectively, owing to both Escher's manipulations and the observer's shifting attention. In his *Mondschein Sonata*. Beethoven uses a typical ground texture as a pervasive figure (used as background in Mozart's *Don Giovanni*). Performers too may manipulate the listener's attention. In his works for solo string instruments, Bach fools his listeners, with the help of the gestalt principles of grouping, into perceiving simultaneous melodies or figures and grounds. While in the visual arts there can be no figure without ground, Tsur argues that in music and literature figures can occur without ground. Pervasive as they may be, figure-ground relationships in literature are extremely complex phenomena and attempts to use such notions as "trajector" and "landmark" as foolproof diagnostic signs of figure-ground are, according to Tsur, doomed to failure. A herald of foregrounding theory, **Tsur** speaks not of cognitive linguistic "form-meaning pairings" but assumes another pair that cuts across form and meaning, to know, materials (phonetic, semantic, metric...) organized in structures (see Wellek and Warren 1949). Poetry often presents free-floating ("gestalt-free") materials which can become structured in one way or another. Instead of iconicity between form and meaning, Tsur finds that structured materials create emergent gestalt qualities of many complexly interacting sorts. On the one hand, Freeman's precategorial poetic iconicity and Tsur's gestalt-free qualities bear obvious resemblances. On the other hand, in being explicitly non-CL, Tsur's cognitive poetics reminds us (just like **Culpeper's** chapter) not only of the goals and gains of cognitive literary studies, but also of the many gaps that remain and the challenges that will have to be faced, if cognitive poetics wants to grow into a truly successful interdisciplinary enterprise (see also section 4 of this introduction).

Tony Veale's commentary ludically (and ironically) foregrounds what was merely an introductory idea in Tsur's essay, to know, the humorous potential of figure-ground reversals – here, a Soviet joke on the theft of straw in/and wheelbarrows. He contends that "humour is the ideal laboratory in which to study figure-ground distinctions, since, in a joke (as opposed to a poem, or a piece of music), [...] tiny movements can yield disproportionately large and obvious effects". Second, and also ironically, he contends that figure-ground reversal is not some of humour's "straw" (as Attardo's General Theory of Verbal Humor views it) but the very wheelbarrow of humour. Thirdly, Veale draws attention to a phenomenon which has been given centre stage by literary scholars working with Possible Worlds Theory: transworld relations (see Eco 1979; Ryan 1991 Doležel 1998). Veale explains that the joke deftly makes the factory guard, who looks for stolen goods in the straw, "our representative in the narrative", since both the guard and the listener (reader) are led to believe that the wheelbarrow is merely an *instrument* of the stealer. Reminiscent of Wayne Booth's concept of the "unreliable narrator", Veale's analysis relates figure-ground assumptions to perspective: "Whenever we comprehend a narrative, our critical faculties constantly play the role of such a sentry, applying intuitions about what is salient and important and what is not. Sometimes, as in humour, these intuitions are subverted by a wily jokester, prompting us to comb through worthless straw for a pay-off that lies elsewhere".

As in fiction theory, the inflexibility of Possible Worlds Theory to account for correspondences despite perspectival shifts (mental world shifts) was a major issue for Cognitive Linguistics too: Fauconnier's Mental Space Theory (1994, 1997) and its offshoot Blending Theory (Fauconnier and Turner 1998, 2002) were initially a response to referential problems encountered in Possible Worlds Theory. Instead of conceiving concepts as *sets*, as is done in formal one-world and many-worlds logic, Fauconnier analysed the actual mental working of concepts in real minds and in real communication. Real human minds who are engaged in real communication move in a "base space" (the mutually known world of interlocutors) but also build other spaces for local use: fictional, hypothetical, counterfactual, future, past, etc. spaces. Moreover, actual minds in real communication establish relations between "base" and "imagined" spaces, and between certain entities of these spaces. In the counterfactual construction "If Ted Turner had been born twins, they would have had competing sports networks, but as things are, he has no competition", there are correspondences between *Ted Turner, twins, they*, and *he*, which are not allowed in formal PWT but are nevertheless perfectly understandable (Lakoff 1987: 213). In larger fictional texts these correspondences are complex yet very meaningful (see **Semino**). **Veale** shows these correspondences to be present in short jokes too. At first, listeners think like the sentry in the joke world but then shift to another level. **Sternberg** reminds us of the ontic difference between frame (here: hearer's frame) and inset (sentry) despite the correspondences between frame and inset (see also **Culpeper** on the differences between understanding real-life persons and fictional characters). Finally, Veale does not believe in Tsur's idea of figure without a ground.

The third section of the volume, dealing with "stance" in literature, opens with a contribution by **Eleni Antonopoulou and Kiki Nikiforidou** on the explanatory power of Construction Grammar for the analysis of verbal humour in literary texts. The chapter aims to illuminate satiric meta-linguistic awareness through a principled, fine-grained analysis of the relation between "normal" language use and "marked" discourse which may be humorously interpreted. Antonopoulou and Nikiforidou set out to show how the preoccupation of Construction Grammar with "marked" encodings and their treatment as cases of *coercion* may prove a valuable methodological tool for the analysis of creative or neologistic literary discourse. To that effect they focus on extracts from Kingsley Amis' *Lucky Jim* and Martin Amis' *Dead Babies* which involve coercive constructions, i.e. clashes between the syntactic and/or semantic properties of lexical units and those of the construction in which they are embedded. They discuss the principles that guide coherent, consistent interpretations in such cases of conflict, with the aim to make explicit the cognitive mechanisms involved and their contribution to humorous interpretation. Coercion is viewed as a cognitive (not humour specific) phenomenon, naturally couched in more general phenomena such as the prototype and deviations from it or foregrounding vs. backgrounding. Antonopoulou and Nikiforidou specifically argue that what is foregrounded in such cases is the linguistic discrepancy between the word and its context, illuminating the essence of verbal humour as metalinguistic awareness. Finally, they discuss the humorous exploitation of discoursal or textual ambiguity in literary texts, linking discoursal properties and socially determined conditions with formal constructional properties. In his commentary **Salvatore Attardo** claims that his General Theory of Verbal Humour is not incompatible with Antonopoulou and Nikiforidou's findings, if that is what the authors suggest. Secondly, he does not like the authors to qualify humour as "marked" or even "deviant", for he believes that the logical pre-existence of a serious mode is at best "a pedagogical fiction". Thirdly, he does not like their all too prudent and appeasing rhetoric vis-à-vis literary studies. The authors indeed refrain from commenting on the interaction between the microlevel devices they discuss and the broader generic or cultural embedding of these devices within a full-blown poetics of humour. In her analysis of humour, **Semino** does seem to feel the need for a global framework. She explains for her treatment of *Mrs Midas* that humour "is a central aspect of the way in which the text world is projected, but is difficult to account for in terms of existing approaches to text worlds (possibly with the exception of blending theory)". As **Herman**'s discussion of a joke on Dick Cheney illustrates, a poetics of humour should indeed be cognitive *and* discursive (see e.g. Vandaele 2002 on the social and cognitive aspects of humour).

In their chapter entitled "Judging distances: Mental spaces, distance, and viewpoint in literary discourse", **Barbara Dancygier and Lieven Vandelanotte** propose to distinguish "discourse distance" as distinct from other cases of distance such as temporal, social, metalinguistic and epistemic distance. In distanced discourse, one and the same utterance subordinated to one deictic centre may represent two discourse stances, one of which is not grounded in the speaker's belief world. An example of this is the conditional *If (as you say) she was hired, she doesn't need our help any more*, in which the *if*-clause does not represent the speaker's knowledge, but is essentially a premise temporarily borrowed from another's discourse for the purposes of conditional reasoning. Indeed, Dancygier and Vandelanotte argue that discourse distance borrows or evokes (rather than properly embeds) a thought from another discourse space in the argumentative build-up of the speaker's own space. This phenomenon is discussed across a wide range of constructions in grammar and discourse, including past indicative conditionals, metalinguistic negation, a specifically "distanced" mode of indirect speech and thought, all the way through to distanced discourse in the poetry of Larkin, Szymborska and Reed. In the concluding discussion of Reed's war poem "Judging distances" the different kinds of distance all come together, thus unravelling the poem's message that however hard we may try to fool ourselves in different forms of linguistic distancing, ultimately we can never distance ourselves from our emotions. **Jeroen Vandaele**'s commentary asks whether distance (or emotion in general) is necessarily coded in language and if code-external perspectives cannot always overrule the apparently coded emotion.

The third chapter on "stance" differs from the preceding two in that it presents experimental evidence on the cognitive processing of distancing discourse. **Rachel Giora, Ofer Fein, Ronie Kaufman, Dana Eisenberg and Shani Erez** examine the impact of an "ironic situation" on the interpretation of irony. An unresolved issue within irony research is whether salience-based (e.g., literal) but inappropriate interpretations are construed initially even when contexts strongly benefit ironic interpretations. Do some kinds of contexts benefit ironic interpretations to the extent that comprehenders bypass accessible but incompatible interpretations? According to Gibbs (2002), "ironic situations" are such contexts: he suggests that an "ironic situation" – a context displaying some contrast between a protagonist's expectation and the reality that frustrates it – (a) raises an expectation for ironies and (b) facilitates ironic interpretations to the extent that accessible but incompatible interpretations need not be derived.

A first experiment examines Gibbs' first prediction by comparing "ironic situations" with ironic contexts featuring fulfilled expectations. Results show *no* preference for ironic interpretations in any of the contexts, which, instead, favoured literal interpretations. A second experiment tests the predicted facilitative effects of "ironic situations". In addition to a new set of contexts featuring frustrated vs. fulfilled expectations, contexts exhibiting no expectation were also used. All the contexts ended in an identical target (=expression to be understood) which had a literal reading only in the no-expectation condition. Pretests controlled for degree of "ironiness" and protagonists' expectations. Again, reading times of targets show *no* facilitation of ironic interpretations compared to salience-based interpretations. While the ironic targets, on their own, did not differ from each other, they took longer to read than the literal targets. The findings reported by Giora and her collaborators argue against the view that a context featuring an "ironic situation" favours an ironic interpretation (Experiment 1) which, in turn, facilitates its interpretation compared to a salience-based alternative (Experiment 2). Instead, they replicate previous results showing that, regardless of context bias, interpreting irony takes longer to process than equivalent salience-based interpretations. **Albert Katz** sees Giora et al.'s chapter as a deconstruction of the well-known claim that context ("ecology") facilitates irony production and comprehension. On the other hand, Katz hypothesizes that other factors (e.g. absence of negative attitude) might explain why the putative ironic "situations" did not favour irony production and reception. Another problem, namely that most materials were "not situationally real", is similar to the main objection made by **Edmond Wright** in a second commentary on Giora et. al. For reasons he explains, he does not feel that Giora et al.'s examples "sustain the extension to actual examples more characteristic of its occurrence, whether in life or literature". Since irony is such a broad research topic, an editorial choice was made to add Wright's philosophical and cultural perspective to Giora et al.'s and Katz' experimental viewpoints.

The fourth and last section of the volume is intended as a critical reflection on current cognitive poetic practice. **Max Louwerse and Willie Van Peer**'s chapter entitled "How Cognitive is Cognitive Poetics? Adding a Symbolic Approach to the Embodied One", starts with the observation that in theories of language comprehension a bias can be observed in support of strict embodiment. According to this embodiment view of language comprehension, words and sentences activate perceptual and embodied experiences. Louwerse and Van Peer contend that the same embodiment bias can be found in cognitive poetics. They counter this bias by showing how language comprehension is both symbolic and embodied: embodied representations do not always have to be activated, and language has encoded many embodied relations. The authors take examples from Stockwell (2002) and analyze them, using Latent Semantic Analysis, a statistical technique that identifies semantic relations between language units. By taking examples ranging from figure and ground, prototypes, cognitive deixis and conceptual metaphor, Louwerse and Van Peer illustrate how LSA analyses can shed light on the processes of meaning construction just as well as embodiment theory does, arguing that adding a symbolic approach augments the theoretical and methodological validity of cognitive poetics. If Louwerse and Van Peer suggest that there is a necessary link between method and theory (possibly suggesting a qualitative-embodied cluster versus a quantitative-symbolic cluster), then **Dirk Geeraerts** disagrees in his commentary. Moreover, Geeraerts argues, "Louwerse and Van Peer are wrong by identifying embodied meanings with indexical or iconic meanings".

The volume closes off with a critical and – so we expect – highly controversial epilogue by **Meir Sternberg**, a leading scholar in narratology and a renowned critic of cognitive poetics. Sternberg's essay was originally intended as a commentary on Herman's chapter but grew into a broad critique of cognitive literary studies, thus curbing the enthusiasm of many of the students in this field. Although the epilogue presents a review of cognitive poetics – and Cognitive Linguistics in general – that many will in some respects disagree with (including the editors), we feel that it may serve as an incentive for cognitive poeticians to further develop the field towards a full-fledged interdisciplinary endeavour on the interface between cognitive science and literary studies.

Among the many issues taken up by Sternberg are the topics of "role" and "focalization" developed in Herman's chapter. Sternberg disputes Herman's claim that these topics have been long-time cruxes of narrative genre. Cognitively speaking, he sees narrative as a "unique discourse-length processual activity and experience" requiring other focal concepts. He initially defines narrative discourse by contrasting it to descriptive discourse. Whereas descriptive discourse represents static space, narrative represents dynamic space*time*. This spacetime world is dynamized on/by two interconnected levels: narrated time and narrating time. Narrative's second time line, narrating time (or, from the receiver's end, processing time), is an inevitable consequence of the linearity of verbal communication. Although it is generally overlooked by "cognitivism" – even by Schank and Abelson (1977) – it is no less crucial to narrative than narrated time, Sternberg explains. Both times together are "narrative's two definitional and infinitely twinnable sequences – the told vs. the telling, what happened vs. how the what's unfold before us, the reconstructed chronology vs. the given temporal order". Narrative's universal triple effect – suspense, curiosity and surprise – cannot be explained in terms of narrated time only: a plot summary of a story world has no emotional impact because it refers only to narrated time, to the temporal evolution within the narrated world. Instead, a "poetics of impact" regarding narrative has to analyze to no lesser degree who-discloses-what-how-when-why on the level of the tale (or telling, or narrating time). Narrating time thus constitutes a first (and inevitable) framing of the narrated world.

But Sternberg's critique moves beyond Herman's chapter. He identifies seven general flaws in cognitive narrative theory: (1) it leaves story and storyhood undefined (cf. narrative's triple effect); (2) it erases the difference between real-life events and represented events: it ignores quotation theory (dialogue in novels differs e.g. from talk in the first-order world); (3) it tends to focus on mini-stories; (4) it reifies story interest by preloading with "absolute interest" such representable objects as death, danger, power, sex, money, risk, trouble, conflict, unusualness; (5) it reduces the mind to emotionless cognition; (6) it does not appreciate the importance of narrative gaps for human beings.

Next, Sternberg contends that Talmy's and Langacker's concepts of perspective concern language's space, not narrative's double time. For Sternberg, the basic questions of narrative perspective are: Whose frame is it? Whose frame are we in or dealing with? Who says this? At what point? Was this frame wrong? Do we still know what we thought we knew? What does this mean for the future of the story world? Does this change our past understanding of the story world? Why did I not see it coming? Etc. "Every [...] perspectivizing event (of telling, viewing, quoting, hearing, remembering) intersects as well as co-extends with the events perspectivized, so that they can always dynamize each other. [...] Once narrativized, perspective uniquely happens, evolves, twists". This is, for Sternberg, what is properly narrative about narrative perspective. All of this goes back to "an asymmetry in perspective: knowing (because self-knowing) speaker vs. groping addressee, I-insider vs. you-outsider. Though built into earthly communication, the asymmetry is ignored by the grammar". Furthermore he criticizes the preverbal model of Cognitive Linguistics ("percept and concept before verbalization"), for discourse proper can also trigger more discourse.

Sternberg holds against linguistics its paradigmatic desire to bring all meaning-making mechanisms into coded systems. Instead, he argues that the mind is protean, infinitely flexible, not necessarily restricted by the do's and don'ts of grammar or "usual behaviour" in general. Given this Proteus Principle, the mind can map any form/meaning – linguistic or otherwise – on any function in a given (or constructed) frame. When operating within the narrative frame of mind, the protean mind can even narrativize nonnarrative forms (static nouns, adjectives) by assimilating it to a certain narrative teleology. Trained minds are especially good at flexible reinterpretation according to a repertoire of teleologies. It is true that knowledge of genres and even low-level language forms can help to determine discourse goals. However, such forms cannot carry their full-fledged (framed) meaning. Instead, an infinite amount of discursive elements come into play (or even into conflict). Thus, although certain linguistic forms (verbs, most notably) contribute to narrative, narrativity as such does not reside mainly in coded forms: narrative is a general framing which need not be manifest, linguistically or otherwise. "The perspectival range of discourse – as against its surface encoding – only begins with the senses. Even beyond eye-to-eye contact, as on the telephone or the internet or the novelistic page, there always re-main nonverbal, possibly never verbalized features and axes of viewpoint: knowledge horizons, perceptual factors, ontic distances, emotive attitudes, cultural markers or lenses, value schemes, self-awareness, communicativeness, intentionalities, ideologies, abilities, liabilities, and so forth". Sternberg's critique naturally leads us to the final section of our introduction, which deals with the gaps in cognitive poetics.

4.   Gaps and bridges in cognitive poetics

Despite its laudable goals and potential gains, cognitive poetics still needs to overcome a number of significant challenges, if it wants to develop into a truly successful interdisciplinary enterprise. Its main selling point is also its main problem: the multiple directionality that cognitive poetics is facing and the mutual distrust of what is happening in other disciplines and paradigms.

First, in some areas of literary studies there is fear of empiricism, with its formalization procedures and/or quantitative approaches. Cognitive analysts who talk of "facts" of literary interpretation will be suspect from the outset. This fear is partly warranted since introspection and observation are so distinct as methods that they yield distinct data calling for distinct concepts and theories. The debate on irony between **Giora et al., Wright** and **Katz** perfectly illustrates that empirical and introspective research can be worlds apart. Whereas Giora and her collaborators probe introspective concepts of figurative speech and thought via well-controlled observations, Wright criticizes the experimental design for being too stripped of their rich discursive context. This is the classical divide between experimental and cultural studies (cf. Sternberg 2003a: 310). However, despite its necessary methodological restrictions of operationalization, Giora et al.'s study does stimulate poeticians' reflections on the relationship between ironic situations and verbal irony, and may therefore have relevance beyond the boundaries of the reported experiments. The same argument applies to the chapters by Steen and Louwerse and Van Peer. **Steen's** five-step technical procedure for the identification of metaphorical structures in discourse may be, as he puts it, "relatively independent of the analysis of people's text processing and its products", but it does provide an important insight into the complexities involved in mapping linguistic form onto underlying conceptual structures and in making metaphorical thinking explicit. **Louwerse and Van Peer**, on their part, criticize cognitive poetics for its selective borrowing of insights from cognitive science, mainly in function of its own research agenda. The (almost) exclusive focus on the embodied approach to cognition in cognitive poetics, the authors argue, does not do justice to the potential of the interdisciplinary endeavour that is cognitive science. Fear of empiricism and formalism may in fact be at the bottom of the near-absence of insights from computer science and computational linguistics (as valued partners in cognitive science) in cognitive poetics. Their study does constitute a significant challenge to the methodology as well as the claimed innovative insights of cognitive poetics. Their plea for a cognitive poetics broadly conceived – both theoretically and methodologically – forces cognitive poeticians (including the editors and authors in this volume) to be aware of the potential drawbacks of bilateral (instead of multilateral) interdisciplinarity.

Second, and on the other side of the spectrum, there is fear of idealism, with its uncontrollable theorizing, exempt from strictly empirical evidence. Proponents of stricter empirical methods in cognitive science argue that introspective analysis, which is common practice in large sections of poetics and hermeneutics, does not meet the standard of modern scientific research (see e.g. Geeraerts [1999] 2006 for a staged Socratic dialogue on this debate). For those empiricists, the majority of studies in cognitive poetics (including most chapters in the present volume) will lack the methodological precision to be of true scholarly significance. Although such criticism may be founded for particular research questions, phenomenological accounts remain adequate for other cognitive scientific issues (see Gallagher and Zahavi 2007), as is illustrated by some of the contributors. **Semino**'s text world approach e.g. presents a convenient and practicable first-person method for the analysis of the potential meaning and actual processing of fictional worlds, despite the criticism of Possible Worlds Theory by proponents of Mental Space Theory and despite Gibbs' (2000) criticism of Mental Space Theory and Blending Theory as empirical research models. In a similar vein, **Culpeper** appeals to nonformalized, frame-related text research (delving into the character's situations, genres, world types) as a necessary step in understanding characters. **Herman** draws on not strictly empirical approaches like position theory, focalization and emotionology in his attempt to capture some of the most basic cultural and phenomenological aspects of the narrative.

In any case, methodological distrust leads to mutual ignorance and caricature. If we want to start understanding why it is that our human minds react in certain ways to poetic language, we need to ponder all resources available in as many areas as possible. When he applies scheme theory to characterization, **Culpeper** therefore pleads – *pace* this volume's editors – for more cognitive science and less narrow-minded Cognitive Linguistics (cf. also **Louwerse and Van Peer**). **Tseng**, a stylistician like Culpeper, brings under attention the "integrationist approach" to literary and nonliterary language, as advocated by Toolan (1997).

To conclude, then, let us return to the most general question of our enterprise: Can the epistemic project of cognitive poetics be truly interdisciplinary? While methodological distrust is understandable and mutual ignorance dissolvable in time, the basic epistemic projects of all fields involved may of course be very different and thus hinder fruitful collaboration, for research is not just about objects – "poetic language" – but also about goals or research perspectives – what does poetic language mean *in our theory*? Theories and paradigms have different goals, different interests and perspectives. Let us try to nail down some basic tensions and possibilities of interdisciplinarity from the viewpoint of the two fields most represented in this volume, CL and Poetics.

On the one hand, we have a view on cognitive poetics from the perspective of Cognitive Linguistics: Poetic language (= Poetics' object), as part of language (= CL's object), informs CL hypotheses about language as part of our general mental faculties (CL's research goal). As Adler and Gross point out, "[t]he study of literature, in this model, is merely a sub-discipline of the study of the human mind" (2002: 199). On the other hand, we have a view on cognitive poetics from the viewpoint of Poetics: Language as a mental faculty (= CL's object), as part of artful meaning making mechanisms (= Poetics' object), informs Poetics' hypotheses on how artful meaning is mentally (emotionally and rationally) institutionally, contingently, historically, and individually constructed.

Even these cursory descriptions show how each field yields a different conception of cognitive poetics, according to its own needs. The supposedly common object of investigation, poetic language, is split into "artful meaning making mechanisms on any level" and "poetic language as part of language as part of our mental faculties". That is, poetic language can either illustrate cognitivized language or be an end in its own right. Therefore, both disciplines will have to convince each other of the necessity to take over (part of) the other's research perspective. In one direction, CL will have to convince poeticians that, if they want to better understand an important aspect of artful discourse, they should for very specific reasons theorize the mind and language as CL does. This will have to be done in constant practice. In the other direction, Poetics will have to convince cognitive linguists that the mind is but one factor in a discursive configuration that has been well mapped by descriptive poetics: genres, institutions, events, agency, history, contingency, nonformalizable frames at large. If Poetics is willing to accept that the CL concept of "mind" does not imply determinism and/or reductionism and if CL is willing to accept that "discourse" at large is not to be disposed of as unscientific, we will have moved a long way toward real interdisciplinarity.

Mapping out the goals, gains and gaps of cognitive poetics certainly shows that, while this interdisciplinary endeavour is still in its infancy, it will raise as many questions as it helps to answer. Nevertheless, the rapidly growing body of publications sprouting from the epistemic marriage of literary studies and cognitive science suggests that these questions are worth asking, and partial answers are worth sharing. We hope that the chapters and commentaries in the present volume will contribute to the further development of the cognitive poetic enterprise.

References

Adler, Hans and Sabine Gross
 2002   Adjusting the frame: Comments on cognitivism and literature. *Poetics Today* 23: 195–220.
Bal, Mieke
 1997   *Narratology: Introduction to the Theory of Narrative.* 2nd edition. Toronto: University of Toronto Press.
Bizup, Joseph M. and Eugene R. Kintgen
 1993   The cognitive paradigm in literary studies. *College English* 55(8): 841–857.
Brône, Geert, Kurt Feyaerts and Tony Veale
 2006   Humor research and Cognitive Linguistics: Common grounds and new perspectives. *Humor. International Journal of Humor Research* 19(3): 305–339.
Culler, Jonathan
 1997   *Literary Theory: A Very Short Introduction.* Oxford: Oxford University Press.
Culler, Jonathan
 2001   Preface to the Cornell Paperbacks Augmented Edition. *The Pursuit of Signs. Semiotics, Literature, Deconstruction*, Ithaca, NY: Cornell University Press, vii-xv.
Dancygier, Barbara
 2005   Blending and narrative viewpoint: Jonathan Raban's travels through mental spaces. *Language and Literature* 14(2): 99–127.
Doležel, Lubomír
 1998   *Heterocosmica. Fiction and Possible Worlds.* Baltimore/London: The Johns Hopkins University Press.
Eco, Umberto
 1979   *The Role of the Reader: Explorations in the Semiotics of Texts.* Bloomington and London: Indiana University Press.
Eco, Umberto
 1989   Unlimited Semiosis and Drift. In: Umberto Eco. *The Limits of Interpretation.* Bloomington: Indiana University Press.
Fauconnier, Gilles
 1994   *Mental Spaces: Aspects of Meaning Construction in Natural Language.* Cambridge (MA): MIT Press.
Fauconnier, Gilles
 1997   *Mappings in Thought and Language.* Cambridge: Cambridge University Press.
Fauconnier, Gilles and Mark Turner
 1998   Conceptual integration networks. *Cognitive Science* 22(2), 133–187.
Fauconnier, Gilles and Mark Turner
 2002   *The Way We Think. Conceptual Blending and the Mind's Hidden Complexities.* New York: Basic Books.

Flanagan, Owen J.
1989   *The Science of the Mind*. Cambridge (Mass.): MIT Press.
Gallagher, Shaun
2004   *How the Body Shapes the Mind*. Oxford: Oxford University Press.
Gallagher, Shaun and Dan Zahavi
2007   *The Phenomenological Mind. An Introduction to Philosophy of Mind and Cognitive Science*. London/New York: Routledge.
Gavins, Joanna and Gerard Steen (eds.)
2003   *Cognitive Poetics in Practice*. London and New York: Routledge.
Geeraerts, Dirk
[1999] 2006 Idealist and empiricist tendencies in Cognitive Linguistics. In: Theo Janssen and Gisela Redeker (eds.), *Cognitive Linguistics: Foundations, Scope, and Methodology*, 163–194. Berlin: Mouton de Gruyter. Reprinted in: Dirk Geeraerts, *Words and Other Wonders: Papers on Lexical and Semantic Topics*. Berlin/New York: Mouton de Gruyter, 416–444.
Genette, Gérard
[1972] 1980 *Narrative Discourse: An Essay in Method*. Ithaca: Cornell University Press.
Gibbs, Raymond W. Jr.
2000   Making good psychology out of blending theory. *Cognitive Linguistics* 11(3/4): 347–358.
Glicksohn, Joseph and Chanita Goodblatt
1993   Metaphor and Gestalt: Interaction Theory Revisited *Poetics Today* 14(1): 83–97.
Glucksberg, Sam
2001   *Understanding Figurative Language. From Metaphors to Idioms*. Oxford: Oxford University Press.
Gonzalez-Marquez, Monica, Irene Mittelberg, Seana Coulson and Michael J. Spivey (eds.)
2007   *Methods in Cognitive Linguistics*. Amsterdam/Philadelphia: John Benjamins
Goodman, Nelson
1978   *Ways of Worldmaking*. Indianapolis: Hackett.
Haiman, John
1999   Action, speech, and grammar: The sublimation trajectory. In: Max Nänny and Olga Fischer (eds.), *Form Miming Meaning: Iconicity in Language and Literature*, 37–57. Amsterdam/Philadelphia: John Benjamins.
Hogan, Patrick Colm and Lalita Pandit (eds.)
2006   *Cognitive Shakespeare: Criticism and Theory in the Age of Neuroscience*. Special issue of *College Literature* 33(1).
Ingarden, Roman
1973   *The Cognition of the Literary Work of Art*. Trans. Ruth Ann Crowley and Kenneth R. Olson. Evanston, IL: Northwestern University Press.

Jackson, Tony E.
  2002   Issues and problems in the blending of cognitive science, evolutionary psychology, and literary study. *Poetics Today* 23(1): 161–179.
Jackson, Tony E.
  2005   Explanation, interpretation, and close reading: The progress of cognitive poetics. *Poetics Today* 26(3): 519–33.
Jahn, Manfred
  1999   'Speak, friend, and enter': Garden Paths, Artificial Intelligence, and Cognitive Narratology. In: David Herman (ed.), *Narratologies: New Perspectives on Narrative Analysis*, 167–194. Ohio: Ohio State University Press.
Jahn, Manfred
  2003   'Awake! Open your eyes!' The Cognitive Logic of External and Internal Stories. In: David Herman (ed.), *Narrative Theory and the Cognitive Sciences*, 195–213. Stanford: CSLI Publications.
Lakoff, George
  1987   *Women, Fire, and Dangerous Things*. Chicago: University of Chicago Press.
Lakoff, George and Mark Johnson
  1980   *Metaphors We Live By*. Chicago/London: The University of Chicago Press.
Ricoeur, Paul
  1975   *La métaphore vive*. Paris: Le Seuil.
Ricoeur, Paul
  1983   *Temps et récit. Tome I: L'intrigue et le récit historique*. Paris: Le Seuil.
Ricoeur, Paul
  1984   *Temps et récit. Tome II: La configuration dans le récit de fiction*. Paris: Le Seuil.
Ricoeur, Paul
  1985   *Temps et récit. Tome III: Le temps raconté*. Paris: Le Seuil
Rohrer, Tim
  2005   Mimesis, artistic inspiration and the blends we live by *Journal of Pragmatics* 37(10): 1686–1716.
Rumelhart, David E.
  1975   Notes on a schema for stories. In: D.G. Bobrow and A.M. Collins (eds.), *Representation and Understanding: Studies in Cognitive Science*, 211–236. New York: Academic Press.
Rumelhart, David E.
  1977   Understanding and summarizing brief stories. In: D. Laberge and S. Samuels (eds.), *Basic Processes in Reading: Perception and Comprehension*, 265–303. Hillsdale, NJ: Lawrence Erlbaum Associates.
Ryan, Marie-Laure
  1991   *Possible Worlds, Artificial Intelligence and Narrative Theory*. Bloomington: Indiana University Press.

Schank, Roger C. and Robert P. Abelson
  1977   *Scripts, Plans, Goals, and Understanding: An Inquiry into Human Knowledge Structure*. Hillsdale, NJ: Erlbaum.
Semino, Elena and Jonathan Culpeper (eds.)
  2002   *Cognitive Stylistics: Language and Cognition in Text Analysis*. Amsterdam/Philadelphia: John Benjamins.
Shen, Dan
  2005   How stylisticians draw on narratology: Approaches, advantages and disadvantages. *Style* 39(4): 381–395.
Simons, Peter
  1995   Meaning and Language. In: B. Smith and D. Woodruff Smith (eds.), *The Cambridge Companion to Husserl*, 106–137. Cambridge: Cambridge University Press.
Stanzel, Franz K.
  2004   The "complementary story": Outline of a reader-oriented theory of the novel. *Style* 38(2): 203–220.
Sternberg, Meir
  2003a   Universals of narrative and their cognitivist fortunes (I). *Poetics Today* 24(2): 297–395.
Sternberg, Meir
  2003b   Universals of narrative and their cognitivist fortunes (I. *Poetics Today* 24(3): 517–638.
Stockwell, Peter
  2002   *Cognitive Poetics: An Introduction*. London: Routledge.
Talmy, Leonard
  2000   *Toward a Cognitive Semantics*, vols. 1 and 2. Cambridge, MA: MIT Press.
Toolan, Michael
  1997   *Language in Literature: An Introduction to Stylistics*. London: Arnold.
Turner, Mark
  1991   *Reading Minds: The Study of English in the Age of Cognitive Science*. Princeton: Princeton University Press.
Turner, Mark
  1996   *The Literary Mind*. New York: Oxford University Press.
Vandaele, Jeroen
  2002   Humor mechanisms in film comedy: Incongruity *and* superiority. *Poetics Today* 23(2): 221–249.
Van Oort, Richard
  2003   Cognitive science and the problem of representation. *Poetics Today* 24(2): 237–295.
Wellek, René and Austin Warren
  1949   *Theory of Literature*. New York: Harcourt, Brace & Co.

Part I: Story

Text worlds

Elena Semino

1. Introduction

An important aspect of literary interpretation (and of text comprehension generally) is the construction of the "world" projected by a text, i.e. the sets of scenarios and type of reality that the text is about. In this chapter I will discuss different approaches to the study of text worlds from narratology and cognitive poetics by demonstrating their application to two specific texts: Carol Ann Duffy's poem *Mrs Midas* and (an English translation of) the story of King Midas in Ovid's *Metamorphoses*. The texts will be introduced in the next section. I will then discuss, in turn, possible-worlds approaches to fictional worlds from narratology and a selection of relevant theories from cognitive linguistics and poetics. I will finish by reflecting on what are, in my view, the main challenges for future work on text worlds.

2. The Midas myth in Carol Ann Duffy's *Mrs Midas* and Ovid's *Metamorphoses*

Born in Glasgow in 1955, Carol Ann Duffy is one of the foremost contemporary British writers. She is best known for her poetic production, which includes the collection *The World's Wife*, published in 1999. The title of the collection plays on the sexist English expression *the world and his wife*, which mirrors the convention of referring to married couples as *Mr X and his wife*, and is commonly used to refer hyperbolically to large numbers of people (e.g. *It seemed that all the world and his wife were in Madrid*, from the British National Corpus).[1] In the title of the collection,

---

1. The expression *the world and his wife* can be analysed both as a metaphor and as a metonymy: the noun phrase *the world* can be seen as a personification of the world as a male human being, or as a metonymic reference to all males in the world. Either way, women are referred to in their role as wives, and paradoxically excluded from the referent of *world* (whether interpreted as a metaphor or a metonymy).

Duffy has modified the idiomatic expression by making *wife* the head of the noun phrase, thereby foregrounding the female member of the couple. The titles of each of the thirty poems included in the collection refer to the (real or imaginary) wives or sisters of famous men of history, myth, or the Bible, such as *Mrs Darwin, Elvis's Twin Sister, Mrs Tiresias, Mrs Icarus, Queen Herod,* and *Pilate's Wife.* In the poems, each of these women speaks in the first person about how her life was affected by the behaviours and actions that made her husband or brother famous.[2] In line with a well-established tradition in feminist writing, the poems expose the male bias in the "stories" that dominate Western culture, and present the famous men of history and fantasy as weak, idiosyncratic, irrational, and, most of all, entirely self-centred. In the majority of the poems, however, the women's expression of irritation, anger, miscomprehension and regret tends to be tempered by a pervasive tone of amused disenchantment with the behaviours and foibles of men. Most importantly, the women in Duffy's poems are presented as survivors: even though their husbands and brothers make their lives difficult or downright impossible, they cope with humour and resilience, and often rebuild new lives without their men. *Mrs Midas,* which is quoted in full below, exemplifies all these different aspects of the collection.

Mrs Midas

It was late September. I'd just poured a glass of wine, begun
to unwind, while the vegetables cooked. The kitchen
filled with the smell of itself, relaxed, its steamy breath
gently blanching the windows. So I opened one,
then with my fingers wiped the other's glass like a brow.
He was standing under the pear-tree snapping a twig.

Now the garden was long and the visibility poor, the way
the dark of the ground seems to drink the light of the sky,
but that twig in his hand was gold. And then he plucked
a pear from a branch – we grew Fondante d'Automne –
and it sat in his palm like a light-bulb. On.
I thought to myself, Is he putting fairy lights in the tree?

---

2. A few of the poems (e.g. *Little Red Cap, Circe, Queen Kong*) do not fall exactly within this general pattern, but they still present a fresh version of well-known stories from the perspective of a female protagonist.

He came into the house. The doorknobs gleamed.
He drew the blinds. You know the mind; I thought of
the Field of the Cloth of Gold and of Miss Macready.
He sat in that chair like a king on a burnished throne.
The look on his face was strange, wild, vain; I said,
What in the name of God is going on? He started to laugh.

I served up the meal. For starters, corn on the cob.
Within seconds he was spitting out the teeth of the rich.
He toyed with his spoon, then mine, then with the knives, the forks.
He asked where was the wine. I poured with a shaking hand,
a fragrant, bone-dry white from Italy, then watched
as he picked up the glass, goblet, golden chalice, drank.

It was then that I started to scream. He sank to his knees.
After we'd both calmed down, I finished the wine
on my own, hearing him out. I made him sit
on the other side of the room and keep his hands to himself.
I locked the cat in the cellar. I moved the phone.
The toilet I didn't mind. I couldn't believe my ears:

how he'd had a wish. Look, we all have wishes; granted.
But who has wishes granted? Him. Do you know about gold?
It feeds no one; aurum, soft, untarnishable; slakes
no thirst. He tried to light a cigarette; I gazed, entranced,
as the blue flame played on its luteous stem. At least,
I said, you'll be able to give up smoking for good.

Separate beds. In fact, I put a chair against my door,
near petrified. He was below, turning the spare room
into the tomb of Tutankhamun. You see, we were passionate then,
in those halcyon days; unwrapping each other, rapidly,
like presents, fast food. But now I feared his honeyed embrace,
the kiss that would turn my lips to a work of art.

And who, when it comes to the crunch, can live
with a heart of gold? That night, I dreamt I bore
his child, its perfect ore limbs, its little tongue
like a precious latch, its amber eyes
holding their pupils like flies. My dream-milk
burned in my breasts. I woke to the streaming sun.

So he had to move out. We'd a caravan
in the wilds, in a glade of its own. I drove him up
under cover of dark. He sat in the back.

And then I came home, the woman who married the fool
who wished for gold. At first I visited, odd times,
parking the car a good way off, then walking.

You knew you were getting close. Golden trout
on the grass. One day, a hare hung from a larch,
a beautiful lemon mistake. And then his footprints,
glistening next to the river's path. He was thin,
delirious; hearing, he said, the music of Pan
from the woods. Listen. That was the last straw.

What gets me now is not the idiocy or greed
but lack of thought for me. Pure selfishness. I sold
the contents of the house and came down here.
I think of him in certain lights, dawn, late afternoon,
and once a bowl of apples stopped me dead. I miss most,
even now, his hands, his warm hands on my skin, his touch.

(Duffy 1999: 11–13)[3]

The title of the poem presents the poetic speaker as the wife of Midas, the well-known mythological character who was granted the wish of turning to gold everything he touched, only to discover that, as a result of his new power, he could no longer eat or drink. The setting of the poem, however, is contemporary, and the development of the plot diverges from that of the original myth. I will therefore discuss the text world projected by the poem in comparison with the classical version of the myth provided by the Roman poet Ovid in *Metamorphoses*.

The myth of Midas originated in ancient Greece, but, like other Greek myths, became known throughout the centuries partly via the writings of Roman poets, including particularly Ovid (43BC-17AD). *Metamorphoses* is a 15-book collection of mythological stories involving some sort of transformation, written in dactylic hexameters. Below is a prose English translation of the Midas story, from book 11. The immediately preceding text tells of how Bacchus's tutor, the satyr Silenus, had been captured by Phrygian peasants and handed over to Midas (the king of Phrygia), who, after organising ten days of festivities in his honour, took him back to Bacchus in Lydia.

---

3. The author and editors are grateful to Macmillan Publishers Ltd. for permission to reproduce Carol Ann Duffy's poem *Mrs Midas*.

The god was glad to have his tutor back, and in return gave Midas the right to choose himself a gift – a privilege which Midas welcomed, but one which did him little good, for he was fated to make poor use of the opportunity he was given. He said to the god: 'Grant that whatever my person touches be turned to yellow gold.' Bacchus, though sorry that Midas had not asked for something better, granted his request, and presented him with this baneful gift. The Phrygian king went off cheerfully, delighted with the misfortune which had befallen him. He tested the good faith of Bacchus' promise by touching this and that, and could scarcely believe his own senses when he broke a green twig from a low-growing branch of oak, and the twig turned to gold. He lifted a stone from the ground and the stone, likewise, gleamed pale gold. He touched a sod of earth and the earth, by the power of his touch, became a lump of ore. The dry ears of corn which he gathered were a harvest of golden metal, and when he plucked an apple from a tree and held it in his hand, you would have thought that the Hesperides had given it him. If he laid his finger on the pillars of his lofty doorways, they were seen to shine and glitter, and even when he washed his hands in clear water, the trickles that flowed over his palms might have served to deceive Danae. He dreamed of everything turned to gold, and his hopes soared beyond the limits of his imagination.

So he exulted in his good fortune, while servants set before him tables piled high with meats, and with bread in abundance. But then, when he touched a piece of bread, it grew stiff and hard: if he hungrily tried to bite into the meat, a sheet of gold encased the food, as soon as his teeth came in contact with it. He took some wine, itself the discovery of the god who had endowed him with his power, and adding clear water, mixed himself a drink: the liquid could be seen turning to molten gold as it passed his lips.

Wretched in spite of his riches, dismayed by the strange disaster which had befallen him, Midas prayed for a way of escape from his wealth, loathing what he had lately desired. No amount of food could relieve his hunger, parching thirst burned his throat, and he was tortured, as he deserved, by the gold he now hated. Raising his shining arms, he stretched his hands to heaven and cried: 'Forgive me, father Bacchus! I have sinned, yet pity me, I pray, and save me speedily from this disaster that promised so fair!' The gods are kind: when Midas confessed his fault, Bacchus restored him to his former state, cancelling the gift which, in fulfilment of his promise, he had given the king. 'And now,' he said, 'to rid yourself of the remaining traces of that gold which you so foolishly desired, go to the river close by the great city of Sardis. Then make your way along the Lydian ridge, travelling upstream till you come to the water's source. There, where the foaming spring bubbles up in great abundance, plunge your head and body in the water and, at the same time, wash away your crime.' The king went to the spring as he was bidden: his power to change things into gold passed from his person into the stream, and coloured its waters. Even to-day, though the vein of ore is now so ancient, the soil of the fields is hardened by the grains it receives, and gleams with gold where the water from the river moistens its sods.

Midas, hating riches, made his home in the country, in the woods, and worshipped Pan, the god who always dwells in mountain caves: but he remained a foolish person, and his own stupidity was to injure its owner again, as it had done before.

(Ovid, *Metamorphoses*, translated by Innes 1955: 248–50)

The title of Duffy's poem clearly signals its intertextual connection with the Midas myth. However, as is often the case with contemporary re-writings, the effect of the poem relies on its *contrasts* with the classical version. Focusing particularly on Ovid's version quoted above, these contrasts can be summarised as follows:

– Ovid's story has a third-person heterodiegetic narrator; the poem has a first-person homodiegetic narrator.
– The narrator in Ovid's story provides some internal access to the mental states of both Bacchus and Midas (e.g. *though sorry that* and *he dreamed of ... and his hopes soared ...*); the first-person narrator in the poem focuses on her own internal states, both at the time of the narrated events (e.g. *I thought to myself ...*), and in the current narrative present (e.g. *I think of him ...*).
– Ovid's story is set in a mythical world populated by human beings and gods; the poem is set in a world that appears to correspond to a contemporary Western country.
– In Ovid's story, King Midas and Bacchus are the main participants; in the poem, the protagonists are a woman, "Mrs Midas", and her husband.
– In Ovid's story, the gold touch is explicitly granted by Bacchus; in the poem, it is not made explicit how the wish was granted.
– In Ovid's story, the gold touch is eventually removed; in the poem, the gold touch is not removed, and the male protagonist ends up living in isolation, while his wife moves elsewhere.
– In Ovid's story, Midas is stigmatised for his foolishness and greed; in the poem, the first-person narrator feels more hurt by her husband's *lack of concern* for her than by what she calls *the idiocy or greed*.

This brief summary suggests that the intertextual relationship between *Mrs Midas* and the classical myth lies primarily in the similarities and differences between the world of the poem and that of the myth, rather than in stylistic or textual allusions. Indeed, an appreciation of the intertextuality of the poem does not depend on knowledge of any specific version of the myth, but simply on knowledge of the classical story in terms of characters and plot. As Doležel (1998: 202) has put it, literary works can be intertextually linked "not only on the level of texture but also, and no less importantly, on the level of fictional worlds."[4]

In the rest of this chapter, I will discuss the scope of different approaches to the study of text worlds by applying them to the analysis of the text worlds of *Mrs Midas* and Ovid's story, and their mutual relationship. My aims are (1) to discuss the current state of the art in the study of text worlds, and (2) to elucidate further the relationships between the two texts, and particularly the ways in which Duffy has exploited and modified the mythological story.

3.   Possible-worlds approaches to text worlds

"Possible worlds" theory is a prominent approach to the study of literary and fictional text worlds, which has led to important advances in narratology and literary semantics (see Allén 1989; Doležel 1998; Eco 1979, 1990; Maitre 1983; Pavel 1986; Ronen 1994; Ryan 1991; Semino 1997). The theory relies on the basic notion, which is usually traced back to the German philosopher Leibniz, that the world we call "actual" is only one of an infinite constellation of possible worlds, or alternative sets of states of affairs (Bradley and Swartz 1979: xv). This idea was initially exploited by logicians and philosophers to account for a number of important and previously intractable logical problems, such as the difference in the truth values of the propositions expressed by the following sentences: (a) *Human beings are routinely cloned to act as organ donors*; (b) *The earth is round and the earth is not round*. The former sentence is false in relation to the current state of the "actual" world, but may be true in an alternative possible world which differs from the actual world in terms of what is medically possible and ethically acceptable. The world projected by Kazuo Ishiguro's novel *Never Let Me Go* (2005) is one such world, for example. As a consequence, within a possible-worlds approach to logic, sentence (a) would be described as "possibly false". Sentence (b), on the

---

4. My decision to compare Mrs Midas with Ovid's story in particular was due to the fact that the versions of ancient myths included in *Metamorphoses* have been particularly influential. I am not of course claiming that Duffy took Ovid's version as her primary intertextual referent, nor that readers need to be aware of that particular version to appreciate the poem.

other hand, projects two contradictory states of affairs and thereby violates the logical rule of non-contradiction. As such, from a logical point of view, it would be described as "necessarily false", since the possible worlds of logic are sets of states of affairs that do not violate logical laws (see Bradley and Swartz 1979; Divers 2002; Kripke 1971).

The extension of the notion of possible worlds to the semantics of fiction has involved a substantial redefinition both of the notion of "world" and of the notion of "possibility". In fact, some important insights into the nature of the fictional text worlds have resulted precisely from an explicit consideration of how they differ from the possible worlds of logic.

3.1. Furnished, parasitical and incomplete worlds

The possible worlds of logic are abstract sets of states of affairs which are postulated in order to carry out logical operations and solve logical problems. As such, they are both non-contradictory (i.e. two contradictory propositions cannot be true at the same time in a particular world) and complete (i.e. they assign a truth value to any given proposition). In contrast, the text worlds of fiction and literature are cognitive and cultural constructs that are imagined by speakers or writers in text production and by listeners or readers in text comprehension (Doležel 1998: 23–4; Eco 1979: 220–21; Ronen 1994: 48).[5] The text world we imagine in reading *Mrs Midas*, for example, is a dynamic mental representation that results from our active engagement with the poem. When many different texts tell the "same" story, as in the case of the myth of King Midas, a particular fictional world may become partly independent from any specific textual realisation, and gain the status of a widely shared cognitive construct within a particular culture, regardless of individuals' familiarity with a particular literary work.

The status of text worlds as cognitive rather than logical constructs results in a range of further differences from the possible worlds of logic. The possible worlds considered by logicians are abstract, theoretical models which are conceived in order to carry out logical operations. In contrast, the text worlds of fiction and literature are rich, dynamic, "furnished" worlds (Eco 1990: 65): they are inhabited by concrete individuals who are endowed with specific properties and involved in specific events

---

5. Although I am focusing on texts here, fictional worlds can of course be projected via other media, such as ballet or film.

unfolding in specific settings. Both *Mrs Midas* and Ovid's story project text worlds in which concrete, individual characters with specific properties go through particular experiences that, in some cases, lead to changes to their properties (e.g. Ovid's Midas goes from not having the gold touch to having it and back again). Indeed, one of the differences between the two texts (and the genres they belong to) lies in the *way* in which their text worlds are furnished: the third-person narrator in Ovid's story tells us about locations, characters, entities and actions, but does not describe settings in much detail, nor provide detailed descriptions of thoughts and internal states. In *Mrs Midas*, the individuality and concreteness of the life and experience of the female protagonist is much more foregrounded: as first-person narrator, she tells us in detail about her house, her garden, the physical intimacy she used to enjoy with her husband, and her feelings and actions after the discovery of her husband's acquisition of the "gold touch".[6]

At the same time, however, text worlds such as those of Ovid's story and *Mrs Midas* are not maximal, complete and autonomous sets of states of affairs like the possible worlds of logic: they are both ' parasitical" on other worlds for their contents and structure (Eco 1990: 65), and incomplete, i.e. they do not assign a truth value to any conceivable proposition (Doležel 1998: 22). The "parasitical" nature of text worlds results from the fact that texts can only explicitly provide a limited amount of information about the worlds they project. For example, in Ovid's story we are told that Midas *went to the spring* as Bacchus had ordered, but we are not told whether he had two legs and could walk: we assume that this is the case on the basis of our general knowledge of the actual world. Similarly, at the beginning of the fourth stanza of *Mrs Midas* we are told that the female protagonist

> [...] served up the meal. For starters, corn on the cob.
> Within seconds he was spitting out the teeth of the rich.

We are not explicitly told that the husband tried to eat the corn on the cob, but we assume this must have been the case from our general knowl-

---

6. The specificity and concreteness of the inhabitants of fictional text worlds does not deny, of course, that literary characters such as these can be interpreted as symbols of universal human conditions and experiences: in fact, it could be argued that only fully particularised individuals can be effective and powerful enough to acquire universal significance.

edge about what people do in the actual world when a meal is served. Without that inference, we would not be able to understand why he is described as *spitting out the teeth of the rich* in the following line.

This phenomenon, which applies to text comprehension generally, has been captured by Ryan (1991: 48ff.) via what she calls the "principle of minimal departure":

> we reconstrue the central world of a textual universe [...] as conforming as much as possible to our representation of AW [actual world]. We will project upon these worlds everything we know about reality, and we will make only the adjustments dictated by the text. (Ryan 1991: 51)

This applies even when we are faced with impossibilities such as a man being able to turn into gold everything he touches: we still assume this man is subject to the law of gravity, needs to eat and drink in order to survive, and so on. However, our knowledge of the actual world is not the only possible frame of reference for the operation of the principle of minimal departure:

> As a part of reality, texts also exist as potential objects of knowledge, and this knowledge may be singled out as relevant material for the construction of a textual universe. The principle of minimal departure permits the choice, not only of the real world, but also of a textual universe, as a frame of reference. This happens whenever an author expands, rewrites or parodies a preexisting fiction [...]. (Ryan 1991: 54)

Eco (1979: 20ff) similarly points out that readers construct text worlds by drawing both from the general frames that make up their "encyclopaedia" and from "intertextual frames", namely knowledge about language, texts, genres, and so on (see also Doležel's [1998: 177] notion of "fictional encyclopaedia").

Even the original readers of Ovid's *Metamorphoses* might have already heard or read other versions of Midas's story. They may also have been familiar with historical accounts of a King Midas who is believed to have lived in Phrygia around 700BC. However, Eco's "intertextual frames" are particularly relevant to the interpretation of Duffy's poem. The title of the poem explicitly sets up an intertextual connection with the Midas myth. In the context of the collection in which the poem appeared, the specific reference to *Mrs Midas* sets up as protagonist an imaginary woman who is married to (someone like) Midas. The use of *Mrs*, however, suggests a contemporary setting, in which the woman's husband is not a king and in which married women are referred to by means of the title *Mrs* and their husband's surname.[7] Interestingly, the two characters are not named inside the text, but the title (coupled with the context of the collection) suffices to set up the male protagonist as a counterpart of Midas in the Greek myth. In possible-worlds approaches to narratology, counterparts are defined as individuals who inhabit different worlds, but who are linked by a relationship of similarity, and, normally, share the same proper name (Doležel 1998: 225–6; Lewis 1968, 1986: 20ff.). More specifically, counterparts share "essential" properties (Rescher and Parks 1973): in our case, the husband in *Mrs Midas* shares with the mythological Midas the property of maleness, the acquisition of the gold touch, and, possibly, the name Midas. The two characters are quite different, however, in terms of other "accidental" properties: their social status, the historical period they live in, and so on.

The intertextual reference made in the title of the poem, in other words, signals that the world it projects is parasitical on the world of the myth, as well as on the readers' knowledge of the *contemporary* state of the actual world (the relevance of the latter is immediately relevant from the use of *Mrs* in the title and from the opening lines of the poem). In section 4 below, I will argue that the poem's text world can be seen as a "blend" of the world of the myth and contemporary reality (Fauconnier and Turner 2002). In possible-worlds terms, readers furnish the world of the poem by combining elements from their knowledge of the world of the myth with their knowledge of the world they live in. This results in a world where a man who has acquired the gold touch is driven by car to a caravan in a remote location so that his "gift" will be kept private and relatively under control. More crucially, the narrator in the poem never explicitly refers to her husband's acquisition of the gold touch: even in the sixth stanza, there are only relatively vague references to the granting of a wish and to gold. Readers, however, can import some of the details about Midas's wish for the gold touch from their knowledge of the myth. In fact, thanks to the title of the poem, they are likely to do this right from the beginning of the poem. This may lead to some degree of dramatic irony when the narrator initially describes the strange effects of her husband touching the tree in the garden, the doorknob, the blinds, and then sitting down to eat corn on the cob. Indeed, our understanding of the sequence of events at the dinner

---

7. Both the mythological and historical Midas probably had Midas as their first name, of course, but here this first name is used in the slot normally occupied by a surname.

table in the lines I quoted above (the first two lines of the fourth stanza) relies on a combination of our general knowledge of reality (when a meal is served, people start eating) and on our intertextual knowledge of the world of the myth (the corn on the cob turns into gold as soon as the husband touches it).

The fact that we imagine text worlds by importing knowledge from a wide range of relevant sources does not mean, however, that they are complete sets of states of affairs, which assign a truth value to any given proposition. While default information can be imported on the basis of the principle of minimal departure (whether from the actual world or from other fictional worlds), many "gaps" are left, as Doležel (1998) puts it, in our knowledge of individual text worlds. For example, we do not know whether Ovid's King Midas had a wife, nor do we know how long the husband in Duffy's poem managed to survive living in the caravan.[8] The extent and nature of these gaps vary depending on the text and genre (Doležel 1998: 169ff.). Mythological stories such as Ovid's do not dwell on the mental and personal lives of characters, so that we know little or nothing about Midas's thoughts and feelings, his domestic routines, his sex life, and so on. Poems such as *Mrs Midas* are more introspective, but leave gaps in other areas: for example, as I mentioned earlier, there is no specification of the geographical area or town in which the narrated events take place.

In fact, I would argue that a combination of the parasitical nature of fictional worlds and of their inevitable incompleteness explains how Duffy avoids potentially jarring incongruities in the world of *Mrs Midas*, and in several other poems in the collection. The world of the poem appears to correspond in all respects with our contemporary "actual" world, apart from the crucial detail of containing an individual who possesses the gold touch as a result of the realisation of a wish. No detail is provided about who granted the wish or how. Readers can, of course, fill

---

8. Literary theorists differ on whether these "gaps" are purely epistemological (e.g. we do not know whether the King Midas of the myth had children) or, at least in part, ontological (e.g. there is no answer to the question of whether the King Midas of the myth had children). I hold the latter position. Significantly, Ryan (1991: 48ff.) runs into difficulties when she argues that, as a result of the application of the principle of minimal departure, text worlds are ontologically complete, and has to introduce a series of supplementary rules in order to exclude computers from the world of Jabberwocky, or the writings of Thomas Aquinas from the world of Little Red Riding Hood.

this gap by importing material from the world of the Midas myth, and include a god or supernatural entity who granted the wish. On the other hand, they do not have to, as no supernatural presence is explicitly mentioned, or, in Doležel's (1998) terms, "authenticated" as existing in the text world: the sudden appearance of Bacchus in the protagonists' garden would clash considerably with the contemporary setting of the poem. Different readers will furnish the text world differently in this respect, but it is possible to accept that the husband had a bizarre and extraordinary wish granted while leaving indeterminate the exact details of how this happened. This indeterminacy is further allowed by the fact that, in the poem, the gold touch is not removed, and no reference is made to anybody the husband could go back to in order to cancel his wish.[9]

As Eco (1990: 78–9) puts it, the construction of fictional text worlds requires some degree of "flexibility and superficiality" on the part of readers. We do not need to know who granted the husband's wish in order to interpret and appreciate *Mrs Midas*. Furthermore, in imagining both text worlds, we also need to accept that a human being can acquire the gold touch without expecting to understand how this changed his biology, or the exact chemical composition of the objects he touched. In constructing the text world of *Mrs Midas*, we have to accept that the husband managed to carry on living even though, strictly speaking, he should not be able to eat or drink. In other words, we tend to focus on the intelligible aspects of fictional worlds, and we do not pursue the unintelligible ones in all their details and possible implications (Maitre 1983: 17). Among other things, this relative flexibility and superficiality explains why fictional worlds can include logical impossibilities, such as contradictory states of affairs (e.g. an event is presented as both having happened and not having happened) or the violation of ontological boundaries (e.g. characters being aware of the presence of the author who created them) (see Ashline 1995; Eco 1990; Doležel 1998; Ronen 1994; Ryan 1991).

Differences in the nature and amount of knowledge available to readers will result in differences in their interpretation and appreciation of the

---

9. It is interesting that the first two stanzas of the poem contain three striking and novel instances of personification: the kitchen is personified in lines 3–4 (*relaxed, its steamy breath ...*); the window is personified in line 5 (*wiped the other's glass like a brow*); and the ground is personified in lines 7–9 (*The way the dark of the ground seems to drink ...*). These personifications can potentially be interpreted as hinting at some kind of awareness of a supernatural presence, but without referring to it explicitly.

text. Any readers of *Mrs Midas* who are completely unfamiliar with the Midas myth would probably have difficulties in constructing the world of the poem, at least initially, due to the rather inexplicit way in which the acquisition of the gold touch is narrated. They would of course also be unable to perceive the similarities and differences between the poem's text world and the world of the myth, and the subtle irony in the way in which parallels and contrasts are set up. Conversely, the greater the reader's knowledge of the original myth, the greater their ability to notice multiple connections between the two text worlds, such as between the twig in Ovid's story and the pear tree twig in the poem, between Midas's devotion to Pan in Ovid's story and the husband's claim that he can hear the music of Pan in the poem, and so on.

Finally, it is important to mention that there are also cases where the construction of a text world requires knowledge that is not yet included in the readers' encyclopaedia, so that readers will, for a time at least, find it difficult to construct a text world while reading. For example, at the beginning of Kazuo Ishiguro's novel *Never Let Me Go*, which I mentioned earlier, the first-person narrator takes for granted knowledge about a world where human beings are cloned and raised in institutions so that, when they reach adulthood, they can start donating organs to "ordinary people". Initially, the world described by the narrator is relatively unfamiliar and opaque, but the reader gradually acquires the knowledge and the vocabulary to imagine it as a disturbing potential alternative of the "actual" world.

3.2. The characteristics and internal structure of text worlds

The possible-worlds framework has been exploited to account for a number of fictional phenomena, including the definition of fiction itself. Ryan (1991: 21ff), in particular, describes the production of fictional texts as a kind of "gesture", which shifts the relevant frame of reference from a system of worlds centred on the "actual" world to a system of worlds centred on an alternative possible world. The use of the expression "system of worlds" is crucial here. Although I have so far referred to the "text world" of Ovid's story and the "text world" of *Mrs Midas*, those worlds, like fictional worlds generally, are better seen as "universes", consisting of multiple worlds. One of these worlds counts as the "actual domain" of the story, while other worlds are non-actual, i.e. they are desired, imagined, etc. by characters. In *Mrs Midas*, for example, the husband's acquisition of the gold touch occurs in the actual domain, while the woman only gives birth to a "golden" child in a dream world. Possible-worlds theorists have produced useful typologies of fictional worlds by exploring the potential variation in the internal structure of text worlds (I will continue to use this term for simplicity's sake), and their relationship with the actual world.

For example, mythological stories such as Ovid's project text worlds in which the actual domain is split into two spheres, the human sphere inhabited by human beings and the supernatural sphere inhabited by the gods. The two spheres are different and separate, but there is constant interaction between their inhabitants, and the gods regularly interfere with the lives of human beings, as in the case of Midas. Such worlds have been described as "dyadic" worlds (Doležel 1998: 128ff.) or "salient" structures (Pavel 1986: 54ff.). Because of the indeterminacy surrounding the granting of the wish in the world of *Mrs Midas*, however, it is not clear whether the actual domain of the poem can be described as a dyadic structure. As I mentioned earlier, the explicit insertion of a supernatural domain would clash with an otherwise realistic and contemporary setting, and the intertextual reference to the myth is sufficient to import the granting of the gold touch without specifying any further details.

3.3. Types of impossibility

What the text worlds of the poem and Ovid's story definitely share, however, is the "impossible" event around which both stories revolve, namely the acquisition of the gold touch on the part of a male human being as a result of a wish. In logic, a world is regarded as "possible", and therefore accessible from the "actual" world, if it complies with the laws of logic. Narratologists working within a possible-worlds framework have extended the logical notion of possibility to account for the different types of impossibility that may occur in fictional worlds. Ryan (1991), in particular, has proposed a typology of fictional and non-fictional genres based on nine types of accessibility relations between the actual world and the world that counts as actual within a textual universe: *identity of properties, identity of inventory, compatibility of inventory, chronological compatibility, physical compatibility, taxonomic compatibility, logical compatibility, analytical compatibility* and *linguistic compatibility* (Ryan 1991: 32ff.). Non-fictional texts project worlds that are supposed to correspond to the "actual" world, and therefore fulfil all these criteria. Different fictional genres project worlds that break different combinations of accessibility relations.

Both Ovid's story and *Mrs Midas* project worlds that break the relation of physical compatibility, since the existence of the "gold touch" is incompatible with the natural laws of the actual world. As such, in Ryan's terms, both worlds are physically impossible. From the perspective of modern readers, both text worlds also break the relation of identity of inventory: the "actual" world does not contain Bacchus or Silenus (although it might have contained a King Midas without the gold touch); it also does not contain the two main characters in *Mrs Midas*. However, the inclusion of the god Bacchus and the satyr Silenus also makes the world of Ovid's story taxonomically impossible, for modern readers at least, since these types of entities are not part of the actual world. In contrast, as I have said before, the poem leaves the presence of supernatural entities indeterminate. If the King Midas of the myth is seen as a counterpart of a historical Midas, the world of the myth also breaks the relation of identity of properties, since the "same" individual has different properties in the text world as opposed to the real world.

Ryan's other accessibility relations can account for the characteristics of a variety of other genres. For example, realistic novels, and historical novels in particular, project worlds that only break the relation of identity of inventory, by including individuals who do not exist in the actual world. The worlds of science fiction tend to be both chronologically and taxonomically impossible: they are normally located at a point in time that is future with respect to the relevant state of the actual world, and they typically include a variety of objects that do not (yet?) exist in the actual world. The relation of logical compatibility accounts for fictional worlds that break logical laws, for example by presenting two contradictory states of affairs as simultaneously true. This is the case in Robert Pinget's novel *Le Libera*, where a character is described as being both dead and alive. Logical impossibilities may also result from the existence of time travel within a fictional world. In J. K. Rowling's *Harry Potter and The Prisoner of Azkaban* (2000), for example, Harry travels back in time and therefore ends up being simultaneously agent and observer of his action of conjuring up a Patronus. The types of impossibility that most characterise the Harry Potter novels, however, are physical and taxonomical, whereas some postmodernist works are primarily characterised by a variety of violations of logical laws (see Ashline 1995).

3.4. The structure and development of the textual universe

As I mentioned earlier, possible-worlds approaches to fiction and literature also include accounts of the internal structure of text worlds. Building on earlier models (notably Doležel 1976), Ryan has suggested that texts project "universes" or systems of worlds, where a world functioning as the "actual" domain is surrounded by a variety of alternative possible worlds that primarily correspond to the beliefs, desires, obligations and dreams of characters. More specifically, Ryan (1991: 114ff.) has proposed four main types of "sub-worlds" or "private" worlds, namely:

- *Knowledge/belief worlds*: alternative versions of the actual domain that a character believes to be true;
- *Obligation worlds*: alternative versions of the actual domain that a character feels obliged to bring about or prevent as a consequence of his or her moral principles or awareness of social rules;
- *Wish worlds*: alternative versions of the actual domain that a character wishes to realise in order to fulfil his or her desires, or those of a group he or she belongs to;
- *Fantasy worlds*: alternative versions of the actual domain that a character dreams, fantasizes or hallucinates about; these also include fictions invented by characters.

Ryan (1991: 119ff.) shows how this kind of approach to the description of the internal structure of text worlds can account for plot development, and for some aspects of the "tellability" of stories. In order for a plot to get going, there needs to be some kind of conflict between at least two of the worlds within the textual universe. The plot in both our versions of the Midas story starts because of the formation of a wish world on the part of Midas/the male protagonist where he has the gold touch, and can therefore become immensely rich. In Ovid's version, this wish world is explicitly realised by Bacchus, while in *Mrs Midas* it is simply presented as having been realised. At this point, there is no longer a conflict between the wish world and the actual domain, but other conflicts arise which the male protagonist had not anticipated, and which require action. In Ryan's terms (1991: 124ff.), a plot is constituted by a series of successive states of the system of worlds that make up the textual universe. Although the plots of our two texts arguably start with the realisation of similar wish worlds, they proceed in different ways, both in terms of what sub-worlds are focused on and in terms of the successive changes in the content and mutual relationships of these sub-worlds.

In Ovid's story, Midas realises that the new state of the actual domain (in which he has the gold touch) makes it impossible for him to realise a more fundamental wish world, namely one in which he is able to satisfy his hunger and thirst, and, ultimately, to survive. He then expresses, in the form of a prayer to Bacchus, a new wish world, in which he no longer has the gold touch. His admission that he has sinned can be seen as a belated realisation that his initial wish world clashes with an obligation world in which one is supposed to be content with what he has. Bacchus brings about this new wish world and imposes on Midas a new obligation world, in which he washes himself in the waters of the river Pactolus. Midas realises this obligation world and then changes his life in the actual domain, by going to live in the woods and worshipping Pan. Although the narrator warns us that Midas will again be harmed by his foolishness in the future, this episode ends with equilibrium within the textual universe, i.e. with no obvious conflicts among the worlds that make up the textual universe. Throughout, we are given access to the private sub-worlds of Midas and, to a lesser extent, Bacchus, but these sub-worlds are relatively sketchy in their content. For example, the sentence *He dreamed of everything turned to gold, and his hopes soared beyond the limits of his imagination* arguably refers to imagined states of affairs that can be described either as fantasy worlds or wish worlds, but these worlds are not furnished or explored in much detail within the narrative.

In the poem, the story is narrated in the first person by "Mrs Midas" and there is therefore no direct access to the husband's private worlds. In the sixth stanza, however, he is reported as talking about the expression and realisation of his wish world, which is of course the crucial plot development in both texts. Although we can infer (from both general and intertextual knowledge) that the husband belatedly realises how the granting of the wish contrasts with other more basic wish worlds (where he lives easily, comfortably, etc.), there is no reference to him formulating a "counter" wish world, let alone obtaining the cancellation of his gift. In the penultimate stanza, he is reported as saying that he can hear *the music of Pan in the woods*, which is clearly perceived by the female protagonist as some kind of delusion or hallucination, signalling her husband's descent into madness. In Ovid's story, Pan is part of the supernatural sphere within the actual domain, and Midas appears to achieve some degree of (temporary) redemption by giving up his wealth and worshipping him. In *Mrs Midas*, Pan seems to be part of the actual domain in the husband's knowledge world, but is viewed as part of a fantasy world by the female protagonist. Hence, the husband's reference to Pan turns out to represent the final straw for her, resulting in permanent loss of contact between the two characters.

The whole point of the poem, however, is to introduce the voice and perspective of Midas's hypothetical wife. The poem therefore focuses on the way in which the text's "actual domain" contrasts in various ways with her own private sub-worlds. In the first few stanzas, the narrator describes her initial puzzlement and incomprehension at the strange effects that her husband seems to have on the objects he touches. At the end of the second stanza, there is a specific reference to a (mistaken) knowledge world in which he is putting fairy lights in the pear tree. Here the character's interpretation humorously contrasts with what readers have already been able to infer about the actual domain from the title of the story (i.e. that the husband is turning into gold everything he touches). There is also some irony in the contrast between what we know has happened and the thoughts the woman remembers to have had in line 15, which also involve intertextual references to a historical event (*the Field of the Cloth of Gold*) and a fictional character (Mrs Macready, the Professor's housekeeper in C. S. Lewis's *The Chronicles of Narnia*, who tells the Pevensie children not to touch anything in the house). After discovering what has actually happened, the female protagonist presents herself as acting rationally and efficiently in the actual domain, for example by moving the cat out of harm's way, refusing to share a bed with her husband, and finally moving him permanently into their caravan in the country. On the other hand, the fact that we have access to her mental life shows how the realisation of her husband's wish has created some irresolvable conflicts between the actual domain and her private worlds. After narrating how she relegated her husband to the spare room, she tells of their passionate sex life in stanza seven, and, at the end of the poem, poignantly declares that what she misses most is *his hands, his warm hands on my skin, his touch*. In Ryan's terms, this suggests that the woman is left with an unrealisable wish world: she still desires a situation where her husband can touch her, but knows that his touch would now kill her. Interestingly, in stanza eight the narrator reports a dream in which she gives birth to a golden child, and her breasts are filled with burning (molten gold?) milk. This is a fantasy world which can be seen as having been triggered by the memory and/or desire for sex with a man who now has the gold touch. On the basis of their background knowledge, readers may also attribute to the woman a desire to have children with her husband, which would constitute another unrealisable wish world in the new state of the actual domain.

Overall, the point of the Midas myth in its classical version was to condemn and expose as foolish an excessive desire for wealth. It can be argued that, in Ovid's story, Midas belatedly understands that a realisation of his "gold touch" wish world makes other, more important wish worlds impossible, so that he has to review a previous belief world in which wealth makes people happy. In *Mrs Midas*, all of this is also present, partly via the importation of material from the readers' relevant intertextual frame, and partly due to explicit comments: in stanza six, for example, the woman is presented as reminding her husband that, in spite of its perceived value, gold *feeds no one [...] slakes no thirst*. As I mentioned earlier, however, the narrator later declares that what she resents the most is not *the idiocy or greed, but lack of thought for me*. This implies that, in her own world view, her husband's "gold touch" wish world should have clashed, amongst other things, with an obligation world in which he should not do anything that would harm her and their relationship. However, she now realises that the husband did not have such an obligation world, or, in any case, put his personal, private wish world first, and acted (or rather wished) accordingly. The poem, therefore, emphasizes the conflicts between the woman's private sub-worlds and her husband's private sub-worlds on the one hand, and between the woman's private sub-worlds and the new state of the actual domain on the other. This shifts the emphasis from a stigmatisation of foolishness and greed in the myth to a stigmatisation of male self-centredness in the poem, and foregrounds female experience.

Ryan (1991: 148 ff.) interestingly argues that what makes stories "tellable" is the richness of the domain of the "virtual" within the system of worlds projected by a text, namely the presence of a variety of private sub-worlds which remain unrealised. These private sub-worlds can form "embedded narratives" in the minds of characters, corresponding to events that are imagined, desired or feared but not realised in the actual domain. Ryan expresses this view of tellability via her "principle of diversification": "seek the diversification of possible worlds within the narrative universe" (Ryan 1991: 156). In the case of Ovid's story, it can be argued that Midas's initial wish world represents an embedded narrative in which the gold touch makes him happy, rich, and powerful for the rest of his life. The realisation of the wish world, however, leads to very different consequences, so that he has to ask for its cancellation and ends up living a very different life to what he had expected. The challenge for poems such as *Mrs Midas* is to justify the re-telling of the story. In Ryan's terms, Duffy achieves this by expanding the domain of the virtual to include the private sub-worlds and embedded narratives of Midas' wife. Indeed, the constellation of worlds projected by the poem is not just different from that of Ovid's story but larger and more diversified. The contrasts between subworlds in the world of the myth remain in the new version, but, as I have shown, new sub-world contrasts are included, resulting in quite a different story with a different overall message. While Ovid's story ends with (temporary) harmony amongst the worlds that make up the textual universe, Duffy's poem ends with the expression of a wish world that will never be realised, namely a state of affairs where the woman can still experience and enjoy her husband's touch. This is arguably a crucial factor in the poem's potential for emotional involvement on the readers' part: in Ovid's story, Midas is rescued from the consequences of his own foolishness, while in the poem the woman ends up living in sadness and regret as a result of somebody else's foolishness.

3.5. Possible-worlds theory and further contrasts between the two texts

The concepts I have discussed so far capture a number of central characteristics of the text worlds of Ovid's story and *Mrs Midas*, and several important aspects of the relationship between the poem and the classical myth. However, this kind of analysis does not exhaust the richness and complexity of the two texts. More specifically, it does not successfully account for the many subtle manifestations and consequences of intertextuality in Duffy's poem.

After presenting her typology of genres based on her nine accessibility relations, Ryan (1991: 43) goes on to add that some "additional factors of semantic diversification" need to be considered in order to account for "accepted generic labels". The three factors she considers (thematic focus, stylistic filtering and probabilistic emphasis) are all relevant to the contrasts between the two text worlds and the ways in which they are linguistically projected. "Thematic focus" is to do with the selection of "setting, characters, and events from the history and inventory of the textual universe to form a plot or a message" (Ryan 1991: 43). This factor can account for how the poem contrasts with the mythological narrative by focusing in more detail on objects and settings (the steamy kitchen, the cat, the golden animals in stanza ten) and on the female protagonist's mental life. "Stylistic filtering" "determines in which light these objects will be presented, the impression they will create on the reader" (Ryan 1991: 43). This can account for the stylistic contrasts between the two texts: Ovid's story was written in dactylic hexameters, and the narrative has the elevated and rather moralistic and detached tone that is characteristic of the genre. *Mrs Midas* is both more introspective and more humorous. Some potential for humour results from the fact itself that a physically impossible event is placed within a realistic contemporary setting. This potential is exploited throughout via the addition of humorous detail, such as the reference to the fact that the female protagonist *did not mind* if the toilet was turned into gold, or her claim that her husband would turn their spare room into *the tomb of Tutankhamun*. Finally "probabilistic emphasis" is to do with whether texts focus on plausible or implausible events. While the presence of the supernatural and physically impossible transformations are very much at the centre of the mythological story, the poem, as I have already explained, does not explicitly mention any supernatural intervention, and focuses of the aftermath of the impossible transformation, both in practical and emotional terms.

Doležel's (1998: 199 ff.) work on intertextuality can also add a further edge to the analysis of *Mrs Midas*. In discussing "postmodernist rewrites" of classic works, he says that they

> *re*design, *re*locate, *re*evaluate the classic protoworld. Undoubtedly, this *re*making is motivated by political factors, in the wide, postmodernist sense of "politics". (Doležel 1998: 206; emphases in original)

Mrs Midas displays elements of all three types of postmodernist rewrites identified by Doležel: the "transposition" of the world of the myth to a different temporal and spatial setting; the "expansion" of the protoworld by filling in and developing the role of Midas's wife, who reacts both rationally and creatively to the consequences of the realisation of her husband's wish; and the polemical construction of a different text world, in which Midas is not relieved of the gold touch, and his wife ends up abandoning him to his lonely fate. These transformations of the original world of the myth convey the kind of political message that Doležel associates with postmodernism: on the one hand, they expose the male-centeredness of Western culture and the weaknesses of men, while on the other hand they foreground the suffering and resilience of women. As Pavel (1986: 145) has put it, "literary artefacts often are not projected into fictional distance just to be neutrally beheld but [...] they vividly bear upon the beholder's world".

While a possible-worlds analysis often needs to be complemented by a detailed textual analysis, it is clear that possible-worlds theory provides the concepts and terminology to account for some central aspects of the relationship between the worlds of *Mrs Midas* and Ovid's story. I will now move on to consider some approaches to the analysis of text worlds that are more explicitly "cognitive" in orientation, and that account more successfully for particular phenomena, such as the online construction of "worlds" as mental representations during text processing, the progressive tracking of characters in plot development, and the way in which *Mrs Midas* merges the Midas myth with some aspects of contemporary reality.

4.   Cognitive poetic approaches to text worlds

Over the last few decades, the study of text worlds has been enriched by developments in cognitive linguistics, and particularly by research in an area at the interface between linguistics, literary studies, and cognitive science, which has come to be known as "cognitive poetics" or "cognitive stylistics" (see Gavins and Steen 2003; Semino and Culpeper 2002; Stockwell 2002; Tsur 1992, 2003). In contrast with other areas of literary studies, the goals of cognitive poetics include providing accounts of *how* readers comprehend and interpret (literary) texts, namely how they imagine text worlds and characters, how they respond to incongruities and ambiguities, how they perceive sound patterns, and so on. As a consequence, cognitive poetics is sometimes criticised as just another complex metalanguage for text analysis, especially by those literary scholars who primarily value research that proposes new interpretations of texts or literary phenomena (e.g. Jackson 2005; Hall 2003).

As I showed in the previous section, possible-worlds theory approaches text worlds as the "product" of comprehension, namely as the relatively stable outcome of processes of interpretation. Possible-worlds theorists do not, in other words, aim to account for how text worlds are incrementally constructed by readers or listeners during online text processing. Some recent work in cognitive linguistics and cognitive poetics has attempted to tackle precisely this complex phenomenon. Since, for reasons of space, I cannot do justice to all the work that has been conducted in this area, I will briefly discuss three approaches that are currently particularly influential in literary text analysis, namely Fauconnier's (1994, 1997) theory of mental spaces, Werth's (1999) text worlds theory, and Emmott's (1997) contextual frames theory. I will then discuss in more detail the relevance of Fauconnier and Turner's (2002) theory of "blending" or "conceptual integration", by applying it to the world projected by *Mrs Midas*.

4.1. The incremental construction of text worlds

Fauconnier's (1994, 1997) theory accounts for text processing in terms of the construction of networks of mental representations known as "mental spaces", which are defined as "small conceptual packets constructed as we think and talk, for purposes of local understanding and action. They are interconnected, and can be modified as thought and discourse unfold" (Fauconnier and Turner 1996: 113). Mental spaces are constructed on the basis of background knowledge on the one hand and textual references to time, place, modality, entities and actions on the other. In Fauconnier's (1997: 35) terms, "linguistic forms" are "(partial and underdetermined) instructions" for constructing interconnected sets of mental spaces.

Within mental space theory, for example, the first sentence of *Mrs Midas* (*It was late September*) functions as a "space builder", which sets up two mental spaces: a "base space" which corresponds to the time and place in which the narration takes place, and which includes the narrator; and another space which is temporally anterior to the base space (due to the use of the past tense) and located at an unspecified time towards the end of an unspecified September. The rest of the stanza indicates that this space contains a counterpart of the narrator in the base space (referred to via the deictic pronoun *I*) and adds further material to the space, in terms of location, entities, and so on.

The progressive construction of the poem's text world involves the development of existing spaces and the addition of new ones, which will be connected to each other via relationships of temporal, spatial or epistemic distance. A number of temporal space builders indicate the connections between the various mental spaces that make up what Fauconnier (1997: 50) has called the "'reality' within fiction" (and which corresponds to the text's "actual domain" of possible-worlds theory): *after we'd both calmed down, that night, and then, now*. Other space builders trigger the construction of mental spaces that are epistemically distant from the base. For example, *I dreamt* in stanza eight triggers the construction of a "dream" space that is ontologically distant from the base and from the other spaces that are temporally linked to the base. This space contains a counterpart of the character/narrator, as well as an entity (the golden baby) and an event (giving birth) that are not included in the networks of spaces that make up the reality within the fiction set up by the poem.

I cannot do justice to the richness and complexity of Fauconnier's theory, nor to its multiple applications. For the purposes of this chapter, the crucial point is that, in mental space theory, a text world corresponds to the network of mental spaces that readers construct while reading a text.

Whereas mental space theory was developed in order to account for general linguistic and cognitive phenomena, Werth's (1999) text worlds theory is more focused on the analysis of fiction and literature, even though it also aims to apply to text comprehension generally. Werth makes a distinction between what he calls the "discourse world" and the "text world": the discourse world is the context in which communication takes place (whether face-to-face or otherwise), and is inhabited by participants in communication (e.g. author and reader); the "text world" is a mental representation that is constructed on the basis of the discourse, and is inhabited by characters and other entities. A text world normally includes many interconnected sub-worlds, i.e. mental representations of specific situations in specific settings (e.g. the kitchen vs. the car in the text world of *Mrs Midas*). Werth proposes three main types of sub-worlds: "deictic" sub-worlds, which result from switches in time and place from the situation that functions as the starting point of the text world (e.g. the switch from the kitchen to the bedroom in *Mrs Midas*); "attitudinal" sub-worlds, which correspond to the desires, beliefs and purposes of characters (e.g. the scenario desired by King Midas at the beginning of Ovid's story); and "epistemic" sub-worlds, which correspond to scenarios that are presented as hypothetical, probable, possible, and so on (Werth 1999: 216ff.).

In Werth's approach, the construction of text worlds relies on the participants' exploitation of relevant background knowledge, and is linguistically triggered by what Werth calls "world-building elements" and "function-advancing propositions" (Werth 1999: 180ff.). The former (which include Fauconnier's space builders) are used to "furnish" sub-worlds within text worlds, and consist of references to time, space, characters and entities (e.g. expressions such as *It was late September, the kitchen* and *he* in *Mrs Midas*). Function-advancing propositions, on the other hand, are expressions that indicate the states, actions and events that the story is about (e.g. *Bacchus ... granted his request, and presented him with his baneful gift* in Ovid's story). The totality of a text world normally includes a complex network of interconnected sub-worlds.

Emmott's (1997) theory of contextual frames is particularly concerned with the comprehension of narrative texts. Contextual frames are defined as mental representations that provide "'episodic' information about a configuration of characters, location, and time at any point in a narrative" (Emmott 1997: 104). They are "built up from the text itself and from inferences made from the text" (Emmott 1997: 121). The comprehension of Ovid's story, for example, involves the construction of a series of successive contextual frames, including: a frame involving Bacchus and Midas, and in which Bacchus grants Midas the gold touch; a frame involving Midas and his servants, and in which Midas finds he cannot eat or drink, a frame in which Midas washes himself in the river Pactolus, and so on.

Emmott's central argument is that

> a reader needs to monitor contextual information in order to keep track of continuity and change within a fictional world. I also suggest that a reader needs to be actively conscious of contextual information all the time, rather than having to stop and access information when each new sentence is read. (Emmott 1997: 104)

Within Emmott's theory, the frame that is focused on by the stretch of text one is reading at a particular point is the "primed" frame, and all the entities contained in the frame (notably the characters) are also primed. This means that we are aware of their presence even when they are not explicitly mentioned. In the first four sentences of the fourth stanza of *Mrs Midas*, for example, the husband is the "overt" character, since he is explicitly mentioned. The wife is "covert", but she is primed nevertheless, as she is part of the primed "mealtime" frame. This explains why, although she is not explicitly mentioned, we are aware of her presence, and we imagine her likely reaction in observing what is happening to her husband.

As we read, Emmott argues, we build up a "central directory" of the characters in the text world, and we become progressively aware of many contextual frames, only one of which is primed at each particular point in text processing (Emmott 1997: 121 ff.). Some frames may of course be disbanded when we know that characters have left a particular location. For example, in *Mrs Midas* the sentence *He came into the house* signals that the frame in which the husband is in the garden is no longer current. However, other frames may persist, so that readers can switch between frames while reading. For example, the second sentence of the seventh stanza in *Mrs Midas* (*I put a chair against my door*) sets up a primed frame in which the female protagonist is alone in her bedroom. The following sentence switches to a contextual frame in which the husband is in the spare room. This is followed by some "unframed text" which provides information about the two characters' previous sex life (lines 3–6 in stanza six) and about the narrator's attitude to living *with a heart of gold* (lines 3–5 in stanza seven).[10] Then in the second sentence of the eighth stanza (*That night I dreamt*) we switch back to the frame in which the woman is in her bedroom, which was still available, although temporarily "unprimed". This is in turn followed by a new "dream" frame, which is part of the character's imagination (Emmott 1997: 149).

Text belonging to different genres may exhibit different kinds of phenomena in relation to contextual frames. In realistic genres, characters can only be "bound in" or "out" of frames via references to their movement from one location to another. For example, the sentence *He came into the house* in *Mrs Midas* binds the husband out of the previous "garden"

---

10. Emmott (1997: 238) uses the term "unframed" to describe stretches of text that do not refer to specific occasions, and hence do not need to be monitored by a contextual frame.

frame and into the "kitchen" frame in which the female character was previously alone. In contrast, in Ovid's story Bacchus suddenly appears in the "meal" scene when Midas utters a prayer to him: stories with a supernatural element, in other words, have different conventions for binding characters in and out of contextual frames (Emmott 1997: 153). There may also be ambiguity in the content of contextual frames (Emmott 1997: 212). For example, in *Mrs Midas* the use of the passive *granted* in relation to the realisation of the husband's wish in stanza six leads to "frame participant ambiguity": we do not know who else (if anyone) was present in that particular frame.

The strength of cognitive linguistic approaches such as those proposed by Fauconnier, Werth and Emmott is that they account for text worlds as complex mental representations that are incrementally set up by readers (or listeners) during text processing. While possible-worlds theorists such as Ryan have proposed typologies of sub-worlds within fictional worlds, cognitive linguists provide detailed classifications of the kinds of linguistic expressions that act as triggers for the online construction of mental representations. My brief overview shows how all three approaches can account for the progression of the plot in the actual domains of both texts, as well as for imaginary scenarios such as dreams and wishes. They can also elegantly show how *Mrs Midas* triggers the construction of a more complex constellation of spaces, sub-worlds or frames than Ovid's story, and how the poem differs from the classical story by being focused on the woman, who is present in most scenes. Although I have not been able to show this, all three approaches cater for the deictic shifts involved in the use of direct speech or thought presentation, and for a variety of other phenomena. Indeed, all three approaches have been successfully applied to the analysis of a variety of texts (e.g. Dancygier 2004, 2005; Emmott 2003; Gavins 2003, 2007).

On the other hand, as I have mentioned earlier, cognitive poetic approaches to text worlds often do not appeal to literary scholars who are interested in novel interpretations of texts, or in aspects of interpretation such as allusion, political undertones, and so on. All three approaches (and particularly Fauconnier's and Werth's) also involve quite a complex analytical machinery, with visual representations that often become impossibly complicated when applied to stretches of text longer than a few sentences (see also Semino 2003). However, as I mentioned earlier, it is important to distinguish between different research goals in literary studies: accounting for *how* readers understand (literary) texts is a different enterprise from proposing new interpretations of texts. Nonetheless, it is desirable that existing approaches in cognitive poetics are refined and extended to account more systematically for a wider range of phenomena, such as humour, emotional involvement, ideological messages, and so on.

4.2. "Blending" and text worlds

Mental space theorists have discussed a variety of mental operations involving the "mapping" or "projection" of material across mental spaces (Fauconnier 1997). These operations include particularly "conceptual blending" or "conceptual integration", which is described as a basic and fundamental cognitive process whereby material from two or more "input" mental spaces is projected into a separate space, the "blend". This blended space inherits structure from the input spaces and also develops its own "emergent" structure (Fauconnier and Turner 2002). One of Fauconnier and Turner's (2002) examples is a humorous counterfactual statement that apparently circulated in Washington D.C. in 1998, a year after the release of the blockbuster film *Titanic*, and in the early stages of a new sexual scandal involving the US President Bill Clinton: "If Clinton were the *Titanic*, the iceberg would sink". This counterfactual statement clearly compares the US President to the ship that famously sank in 1912 after colliding with an iceberg, but suggests that Clinton's presidency will survive the sexual scandals (which indeed it did). Fauconnier and Turner use the notion of blending to explain how we make sense of this statement:

> The counterfactual blend has two input mental spaces – one with the *Titanic* and the other with President Clinton. There is partial cross-space mapping between these inputs: Clinton is the counterpart of the *Titanic* and the scandal is the counterpart of the iceberg. There is a blended space in which Clinton is the *Titanic* and the scandal is the iceberg. This blend is double-scope. It takes much of its organizing frame structure from the *Titanic* input space – it has a voyage by a ship towards a destination and it has the ship's running into something enormous in the water – but it takes crucial causal structure from the Clinton scenario: Clinton is not ruined but instead survives. [...] There is a generic space whose structure is taken as applying to both inputs: One entity involved in an activity motivated by some purpose encounters another entity that poses a threat to that activity. In the generic space, the outcome of that encounter is not specified. (Fauconnier and Turner 2002: 221–22)

Fauconnier and Turner (2002: 4) argue that, at the neural level, "mental spaces are sets of activated neuronal assemblies" and the mappings across spaces are "co-activation bindings of a certain kind". While the authors' optimistic claims about the psychological validity of the model in its current form has received some criticism (e.g. Gibbs 2000; Ritchie 2004), the theory does have considerable explanatory power. Fauconnier and Turner (2002) use it to explain a wide range of phenomena, including not only counterfactuals, but also metaphor, a variety of grammatical constructions, higher-level reasoning, mathematical thinking, and so on. More generally, they explain the phenomenon of human creativity in terms of the basic ability to bring together material from different mental spaces in order to arrive at new meaning. Indeed, blending theory is increasingly being applied to the analysis of literature and fiction, (e.g. the papers in *Language and Literature*, 15, 1, 2006), and has been used particularly to account for texts that bring together and merge different "stories" or situations (e.g. Freeman 2000; Semino 2006; Turner 2003). *Mrs Midas*, I will argue, can be described as one such text.

The text world projected by the poem can be seen as a blend that arises from the merging of two input spaces: the classical Midas story (which I will call input space 1), and a space that contains a prototypical representation of contemporary married life (which I will call input space 2).[11] As with the "Clinton/*Titanic*" example, material from *both* input spaces is projected into the blend, resulting in what Fauconnier and Turner call a "double-scope" blend (Fauconnier and Turner 2002: 131 ff.). The blend, however, also contains "emergent" structure that is not projected from either input space. This emergent structure arises from the interaction of material from the two input spaces and from what Fauconnier and Turner call the "running" of the blend, i.e. from actions and events that are imagined as happening in the blend itself. I will now try to explain this in more detail. A (tentative) representation of the conceptual integration network is provided in figure 1.[12]

For the purposes of my analysis, I have modelled input space 1 on the version of the Midas myth provided by Ovid. This space contains Bac-

---

11. Strictly speaking, both Ovid's story and Duffy's poem project texts worlds that consist of multiple mental spaces, as I have already explained. In this analysis, however, I am using the notion of "space" for mental representations corresponding to whole text worlds. Turner (2003) also uses the notion of space in this way in his analysis of a variety of blended narratives.

12. I have not included the generic space as it does not crucially contribute to the analysis of the poem's text world as a blended space (see also Ritchie 2004).

INPUT SPACE 1: THE MIDAS MYTH IN OVID	INPUT SPACE 2: MARRIED LIFE IN CONTEMPORARY WORLD

1 Midas
2 Bacchus
3 Midas returns Silenus to Bacchus
4 Bacchus grants Midas a wish
5 Midas wishes for the 'gold touch'
6 Midas obtains the gold touch
7 Midas initially enjoys the gold touch:
    7.1 Twig
    7.2 Stone
    7.3 Earth
    7.4 Corn
    7.5 Apple
    7.6 Doorways
    7.7 Water
8 Midas dreams of turning everything to gold
9 The gold touch makes Midas's life impossible:
    9.1 Bread
    9.2 Meat
    9.3 Wine
10 Midas prays that the gold touch is removed
11 Bacchus removes the gold touch
12 Midas has to wash himself in river
13 River gleams with gold thereafter
14 Midas moves to the country
15 Midas worships Pan
	A Wife
	B Husband
	C Marital life
	D Physical intimacy, sex
	
	E Modern house, including:
	    E.1 Kitchen
	    E.2 Door knob
	    E.3 Blinds
	    E.4 Chairs
	    E.5 Toilet
	    E.6 Spare room
	
	F Domestic garden, including:
	    F.1 Pear trees (with twigs)
	
	G Possessions and activities, including:
	    G.1 Cooking
	    G.2 Food (corn-on-thecob)
	    G.3 Drink (wine)
	    G.4 Phone
	    G.5 Cigarette
	    G.6 Caravan
	    G.7 Car
	
	H Other: Italy, British history, Greek myths (Pan), etc.

BLEND: THE POEM'S TEXT WORLD

1/B Husband/Midas *A Wife/Midas's wife (Mrs Midas)* *C Marital life* *D Physical intimacy, sex* *E Modern house* *E.1 Kitchen* *F Domestic garden* *G Possessions and activities* *H Other: : Italy, British history, Greek myths (Pan), etc.*	Gold touch makes everyday marital life impossible (9 and C)
	Gold touch makes physical intimacy/sex impossible (9 and D)
	Wife locks cat in cellar and makes husband sleep in spare room, but allows him to go to the bathroom.

5(+B) Husband wishes for gold touch
6(+B) Husband obtains gold touch:
    7.1/F.1 Pear tree and twig
    7.6/E.1 Door knob
    E.2 Blinds
    E.4 Chair
9(+B) Gold touch makes husband's life impossible:
    G.2 Corn on the cob
    9.3/G.3 Wine
    G.5 Cigarette
	Wife dreams of giving birth to a golden child (8 and A)

	Wife drives husband to the country where he is going to live in their caravan on his own (14 and A, B, G6 and G7)
	Husband gets thin
	Wife visits for a while (and sees golden animals on the way)
	Husband says he can hear the music of Pan (15)
	Wife stops visiting
	Wife sells contents of house and moves somewhere else on her own
	Wife is particularly aggrieved by the husband's lack of concern for her
	Wife misses husband's touch

Figure 1. Conceptional integration network for *Mrs Midas*

chus and Midas as main characters, and all the entities and events mentioned by Ovid. In figure 1, the contents of input space 1 are numbered and presented in bold typeface. Input space 2, as I conceive of it, is modelled on a particular "slice" of our knowledge of contemporary reality, namely our schema for married life. It contains a husband and a wife, their marital life (including their sex life), and the entities and objects associated with modern living (contemporary house and garden, food, drink, possessions, etc.). It also potentially includes other aspects of reality, such as British history, Greek mythology, etc. In figure 1, the elements of input space 2 are italicised, and identified via the letters of the alphabet. The most crucial counterpart relation between the two input spaces is that between King Midas in input space 1 and the husband in input space 2. The wife, of course, has no counterpart in input space 1.

In my analysis, the poem's text world is a blend that results from the selective projection of material from both input spaces. Input space 2 provides the overall structure of the blend, which contains a wife and a husband living in the contemporary world. They have a house, a garden a sex life and a fairly typical lifestyle and set of possessions. Input space 1 provides the crucial elements of the first part of the Midas story, namely Midas himself, the granting of the gold touch, the initial enjoyment of the gold touch, the subsequent impossibility to eat and drink and the final move to the country. In Fauconnier and Turner's terms, projection from input space 1 is "selective": as I mentioned earlier, Bacchus is not explicitly projected, and, more importantly, the subsequent appeal to the god and the removal of the gold touch are not projected at all. In other words, only the elements that most characterise the Midas story are projected: the acquisition of the gold touch and its consequences. In all other respects, the blend is structured on the basis of input space 2. In figure 1, I have emboldened the material projected from input space 1, italicised the elements projected from input space 2, and combined bold and italics for those elements that can be seen as counterparts, namely Midas and the husband, and some smaller details that can be seen as being part of both input spaces (the tree/twig, the house door, etc.).[13]

The construction of a blend in which a contemporary married man is permanently granted the gold touch creates the potential for the addition of further material, which is not projected from either input space (see under-

---

13. In fact, the title of the poem itself can be seen as a blend: the name *Midas* comes from input space 1, while the role of wife signalled by *Mrs* comes from input space 2.

linings in figure 1). In input space 1, King Midas has the gold touch removed, while in input space 2 the gold touch does not exist. In the blend, the gold touch makes it impossible for the husband to carry on living normally, and for his wife to carry on living with him (including having sex with him). On the one hand, this leads to some practical actions aimed at minimising the consequences of the husband's new state. To begin with, the wife locks the cat in the cellar and makes the husband sleep in the spare room. Then she drives him to their caravan in the country, where she visits him until he starts telling her that he can hear the music of Pan. She then sells the contents of the house (presumably including several gold objects!) and moves to another place, but continues to miss their sex life and particularly his touch. As a consequence of this, she comes to resent her husband's lack of concern for her, more than his greed and foolishness. In Fauconnier and Turner's (2002) terms, this is the "emergent" structure that arises in the blend, and that characterises Duffy's particular "re-telling" of the classical myth.[14] The *contrast* between the two input spaces also generally accounts for the humorous potential of transposing a classical story to a contemporary setting, which Duffy exploits at various points.

In Fauconnier and Turner's model of conceptual integration, the blended space remains dynamically connected with the input spaces. This allows the further projection of material from the inputs to the blend, as well as, crucially, "backward projection" (Fauconnier and Turner 2002: 308), namely the modification of the inputs themselves as a result of inferences arising from the blend. This aspect of the theory can account for the general significance and potential effects of Duffy's poem. On the one hand, the blended story may lead to inferences concerning the absence of women from the world of the Midas myth in input space 1, and from myth generally. This may affect readers' perceptions and evaluations of the mythological story and of other texts, genres and traditions which ignore or background women's lives and experiences. On the other hand, the blended story constructs the husband as greedy, self-centred and rather pathetic, and the wife as sensitive and resourceful. It also shows how the consequences of the husband's greed do not just affect him, but also his

---

14. In figure 1, I have underlined as part of emergent structure some elements of the blended space that do have some relation with material from the input spaces. In such cases, however, the material was so radically transformed in the blend that I did not think it could be simply explained in terms of projection from the input spaces. I have, however, indicated the relations with elements from the input spaces in round brackets.

wife. This potentially leads to inferences that are projected back onto input space 2 and the "real-world" frames about men, women and marriage that are linked with it. These inferences may include, for example, the realisation that greed is not just foolish but also selfish, and that it potentially destroys personal relationships.[15] However, all of this obviously depends on the readers' previous assumptions and attitudes.

In the terms used in Cook (1994) and Semino (1997), the blending of two very different situations into a single text world results in a potential for "schema refreshment", i.e. the modification of readers' existing schemata. Schema refreshment would be rather dramatic for readers who had never thought of traditional stories as sexist, or of husbands as (sometimes) insensitive to their wives' needs. A less dramatic form of schema refreshment would be experienced by readers who, as a result of reading the poem, become more keenly aware of some aspects of "reality", including for example the dominance of male characters in traditional stories. Some readers may of course not experience schema refreshment at all: this will include both readers who share the assumptions that underlie Duffy's rewriting of the Midas myth, and readers who reject these assumptions altogether. For the latter kind of reader, the poem may in fact confirm existing (negative) assumptions about "feminism" or "political correctness".

Overall, I would argue that an analysis in terms of blending theory provides a satisfactory account of the intertextuality of the poem, and of the way the text world is constructed. It also usefully links the particular kind of creativity exhibited by Duffy's re-telling with more general and basic cognitive processes.

5.   Concluding remarks: future challenges for text world theory

Throughout this chapter I have shown how different approaches to the analysis of text worlds can account for a variety of important phenomena. The challenge for the future is to build on existing work in order to arrive at approaches that are both cognitively plausible on the one hand and able to cater for the nuances and complexities of fiction and literature on the other. In these concluding remarks, I will outline some of these challenges.[16]

---

15. In figure 1, I have not attempted to represent backward projection.
16. Gavins's *Text World Theory* (2007), which extends Werth's (1999) model, begins to tackle some of these challenges and raises some further issues. Unfortunately, Gavins's book was published just before this chapter went to press, and could not therefore be given the attention it deserves.

My analysis of *Mrs Midas* in relation to Ovid's story lends support to Doležel's observation that intertextuality may, in some cases, primarily involve the level of fictional worlds, rather than that of "texture" (Doležel 1998: 202). The intertextuality of Duffy's poem does not depend on familiarity with another text in particular, let alone with the specific way in which another text is written. Readers simply need to be familiar with the skeleton of the Midas myth (the acquisition of the gold touch and its consequences) in order to understand and appreciate the poem, at least in general terms. However, the more familiar readers are with the world of the myth, the greater their ability to notice and appreciate the many parallels that Duffy sets up with the mythical story (e.g. the twig, the meal, Pan, etc.). This kind of intertextuality is not a marginal phenomenon (think, for example, of the many different versions of traditional tales such as *Little Red Riding Hood*), but has not received as much attention as the kind of intertextuality that manifests itself primarily in the linguistic and stylistic make-up of texts.

The fact that intertexuality may involve parallels between texts worlds should not, however, obscure the fact that the particular *way* in which a reader imagines the text world projected by a particular text depends on the local and cumulative effects of specific linguistic choices and patterns. This is an area where existing approaches to text worlds are somewhat limited. The analyses of possible-worlds theorists are carried out at such a level of generality that they are largely independent of linguistic choices and patterns, or even of individual textual realisations. This is an advantage when considering "texts" in different media (e.g. film and ballet as well as written texts), but a disadvantage when trying to account for the workings of individual literary texts. Cognitive linguists do focus on linguistic choices as prompts for the construction of mental representations in the readers' minds, but they seldom consider the effects of variant linguistic realisations and textual patterns. As a consequence, an analysis of a prose summary of *Mrs Midas*, for example, could yield the same result both in terms of Ryan's (1991) possible-worlds approach and in terms of Fauconnier and Turner's (2002) blending theory.

I readily acknowledge, of course, that these analytical frameworks do not *aim* to account for stylistic differences and nuances in linguistic expression. However, this means that they cannot do full justice to many important aspects of interpretation that are inextricably linked with the construction of text worlds, such as attitudes, evaluations, associations, emotional impact, empathy, and so on. The undercurrent of humour in *Mrs Midas*, for example, is a central aspect of the way in which the text world is projected, but is difficult to account for in terms of existing approaches to text worlds (possibly with the exception of blending theory). Similarly, the use of a variety of expressions referring to gold and golden colours in the poem (e.g. *aurum, luteous, honeyed, lemon*) arguably plays a role in the projection of the poem's text world, but is not easy to include within current analytical approaches. Minimally, a text world analysis needs to be combined with a detailed stylistic analysis, in order to account more fully for the meaning potential of texts. However, it is also desirable that, as we refine and develop existing models, we increasingly strive to include more systematically the role of linguistic choices and patterns in the projection of text worlds.

Another challenge for text world theory is that of providing an adequate account of the "minds" of characters. Narratologists are increasingly emphasizing the centrality of fictional minds to the interpretation of narratives. Fludernik (1996), for example, has argued that:

> Experientiality in narrative as reflected in narrativity can [...] be said to combine a number of cognitively relevant factors, most importantly those of the presence of a human protagonist and her experience of events as they impinge on her situation and activities. [...] [S]ince humans are conscious human beings, (narrative) experientiality always implies – and sometimes emphatically foregrounds – the protagonist's consciousness. (Fludernik 1996: 30)

Similarly, Palmer has recently argued that "narrative fiction is, in essence, the presentation of fictional mental functioning' and that "the study of the novel is the study of fictional mental functioning" (Palmer 2004: 5; see also Margolin 2003). In understanding both our versions of the Midas story, we need to imagine the fictional mental functioning of characters, in order to make sense of their actions, reactions, and feelings (see Zunshine 2006). As I have shown, the two texts also differ considerably in terms of whose minds they focus on, and how much access they provide into the characters' mental lives.

The different approaches to text worlds I have discussed do take characters' minds into account. Characters' wishes, hypotheses, obligations, dreams, etc. are described as private sub-worlds in possible-worlds theory, as attitudinal sub-worlds in Werth's theory, and as different types of contextual frames and mental spaces in Emmott's and Fauconnier's theories respectively. However, texts such as *Mrs Midas* require a more fundamental inclusion of mind into a text-world analysis: we access the text world via the female protagonist only, both as a narrator (whose "voice" we "hear") and as a character (whose experiences we are exposed to). This crucially affects the particular *way* in which the text world is presented, including, for example, the many metaphors and similes in the poem, which reflect the female protagonist's experience (e.g. the personifications in the first two stanzas). The importance of viewpoint and mind is even more evident in narratives that are filtered through characters with limited or partly mistaken world views, such as Lok in Golding's *The Inheritors* or Bromden in Kesey's *One Flew Over the Cuckoo's Nest*. This kind of phenomenon is recognised in different approaches to text world theory. Doležel (1998: 152 ff.) discusses various degrees of "authentication" of entities and events in fictional worlds, and considers cases where the possibility of authentication fails altogether. Ryan (1991: 39–40) talks about texts that only give us access to a character's version of the actual domain, and points out how the actual domain may be difficult to construct, particularly in cases of unreliable narrators (Ryan 1991: 27). Fauconnier's mental space theory includes the idea that a mental space functions as "viewpoint" for the construction of other spaces, and this notion has started to be applied to narratological issues (see Dancygier 2004, 2005; Sanders and Redeker 1996). However, no existing approach caters fully for the potential complexity and variety of the relationships between fictional minds and text worlds in fiction and literature.

In conclusion, much important work on text worlds already exists, and many interesting challenges need to be met in future work.

References

Allén, Sture (ed.)
  1989   *Possible Worlds in Humanities, Arts and Sciences: Proceedings of Nobel Symposium 65*. New York/Berlin: de Gruyter.
Ashline, William L.
  1995   The problem of impossible fictions. *Style* 29: 215–34.
Bradley, Raymond and Norman Swartz
  1979   *Possible Worlds: An Introduction to Logic and its Philosophy*. Oxford: Basil Blackwell.
Cook, Guy
  1994   *Discourse and Literature*. Oxford: Oxford University Press
Dancygier, Barbara
  2004   Visual viewpoint, narrative viewpoint, and mental spaces in narrative fiction. In: Augusto Soares da Silva, AmadeusTorres and Miguel Goncalves (eds.), *Linguagem, Cultura e Cognicão: Estudos de Linguistica Cognitiva* vol. 1/2, 347–362. Coimbra: Livraria Almedina.

Dancygier, Barbara
2005 Blending and Narrative Viewpoint: Jonathan Raban's Travels through Mental Spaces. *Language and Literature* 14(2): 99–127.

Divers, John
2002 *Possible Worlds.* London: Routledge.

Doležel, Lubomir
1976 Narrative modalities. *Journal of Literary Semantics* 5: 5–14.

Doležel, Lubomir
1998 *Heterocosmica: Fiction and Possible Worlds.* Baltimore/London: The John Hopkins University Press.

Duffy, Carol Ann
1999 *The World's Wife.* London: Picador.

Eco, Umberto
1979 *The Role of the Reader.* London: Hutchinson.

Eco, Umberto
1990 *The Limits of Interpretation.* Bloomington/Indianapol s: Indiana University Press.

Emmott, Catherine
1997 *Narrative Comprehension: A Discourse Perspective.* Oxford: Oxford University Press.

Emmott, Catherine
2003 Reading for pleasure: a cognitive poetic analysis of "twists in the tale" and other plot reversals in narrative texts. In: Joanna Gavins and Gerard Steen (eds.), *Cognitive Poetics in Practice*, 145–160. London: Routledge.

Fauconnier, Gilles
1994 *Mental Spaces.* New York: Cambridge University Press.

Fauconnier, Gilles
1997 *Mappings in Thought and Language.* Cambridge: Cambridge University Press.

Fauconnier, Gilles and Mark Turner
1996 Blending as a Central Process of Grammar. In: Adele Goldberg (ed.), *Conceptual Structure, Discourse, and Language*, 113–130. Stanford: Center for the Study of Language and Information (CSLI).

Fauconnier, Gilles and Mark Turner
2002 *The Way We Think: Conceptual Blendings and the Mind's Hidden Complexities.* New York: Basic Books.

Fludernik, Monika
1996 *Towards a "Natural' Narratology.* London: Routledge.

Freeman, Margaret H.
2000 Poetry and the scope of metaphor: Toward a cognitive theory of literature. In: Antonio Barcelona (ed.), *Metaphor and Metonymy at the Crossroads: A Cognitive Perspective*, 253–281. Berlin: Mouton de Gruyter.

Gavins, Joanna
  2003   Too much blague? An exploration of the text worlds of Donald Bar-
          thelme's *Snow White*. In: Joanna Gavins and Gerard Steen (eds.), *Cog-
          nitive Poetics in Practice*, 129–144. London: Routledge.
Gavins, Joanna
  2007   *Text World Theory: An Introduction*. Edinburgh: Edinburgh University
          Press.
Gavins, Joanna and Gerard Steen (eds.)
  2003   *Cognitive Poetics in Practice*. London: Routledge.
Gibbs, Raymond
  2000   Making Good Psychology out of Blending Theory. *Cognitive Lin-
          guistics* 11(3/4): 347–58.
Hall, Geoff
  2003   The year's work in stylistics: 2002. *Language and Literature* 12(4):
          353–70.
Jackson, Tony E.
  2005   Explanation, interpretation, and close reading: the progress of cogni-
          tive poetics. *Poetics Today* 26(3): 519–32.
Kripke, Saul
  1971   Semantical considerations on modal logic. In: Leonard Linsky (ed.),
          Reference and Modality, 63–72. Oxford: Clarendon Press.
Lewis, David
  1968   Counterpart theory and quantified modal logic. *The Journal of Philos-
          ophy* 65(5): 113–26.
Lewis, David
  1986   *Philosophical Papers*, Volume II. New York/Oxford: Oxford University
          Press.
Maitre, Doreen
  1983   *Literature and Possible Worlds*. London: Middlesex Polytechnic Press.
Margolin, Uri
  2003   Cognitive science, the thinking mind, and literary narrative. In:
          David Herman (ed.), *Narrative Theory and the Cognitive Sciences*,
          271–294. Stanford, Ca.: Center for the Study of Language and In-
          formation.
Ovid
  1955   *Metamorphoses*, translated by Innes, M. M. (1955). London: Penguin
          Books.
Palmer, Alan
  2004   *Fictional Minds*. Lincoln/London: University of Nebraska Press.
Pavel, Thomas G.
  1986   *Fictional Worlds*. Cambridge (Mass.)/London: Harvard University
          Press.
Rescher, Nicholas and Zane Parks
  1973   Possible individuals, trans-world identity, and quantified modal logic.
          Noûs, 7: 330–50.

Ritchie, David
  2004   Lost in *"conceptual space"*: metaphors of conceptual integration. *Metaphor and Symbol*, 19(1): 31–50.
Ronen, Ruth
  1994   *Possible Worlds in Literary Theory.* Cambridge: Cambridge University Press.
Ryan, Marie-Laure
  1991   *Possible Worlds, Artificial Intelligence and Narrative Theory.* Bloomington/Indianapolis: Indiana University Press.
Sanders, José and Gisela Redeker
  1996   Perspective and the representation of speech and thought in narrative discourse. In: Gilles Fauconnier and Eve Sweetser (eds.), *Spaces, Worlds, and Grammar*, 290–317. Chicago: The University of Chicago Press.
Semino, Elena
  1997   *Language and World Creation in Poems and Other Texts.* London: Longman.
Semino, Elena
  2003   Discourse worlds and mental spaces. In: Joanna Gavins and Gerard Steen (eds.), *Cognitive Poetics in Practice*, 83–98. London: Routledge.
Semino, Elena
  2006   Blending and characters' mental functioning in Virginia Woolf's *Lappin and Lapinova*. *Language and Literature* 15(1): 55–72.
Semino, Elena and Jonathan Culpeper (eds.)
  2002   *Cognitive Stylistics: Language and Cognition in Text Analysis.* Amsterdam: John Benjamins.
Stockwell, Peter
  2002   *Cognitive Poetics: An Introduction.* London: Routledge.
Tsur, Reuven
  1992   *Toward a Theory of Cognitive Poetics.* Amsterdam: Elsevier.
Tsur, Reuven
  2003   *On the Shores of Nothingness: A Study in Cognitive Poetics.* Charlottesville, VA.: Imprint Academic.
Turner, Mark
  2003   Double-scope stories. In: David Herman (ed.), *Narrative Theory and the Cognitive Sciences*, 117–142. Stanford, Ca.: Center for the Study of Language and Information.
Werth, Paul
  1999   *Text Worlds: Representing Conceptual Space in Discourse.* London: Longman.
Zunshine, Lisa
  2006   *Why We Read Fiction: Theory of Mind and the Novel.* Columbus: The Ohio State University Press.

The way in which text worlds are furnished: response to Elena Semino's *Text Worlds*

Shweta Narayan

Elena Semino's *Text Worlds* looks at intertextuality, and the construction of fictional worlds, from several theoretical perspectives, using Ovid's *Metamorphoses* and Carol Ann Duffy's *Mrs Midas* to make a number of interesting points about the frameworks she discusses. Since this is a brief response, I will focus on one problem she raises and propose a possible solution.

Semino notes that literary analysts have a range of goals, which affect the choice of analytic framework:

1. Proposing novel interpretations of literary texts – this is essentially outside the scope of Semino's paper.
2. For accepted interpretations, describing a network of interconnected fictional worlds and the progression of a plot in terms of their buildup and interrelations – Semino shows elegantly how both Possible Worlds and a number of different cognitive approaches can do this. She also notes that cognitive linguistic approaches can "account for text worlds as complex mental representations that are incrementally set up by readers".
3. Accounting for a range of phenomena in literary texts, including humor, allusion, political undertones, and emotional involvement – Semino says that cognitive poetic approaches need to account for these systematically in order to appeal more to literary scholars. While I agree that there needs to be more such work, cognitive linguists have in fact done some work on humor (e.g. Coulson 2001) and on indirect cues to cognitive structure (e.g. Sweetser 2006). In addition, I would like to claim that a Conceptual Integration (Blending) analysis that focuses on the dynamic creation of mental spaces, and the long-term cognitive structure brought into them, will account for readers' emotional involvement.

1.   Theory and diagrams

Mental Spaces theory is inherently dynamic. Mental spaces are dynamically created and blended as people think and speak. Mental space *diagrams,* however, are static in nature and, as Semino notes, "become impossibly complicated when applied to stretches of text longer than a few sentences". This is not a failure of the theoretical framework; it is merely a difficulty posed by the diagramming method.[1] However, it sometimes leads analysts to focus too much attention on single final-state blending diagrams instead of their dynamic construction from the cues provided – making blending theory look, perhaps, more like Possible World Semantics than it really is.[2]

Fortunately for us, it is possible for an analysis to make use of the insights of blending theory without drawing out the diagrams at every stage. I present prose-only blending analyses of part of the Ovid and *Mrs Midas* texts, showing how the differences in the dynamic construction of meaning might account for differences in the reader's experience of the stories.[3] As Semino says, the texts "differ considerably in terms of whose minds they focus on, and how much access they provide into the characters' mental lives". In Mental Spaces terms, the two texts differ in the specific linguistic forms which cue meaning construction, and in the viewpoint space from which these cues are presented. What a blending analysis can add to Semino's insight is the idea that this affects the cognitive work readers need to do to interpret the Ovid and *Mrs Midas,* which in turn affects their degree of involvement and empathy. We can start to get at *why* the way in which a text world is furnished might affect the reader's experience of it.

2.   Ovid

Let us look at the first part (of the English prose translation) of Ovid that Semino quotes: "The god was glad to have his tutor back, and in return gave Midas the right to choose himself a gift". This provides three en-

---

1. Coulson's alternative blending diagrams, which are in table form, allow for more dynamic representations.
2. Earlier work (e.g. Fauconnier 1997) focused more on dynamic buildup – but the complexity of those diagrams underscores Semino's point.
3. These are only partial sketches – in particular, I have tried not to repeat too much of what Semino has said.

tities – Midas, a tutor, and a god, Bacchus. Readers can infer two input spaces from this – the human realm, which contains the human entity Midas, and the divine realm, which contains the god Bacchus. Readers have rich experiential knowledge of the human realm, and the divine realm is a previously established and accessible blend, which shares some qualities with the human realm (it is inhabited by people, who have intents that affect their actions), but also differs from the human realm in that entities in the divine realm can affect the human realm, while the opposite is less true.

These inputs are overtly set up, with one entity coming from each. Shared structure is clear from knowledge of the spaces, and the sentence structure evokes an *interaction* frame to structure the encounter between Midas and Bacchus.[4] The plot of the encounter is also provided: readers are told about Bacchus's mental state, the reason for it, and how it affects that entity's actions (which, in the blend, affect Midas).

The reader, then, is given the inputs, the entities in them, information about how to link them up and how to run the blend. The reader does not need to bring in much additional structure to make sense of the scene – what they need is evoked by the names of the entities, and the long-term cognitive structure associated with them. The reader does not need to bring in rich imagery and create a vivid imagined scene in order to build a coherent narrative, and is not prompted to by the text.[5]

Information is presented as past with relation to the viewpoint space, which is not clearly connected to the story network by any relation other than the temporal. The viewpoint space is distant from the narrative network, therefore, which keeps the reader's cognitive viewpoint distant from the characters.

3. Mrs Midas

Semino notes that the poem can cause a great deal of emotional involvement on the reader's part, which is not true of the Ovid. she notes some factors that cause it to be so, including Midas' cited "lack of thought" for

---

4. Mappings between entities are based in shared cognitive structure – either semantic (frame structure, image schematic structure, etc.) or formal (e.g. rhyme) – whether one wants to put that in a generic space or not.

5. A reader could, of course. This is presumably part of what causes differences in readers' experience of texts.

the narrator, and the ending, in which she continues to experience unhappiness. But reader involvement starts well before the plot of *Mrs Midas* diverges from the original myth in these ways. What causes it is a combination of the types of cues presented, and the viewpoint space they are presented from.

The title provides us with two entities: a wife and (by frame completion) her husband, whose name is Midas. This name evokes the space of the Midas myth (itself a complex blend with temporal and causal structure) in the reader's mind. "Mrs" evokes a relatively modern, non-noble wife from an English-speaking country – someone readers can empathize with, whose concerns are understandable. The two inputs, then, are evoked by the title – but readers are given only one relation: a marriage between Midas and Mrs Midas.

The first stanza gives the reader vivid details about the world evoked by "Mrs", but no information about what to map into the blend from the Midas myth – merely that it should be integrated into the narrative somehow.[6] Readers are bombarded with cues for rich sensory and motor experience of wine, cooking vegetables, fruit, and foggy windows.

Another important contributor to the vividness of the poem is the information readers are *not* given. Unlike the Ovid, *Mrs Midas* does not provide an entire network of spaces and connections. Some motivations, intents, belief spaces, and connections are left entirely unspecified, and readers must create this structure and incorporate it into the blend in order to create a coherent story. It is not possible to do this much cognitive work without actively engaging with the narrative.

The network the reader is creating is (until the last stanza) past with relation to the viewpoint space, as in the Ovid, but the reader knows how this space fits into the network; it is the memory/belief space of the narrator, who is closely involved with the events and affected by them.

In understanding the poem, the reader is re-creating the narrator's internal experience, through sensory detail and the filling-in of cognitive structure, building up a network from a viewpoint space that is closely connected to it. The reader creates the blend, and runs it; to some extent, then, they live it. This is why readers can be deeply engaged with *Mrs Midas*. Literary analysis is in many ways an ideal environment for

---

6. Though as Semino notes, they are given a few hints: the pear twig, the personification metaphors. Personification metaphors also evoke aspects of the domain of human action which readers have experience of; this adds to the richness of the blend.

study of people's internal experience and the cues which evoke it; I join Semino in looking forward to more work in this exciting area.

References

Coulson, Seana
  2001   *Semantic Leaps: Frame-Shifting and Conceptual Blending in Meaning Construction.* Cambridge: Cambridge University Press.
Fauconnier, Gilles
  1997   *Mappings in Thought and Language.* Cambridge: Cambridge University Press.
Sweetser, Eve
  2006   Whose Rhyme is Whose Reason? *Language and Literature* 15(1): 29–54.

Cognitive approaches to narrative analysis

David Herman

1.   Introduction: toward a cognitive narratology

Study of the cognitive dimensions of stories and storytelling has become an important subdomain within the field of narrative analysis. Concerned both with how people understand narratives and with narrative itself as a mode of understanding, studies range from attempts to establish empirical methods for testing correlations between textual features and the processing strategies triggered by those features (Bortolussi and Dixon 2003; Gerrig 1993; van Peer and Chatman 2001); to inquiries into narrative as a resource for navigating and making sense of computer-mediated environments (Ryan 2001); to intermedial research suggesting that narrative functions as a cognitive "macroframe" enabling interpreters to identify stories or story-like elements across any number of semiotic media, literary, pictorial, musical, and other (Wolf 2003). Further, analysts working in this area borrow descriptive and explanatory tools from a variety of disciplinary traditions. Source disciplines include cognitive linguistics; pragmatics; discourse analysis; narratology; communication theory; anthropology; stylistics; cognitive, evolutionary, and social psychology; rhetoric; computer science; literary theory; and philosophy.

It should not be surprising that, given the range of artifacts falling under their purview, their richly interdisciplinary heritage, and the varying backgrounds and interests of their practitioners, cognitive approaches to narrative analysis at present constitute more a set of loosely confederated heuristic schemes than a coordinated research program. In an effort to promote greater synergy among the various initiatives within this domain – to delineate focal concerns on which theorists working in different disciplines might converge – the present chapter discusses three key aspects of stories that promise to be illuminated by bringing narrative inquiry into dialogue with research in the cognitive sciences.[1] Section 2

---

1. Here and throughout, in referring to the cognitive sciences (in the plural) I have in mind Wilson and Keil's (1999) taxonomic scheme, in which six

reviews explanatory frameworks concerned with the concept of **character** or **narrative role**. This section outlines role-theoretic frameworks deriving from models of discourse processing as well as the idea of "positioning", an idea that was developed in the subdomain of social psychology sometimes called *discursive psychology* (see, e.g., Harré and Gillett 1994; Edwards 1997) and that opposes itself to standard conceptions of roles. Section 3 also draws on discursive psychology, but this time to explore **emotion discourse** in narrative contexts – more specifically, how stories both rely on and help generate systems of emotion terms and concepts. Lastly, section 4 uses ideas from cognitive linguistics to explore the structure and dynamics of **narrative perspective**. Here I suggest the advantages of supplementing narratological accounts of *focalization* with cognitive-grammatical research on *construal* or *conceptualization*. In an integrative approach of this sort, perspective takes its place among a wider array of construal operations that may be more or less fully exploited by a given narrative.

My chapter thus draws on a range of cognitively oriented paradigms for study, including theories of text processing, social psychology, discourse analysis, and cognitive grammar. But the chapter has an overarching goal: namely, to suggest that by incorporating into the domain of narrative analysis research exploring the nexus of language, mind, and world, theorists can help promote the development of cognitive narratology as one of a number of "postclassical" approaches to narrative inquiry. At issue are frameworks for narrative study that build on the work of classical, structuralist narratologists but enrich that work with concepts and methods that were unavailable to story analysts such as Roland Barthes, Gérard Genette, A. J. Greimas, and Tzvetan Todorov during the heyday of the structuralist revolution.[2] Cognitive narratology constitutes one such framework, or rather cluster of frameworks, and in the present essay I focus on the three problem domains just mentioned to suggest directions for research in this emergent area.[3] Further, my chapter tests the descrip-

---

"confederated disciplines" can be grouped together under this umbrella field: philosophy; psychology; the neurosciences; computational intelligence; linguistics and language; and culture, cognition, and evolution.

2. For a fuller account of classical versus postclassical approaches to narrative theory, see Herman (1999). For accounts of the structuralist revolution and of the way it shaped structuralist theories of narrative in particular, see, respectively, Dosse (1997) and Herman (2005a).

3. See Jahn (2005) for a synoptic account of developments in cognitive narratology; see also Herman (2003b) and Palmer (2004).

tive and explanatory power of cognitive approaches by using as case studies a range of narrative texts, from *The Incredible Hulk* comics, to a television interview, to a tape-recorded narrative told in face-to-face interaction, to short stories from James Joyce's 1914 collection, *Dubliners*. By focusing on cognitive dimensions of multiple kinds of narrative practices, I suggest, story analysts can overcome limitations arising from the restricted corpora on which scholars working in separate traditions of research have based their concepts and methods.

2.   Cognitive dimensions of character: From narrative roles to positions in storylines

Analysts of stories have long been concerned with the concept of "role". Aristotle (1971) made roles parasitic on plot (*muthos*), arguing that characters' qualities and functions derive from the unfolding structure of action in which they participate. Some 2,500 years later, the novelist Henry James sketched a more complicated model, suggesting a tight reciprocity between roles and plots. As James famously put it, "What is character but the determination of incident? What is incident but the illustration of character?" (Miller 1971: 37). The pendulum shifted back toward Aristotle's position with the advent of structuralist narratology, which drew on Propp's ([1928] 1968) groundbreaking analysis of the "functions" performed by characters in Russian folktales. Describing the function as "an act of character, defined from the point of view of its significance for the course of the action" (1968: 21), Propp argued that many seemingly diverse functions join together to create a few, typifiable "spheres of action". He developed a typology of seven general roles (the villain, the donor, the helper, the sought-for-person and her father, the dispatcher, the hero, and the false hero) that correspond to the ways in which characters can participate in the plot structures found in the genre of the folktale (Propp 1968: 79f.). This typology became the basis for Greimas's theory of *actants*, or deep-structural roles underlying the specific, particularized characters (or "actors") populating storyworlds.

After reviewing the structuralist conception of roles as actants in somewhat more detail, the remainder of this section suggests how another strand of structuralist research – namely, Barthes' ([1966] 1977) account of the design and interpretation of narrative sequences – anticipates Catherine Emmott's (1997) later, cognitively oriented approach to roles as elements of contextual frames. For Emmott, contextual frames are mental models containing information about the spacetime coordinates of narrated events and about the number, identity, and configuration of participants involved in those events.[4] Whereas Emmott's theory is designed to account for how readers use role-based mental models to process written narrative texts, I conclude this section by reviewing discursive psychologists' reconceptualization of roles as positions. Or rather, positioning theory rejects the very idea of "role" as overly static and reified, making a case instead for dynamic, interactionally accomplished positions assigned by participants in discourse, which thus becomes the means by which people ascribe to themselves and others presuppositions, beliefs, inferences, attitudes, and other (socio)cognitive attributes. From this perspective, a "character" is less a fixed type or substrate for identity than an agent-position pairing achieved (or undermined) through the utterance of speech acts during the sometimes conflictual process of constructing larger "storylines". These storylines, or more or less extended narrative arcs that are built up when speakers assign positions to themselves and others, and that reciprocally provide context for understanding any local speech act with a position-assigning force, can operate at multiple narrative levels simultaneously – not only at the primary diegetic level created by the process of narration but also at subordinate levels created when characters are in turn portrayed as assigning positions to themselves and others over the course of a represented interaction or "scene of talk" (Herman 2006). During such scenes, different characters may seek to promote different, even radically inconsistent storylines, suggesting the extent to which acts of narration emerge from a larger discourse context in which competing stories, and the competing logics of positioning that they entail, struggle for dominance.

2.1 Roles as actants

One of the first projects of structuralist narratology was the attempt to create a systematic framework for describing how characters participate in the narrated action. Building on the ideas of Saussure, the narratol-

---

4. Dancygier (2006) outlines another cognitively grounded approach to narrative roles, using Fauconnier's (1994) concept of role-value mapping to explore the structure of narratives with multiple diegetic levels. To paraphrase: each diegetic level can be conceived as a mental space that specifies a constellation of roles, and roles that are more or less parallel across levels may be instantiated by different characters (= value assignments for the roles), just as a single character (= value) may instantiate multiple roles across narrative levels.

ogists posited a distinction between narrative *langue* (or the system in terms of which individual stories are understood *as* stories) and narrative *parole* (or the individual narrative "messages" made possible and intelligible by that system). Specific characters are constituents of narrative *parole*; but roles, defined as invariant semantic functions instantiated by any number of particularized individuals, are constituents of narrative *langue*. Conceived as "fundamental role[s] at the level of narrative deep structure" (Prince 2003: 1), "*actants* are general categories [cf behavior or doing] underlying all narratives (and not only narratives) while [*actors*] are invested with specific qualities in different narratives" (Rimmon-Kenan 1983: 34). Narrative processing, from this structuralist perspective, depends on reducing or normalizing the heterogeneity of specific actors by matching each such character with a limited repertoire of basic and general roles.

Greimas drew on the syntactic theories of Lucien Tesnière (1976) to re-characterize Propp's spheres of action as actants.[5] Further, associating actants with "narrative syntax" (Greimas 1987: 106), Greimas argued that whereas "an articulation of actors constitutes a particular *tale*; a structure of actants constitutes a *genre*" ([1966] 1983: 200). In refining Propp's typology, Greimas initially identified a total of six actants to which he thought all particularized narrative actors could be reduced: Subject, Object, Sender, Receiver, Helper, and Opponent (see Figure 1).

Sender — Object → Receiver

↑

Helper → Subject ← Opponent

Figure 1. Greimas's (1983) Actantial Model

He explicated this scheme as follows: "[i]ts simplicity lies in the fact that it is entirely centered on the object of desire aimed at by the subject and situated, as object of communication, between the sender and the receiver – the desire of the subject being, in its part, modulated in projections from the helper and opponent" (1983: 207). In later work, however, Greimas demoted Helpers and Opponents to positive and negative "auxiliants",

---

5. See Kafalenos (2006) for an account that builds both on Propp's function-analytic scheme and on Greimas's concept of actants to explore how the interpretation of events is shaped by their place within larger narrative sequences.

thereby raising questions about the internal coherence and modeling adequacy of the actantial framework (Herman 2002: 128 ff.).

At issue is the appropriate number and kinds of actants for all narrative genres and subgenres, as well as the procedure for matching general actantial roles with particularized actors. The link between actors and actants, after all, is both one-many and many-one. On the one hand, a given character may embody more than one actantial role. Take, for example, the complex actantial structure of *The Incredible Hulk* comics. Centering on a character originally created in 1962, these comics portray the experiences of Robert Bruce Banner, a nuclear physicist from Dayton, Ohio, who grew up in an abusive home and whose exposure to gamma radiation has led to his bifurcation into the normal human Banner and his alterego, the creature known as the Hulk – a creature into whom Banner is transformed by sudden surges of adrenaline and who can lift 100 tons and withstand up to 3000 degrees of heat (Fahrenheit). Figure 2 reproduces a page taken from the first issue of volume 2 of the *Hulk* comic book series. Published in April 1968, this issue postdates the six issues of the first volume of *Hulk*, published in 1962, as well as the Hulk's appearances among the ensemble of characters featured in the *Tales to Astonish* series, including Giant Man, The Wrecker, Madam Macabre, The Sub-Mariner, and others.[6]

Depending on circumstances, the Hulk may be Subject, who seeks to eliminate a threat or irritant in his environment, or merely to display his indomitable strength, as suggested in the final panel of figure 2; Helper, when the superhuman strength mentioned by the Hulk in the final two panels on the page, and evident from Banner's altered appearance, enables the Hulk to accomplish feats that Banner the scientist could not bring about on his own power; or Opponent, vis-à-vis Banner's desire for a normal existence, via-à-vis Rick, the slang-speaking teenager saved by Banner from gamma ray exposure but pushed roughly aside by the Hulk in the final panel, or vis-à-vis the intentions and goals of various Opponents ranging from Giant Man to the big-brained Leader to The Abomination, another mutant hailing from Zagreb, Yugoslavia. On the other hand, a given actantial role may be realized by more than one character in a narrative. Thus multiple characters function as Opponents to the Hulk over the course of the series, from the Abomination, Zzzax, and Bi-Beast,

6. For more on the history and special capabilities of the Hulk, see http://www.hulklibrary.com/hulk/info/profile.asp and http://en.wikipedia.org/wiki/Hulk_(comics)

to Doctor Strange and Silver Surfer (who are also Helpers in other contexts), to the environmental impediments and injuries the Hulk must overcome in order to accomplish situation-specific goals.

Indeed, around the same time Greimas proposed his model, William O. Hendricks (1967) argued that the one-many and many-one mappings among actors and actants revealed problems with the conceptual underpinnings of the Proppian tradition from which the model derived. An early contribution to the then-nascent field of discourse analysis, Hendricks' study sought to distinguish between legitimate and illegitimate extensions of linguistic paradigms "beyond the sentence". For Hendricks, Propp's function analysis constitutes an illegitimate extension because functions (e.g., "act of villainy"), like the spheres of action that informed Greimas' actantial model, are byproducts of a prior unstated gloss of the story being analyzed, rather than constituents of narrative discourse in the way that morphemes are constituents of words and phrases are constituents of clauses and sentences. What the structuralists left unspecified, in other words, is the procedure by which the analyst builds an initial global interpretation of the narrative being analyzed. Actantial roles, supposedly encoded in a story's structure, are in actual fact the product of an implicit theory of what the story is *about* – e.g., a theory according to which his own recurrent transformations into the Hulk thwart Banner's desire for a normal existence. The model thus begs questions that it was designed to help answer.

A paradox, related to the classic bootstrapping problem, emerges: a processor cannot assign a role to a character without already having knowledge of the overarching plot-structure of which the character is an element. Roles are needed to build up an understanding of this larger configuration, i.e., the plot; yet roles can be matched with participants only after the fact, on the basis of a fully developed plot-model that allows roles to be (retrospectively) attributed to characters in a given time-slice of the unfolding storyworld. As my next subsection discusses, however, another strand of work in the structuralist tradition suggested how this paradox might be transformed into a viable model for text processing, construed as an interplay between top-down and bottom-up strategies for interpreting narrative texts.

Figure 2. Page 7 of the First Issue of *The Incredible Hulk*, Volume 2 (Marvel Comics Group, Issue 102, April 1968, created by Stan Lee, written by Gary Friedrich and Marie Severin, inked by George Tuska, lettered by Artie Simek). Reproduced with permission of Marvel Entertainment, Inc.

2.2   From actantial roles to processing heuristics

As a rule, first-wave narratologists did not question the scalability of the linguistic paradigms that they used; they worked in a bottom-up fashion, attempting to map sentence-level units and structures on to units and structures at the level of narrative discourse. Thus Greimas (1983) tried to move directly from Tesnière's syntactic theory to a theory of discourse-level roles. Likewise, Todorov (1969) sought to correlate nouns, verbs, and predicates with characters, their actions, and their attributes.

By contrast, although he too made a structuralist category-mistake when he argued that a narrative is merely a long sentence (Barthes 1977: 83), Barthes (1971, 1977) also presciently suggested that roles are inferential constructs that derive from an interplay of top-down and bottom-up processing strategies. For Barthes, people's stereotypical knowledge about the world allows them to chunk narrative discourse into action-sequences; these sequences are elements of a broader experiential repertoire based on recurrent patterns of behavior (*quest, betrayal, revenge*, etc.).[7] Hence action-sequences afford heuristics for assigning roles to characters whose doings trigger the inference that the characters are engaged in some culturally salient behavioral pattern or another. When the Incredible Hulk's behavior assumes the form of a struggle with a villainous opponent, such as Bi-Beast or The Abomination, the classification of the unfolding events as part of a *violent struggle* in turn generates mapping principles by which participants in the narrated action can be slotted into a configuration of roles. By contrast, if what initially seemed to be a struggle instead proves to be a *playful contest*, then different mapping principles will be generated by the heuristics of this alternative sequence-type. In figure 2 the heuristic construct of *transformation* affords principles of this same kind – principles that allow interpreters to make sense of local textual details (verbal as well as visual) by engaging in character-to-character and role-to-role mappings. Here the mapping relationships form an almost perfect chiasmus: Banner's painful enfeeblement is the gateway to the Hulk's unconquerable strength, which at this point in the Hulk's history comes at the cost of a cognitive capacity manifestly inferior to Banner's – as signaled by truncated, nonidiomatic syntax and dropped lexical items or nonstandard orthography (e.g., *too* spelled as *to* in the left-

---

7. See Herman (2002: 85ff.) for an account of the parallels between Barthes' account of action-sequences and early Artificial Intelligence research on the dynamic knowledge representations characterized as scripts

hand speech balloon in the final frame). Thus readers make sense of the sequence of panels in figure 2 by hypothesizing that the character Banner instantiates a role whose constituent features include +intelligence and -superhuman strength, whereas the Hulk instantiates a converse role marked by –intelligence and +superhuman strength. My larger point is that, in the post-actantial model at least hinted at by Barthes, character-to-role mappings are dynamically enabled by ongoing, moment-by-moment inferences about action-sequences, rather than deriving from unstated glosses of whole texts – i.e., from necessarily *ex post facto* assessments of how a particular character's action relates to the plot as a whole. Localized roles and larger plot-configurations are thus reciprocally, rather than circularly, related to one another.[8]

In moving beyond the actantial models of the structuralists, later story analysts have built on Barthes's intuition that roles are the output of heuristics brought to bear on the processing of narrative texts. But these theorists have developed analytic paradigms using ideas that were not available to Barthes himself. I now turn to one such explanatory paradigm: the contextual frame theory proposed by Catherine Emmott (1997).

2.3   Roles as elements of contextual frames

Drawing on models of discourse processing (cf. Webber 1979; Garnham and Oakhill 1996), Emmott (1997) has developed a theory of narrative comprehension oriented toward the process by which readers of written narratives decode references to participants in the narrated action, that is, to storyworld inhabitants. More specifically, the framework was designed to account for how pronominal references can be disambiguated across more or less extended stretches of narrative discourse. At issue is how

---

8. In this connection, compare Jahn's (1997) account of how higher-order knowledge representations or frames enable interpreters of stories to disambiguate pronominal references, decide whether a given sentence serves a descriptive or a thought-reporting function (e.g., depending on context *the train was late* might either be a thought mulled over by a character or part of the narrator's own account the narrated world), and, more generally, adopt a top-down as well as a bottom-up approach to narrative processing. A frame guides interpretation until such time as textual cues prompt the modification or abandonment of that frame. Compare also classical accounts of the hermeneutic circle (Bontekoe 1996), whereby understanding of a textual whole affects interpretation of its parts and interpretation of the parts in turn (re)shapes understanding of the whole.

even the most skeletal textual cues (*he, she, it*) allow specific participants to be selected from among a pool of candidate referents. As I discuss below, in order to map Emmott's theory onto graphic narratives like *The Incredible Hulk*, one needs to account for the way visual cues with varying degrees of detail or specificity can supplement verbal cues to serve participant-indexing functions in multimodal narratives. For example, the rendering of a character's appearance or of the setting can suggest the position of a given scene on an overarching time-line of events.

For Emmott "contexts", or spatiotemporal nodes inhabited by configurations of participants, constrain pronoun interpretation. Actions and events are necessarily indexed to a particular context and must be viewed within that context, even if the context is never fully reactivated (after its initial mention) textually. Shifts in context – e.g., shifts from a flashback to the main narrative – alter the pool of potential referents for a pronoun and may enable a pronoun to be interpreted without an antecedent. Further, information about contexts attaches itself to mental representations that Emmott terms *contextual frames*. A participant is said to be *bound* to a contextual frame, and when one particular contextual frame becomes the main focus of attention for the reader, it is said to be *primed*. In the case of *frame modification*, the same contextual frame remains primed but the frame has to be altered to reflect a change in the participant group. In *frame switch*, one contextual frame replaces another, while in *frame recall* a previously primed frame is reinstated. Note that in comics like *The Incredible Hulk* and graphic narratives more generally, Emmott's notion of frame moves from being a metaphor for narrative processing to a literal feature of the narrative text: processes of frame priming, modification, switch, and recall are enacted by semiotic means available within the medium, namely, the use of word-image combinations to evoke bounded "snapshots" of time-slices of the storyworld. Hence graphic narratives can serve as an important test-bed for Emmott's model, and in particular for its ability to explain referential processes by which interpreters use textual cues to generate inferences about which storyworld participants are doing what, where, and when (see Bridgeman 2005).

For example, in figure 2, the background in the sixth panel has the same watermelon color and striated texture as that contained in the first panel, while the purple color of the Hulk's pants in the final three panels recalls the purple pants Banner is wearing in the third panel while he is being examined by the doctor. In this way, the visual logic of the page reinforces the causal and chronological links articulated or implied by Oldar the witch in the framing narration she provides via rhyming couplets – couplets set off in yellow, rectangular boxes from the white, rounded speech balloons reporting the characters' utterances at the embedded or hypodiegetic level evoked through Oldar's story.[9] The panel representing Banner's transformation into the Hulk (panel six) visually recalls the panel in which Banner is exposed to the gamma rays that *caused* the transformation, while the purple pants establish participant continuity: the color marks Hulk as a different version of Banner, linked to him through a process of transformation, rather than as an altogether different participant. For her part, Emmott uses the term *enactors* to name the different versions of participants encountered in narrative flashbacks or embedded stories like Oldar's. Contextual monitoring is necessary to keep track of the current enactor because flashback time in written texts is not always signaled by changes in verb tense. There can thus be *frame participant ambiguity* – that is, uncertainty about who (or which enactor) is present in a given context. Another challenge is monitoring covert participants in the action, that is, participants whose presence can be inferred but is not explicitly marked by textual cues. For instance, in an individual panel within a *Hulk* comic, such as the first panel in figure 2, even though the Hulk's facial or bodily response to surrounding circumstances may fill the panel, the continuing presence of those environmental triggers can nonetheless be inferred – in this case, the continuing presence of the gamma rays to which Banner is being agonizingly exposed at this moment.

In effect, Emmott's approach focuses on the referential basis for drawing inferences about the roles of participants in storyworlds. Before a role can be mapped on to a particular participant, the identity of the participant needs to be established within the flow of discourse. At the same time, Emmott's model allows for the possibility that in some instances roles may serve as a criterion for participant identity, as when a character's behavior suggests that a given textual segment concerns enactor$_x$ rather than enactor$_y$. For example, the role being instantiated by Banner at a given point in a *Hulk* comic can serve to identify whether the narrative is flashing back to an earlier, pre-mutated version of Banner or whether the Banner being referred to is the one who has already been exposed to gamma rays.

---

9. Oldar's framing story, which provides an opportunity for retelling the origins of the Hulk in this inaugural issue of the second volume of the Hulk series, takes place in the context of a dispute between warring factions of the Asgardians, a race of immortals among whom Banner/the Hulk finds himself as the issue opens.

The positioning theory discussed in my next subsection likewise focuses on the dynamic, variable relation between participants and their attributes, but it subsumes both of those concepts under the idea of position, defined as a region of sociocommunicative space whose coordinates are established by way of illocutionary acts – more precisely, by the bearing of those acts on the larger "storylines" to which they contribute, or against which they militate in favor of other, competing storylines.

2.4 From roles to positions

In Harré and van Langenhove's (1999: 1ff.) account, one can position oneself or be positioned in discourse as powerful or powerless, admirable or blameworthy, etc. In turn, a position can be specified by characterizing how a speaker's contributions are taken as bearing on these and other "polarities of character" in the context of an overarching storyline – a narrative of self and other(s) being jointly elaborated (or disputed) by participants, via self-positioning and other-positioning speech acts. Hence positions are selections made by participants in discourse, who use position-assigning speech acts to build "storylines" in terms of which the assignments make sense. Reciprocally, the storylines provide context in terms of which speech acts can be construed as having a position-assigning force.

For example, in a recent television interview the comedian Jon Stewart other-positioned U.S. Vice President Dick Cheney by comparing him with the Incredible Hulk. Although Stewart deployed a metaphor rather than a full-fledged narrative, the metaphor sets up a proportion (in Fauconnier and Turner's 2002 terms, a conceptual blend) that serves to position Cheney by mapping his position onto Banner's. In fuller terms, just as Banner presents a mild-mannered appearance in comparison with the monster into which he is transformed given the existence of triggering circumstances, the calm, controlled figure that Cheney presents in public should not be taken as a reliable indicator of the far-different behavior of which he is capable at other times. Hence Stewart's use of a metaphor to equate Cheney with Banner also situated the Vice President in a recurrent storyline associated with the Hulk. That storyline suggests inner tendencies toward aggression and rage on Cheney's part – tendencies that might "break out" uncontrollably at a moment's notice. Inversely, the Hulk storyline afforded a context in which Stewart, his interviewer, and the wider television audience could match a particular kind of illocutionary force – namely, a position-assigning force – with Stewart's speech acts.

Further, the storyline in which Stewart's joke positioned Cheney recast the broader American political scene in comic-book terms, ironically embedding the storyline of recent U.S. politics within the storyline of uncontrollable "acting-out" used to position the Hulk himself. A metaphor thus gave birth to a storyline that in turn functioned synecdochically, creating another conceptual blend between Cheney the individual politician and the whole tenor of recent U.S. foreign policy. Given the chance, Cheney would no doubt dispute Stewart's other-positioning strategy and mode of storyline construction; a Stewart-Cheney debate would result not just in a battle of positions, but also in a war over what constitutes a legitimate way of constructing storylines and assigning positions in this context.

Positions are thus interactional achievements grounded in the production and interpretation of discourse. They are also Janus-faced. On the one hand, positions derive from inferences about what sort of storyline is being constructed by way of illocutionary acts; a given storyline entails specific positions. On the other hand, by monitoring an unfolding discourse for position-assigning speech acts, participants can infer what sort of storyline is being constructed, on a moment-by-moment, turn-by-turn basis. Although positioning theory thus relies, like Barthes' account of processing heuristics, on an interplay between top-down and bottom-up interpretive strategies, positioning theorists use that interplay to pose questions of a sort that Barthes never formulated. Barthes focused on the reciprocal relation between inferences about textually inscribed roles and inferences about larger narrative sequences in the texts in which they figured. By contrast, positioning theory redescribes identity formation itself as a process whereby discourse producers inscribe self and other within a network of convergent as well as divergent storylines. Positioning theorists can thus ask: How do the stories we tell about ourselves and others, as well as written literary narratives, position us, our interlocutors, authors, narrators, characters, and readers in networks of presuppositions and norms? Conversely, how do storylines emerge over the course of sequences of position-assignments? Can stereotypes and ideologies (e.g., those bound up with race, ethnicity, or gender) be redefined as entrenched storylines, master narratives that arise through an iterative process of assigning the same position, repeatedly, to the same kind of agent, until the agent and his or her position appear to be indissolubly linked? In short, this work suggests not just that narrative comprehension is inextricably bound up with the understanding of positions, but also that, conversely, stories are essential for fundamental aspects of social cognition, including the self-other dialectic.

3.   Emotion discourse in narrative contexts

Exploring the role of emotion discourse in narrative – that is, how the discourse of emotions is both a foundation for and an achieved result of storytelling practices – this section uses as a case study a story told in a different narrative medium. My illustrative narrative in this instance is *UFO or the Devil*, which was told during a sociolinguistic interview. The Appendix contains a full transcript of the story, which I have segmented into numbered clauses for the purposes of analysis; the Appendix also lists the transcription conventions used to annotate the story.

The story, *UFO or the Devil*, was told by Monica, a pseudonym for a 41-year-old African American female, to two white female fieldworkers in their mid-twenties, CM and RC. It was recorded on July 2, 2002, in Texana, North Carolina, near where the events recounted are purported to have occurred.[10] Located in Cherokee County, which is otherwise nearly totally white, Texana is a community consisting almost exclusively of African Americans; indeed, with about 150 residents, only 10 of whom are white, Texana is the largest black Appalachian community in western North Carolina (Mallinson 2006: 69, 78). (Figures 3 and 4 indicate, respectively, the location of North Carolina in the U.S. and of Cherokee County within North Carolina.) The narrative concerns not only Monica's and her friend's encounter with what Monica characterizes as a supernatural apparition – a big, glowing orange ball that rises up in the air and pursues them menacingly – but also Monica's and Renee's subsequent encounter with Renee's grandmother, who disputes whether the girls' experience with the big ball really occurred. In the remainder of this section, I again draw on ideas from discursive psychology to explore how Monica uses emotion discourse to construct her own and others' minds in the context of the storyworld. To pick back up on ideas from section 2.4, Monica's rhetorical deployment of emotion terms and concepts allows her to position herself as a frightened experiencer of actual events, thus undercutting the storyline in terms of which the grandmother seeks to other-position her and Renee as overwrought imaginers, hysterically deluded about what they encountered.

---

10. NSF Grant BCS-0236838 supported research on this narrative. I am indebted to Christine Mallinson for her collegiality and willingness to share insights about Monica's narrative, background, and attitudes toward issues of race and ethnicity.

Figure 3. Location of the state of North Carolina within the U.S.
Mapping software provided courtesy of John Adamson, Management
Information Specialist, Texas AgriLife Extension, Texas A&M Univer-
sity System. <http://monarch.tamu.edu/~maps2/>.

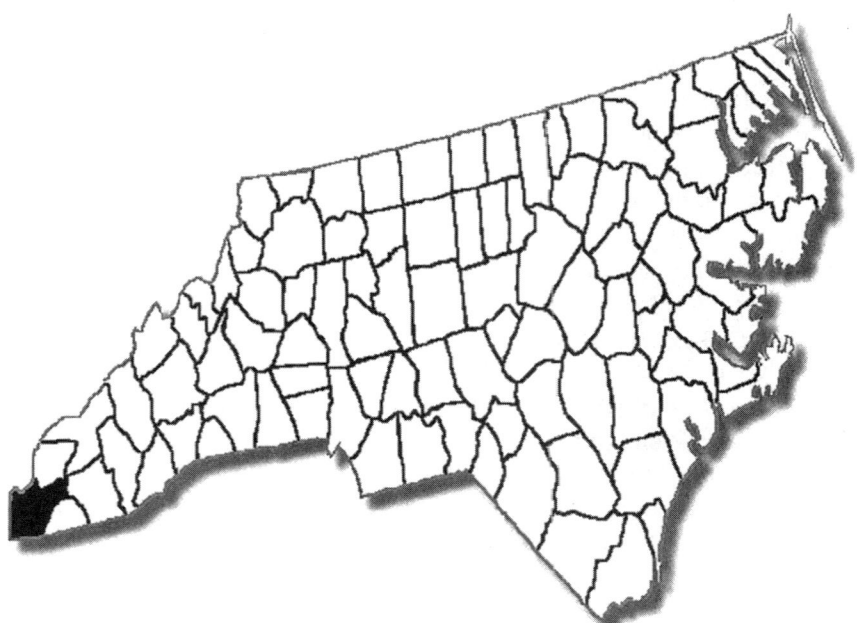

Figure 4. Location of Cherokee County within North Carolina
Mapping software provided courtesy of John Adamson, Management
Information Specialist, Texas AgriLife Extension, Texas A&M Univer-
sity System. <http://monarch.tamu.edu/~maps2/>.

3.1 Emotion, emotionology, and narratology

As Stearns (1995) points out, there is a basic tension between naturalist and constructionist approaches to emotion. Naturalists argue for the existence of innate, biologically grounded emotions that are more or less uniform across cultures and subcultures. By contrast, constructionists argue that emotions are culturally specific – that "context and function determine emotional life and that these vary" (41).[11] Squarely constructionist in orientation and methodology, discursive-psychological approaches follow the protocol identified by Stearns: "the initial basic step in investigating an emotion involves exploring the culture, not venturing general hypotheses about characteristics and functions" (45). Given that, as Edwards (1997) notes, "[e]motion discourse is an integral feature of talk about events, mental states, mind and body, personal dispositions, and social relations", the question is how "various emotion categories contrast with alternative emotions, with non-emotional states, with rational conduct, and so on, within the discursive construction of reality and mind" (170).

In studying the cultural and rhetorical grounding of emotion discourse, discursive psychologists have drawn on the concept of "emotionology", which was proposed by Stearns and Stearns (1985) as a way of referring to the collective emotional standards of a culture as opposed to the experience of emotion itself.[12] (The term is used in parallel with recent usages of *ontology* to designate a model of the entities, together with their properties and relations, that exist within a particular domain.) Every culture and subculture has an emotionology, a system of emotion terms and concepts, that people deploy rhetorically in discourse to construct their own as well as other minds. At issue is a framework for conceptualizing emotions, their causes, and how participants in discourse are likely to display them. Narratives at once ground themselves in and help build frameworks of this sort. Everyday storytelling as well as literary narratives use and in some cases thematize emotion terms and concepts; for example, spy thrillers and romance novels are recognizable as such because of the way they link particular kinds of emotions to recurrent narrative scenarios. More

---

11. For a study that uses the world's narrative literature to develop an account of emotions as innate and universal, see Hogan (2003).
12. See, in addition to Stearns and Stearns (1985), Kotchemidova (2005); Edwards (1997: 170ff.); Harré and Gillett (1994: 144ff.); Lee (2003); and Stearns (1995). For an account of emotion that derives from the tradition of narrative semiotics, see Greimas and Fontanille (1993).

generally, stories provide insight into a culture's or subculture's emotionology – and also into how minds are made sense of via this system.

3.2   Emotion discourse in UFO or the Devil

Emotion discourse is a prominent dimension of *UFO or the Devil*. Throughout her narrative, Monica draws on the vocabulary of emotion, reports behaviors conventionally associated with extreme fear, and makes skillful use of the evaluative device that Labov (1972) called "expressive phonology", which encompasses a range of prosodic features, from changes in pitch, loudness, and rhythm, to emphatic lengthening of vowels or whole words, etc.[13] To take the issue of prosody first, and to dwell for a moment on the synergy between emotion discourse and the logic of positioning, note how Monica uses rhythm and intonation in line 53 (*bah bah ^bah ^bah*) to reposition herself: despite its stripped-down semantic profile, this speech production effectively dismisses as so much nonsense the storyline by means of which Renee's grandmother tries to other-position Monica as an hysterical imaginer of nonactual events. But beyond this, Monica interweaves shifts in volume with emphatically lengthened speech productions throughout her narrative, thereby foregrounding aspects of the encounter that carry the strongest emotional weight. In other words, Monica draws on the expressive resources of spoken discourse not only to highlight events (and features of events) that were the most emotionally salient, but also to construct herself as an accountably frightened experiencer of those events. Monica's emphatic production of *big ball* in line 10, for example, underscores the impact of her first glimpse of the apparition. Equally, her emphasis on *risen* in line 17 and *shit* in line 18, variably accomplished by changes in loudness or duration, throws into relief the frightening quality of the ball's movement as well as the intensity of her own fearful response. Similarly, in lines 38 and 39, Monica again uses these prosodic resources to indicate what makes the ball's manner of progress so frighteningly anomalous:

(37)   It's just a-bouncin behind us
(38)   It's NOT touchin the ^ground.
(39)   It's bouncin in the ^air.

---

13.   See Wennerstrom (2001) for a study of some of the discourse functions of prosody.

In narrative contexts, then, the sound properties of spoken discourse constitute a key emotionological resource, allowing first-person narrators like Monica to index percepts as more or less emotionally charged and to account for their own actions by situating them within this array of emotional valences. More than this, prosody allows first-person narrators to animate in the present their previous emotional responses; storytellers can thus establish a performative link between different phases of the self whose coherence and continuity derive in part from this ongoing process of re-performance – a process that more traumatic experiences, by splitting off the past from the present, can disrupt.

Further, *UFO or the Devil* grounds itself in an emotionology not just through prosodic performances but also at the level of individual words and more complex speech-act sequences. At the lexical level, Monica's story mirrors the way, in everyday discourse more generally, people draw on a vocabulary of emotion to make sense of one another's minds *as* minds. Thus, in lines 30 and 47, Monica uses an explicit emotion term (*scared*) to attribute the emotion of fear to Renee and herself. In addition, as the following excerpts suggest, Monica uses a number of locutions that imply a frightened emotional state. In line 14, Mary reports an attempt on her part to quell her own fears; line 18 involves another self-attribution, this time one involving both surprise and fright; and lines 30–33 report a speech act produced simultaneously by Monica and Renee in response to the fear-inducing apparition:

> (14) "nah..you know just..nah it ain't nothin", you know.
> [...]
> (18) And I'm like "SHIT!"..you know.
> [...]
> MW: (30) We like..we were scared and..
> (31) ^"Aaahhh!" you know=
> [
> CM: (32) (laughs)
> MW: (33) =at the same time.

What is more, Monica recounts actions that are, in the cultural, generic, and situational contexts in which her discourse is embedded, conventionally linked with the emotion of fear. These actions include running away from a threatening agent or event as fast as possible (34); running nonstop while being pursued (42); crying and screaming and feeling unable to breathe (45f.); and making a permanent change in one's routine in order to avoid the same threat in the future (57ff.). On the one hand, these behaviors are intelligible because of the emotionology in which Monica's story is grounded. That emotionology specifies that when an event X inducing an emotion Y occurs, an agent is likely to engage in Z sorts of behaviors, where Z constitutes a fuzzy set of more or less prototypical responses.[14] Thus a discourse such as Monica's acquires (suprasentential) coherence by virtue of its relationship to the broader emotionological context from which it emerges. The behaviors reported in the narrative can be construed as more than an agglomeration of individual acts because of the assumption, licensed by the emotionology in which Monica and her interlocutors participate, that actions of that sort constitute a coherent *class* of behaviors – namely, a class of behaviors in which one is likely to engage when motivated by fear.

But on the other hand, although emotionology constitutes a major resource for both the production and the understanding of narrative, stories also have the power to (re)shape emotionology itself. Narrative therapy, for example, involves the construction of stories about the self in which the emotional charge habitually carried by particular actions or routines can be defused or at least redirected (Mills 2005). Generic innovation in literary narratives can likewise entail the creation of new emotionological paths and linkages among events: consider the different logics of action in picaresque eighteenth-century fictions versus Gothic novels – e.g., the one-after-another-thing progression of something like Smollet's *Roderick Random* versus the enigma-fueled plot of Ann Radcliffe's *The Italian*, with its atmosphere of mysteriousness and danger. For its part, *UFO or the Devil* suggests how narrative provides a means for reassessing the emotion potential of whole sectors of experience; if narrative therapy allows people to uncouple counterproductive emotions from particular actions, other modes of storytelling bind emotional responses (e.g., fear) to regions of social or physical space hitherto uninvested with such emotions. Hence stories do not just emanate from emotionologies but also constitute a primary instrument for adjusting those systems of emotion terms and concepts to lived experience – whose broader profile is configured, in turn, through collaborative discourse practices. In species terms, narrative would presumably constitute a distinct evolutionary advantage, promoting more fear in potentially threatening circumstances and less fear in circumstances whose probable harmlessness multiple storytelling acts have

---

14. For example, in an investigative report recently broadcast on television, police detectives were led to conclude that a mother had played a role in her own children's death because of her atypically gleeful behavior at their gravesite.

cumulatively revealed. More generally, to follow the discursive psychologists and ground the mind in sociocommunicative practices is not to dissociate the mind from its physical or material contexts; rather, it is to
point to ways in which such contexts are enmeshed with discourse processes, including those supporting the design and interpretation of stories.

4. Cognitive grammar and focalization theory

My final case study in cognitive narratology concerns the issue of narrative perspective – that is, how vantage-points on situations and events in
the storyworld are encoded in narrative discourse and interpreted as such
during narrative processing. In this section, I hope to suggest ways in
which ideas from cognitive grammar might, by shifting the terms of analysis, enable narrative scholars to circumvent impasses created by classical
narratological theories of focalization.[15] To illustrate the advantages of
moving from talk of focalization to talk of conceptualization, I shift again
to another narrative medium, this time literary narrative – in particular,
three stories from Joyce's *Dubliners* (Joyce [1914] 1967). All of them completed between 1904 and 1906, the three stories form something of a comparison set; I use them to redescribe contrasting modes of focalization as,
instead, alternative patterns of construal or conceptualization. Narrative
perspective, in other words, can be interpreted as a reflex of the mind or
minds conceptualizing scenes represented in narrative texts. Further,
treating construal as the common root of voice and vision – as the common denominator shared by modes of narrative mediation – has wide-
ranging consequences for previous accounts of perspective in stories.[16]

---

15. See Jahn (1996) and (1999) for another approach to focalization that draws
    on ideas from the cognitive sciences.
16. Likewise, Grishakova (2002, 2006) richly synthesizes semiotic, narratologi-
    cal, and cognitive linguistic research to argue that "Genette's 'voice' and 'vi-
    sion' ('perception') are the two sides of the same process of sense-generation"
    (2002: 529) – that "perception is the common root of different modes of
    sense-production (verbal, visual and others)" (2002: 529). As I do in the pres-
    ent study, Grishakova draws on Langacker's ideas to underscore the parallel-
    ism of perception and conception and to challenge "Genette's understanding
    of 'focalization' as pure perception, on the one hand, and the existence of…
    'non-focalized' narration, on the other" (2006: 153). See Broman (2004) for a
    comparable critique of Genette's attempt to drive a wedge between narration
    and focalization.

Among other consequences, the focus of analysis shifts from taxonomy building, or the classification of types of focalization, to a functionalist account of perspective as sense-making strategy.

In the remainder of this section, I use three stories from *Dubliners* as case studies: "Araby", "Ivy Day in the Committee Room", and "The Dead". Although I refer to these stories in their entirety, initially my discussion will use the following three passages as "touchstones" or specific illustrative examples:

(a) Mr Hynes sat down again on the table. When he had finished his recitation [of "The Death of Parnell"] there was a silence and then a burst of clapping: even Mr Lyons clapped. The applause continued for a little time. When it had ceased all the auditors drank from their bottles in silence. ("Ivy Day", p. 135)

(b) I watched my master's face pass from amiability to sternness; he hoped I was not beginning to idle. ("Araby", p. 32)

(c) The piano was playing a waltz tune and he [Gabriel Conroy] could hear the skirts sweeping against the drawing-room door. People, perhaps, were standing in the snow on the quay outside, gazing up at the lighted windows and listening to the waltz music. The air was pure there. In the distance lay the park where the trees were weighted with snow. ("The Dead", p. 202)

Then, in the final part of the section, I draw on another passage from "The Dead", represented as (d), to draw together further the strands of my discussion and underscore the advantages of moving from classical narratological theories of focalization to a postclassical account informed by Langacker's cognitive grammar and Talmy's cognitive semantics:

(d) When he saw Freddy Malins coming across the room to visit his mother Gabriel left the chair free for him and retired into the embrasure of the window. The room had already cleared and from the back room came the clatter of plates and knives. Those who still remained in the drawing-room seemed tired of dancing and were conversing quietly in little groups. Gabriel's warm trembling fingers tapped the cold pane of the window. How cool it must be outside! How pleasant it would be to walk out alone, first along by the river and then through the park! The snow would be lying on the branches of the trees and forming a bright cap on the top of the Wellington Monument. How much more pleasant it would be there than at the supper-table! ("The Dead", p. 192)

4.1 Narrative perspective: classical accounts

In the narratological literature, the concept of focalization, originally proposed by Genette as a way to distinguish between who sees and who speaks in a narrative, has generated considerable debate. In the Genettean tradition, focalization is a way of talking about perceptual and conceptual frames, more or less inclusive or restricted, through which participants, situations, and events are presented in a narrative (Prince 2003: 31 f.; Herman 2002: 301 ff.). Thus, in what Genette ([1972] 1980) calls internal focalization, the viewpoint is restricted to a particular observer or "reflector" whereas in what he calls zero focalization (which Bal 1997 and Rimmon-Kenan 1983 term external focalization) the viewpoint is not anchored in a localized position. Also, internal focalization can be fixed, variable, or multiple. Hence the focalization in "Araby" and "The Dead" is, in Genette's terms, internal: as suggested by passages (b) on the one hand and (c) and (d) on the other hand, the younger, experiencing-I is the focalizer in "Araby" whereas in "The Dead" Gabriel Conroy provides the vantage-point on situations and events in the storyworld. Meanwhile, "Ivy Day" (a), which focuses on a group of election workers commemorating the anniversary of the death of the Irish political leader Charles Parnell, relies mainly on externalized views of the action. Hence, whereas the focalization is fixed and internal in "Araby" and "The Dead", "Ivy Day" uses what Genette (as opposed to Bal and Rimmon-Kenan) would term external focalization, in which "what is presented [is] limited to the characters' external behavior (words and actions but not thoughts or feelings), their appearance, and the setting against which they come to the fore" (Prince 2003: 32). There is, however, a departure from (what Genette might call an "infraction against") this dominant code of focalization when the narration dips briefly into the contents of Mr Crofton's mind and reveals that he refrains from speaking because "he considered his companions beneath him" (Joyce [1914] 1967: 142).

So far, so good: the structuralist approach to focalization yields important insights into the contrasts and commonalities among texts like Joyce's – and, in principle, among all texts categorizable as narratives. Yet the classical picture of narrative perspective is complicated both by (1) tensions between different approaches within the Genettean framework and by (2) a separate tradition of research stemming from the work of F. K. Stanzel ([1979] 1984) on "narrative situations", which is inconsistent with or at the very least orthogonal to Genette's approach. With respect to (1), Shlomith Rimmon-Kenan (1983) and Mieke Bal (1997) are among the narratologists who argue for a baroque ontology of focalizer and focalized (which can in turn be focalized both from without and from within). Notably, Genette ([1983] 1988) himself disputes these elaborations of his original account. Invoking Occam's razor, Genette maintains that only the gestalt concept of focalization is needed to capture the modalities of narrative perspective.[17]

With respect to (2), Stanzel assimilates narrative perspective to the more general process of narratorial mediation, which he characterizes in terms of three clines or continua: internal vs. external perspective on events, identity vs. non-identity between narrator and narrated world, and narrating agent (or teller) vs. perceptual agent (or reflector). For example, the figural narrative situation, exemplified by "The Dead" globally and also locally in passages (c) and (d) above, obtains when a given stretch of narrative discourse is marked by an internal perspective on events, a position toward the reflector end of the teller-reflector continuum, and non-identity between narrator and storyworld. Authorial (= distanced third-person) narration, exemplified by passage (a), obtains when the discourse is marked by an external perspective, a position toward the teller end of the teller-reflector continuum, and, again, non-identity between narrator and storyworld. More generally, whereas Genette and those influenced by him strictly demarcate who speaks and who sees, voice and vision, narration and focalization, the Stanzelian model suggests that the voice and vision aspects of narratorial mediation cluster together in different ways to comprise the different narrative situations. Furthermore, for Stanzel, these aspects are matters of degree rather than binarized features. As the gradable contrast between the authorial and figural narrative situations suggests, the agent responsible for the narration can in some instances, and to a greater or lesser degree, fuse with the agent responsible for perception – yielding not an absolute gap but a variable, manipulable distance between the roles of teller and reflector, vocalizer and visualizer (cf. Shaw 1995; Nieragden 2002; Phelan 2001). Contrast Kate Chopin's *The Awakening*, which shuttles back and forth

---

17. Broman (2004) notes a further division among researchers working within the Genettean tradition: namely, between those who follow Genette himself in developing a global, typological-classificatory approach, whereby differences among modes of focalizations provide a basis for categorizing novels and short stories, and those who follow Bal in developing "the minute analysis of shifts in points of view between text passages and sentences, and in certain cases even within the same sentence" (71).

between the authorial and figural modes in order to extrapolate general truths from internal views of Edna Pontellier's situation, with Franz Kafka's *The Trial*, which suggests the impossibility of any such extrapolation by remaining scrupulously close to Josef K's position as reflector.

As even this cursory overview suggests, the lack of consensus or even convergence among researchers after several decades of research in this area, as well as the problematic incommensurability of the Genettean and Stanzelian paradigms, points up the need to rethink foundational terms and concepts of focalization theory itself. Tools required for this reconceptualization, I argue in my next subsection, can be found in cognitive grammar. Building on studies by Langacker (1987) and Talmy (2000), among others, narrative analysts can move from classical theories of narrative perspective toward a unified account of *construal* or *conceptualization processes* and their reflexes in narrative. Such construal operations, which underlie the organization of narrative discourse, are shaped not just by factors bearing on perspective or viewpoint, but also by temporal, spatial, affective, and other factors associated with embodied human experience.

4.2   From focalization to conceptualization

4.2.1. *Narrative perspective and modes of construal*

The basic idea behind conceptualization or construal is that one and the same situation or event can be linguistically encoded in different ways, by means of locutions that are truth-conditionally equivalent despite more or less noticeably different formats (for a more detailed overview, see Croft and Cruse 2004: 40ff.). Langacker (1987) suggests that a range of cognitive abilities, including comparison, the deployment of imagery, the transformation of one construal into another or others, and focal adjustment, support the processes of conceptualization that surface as dimensions of semantic structure. In other words, these cognitive abilities are also design parameters for language. A subset of the parameters at issue – namely, those associated specifically with *focal adjustment* – derives from the enabling and constraining condition of having an embodied, spatiotemporally situated perspective on events.

A brief thought-experiment can illustrate the general processes at issue. Assuming that (i) – (vi) all truly apply to the same spatiotemporal configuration of participants and circumstances, differences among them reflect humans' ability to mentally "construe" one and the same situation in alternative ways.

(i)   The family of raccoons stared at the goldfish in the pond
(ii) The goldfish in the pond were stared at by the family of raccoons
(iii) A family of raccoons stared at some goldfish in a pond
(iv) The family of raccoons stared at the goldfish in the pond over there
(v)   That damned family of raccoons stared at the goldfish in the pond
(vi) The family of raccoons stared at those damned goldfish in the pond

(i) and (ii) show how alternate figure-ground relationships afford contrasting conceptualizations; (i) and (iii) how different locutionary formats can represent different construals of hearer knowledge; (i) and (iv) how conceptualizations can be more or less subjective in Langacker's sense of that term, i.e., include the situation of utterance more or less prominently in the scene being construed; and (i), (v), and (vi) how different affective registers can surface in alternative construals. Although cognitive grammarians tend to study such construal operations at the clause and sentence level, my claim is that the operations themselves are scalable and can be mapped onto discourse-level structures in narrative.

To return to the parameter of focal adjustment in particular, Langacker (1987) identifies a number of sub-parameters relevant for the study of how perspective shapes the construal of events. Combined with Talmy's (2000) account of perspective as a "conceptual structuring system", Langacker's account yields a rich framework for studying perspective-taking processes in narrative contexts. Langacker decomposes focal adjustment into the following sub-parameters (and sub-sub-parameters):

– Selection (concerns the scope of a predication, i.e. how much of the "scene" one is construing is included in the conceptualization)
– Perspective, which includes
  – figure-ground alignment, i.e., foreground-background relations; see also Talmy (2000, 1: 311 ff.)
  – viewpoint (= vantage point + orientation within a directional grid consisting of vertical and horizontal axes)
  – deixis (deictic expressions include some reference to the "ground" or situation of utterance in their immediate scope of predication)
  – subjectivity/objectivity (for Langacker, the degree of subjectivity of a construal varies inversely with the degree to which the ground is included in the immediate scope of a predication: the more the ground is included, the more objectivized the construal)
– Abstraction, which pertains to the level of specificity of a construal, i.e., its degree of granularity (how much detail is included)

Meanwhile, in Talmy's (2000) cognitive semantics, perspective constitutes a schematic system. On the basis of this system, languages establish "a conceptual perspective point from which [a referent entity can be] cognitively regarded" (1: 68). In parallel with Langacker's model, Talmy's account of the perspective system encompasses several categories or parameters that find reflexes in the semantic system of a given language (1: 68 ff.), including

- the location of a perspective point within a "referent scene"
- the distance of a perspective point from the regarded scene (distal, medial, proximal)
- perspectival mode, including motility, i.e. whether the perspective point is stationary or moving, and mode proper, i.e., synoptic versus sequential viewing
- direction of viewing, i.e., "sighting" in a particular direction (spatially or temporally) from an established perspective point

My larger point here is that classical theories of focalization, deriving from the work of Genette and Stanzel, capture only part of this system of perspective-related parameters for construal.

By shifting from theories of focalization to an account of the processes and sub-processes involved in conceptualization, story analysts can explore how narratives may represent relatively **statically** (synoptically) or **dynamically** (sequentially) scanned scenes (or event-structures). These will have a relatively wide or narrow **scope, focal participants** and **backgrounded elements**, varying **degrees of granularity**, an **orientation** within a horizontal/vertical dimensional grid, and a more or less **objective** profile (i.e., encompass the ground of predication to a greater or lesser extent). Scenes are also **"sighted"** from particular temporal and spatial directions, and viewpoints on scenes can be **distal, medial,** or **proximal**. Each such distance increment, further, may carry a default expectation about the **level of granularity** of the construal.

Passage (a), for example, can be redescribed as an instance of narrative discourse in which the conceptual perspective point is static rather than dynamic and situated at a medial distance from the regarded scene, yielding a medium-scope construal of the characters and their environment. Yet, despite the constant distance between the vantage-point on the scene and the scene itself, there is a shift in the level of granularity of the representation: over the course of the passage, the focal participants move from particularized individuals (Mr Hynes, Mr Lyons) to the characters viewed as a group ("all the auditors"). Conversely, passage (c) (and also, as I discuss below in 4.2.2, passage d) is remarkable for the way fluctuations in perspectival distance do not affect the relative granularity of the construal. Gabriel is at a proximal distance from the drawing room, but as the sentential adverb *perhaps*[18] indicates, his vantage-point is distally located vis-à-vis the scenes he *imagines* to be outside: namely, the quay and, still farther away, the park. Yet there is no appreciable difference in the granularity of the construals afforded by shifts along this chain of vantage-points. Working against default expectations about how much granularity is available from what perspectival distance, Joyce's text evokes the power of the imagination to transcend the constraints of space and time – both here and again at the end of story, when Gabriel imagines how the snow is general all over Ireland. The conceptualization processes portrayed in the story thus emulate the spatiotemporal transpositions accomplished by Joyce's own fictional discourse; the concern in both contexts is the process by which one set of space-time parameters can be "laminated" within another, to use Goffman's (1974) term. In other words, the scene outside the party becomes proximate to Gabriel's mind's eye through the same process of transposition that allows readers to relocate, or deictically shift (Zubin and Hewitt 1995), to the spatial and temporal coordinates occupied by Gabriel as the reflector through whom perceptions of the fictional party are filtered.

In passage (b), meanwhile, what is noteworthy are the cross-cutting directions of *temporal* sighting: the older, narrating-I looks back on the younger, experiencing-I, whose observation of the increasingly dissatisfied expression on his schoolmaster's face is in turn forward-oriented. This bidirectional temporal sighting, the signature of first-person retrospective narratives (whether fictional or nonfictional), is complemented by a combination of synoptic and sequential scanning. The passage reveals a construal of the master's face as undergoing change over time, but the construal itself is summative, compressing into a single clause an alteration that one can assume unfolded over a more or less extended temporal duration.

---

18. In Fauconnier's (1994) terms, *perhaps* functions here as a space-builder, opening within the storyworld an embedded mental space constructed by Gabriel's imagination. This space could also be characterized, in Paul Werth's (1999) terms, as a subworld within the text world evoked by Joyce's story as a whole.

4.2.2. Underscoring the advantages
of a cognitive-grammatical approach

Drawing on the enriched analytic framework outlined in this section, theorists can ask questions about narrative perspective that could not even be formulated within the classical models, while still preserving the (important) insights afforded by Genettean and Stanzelian focalization theory. The approach thus affords a more unified, systematic treatment of perspective-related aspects of narrative structure that previous narratological research treats in a more piecemeal or atomistic way.

In passage (d), the Genettean analyst would speak of internally focalized narration; the Stanzelian, of narration in the figural mode. Further, drawing on the "speech-category" approach to consciousness representation (Cohn 1978; Palmer 2004: 53 ff.), the classical narratologist interested in tracing moment-by-moment shifts in the perspective structure of the passage would be able to note the movement from actual to imaginary perceptions in the second half of the passage. The exclamation marks suggest sentiments or thoughts that have forcibly struck Gabriel, and that are therefore linked to his subjectivity rather than the neutral, non-exclamatory discourse of the narrator. In Stanzelian terms, these exclamation marks signal that the mode of narration has shifted even closer to the reflector end of the continuum than it was in the first part of the passage – as do the modal auxiliary verbs ("How cool it *must be* ..", "The snow *would be* lying...", "How pleasant it *would be*...") indexing Gabriel's probabilistic reasoning about the outside world to which he does not currently have direct access.

However, recruiting from Langacker's and Talmy's frameworks allows the analyst to capture how the factor of perspective bears on a wider range of textual details, and to uncover systematic interconnections among those details that remain hidden when classical narratological approaches are used. In Talmy's terms, passage (d) reveals how Gabriel's perspective constitutes a conceptual structuring system, in which Freddy Malins and his mother are, initially, the focal participants in a sequentially scanned scene. The past-tense indicative verbs mark the scene as one that is being sighted from a temporal viewpoint located later on the time-line than the point occupied by the represented events. Spatially, the scene is sighted from a viewpoint situated on the same plane as the represented action: Gabriel is not observing the scene from below, for example, as is the case when he construes Gretta as "a symbol of something" at the top of the stairs (Joyce [1914] 1967:

210).[19] Further, Gabriel's initial medium-distance viewpoint on the scene (from the chair next to Mrs Malins) affords a medium-scope representation with a corresponding, mid-level degree of granularity or detail.

Then, when Gabriel takes up his new position in the embrasure of the window, his distance from the scene increases, producing a wider-scope conceptualization of the scene that has a correspondingly lower degree of granularity: Gabriel construes the scene in terms of groups rather than individuals. As they did in passage (c), then, the factors of distance, scope, and granularity of construal co-vary systematically: generally speaking, as you get farther away from something, you see more of the context that surrounds it but with less overall detail, and these perspectival constraints on people's mental lives also shape how they use language – for example, how they produce and interpret narratives. Meanwhile, Gabriel has now moved much closer to the window, his position affording a proximal, narrow-scope, and highly granular, detailed representation of his own fingers tapping the cold pane. The shift to free indirect thought in "How cool it must be outside!" marks the onset of a new conceptualization – this time of an imagined scene outside. As the new construal gets underway, distance, scope, and granularity again co-vary: the hypothetical scene is farther away than the window, encompasses the whole area by the river and through the park, and is not envisioned in any detailed way. But then Gabriel imagines specific features of the scene, the degree of granularity increasing dramatically to the point where the snow on the branches of trees and on the top of the Wellington monument comes into focus. Working against default expectations about how much granularity is available from what perspectival distance, Joyce's text once again evokes, structurally as well as thematically, the power of the imagination to transcend the constraints of space and time.

In short, in contrast with earlier focalization theory, a cognitive-grammatical approach points the way toward a more unified, integrative account of perspective and its bearing on other aspects of narrative production and processing, including stylistic texture (e.g., verb tenses and moods), the spatio-temporal configuration of storyworlds, the represen-

---

19. Likewise the factors of orientation and (spatial) sighting come into play in passage (c). Gabriel first imagines others looking up at the lighted windows and listening to the music in the house; then, mentally shifting to the deictic coordinates occupied by those hypothetical outside observers, he imaginatively takes up their vantage-point and sights the imagined scene in the park along a horizontal rather than vertical axis.

tation of consciousness, and narrative thematics. A task for future research is to consider other ways in which the idea of construal might afford new foundations for narrative inquiry – for the study of how strategies for telling are inextricably interlinked with strategies for conceptualizing the world told about.

5.   Conclusion: narrative inquiry beyond the two cultures

As I have characterized them here, cognitive approaches to narrative analysis constitute a domain of inquiry that falls under the broader rubric of postclassical narratology. In turn, a crucial aspect – indeed, a precondition – of the shift from classical to postclassical frameworks is the attempt to heal the rift between humanistic and (social-)scientific approaches to narrative study. Unfortunately, these approaches began to bifurcate from the very inception of sustained inquiry into stories (Herman 2004; cf. Jackson 2005 and Sternberg 2003a, 2003b, 2004). Yet as I have tried to suggest through my examination of case studies in different media (including multimodal texts, spoken language, and literary narrative), by shifting the focus of research to cognitive dimensions of narrative practices, analysts can overcome limitations arising from the restricted corpora on which scholars working in different traditions have based their concepts and methods. Indeed, it is a central aim of cognitive narratology and of related endeavors whose scope extends beyond narrative, including cognitive semiotics (Fastrez 2003), cognitive poetics (Stockwell 2002; Gavins and Steen 2003), and cognitive stylistics (Semino and Culpeper 2002), to discover ways of reconnecting the study of narratives and other semiotic artifacts with the study of language and mind (cf Turner 1991) – to rejoin the study of narrative art with the study of the dispositions and abilities that both bring it into being and make it intelligible as such. The more that theorists can do to promote synergies of this kind, the more likely that cognitive approaches to narrative inquiry will afford a bridge between C.P. Snow's ([1959] 1993) two cultures, uniting story analysts from across the arts and sciences.[20]

---

20. I am grateful to Jeroen Vandaele, Geert Brône, and the anonymous reviewers for their productive comments and criticisms on an earlier draft of this chapter. Also, my special thanks go to my colleague Jared Gardner, for his willingness to share his extensive expertise on comics and graphic novels – expertise that informs my discussion of *The Incredible Hulk* in section 2.

Appendix: *UFO or the Devil*

Transcription Conventions (adapted from Tannen 1993 and Ochs et al. 1992)

... represents a measurable pause, more than 0.1 seconds

.. represents a slight break in timing

. indicates sentence-final intonation

, indicates clause-final intonation ("more to come")

Syllables with ~ were spoken with heightened pitch

Syllables with ^ were spoken with heightened loudness

Words and syllables transcribed with ALL CAPITALS were emphatically lengthened speech productions

[indicates overlap between different speakers' utterances

= indicates an utterance continued across another speaker's overlapping utterance

/ / enclose transcriptions that are not certain

( ) enclose nonverbal forms of expression, e.g. laughter unaccompanied by words

(( )) enclose interpolated commentary

[...] in short extracts indicates omitted lines

M: (1) So that's why I say.. UFO or the devil got after our ^black asses,
        (2) for showing out.
        (3) I don't know what was it
        (4) we walkin up the ^hill,
        (5) this ^way, comin up through here.
CM: (6) Yeah.
M: (7) And.. I'm like on ^this side and Renee's right here.
        (8) And we ^walkin
        (9) and I look over the ^bank,
        (10) and I see this.. ^BIG ^BALL.
        (11) It's ^glowin..
        (12) and it's ^orange.
        (13) And I'm just like..
        (14) "nah.. you know just.. nah it ain't nothin", you know.
        (15) And I'm still ^walkin, you know.
        (16) Then I look back over my side ^again,
        (17) and it has ^risen up.
        (18) And I'm like "SHIT!".. you know.
        (19) So but ^Renee.. I still ain't say nothin to her

(20) and I'm not sure she see it or ^not.

(21) So I'm still not ^sayin anything.

(22) We just ^walkin.

(23) Then I look over the bank ^again

(24) and I don't see it.

(25) Then I'm like "well, you know."

(26) But then..for some reason I feel some heat or somethin other

(27) and I look ^back

(28) me and Renee did at the same time

(29) it's right ^behind us.

(30) We like..we were scared and..

(31) ^"Aaahhh!" you know=

[

RC: (32)   (laughs)

M: (33) =at the same time.

(34) So we take off ^runnin as ^fast as we can

(35) And we still lookin ^back

(36) and every time we look back it's with us.

(37) It's just a-bouncin behind us

(38) it's NOT touchin the ^ground.

(39) It's bouncin in the ^air.

(40) It's like this..behind us

(41) as we ^run.

(42) We run ^all the way to her grandmother's

(43) and we ^open the door

(44) and we just fall out in the floor,

(45) and we're cryin and we screamin

(46) and we just can't ^BREATHE.

(47) We that ^scared.

(48) "What's ^wrong with you all" you know

(49) and we ^tell them..you know..what had ^happened.

(50) And then her grandmother tell us

(51) it's some mineral.. this or that

(52) they just form

(53) bah bah ^bah ^bah

(54) and..the way we ^ran..it's the ^heat

(55) and..you know..Bullshit.

(56) You know..but so I never knew in my ^life. about that

(57) but we didn't ^do that anymore.

CM: (58) Right.

M: (59) When dark goddamn came
      (60) our ass was at ^home.

References

Aristotle
    1971   *Poetics.* In: Hazard Adams (ed.), *Critical Theory Since Plato*, 48–66. San Diego, CA: Harcourt Brace Jovanovich.
Bal, Mieke
    1997   *Narratology: Introduction to the Theory of Narrative.* 2nd edition. Toronto: University of Toronto Press.
Barthes, Roland
    [1966] 1977   Introduction to the structural analysis of narratives. In: Stephen Heath (trans.), *Image-music-text*, 79–124. New York: Hill and Wang.
Barthes, Roland
    1971   Action sequences. In Joseph Strelka (ed.), *Patterns of Literary Style*, 5–14. University Park, PA: Pennsylvania State University Press.
Berman, Ruth A. and Dan I. Slobin (eds.)
    1994   *Relating Events in Narrative: A Crosslinguistic Developmental Study.* Malwah, NJ: Lawrence Erlbaum.
Bontekoe, Ronald
    1996   *Dimensions of the Hermeneutic Circle.* Atlantic Highlands, NJ: Humanities Press International.
Bortolussi, Marisa and Peter Dixon
    2003   *Psychonarratology: Foundations for the Empirical Study of Literary Response.* Cambridge: Cambridge University Press.
Bridgeman, Teresa
    2005   Figuration and configuration: Mapping imaginary worlds in bande dessinee. In: Charles Forsdick, Laurence Grove and Libbie McQuillan (eds.), *The Francophone Bande Dessinee*, 115–136. Amsterdam: Rodopi.
Broman, Eva
    2004   Narratological focalization models – A critical survey. In: Göran Rossholm (ed.), *Essays on Fiction and Perspective*, 57–89. Bern: Peter Lang.
Croft, William and D.A. Cruse
    2004   *Cognitive Linguistics.* Cambridge: Cambridge University Press.
Dancygier, Barbara
    2006   Authors and narrators: Levels of conceptual integration. Paper presented at the UConn Conference on Literature and the Cognitive Sciences; Storrs, Connecticut, April 2006.
Dosse, François
    1997   *History of Structuralism,* vol. 1, Deborah Glassman (trans.). Minneapolis: The University of Minnesota Press.

Edwards, Derek
   1997   *Discourse and Cognition.* London: Sage.
Emmott, Catherine
   1997   *Narrative Comprehension: A Discourse Perspective.* Oxford: Oxford University Press.
Fastrez, Pierre (ed.)
   2003   *Sémiotique Cognitive – Cognitive Semiotics.* Special issue of *Recherches en communication* 19.
Fauconnier, Gilles
   1994   *Mental Spaces: Aspects of Meaning Construction in Natural Language.* Cambridge: Cambridge University Press.
Fauconnier, Gilles and Mark Turner
   2002   *The Way We Think: Conceptual Blending and the Mind's Hidden Complexities.* New York: Basic Books.
Garnham, Alan and Jane Oakhill
   1996   The mental models theory of language comprehension. In: Bruce K. Britton and Arthur C. Graesser (eds.), *Models of Understanding Text,* 313–39. Mahwah, NJ: Lawrence Erlbaum.
Gavins, Joanna and Gerard Steen (eds.)
   2003   *Cognitive Poetics in Practice.* London: Routledge.
Genette, Gérard
   [1972] 1980 *Narrative Discourse: An Essay in Method,* Jane E. Lewin (trans.). Ithaca: Cornell University Press.
Genette, Gérard
   [1983] 1988 *Narrative Discourse Revisited,* Jane E. Lewin (trans.). Ithaca: Cornell University Press.
Gerrig, Richard J.
   1993   *Experiencing Narrative Worlds: On the Psychological Activities of Reading.* New Haven: Yale University Press.
Goffman, Erving
   1974   *Frame Analysis: An Essay on the Organization of Experience.* New York: Harper.
Greimas, A. J.
   [1966] 1983 *Structural Semantics: An Attempt at a Method,* Daniele McDowell, Ronald Schleifer and Alan Velie (trans). Lincoln: University of Nebraska Press.
Greimas, A.J.
   1987   Actants, actors, and figures. In: Paul F. Perron and Frank H. Collins (eds.), *On Meaning: Selected Writings in Semiotic Theory,* 11–36. Minneapolis: University of Minnesota Press.
Greimas, A. J. and Jacques Fontanille
   1993   *The Semiotics of Passions: From States of Affairs to States of Feeling,* Paul Perron and Frank Collins (trans.). Minneapolis: University of Minnesota Press.

Grishakova, Marina
    2002   The acts of presence negotiated: Towards the semiotics of the observer. *Sign Systems Studies* 30(2): 529–53.

Grishakova, Marina
    2006   *The Models of Space, Time and Vision in V. Nabokov's Fiction: Narrative Strategies and Cultural Frames.* Tartu: Tartu University Press.

Harré, Rom and Grant Gillett
    1994   *The Discursive Mind.* London: Sage

Harré, Rom and Luk van Langenhove (eds.)
    1999   *Positioning Theory.* Oxford: Blackwell.

Hendricks, William O.
    1967   On the notion "beyond the sentence." *Linguistics* 37: 12–51.

Herman, David
    1999   Introduction. In: David Herman (ed.), *Narratologies: New Perspectives on Narrative Analysis*, 1–30. Columbus: Ohio State University Press.

Herman, David
    2002   *Story Logic: Problems and Possibilities of Narrative.* Lincoln: University of Nebraska Press.

Herman, David
    2003a   Stories as a tool for thinking. In: David Herman (ed.), *Narrative Theory and the Cognitive Sciences*, 163–92. Stanford, CA: Publications of the Center for the Study of Language and Information.

Herman, David (ed.)
    2003b   *Narrative Theory and the Cognitive Sciences.* Stanford, CA: Publications of the Center for the Study of Language and Information.

Herman, David
    2004   Toward a transmedial narratology. In: Marie-Laure Ryan (ed.), *Narrative across Media: The Languages of Storytelling*, 47–75. Lincoln: University of Nebraska Press.

Herman, David
    2005a   Histories of narrative theory (I): A genealogy of early developments. In: James Phelan and Peter J. Rabinowitz (eds), *The Blackwell Companion to Narrative Theory*, 19–35. Malden: Blackwell.

Herman, David
    2005b   Quantitative methods in narratology: A corpus-based study of motion events in stories. In: Jan Christoph Meister, in cooperation with Tom Kindt, Wilhelm Schernus and Malte Stein (eds.), *Narratology Beyond Literary Criticism*, 124–49. Berlin: Walter de Gruyter.

Herman, David
    2006   Dialogue in a discourse context: Scenes of talk in fictional narrative. *Narrative Inquiry* 16(1): 79–88.

Hogan, Patrick Colm
    2003   *The Mind and Its Stories: Narrative Universals and Human Emotion.* Cambridge: Cambridge University Press.

Jackson, Tony E.
2005   Explanation, interpretation, and close reading: The progress of cognitive poetics. *Poetics Today* 26(3): 519–33.

Jahn, Manfred
1996   Windows of focalization: Deconstructing and reconstructing a narratological concept. *Style* 30(3): 241–67.

Jahn, Manfred
1997   Frames, preferences, and the reading of third-person narratives: Towards a cognitive narratology. *Poetics Today* 18: 441–68.

Jahn, Manfred
1999   More aspects of focalization: Refinements and applications." *GRAAT* 21 (Groupes de Recherches Anglo-Américaines de Tours) [Issue Topic: "Recent Trends in Narratological Research"]: 85–110.

Jahn, Manfred
2005   Cognitive narratology. In: David Herman, Manfred Jahn and Marie-Laure Ryan (eds.), *Routledge Encyclopedia of Narrative Theory*, 67–71. London: Routledge.

Joyce, James
[1914] 1967   *Dubliners*. New York: Penguin Books.

Kafalenos, Emma
2006   *Narrative Causalities*. Columbus: Ohio State University Press.

Kotchemidova, Christina
2005   From good cheer to "drive-by smiling": A social history of cheerfulness. *Journal of Social History* 39(1) <http://www.historycooperative. org/journals/jsh/39.1/kotchemidova.html>.

Labov, William
1972   The transformation of experience in narrative syntax. In: William Labov, *Language in the Inner City*, 354–96. Philadelphia: University of Pennsylvania Press.

Labov, William and Joshua Waletzky
1967   Narrative analysis: Oral versions of personal experience. In: June Helm (ed.), *Essays on Verbal and Visual Arts*, 12–44. Seattle: University of Washington Press.

Langacker, Ronald W.
1987   *Foundations of Cognitive Grammar*, vol. 1. Stanford: Stanford University Press.

Lee, Penny
2003   "Feelings of the mind" in talk about thinking in English. *Cognitive Linguistics* 14(2/3): 221–49.

Mallinson, Christine
2006   The dynamic construction of race, class, and gender through linguistic practice among women in a black Appalachian community. Unpublished Ph.D. dissertation. Department of Sociology, North Carolina State University.

116   *David Herman*

Meister, Jan Christoph (ed.)
2005   *Narratology Beyond Literary Criticism*. Berlin: Walter de Gruyter.
Miller, James E., Jr. (ed.)
1971   *Theory of Fiction: Henry James*. Lincoln: University of Nebraska Press.
Mills, Linda
2005   Narrative therapy. In: David Herman, Manfred Jahn and Marie-Laure Ryan (eds.), *Routledge Encyclopedia of Narrative Theory*, 375–76. London: Routledge.
Nieragden, Göran
2002   Focalization and narration: theoretical and terminological refinements. *Poetics Today* 23(4): 685–97.
Ochs, Elinor, Carolyn Taylor, Dina Rudolph and Ruth Smith
1992   Storytelling as theory-building activity. *Discourse Processes* 15: 37–72.
Palmer, Alan
2004   *Fictional Minds*. Lincoln: University of Nebraska Press.
Phelan, James
2001   Why narrators can be focalizers – and why it matters. In: Willie van Peer and Seymour Chatman (eds.), *New Perspectives on Narrative Perspective*, 51–64. Albany: State University of New York Press.
Prince, Gerald
2003   *A Dictionary of Narratology*, 2nd edition. Lincoln: University of Nebraska Press.
Propp, Vladimir
[1928] 1968 *Morphology of the Folktale*, Laurence Scott (trans.; revised by Louis A. Wagner). Austin: University of Texas Press.
Rimon-Kenan, Shlomith
1983   *Narrative Fiction: Contemporary Poetics*. London: Methuen.
Ryan, Marie-Laure
2001   *Narrative as Virtual Reality: Immersion and Interactivity in Literature and Electronic Media*. Baltimore: Johns Hopkins University Press.
Schiffrin, Deborah
1987   *Discourse Markers*. Cambridge: Cambridge University Press.
Semino, Elena and Jonathan Culpeper (eds.)
2002   *Cognitive Stylistics: Language and Cognition in Text Analysis*. Amsterdam: John Benjamins.
Shaw, Harry
1995   Loose narrators. *Narrative* 3: 95–116.
Snow, C. P.
[1959] 1993 *The Two Cultures*. Cambridge: Cambridge University Press.
Stanzel, F. K.
[1979] 1984 *A Theory of Narrative*, Charlotte Goedsche (trans.). Cambridge: Cambridge University Press.
Stearns, Peter
1995   Emotion. In: Rom Harré and Peter Stearns (eds.), *Discursive Psychology in Practice*, 37–54. Thousand Oaks, CA: Sage.

Stearns, Peter and Carol Stearns
    1985   Emotionology: Clarifying the history of emotions and emotional stan-
           dards. *American Historical Review* 90: 13–36

Sternberg, Meir
    2003a   Universals of narrative and their cognitivist fortunes (I). *Poetics Today*
           24(2): 297–395.

Sternberg, Meir
    2003b   Universals of narrative and their cognitivist fortunes (I). *Poetics Today*
           24(3): 517–638.

Sternberg, Meir
    2004   Narrative universals, cognitivist story analysis, and interdisciplinary
           pursuit of knowledge: An omnibus rejoinder. http://www.arts.ualberta.
           ca/igel/igel2004/debate/Sternberg.htm

Stockwell, Peter
    2002   *Cognitive Poetics: An Introduction.* London: Routledge.

Talmy, Leonard
    2000   *Toward a Cognitive Semantics*, vols. 1 and 2. Cambridge, MA: MIT
           Press.

Tannen, Deborah (ed.)
    1993   *Framing in Discourse.* Oxford: Oxford University Press

Tesnière, Lucien
    1976   *Éléments de syntaxe structurale.* 2nd edition. Paris: Klinksieck.

Todorov, Tzvetan
    1969   *Grammaire du "Décaméron."* The Hague: Mouton.

Turner, Mark
    1991   *Reading Minds: The Study of English in the Age of Cognitive Science.*
           Princeton: Princeton University Press.

Van Peer, Willie and Seymour Chatman (eds.)
    2001   *New Perspectives on Narrative Perspective.* Albany: State University of
           New York Press.

Webber, Bonnie Lynn
    1979   *A Formal Approach to Discourse Anaphora.* New York: Garland.

Wennerstrom, Ann
    2001   *The Music of Everyday Speech: Prosody and Discourse Analysis.* Ox-
           ford: Oxford University Press.

Werth, Paul
    1999   *Text Worlds: Representing Conceptual Space in Discourse.* London:
           Longman.

Wilson, Robert and Frank Keil (eds.)
    1999   *The MIT Encyclopedia of the Cognitive Sciences.* Cambridge, MA: MIT
           Press.

Wolf, Werner
    2003   Narrative and narrativity: A narratological reconceptualization and its
           applicability to the visual arts. *Word & Image* 19: 180–97.

Young, Kay and Jeffrey Saver
    2005   Narrative disorders. In: David Herman, Manfred Jahn and Marie-Laure Ryan (eds.), *Routledge Encyclopedia of Narrative Theory,* 352–53. London: Routledge.
Zubin, David A. and Lynne E. Hewitt
    1995   The Deictic Center: A Theory of Deixis in Narrative. In: Judith F. Duchan, Gail A. Bruder and Lynne E. Hewitt (eds.), *Deixis in Narrative: A Cognitive Science Perspective,* 129–55. Hillsdale, NJ: Lawrence Erlbaum.

Situating cognitive approaches to narrative analysis

Peter Stockwell

Let's begin with a story.

> In the middle of the last decade of the twentieth century, the Literary-Linguist was travelling on a bus across the Hungarian central plain towards a large academic conference in the town of Debrecen. The hours rolled by with the vast fields of crops, scrub and sandy tracks, and the conversation, which had been sparkling and erudite at the start of the journey leaving Budapest, dwindled to a low buzz. In the seats in front of him, the Pragmaticist and the Critical Theorist were discussing narratology.

> "Fundamentally, I think that, as a discipline, it's finished. In the sense of being completed", opined the Pragmaticist.

> "Mined out, you mean?" added the Critical Theorist.

> "Yeah. A victim of its own success. Narratology has pretty much done everything it set out to do. All the main questions answered, and it even has an obvious set of solutions for any possible questions that might be asked in the future."

> The Critical Theorist looked out at the poor rows of vegetation stretching into the distance. "So", he mused, after a moment. "Essentially it s stopped being a research programme and has become a technique. A settled paradigm, with agreed methods?'

> "Mmm". The Pragmaticist agreed. And they both fell into silence. Outside, the fields of central Europe rolled past.

The view perhaps did look bleak for narratology only these few years ago, and the conclusions of those colleagues on that bus trip might easily have been seen as reasonable at the time. However, it is clear to us now that, in fact, narratology has been revolutionised as a research programme, and the driver behind that paradigm-rejuvenation has been cognitive science.

David Herman's chapter in this book has the over-arching aim of redirecting the attention of his colleagues towards cognitive narratology. What is particularly successful in his paper is his move beyond polemic to demonstration, even as he calls for a closer future engagement between narrative studies and attention to productive and interpretative dynamic processes. The claims for cognitive poetics towards democratisation echoed from Turner (1991) are enacted here across a wide range of sites: from the most canonical works of high modernism to the most populist texts of sci-fi culture, from verbal literary art to oral sociolinguistic transcript. Of course, democratisation does not entail demoticisation, and though Herman's argument is clear, engagement with his thinking requires a disciplined analysis and technical vocabulary that aims for rigour and systematicity.

By his own analytical example, Herman asserts the continuities between the study of the felt effects of narratives (and how narratives play a part in generating these effects) and readers' articulations of their emotional and aesthetic responses. Both areas, as he points out, are connected for the cognitivist since readers' forms of self-expression and narratives existing in the culture both draw on the same patterns of embodied conceptual metaphor. There is increasingly an identifiable research project across the world in exploring emotion in all its manifestations, but in fact it is *aesthetics* itself that is the intellectual zeitgeist of the last few years. Aesthetics comprises – among other dimensions – emotional expression in narrative, emotional articulation in response to narrative, and the texture of shifts in perspective that are explored in the latter part of Herman's chapter.

The new aesthetics is innovative because it involves cognitive scientists and narratologists, as well as the traditional interest of philosophers and literary critics. It is important, however, that the move to aesthetics and "emotionology" occurs in a dialectic with classical narratology, rather than as a pendulum swing away from an exclusive concern with meaning. For political, ideological, and personal texts with social significance, meaningfulness is still as important as intensity of feeling. Herman achieves this integration, I think, because he does not lose sight of sociolinguistics. Edwards (1997), quoted by Herman, launched an early corrective for cognitive linguistics not to neglect social and ideological factors, and Herman exemplifies this approach.

It is also refreshing, writing as a literary-linguist, to see Herman paying attention to the stylistic texture even as he discusses both the cognitive and ideological trajectories in the "narrative arc". Ideologically-driven stylistic choices are explored directly, and here Herman does a better job than earlier discussions of ideology that remained at the abstract and idealised level. It is significant that Herman's first sketch is Emmott's (1997) model of narrative comprehension, an early integration of cognitive narratology with an eye on stylistics.

Herman's route out of the classical narratological blind-alley of focalisation by broadening the view to narrative perspective in general is inspired. It is worth noting that in effecting this manoeuvre, Herman opens the field to much of the interesting recent work developing in literary linguistics: he cites van Peer and Chatman's (2001) collection, and the influential papers in Duchan, Bruder and Hewitt (1995); I could add Bray (2003), McIntyre (2006) and note the recent heightened interest from literary stylisticians such as Lodge (2002). A renewed concern for "mind-style" and "intermental communication" (Palmer 2004) once more returns academic discourse to coincide with "natural" readers' talk about characters, empathy and their emotional connections with literary narratives. Opening up narrative perspective requires an engagement with theories of consciousness and subjectivity, and this in turn further reconnects narrative study away from the "baroque ontology" of its tradition and towards the concerns of non-academic readers. Fundamentally, narratives are acts of communication that share experience.

The use of Langacker and Talmy's cognitive grammar in the last part of Herman's chapter is convincing as an analytical demonstration. Again, it works because it connects conceptualisation with stylistic expression, and it lays its arguments open and transparent for verification. Herman invites the reader to agree that cognitive grammar can be "scaled up" to the narratological level, and he has already raised awareness of the dangers involved in his criticism of Barthes' (1977) similar manoeuvre: it is a persuasive move, here, however, since cognitive grammar is founded on image-schemas that operate across discourse. I have pointed out elsewhere (Stockwell 2002: 70–72, 2005) the parallels between cognitive grammar (Langacker 1987, 1990, 1991) and systemic-functional linguistics (Halliday 2004), and Herman's discussion reminds me very much of the powerful analyses of political, institutional and other ideological discourses that draw on the latter framework. Though various other construction grammars have multiplied in recent years, cognitive grammar is now a mature and established paradigm, and there is evidence that a virtuous feedback loop is in operation, whereby analytical explorations serve to refine the grammar further.

In conclusion, Herman's chapter serves as a useful piece of navigation for future researchers, both in his general thinking and in the suggestive directions for exploration that his work creates. There is much here to concern the narratologist, the stylistician, the sociolinguist, and the discourse analyst. Looking back at that narrativised bus journey a decade later, the Pragmaticist has retired, his discipline largely moribund through its own success, just as he thought narratology had been; the Critical Theorist passed away a few years ago, with his area subject to increasing abstruseness, mystification and irrationality; and the eavesdropping Literary-Linguist struggles to keep up with the myriad of new research threads arising out of the fruitful collision of narratology, cognition and stylistics.

References

Barthes, Roland
   [1966] 1977 Introduction to the structural analysis of narratives. In: Stephen
          Heath (trans.), *Image-music-text*, 79–124. New York: Hill and Wang.

Bray, Joe
   2003   *The Epistolary Novel: Representation of Consciousness.* London: Rout-
          ledge.

Duchan, Judith F., Bruder, Gail A. and Hewitt Lynne E. (eds.)
   1995   *Deixis in Narrative: A Cognitive Science Perspective.* Hillsdale, NJ:
          Lawrence Erlbaum.

Edwards, Derek
   1997   *Discourse and Cognition.* London: Sage.

Emmott, Catherine
   1997   *Narrative Comprehension: A Discourse Perspective.* Oxford: Oxford

Halliday, Michael A.K.
   2004   *An Introduction to Functional Grammar* (ed. Christian Matthiesson).
          London: Arnold.

Langacker, Ronald W.
   1987   *Foundations of Cognitive Grammar, vol. 1. Theoretical Prerequisites.*
          Stanford, CA: Stanford University Press.

Langacker, Ronald W.
   1990   *Concept, Image, and Symbol: The Cognitive Basis of Grammar.* Berlin:
          Mouton de Gruyter.

Langacker, Ronald W.
   1991   *Foundations of Cognitive Grammar, Vol. II: Descriptive Application.*
          Stanford, CA: Stanford University Press.

Lodge, David
   2002   *Consciousness and the Novel.* London: Secker and Warburg.

McIntyre, Dan
   2006   *Point of View in Plays.* Amsterdam/Philadelphia: John Benjamins.

Palmer, Alan
   2004   *Fictional Minds.* Lincoln, NE: University of Nebraska Press

Stockwell, Peter
   2002   *Cognitive Poetics: An Introduction.* London: Routledge.

Stockwell, Peter
  2005   Stylistics and cognitive poetics. In: Harri Veivo, Bo Pettersson and
          Merja Polvinen (eds.), *Cognition and Literary Interpretation in Practice*,
          Helsinki: University of Helsinki Press.
Turner, Mark
  1991   *Reading Minds: The Study of English in the Age of Cognitive Science.*
          Princeton: Princeton University Press.
Van Peer, Willie and Seymour Chatman (eds.)
  2001   *New Perspectives on Narrative Perspective.* Albany: State University of
          New York Press.

Reflections on a cognitive stylistic approach to characterisation

Jonathan Culpeper

1.   Introduction

What might a cognitive stylistic approach to characterisation consist of? In our earlier collection of papers with that label, Elena Semino and I suggest that cognitive stylistics is:

> a rapidly expanding field at the interface between linguistics, literary studies and cognitive science. Cognitive stylistics combines the kind of explicit, rigorous and detailed linguistic analysis of literary texts that is typical of the stylistics tradition with a systematic and theoretically informed consideration of the cognitive structures and processes that underlie the production and reception of language. (2002: ix)

Some use the term "cognitive poetics", but we prefer "cognitive stylistics", because it emphasizes a concern for close attention to the language of texts. So, a cognitive stylistic approach to characterisation aims at combining linguistic analysis with cognitive considerations in order to shed light on the construction and comprehension of fictional characters. In fact, I would go further and argue that the words "cognitive stylistic" in the title of this chapter are redundant: any adequate account of characterisation has to be both linguistic and cognitive. Scholars who consider their work to be part of the cognitive stylistic (or cognitive poetic) enterprise have somewhat different "takes" on the nature of that enterprise, some leaning towards conceiving cognitive stylistics as part of the Cognitive Linguistic paradigm, but others taking the view that a variety of cognitive theories or paradigms can feed into cognitive stylistics. The problem with the former position is that Cognitive Linguistics (with capitals) is generally narrowly conceived, being strongly dominated by work of such scholars as Langacker, Lakoff, Fauconnier and Turner, and focused on such topics as semantic categories, grammatical constructions and metaphor (a skim through a Cognitive Linguistics textbook, such as Evans and Green 2006, illustrates this point). Such a conception excludes, for example, much of the voluminous literature on discourse processing /

text comprehension literature. Thus, it is not currently well-suited to the work to be outlined in this chapter, as my approach to characterisation draws upon work in text comprehension and social cognition.

With regard to the wider academic community, some myths seem to be circulating about both the nature and the purpose of cognitive stylistics. Some scholars are concerned that the cognitive input into cognitive stylistics means that cognitive stylistics will be (a) overly deterministic in the way it constrains reader interpretation and (b) asocial (or at least not sufficiently social) (see, for example, Jeffries 2001: 341, and also Semino 2001 for a response). I will address both these issues, especially in section 2. Others seem concerned that cognitive stylistics will not offer sufficient literary interpretive reward: "the endeavour can at best offer retrospective accounts of how readings arose, it seems, which will not be quite enough for some" (Hall 2003: 355). In an earlier publication, Hall (2002) rightly suggests that reactions to my own characterisation work, and indeed cognitive stylistics generally, will partly be determined by what one thinks the purpose of stylistics is. In common with other stylistics work at Lancaster University (e.g. Leech 1969; Leech and Short 1981; Short 1996; Semino 1997), I take the view that it is not the specific job of stylistics to come up with new interpretations. Short (1996: 27) proposes that "stylistic analysis is a method of linking linguistic form, *via* reader inference, to interpretation in a detailed way and thereby providing as much explicit evidence as possible for and against particular interpretations of text". Note both the emphasis on supporting interpretations rather than creating them, and the fact that even in this definition of stylistics a cognitive element can be seen (cf. "inference", "interpretation"). In a later publication, Short (2001: 339 f.) elaborates on the issue of new interpretations:

> The easiest way to be newsworthy in literary criticism is to provide a new interpretation of an established text [...] But to investigate how readers interact with texts in order to understand them, narratologists, text-analysts, and those involved in informant-based research usually need to start with less outlandish interpretations and texts, precisely because linguistic, perceptual, and interpretive norms need to be established and explained (often using relatively simple texts and constrained perceptual and interpretive contexts) before the more extraordinary can be tackled. This in turn lays such careful work open to the charge of not being "interesting" (i.e. newsworthy in terms of new texts or interpretations examined) [...]

In this chapter I shall address the issues mentioned above and expand on some of the key features of my theory of characterisation, taking the opportunity to update aspects of my work, notably Culpeper (2001), both with respect to the literature in cognition and the literature in stylistics/narratology. The emphasis will be on what cognitive research can do for characterisation; I give much less attention to the role of language. This should not be taken to mean that language is any less important in characterisation, rather it is a reflection of the fact that traditional stylistic analyses have focused on the language of character. The more newsworthy aspect of what I have to say is thus what cognition can do for the understanding of characterisation in text. With respect to a cognitive stylistic approach to characterisation specifically, I consider my work as following the path first adumbrated in Gerrig and Allbritton (1990). More recently, Schneider (2001) and Bortolussi and Dixon (2003, particularly chapter 5) have travelled similar paths.[1] I shall concentrate mainly on readers forming impressions or conceptions of characters. As Schneider (2001: 608) indicates, this means that the main issue will not be what characters *are* but what they *appear* to be to readers (thus invoking the empirical study of actual readers and how they respond to the text). For the purposes of brief illustration, during the course of this chapter I shall draw on an array of characters from various genres. The point behind the wide array is that what is proposed here is a *general* theory of characterisation, it is not limited to a particular genre. In particular, the cognitive fundamentals are the same. That is not to say, of course, that the way characterisation works is identical in every genre. There are crucial stylistic or narratological differences between genres that affect the way characterisation proceeds (e.g. the general absence of narration in play-texts), but I lack the space to discuss these here.[2]

---

1. My understanding of characterisation was mainly formulated between 1990 and 2000, resulting in a doctoral thesis, various articles and finally a book in 2001. Unfortunately, it was only after this that I discovered Schneider (2001), an article in English which summarises his 2000 book in German. It also seems that Schneider had no knowledge of my work, given the absence of citations in the 2001 publication. Our work is mutually supportive of a number of the fundamentals we propose, though there are numerous differences in the detail.
2. Examples drawn from drama (or film) are with respect to the play-text (or screenplay) only. Performances of plays involve a raft of complications that I cannot deal with here. See Culpeper (2001: 39ff.), for my views, and Short (1989) and (1998), for a discussion of the general issues. An interesting, though brief, perspective from Cognitive Linguistics, specifically blending theory, is articulated in Fauconnier and Turner (2002: 266f.).

2.   Schema theory and characterisation

Schema theory has been used to account for how people comprehend, learn from and remember meanings in texts. Essentially, the idea is that knowledge is retrieved from long-term memory and integrated with information derived from the text to produce an interpretation. The term "schema/schemata" refers to the "well integrated chunks of knowledge about the world, events, people, and actions" (Eysenck and Keane 2000: 352). They are usually taken to be relatively complex, or higher-order, clusters of concepts, with a particular network of relationships holding those concepts together, and are assumed to constitute the structure of long-term memory (an overview of schema theory and other aspects of cognition, as well as many references, can be found in Culpeper 2001: chapter 2). Other terms, such as "frames", "scripts" and "scenarios", have been used in the literature, each within a somewhat different tradition and with a somewhat different emphasis. However, schema/schemata is the term used in social cognition, a field of particular importance to my discussion (see in particular, section 2.2). Schema theory has been applied to the study of literature, most notably by Cook (1994) and Semino (1997), and continues to be so (e.g. Stockwell 2003). In this section, I focus on schemata made up of knowledge about people – social schemata (or what are sometimes referred to as "cognitive stereotypes" in the social cognition literature) – and the implications this has for characterisation. Note that I assume that knowledge about real-life people is brought into play in the *interpretation* of fictional characters, and not just knowledge about fictional characters. As Margolin (2001: 281) points out, it is difficult to imagine that either the author in the act of creating the characters or the reader in the act of interpreting them could switch off the mental apparatus used for non-fictional people (see also, Bortolussi and Dixon 2003: 134 ff.). An interesting issue is the extent to which real-life people knowledge is used by readers compared with fictional character knowledge. Empirical investigations of this issue are, as far as I know, lacking, though one might note Livingstone's (1998) study of people's perceptions of TV soap opera characters. She found that knowledge of structural aspects of the genre (e.g. a character's moral stance – "goody" or "baddy" – within the moral narrative) took precedence over real-life social knowledge.

2.1. Variability in interpretation of character

Writers do not write all there is to be known about a character: they mean more than they say. Often the larger part of our impression of a character is not in the text at all but has been inferred. Toolan (1988) usefully refers to this as the "iceberg" phenomenon in characterisation. Schema theory helps explain how that larger chunk below the waterline might be inferred. The important point to note is that not everybody will make the same assumptions about what lies below the waterline.

Andersen et al. (1977) conducted an experiment which conveniently illustrates characterisation issues. They asked people to read the following fictional passage:

> Rocky slowly got up from the mat, planning his escape. He hesitated a moment and thought. Things were not going well. What bothered him most was being held, especially since the charge against him had been weak. He considered his present situation. The lock that held him was strong but he thought he could break it. He knew, however, that his timing would have to be perfect. Rocky was aware that it was because of his early roughness that he had been penalised so severely – much too severely from his point of view. The situation was becoming frustrating; the pressure had been grinding on him for too long. He was being ridden unmercifully. Rocky was getting angry now. He felt he was ready to make his move. He knew that his success or failure would depend on what he did in the next few seconds.

Who is Rocky? The text tells us about, for example, his spatial circumstances (he is on a "mat", and "held" by a "lock"), his goal ("planning his escape"), his evaluation of the situation ("things were not going well"), his history ("his early roughness", "the pressure had been grinding on him for too long"), his evaluation of his plan to achieve his goal ("He felt he was ready to make his move. He knew that his success or failure would depend on what he did in the next few seconds"). We also, of course, learn that Rocky is his name, and from this we might infer that he is male (and quite possibly North American rather than British). But it does not really tell us who Rocky is or even where he is. What readers will generally try to do is to activate a schema which will provide a scaffold for the incoming textual information. The alternative – keeping all the separate bits of textual information in the cognitive air – would be mentally taxing to say the least, and would not constitute an understanding of the passage. Once the reader has decided on which is the most relevant schema for accommodating the textual information, they are in a position to generate knowledge-based inferences about Rocky. The case of fictional characters in literary texts is exactly the same. Consider Katherina, the protagonist in Shakespeare's play *The Taming of the Shrew.* Much of that play revolves around deciding whether Katherina really is a "shrew" (broadly, a talkative, evil-intentioned, ill-tempered woman). As I argued in Culpeper (2001: chapter 6), a shrew is a particular type of person – a particular schema. In the first part of the play, there is overwhelming evidence that Katherina is a shrew (she talks a lot, beats other characters, ignores her father, etc), and so the SHREW SCHEMA is a likely schema upon which to hang such text-derived information. This then allows us to generate knowledge-based inferences, such as that Katherina is evil-intentioned, despite the fact that we are not explicitly informed of this in the text.

Andersen et al. (1977) discovered that most of their informants thought the passage was about a convict planning his escape from prison. However, one group of people had an entirely different interpretation of whom Rocky was: men who had been involved in wrestling assumed that it was about a wrestler caught in the hold of an opponent. Most subjects gave the passage one distinct interpretation and reported being unaware of other perspectives whilst reading. This illustrates the point that the particular schema (or schemata) deployed in interpretation depends upon the cultural life experiences of the interpreter. A person's experiences constitute the basis of their schemata. Fredric Bartlett's (1932 [1995]) early pioneering work in schema theory was partly designed to explore cultural differences in interpretation (see also the experiment by Steffenson et al. 1979), and schema theory is used today in the context of cross-cultural pragmatics (e.g. Scollon and Scollon 1995). The argument here also accounts for diachronic variation in interpretation as well as synchronic. Today's reader or audience of Shakespeare's plays will have a very different understanding of them compared with the reader or audience of the past, because they have acquired different schemata. Consider Katherina once more. It is unlikely that today's reader/audience would have exactly the same kind of SHREW SCHEMA, despite the fact that stereotypes of the nagging woman have proved durable. As I pointed out in earlier work (Culpeper 2001: 268), Katherina's challenge to her father's authority may not now be perceived as a constituent of the SHREW SCHEMA, as would almost certainly have been the case for the Elizabethans, but as a spirited rebellion against an unfair and repressive patriarchal system. Hence, the same information generated by the text could trigger a completely different and more positive kind of schema, such as a feminist non-conformist who is frustrated, not evil-intentioned. Indeed, in a recent film version of the play, *10 Things I Hate About You* (directed by Gil Junger 1999), Katherina drives an old banger, reads feminist literature, plays football aggressively, and despises boys and the dating game. Note here that schema theory accounts not just for reader comprehension but also writer production. The author of the film-script presumably had in mind a certain set of schemata when typing the script of the film, just as Shakespeare had had in mind a certain and somewhat different set of schemata when penning the script of the play. In this paragraph I have touched on the notion of stereotypes and also hinted that schemata can include evaluations of those schemata; I will return to these issues in section 2.2.

Before leaving this section, it is worth elaborating on the point that difference in the nature of schemata is not the only factor that causes interpretive variability. Many people who interpreted the Rocky passage as a convict in a prison would surely have known about the sport of wrestling, including the fact that it takes place on mats, that arm locks are used, and so on – they would have had a WRESTLING SCHEMA. So why did they not use it? Researchers in social cognition have argued that the precise schema that is activated depends on the following factors: recency, frequency, observational purpose and situational context (see Fiske and Taylor 1991: 145 f.; Zebrowitz 1990: 50; Fiske and Neuberg 1990: 9 ff., where many supporting references can be found). The more recently and more frequently a particular schema has been activated the more accessible it is. Thus, people involved in the sport of wrestling would have found it easier to access schemata that led to the conclusion that Rocky was a wrestler. From this, one might predict, for example, that parents of autistic children may arrive at the conclusion that Christopher, the child protagonist of Mark Haddon's novel *The Curious Incident of the Dog in the Night-Time* (2003), has Asperger's, a form of autism, before other parents without such immediate and frequent experiences. Regarding observational purpose, people make sense of the world strategically, not least of all because comprehension is effortful and mental resources are limited. This point has also been made by researchers within the field of text comprehension, where they emphasise that the activation of schematic knowledge is related to the reader's goals (e.g. van Dijk and Kintsch 1983: 13; Graesser et al. 1994: 377 f.). A reader may aim at predicting a character's particular behaviour, trying to construct their perspective, or, less consciously, may focus on aspects relevant to particular interests or simply on characters with whom they empathise – all of which will result in variable interpretations of character. Finally, situational context may prime the activation of certain schemata. For example, seeing somebody on a running-track is much more likely to activate an athlete category than seeing that person at a desk. The relationship between people and contexts is something which, whilst I have not ignored it in my own work, has not received sufficient attention, both in terms of cognition and the text. For this reason I will devote section 4 to this topic.

2.2. The social interpretation of character

Jeffries (2001: 341) quite rightly proposes that what is needed in literary comprehension is "a model of meaning that incorporates a range from the most general shared understanding of texts to the most individual experience-based meanings", and not, as seems to be the case with schema-theoretic readings, a model that tends to privilege the more general. One might argue that the fact that schema-theoretic readings gravitate towards the general is not just a feature of schema-theoretic readings but also stylistic readings. Remember the quotation from Mick Short in section 1, stylistics tends to deal with those "less outlandish interpretations", and for good reason. With regard to the Rocky text above, consider if I had told you about Tony, who runs the Wrestling World sports equipment mail-order company based in the UK. Having arrived at work, Tony discovered that the wrestling mats had sold out, and had to re-order another hundred. Yesterday had been particularly busy; Tony had gone to Reading prison to help advise on equipment for their new gym. The only moment of mild amusement had been when the prison governor, who insisted on showing-off the new prison cells, cut his thumb on the new safety lock of the cell door. When Tony read the Rocky text, the appearance of "mat" in the very first sentence triggered knowledge about the wrestling world. Moreover, as Tony had been given a glimpse of some of the prison cells yesterday and no mats were in evidence, only bunk beds, the idea of a prison cell did not spring to mind. The point behind my (fictional) account of Tony and his reading is that you the reader of this very text get bogged down in specific information about Tony that will be of little use in helping you understand other readings, and you cannot very easily relate (I assume!) to Tony's life experiences.

Nevertheless, as Jeffries points out, a model of reading needs to be able to account for various types of reading. There is in fact a well-established cognitive distinction that helps account for the more "general" and "shared" as opposed to the more "individual" and "experience-based". Schema-theoretic accounts tend to focus on just one type of knowledge in long-term memory. Tulving (1972) made a distinction between "semantic memory" and "episodic memory". Semantic memory contains more general, abstract knowledge or schemata, such as Tony's journey to work every morning. Episodic memory contains episodes: personal experiences associated with a particular time and place; in other words, specific autobiographical experiences. Tony's experience of visiting Reading prison yesterday and getting a glimpse of a prison cell was one such experience. The two memory types are linked: episodic memory is assumed to feed semantic memory, as an accumulation of related experiences leads to generalisation and abstraction. In sum, current or recent experiences are stored as episodes in memory (e.g. Tony's first trip to Reading prison); some experiences may remain as personal episodes in memory (e.g. Tony's vision of the prison governor cutting his thumb); whilst others blur into semantic memory (e.g. Tony can't remember the individual episodes that represent each time he arrives at work). Episodic memories can, of course, play an important role in the variability of interpretation.

As semantic memory is "general" and "shared", it is obviously more social than episodic memory. In the construction of a text, it constitutes the kind of knowledge that an author can assume to be shared amongst a particular readership. The shared nature of semantic memory has led van Dijk (e.g. 1987, 1990) to suggest that it be called "social memory". It is the role of semantic or social memories that have been the focus of research in social cognition, a field that largely developed in North America, and focuses on the study of "how people make sense of other people and themselves" (Fiske and Taylor 1991: 1). It is thus an obvious field to draw upon for any cognitive approach to characterisation. In turn, much of the cognitive theoretical input to social cognition is drawn directly from cognitive psychology, and this includes schema theory. Schema theory has a contribution to make to the study of both stereotypes and stereotyping, a key topic in social cognition. If stereotypes are "highly organised social categories that have the properties of schemata" (Andersen et al. 1990: 192), they "can then influence subsequent perceptions of, and behaviors toward, that group and its members" (Hamilton and Sherman, 1994: 15). Note then, that schemata are not simply social in nature but account for social functions. As Leyens et al. (1994: 84) point out, the schema-theoretic view of people, or indeed of anything, is biased, as schemata are thought to guide the way information is processed. People more easily pay attention to, memorise and recall information that is consistent with expectations derived from their schemata, and, given that schemata are probabilistic, exceptions can be ignored (though if that effort is made, the information may be well remembered) (e.g. Taylor et al., 1978; Fiske and

Taylor, 1984: 149; Hamilton and Sherman, 1994: 33ff.).[3] Clearly, if schemata bias perception toward schema-consistent information, then that
factor operates as a self-perpetuating bias for the stereotype: it explains
their durability. From the point of view of characterisation, the important
point is that social schemata explain the basis of expectations about characters – expectations that can be manipulated for particular effects, as
I shall illustrate below.

In order to analyze and explain particular character expectations, the
contents of social schemata can be grouped on the basis of type of knowledge. In Culpeper (2001: 75f.), I suggested three groupings:

- Personal categories: e.g. preferences, interests, traits, goals
- Social role categories: e.g. kinship roles, occupational roles, relational
  roles
- Group membership categories: e.g. gender, race, class, age, nationality,
  religion

Note that these vary from the more individual to the more general, and
constitute a three-level hierarchy of categories of the kind suggested by
Rosch et al. (1976). The cognitively important base level is the one in the
middle, social roles, as such categories are rich in attributes but not overwhelming, and also well differentiated from each other (Holyoak and
Gordon 1984: 50; Fiske and Taylor 1991: 143). Social roles, then, are crucial to the description of both real-life people and, I would argue, fictional
characters. Note that in the Rocky text above one can infer possible personal category features (e.g. his goals and feelings) and group membership categories (e.g. that he is male), but it is the lack of role information
(e.g. convict, wrestler) that makes one's understanding of him so incomplete. The important point, however, is that these three types of social information are linked within a schematic network: an application of part
of the network to a character allows the knowledge-based inference of
other parts of the network. Agatha Christie's early detective novel *And
then there were none* (1939) illustrates this point.[4] The murderer turns out
to be – and I apologise to readers here for ruining the denouement of the
novel – the retired judge, Lawrence Wargrave. Knowing the social role of

---

3. This, needless to say, is something of a simplified summary. See Fiske and Taylor's (1991: 126ff.) overview of some of the complexities.
4. It originally had the potentially offensive titles "10 Little Niggers" in the U.K.
   and "10 Little Indians" in the U.S.

"judge" the reader can generate certain expectations about group membership, such as that the judge is likely to be male and fairly advanced in years. More significantly, they can also generate expectations about personal categories, namely, that the judge is moral and aims not only to be law-abiding but to maintain the law. Such expectations help put the reader off the scent, as the schematic bias means that they will tend to ignore information that does not quite fit the schema. Of course, the way the culprit is constructed and comprehended in detective novels is not simply determined by real-life social knowledge but also by our knowledge of the dramatic types that are associated with particular genres. We will return to this issue in section 4.2.

A final point to be made about the social interpretation of character relates to ideology. I pointed out in my discussion of *The Taming of the Shrew* that conceptions of Katherina could vary according to attitudes towards her: negative evaluations of a rebel versus positive evaluations of principled non-conformist. Sack's (2001) way of approaching ideological point of view is to make links between "actors" (i.e. participants in the story) and "roles", giving the real-life example of Oliver North, who was involved in the Iran-Contra scandal in the USA, being paired with either "patriot" or "criminal", each pairing representing a different ideology. This is the same for my example of Katherina. However, ideology itself is not simply a matter of a linking people with roles, but involves shared evaluative beliefs. Van Dijk (e.g. 1987, 1988, 1990) has suggested that social schemata may include "attitude schemata"; in other words, attitudes towards some other part of the schema (i.e. evaluative beliefs, positive or negative, about a social group). Clusters of attitudes shared amongst members of a social group constitute ideologies. Thus, a conservative and/or patriarchal reading of Katherina may result in a negative interpretation of her as a rebel, whereas a liberal or feminist reading may result in a positive interpretation of her as spirited, independent non-conformist.

3.   Characterisation beyond schema theory

A schema-theoretic approach to characterisation is not enough. Schema theory is a "top-down" theory, applying cognitive concepts to the understanding of something in the world. However, most scholars take the view that understanding is in some sense constructionist, that is to say, it involves the integration of "bottom-up" information from the stimulus input with the "top-down" information retrieved from schematic knowledge.

This means that schema theory does not account very well for situations in which no obvious schema fits the incoming information or in which a lack of fit develops during the course of a reading. Moreover, schema theory is not a complete theory of reader comprehension: it does not offer a full account of how information is extracted from the text and how some of that information will end up in one's understanding of the text.

The idea that social schemata do not always suffice for impressions of people has been addressed within social cognition. The alternative to a schema-driven or category-based impression is a person-based impression. The latter is made up of the individual attributes of the target person; it is richer and more personalised than a schema-driven impression, and also requires more cognitive effort on the part of the person forming the impression. Fiske and Neuberg (1990) present a model that attempts to include both kinds of impression, one at each end of a continuum. They identify four stages on the continuum that we might go through in forming an impression of someone we encounter:

An *initial categorisation* of the person takes place.
If the information fits the initial categorisation, then *confirmatory categorisation* occurs.
If the information does not fit the initial categorisation, but is categorisable (by accessing, for example, a new category or subcategory), then *recategorisation* occurs (e.g. in the case of switching to a new category, from somebody who has a job to somebody who does not, or, in the case of subcategorisation, from somebody who has the job, to a university employee, to a member of academic staff, to a professor of English).
If the information does not fit any particular category, then *piecemeal integration* occurs; in other words, the person's attributes are averaged or added up in order to form an impression.

Note that schematic categorisation processes take precedence over person-based processes. One of the reasons for this is that they require less effort. There is no reason to suppose that similar processes are not involved in forming an impression of fictional characters. Indeed, in the field of literary criticism, Forster ([1927] 1987) proposes a distinction between "flat" and "round" characters. Flat characters are "constructed around a single idea or quality" (1987: 73). I would suggest such characters are constructed round a single schema; they have not progressed beyond stage two on the continuum – they do not develop. Round characters have more than a "single idea or quality", and must be "capable of surprising" (1987: 81).

Round characters correspond to stage four on the continuum, and their ability to surprise can be explained in terms of the fact that they could not meet the expectations of a schema. They are relatively dynamic characters, both with respect to their formation, as movement along the continuum is required, and the final piecemeal impression, which lacks the relative fixity of a schema. Thus, Agatha Christie's Judge Wargrove is a rather surprising judge in that he is also a murderer; the pieces of information that pertain to his character cannot be matched to a schema. Stage three processes result in an impression based on a single schema, and thus constitute a flat character. They do not develop like round characters, as the reader simply switches categories in forming an impression of them, rather than departing from a category-based view, as with piecemeal integration. Nevertheless, they are of importance in achieving dramatic characterisation effects. More precisely, it is the switch from one category to a wholly different category that has dramatic importance. This is because the author constructs the text so that it plays "garden path" tricks on the reader: we are led to believe that the target is one particular kind of character, only to discover that they are in fact a completely different kind of character. Bianca, Katherina's sister in *The Taming of the Shrew*, is a good example. In the first half of the play Shakespeare leads the reader to think that she is the goodly daughter (a reflection of her name). In the latter half of the play, we are led to believe that this is all a sham and that she is the truly bad daughter. Note that the fact that her previous behaviour is a sham means that we can dismiss it; if we thought that both her good behaviour and her bad behaviour reflected her character we would have a more complex characterisation – one that suggests piecemeal integration.

The idea that schemata do not always suffice has also been considered within text comprehension. In Culpeper (2001: 28ff.), I outlined a model of characterisation largely based on van Dijk and Kintsch (1983). At the heart of the model lies the "situation model", where information from prior knowledge (i.e. schemata) and the text combine to create a representation of the meaning of the text (i.e. what the text is about). This situation model will include inferences about characters. The situation model is the outcome of the integration of top-down and bottom-up information inputs; it is not limited to more top-down focused schema-theoretic approaches to text comprehension. Regarding the bottom-up input from the text, the idea is that readers first form a representation of the surface structure of the text. This surface representation is thought to be lost after only a few seconds (see references in Long 1994; and also Kintsch et al. 1990). However, syntactic and semantic processing of this surface structure can give rise to a textbase representation, which is thought to last longer in memory (Kintsch et al. 1990). The textbase consists of propositions. For literary characterisation, this means that as readers move towards piecemeal integration, they move towards the textbase, and that writers can create characters whose essence involves importing aspects either of the surface structure or the textbase into the situation model, rather than processing these and forgetting them. To illustrate the latter point, consider that any character known for a catchphrase is one for whom the surface structure has been imported into their characterisation. For example, the (nauseating!) protagonist of the film *Forrest Gump* (1994) has the line "life is a box of chocolates" as a memorable part of his characterisation; or, less prosaically, many of Shakespeare's protagonists are strongly associated with particular lines, as is the case with Hamlet and the "to be or not to be" speech. The writer can use linguistic strategies to foreground textual aspects, making it more likely that the reader will dwell on them and import them into the situation model (see also Zwaan 1996: 245). Similarly, propositions constituting the textbase can be imported into the situation model. The best example of this relates to allegorical characters: their meaning in the textbase – "Sloth", "Pride", "Gluttony", "Lust", etc. – is imported into the situation model where it constitutes a key part of their character. It is worth briefly noting here that van Dijk and Kintsch (1983) suggest that the propositions of the textbase can receive a degree of organisation on the basis of prior knowledge, even before they are integrated within the situation model, and thus form a "macropropositional" textbase. The important point for characterisation is that genre knowledge, as well as other types of world knowledge such as a script for a restaurant, can organise this information. It is here that characters can be defined with respect to their function within a basic semantic frame.

Before leaving this section, I should draw attention to the fact that the movement away from schema-driven characterisation towards piecemeal integration is paralleled by increasing cognitive effort on the part of the reader. Why would readers bother? People working in social cognition tend to focus on external motivation (e.g. arriving at an accurate impression of a candidate for a job interview). This is largely irrelevant to most encounters of literary texts, where internal motivation (i.e. the reading of the text is self-motivating) is important. Researchers working on motivation from reading, often within an educational context, have identified intrinsic motivational factors such as curiosity or interest, involvement and challenge (see, for example, Guthrie et al. 2004 and references therein).

Clearly, if a writer can generate reader curiosity or interest through the text, then that will motivate greater attention and increase the likelihood that a character will be understood in terms of piecemeal integration. (Of course, a writer may wish to do the opposite: in a detective novel, the writer may not wish to motivate attention for the culprit). Brewer (1988) suggested that self-involvement may play a role in determining the kind of processing involved. Self-involvement is when "the perceiver feels closely related to or interdependent with the target person, or feels ego-involved in the judgement task" (Brewer 1988: 9). Hence, one might predict that sympathetic (or antipathetic) characters receive more attention than characters one feels more neutral about, with the consequence that those characters are more likely to be treated in a non-schema-based way. Challenge refers to the enjoyment derived from tackling difficult or complex information. Round characters, constructed via piecemeal integration, are by definition informationally difficult and complex. Also, one might note that the whole point of characterisation in crime fiction is to present a "character puzzle" of some kind. The issues I have been discussing in this paragraph also account for some of the variation in interpretation of character.

4. Constructing characters in context and contexts in characters

The above description of characterisation said almost nothing about context. Yet, people are understood in context (Cantor and Mischel 1979). Consider the Rocky passage above. It is very difficult to understand that he is a convict without simultaneously understanding that his situation is that of a prison. It cannot be overemphasised that characters are always understood in context, and thus part of the study of characterisation must be to understand the way writers construct characters and contexts, as well as the way they interact and the way readers comprehend those interactions. In the first section below, I consider a fundamental aspect of characterisation: how information inferred from text is attributed to an aspect of character as opposed to an aspect of the character's context. Note that traditional stylistics work on characterisation makes little or no attempt, beyond an appeal to intuition, to explain why a linguistic feature provides character information as opposed to contextual information. In my earlier work (notably 1996; but also 2001: chapter 3), I argued that "attribution theories", developed over a number of decades to account for how people infer real-life personality information in context, are relevant to fictional characterisation. In the following section, I summarise this work, discussing how characters might interact with contexts in different ways, thereby affording the potential for various impressions of character. In the final section, I consider the idea that we need a flexible notion of context, and one that can include contexts within contexts.

4.1 Character or context?

In order for characterisation to proceed, at some point the reader must decide that information arising from the text has something to do with character as opposed to something else in the context. This decision is a matter of *character inferencing*. Even if a narrator or character tells us something about him or herself or about another character, theoretically, we still must decide that this is a true reflection of the target character, and not simply a reflection of the teller's strategy in telling it (e.g. they claimed someone was something they are not in order to upset them), before we can ascribe that characteristic. Although we should note that in practice readers are more likely to accept characterising statements at face value in the absence of reasons not to do so, as to do otherwise requires more complex processing (Gilbert 1989; see also Jones 1990: 154, for practical and social justifications). Surprisingly, such fundamental issues have escaped the attention of most literary critics and narratologists, with the notable exception of Uri Margolin (particularly 1983) whose work echoes some of the points I will be making here. My approach draws insights from studies on real-life person inferencing, and in particular from classic attribution theories in social psychology (see also Bortolussi and Dixon 2003: 142 ff., who take a similar line).

The key issue in classic attribution theories is where to attribute the causes of behaviour: is behaviour internally driven (i.e. is it a result of the personality of the person doing it) or is behaviour externally driven (i.e. is it a result of the context in which that person is doing it)? If it is internally driven, we are in a position to infer that characteristics of the behaviour reflect characteristics of the person (e.g. a "good" act reflects a "good" person). This is a "correspondent inference" (i.e. an inference that the description of behaviour and of character correspond), and such inferences vary in strength (e.g. Jones 1990). Correspondent inferences rely on the assumption that people act in ways consistent with their personalities. This assumption is only tenable in such conditions where they have freedom of choice. In other words, if you are pressured or constrained to act in a particular way, your acts do not say something about you as much as the context in which you are. The role of the context in discounting correspondent inferences has been called the "discounting principle" (Kelly 1972). Such assumptions and principles behind attribution apply to fictional characters. King Lear's conceited and mean behaviour to Cordelia at the beginning of the play leads to the correspondent inference that he is conceited and mean in character, and there are no obvious discounting factors, something that is often the case at the beginning of a fictional work where we have a less comprehensive appreciation of the context. In contrast, Macbeth's fearful behaviour in the banquet scene where the ghost of Banquo appears cannot give rise to a correspondent inference such that Macbeth is characteristically fearful, for the reason that the presence of the ghost in the context is clearly a powerful discounting factor. Of course, part of the drama of this scene is that Lady Macbeth cannot see the ghost, only Macbeth and the audience can, and so she is unable to bring the discounting principle into play, thus dismissing her husband as a shameful coward fearful of figments of his imagination.

There is an important complication that behaviours are not hot-wired to specific characteristics – they are by nature ambiguous, and ambiguity weakens the strength of correspondent inferences. For example, a shaking hand could mean somebody is nervous, is stressed, has just had a workout at the gym, and so on. How do we know what corresponds with what? Rather different solutions are offered by two classic attribution theorists. Jones (e.g. Jones 1990; Jones and Davies 1965) points out that behaviours vary in their ambiguity, and obviously less ambiguous behaviours are likely to be more informative about a person (they are likely to be more correspondent). He suggests that unusual behaviours, particularly socially undesirable behaviours, tend to be more informative about people. For example, saying thank you for the receipt of a gift is the socially desirable and conventional choice which has little personality information, beyond the observation that the speaker is following the convention. Conversely, deliberately not saying thank you to the receipt of the gift is likely to focus attention, trigger greater inferential effort to find a reason for the act, and – context permitting – allow a strong inference about the person. Kelley (1967), another attribution theorist, had a somewhat different view, suggesting that we consider the covariation of causes and effects over time. The key factor in attributing characteristic X to person Y is that the target person must act in a similar way *despite* different contexts. Thus, cheerfulness when the sun is shining and cheerfulness when it is raining begins to set up a covariation pattern in which a person is reacting to different contexts in a similar way, lending the potential for support of an inference that they really are cheerful by nature. These two attribution theories are not in fact incompatible. In Culpeper (2001) I argue that they were reminiscent of the different facets of foregrounding theory (e.g. Mukařovský 1970; Leech 1969, 1985), a theory that is prominent in stylistics. Foregrounding can arise from unexpected irregularity (the breaking of norms) or unexpected regularity (the establishment of patterns), the first being frequently termed "deviation" and the second "parallelism". Furthermore, foregrounded aspects of the text are regarded as more important for interpretation (van Peer 1986). Jones seems to be focusing on deviation, and Kelley parallelism. To illustrate, Capulet in Shakespeare's *Romeo and Juliet* has a particular fondness for directive speech acts, and above all the word "go", which he uses to direct other members of the household in various ways and situations (e.g. Tybalt I.v.82, Paris III.iv.31, the Nurse III.v.171, his servants IV.11.2, and Juliet IV.ii.9). Thus, his speech acts form an unexpectedly regular pattern which triggers the inference that he is the head of the household and imbued with power. And later in the play, of course, Shakespeare dramatises this character inference, as it is Capulet's spectacular inability to direct Juliet that marks him as a tragic figure.

Expectations about the real-world causes of behaviour are applied by readers to the fictional text world (Trabasso et al. 1989; van den Broek 1990). But there are differences: person attribution is not identical to character attribution. Firstly, the text gives us the complete and explicit record of character evidence. No parallel exists with real people (even biographies are but a small, filtered selection of a person's total life). Since in fictional works we have the whole, stronger inferences can be made about any part. Moreover, fictional works need to be considered within their communicative context: a writer conveys the reader a message, and often via what a character does (see Short 1989: 149). Thus, character behaviours have more significance as they are put there on purpose by the writer. Consider this real-life event. Whilst reversing a car, I nearly ran over my wife, who happened to be standing behind it. Anybody witnessing the event might well assume that I had not been paying attention or perhaps that I was careless. If the same event were placed in a fictional work, I would suggest that witnesses – the readers – would assume the event had greater significance for character and plot. For example, they might assume that I was conspiring to "bump off" my wife, particularly in the context of the genre of crime fiction. I shall pursue the issue of context further in the following section, where I will also note further ways in which person attribution is different from character attribution.

4.2. Interactions between characters and contexts

It is important to note that attribution processes do not always proceed on the basis of the inferences discussed above. For reasons of cognitive economy, we may well resort to "causal schemata". Certain acts may become associated with certain causes and this association is stored in our memories as a causal schema. So, the economic way of understanding what is causing what is simply to remember what in the past has tended to cause what (i.e. to recall the relevant causal schema). This way we generate expectations about causes, including expectations about the kind of personalities causing particular behaviours. This then connects back to the top-down schema approach to characterisation, as discussed in section 2. In this section, I shall first consider interactions between characters and three different kinds of context: I will examine how situations drive expectations about causes, how fictional genres drive expectations about causes, and then I will briefly note characters in the context of impossible worlds. I shall then consider the implications of the fact that the interaction between character and context may not always be evenly weighted in that either character or context may, in some circumstances, exert a more powerful influence in forming an impression of character.

In Culpeper (2001), I argued that characters who are in some sense caricatures can be explained as prototypicality distortions. Perhaps an analogy can be drawn with visual caricature, in so far as a caricature relies on the unusual prominence of one (physical) feature (or more) relative to others (e.g. ears that are too big for the size of the head). But how is unusual prominence achieved for the abstract properties of a character? Cantor and Mischel (1979), working on real-life person perception, applied prototype theory (Rosch 1976, 1978) to categories of people. Within prototype theory, a category is not rigid, well-defined and constituted by necessary and sufficient conditions, but rather is fuzzy-edged, and conceived of "in terms of its *clear cases* rather than its boundaries" (Rosch 1978: 36).[5] Thus, some types of people are better examples of that type than others. For example, an Italian who has blonde hair or who does not speak Italian is a less prototypical example of an Italian. A prototypical instance of a social category would be someone who is in some sense aver-

---

5. Like schema theory, prototype theory is a theory of knowledge, and to a degree they overlap. Prototype theory differs from schema theory in that it is usually applied to simpler concepts, and used for the discussion of categorisation processes, rather than interpretation and inferencing.

age or normal. But this does not constitute a caricature in any way, since by definition caricatures are abnormal with respect to an overly prominent feature. However, the key point is that the unusual prominence of a behavioural characteristic can be achieved by manipulating the interaction between behaviours and situations. As Cantor and Mischel (1979: 36 ff.) noted, how prototypical of their type a person seems to be depends on the *interaction* between behaviours and situations. All people or characters are expected to orientate, at least to some degree, to some contexts; in other words, they vary to an extent with contexts. If people or characters repeatedly fail to exhibit contextually sensitive behaviour and/or they repeatedly appear in situations where they are not expected, they will be perceived as excessively prototypical with respect to some characteristics. Allegorical figures or fictional stock figures often provide good examples, but it is in the world of comedy that many prototypicality distortions can be found. Whether it is Bottom in William Shakespeare's *A Midsummer-Night's Dream*, Mrs Bennett or Mr Collins in Jane Austen's *Pride and Prejudice*, or Inspector Clouseau in the Pink Panther films, they represent the prototype of a category that fails to vary with context, and thus the features of that category become unusually prominent relative to normal variation. Of course, in fictional worlds, these prototypicality distortions can be remembered and may become a particular schema (or fictional stock figure) in their own right.

Situations, whether real-world or the fictional world, are of course not the only kind of context. The fictional world is partly shaped by the context of its genre, and people have expectations based on genres. For example, in the real world, "good" people, like retired judges, are not usually the cause of murders. Hence, part of the shock in the UK at the murders committed by Harold Shipman – a doctor who might have been expected to save lives. But the causal schemata we apply to fiction are not simply drawn from one's knowledge of real-life people but also from knowledge of characters in fiction. In reading classic crime fiction, we may well have developed a causal schema such that the least likely person to have committed the murder on the basis of real-world knowledge is in fact the most likely person to have committed the murder in the fictional text world. The fictional causal schema includes knowledge about how a character's actions might be discounted by the fictional genre of which they are a part. Thus, we might know that in crime fiction the "good" character does not strongly correspond with good deeds, whilst, conversely, in Westerns the "good" character does strongly correspond with good deeds. Writers of crime fiction must perform something of a tricky balancing act: expectations generated from real-life contexts may suggest that one particular character did not do the murder, whereas expectations generated from a particular fictional genre may suggest that that particular character did do the murder. A solution may be to select a character for which expectations are fairly neutral.

A further context in which characters depart from the expectations we might have about real-life people is when they inhabit impossible worlds or are in some sense impossible themselves. It is the latter that I labelled "possibility distortions" in Culpeper (2001). In this case, part of the information about a character can be matched to a real-life social schema, but the rest of the information clashes with expectations generated by other parts of the schema and indeed what we know to be possible in the real world. Consider science fiction. Here we can find robots (physically non-human), androids (physically non-human) and cyborgs (physically non-human and human). All of these, even the robots, have human-like characteristics, and sometimes they have human-like personalities. They may even have goals, plans, emotions and moral scruples just like human beings. Perhaps the most interesting case are androids: physically non-human but strongly like humans in appearance and behaviour. The term android was first used by Auguste Villiers de l'Isle-Adam of characters in his novel *L'Ève future* ("Tomorrow's Eve") (1886), and has been popularised by Philip K. Dick's novel *Do Androids Dream of Electric Sheep?* (1968), which was the basis for the film *Blade Runner* (1982). In forming an impression of these characters we can apply our real-world social schematic knowledge and there is a good fit, but part of the impression – they are not actually organically human – clashes with what we know to be possible in the real-world, giving rise to a "possibility distortion". Philip K. Dick achieves some of his key effects by exploiting the readers understanding of "human but not human" androids: if they are human, killing them is shocking; if they are not human, killing them is not so shocking.

With regard to attributing causes to people's dispositions as opposed to the context, attribution processes do not always proceed on a level playing field. Empirical work relating to attribution theory has shown repeatedly that observers have a tendency not to take the context into account in the way the theory predicts it should be (i.e. they do not always apply the discounting principle where it should be applied) (Jones 1990: 164). Ross (1977: 183) labelled "the tendency to underestimate the impact of situational factors and to overestimate the role of dispositional factors in controlling behaviour" the *fundamental attribution error.* This ties in with what Heider (1958: 54) noted as the tendency of behaviour to be more salient in context: "it tends to engulf the field rather than be confined to its proper position as a local stimulus whose interpretation requires the additional data of the surrounding field – the situation in social perception". Also, it has been noted that the act and actor are more automatically seen as a causal unit and that taking account of situational factors seems to require a more complex kind of processing (Gilbert 1989). Gerrig and Allbritton (1990: 382f.) have used the fundamental attribution error to explain why a predictable plot, such as that of the James Bond books, does not destroy the reader's interest in the outcomes of events:

> [...] the illusion that even the most formulaic outcomes are brought about – afresh – by the internal properties of characters [...] readers are so solidly predisposed to find the causes of events in the characters rather than in the circumstances that reflection upon the "formula" plays no role in their immediate experience of the novel: when events can be explained satisfactorily with recourse to dispositions, we have no reason to look elsewhere.

Of course, other factors are involved in maintaining suspense (e.g. the short-term issue of how a character gets out of a difficult situation, rather than just the long-term issue of whether the character is all right at the end), but the fundamental attribution error can plausibly be a contributory factor in maintaining reader interest.

There are other perceiver biases. Perceivers tend to make different kinds of attributions according to whether they subsume the role of "actor" or "observer" (Heider 1958: 157). Jones and Nisbett (1972: 80) label this the "actor-observer effect" and describe it thus: "[t]here is a pervasive tendency for actors to attribute their actions to situational requirements, whereas observers tend to attribute the same actions to stable personal dispositions" (note that the second half of this statement is in fact the fundamental attribution error). For our purposes, of particular interest is a group of studies (e.g. Storms 1973; Taylor and Fiske 1975) that attempt to explain the actor-observer bias in terms of differences of perspective. The issue is one of perceptual salience (cf. Heider's remark on behaviour filling the field). The argument is well put by Augoustinos and Walker (1995: 82) (see also, Fiske and Taylor 1991: 73):

> Observers see the actor acting, but don't see a situation. The actor is salient; the situation is not. Actors, though, don't see themselves acting. They see the situation around them, and are aware of responding to invisible situational forces. Thus, when actors and observers are asked to explain the same event, they give different accounts because different facets of the same event are salient to them.

Perspective or point of view is, of course, also a textual or narratological issue. The intriguing issue is whether this too can be linked to the actor-observer bias, as indeed Graumann (1992) and Pollard-Gott (1993) have claimed. The hypothesis is that an internal perspective is more likely to result in contextual explanations for behaviour, whereas an external perspective is more likely to result in dispositional explanations for behaviour. Writers may bias their readers simply by using first-person narration, as opposed to third-person, and by using internal focalisation (i.e. the expression of a character's thoughts and feelings), as opposed to external (cf. Fowler 1986) (which would also imply using more direct speech and thought presentation, as opposed to less [cf. Leech and Short 1981]). Thus in theory, and simplifying somewhat, by looking through a character's eyes (including their mind's eye) a reader gets to view the fictional world as if they were that character, thus becoming more of an actor in that world than an observer of it. Consider the Rocky passage above. Numerous words and phrases relate to Rocky's thinking ("planning", "thought" (x2), "bothered", "considered", "knew" (x2), "aware", "frustrating", "felt"), and there are instances of "free indirect thought" ("things were not going well"), as well as of other less direct categories of thought presentation (cf. Leech and Short 1981). The effect of this is that the reader is presented with the world from the perspective of Rocky, but not presented with Rocky from the perspective of (somebody else in) the world. Hence, the theory would predict that we see better how the world impinges upon Rocky as opposed to how Rocky impinges upon the world The important point in all this is that the language of fictional texts has the potential to affect readers' understanding of the causes of behaviours in the text world. Gerrig (2001) provides some experimental evidence for this, though points out a number of important complexities. This is certainly an area that could benefit from further research.[6]

4.3   Contexts in characters

As I pointed out in Culpeper (2002: 273), the characterisation model I had developed in Culpeper (2001) did not capture sufficiently some of the complexities of characterisation. Characterisation is dynamic: as we read, we perform inferencing to keep track of characters in the context con-

---

6. One of the reviewers of this chapter suggests that some of the claims in this section could find independent support in the subjectivity literature within Cognitive Linguistics, specifically noting Sanders and Spooren (1997).

structed by the text. Emmott (e.g. 1997, 2003) put forward "contextual frame theory" in order to account the way in which readers gain a certain amount of information from the text but have to fill in the rest of the context created by the text from information in their heads. A "contextual frame" stores information about characters co-present in a particular place and time. This is not unrelated to the "situation model" of van Dijk and Kintsch (1983). However, the emphasis on the dynamics of co-presence is a distinctive feature of contextual frame theory, and contextual frame theory offers much more guidance with regard to how readers gather information from the text to create fictional contexts. The importance of the co-presence of characters in fictional worlds was not adequately emphasised in my own work. As Emmott points out (2003: 304), "[e]very action and speech utterance by characters in a context can generally be inferred to have an effect on the co-present participants". What this means is that in our understanding of a text we are constructing a mental representation not only of each character, but also a representation of each character's representation of co-present characters, and a representation of the co-present characters and their representation of the other characters, not to mention a representation of the time and space within which the characters appear, as well as a representation of what the writer of the text intends us to understand by the text. And all these representations are linked, allowing further inferencing. Keeping all these balls in the cognitive air may sound like a tall order, but there is some research which suggests that readers are quite good at it. Graesser et al. (2001) conducted experiments which suggested that readers were reasonably good at keeping track of which character had said what and which character knew what.

A corollary of perspective or point of view discussed in the previous section is the idea that our impression of a character must include that character's impression of their context, including other characters that are part of that context. Perspective here does not simply mean matters of focalisation in narrative, but "more generally a character's or narrator's subjective worldview" (Nünning 2001: 207) or the "subjective belief worlds" (Margolin 1990: 850) of characters. Needless to say, this is not just an issue for characterisation in narrative, but for the characterisation of any character in any text (including non-fictional texts). Consider, for example, that an impression of Othello minimally involves constructing a representation of his evaluation of Desdemona, a representation of his feelings, and a representation of his plan for vengeance (see McIntyre 2006, for an elaboration on the importance of point of view for characterisation in drama). Note that, somewhat in the manner of Russian dolls, contexts can be multiply embedded, particularly in narrative. Thus, minimally, third-person omniscient narrative involves a character's perspective of the text world embedded in the narrator's perspective (see Nünning 2001, for elaboration of different types of perspective embeddings and structures in different types of narrative).

Perspective, particularly one character's perspective of another, is of the utmost importance in conversation (see Schober 1998, for a more general discussion of perspective in conversation). For conversation to work, people must orientate their conversational contribution to others. The case of dramatic dialogue is no different. However, both in real life and in fiction, conceptions of others run into a particular problem: theoretically, there is infinite regress. Thus, one character may have an impression of another character which includes that character's impression of another character which includes that character's impression of another character, and so on. Infinite regress is perhaps more of a philosophical problem than anything else, as increasing cognitive effort and decreasing cognitive/ social reward acts as a brake (cf. Sperber and Wilson 1995). Nevertheless, at least some of the lower levels of co-representation need to be taken into consideration in a model of characterisation.

5. Conclusion

The key aim of this chapter has been to show the ways in which research in cognitive psychology can be fruitfully deployed in accounting for how characterisation works. A theory of characterisation must account for:

- the reader's cognitive operations involved in conceptualising and distinguishing the wide range of character types available in literature (e.g. flat characters, round characters, caricatures, more textually-based characters, allegorical characters, genre-based characters),
- the fact that some conceptions of characters are shared to some degree within particular communities of readers (i.e. they have a social basis), whilst others are not (i.e. they are the more idiosyncratic conceptions of particular readers),
- the fact that a conception of character can be informationally richer than the information provided by the text, and
- the fact that conceptions of characters are dynamic to varying degrees, that some can develop and even surprise the reader in that development.

These points, however, only explicitly account for the reader's role in characterisation. In this chapter, I have largely concentrated on what the reader does, periodically noting aspects of what the writer does. That I was able to switch from reader to writer so easily reflects the fact that what the reader does is not so remote from what the writer does, at least from a cognitive point of view. Processes of text production use the same cognitive components as text comprehension but in reverse order: a representation is constructed from fragments of memory which in turn is rendered into language (see, for example, van Dijk and Kintsch 1983). Moreover, writers can assume the readerly operations involved in the points above, and can construct and manipulate characters accordingly. What the points above do not cover are the specific linguistic strategies that may be used in those character constructions, as well as the specific cognitive effects those strategies may produce in readers. As I pointed out at the outset of this chapter, my focus here has been on the cognitive in a cognitive stylistic approach to characterisation. Chapters 4 and 5 of Culpeper (2001) present a comprehensive discussion of such linguistic strategies used in play-texts, and pages 99–110, 149–153, and 251–254 present the results of a small-scale study designed to investigate the impact on readers of such strategies. Regarding effects on readers, a particular study of note is Bortolussi and Dixon (2003), which submits the major claims of narratology, including claims about characterisation, to experiments with readers in order to test their psychological reality.

Whilst it is difficult to see how anything other than a *cognitive* stylistics approach could further the understanding of the characterisation issues dealt with in this chapter, the main field of input, cognitive psychology, is in some ways not entirely up to the job. In section 4.3 in particular, I emphasised some of the complexities of understanding characters in context. Cognitive models of narrative comprehension have until relatively recently ignored much of this complexity. Typically, research has considered a single aspect in the construction of a situation model, such as time, causality or motivation (see references in Magliano et al. 1999: 219). However, more recently we have seen the advent of the "event-indexing model" (Zwaan et al. 1995, see also Magliano et al. 1999), which proposes that readers simultaneously monitor aspects such as these. This is not to say that they claim that all these aspects are equally important in one's understanding. In fact, they make a case for the central importance of causal and intentional dimensions of understanding in narrative (Magliano et al. 1999: 242). Interestingly, this would justify approaches in stylistics that argue for the importance of the speech act analysis of character talk, given that speech acts theoretically encapsulate the speaker's intentions (see also Culpeper 2001: 122 ff.). The event-indexing model also proposes that discontinuities between the situation model and the discourse attract additional processing. This has obvious importance in literary discourse where, for example, flashbacks and flashforwards in the discourse can disrupt temporal continuity between the discourse and the situation model, with the result that readers may divert resources from maintaining the main situation model to building a sub-structure in order to monitor the discontinuity. Similarly, van Dijk has recognised that the scheme proposed in van Dijk and Kintsch (1983) needs further development. He suggests the addition of the notion of "context model", a dynamic representation that participants construct to understand and manage communicative situations (see van Dijk 1999). The details have yet to be worked out; for example, the context model seems to act as an interface between the more static situation model and the flow of discourse, but van Dijk is vague about the precise relationship. Nevertheless, this seems to be a step in the right direction (see Fanlo Pinies 2006 for an application of context models to the minds of characters). Incidentally, both of the models mentioned in this paragraph emphasize episodic memory, not the semantic memory of schema theory. In fact, apart from lack of complexity and being somewhat too static, cognitive psychology generally suffers from another potentially more serious problem: models and theories in cognitive psychology have largely been developed in laboratory conditions with simplified and constructed texts, such as the Rocky text in this chapter. A challenge for cognitive stylistics is to validate cognitive models and theories in the light of complex and messy literary data, and not to assume they are necessarily valid.

Finally, let us briefly consider what Cognitive Linguistics could have offered with regard to the issues covered in this chapter. Fauconnier and Turner (2002) do indeed have a short chapter on "Identity and Character" (chapter 12). They devote some space to the relationship between characters and frames (which roughly correspond to the situational context I discussed above), and suggest two perspectives: frames remaining relatively stable across different characters (their example being a buying-selling frame) and characters remaining relatively stable across different frames (their example being Odysseus). They suggest two "general patterns":

> First, we are able to extract regularities over different behaviours by the same person to build up a generic space for that person – a personal character. Second, we are able to extract regularities over different behaviours by many

people to build up a generic space for a kind of behaviour. They interact. The phrase "he's the kind of guy who does X" asks us to do both: to establish a generic for him and a generic for the kind of behaviour exemplified by X. There is a further kind of extraction, the kind Theophrastus and his successor La Bruyère do in their works on character, where we create a generic space for a "kind of person" – the Vain Man, the Liar, the Social Climber – who is a blend of several of these kinds of generic behaviour. (2002: 251f.)

One can see strong echoes here of attribution theory, specifically, the classic theory according to Kelley, which emphasises consistency across situations. Notice also that "generic spaces" for kinds of character and kinds of behaviour are analogous to my discussion of causal schemata, where I pointed out that causal schemata enable us to "generate expectations about causes, including expectations about the kind of personalities causing particular behaviours". Furthermore, "piecemeal integration", as discussed in section 3, could be accounted for within blending theory. An understanding of Katherina in *The Taming of the Shrew*, for example, does not involve a rejection of her characteristics exhibited in the first third of the play, but the integration of those characteristics with those exhibited in the latter part of the play. This could be analysed as a blend of her former self with her latter self (see Fauconnier and Turner 2002: 259, for a similar example). Clearly, then, there is the potential for the application of blending theory to issues of characterisation. However, Fauconnier and Turner (2002: chapter 12) provide at best a few pointers with regard to the general direction in which one might go. The issues that they allude to have been scrutinised and discussed for decades within social cognition. For example, Solomon Asch, one of the founders of social psychology, was arguing that traits form a "gestalt", which is not simply an average of the traits, back in 1946; and Fritz Heider, one of the founders of attribution theory, published his classic work on attribution in which he considered the interaction between personality and situations in 1958. Relevant proposals and theories in social cognition have been subjected to extensive testing and consequent revision. It would seem positively churlish to ignore this work and head off down the less certain paths presented within the relatively narrow Cognitive Linguistics paradigm. To return to the point I made in my introduction, cognitive linguistics should encompass any enterprise that involves an interaction between cognition and language.

References

Andersen, Richard C., Ralph E. Reynolds, Diane L. Schallert and Ernest T. Goetz
    1977   Frameworks for comprehending discourse. *American Educational Research Journal* 14(4): 367–381.
Andersen, Susan M., Roberta L. Klatsky and John Murray
    1990   Traits and social stereotypes: Efficiency differences in social information processing. *Journal of Personality and Social Psychology* 59(2): 192–201.
Asch, Solomon E.
    1946   Forming Impressions of Personality. *Journal of Abnormal and Social Psychology* 41: 258–90.
Augoustinos, Martha and Iain Walker
    1995   *Social Cognition: An Integrated Perspective.* London: Sage.
Bartlett, Frederic C.
    [1932] 1995 *Remembering: A Study in Experimental and Social Psychology.* Cambridge: Cambrige University Press.
Bortolussi, Marisa and Peter Dixon
    2003   *Psychonarratology: Foundations for the Empirical Study of Literary Response.* Cambridge: Cambridge University Press.
Brewer, Marilyn B.
    1988   A Dual Process Model of Impression Formation. In: Thomas K. Srull and Robert S. Wyer (eds.), *Advances in Social Cognition* (Vol. 1), 1–36. Hillsdale, NJ: Lawrence Erlbaum.
Cantor, Nancy and Walter Mischel
    1979   Prototypes in person perception. In: Leonard Berkowitz (ed.), *Advances in Experimental Social Psychology*, Vol. 12, 3–52. New York: Academic Press.
Cook, Guy
    1994   *Discourse and Literature.* Oxford: Oxford University Press.
Culpeper, Jonathan
    1996   Inferring character from text: attribution theory and foregrounding theory. *Poetics* 23: 335–61.
Culpeper, Jonathan
    2001   *Language and Characterisation: People in Plays and other Texts.* Pearson Education: Harlow.
Culpeper, Jonathan
    2002   A cognitive stylistic approach to characterisation. In: Elena Semino and Jonathan Culpeper (eds.), *Cognitive Stylistics: Language and Cognition in Text Analysis*, 251–277. Amsterdam; Philadelphia: John Benjamins.
Emmott, Cathy
    2003   Constructing social space: Socio-cognitive factors in the interpretation of character relations. In: David Herman (ed.), *Narrative Theory and the Cognitive Sciences*, 295–321. Stanford, California: CSLI Publications.

Emmott, Cathy
    1995   *Narrative Comprehension: A Discourse Perspective.* Oxford: Oxford
            University Press.
Evans, Vyvyan and Melanie Green
    2006   *Cognitive Linguistics: An Introduction.* Edinburgh: Edinburgh Univer-
            sity Press.
Eysenck, Michael W. and Mark T. Keane
    2000   *Cognitive Psychology: A Student's Handbook.* 4th ed. Hillsdale, N.J.:
            Lawrence Erlbaum.
Fauconnier, Gilles and Mark Turner
    2002   *Conceptual Blending and the Mind's Hidden Complexities.* New York:
            Basic Books.
Fanlo Pinies, Maria
    2006   The minds and mental selves of characters in prose fiction. Ph.D. dis-
            sertation. Department of Linguistics and English Language, Lancaster
            University.
Fiske, Susan T. and Steven L. Neuberg
    1990   A continuum of impression formation, from category-based to indi-
            viduating processes: Influences of information and motivation on
            attention and interpretation. In: Mark P. Zanna (ed.), *Advances in
            Experimental Social Psychology*, Vol. 23, 1–74. New York: Academic
            Press.
Fiske, Susan T. and Shelley E. Taylor
    1984   *Social Cognition.* Reading, Massachusetts: McGraw-Hill.
Fiske, Susan T. and Shelly E. Taylor
    1991   *Social Cognition.* 2d ed. New York: Addison-Wesley.
Forster, Edward M.
    [1927] 1987 *Aspects of the Novel.* Middlesex: Penguin.
Fowler, Roger
    1986   *Linguistic Criticism.* Oxford and New York: Oxford University Press.
Gerrig, Richard J.
    2001   Perspective as participation. In: Willie van Peer and Seymour Chatman
            (eds.), *New Perspectives on Narrative Perspective*, 303–323. New York:
            State University of New York Press.
Gerrig, Richard J. and David W. Allbritton
    1990   The construction of literary character: A view from cognitive psychol-
            ogy. *Style* 24(3): 380–91.
Gilbert, Daniel T.
    1989   Thinking lightly about others: Automatic components of the social in-
            ference process. In: James S. Uleman and John A. Bargh (eds.), *Unin-
            tended Thought: Limits of Awareness, Intention, and Control*, 189–211.
            New York: Guilford.
Graesser, Arthur C., Cheryl Bowers, Ute J. Baten and Xiangen Hu
    2001   Who said what? Who knows what? Tracking speakers and knowledge
            in narratives. In: Willie van Peer and Seymour Chatman (eds.), *New*

Perspectives on Narrative Perspective, 255–272. New York: State University of New York Press.

Graesser, Arthur C., Murray Singer and Tom Trabasso
1994   Constructing inferences during narrative text comprehension. *Psychological Review* 101(3): 371–95.

Graumann, Carl F.
1992   Speaking and understanding from viewpoints: Studies in perspectivity. In: Gün R. Semin and Klaus Fiedler (eds), *Language, Interaction and Social Cognition*, 237–255. Newbury Park: Sage.

Guthrie, John T, Wigfield, Allan, Metsala, Jamie L. and Kathleen E. Cox
2004   Motivational and cognitive predictors of text comprehension and reading amount. In: Robert B. Ruddell and Norman J. Unrau (eds.), *Theoretical Models and Processes of Reading*, 929–953. (5th ed.). Newark: International Reading Association.

Hall, Geoff
2002   Review article: The years work in stylistics: 2001. *Language and Literature* 11(4): 357–372.

Hall, Geoff
2003   Review article. The years work in stylistics: 2002. *Language and Literature* 12(4): 353–370.

Hamilton, David L. and Jeffrey W. Sherman
1994   Stereotypes. In: Robert S. Wyer and Thomas K. Srull (eds.), *Handbook of Social Cognition, Volume 2: Applications*, 1–68. 2nd ed. New Jersey: Lawrence Erlbaum Associates.

Heider, Fritz
1958   *The Psychology of Interpersonal Relations*. New York: Wiley.

Holyoak, Keith J. Peter C. Gordon
1984   Information processing and social cognition. In: Robert S. Wyer and Thomas K. Srull (eds.), *Handbook of Social Cognition. Vol.1*, 39–70. Hillsdale, NJ: Lawrence Erlbaum.

Jeffries, Lesley
2001   Schema affirmation and White Asparagus: Cultural multilingualism among readers of texts. *Language and Literature* 10(4): 325–343.

Jones, Edward E.
1990   *Interpersonal Perception*. New York: W.H. Freeman.

Jones, Edward E. and Davis, K.E.
1965   From acts to dispositions: The attribution process in person perception. In: Leonard Berkowitz (ed.), *Advances in Experimental Social Psychology*, Vol.2, 219–266. New York: Academic Press.

Jones, Edward E. and Richard E. Nisbett
1972   The actor and the observer: Divergent perceptions of the causes of behavior. In: Edward E. Jones, David E. Kanouse, Harold H. Kelley, Richard E. Nisbett, Stuart Valins and Barnard Weiner (eds.), *Attribution: Perceiving the Causes of Behaviour*, 79–94. Morristown, NJ: General Learning Press.

Kelley, Harold H.
   1967   Attribution theory in social psychology. In: David Levine (ed.), *Nebraska Symposium on Motivation*, 192–238. Lincoln, Nebraska: University of Nebraska Press.

Kelley, Harold H.
   1972   Attribution in social interaction. In: Edward E. Jones, David E. Kanouse, Harold H. Kelley, Richard E. Nisbett, Stuart Valins and Barnard Weiner (eds), *Attribution: Perceiving the Causes of Behaviour*, 1–26. Morristown, NJ: General Learning Press.

Kintsch, Walter, Schmalhofer, Franz, Welsch, David and Susan Zimny
   1990   Sentence memory: A theoretical analysis. *Journal of Memory and Language* 29: 133–59.

Leech, Geoffrey N.
   1969   *A Linguistic Guide to English Poetry*. London: Longman.

Leech, Geoffrey N.
   1985   Stylistics. In: Teun A. van Dijk (ed.), *Discourse and Literature*, 39–57. Amsterdam/Philadelphia: John Benjamins.

Leech, Geoffrey N. and Short, Mick
   1981   *Style in Fiction*. London: Longman.

Leyens, Jacques-Philippe, Vincent Yzerbyt and Georges Schadron
   1994   *Stereotypes and Social Cognition*. Sage: London.

Livingstone, Sonia
   1998   *Making Sense of Television: The Psychology of Audience Interpretation*. 2d edn. London/New York: Routledge.

Long, Debra L.
   1994   The effects of pragmatics and discourse style on recognition memory for sentences. *Discourse Processes* 17: 213–234.

Magliano, Joseph P., Rolph A. Zwaan and Arthur Graesser
   1999   The role of situational continuity in narrative understanding. In: Herre van Oostendorp and Susan R. Goldman (eds.), *The Construction of Mental Representations during Reading*, 219–245. Mahwah, N.J.: Lawrence Erlbaum Associates.

Margolin, Uri
   1983   Characterization in narrative: Some theoretical prolegomena. *Neophilologus* 67: 1–14.

Margolin, Uri
   2001   Collective perspective, individual perspective, and the speaker in between: On "we" literary narratives. In: Willie van Peer and Seymour Chatman (eds.), *New Perspectives on Narrative Perspective*, 241–253. New York: State University of New York Press.

McIntyre, Daniel
   2006   *Point of View in Plays: A Cognitive Stylistic Approach to Viewpoint in Drama and Other Text-types*. Amsterdam/Philadelphia: John Benjamins.

Meutsch, Dietrich
   1986   Mental models in literary discourse: Towards the integration of linguistic and psychological levels of description. *Poetics* 15: 307–31.

Mukařovský, Jan
   1970   Standard language and poetic language, ed. and trans. by Paul L. Garvin. In: Donald C. Freeman (ed.), *Linguistics and Literary Style*, 40–56. New York: Holt, Rinehart and Winston.

Nünning, Ansgar.
   2001   On the perspective structure of narrative texts: steps towards a constructivist narratology. In: Willie van Peer and Seymour Chatman (eds.), *New Perspectives on Narrative Perspective*. 207–223. New York: State University of New York Press.

Pollard-Gott, L.
   1993   Attribution theory and the novel. *Poetics* 21: 499–524.

Rosch, Eleanor
   1978   Principles of categorization. In: Eleanor Rosch and Barbara B. Lloyd (eds.), *Cognition and Categorization*, 27–48. Hillsdale, N.J.: Lawrence Erlbaum.

Rosch, Eleanor, Carolyn B. Mervis, Wayne D. Gray, David M. Johnson and Penny Boyes-Braem
   1976   Basic objects in natural categories. *Cognitive Psychology* 8: 382–439.

Ross, Lee
   1977   The intuitive psychologist and his shortcomings: Distortions in the attribution process. In: Leonard Berkowitz (ed.), *Advances in Experimental Social Psychology*, Vol. 10, 173–220. New York: Academic Press.

Sack, Warren
   2000   Actor-role analysis: ideology, point of view, and the news. In: Willie van Peer and Seymour Chatman (eds.), *New Perspectives on Narrative Perspective*, 189–204. New York: State University of New York Press.

Sanders, Ted and Wilbert Spooren
   1997   Perspective, subjectivity, and modality from a cognitive linguistic point of view. In: Wolf-Andreas Liebert, Gisela Redeker and Linda Waugh (eds.), *Discourse and Perspective in Cognitive Linguistics*, 85–114. Amsterdam; Philadelphia: Benjamins.

Schneider, Ralph
   2000   *Grundriß zur kognitiven Theorie der Figurenrezeption am Beispiel des viktorianischen Romans*. Tübingen: Stauffenburg.

Schneider, Ralph
   2001   Toward a cognitive theory of literary character: The dynamics of mental-model construction. *Style* 35(4): 607–40.

Schober, Michael F.
   1998   Different kinds of conversational perspective-taking. In: Susan R. Fussell and Roger J. Kreuz (eds.), *Social and Cognitive Approaches to Interpersonal Communication*, 145–174. Mahwah, N.J.: Lawrence Erlbaum Associates.

Scollon, Ronald and Suzanne Scollon
   1995   *Intercultural Communication: A Discourse Approach*, Language in Society 21. Oxford: Blackwell.

Semino, Elena
   1997   *Language and World Creation in Poems and Other Texts*. London: Longman.
Semino, Elena
   2001   Notes and discussion. On readings, literariness and schema theory: a reply to Jeffries. *Language and Literature* 10(4): 345–355.
Semino, Elena and Jonathan Culpeper (eds.)
   2002   *Cognitive Stylistics: Language and Cognition in Text Analysis*. Amsterdam/Philadelphia: John Benjamins.
Short, Mick
   1989   Discourse analysis and the analysis of drama. In: Ronald Carter and Paul Simpson (eds.), *Language, Discourse and Literature: An Introductory Reader in Discourse Stylistics*, 139–168. London: Unwin Hyman.
Short, Mick
   1996   *Exploring the Language of Poems, Plays and Prose*. London: Longman.
Short, Mick
   1998   From dramatic text to dramatic performance. In: Jonathan Culpeper, Mick Short and Peter Verdonk (eds.), *Exploring the Language of Drama: From Text to Context*, 6–18. Routledge: London.
Short, Mick
   2001   Epilogue: research questions, research paradigms, and research methodologies in the study of narrative. In: Willie van Peer and Seymour Chatman (eds.), *New Perspectives on Narrative Perspective*, 339–355. New York: State University of New York Press.
Sperber, Dan and Deidre Wilson
   1995   *Relevance: Communication and Cognition* (2nd edition). Oxford: Blackwell.
Steffensen, Margaret S., Chitra Joag-Dev and Richard C. Andersen
   1979   A cross-cultural perspective on reading comprehension. *Reading Research Quarterly* 15: 10–29.
Stockwell, Peter
   2003   Schema poetics and speculative cosmology. *Language and Literature* 12(3): 252–271.
Storms, Michael D.
   1973   Videotape and the attribution process: Reversing actors' and observers' points of view. *Journal of Personality and Social Psychology* 27: 165–75.
Taylor, Shelley E. and Susan J. Fiske
   1975   Point-of-view and perceptions of causality. *Journal of Personality and Social Psychology* 32: 439–445.
Taylor, Shelley E., Susan J. Fiske, Nancy L. Etcoff and Audrey Ruderman
   1978   Categorical bases of person memory and stereotyping. *Journal of Personality and Social Psychology* 36: 778–93.
Toolan, Michael J.
   1988   *Narrative: A Critical Linguistic Introduction*. London: Routledge.

Trabasso, Tom, Paul van den Broek and So Young Suh
  1989   Logical necessity and transitivity of causal relations in the representation of stories. *Discourse Processes* 12: 1–25.
Tulving, Endel
  1972   Episodic and semantic memory. In: Endel Tulving and William Donaldson (eds.), *Organisation of Memory*, 382–403. New York: Academic Press.
van den Broek, Paul
  1990   Causal inferences and the comprehension of narrative texts. In: Arthur C. Graesser and Gordon H. Bower (eds.), *Inferences and Text Comprehension*, 175–196. New York: Academic Press.
van Dijk, Teun A.
  1987   *Communicating Racism: Ethnic Prejudice in Thought and Talk*. Newbury Park: Sage Publications.
van Dijk, Teun A.
  1988   Social cognition, social power and social discourse. *Text* 8(1–2): 129–157.
van Dijk, Teun A.
  1990   Social Cognition and Discourse. In: Howard Giles and William P. Robinson (eds.), *Handbook of Language and Social Psychology*, 163–183. Chichester: John Wiley.
van Dijk, Teun A.
  1999   Context models in discourse processing. In: Herre van Oostendorp and Susan R. Goldman (eds.), *The Construction of Mental Representations during Reading*, 123–148. Mahwah, N.J.: Lawrence Erlbaum Associates.
van Dijk, Teun A. and Walter Kintsch
  1983   *Strategies of Discourse Comprehension*. London: Academic Press.
van Peer, Willie
  1986   *Stylistics and Psychology: Investigations of Foregrounding*. London: Croom Helm.
Zebrowitz, Leslie A.
  1990   *Social Perception*. Milton Keynes: Open University Press.
Zwaan, Rolf A.
  1996   Toward a model of literary comprehension. In: Bruce K. Britton and Arthur C. Graesser (eds.), *Models of Understanding Text*, 241–255. Mahwah, NJ: Lawrence Erlbaum.
Zwaan, Rolf A., Mark C. Langston and Arthur Graesser
  1995   The construction of situation models in narrative comprehension: An event-indexing model. *Psychological Science* 6: 292–297.

Comments on Culpeper

Uri Margolin

In his rich and nuanced essay, Culpeper provides valuable insights on four interrelated topics:

- The reader's construction of character (=RCC) from a narrative or dramatic text, and the elements, factors and operations involved in this process, i.e. the cognitive dimension.
- (Some) of the major differences between RCC on the basis of factual and fictional texts i.e. the cognitive-literary nexus.
- Explication or explanation in terms of cognitive psychology of some aspects of RCC recognised, but described only vaguely and intuitively, in traditional literary criticism, i.e. literary into cognitive.
- The influence of textual surface features on RCC, i.e. cognitive stylistics proper.

As for the first topic, let us note that both "character" and "characterisation" are hopelessly ambiguous in English. "Character" may thus designate a literary figure, story world participant, or narrative agent as opposed to an actual person, or the personality of a real or fictional individual. "Characterisation" can designate the ascription of any features whatsoever or just personality ones to an actual or fictional individual, this ascription being explicitly formulated in the text or carried out by the reader. To be sure, Culpeper's essay is on the readerly attribution of personality features to fictional individuals, that is, the reader's construction of character in the narrow sense. Following an established tradition in cognitive studies, the author points out the crucial role of personality schemata stored in the reader's long term memory in the construction of character, and points out some of the factors involved in the reader's activation of a particular schema in a given case: textual data, the reader's cultural experience, and specific contextual factors such as the reader's current situation and goals in reading, as well as the frequency and recency of schemata to which s/he has been earlier exposed. The uses of schemata are pointed out in detail: integrating data into a coherent pattern, guiding of inferences ("filling in"), and formulation of expectations. Person schemata can be of three levels of generality: the individual person, a social role, that is, one's station and the personal properties normally associated with it, and a wide group, such as race of gender. Following Ellen Rosch's prototype theory, Culpeper attributes special importance to the mid-level social category and points out that one may have positive or negative attitude towards a particular role.

Since textual cues/clues about any literary figure are necessarily provided sequentially, several possibilities of readerly characterization immediately arise. Initial data lead to a categorization which stays the same throughout the text; initial categorization is undermined by later dissonant information, requiring category modification or re-categorisation; the given clues do not fit any schema available to the reader, necessitating a piecemeal, bottom-up construction of the character of the literary figure, yielding an individual portrait of a new and unfamiliar kind. Culpeper further points out an inherent difficulty of any RCC *cum* inference or computation: all human behaviour occurs in some context or situation. Given that an individual behaves in a certain way in a particular situation, is it indicative of one's personality or of situational constraints? One factor in deciding this question would be the availability of choice or alternatives in the situation. In general, one should further check whether the individual's behaviour deviates from standard expectations, and whether this individual manifests the same behaviour in very different situations. If the answer to either question is positive, then this would provide a good reason for inferring from behaviour to personality traits.

Everything said so far applies equally to cases of readerly attribution of personality features to actual persons on the basis of non-fictional texts, employing life-world schemata. This indicates on the one hand the continuity of readerly mental operations between the actual and the make-believe, and on the other the potentially significant contribution of literary studies to general theories of textual processing. But we all feel there must be some specifics, limited to the processing of fictional texts, and Culpeper indeed lists some of them clearly and eloquently. In the first case, in fictional contexts "all the evidence is in". Consequently, we are inclined to interpret any detail of a character's behaviour as significant and indicative of his personality, intentions, state of mind, etc. Secondly, there are numerous character-kinds created specifically by literary genres, and in such cases the appropriate schema for RCC belongs to the literary rather than life-world knowledge inventory. Literary character-kinds may manifest a clash or incongruity of features as regards actual world categories, as in the case of androids (organic or inorganic, man or machine), leading to hesitation on part of the reader how to judge them.

Even more interesting, although staying within the actually possible, are cases where a literary genre deliberately endows an individual with features which contradict some of the basic features associated with this individual's social role according to the standard schema. Agatha Christie, for example, has a novel in which a judge turns out to be the murderer. The stereotypical actual-world image of a judge and our actual-world expectations about his nature and behaviour are thus inverted. But this initially surprising or shocking inversion, if sufficiently repeated, may itself in due course give rise to a judge-in-detective-fiction schema, where the inversion will be built into the new schema, and thus lose its surprise effect. So how should a detective-story writer choose his murderer? As Culpeper aptly suggests, the optimal solution would be to select a character for whom both actual-world and genre-based expectations are fairly neutral. In general terms, the interplay between actual-world based schemata and genre-based ones in the process of RCC, and the factors influencing the reader's choice of the optimal schema (or his inability to choose, hesitation, double vision, oscillation between a life world and a literary one) is a fundamental issue meriting further study based on a wider range of genres and periods.

Numerous pre-theoretical literary insights regarding literary characters find their explication or explanation within a cognitive framework. The facts that different readers possess different inventories of schemata and read in different contexts and with different goals in mind, and that any collection of data could fit (to some degree at least) more than one schema provide a clear explanation of the different "understandings" of the same literary figure by different reader groups or generations. It further explains the intuitive claim that "one can see literary characters in different ways". The traditional typology of literary characters is also given a firm footing by associating them with schemata. Thus a stock figure, especially in comedy, is one who behaves in the same manner in all contexts and a flat (and I would add static) character is one where the initial categorization stays valid throughout. Conversely, a round (and I would add dynamic) character is precisely one where the initial schema selected needs to be modified or replaced at least once in the course of our reading. Finally, the unprecedented kinds of characters, where we need to proceed bottom-up, are those which we find difficult but also challenging, interesting and requiring greater involvement on our part. Here it is the aesthetic effect of a character that is explained in cognitive terms.

Culpeper states that in this essay he tends to emphasise cognitive research, giving much less attention to the role of language. Yet he still provides some insights that definitely belong to cognitive stylistics. Now a discipline is what its practitioners make it to be, and there are always several, only partially overlapping conceptions of a discipline on offer from its practitioners. In our particular context, cognitive stylistics would, in my view, consist of the enquiry how surface features of language, style and expression, together with particular devices, techniques and methods of portrayal, influence or steer the RCC. Culpeper indicates that in literary contexts surface features are not always forgotten after a few seconds, but may be retained and enter the portrait of a character. Examples are repeated phrases like "I will never leave Mr. Micawber", significant names and others. As we have seen earlier, it is often difficult to determine whether an individual's behaviour is dictated by his personality or by situational factors. A stylistic clue would be the perspective or point of view from which things are presented. If it is internal, that is, the character's, then the situation would likely be regarded as the cause, while an external perspective would tend to regard the agent's personality as the cause. Finally, there is the interesting analogy drawn between repeated identical behaviour in different situations and failure to obey standard situational norms or expectations on one hand and the overcoding (parallelism) and deviation of textual patterns. I guess the analogy could be motivated by the fact that in both cases we are dealing with semiotic or symbolic activities which can manifest similar formal features regardless of the substance they are embodied in.

As one can see, I am in agreement with Culpeper's overall approach and with most of his specific claims. There are nevertheless a few points where I believe further clarification, or even correction, are called for. To begin with, Culpeper notes that, as we proceed along the text continuum new, unexpected information may be provided which forces us to re-categorise a given character, and I agree. But a further distinction should be made concerning the chronology of the story world. The new information may be associated with a *new temporal phase* in the character's life, in which case the initial category is not rejected, but only temporally restricted. Up to a certain point in time the individual had this character, but beyond it his character changed markedly, requiring a new, again temporally demarcated, schema to describe it. Only in this case can we speak of a dynamic or changing character. The other case is when new, incompatible information concerning *the same time period* is provided later in the text, forcing us to discard the categorization we have been using so far and replace it with a different, more appropriate one. In this case the character need not have changed at all; it is rather our knowledge about him that has changed. Only in this case can we speak of authorial garden paths, authors withholding information and playing tricks, readerly surprise, retrospective revisions and so on.

Although it is a minor point, I cannot agree with the author's argument in 4.2 equating someone who behaves the same in all situations with a stock figure and with exaggeration and caricature. Insensitivity to context may or may not be comic, depending on genre and circumstances. It is surely not comic in the case of Dostoevsky's Prince Myshkin in *Idiot*. To turn Culpeper's argument against him, context itself seems to be in need of contextualisation. Moreover, unchanging behaviour does not equal exaggeration and certainly not the distortion and disproportionate detail normally associated with caricature.

The list of phenomena which a model of characterisation should account for (Conclusion) consists of a mixed bag in need of further clarification. To begin with, what we are concerned with is a theory, not a model, since only arguments or claims can account for anything. Moreover, a theory of RCC does not have to account for the wide range of character types available in literature, but rather for the variety of readerly cognitive operations involved in distinguishing and modelling them. The distinction between shared and unshared conceptions of character is ambiguous: does it mean the same as the personal category vs. the social role and group ones (2.2), or does it mean that some RCC are shared by a group of readers while others are idiosyncratic? The fact that an impression of character may be richer than what the text provides is of course the key issue of reader filling-in through categorization, inferencing, supplementation through literary or world knowledge, etc. to which most of the article is clearly devoted. Finally, as for accounting for ways in which *writers* can manipulate readers' impression of characters, this has traditionally been dealt with in the poetics of narrative, especially the rhetorical approaches (Booth, Sternberg and many others). Since such studies link textual features with cognitive and emotional effects, they constitute cognitive stylistics par excellence. But to go beyond theoretical surmises, one needs empirical work studying the impact on actual readers of the devices singled out by poetics. One experimental method, for example, consists of rewriting the same short text in various ways and checking for the differences in resultant readers' reactions.

Part II: Figure

Minding: feeling, form, and meaning in the creation of poetic iconicity

Margaret H. Freeman

The recognition that significant meaning cannot occur without form-in-feeling and feeling-in-form is what is lacking in the practice of most cognitive linguistics today (Sternberg 2003). Cognitive Linguistics will never come of age until it can account for the human sign ficance of the language utterance – and that can only occur when cognitive linguists discover the principles that enable feeling (sensation, emotion) to motivate expression. But to do this, they don't have to reinvent the wheel. A long tradition of aesthetics exists which, however flawed in its details, has been examining both form and feeling in works of art – music, dance, sculpture, architecture, art, literature, and so on. Susanne K. Langer (1967: xviii–ix) believed that the study of works of art as "images of the forms of feeling" would enable her to construct "a biological theory of feeling that should logically lead to an adequate concept of mind".

I suggest that literary study can help to develop a working model of what I call "minding" by establishing the role of the forms of feeling in language use. You might ask, why can't one create the model directly from the nonfictional language of everyday discourse? Why do we need to turn to non-discursive poetic language? Langer (1953: 40) points out that form is elusive in actual felt activity whereas "[a]rt is the creation of forms symbolic of human feeling". A symbol, she says (1967: 244), "always presents its import in simplified form, which is exactly what makes that import accessible for us. No matter how complex, profound and fecund a work of art – or even the whole realm of art – may be, it is incomparably simpler than life. So the theory of art is really a prolegomena to the much greater undertaking of constructing a concept of mind adequate to the living actuality". Langer (1953: 241) notes elsewhere that non-discursive form in art articulates "knowledge that cannot be rendered discursively because it concerns experiences that are not *formally* amenable to the discursive projection" – that is, such experiences are the rhythms of life, organic, emotional and mental (the rhythm of attention is an interesting link among them all), which are not simply periodic, but endlessly complex, and sensitive to every sort of influence. All together, they compose the dynamic pattern of feeling. It is this pattern that only non-discursive symbolic forms can present, and that is the point and purpose of artistic construction.

For the cognitive linguist then, the study of literary texts can help illuminate the way in which human language is motivated by and expresses the forms of the mind feeling. The mechanism by which these forms of feeling are symbolized in language is iconicity. What has not yet been fully explored in iconicity studies of language and literature so far are two aspects of iconic representation: its phenomenological status and the role of feeling. In this paper, I suggest ways in which these iconic representations can be seen to be especially prominent in the literary arts and thus create what I call poetic iconicity. (Freeman 2007)

1.   Theoretical framework

My exploration of "minding" in the ways feeling, form, and meaning interact in creating poetic iconicity is drawn from my understanding of three philosophical approaches: Merleau-Ponty's existential phenomenology, Charles Sanders Peirce's semiotic theory of the sign, and Susanne K. Langer's theory of the mind feeling. In this section, therefore, I outline a brief sketch of some of the ways these approaches apply to my concept of poetic iconicity.

1.1. Iconicity

Art is the semblance of felt life (Langer 1953). Art's semblance is brought about through the mechanism of iconicity. The different varieties of artistic expression tend to focus on one of the five senses. That is, although the arts may involve several senses at once – like texture in the visible arts or sight in the musical – one of the senses dominates, as in sight for visual art or sound for music. This truism accords with Charles Sanders Peirce's (1955) theory of the sign. The *icon* is that which is closest to the concrete experiences of our senses, the *index* one step removed, and the *symbol* the most abstract. All three may occur in artistic expression (for example, in Renaissance art, the image of a human skull often appears in scenes of arcadia. The skull iconically signifies the living person, it points to the fact of human mortality, and it symbolizes Death).[1] However, literature differs from the other arts because its means of expression is language, itself a symbolic form. Thus the semblance of felt life in literature, appearing through the medium of language, may incorporate any of the five senses, but less directly than those of its sister arts.

The idea that language is almost totally symbolic or arbitrary has been challenged in recent studies of iconicity, evidenced primarily in the work of the Iconicity Project (http://es-dev.uzh.ch/), special issues of the *Journal of Pragmatics* (1994, 22:1) on Metaphor and Iconicity in Language and the *European Journal of English Studies* (2001, 5.1) on Iconicity, and Masako Hiraga's (2005) volume on *Metaphor and Iconicity: A Cognitive Approach to Analysing Texts*. Such studies have found a much closer connection between form and meaning in conventional and poetic language use than had previously been assumed. As Nänny and Fischer (1999: xxii) have noted, iconicity can be imagic and diagrammatic, and diagrammatic iconicity can be structural and semantic (Fig. 1).

Terminology that links form to meaning (as in the title of the first volume in the Iconicity Project, *Form Miming Meaning*) introduces a misleading element into the cognitive processes at work. It implies that form is separable from content, that form can somehow be applied "after the fact" on a pre-existing content. In western literary tradition, this separation gave rise to the notion of "figures of speech", to the notion that literary texts, especially poetry, were differentiated from conventional language by the ornaments and embellishments of special forms. What is missing from this perspective is the realization that meaning arises from the form *of* content and the content *of* form. In other words, symbols are indivisible. As Langer (1953: 369) notes: "They only occur in a total form; as the convex and concave surfaces of a shell may be noted as characterizing its form, but a shell cannot be synthetically composed of 'the concave' and 'the convex'. There are no such factors before there is a shell".

---

1. Note that it is a skull and not some other skeletal part of the human body that is featured (like a leg or an arm). When Hamlet sees the skull the gravedigger has unearthed, he cries "Alas, poor Yorick!" thus identifying the object with the person. Whether or not we can actually identify the living person from the skeletal head, it seems a more likely association than identification by other body parts, since it is the seat of our cognition.

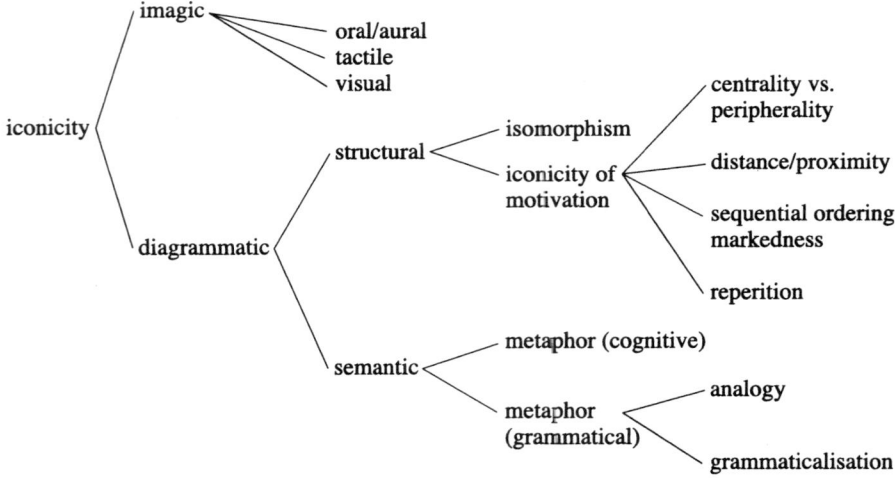

Figure 1. Types of Iconicity. (Based on Nänny and Fischer 1999: xxii.)

Peirce noted that the icon has a complex structure, composed of image, diagram, and metaphor. "Image" refers to the forming of a concept in the mind as in "imagination", and can thus denote mental concepts arising from external stimuli (through the senses) or internal stimuli (through the emotions and memory).[2] "Icon", in its rudimentary meaning, refers to the representation of an image. "Diagram" refers to the abstraction of the structure of the image, serving to symbolize the mental processes of creating concepts in the mind. This structure includes the morphological, phonological, and syntactical forms of language. At the level of discourse, structure also includes patterning of image, such as repetition, alliteration, rhyme, meter, and so on. The relation of image to diagram is one of

---

2. As Langer (1967: 59) notes: "An image does not exemplify the same principles of construction as the object it symbolizes but abstracts its phenomenal character, its immediate effect on our sensibility or the way it presents itself as something of importance, magnitude, strength or fragility, permanence or transience, etc. It organizes and enhances the impression directly received. And as most of our awareness of the world is a continual play of impressions, our primitive intellectual equipment is largely a fund of images, not necessarily visual, but often gestic, kinesthetic, verbal or what I can only call "sitational." [...] [W]e apprehend everything which comes to us as impact from the world by imposing some image on it that stresses its salient features and shapes it for recognition and memory".

total integration. When diagram takes on the characteristics of image, then iconicity at the more abstract level occurs. Peirce apparently did not elaborate on the processes by which iconicity in this sense occurs, although his linking of metaphor with image and diagram as components of the icon is suggestive in this direction (Hiraga 2005).[3]

Halliday (1994: 143) identifies three kinds of iconic correlation between grammar and concept: linear order, nominalization, and the combination of the two. Hiraga (2005: 42–43) recognizes the metaphorical nature of Halliday's iconic representations. Syntax becomes metaphoric when it maps the movement of theme-background to rheme-foreground (these are Halliday's terms) onto the "periodic flow of information". Nominalizations are metaphoric when they reify, or make objective entities, out of processes or events. As Langer (1967: 20f.) notes:

> The fact that we call something by a name, such as "feeling", makes it seems like a kind of thing, an ingredient in nature or a product. But "feel" is a verb, and to say that what is felt is a "feeling" may be one of those deceptive common-sense suppositions inherent in the structure of language which semanticists are constantly bringing to our attention. "Feeling" is a verbal noun – a noun made out of a verb, that psychologically makes an entity out of a process.

"Mind", I suggest, may also be seen as a metaphoric reification of the process of minding.

1.2. Minding

For Langer (1953, 1967), the relation of form to feeling lies at the basis of all art. In her definition of the arts (and especially poetry) as the semblance of felt life, Langer points to iconicity as a structuring principle of art. Not "representation", note, or even "resemblance", but "semblance". As Langer (1953: 49) notes, semblance (or *Schein*) "liberates perception –

---

3. Hiraga follows traditional thinking about form and content by analyzing metaphor as linking form to meaning. However, her idea that metaphor is the icon's connecting bridge is worth exploring. If one substitutes "image" and "diagram" for "form" and "meaning", Peirce's notion of the structure of the icon as being composed of image, diagram, and metaphor makes more sense. It is beyond the scope of this study to pursue the idea further, but it may provide philosophical justification for the cognitive linguistic approach to metaphor (Lakoff and Johnson 1980, 1998; Fauconnier and Turner 2002; Brandt and Brandt 2005).

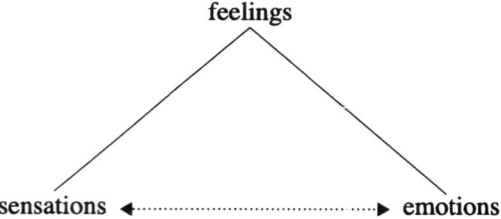

Figure 2.

and with it, the power of conception – from all practical purposes, and lets the mind dwell on the sheer appearance of things". Not likeness or similarity but the image of. And not simply the image of life, but the image of *felt* life.

Feelings arise from two sources: sensations, from interaction with the external world through the five senses, and emotions, which are internally generated. Sensations and emotions may themselves interact bidirectionally, with sensations triggering emotions and emotions coloring sensations (Fig. 2).

In this way, we both act upon and are acted upon by our environment as we develop mental concepts through interaction with the physical and intersubjective social world that makes up the phenomenological world of our experience. Feeling, form, and meaning are all intertwined components of the cognitive processes of the embodied human mind or "minding" in language and literature. "Minding" is the term I use for the cognitive processes of the embodied human mind that include not just conceptualizing, but form[ing] and feeling too.[4] Because "minding" is an activity, not an object, and because it primarily means "caring for or about", it is my attempt to capture Langer's idea of the mind forming, feeling, and meaning.[5]

---

4. Louise Sundararajan notes that in Chinese, the seat of emotion and reason is the same, with one word in Chinese to represent mind and heart (e-mail communication 1/31/06). Kang Yanbin (e-mail communication 1/27/06) informs me that there are two words for mind and feeling: "Mind refers to the intellect, *zhi*, while feeling refers to emotions, *qing*. But we do have a more encompassing word which might include the two levels of meaning. That is *xin* […] The word *xin* can be put together with *zhi* and *qing*, reinforcing the two ideas respectively".

5. Langer's philosophical project to equate mind and feeling, in spite of their separation in the English lexicon, can be seen in the title of her second volume: *Mind: An Essay on Human Feeling*.

Form and feeling have long been recognized as particular attributes of poetic expression. However, it would be misleading to think of them as separate attributes, just as it is misleading to think of form and meaning as separate entities. Form, feeling, and meaning (or, more specifically concept) are rather aspects of the phenomenon that creates "meaning" in the sense of significance or understanding.[6] These aspects are experienced differentially in the acts of composing and interpreting a literary text. That is, the writer conceives the feeling from which form-meaning emerges: feeling of sense-emotion creates form-meaning which is embodied or employed in the language of the text, in the representation of sound (and sight in the case of the written text). The reader experiences this form-meaning in the text from which the recognition of the writer's conceived feeling emerges: form-meaning in sound (and sight) embodies feeling of sense-emotion. The task of the literary scientist then becomes to model these relations as they are employed in the text itself. I think one of the most challenging tasks facing cognitive poetics in the foreseeable future is to find ways to articulate these connections.

1.3. Embodiment

Merleau-Ponty's (1962) work, in steering between the Scylla of rationalism and the Charybdis of empiricism, anticipated cognitive linguistics' notion of embodied realism (Freeman 2004). Although his untimely death in 1961 cut short the development of his ontology of the flesh (1968), enough remains to give a sense of where he was heading in his understanding of our phenomenological world. As I understand his thought, the world is real, not because it exists independently of the mind, but because our being is in the world and is part of the world. Our bodies are synthetic unities of sensations, thoughts, and emotions, so that they should be compared, Merleau-Ponty (1962: 150) claims, "not to a physi-

---

6. The ambiguity of the term "meaning" creates a confusion between the content of a linguistic expression and its sense or significance. Use of the term "sense" produces a different kind of confusion, between the sensations arising from the five senses and what is indicated by the phrase "making sense" of something. The challenge for scholars of cognitive poetics is how to use such natural language terminology to describe phenomena that go beyond it, a challenge that parallels the attempt of a poetic text to capture the nature or essence of the phenomenological experience in language that, because of its own nature, obscures or conceals it.

cal object, but rather to a work of art". A poem cannot exist apart from its existence on the page:

> Its meaning is not arbitrary and does not dwell in the firmament of ideas: it is locked in the words printed on some perishable page [...] A novel, poem, picture or musical work are individuals, that is, beings in which the expression is indistinguishable from the thing expressed, their meanings accessible only through direct contact, being radiated with no change of their temporal and spatial situation (1962: 151).

The body thus exists in an organic relationship with the world. What is invisible to it does not *not* exist, but is rather "in-visible", lying latent, hidden, as another dimensionality. The negation of the visible is not Sartrean absence or abyss but, as Merleau-Ponty (1968: 257) says in his Working Notes: "what, relative to the visible, could nevertheless not be seen as a thing (the existentials of the visible, its dimensions, its nonfigurative inner framework)". What this mean is that "Nothingness is nothing more (nor less) than the invisible", that is, the existing flux before objectification into concepts (1968: 258). It is this sense of nothing that I think Wallace Stevens (1961: 10) captures in the closing lines of "The Snowman":

> For the listener, who listens in the snow,
> And, nothing himself, beholds
> Nothing that is not there and the nothing that is.

In these lines, Stevens breaks through the veil of our conceptualizing the world as a positive artifact that we can hear and see in order to articulate the dimensionality of the invisible. The invisible is the primordial precategorial, that which exists before our conceptualizing minds bring experience into consciousness: "what exists only as tactile or kinesthetically, etc." (Merleau-Ponty 1968: 257).

These two ideas – of nothingness existing in an invisible dimension, and the primordial experience of the precategorial – are what poets attempt to encapsulate through the mechanism of iconicity.

1.4. Poetic iconicity

Although Reuven Tsur's (1992, 2003) work in cognitive poetics never explicitly refers to the notion of iconicity, his approach incorporates the relation of feeling and form that I consider a necessary element in poetic iconicity. He argues that the effect of poetry is to slow down or disrupt the conceptual processes that lead to constancy and coherence (cognitive stability) and efficient coding of information (cognitive economy), those elements of the mind that enable us to function "normally ' in the world. Under this view, what poetry is doing, like all the arts, is to bring us, for at least a little while, into a certain relation with the world. This relation is variously described in the arts, in different philosophies and religions, as expressing the inexpressible, stopping to smell the roses, becoming one with the universe, to capture, in Merleau-Ponty's terms, the primordial experience of the invisible.

Poetic iconicity creates in language sensations, emotions, and images that enable the mind to encounter them as phenomenally real. As Merleau-Ponty (1962: 404) notes, moments of great danger and great love can trigger this response. It is what it means to live wholly in the present moment, to grasp the phenomenally real. Anyone who has experienced this phenomenon will know what I mean. The Persian word for this experience is *ghayb*: the unseen world "from which the soul receives its most rarefied nourishment. Everything existing in the visible world is the imperfect mirror of this hidden reality" (Wheeler 2006: 23). Unlike the corresponding Platonic notion of Forms that exist in an idealized state, however, this "hidden reality" is the flip side of our everyday experience and may be accessed at any moment. John Burnside (2005: 60) describes it well as an excursion "into the quotidian", into Paul Eluard's

> *autremonde* – that nonfactual truth of being: the missed world, and by extension, the *missed self* who sees and imagines and is fully alive outside the bounds of socially-engineered expectations – not by some rational process (or not as the term is usually understood) but by a kind of radical illumination, a re-attunement to the continuum of objects and weather and other lives that we inhabit.

Most important, here, is Langer's understanding of an art object. It is not the *resemblance* of life that is represented in an art work, but the *semblance*, the illusion of vital life in its rhythms, sensations, emotions: what Henry James called "felt life". That is, as Langer (1953: 245) puts it, "every successful work of literature" is not a representation, expression, or imitation of life, but "is wholly a creation... an *illusion of experience*": "What [the author] makes is a symbol – primarily a symbol to capture and hold his own imagination of organized feeling, the rhythms of life, the forms of emotion" (1953: 392).

I want to make it clear here what we are talking about. We need to distinguish the emotion arising from the semblance of felt life in a literary work from both the personal feelings of the author or the personal feelings of the reader. It is not the author's feelings that are created in a literary work, but feelings that are *conceived* by the author in creating the semblance of felt life. With respect to reading, critics often speak of the emotion *evoked* by a literary text, the fact that a literary work can "move" us, what Meir Sternberg (2003: 355) calls "affect-bound reduction". That is not at all what I mean or what I think Langer is referring to. Readers of a literary text are not experiencing these conceived feelings directly. I am not angry or frustrated at Casaubon's treatment of Dorothea in George Eliot's novel, *Middlemarch*, though one of the characters, Will Ladislaw, is. Instead I recognize these feelings of anger and frustration in Will, and empathize with him. This is aesthetic attitude or what Edward Bullough termed "psychical Distance" (quoted in Langer 1953: 318f.). The actual feelings expressed in the text are rather a state of emotional knowledge, what Indian scholars call *rasa*, communicated through suggestiveness or *dhvani* (Hogan 2003: 156).[7] Aesthetic distance allows the experience of emotions emerging from the text, not from the author or the reader. And that is what enables us to recognize the role of the emotions in nondiscursive, literary language, and suggests a way in which we might also account for the role of emotion in discursive, actual language use.

In poetry, the relation between form and feeling is stylized into deliberate word choice and order. For example, consider the (nonpoetic) sentence "the flowers blossomed yesterday and withered today". The order of events is iconically chronological: yesterday comes before today, first the flowers blossom, then they wither. The verbal actions of blossoming and withering are presented in parallel, conjoined by the grammatical conceptual metaphor of equality, making the blossoming and withering on a par with each other. The sentence holds no surprises; it reflects something that is part of our everyday experience. If I adjust the sentence slightly, by changing the conjunctive metaphor of conceptual equality to subordinate one of the clauses in "the flowers that blossomed yesterday withered today", more emphasis is placed on the withering, since the opening clause, being subordinate, is incomplete and therefore demands what Tsur (1972, 1992) calls "requiredness". The feeling engendered by the idea of withering is heightened through the suspense created by the incomplete clause, bringing this sentence closer to poetic expression. Both sentences, though different in their import, are still in discursive mode,

---

7. See Patrick Colm Hogan (2003) for an extensive discussion of this question.

they tell us something about what the flowers do. However, by reversing the order of events, the Chinese poet Tong Cui Hui makes us see first the withered flowers and then makes us reflect on their earlier blossoming: "withered flowers today blossomed yesterday" (quoted in Du 1976: 491).[8] By deverbalizing the action of withering, the line emphasizes the underlying nature of the verbal actions as inchoative, which, as Donald C. Freeman (1978: 6) explains, "denote some state which is in the process of coming about."[9] By making "withered" an adjective, the line also has the effect of freezing the image of the flowers in their state of witheredness. Tong's line captures not just the event and the idea of decay but highlights the emotion aroused in the *contemplation* of decay It adcs value to the everyday meaning of the first sentence; it makes us feel the effects of decay at the same time that it makes us mourn the memory of past blossoming.[10] That is what poetic iconicity is. It makes language work to create the semblance of felt life. All successful art is iconic in this sense.

2.   Two case studies

Poetic iconicity differs from discursive iconicity in at least two ways. It creates the feeling of form and it breaks through or transcends the abstracting tendency of conceptual language in order to create the immedi-

---

8. I am grateful to Louise Sundararajan for this reference.
9. Freeman was the first to call linguists' attention to what he called "syntactic mimesis" in poetry, what is now described as syntactic iconicity.
10. Two anonymous reviewers questioned my earlier discussion of Tong's line by pointing out that both the nonpoetic line and the poetic one conveyed iconicity. One reviewer asked if it weren't more a matter of foregrounding in the poetic text, and the other asked if it weren't rather iconic of the "capacity to emotionally remember" and therefore convey the mind's nostalgia. I think the difference between discursive iconicity and nondiscursive (or poetic) iconicity lies in the latter's creation of what Langer calls conceived feeling, feeling that is iconically embodied in the text. I don't think, upon reflection, that foregrounding is what makes the difference in Tong's line Preposing "withered" to the beginning of the line makes it the topic focus of the sentence; in its position at the end of the sentence, "blossomed" is given stress emphasis, so that neither predominates over the other as figure against a ground. What is foregrounded in Tong's line is rather the emotion it embodies. For me, Tong's line evokes grief over the past blossoming rather than nostalgia (but see my discussion of the distinction between value and import in the next section). Neither of the discursive sentences embody such conceived feelings.

acy of the present moment in its primordial or "other-world" experience. I explore the first of these in a discussion of a poem by Thomas Hardy; the second discussion shows how Emily Dickinson makes her language phenomenally real.

2.1. Thomas Hardy

In speech situations, participants are attuned to the inflections and mannerisms accompanying the discourse, the tone of voice, the kinesics of gesture, the expressions of facial features, etc., that convey emotion. Certain devices and techniques in written language, such as punctuation, syntactical ordering, meter and rhythm, emphatics and hedges, exploiting the conceptual domains of word choices, symbolize these metalinguistic features. But they do not exhaust the possibilities of conveying the semblance of feeling in written form. Several additional strategies exist that enable us to identify the forms of feeling in a written text. They all serve to enable the feeling mind to select and shape the text's form.

First is the question of focus: grounding the text in a situation that leads to the adoption of perspective. Consider, for example, a poem by Thomas Hardy, "Transformations":[11]

Portions of this yew
Is a man my grandsire knew,
Bosomed here at its foot:
This branch may be his wife,
A ruddy human life
Now turned to a green shoot.

These grasses must be made
Of her who often prayed,

---

11. I am grateful to Donald Hall (personal correspondence) for pointing out a misprint in most editions of the poem, an error that was corrected in Samuel Hynes's (1984: 211) edition of Hardy's poems. As Hall notes: "The first time Hardy printed it, in the Mellstock Edition, he used the word 'vainly' [line 11]. The second time he published it, in Moments of Vision, the error crept in. It is a typical typesetting error (and a typical proofreading error) that a word is reprinted, mistakenly, when it is the same word that has been used in a previous line above it – and which makes sense. The typesetter put 'often' under 'often' – and if Hardy proofread it, he did not notice – again and again. Anyway, 'vainly' is the better word, in connection with a 'fair girl,' and I think it helps to bring out (at least slightly) the Biblical sense of 'know'."

Last century, for repose;
And the fair girl long ago
Whom I vainly tried to know
May be entering this rose.

So, they are not underground,
But as nerves and veins abound
In the growths of upper air,
And they feel the sun and rain,
And the energy again
That made them what they were!

On a communicative, discourse level, the poem may seem to be expressing the belief that people don't really die, but are transformed into another form of life. Beginning students of literature almost always read the poem this way. In fact, so do many experienced readers of literature. The idea is certainly there in the poem. But whose belief is it? Such a reading misses the poem's emotional import. In its reliance on the discursive content, a discursive reading misses the forms of feeling that make this poem a semblance of felt life.[12] As Sternberg (2003: 363) notes, "Not the driest world-making possibly remains value-free, no agent fails to act somehow on our human nature, no movement in time leaves us unmoved". Consider, for example, what we assume about the speaker of the poem. Given its provenance, a Hardy poem at the turn of the last century, the speaker is presumed to be male. Although he is not directly identified as such, the fact that he tells us he "vainly tried to know" a "fair girl" indicates his sex. He is old, since it was "long ago" that he courted the girl. Mention of a "yew" in the first line indicates that he is in a churchyard (yew trees are

---

12. I am indebted to Donald Hall (1992: 45–48), who first drew my attention to the poem's emotional tone. According to Langer (1953: 234) the poet is using the laws of discourse (by using linguistic forms) on a different semantic level: "this has led critics to treat poetry indiscriminately as both art and discourse. The fact that something seems to be asserted leads them astray into a curious study of 'what the poet says,' or, if only a fragment of assertion is used or the semblance of propositional thought is not even quite complete, into speculations on 'what the poet is trying to say'. The fact is [...] that they do not recognize the real process of poetic creation because the laws of imagination, little known anyway, are obscured for them by the laws of discourse. Verbal statement is obvious, and hides the characteristic forms of verbal figment. So, while they speak of poetry as 'creation,' they treat it, by turns, as report, exclamation, and purely phonetic arabesque".

poisonous and in England are planted in churchyards to protect browsing animals from them).[13] So we have an old man, possibly close to the end of his life, contemplating the graves of people who have been dead a long time. What are his conjectures? His feelings? His thoughts lead him to the idea that the dead have been or are being transformed into the living plants around him. But what does he feel?

Sternberg (2003: 364) has alerted us to the fact that "affective and conceptual processing may join forces or join battle [...]: now in harmony, now in disharmony...or now with this balance of power, now with that. The rhetoric of narrative thrives on such protean fact/feeling inter-dynamics". What readers of Hardy's poem who focus on the discursive meaning miss s that the affective forces are at war with the conceptual. That is, the old man *wants* to believe in what he is musing because he is *resisting*, not accepting, the fact that he too must die.

Another strategy that helps us identify the form of feeling in a text is grammatical selection. The grammatical form the poem takes shapes the old man's attitude. Note, for example, the use of the epistemic modals: "this branch *may* be his wife"; "These grasses *must* be made"; the fair girl "*May* be entering this rose". The poem takes the form of a syllogism: if this is true and this is true, then this is also true, as indicated by the "So" of the final stanza. But the logic is false: mays and musts do not lead to factual "are". The old man's feelings that he does not want to lose the experience of feeling the "sun and rain" and "the energy" that makes him what he is leads him to protest too much. The discursive, grammatically well-formed assertion that "they are not underground,/.../And they feel the sun and rain,/ And the energy again" is interrupted by the insertion of the "But as" clause in lines 14–15. The irony of the "But as" construction is that the old man is trying to make it mean "but since", with the idea that nerves and veins of the dead are transformed into the limbs of living plants. (Note that the argument here is not over whether dead bodies provide fertilizer for living plants, which of course they do, but that the elements of life itself, the nerves and veins, are what survive.) The old man's feelings betray him so

---

13. The nature writer Paul Evans (2006: 20) notes: "The greatest lure [for thrushes] is the yew berry. The scarlet, fleshy aril of the yew encloses a poisonous seed and tastes sweet and slimy. The cup-shaped aril is the only part of the yew that does not contain the highly poisonous pseudo-alkaloid taxine. In the old cultures of northern Europe, where the redwings and fieldfares come from, the yew is the 'death-tree'. But, although associated with death and the underworld, the yew also symbolizes resurrection and the persistence of life".

that we understand it rather as an analogy, that it is *his* "nerves and veins" that "abound / In the growths of upper air", not those of the dead. Lines 14–15 disrupt the grammar of the discursive assertion by changing the scope governing the following lines, with the result that there is again a grammatical discordancy, reflecting the tension between the old man's thoughts and desires. Reading "discursive" grammar without recognizing the minding that is being expressed through it misses the living scenario that the poem is creating: the impact of felt (as opposed to reasoned) life. The use of the past tense in the last line is the final betrayal of the old man's false logic: not "That make them what they are", which would support his faith in their still living continuance, but "That made them what they were". The exclamation point at the end adds the final emotional straw to the old man's feelings: to want to believe what he otherwise knows is false.

This discussion raises the inevitable protest that poems exist on several levels, can be protean in meaning. So why should the discursive reading be wrong? I discovered in reading Langer that she also shares my belief that though meanings may multiply on the conceptual level, the forms of feeling in language, whether discursive or nondiscursive, are unitary in nature. That is, unless one is actually struggling with a complex of emotions when uttering a thought, only one feeling predominates. In speaking of the symbolic power of art in creating a pattern of tensions and resolutions, Langer (1953: 373–374) says:

> If feeling and emotion are really complexes of tension, then every affective experience should be a uniquely determined process of this sort; then every work of art, being an image of such a complex, should express a particular feeling unambiguously [...]. I suspect that this is the case, and that the different emotional values ascribed to a work of art lie on a more intellectual plane than its emotional import [...]. The same feeling may be an ingredient in sorrow and in the joys of love. A work of art expressing such an ambiguously associated affect will be called "cheerful" by one interpreter and "wistful" or even "sad" by another. But what it conveys is really just one nameless passage of "felt life" knowable through its incarnation in the art symbol even if the beholder has never felt it in his own flesh.

The emotional *value* placed on a work of art is not the same as its emotional *import*. To use a simple example from actual experience: a person may cry, thus imposing emotional value on an event, but the crying has only emotional import, whether of happiness or sadness. Reuven Tsur (1992, 2003) has shown us how the form of feeling may serve more than one emotional value (or valence) in his discussion of convergent and divergent styles and split and integrated focus.[14] That is, it depends on what is being marked for attention that determines whether a convergent or divergent style or a split or integrated focus supports or destabilizes our cognitive processing. Tsur suggests that divergent style and integrated focus in particular lend themselves to producing an emotional quality. What results in the work of art is its emotional import, its significant form.

2.2. Emily Dickinson

A poem by the nineteenth century American poet Emily Dickinson creates an iconicity that makes its language phenomenally real for the reader (F1268*A*/J1261).[15] Its theme reflects the idea that written words that remain long after their writer has died may still exert power over their

---

14. Tsur (2003: 289) explains convergent and divergent style as follows:

     "Convergent" style is marked by clear-cut shapes, both in contents and structure; it is inclined toward definite directions, clear contrasts (prosodic or semantic) – toward an atmosphere of certainty, a quality of intellectual control. "Divergent" style is marked by blurred shapes, both in contents and structure; it exhibits general tendencies (rather than definite directions), blurred contrasts, an atmosphere of uncertainty, an emotional quality. Convergence appeals to the actively organizing mind, divergence to a more receptive attitude. The two are not solid categories, the differences are of degree, shadings are gradual, along a spectrum.

     Split and integrated focus refers to the ways in which elements are manipulated in a text. As Tsur (1992: 112) explains:

     In non-literary language, the reader tends to 'attend away' from the phonological *signifiant* to the semantic *signifié*. The sound patterns of poetry (meter, alliteration, rhyme and the like) force him to attend back to the sound stratum. Up to a certain point, a mild increase of the cognitive load on the perceptual apparatus caused by the reader's additional attention to these sound patterns is perceived as a more or less vague musical effect, usually of an emotional quality. Beyond that point, however, the focus becomes split, and the perceived quality may be 'witty'.

15. Numbers refer to the Franklin (F) and Johnson (J) editions of the poems. The poem exists in two forms. One is a pencil draft and includes a revision and two variants, as indicated in the text quoted. It resides in the Amherst College Archives (A 121). The other form is a transcript of the first stanza made by Dickinson's Norcross cousins from a letter sent to them. It reads as follows:

     We must be careful what we say. No bird resumes it's [*sic*] egg.
     A word left careless on a page
     May consecrate an eye, When folded in perpetual seam
     The wrinkled author lie.

readers. Iconicity occurs across two dimensions in the poem: within the semiotic world of the poetic text, and within the phenomenal world of actual readers of the poem written by Dickinson. I will distinguish these two domains, the semblance of the poem-world and the semblance of the poet-world, by referring to the maker of the "Word" *in* the poem as "he / author" and the writer of the words *of* the poem as "she / poet":

A Word dropped
careless on a Page
May stimulate an
Eye
When folded in
perpetual seam
The Wrinkled Maker
lie

Infection in the sentence
breeds
~~And~~ we may inhale
Despair
At distances of
Centuries
From the Malaria -

Variants: line 3 stimulate] consecrate; line 7 Maker] Author
Revision: line 11 And] *cancelled*; "may" inserted after "we"

All literature may be said to exist on two planes of perception: the semiotic world of the text and the phenomenological worlds of the author and reader (Johansen 1996).[16] Coleridge's (1817) famous phrase, the "willing suspension of disbelief for the moment, which constitutes poetic faith", describes the process by which the imagined world temporarily replaces the phenomenal (that is, the world of lived experience). In Dickinson's poem, the two worlds are made to intersect through the iconic mapping of the "Word" within the semiotic world of the poem onto the actual word on the page that we as readers see. The moment of intersection occurs as the poem moves from the unspecified "eye" of the first stanza to the introduction of "we" in the second. Since both terms refer to the reader, the eye becomes ours, and the poem suddenly occupies two planes at once. The experience of reading the poem, of subconsciously absorbing

---

16. I thank one of the reviewers for this reference.

its iconic features of image, syntax, and metaphor, leads us to the momentary lifting of the veil between the primordial felt world and the categorial conceptualized one, so that the poem's world becomes phenomenally real to us as we read the poem.

In a letter to her Norcross cousins, Dickinson wrote (F278*A*.2/J1212):

> Thank you for the passage. How long to live the truth is!
> A Word is dead when it is said
> Some say -
> I say it just begins to live
> That day

How is it that a word may live? How is it possible that reading a word can elicit feelings in us that emanate from the formulation created by the person who wrote it? Dickinson's Malaria poem not only tells us that it is possible, but makes it happen in the process of the telling. The main argument of the poem is that careless use of language can be harmful. Put that way, the idea is a common enough, conventional one. But what the poem does is make us feel the force of that harm. It does so by iconic presentation, not just simply blending the ideas of writing and disease to create the metaphor of a word as infection, but by making this metaphor iconically represent ourselves as readers reading Dickinson's text and as a result inhaling the semblance of "Despair".

Each stanza is divided into two syntactic units which parallel their equivalents across the stanzas and bring them into metaphorical relation:

First stanza: the world of the text	*Second stanza:* *the metaphor of disease*
A Word dropped / careless on a Page / May stimulate an / Eye When folded in / perpetual seam / The Wrinkled Maker / lie	Infection in the sentence / breeds / We may inhale / Despair At distances of / Centuries / From the Malaria

Using Brandt and Brandt's (2005) model, the semiotic domains of writing and disease structure the Reference (target) and Presentation (source) spaces of the poem's metaphor (Fig. 3).[17]

---

17. In Brandt and Brandt's (2005) semiotic model of blending, the labels *Reference* and *Presentation* refer to the two input spaces in Fauconnier and Turner's (2002) blending model, and, for metaphorical blends, the target and source spaces, respectively. In this paper, I adopt the Brandts' model because

In the Reference space, we have a writer, words and sentences in a book created by the writer, and readers. In the Presentation space, we have a disease (malaria), infection arising from that disease, and victims. Identity mappings across the two spaces link writer to disease, words to infection, and readers to victims. The virtual space of the blend is structured by means of a time-frame projection from the Presentation space. That is, the fact that malaria, one of the oldest diseases known to man, can cause reoccurrence of its symptoms years after it is first contracted, is mapped onto the image of reading a text, so that the words can still affect the reader centuries after the author is dead.[18]

Structural mappings across the two input spaces link words into pairs to forge the metaphorical blend of writing and disease. There are, for example, six verbs in the poem whose forms match up with each other: two transitive (*stimulate* / *inhale*), two intransitive (*lie* / *breeds*), and two passive past participles (*dropped* / *folded*). The transitive and intransitive pairs reflect the two "sides" of the metaphor. Although the passive past participles appear to refer only to writing (the word dropped, the maker

---

it provides more detail with respect to the semiosis of the text and the dynamic schemas that motivate the various mappings that occur. Dynamic schemas are understood in Johnson's (1987: 19–23) and Talmy's (2000, 1: 40–42) sense, not of scripts and frames but as nonpropositional structures that organize our experience, and are equivalent to Fauconnier and Turner's (2000: 93–102) concept of vital relations. Figure 3 is adapted from Per Aage Brandt's (2004) work, but reflects Line Brandt's (2000) initial formulation. In an email (6-11-07), Line Brandt discusses my adoption of their model as follows: "Situational, argumentational and illocutional relevances are represented separately in the model (as opposed to as components in one mental space), and only argumentational relevance is represented as a „dynamic schema." In some cases, this schema is represented in a mental space, but not necessarily (only when conscious awareness of the schema is required to run the blend). In the example analyzed in 'Making Sense....,' the schema making the presentation relevant to the Reference is one of ethical/unethical acts. In other cases, the relevant schemas may be different ones (that is, the relevant schema is not the same in all cases)."

18. The *Encyclopaedia Britannica* (2005) notes that "Malaria is one of the most ancient infections known. It was noted in some of the West's earliest medical records in the 5th century BC, when Hippocrates differentiated malarial fevers into three types according to their time cycles". That Dickinson envisages malaria as an inhaled disease reflects the nineteenth century belief that the disease was communicated via the miasma of swampy and marshland areas, before scientists established that the infection was caused by the anopheline mosquito.

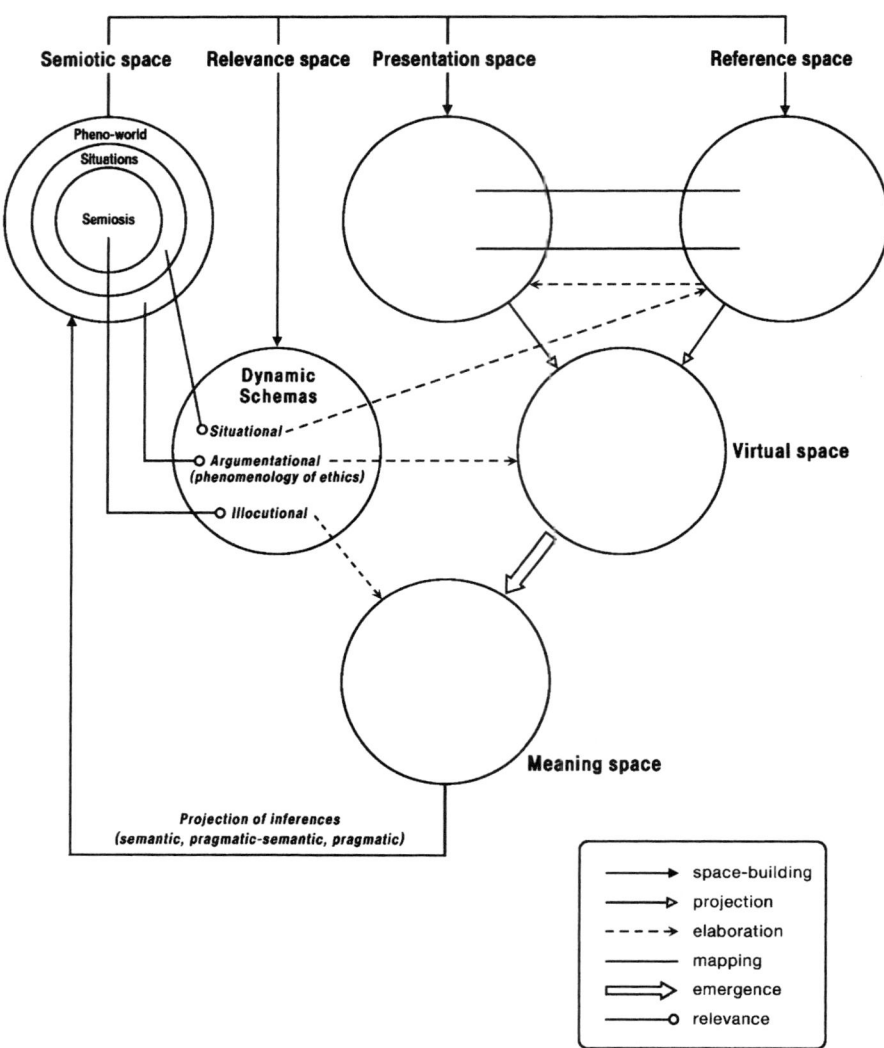

Figure 3. Brandt's (2004) modification of the blending model.

folded), the second is in fact a blend of the Maker as Malaria. The repetition of "may" (lines 3 and 11) before the two transitive verbs reinforces their pairing, and its sound echoes in the words "Maker" and "Malaria". The parallel placement of these two words, the first at the end of the first stanza and the second at the end of the last, bring both author and disease into a relation of causal enablement (that they "may" make something happen). The fact that the words alliterate and are both capitalized also brings them into relation. There are six determiners, three indefinite and three definite (*a* Word / *a* Page / *an* Eye; *the* Maker / *the* sentence / *the* Malaria). The order of their pairing (indefinite to definite) moves from establishment by definition to the establishment of identity.[19] Occurring at the end of the first stanza, the Maker is associated with the author of the words, but he is also associated with both the "sentence" of the second stanza and the Malaria that ends the poem. Thus the word defined becomes the disease identified.

The structure of the poem establishes the form of feeling that causes us as readers to move from the semiotic poem-world to the phenomenological poet-world. The semiotic world set up for the Reference space is that of writers, texts, and readers. Its situation is the event of an eye (metonymically introducing the reader) being stimulated by a word that has been dropped carelessly on a page. The word *stimulate* is well chosen: it means both to animate (to bring to life) and to goad into activity. And this is what the form of the poem – its lack of punctuation, its stanzaic units, and its line breaks – makes us as readers do. The lack of punctuation destabilizes the syntax, creating the phenomenon known in composition circles as garden path reading. Having read the words "dropped /...on a page" in lines 1–2, we may be led by identity of form in the past participles, *dropped* and *folded*, to read lines 5–6 as referring to the word, that is, the event described occurs when the word is "folded in" the "perpetual seam" of a book. However, the following lines stimulate us to rearrange the syntax, so that now the image presented is of an author "folded" in death. What results from this garden path activity is that we are primed to read the image of "The Wrinkled Maker" "folded in perpetual seam" not as one of a corpse wrapped in a burial shroud or lying in a seam of earth, but as a metaphor for the author being folded within the seams of a book. This then creates an affordance whereby the Maker that creates the word is iconically presented as the Malaria that causes the infection.

---

19. See Elżbieta Tabakowska's (1999: 416) discussion of definite and indefinite determiners as establishing identity and definition, respectively.

Dickinson's stanzaic units and line breaks stimulate us into further activity. The poem's two stanzas fall into two parallel units each, separated by *when* in the first stanza and *at* in the second. Each unit has two lines, except for the last unit in the first stanza that has three. What this means is that the odd line occurs right at the center of the poem, with seven lines before it and seven after. This line contains only one word, "lie", appearing as though it had been dropped in as an afterthought, an extra. Its isolated position in the exact center of the poem draws our attention to it and its inherent ambiguity. It can mean "to lie down, be prostrate" describing the way "The Wrinkled Maker" lies prone in death but also metaphorically folded within the pages of his book. It can also mean "to deceive, to misrepresent". In this reading, the operative word is "When" in line 5. That is, the word "when" is ambiguous. It can refer simply to time: words may stimulate eyes after their author has died. However, it also can carry the force dynamic schema of cause, as in the sentence, "When air is removed, people die". Now, it is not so much a question of time as it is of causation. That is, if the author lies, misrepresents, in the word he drops carelessly on the page, then the reader may be affected accordingly.

This reading sets up a further variation in possible syntactic arrangement and prepares the way for the creation of the poem's central metaphor, the blending of the two domains of writing and disease. That is, the "When" clause of lines 5–8 may be read, not as the ending of the first sentence, but as the beginning of the next. When it is read this way, the "When" again carries the possibility of causality as well as time, this time relating the only two intransitive verbs in the poem: when (if) the author lies, infection breeds.

Thus the form of the poem encourages "careless" mis-presentations of syntax at the same time as it encourages us to see the pun on "lie" as the word that has been dropped carelessly. Both meanings may thus be operative: the author lying in death is mapped onto the malaria lying dormant in the body; the lie created by the author becomes an infection breeding in the sentence. Either way, the word "lie", with its tense in the perpetual present, reinforces the notion that the "Word" that has been dropped carelessly lies always at the ready, ready to breed and infect, whenever we read the poem.

Iconicity works also across the dynamic schemas of situation, argument, and illocution. At the situational level, the structural pairings map the imagined world of the maker-author of words onto the actual world of the poet (Dickinson) and her readers. The generalized image of the Reference space (*a* Word / *a* Page / *an* Eye) maps on to the particular image of the Presentation space (*the* Maker / *the* sentence / *the* Malaria). The pairings of the verbs link word to author (*dropped / folded*), author-word to infection (*lie / breeds*), and reader of the author's word to readers of the poet's word (*stimulate / inhale*). The author's feeling, which caused him to use a word without care or consideration, is "folded" into the page as he is "folded" in death, so that the feeling-trace of the word remains to "stimulate", to create a sensation in the reader through seeing the word. Through the dynamic schema of cause and effect, the sensation of seeing the word results in the transmission of feeling, so that the feeling that motivated the author's dropping of the word is identified by the poet as the idea of "Despair", and we as readers of her poem receive its semblance as we read the poem.

At the argumentational level, the dynamic schema is one of "causing harm". However, it was not the author's deliberate intention to cause harm to his reader. The word, after all, is dropped carelessly, without thought or consideration of the effect it might have. The pun on "lie" not only identifies author with word, it also suggests one side of the polarity that is set up by the situation: that careless words deceive or lie because they do not reflect the ethical obligation of a writer to take care, to capture truth. The feeling of despair that is communicated by the infected word is motivated by the negative polarity of the word "careless", represented by the metaphor of disease, that has infected the feeling of the author. Though authors die, the words they leave behind still carry the history of sensations and emotions with which they were first imbued. This latter argument – that words carry memory traces of emotion – moves the argumentational level from the semiotic world of the poem to the phenomenal world of poet and reader, since it is not the author's argument projected from the semiotic base space of his text, but the argument projected from the semiotic base space of the poet's

In the virtual space of the blend, the word becomes the *symptom* of the infection breeding in the sentence that was *caused* by the maker-malaria and which can affect us as readers. The illocutionary force of the meaning of the blend is that authors are ethically responsible for the effect that their words may have on readers. As Dickinson noted in her letter to the Norcross sisters in which she included the first stanza: "We must be careful what we say. No bird resumes it's [*sic*] egg" (see note 15).

Iconicity also occurs at the illocutionary level (Haiman 1999; Tseng 2004).[20] An intriguing possibility arises from the embedding of the im-

---

20. I am grateful to one of the reviewers for these references.

agined scenario into the poem's scenario. In the imagined phenomenological world of the poem, there is no active illocutionary relationship between author and reader, since the author is long dead. In the poet's
phenomenological world, the illocutionary force of her argument is that
words can have a powerful effect, for good or ill, and that therefore "we
must be careful what we say". Just as she identified herself with her
readers in the iconic mapping of the two worlds, as "we" inhale despair
from the author's word, so she identifies her readers with herself as potential authors who may also "say". The irony of the poem for us who read
the poem today is that the poet, too, is "folded in perpetual seam" at "distances of centuries". The illocutionary force that exists in the poem arises
from our emotional response to the feeling of "Despair" that the poet has
made happen through an iconic semblance of the argument that carelessly
used words can harm.

Words have histories. They leave memory traces. They acquire polarities, negative or positive. The authorial trace that is left on the words and
sentences of discourse affects the way in which they are received, both in
affect and meaning. The negative polarities of the words in Dickinson's
poem (*careless, wrinkled, infection,* etc.) cumulate to provide the semblance of the ultimate affect on the reader, "Despair". The force dynamic
schema in this poem is one of cause and effect, and as the metaphors of
the schema blend feeling and form, image and diagram, the illocutionary
effect is cautionary: beware of what you say.

Another Dickinson poem (F930*A*/J883) may serve as an antonym of
her Malaria poem:

The Poets light but
Lamps -
Themselves - go out -
The Wicks they
stimulate
If vital Light

Inhere as do the
Suns -
Each Age a Lens
Disseminating their
Circumference -

The poem conveys a similar idea – of words living after the poet that have
power over their readers. Like the Malaria poem, it uses the same idea of

stimulation and also has a central line, "If vital Light", that is syntactically ambiguous and serves as a pivot between the five lines that precede and the five that follow it. However, the poem develops very different iconicities of form and feeling produced by a very different metaphor. Here, the image of light, associated with the positive polarities of illumination, understanding, and enlightenment, stands as a metaphor for poetry, instead of the negative polarity of infection and disease that carelessly dropped words can evoke. Both poems may be seen as a meditation on the nature of true art, art which captures what Burnside (2005: 61, 64) calls the *plemora* (fullness and plenitude, associated with the divine) in the quotidian, the bridging of the gap between sense and essence, the semblance of felt life. The first poem, ironically, successfully represents the results of *mis*-presenting the truths of the world, thus leading to disease and despair. The other speaks to the results of true presentation through the metaphor of light that, if "vital" (containing life in all its plenitude), will continue to radiate across the centuries.

Literary texts lend themselves to iconic presentations precisely because they engage in the particularities of experience, reflecting the concrete realities that arise from our feelings: our sense experiences and our emotions. These are transformed into the abstract conceptualizations of symbolic language through the processes of metaphor, image, and diagram. Because a poem exists only in the materiality of its language (its sounds, rhythms, meters, its morphology and syntax, etc.), in its physical appearance on the page (its stanzaic form, its line divisions, and so on), feeling is embodied within this materiality of the text. If we wish to explore the ways in which minding makes sense of our phenomenal world, then poetry is a natural place to turn.

Acknowledgment

Emily Dickinson's poems are reprinted by permission of the publishers and the Trustees of Amherst College from THE POEMS OF EMILY DICKINSON, Ralph W. Franklin, ed., Cambridge, Mass.: The Belknap Press of Harvard University Press, Copyright © 1998 by the President and Fellows of Harvard College. Copyright © 1951, 1955, 1979, 1983 by the President and Fellows of Harvard College.

References

Brandt, Line
  2000   Explosive blends: From cognitive semantics to literary analysis. Un-
          published MA thesis. (http://www.hum.au.dk/semiotics/docs2/faculty/
          private_linebrandt.html)
Brandt, Line and Per Aage Brandt
  2005   Making sense of a blend: A cognitive-semiotic approach to metaphor.
          Annual Review of Cognitive Linguistics 3: 216–249.
Brandt, Per Aage
  2004   *Spaces, Domains and Meaning: Essays in Cognitive Semiotics.* Euro-
          pean Semiotics Series No 4. Bern: Peter Lang.
Burnside, John
  2005   Travelling into the quotidian: Some notes on Allison Funk's 'Heart-
          land' poems. *Poetry Review* 95(2): 59–70.
Du, S.B.
  1976   *Chan xue yu Tang Song shi xue* / Zen and poetics of Tang and Song dyn-
          asties. Taibei: Liming.
Evans, Paul
  2006   Nature watch: Blasting through boundaries. *Guardian Weekly* De-
          cember 15–21.
Coleridge, Samuel Taylor
  1817   *Biographia Literaria or Biographical Sketches of My Literary Life and
          Opinions.* Chapter 14.
Fauconnier, Gilles and Mark Turner
  2002   *The Way We Think: Conceptual Blending and the Mind's Hidden Com-
          plexities.* New York: Basic Books.
Freeman, Donald C.
  1978   Keats's "To Autumn": Poetry as process and pattern. *Language and
          Style* 11: 1–17.
Freeman, Margaret H.
  2004   Crossing the boundaries of time: Merleau-Ponty's phenomenology and
          cognitive linguistic theories. In: Augusto Soares da Silva, Amadeu
          Torres and Miguel Gonçalves (eds.), *Linguagem, Cultura e Cognição:
          Estudos de Linguística Cognitiva* 2, 643–655. Coimbra: Almedina.
Freeman, Margaret H .
  2007   Poetic iconicity. In Cognition in Language: Volume in Honour of Pro-
          fessor Elżbieta Tabakowska, Władisław Chłopicki, Andrzej Pawelec,
          and Agnieska Pojoska, (eds.), 472-501. Kraków: Tertium.
Freeman, Margaret H .
  2008   Revisiting/revisioning the icon through metaphor. Poetics Today 29.2:
          353-370.
Franklin, Ralph W. (ed.)
  1998   *The Poems of Emily Dickinson.* 3 vols. Cambridge, MA: The Belknap
          Press of Harvard University Press.

Haiman, John
  1999   Action, speech, and grammar: The sublimation trajectory. In: Max
          Nänny and Olga Fischer (eds.), *Form Miming Meaning: Iconicity in
          Language and Literature*, 37–57. Amsterdam/Philadelphia: John Ben-
          jamins.
Hall, Donald
  1992   To Read a Poem. 2nd edition. New York: Harcourt.
Halliday, Michael A.K.
  1994   The construction of knowledge and value in the grammar of scientific
          discourse, with reference to Charles Darwin's *The Origin of the Species*.
          In: Malcolm Coulthard (ed.), *Advances in Written Text Analysis*,
          136–156. London: Routledge.
Hiraga, Masako K.
  2005   *Metaphor and Iconicity: A Cognitive Approach to Analysing Texts*.
          Houndsmill, Basingstoke, and New York: Palgrave Macmillan.
Hogan, Patrick Colm
  2003   *Cognitive Science, Literature, and the Arts: A Guide for Humanists*. New
          York/London: Routledge.
Hynes, Samuel, ed.
  1984   *The Complete Poetical Works of Thomas Hardy*. Vol. 2. Oxford: Cla-
          rendon Press.
Johansen, Jorgen Dines
  1996   Iconicity in literature. *Semiotica* 110(1–2): 37–55.
Johnson, Mark
  1987   *The Body in the Mind: The Bodily Basis of Meaning, Imagination, and
          Reason*. Chicago/London: The University of Chicago Press.
Johnson, Thomas H. (ed.)
  1955   *The Poems of Emily Dickinson: Including Variant Readings Critically
          Compared with All Known Manuscripts*. Cambridge, MA: The Belknap
          Press of Harvard University Press.
Lakoff, George and Mark Johnson
  1980   *Metaphors We Live By*. Chicago/London: The University of Chicago
          Press.
Lakoff, George and Mark Johnson
  1998   *Philosophy in the Flesh*. Chicago/London: The University of Chicago
          Press.
Langer, Susanne K.
  1953   *Feeling and Form: A Theory of Art 'Developed from Philosophy in a New
          Key.'* New York: Charles Scribner's.
Langer, Susanne K.
  1967   *Mind: An Essay on Human Feeling*. Baltimore: The Johns Hopkins
          Press.
Merleau-Ponty, Maurice
  1962   *Phenomenology of Perception*. C. Smith (tr.). London: Routledge and
          Kegan Paul.

Merleau-Ponty, Maurice
  1968   *The Visible and the Invisible.* Claude Lefort (ed.), Alphonso Lingis (tr.).
          Evanston, IL: Northwestern University Press.
Nänny, Max and Olga Fischer
  1999   *Form Miming Meaning: Iconicity in Language and Literature.* Amster-
          dam/Philadelphia: John Benjamins.
Peirce, Charles Sanders
  1955   *Philosophical Writings of Peirce.* Justus Buchler (ed.) New York: Dover.
Sternberg, Meir
  2003   Universals of narrative and their cognitivist fortunes (1). *Poetics Today*
          24(2): 297–395.
Stevens, Wallace
  1961   *The Collected Poems of Wallace Stevens.* New York: Alfred A. Knopf.
Tabakowska, Elżbieta
  1999   Linguistic expression of perceptual relationships: Iconicity as a prin-
          ciple of text organization (a case study). In: Max Nänny and Olga
          Fischer (eds.), *Form Miming Meaning: Iconicity in Language and Lit-
          erature,* 409–422. Amsterdam/Philadelphia: John Benjamins.
Talmy, Leonard
  2000   Toward a Cognitive Semantics. Vol. I: *Concept Structuring Systems.*
          Vol. II: *Typology and Process in Concept Structuring.* Cambridge, MA/
          London: The MIT Press.
Tseng, Ming-Yu
  2004   A framework for tracing iconicity. *Semiotica* 149: 343–360.
Tsur, Reuven
  1972   Articulateness and requiredness in iambic verse. *Style* 6: 123–148.
Tsur, Reuven
  1992   *Toward a Theory of Cognitive Poetics.* Amsterdam: North Holland.
Tsur, Reuven
  2003   *On the Shore of Nothingness: A Study in Cognitive Poetics.* Exeter, UK:
          Imprint Academic.
Wheeler, Sara
  2006   A portrait of Persia. Review of Jason Eliot, *Mirrors of the Unseen:
          Journeys in Iran* (Picador 2006). *Guardian Weekly,* May 5–11.

From linguistic form to conceptual structure in five steps: analyzing metaphor in poetry

Gerard Steen

Metaphor is clearly one of the areas where cognitive poetics may benefit from the cognitive linguistic enterprise (e.g. Donald Freeman 1993, 1995, 1999; Margaret Freeman 1995, 2000, 2002, 2005; Lakoff and Johnson 1980, 1999; Steen 1994, 1999a; Steen and Gibbs 2004). Following this research, I will assume that metaphor may be fruitfully approached as some form of mapping across two conceptual domains, such as between space and time ("Time is a jet plane, it moves too fast", from Bob Dylan's "You're a big girl now") or journeys and life, as in Robert Frost's famous "The road not taken":

> Two roads diverged in a wood, and I –
> I took the one less traveled by,
> And that has made all the difference.

Cognitive linguists make a distinction between the linguistic expressions of underlying conceptual mappings, and the cross-domain mappings themselves. Thus, the line from Bob Dylan is a classic metaphor in the form of an *A is a B* statement, whereas the Robert Frost poem presents an extended metaphorical comparison (or even a mini-allegory) that only uses language from the source domain of the journey, leaving the target domain of life entirely implicit. Now, the question that arises for the analyst of literature is how we can get from the various linguistic forms of metaphor in the literary text to the underlying conceptual structures that constitute the presumed cross-domain mappings. In fact, I suggest that this is an issue for the analysis of all types of usage, not just literary studies (Steen 2007).

I have proposed a five-step framework for developing a formal analytical technique that can address at least some of the issues involved (Steen 1999b; cf. Semino, Heywood, and Short 2004). The technique aims to identify the conceptual structures of metaphor in discourse in such a way that researchers of talk and text can follow one single procedure in determining what counts as the nature and content of a metaphorical mapping between two conceptual domains in discourse. On the other hand, the

technique is a form of text analysis which should be seen as relatively independent of the analysis of people's text processing and its products: it
may or may not be used in the context of that type of research, depending
on the aims of the researcher. When I talk of conceptual structures, therefore, I refer to the abstract or symbolic structures which may be discerned
by linguists and discourse analysts without necessarily having to make assumptions about their cognitive representation in the processes of writing
and reading of individual people. The latter type of research eventually
requires the analysis of behavioral data instead of textual ones, which is
a different affair (Steen 2007).

The aim of this chapter is to explain this five-step framework and to
develop it somewhat further. The chapter hence addresses a gap which has
been revealed by cognitive linguistic research and aims to show how it can
be bridged. My case study will be literary, as befits the topic of this volume, but as said the method's scope of application is much wider. Literary
communication is just one specific variant of all discourse: we need tools
that can reveal what is common between all types of usage. For this volume, however, I will restrict analysis to a handful of metaphors in a poem
by Lord Alfred Tennyson, which pose various questions to the analyst
(cf. Steen 2002a). The poem may in fact be seen as an exercise in formal
variation of metaphor (reprinted below from Gardner 1972).

Now Sleeps the Crimson Petal

1   Now sleeps the crimson petal, now the white;
Nor waves the cypress in the palace walk;
Nor winks the gold fin in the porphyry font;
The fire-fly wakens: waken thou with me.

5   Now droops the milk white peacock like a ghost,
And like a ghost she glimmers on to me.

Now lies the Earth all Danaë to the stars,
And all thy heart lies open unto me.

Now slides the silent meteor on, and leaves
10 A shining furrow, as thy thoughts in me.

Now folds the lily all her sweetness up,
And slips into the bosom of the lake:
So fold thyself, my dearest, thou, and slip
Into my bosom and be lost in me.

1.   The basic idea: the five steps

The basic idea of the five-step method is simple. If metaphor in discourse can be explained by means of an underlying cross-domain mapping in conceptual structure, then it should be possible to move from the linguistic forms in the text to the conceptual structures that capture their meaning in some ordered fashion. Several issues should be resolved in this analytical movement from language to conceptual structure, and they can be tackled in separate steps. Cognitive linguists have not been overly concerned with these methodological issues, so that this proposal fills a need that has been created but not yet resolved by cognitive linguistic research. And since cognitive linguists claim that metaphor is a matter of all thought and language, the proposal should also be able to handle metaphor in literature (cf. Steen and Gibbs 2004).

Metaphor as a cross-domain mapping implies that we end up with two separate conceptual structures. I will ignore the debate whether these should be labeled as domains (as in Lakoff and Johnson 1980, 1999) or as mental spaces (as in Fauconnier and Turner 1998, 2002) for that distinction is immaterial to the local conceptual structures that will be produced by the analytical procedure: both approaches can make use of the final conceptual output in their own ways. More importantly, the two conceptual domains involved need to be aligned with each other in such a way that they display a number of correspondences between their elements (cf. Gentner and Markman 1993, 1997). Again, these correspondences may be displayed as a series of entailments, as in Conceptual Metaphor Theory, or as a series of arrows, as in Blending Theory. The way in which these conceptual correspondences and their elements may be identified, however, has not received much methodological attention in cognitive linguistics (cf. Steen 2007); the five-step method offers one explicit framework for addressing this problem.

Apart from these issues about the final product of the analysis (crossdomain mappings), there is the initial step of finding the linguistic expressions of metaphor in discourse. Here, too, there has not been much methodological attention to the precise ways in which any text can be analyzed for metaphorical meaning. Work done by the members of the Pragglejaz Group has shown that it is possible to develop tools for the reliable identification of metaphorically used words in discourse, and this work has been partly oriented towards the assumptions of the five-step framework (Pragglejaz Group 2007; Steen 2002, 2005a). However, the Pragglejaz Group deliberately restrict their attention to words which have an obvious metaphorical use, such as "Life is a *jet plane, it moves too fast*" in the line by Bob Dylan. Not all linguistic forms of expression of metaphor are covered by this method: it would be a matter of some debate whether all words in the Robert Frost poem could be taken as metaphorically used in the sense of Lakoff (1986, 1993) or Gibbs (1993, 1994), where indirectness is the prime criterion for metaphorical meaning. Instead, they might also be seen as non-metaphorical language use: the linguistic forms directly express the source domain of the metaphorical mapping, which functions as a relatively independent level of meaning, whereas the target domain is only present in the conceptual structure of the poem – as is typical of allegory (e.g. Crisp 2005). Therefore we need to go beyond Pragglejaz to identify the relevant linguistic forms of metaphor in texts.

Once linguistic expressions of metaphor have been identified in discourse, they still need to be related to the corresponding conceptual structures. Work located in the mainstream of discourse analysis offers a method that is compatible with the spirit of the cognitive linguistic approach as well as generally accepted by discourse analysts and discourse psychologists. This is the work on propositionalization in the tradition of Van Dijk and Kintsch (1983; cf. Weaver, Mannes, and Fletcher 1995; Kintsch 1998). This tradition offers a general technique for turning linguistic forms into conceptual structures which is highly suitable for our needs (cf. Steen 2002b). This may be surprising to those who are aware of Lakoff's (1993) denial that metaphors are propositions, but he made that claim about the general conceptual structure of conventional conceptual metaphors, not about the local conceptual structures of individual metaphors in unique usage events. There is therefore no fundamental contradiction between metaphor and its analytical representation by means of propositional structures.

With the linguistic expressions of metaphor identified in discourse and then turned into propositional structures, we have the beginning of the series of analytical moves that are needed for taking us from metaphor's linguistic form to its conceptual structure. And if we conceive the metaphor's conceptual structure as a mapping between two domains or spaces, we also have a view of the final outcome of such a procedure. What is now still missing is an analytical mechanism to jump from the propositional structures to the cross-domain mapping. I have proposed that this mechanism may be found in George Miller's (1979/1993) chapter on comparison statements, where all linguistic expressions that suggest some form of similarity or comparison, including metaphorical ones, are handled by a uniform approach which turns propositions into analogical structures. Since cognitive linguists have also defined metaphor in discourse with reference to a broad notion of similarity (e.g. Kövecses 2002; Dirven and Pörings 2003), the input to Miller's mechanism is compatible with the first moves of the five-step framework. And since analogical structures have also been discussed in cognitive linguistics as cross-domain mappings (e.g. Fauconnier 1997), the output of Miller's mechanism accords with the last moves of the five-step framework. Miller's contribution gives us precisely what we need to bridge the remaining gap between linguistic form and conceptual structure.

Miller breaks his own proposal down into a number of steps. With the addition of my two initial moves and one final move, my reconstruction of the movement from linguistic form to conceptual structure turns out to have five discrete steps. We shall now analyze the first utterance from the Tennyson poem in terms of this framework.

2. An example: *Now sleeps the crimson petal*

When Tennyson writes *Now sleeps the crimson petal,* it is obvious that the word *sleeps* has been used metaphorically. The Pragglejaz method would say that it is not used in its basic meaning, which pertains to human beings and animals, but displays another meaning in this context, designating some action or state of the crimson petal that cannot be sleep. This indirect contextual meaning is analyzed by setting up some sort of contrast as well as similarity relation with the basic meaning. One candidate for facilitating that analysis is a cross-domain mapping between plants and animate beings. Thus, the analyst would have to find some sort of action or state for the crimson petal that corresponds with the situation where animate beings sleep. One possibility would be to say that the crimson petal is inactive.

Each of these comments points to different aspects of the analytical process that concerns us here: to derive an underlying conceptual structure from the linguistic form of the metaphor. These aspects will now be presented in a more ordered and formalized fashion with reference to the five-step framework. Table 1 shows two columns, with the five steps displayed on the left, and their application to the textual materials on the right. We will take a first look at the five-step method by going through *Now sleeps the crimson petal* again. Further details will be added at later stages in this chapter, when we will look at other examples.

Table 1. Analysis of first half of line 1

Text	*Now sleeps the crimson petal*
1. Identification of metaphor-related words	Sleeps
2. Identification of propositions	P1 (SLEEP$_s$ PETAL$_t$) P2 (MOD P1 NOW$_t$) P3 (MOD PETAL$_t$ CRIMSON$_t$)
3. Identification of open comparison	SIM {∃F ∃a [F (CRIMSON PETAL)]$_t$ [SLEEP (a)]$_s$}
4. Identification of analogical structure	SIM {[BE-INACTIVE (CRIMSON PETAL)]$_t$ [SLEEP (HUMAN)]$_s$}
5. Identification of cross-domain mapping	SLEEP > BE-INACTIVE HUMAN > CRIMSON PETAL *inferences:* GOAL OF SLEEP > GOAL OF BE-INACTIVE: REST TIME OF SLEEP > TIME OF BE-INACTIVE: NIGHT

The first step concerns the identification of the metaphor-related words in the text. This is a deliberately circumspect terminology which will be explained more fully later on, but what should be clarified right here is that metaphor-related words are defined as those words which indicate the source domain of a metaphor. Thus, even though the complete first utterance (*Now sleeps the crimson petal*) is the linguistic expression of a cross-domain mapping, or a metaphor, there is only one word that is metaphorically used, and that is *sleep*. In traditional terminology, it is the focus (Black 1962) or vehicle (Richards 1936) of the metaphor.

When step 1 identifies metaphor-related words, it identifies terms which express the focus, vehicle, or source domain of the metaphor. It does so by finding those words which are somehow indirect or incongruous in context (e.g., Cameron 2003; Charteris-Black 2004). Such words, like *sleep*, therefore form a potential threat to the coherence of the text. However, when it seems possible to integrate them into the overall discourse by some form of comparison or similarity which resolves the incongruity, the words are somehow metaphorical, or related to metaphor.

Step 1 is hence explicitly based on the idea that metaphor is a form of indirect meaning that is based on correspondence or similarity.

Again, it should be noted here that the procedure aims to analyze the semantic structure of the text, and does not make claims about its potential cognitive representation. Thus, to the text analyst it is immaterial that such indirect metaphorical meaning may be more or less conventional and salient (Giora 2003), which might raise questions about the notion of threat to textual coherence. Even though such properties may affect the way in which readers experience metaphorical meanings as more or less incongruous and disruptive during cognitive processing, this is less relevant to the discourse analyst who wishes to capture all metaphor as part of the symbolic structure of the text. In effect, such a general perspective aims to collect all cases of metaphor in order to then examine their varied role in cognitive processing, which may indeed be partly due to their different degrees of conventionality, salience, or aptness (Steen 2007). But that does not lie within the remit of this article.

Step 2 involves the transformation of the linguistic expressions of the text into conceptual structures in the form of a series of propositions. It makes explicit the assumption that metaphor is a matter of thought, not language. This type of conceptual structure for discourse is usually referred to as a text base, which has a linear as well as hierarchical quality (e.g. Kintsch 1998). In order to indicate its conceptual instead of linguistic status, small capitals are used for its technical representation.

There are several formats for this structure, and discourse psychologists are rather practical about the ways in which text bases may be modeled to suit the purposes of their research. In our case, I have followed the format outlined in Bovair and Kieras (1985), for reasons which need not detain us here. I have added subscripts to the word-related concepts so that it is clear which concepts belong to the source domain versus the target domain. This preserves the linguistic analysis in step 1, which made a distinction between source domain and target domain language. The underlining of the concept of SLEEP will be explained later.

The third step transforms the single, complete proposition derived in step 2 into an open comparison between two incomplete propositions which each pertain to another domain. This can be done because the whole procedure assumes, with most cognitive linguists, that there is some form of similarity or correspondence between the two conceptual domains that frame the two sets of concepts involved in steps 1 and 2. Step 3 makes this explicit. It states that, for some activity F in the target domain and some entity a in the source domain, there is some similarity between the activity of the crimson petal on the one hand and the sleeping of some entity on the other hand. Moreover, the labeling of these two domains as target and source, respectively, suggests that the similarity has to be projected from the sleeping of the entity towards the activity of the petal. These assumptions lie at the basis of most metaphor analyses in the literature.

Several issues are implied by step 3. One involves the conceptual separation of the two domains involved in step 2. Another concerns the explication of a basic idea that was there from step 1: the assumption that there is some sort of similarity or correspondence between the two sets of concepts (hence the explicit introduction of the operator SIM). In addition, step 3 also explicates that we need corresponding elements on both sides of the equation, to the effect that there is some activity or state needed for the petal in the target domain, and some agent for the activity of sleeping in the source domain; hence the addition of the open function and argument variables. These are natural additions if we want to align two domains in order to reconstruct the correspondences between them. They are, moreover, minimal assumptions, since no new conceptual elements are added to the comparison except the ones that are implied by the original proposition.

Step 4 turns the open comparison proposed by step 3 into a closed comparison which has the formal structure of an analogy (but in fact does not always need analogical interpretation). The open values indicated by F and a in step 3 have now been interpreted by the analyst. Step 4 thus makes explicit that analysts sometimes have to add new conceptual substance to the mapping between the two domains in order to make the mapping complete. This is often the crucial step of the analysis.

For this particular example, the fourth step also happens to be the least constrained of all steps. Thus, on the side of the source domain, one option is to fill in the logically most encompassing candidate for the agent of sleeping, which would be "animal"; another option is to fill in the most obvious candidate from the perspective of human experience, which is "human". Since the rest of the poem also exploits personification and not animation, the example analysis has preferred the latter option. However, this is just for expository purposes. A similar story can be told for the interpretation of the open target domain value.

Step 5 transforms the analogical structure derived in step 4 into a mapping structure between two separate domains. It explicates what has remained implicit in step 4, the precise correspondences between the separate elements in each of the conceptual domains. This does not seem to be problematic for our current example, but that is not always the case.

Step 5 can also add further correspondences which have remained in the background of the analogy until now. Implicit elements cf the sleeping schema may be projected onto implicit elements cf the crimson petal schema, such as the goal or function of sleeping (rest) which may be projected form source to target to infer that the petal is tired. Or the typical time of sleeping, night, may be projected from source to target to infer something about the time of the real action of the poem. These are examples of inferences which add minimal assumptions about the cross-domain mapping and, if they are accepted, enrich the information that may be derived from it for the overall meaning of the text.

We have now completed our first tour of the five-step method. We have moved from the identification of its linguistic form (step 1) through its propositionalization (step 2) to its transformation into an open comparison (step 3), which was then interpreted as an analogical structure (step 4) and fleshed out into a cross-domain mapping (step 5). This procedure explicates various aspects of what analysts do when they say that particular linguistic expressions in discourse are related to metaphorical mappings. In the next sections, we will examine how the model can be applied to different and more complex examples.

3.   More about step 1: metaphor in language

The first step focuses on the linguistic expression of the underlying cross-domain mapping. The example above is canonical in that it involves the metaphorical use of words. Not only do we have a cross-domain mapping in the conceptual structure of the text, but there is also indirect language use (*sleeps*) which has to be resolved by non-literal comparison. This is metaphor in discourse realized by metaphorically used words, and it has been central in the research done by the Pragglejaz Group and many other researchers inspired by cognitive linguistics.

Yet it is also possible for metaphor in conceptual structure to be expressed by means of language that is not used metaphorically itself. These other forms of metaphor are not based on indirect word use, the canonical example of metaphor in cognitive linguistics (e.g. Lakoff 1986, 1993). One example of this class of metaphor without indirect language use is simile, but there are other illustrations, too. For now, I will concentrate on simile and use it to spell out a number of details of the five-step method.

Simile is illustrated by line 5, *Now droops the milk white peacock like a ghost*. When we take a step back and look at the poem as a whole, it is

Table 2. Analysis of line 5

Text	*Now droops the milk white peacock like a ghost,*
1. Identification of metaphor-related words	a ghost
2. Identification of propositions	P1 (DROOP$_t$ PEACOCK$_t$) P2 (MOD P1 NOW$_t$) P3 (LIKE P1 GHOST$_s$) P4 (MOD PEACOCK$_t$ MILK-WHITE$_t$)
3. Identification of open comparison	SIM {$\exists G$ [DROOP (MILK-WHITE PEACOCK)]$_t$ [G (GHOST)]$_s$}
4. Identification of analogical structure	SIM {EG [DROOP (MILK-WHITE PEACOCK)]$_t$ [DROOP (GHOST)]$_s$}
5. Identification of cross-domain mapping	GHOST > MILK-WHITE PEACOCK DROOP > DROOP *inferences* CAUSE OF DROOPING > CAUSE OF DROOPING: TIREDNESS

quite natural for it to include an utterance about peacocks after the first four lines. Peacocks are within the potential referential and topical scope of the text that has been built up so far. The peacock is depicted as performing the action of drooping, and the verb *droop* may or may not be included as a metaphorically used word, depending on the criteria for analysis of its contextual and basic meanings. Let us assume for the sake of convenience that *droops* is not metaphorically used and that a peacock can literally droop. The point of interest then is that the action of drooping is described in more detail by the addition of the adverbial adjunct *like a ghost*. This adverbial adjunct explicitly expresses a comparison. But the comparison between peacocks and ghosts crosses two distinct domains, which clearly opens up the possibility for a cross-domain mapping creating metaphorical meaning: peacocks can be literally compared with many other animals, but not that easily with ghosts. The text suggests that the peacock droops like a ghost does something, and this cross-domain comparison can be analyzed by applying the five-step method (see table 2).

The critical comment about line 5 is that its potential for metaphorical meaning resides in the conceptual structure of the text, where ghosts and their actions are mapped onto peacocks and their actions. This is captured by steps 2 and 3, which are then elaborated in 4 and 5. In the linguistic form of the text, however, direct reference is made to the ghost: it is explicitly offered to the reader as a distinct object for comparison which needs to be set up and understood as such. The word *ghost* is not used metaphorically. The concept of a ghost is used to set up a metaphorical comparison in the text base, which may be developed by further conceptual analysis. This non-metaphorical use of words is characteristic of most if not all simile.

This is also the reason why step 1 captures "metaphor-related" language. In particular, the use of *ghost* in line 5 shows that some language may be *related* to metaphor (in conceptual structure) but does not have to *be* metaphorical (in the language use itself). That is, such language is used directly, not metaphorically, but it still causes a type of incongruity in the conceptual structure of the discourse which triggers a need for comparison, or semantic transfer by means of similarity. This has to be opposed to the example of *sleep* and other metaphorically used words in the poem, such as *bosom,* and *lie open*: these are all related to metaphor in conceptual structure but are also used indirectly as linguistic expressions – they are also metaphorically used words.

The words *ghost, sleep* and *bosom* all presumably activate their respective concepts of GHOST, SLEEP, and BOSOM. These three concepts, however, do not have identical relations with corresponding referents in the text world that has to be projected by the reader. The concepts SLEEP and BOSOM relate to an indirectly designated activity of a petal and an indirectly designated attribute of the lake, respectively, and these have to be inferred by metaphorical mapping. By contrast, GHOST does relate to a ghost which then has to be incorporated into the intended meaning of the utterance by means of elaborating on its conceptual structure. There is a variable relation between words, concepts, and referents (Steen 2002b).

What the first step does, therefore, is pick out "metaphor-related words", that is, words which point to metaphor in conceptual structure. However, these words are not necessarily metaphorically used as lexical units. That is, they do not necessarily exhibit a form of indirect reference. In particular, in similes the words indicating the source domain are used directly while also being related to metaphor.

These observations are also captured in the analysis displayed by table 2. Thus, the source domain concept GHOST in step 2 is labeled as such by the subscript "s" for source but the concept has not been underlined. The source domain concept SLEEP, in line 1, was marked by "s" but also underlined. This may now be understood as a technical reflection of its indirect, metaphorical use.

Simile is not the only form of metaphor which expresses a cross-domain mapping by non-metaphorical language. Allegory is another. I will discuss a number of further examples from this poem in the next sections. For more information about this aspect of metaphor, see Goatly (1997) and Steen (2007).

4.   More about step 2: metaphor in propositional structure

Step 2 in the procedure aims at turning linguistic expressions into conceptual structures by transforming them into propositions. For many linguistic expressions, this simply involves finding the main clause and the main elements of the main clause, and using this information to build a clause-like structure exhibiting linear and hierarchical relations between concepts. The first utterance of the poem, *now sleeps the crimson petal*, offers a fairly unproblematic illustration of this method of propositionalization, as was shown in table 1.

However, the critical function of step 2 can be aptly explained with reference to the sequel of the first utterance of the poem, that is, the second half of line 1, . . ., *now the white*. Its analysis by the five-step method is shown in table 1. It is a perfect example of the need to make a distinction between the linguistic form of a text on the one hand and its conceptual structure, including a series of propositions, on the other. No reader of Tennyson's poem will be able to understand the poem without creating some sort of text base that contains the equivalent of what has been represented here as the output of step 2.

Not all concepts needed for a text base must be fully expressed in the language of a text. This is a possibility of all natural language use, which is characterized by varying degrees of explicitness or implicitness (e.g. Perfetti 1999). Even metaphor is subject to this general possibility, although this has not been accorded much attention in metaphor research.

As a result, it s possible to have metaphorical meaning in a discourse unit without any material indication of the source domain. In the second half of line 1, there are no words that express the concepts involved in the source domain. They have to be recovered at a conceptual level. Metaphor identification cannot just be a matter of the analysis of linguistic forms, addressed by step 1, but it has to make assumptions about propositions, too (cf. Steen 2005b).

Table 3. Analysis of second half of line 1

Text	*Now the white*
1. Identification of metaphor-related words	
2. Identification of propositions	P1 (SLEEP$_{i,s}$ PETAL$_{i,t}$) P2 (MOD P1 NOW$_t$) P3 (MOD PETAL$_{i,t}$ WHITE$_t$)
3. Identification of open comparison	SIM $\{\exists F \exists a$ $[F$ (WHITE PETAL$_i$)]$_t$ $[$SLEEP$_i$ $(a)]_s\}$
4. Identification of analogical structure	SIM $\{[$BE-INACTIVE (WHITE PETAL$_i$)]$_t$ $[$SLEEP$_i$ (HUMAN)]$_s\}$
5. Identification of cross-domain mapping	SLEEP$_i$ > BE-INACTIVE HUMAN > WHITE PETAL$_i$ inferences: GOAL OF SLEEP > GOAL OF BE-INACTIVE: REST TIME OF SLEEP > TIME OF BE-INACTIVE: NIGHT

When discourse analysts create a text base, they sometimes have to fill in implicit conceptual elements to make the text base coherent. They also sometimes replace personal pronouns and other terms by their intended co-referents to make the text base locally explicit. These additions and re-placements are usually quite explicitly constrained by the instructions of the method. The introduction of concepts like SLEEP and FETAL in step 2 involves a natural application of this general spirit of the method of pro-positionalization to metaphor analysis. These are concepts that have been inferred by the analyst and have been marked as such in the text base by the subscript "i".

Once the implicit parts of a metaphorical utterance have been made explicit by propositional analysis in step 2, the rest of the procedure can treat the metaphor as if it were fully explicit. This may be demonstrated by considering the analysis of the propositional structure for *now the white* by means of its transformation into an open comparison in step 3, an interpreted analogy in step 4, and a fleshed-out mapping in step 5. This analysis does not differ in any respect from the analysis of *now sleeps the crimson petal* in table 1, with the exception of the continued addition of the subscript "i" to two of the concepts as a reminder of their analytically inferred as opposed to textually given status. In principle, implicit metaphor does not have to pose insuperable problems to the five-step method.

There is another implicit metaphor in this poem, which shows the need for the addition of "in principle" in the previous sentence. Lines 9 and 10 exhibit another elliptical expression of metaphor, which is more difficult to analyze:

> Now slides the silent meteor on, and leaves
> 10   A shining furrow, as thy thoughts in me.

The first two clauses in these lines introduce the domain of nature, and the last clause, *as thy thoughts in me*, suggests a comparative link between this domain of nature and the domain of the love relationship that is the theme of the poem. This opens up the possibility of reconstructing a cross-domain mapping between the two domains, which may be analyzed by the five-step method as shown in table 4.

Table 4. Analysis of lines 9–10

Text	*Now slides the silent meteor on, and leaves* *A shining furrow, as thy thoughts in me.*
1. Identification of metaphor-related words	Now slides the silent meteor on, and leaves A shining furrow
2. Identification of propositions	P1 (COMPARISON DU1–2 DU3)
	DU1 P1 (SLIDE$_s$ METEOR$_s$)
	P2 (MOD P1 NOW$_s$)
	P3 (MOD P1 ON$_s$)
	P4 (MOD METEOR$_s$ SILENT$_s$)
	DU2 P1 (LEAVE$_s$ METEOR$_{i,s}$FURROW$_s$)
	P2 (MOD FURROW$_s$ SHINING$_s$)
	DU3a P1 (SLIDE$_{i,t}$ THOUGHTS$_t$)
	P2 (MOD P1 ON$_{i,t}$)
	P3 (POSSESS YOU$_t$ THOUGHTS$_t$)
	DU3b P1 (LEAVE$_{i,t}$ THOUGHTS$_t$ FURROW$_{i,t}$)
	P2 (IN$_t$ P1 ME$_t$)
	P3 (MOD FURROW$_{i,t}$ SHINING$_{i,t}$)
	P4 (POSSESS YOU$_t$ THOUGHTS$_t$)

Text	*Now slides the silent meteor on, and leaves* *A shining furrow, as thy thoughts in me*
3. Identification of open comparison	SIM { [SLIDE-ON$_i$ (THY THOUGHTS) & LEAVE$_i$ (THY THOUGHTS) (SHINING FURROW)$_i$ (IN ME)]$_t$ [SLIDE-ON (SILENT METEOR) & LEAVE (SILENT METEOR) (SHINING FURROW)]$_s$}
4. Identification of analogical structure	SIM { [SLIDE-ON$_i$ (THY THOUGHTS) & LEAVE$_i$ (THY THOUGHTS) (SHINING FURROW)$_i$ (IN ME)]$_t$ [SLIDE-ON (SILENT METEOR) & LEAVE (SILENT METEOR) (SHINING FURROW)]$_s$}
5. Identification of cross-domain mapping	SLIDE-ON > SLIDE-ON SILENT METEOR > THY THOUGHTS Inferences 1 2 3 LEAVE > LEAVE SILENT METEOR > THY THOUGHTS Inferences 1 2 3 SHINING FURROW > SHINING FURROW $_2$IN SKY$_3$ > IN ME Inferences 1 2 3

There are many comments to be made about this analysis, some of which will appear in the next section. One preliminary comment is the need to delineate discourse units in the text, indicated by DU in the text base. Discourse units are independent utterances, often equivalent to main clauses (Steen 2005b). The text base begins with positing a coherence relation between these discourse units, to the effect that a comparison is envisaged between discourse units 1 and 2 on the one hand and 3 on the other. This is a conceptual representation in the text base of the conjunction *as*.

For step 2, however, the main point of interest is the recovery of the presumed meanings and concepts left implicit by the elliptical expression of the metaphorical mapping. As may be seen from table 4, I have assumed that the expression *as thy thoughts in me* mirrors the complete structure of the source domain expressed in the preceding two clauses, leading to the recovery of the implied conceptual structure "as thy thoughts slide on and leave a shining furrow in me". It is possible to argue, however, over the exclusion of the notion of "silent" from the first clause, and over the inclusion of the notion of "shining" in the second clause. Different analysts might hence come up with at least three different solutions to the recovery of meaning in step 2. The recovery of implicit metaphorical meaning is not always as unproblematic as it is for the last part of line 1. It may even be so that decisions about the best solution to this problem in step 2 have to be made on the basis of their effects in steps 3, 4, and 5.

Each of the three different variants of propositionalization leads to a slightly different open comparison, closed analogy, and full-blown mapping. It is conceivable that a full consideration of the consequences of these alternatives can retrospectively motivate a specific representation of lines 9 and 10 in the text base. This is a natural situation for those stretches of discourse that are open to multiple interpretation, as will often happen in poetry. It depends on the aims of the researcher whether all interpretations need to be spelled out in step 2 or not.

In the discussion of lines 9 and 10 I have ignored the fact that the two clauses in line 9 also contain metaphorically used words themselves. The words *slide on* in the first clause and *leaves* and *furrow* in the second clause are clearly metaphorical and require analysis by means of the five-step method independently of what has been presented in table 4 for the entire couplet. These words do not only act as an expression of the source domain (nature) for the target domain (love) in the last clause in line 10; they also function as a target domain (nature) containing source domain language which constitutes a metaphorical expression of parts of that conceptual domain. Unfortunately there is no space to go into these further complications of metaphor embedding, which has to await treatment until another occasion.

5.   More about step 3: metaphor as open cross-domain comparison

Step 3 of the procedure aims to explicate that cross-domain mappings suggested by propositions are a matter of similarity, and that the two domains involved need to be separated from each other in aligned fashion. For this purpose, the analysis of *now sleeps the crimson petal* and of *now the white* introduces the operator SIM which ranges over two separated and open propositions that are related to respectively a source and a target domain. The propositions are open because not all concepts involved in the envisaged alignment and mapping between the two domains are expressed in the language of the text; for instance, the target domain concept corresponding to the concept of sleep in the source domain is linguistically implicit. Consequently, some variables for functions and arguments have to be assumed as open slots in the projected comparison. This creates a skeletal structure for each of the two domains, with closed and open concepts aligned to facilitate the envisaged mapping

However, it is not true that all metaphors leave the assumption of similarity implicit. We have discussed two linguistic expressions of cross-domain mappings above which display an explicit indication that we have to do with a comparison across two domains. First of all, in line 5, there is the preposition *like* which explicitly indicates that there is a similarity between the fact that the peacock droops and the situation where a ghost does something. Secondly, in lines 9 and 10, there is the conjunction *as* which explicitly indicates that there is a similarity between the fact that a silent meteor slides on and leaves shining furrow on the one hand, and some ellipted action by the lover's thoughts with respect to the speaker on the other hand. The words *like* and *as* are turned into concepts which refer to similarity in the text base by step 2. Their transformation into the similarity operator in step 3 does not require any special assumption or addition on the part of the analyst (see tables 2 and 4).

Words such as *like* and *as* are commonly interpreted as potential signals for metaphor in discourse (e.g. Goatly 1997). This is because metaphor and cross-domain mappings have been widely defined as involving some form of non-literal or cross-domain similarity, including in cognitive linguistics. These are facts which provide clear support for the assumption that step 3 requires a SIM operator. Other examples of metaphor lack such clear lexical signals, like our two illustrations from line 1, where the SIM operator was introduced on the basis of an analytical assumption. In simile and analogy and other manifestations of metaphor, however, the use of the similarity operator SIM is not an analytical assumption but a description of the explicitly available materials in the text. This makes the basis of steps 3, and consequently steps 4 and 5, more solid.

The lexical item *as* has been represented by the coherence operator COM-PARISON in the text base (step 2, table 4). This is another general possibility in propositionalization which captures the loose relation between language and propositions. Many coherence relations have received this type of treatment in discourse analysis. A similar approach might be adopted to representing the conceptual force of the conjunction *so* between lines 11 and 12 on the one hand and 13 and 14 on the other. Such an approach reflects the idea that a particular concept, such as COMPARISON, may be expressed in more than one linguistic fashion. It can even account for the charged interpretation of *and* between lines 5 and 6, and between lines 7 and 8: because of the overall structure of the poem, as well as the parallel lexico-grammatical structures of the clauses within the two couplets, the conjunction *and* may clearly be taken as a weak lexical signal, in this context, for comparison by means of matching (e.g. Hoey 2001). (This also implies that all of these words and structures are not always to be taken as signals for metaphor – they simply reflect comparison or matching which may or may not involve two distinct domains, as the case may be.)

Apart from explicating the assumption that metaphor is a matter of similarity between two conceptual domains, step 3 also makes the first move in distinguishing the two domains from each other by separating out the source domain concepts from the target domain concepts in two open propositions. For many metaphors, this is an operation which splits up two sets of concepts originating from one single original proposition in the text base. This is because most metaphors in discourse display one or more metaphorically used words within one otherwise non-metaphorical discourse unit, typically an independent clause (Crisp et al. 2002; Steen 2005b). Since these units would as a rule be represented as one main proposition, step 3 often involves creating two open propositions from this original single text proposition to capture the emerging structure of the mapping between the two domains.

However, some expressions of metaphor in discourse already have driven the source and target domains apart into separate propositions in the text. Our example of lines 9 and 10 provides a case in point. It is characterized by two distinct clauses from the source domain followed by one (albeit elliptical) clause from the target domain. Comparable forms of expression, but with one clause for each domain, may be found in lines 7–8 as well as lines 5–6: the first line of the couplet always contains one clause representing the source domain of nature, and the second line always contains one clause representing the target domain of love. All of these are illustrations of the possibility for metaphor to be expressed as two separate (sets of) propositions in the text which evoke a comparison between their respective conceptual domains or spaces.

As a result, for all of these examples, the source domain propositions and the target domain propositions that are needed for step 3 can simply be copied from the text base constructed in step 2, as may be seen from table 4. Moreover, the comparison that is constructed by step 3 for this specific class of metaphors is typically not an open comparison but a closed one. This can be seen from the empty space behind the SIM operator in step 3: it does not display open functions or arguments, as in tables 1 and 3 for the sleep comparisons. The output of step 3, for these metaphors, can simply be copied wholesale into step 4. This leads us on to the next section.

6.   More about step 4: metaphor as analogy

Since metaphor often involves the use of just one or more source domain words in a target domain context within one sentence, the output of step 3 typically presents two open propositions that are mostly related in analogical fashion. It is the task of step 4 to derive a closed comparison from this skeletal conceptual structure. The two linguistic versions of the "sleep" example show that this may involve two open values, one in each open proposition, that need to be filled. To find the most appropriate concepts for this comparison is the aim of step 4 (tables 1 and 3).

It is interesting to consider how step 4 involves two complementary analytical processes for these types of metaphor. Finding the appropriate values for the source domain may be seen as a matter of vehicle interpretation whereas finding the appropriate values for the target domain concerns tenor or topic interpretation (Reinhart 1976; Steen 1994). The latter is constrained by the specific demands of the utterance in the discourse in context, hinging on local and global referents and discourse topics, whereas the former seems to be guided by more general and typical considerations of meaning and knowledge. Thus, who sleeps or who can sleep is probably first of all decided by encyclopedic knowledge, whereas what the crimson and the white petal do, is probably more affected by what is happening in the situation depicted by the poem. A critical but constructive discussion of some of the difficulties involved in these analytical operations may be found in Semino et al. (2004).

Table 5. Analysis of lines 5–6

Text	*Now droops the milk white peacock like a ghost,* *And like a ghost she glimmers unto me*
1. Identification of metaphor-related words	Now droops the milk white peacock like a ghost,
2. Identification of propositions	P1 (COMPARISON DU1 DU2) DU1 P1 (DROOP$_s$ PEACOCK$_s$) 　　　P2 (MOD P1 NOW$_s$) 　　　P3 (LIKE P1 GHOST$_s$) 　　　P4 (MOD PEACOCK$_s$ MILK-WHITE$_s$) DU2 P1 (GLIMMER$_t$ BELOVED$_t$) 　　　P2 (LIKE P1 GHOST$_t$) 　　　P3 (UNTO$_t$ P1 SPEAKER$_t$)
3. Identification of open comparison	SIM { [DROOP (MILK-WHITE PEACOCK) (LIKE GHOST)]$_t$ [GLIMMER(BELOVED) (UNTO SPEAKER) (LIKE GHOST)]$_s$}
4. Identification of analogy	SIM { [DROOP (MILK-WHITE PEACOCK) (LIKE GHOST)]$_t$ [GLIMMER(BELOVED) (UNTO SPEAKER) (LIKE GHOST)]$_s$}
5. Identification of cross-domain mapping	DROOP > GLIMMER MILK-WHITE PEACOCK > BELOVED MANNER OF DROOPING (LIKE A GHOST) > MANNER OF GLIMMERING (LIKE A GHOST) inferences BELOVED IS MILKWHITE?

Apart from these considerations for these fairly typical metaphors, however, there are other comments that can be made about the five-step procedure which are triggered by our inclusion of other forms of metaphor. Thus, the expression of metaphor by means of a comparison between two or even more propositions across two lines, as in 5–6 and 7–8, is interesting for step 4, too. The analysis for lines 5 and 6 is shown in table 5.

What a metaphor like this shows is that some metaphors do not require any filling of open slots in step 4, as they have been made fully explicit in the text. Their closed form can be copied in full from the output of step 3, where two propositions are linked by the similarity operator. Again, the empty space behind the SIM operator in step 3 is telling. For these metaphors, vehicle and topic interpretation do not have to take place, as both domains are represented by a full proposition. It should be noted that this couplet is also a case where the two domains involved in the mapping have been expressed as two separate propositions. Step 3 consequently does not have to drive the two domains and propositions apart either. In fact, the two propositions can simply be read off from the text base, in step 2, where the two domains can be found as separate discourse units that are connected by a coherence relation COMPARISON (which presents a charged discourse analysis of the conjunction *and*). Finally, with one exception most of the language of lines 5 and 6 is not metaphorical either: both conceptual domains involved in the mapping are expressed directly by the words used in the separate utterances. There is of course the exception of locally embedded metaphorical usage such as *glimmer* in line 6, but that is not the issue.

Similes also often have fewer open slots than classic metaphors. When we focus on line 5 as a separate discourse unit, for instance, we have the open comparison "the peacock droops like a ghost does something", in which only one concept needs filling out in step 4. The structure of such similes often presents an open comparison that is on its way to closure: these similes explicitly contain three of the four terms that are minimally required for an analogy to be reconstructed in step 4.

In sum, the reliability of the identification of the analogical structure in step 4 is rather dependent on the availability of the conceptual materials in the text. Some metaphors in discourse offer much more explication of the underlying metaphor than others. This has a direct effect on the ease with which step 4 can be completed.

7.   More about step 5: metaphor as cross-domain mapping

The function of step 5 is to spell out the aligned and corresponding concepts which are implied by the analogical structure produced by step 4. Thus, for *sleep*, the concept of SLEEP from the source domain is connected with the concept of BE INACTIVE from the target domain (hinting that the expression of the target domain concept by the source domain term adds a dimension of action to the quality of state). And for *crimson petal*, the target domain concept PETAL is explicitly related to the source domain concept of HUMAN, hinting at the possibility of personification. Step 5 also fleshes out whatever other inferences may be connected to the analogy. The selection and identification of these inferences, such as the regular goal and time of sleeping, are probably harder to constrain than the selection and identification of concepts for any open slots in the analogy in step 4. But it is precisely the advantage of employing a mechanism like the five-step procedure that such problematic issues in metaphor analysis are made explicit.

We have seen some other metaphors for which the alignment of the concepts is not based on concepts that have been inferred in step 4. Thus, our analysis of couplet 5–6 displayed a series of correspondences between concepts which were all available from the text. And when such explicit mappings are extended across more than one utterance for either source or target, the analysis becomes more complex, but remains based on the same principles. Consider the structure of the last four lines, as shown in table 6.

Table 6. Analysis of lines 11–14

Text	*Now folds the lily all her sweetness up,* *And slips into the bosom of the lake:* *So fold thyself, my dearest, thou, and slip* *Into my bosom and be lost in me.*
1. Identification of metaphor-related words	Now folds the lily all her sweetness up, And slips into the bosom of the lake:
2. Identification of propositions	P1 (COMPARISON DU1–2 DU3–5) DU1 P1 (FOLD-UP$_s$ LILY$_s$ SWEETNESS$_s$) P2 (MOD P1 NOW$_s$) DU2 P1 (SLIP-INTO$_s$ LILY$_s$ BOSOM$_s$) P2 (OF BOSOM$_s$ LAKE$_s$) DU3 P1 (FOLD$_t$ THOU$_t$ THYSELF$_t$) P2 (VOCATIVE DEAREST$_t$) DU4 P1 (SLIP-INTO$_t$ THOU$_t$ BOSOM$_t$) P2 (POSSESS$_t$ SPEAKER$_t$ BOSOM$_t$) DU5 P1 (BE-LOST$_t$ THOU$_t$) P2 (IN$_t$ P1 SPEAKER$_t$)
3. Identification of open comparison	SIM { [FOLD (THOU) (THYSELF) & SLIP-INTO (THOU) (MY BOSOM) & (BE-LOST (THOU) (IN ME)]$_t$ [FOLD-UP (LILY) (ALL HER SWEETNESS) & SLIP-INTO (LILY) (BOSOM OF LAKE]$_s$}
4. Identification of analogical structure	SIM { [FOLD (THOU) (THYSELF) & SLIP-INTO (THOU) (MY BOSOM) & (BE-LOST (THOU) (IN ME)]$_t$ [FOLD-UP (LILY) (ALL HER SWEETNESS) & SLIP-INTO (LILY) (BOSOM OF LAKE]$_s$}

Text	*Now folds the lily all her sweetness up,* *And slips into the bosom of the lake:* *So fold thyself, my dearest, thou, and slip* *Into my bosom and be lost in me.*
5. Identification of cross-domain mapping	FOLD-UP > FOLD LILY > THOU SWEETNESS > THYSELF inferences 1 2 3 SLIP > SLIP LILY > THOU INTO BOSOM OF LAKE > INTO MY BOSOM inferences 1 2 3 'BE LOST' > BE LOST LILY > THOU 'IN LAKE' > IN ME inferences 1 2 3

I have presented the output of step 5 as three sets of correspondences with open slots for their possible associated inferences, in order to emphasize that this is the conceptual foundation of the cross-domain mapping that needs to be constructed in step 5. The fact that I have left the inferences undecided suggests that this is the most problematic part of doing this type of metaphor identification. More needs to be learned about the mechanisms underlying the cognitive linguistic analysis of conceptual mappings before an explicitly constrained approach to this part of metaphor identification can be proposed.

There is also overlap between the three sets of correspondences. Thus the mapping between the lily in the source domain and the beloved who is addressed in the target domain is constant. It may therefore also be possible to build a more integrated conceptual mapping between these two domains, for instance in a figurative representation between two mental spaces, as in Blending Theory. But the question arises how we can decide that all three sets of correspondences belong to one encompassing mapping or not; in particular, is the sequence of folding up, slipping into, and being lost part of one integrated scenario, or should we see them as a series of three separate actions that each have a mapping of their own which are linked to each other by the target domain, not the same source domain? Similar questions can be asked about the two clauses in lines 9 and 10: does sliding on and leaving a furrow constitute two metaphorical mappings in sequence, which are unified by the target domain; or are they one set of actions which derive from the same source domain, so that they can be integrated, in step 5, into one encompassing mapping? The ways in which these questions can or should be answered require more analysis with reference to the various forms of metaphor that can be distinguished than is available at this occasion, and this issue therefore also needs to be deferred.

In other cases, the elaboration of the analogy critically depends on some special knowledge. Thus, lines 7–8 require knowledge about the story about Danaë for the analyst to be able to draw the appropriate inferences. These have to be added to the list of correspondences which may be derived in relatively formal fashion from the conceptual structure that is explicitly available in the text base, comparison, and analogy produced by steps 2, 3, and 4. That is, there are four obvious correspondences to be derived from the formal structure of the couplet: that *the Earth* corresponds to *all thy heart*, that *lies* corresponds to *lies*, that *all Danaë* corresponds to *open*, and that *to the stars* corresponds to *unto me*. However, the point of (metaphorically) expressing the relationship of the Earth to the stars by means of the reference to Danaë remains unclear without background knowledge, and this, in turn, may affect the mapping between lines 7 and 8 as a source and a target domain (see table 7).

Danaë represents a famous topic in art, with classic paintings by Correggio, Titian, and Rembrandt before the days of Tennyson, and by Burne-Jones and Klimt at the turn of the nineteenth century. The Renaissance paintings all display her in the nude, awaiting Zeus in the form of a golden rain who will impregnate her with Perseus. This is happening against the will of Danaë's father, who has locked her away in order to defend himself against an oracle's prediction that Danaë's son will kill him. This is how it is possible that "Now lies the Earth all Danaë to the stars".

I will again refrain from drawing the appropriate inferences, as these may require more space for their motivation than when we looked at

Table 7. Analysis of lines 9–10

Text	*Now lies the Earth all Danaë to the stars,* *And all thy heart lies open unto me.*
1. Identification of metaphor-related words	Now lies the Earth all Danaë to the stars,

2. Identification of propositions	P1 (COMPARISON DU1 DU2)
	DU1 P1 (LIE_s EARTH_s DANAË_s)
	       P2 (MOD P1 NOW_s)
	       P3 (TO_s P1 STARS_s)
	       P4 (MOD DANAË_s ALL_s)
	DU2 P1 (LIE_t HEART_t OPEN_t)
	       P2 (UNTO_t P1 ME_t)
	       P3 (MOD HEART_t ALL_t)
	       P4 (POSSESS THOU_t HEART_t)

3. Identification of open comparison	SIM { [LIE (ALL THY HEART) (OPEN) (UNTO ME)]_t [LIE (EARTH) (DANAË) (TO STARS)]_s}
4. Identification of analogical structure	SIM { [LIE (ALL THY HEART) (OPEN) (UNTO ME)]_t [LIE (EARTH) (DANAË) (TO STARS)_s]}
5. Identification of cross-domain mapping	LIE > LIE EARTH > HEART DANAË > OPEN STARS > ME *inferences* 1 2 3

sleeps in line 1. This may be disappointing, but it indicates that step 5 is problematic. It offers the beginning of building a conceptual mapping on the basis of the formal structure of the analogy produced by step 4, but its development into a full-blown mapping remains more difficult if that is to remain within the bounds of reliable identification instead of subjective interpretation. Further study is needed of the principles and mechanisms which have been applied by other analysts who produced such mappings in cognitive linguistics and cognitive poetics (cf. Semino et al. 2004).

8.   Conclusion

The five-step procedure offers a mechanism for identifying at least the basis of the conceptual structure of a cross-domain mapping which is realized by some metaphor in discourse. It was originally developed to deal with metaphorically used words, such as *sleeps* in line 1 (cf. Steen 1999b; Semino et al. 2004). However, this chapter has shown that it can also be applied to other forms of metaphor, including simile, analogy, and extended comparisons. Each of these forms of metaphor reveals different aspects of metaphor as a cross-domain mapping, and by implication highlights different problems and difficulties that have to be superseded by the analyst who applies the five-step method.

Difficulties which have had to be left aside include a number of well-known phenomena. We ended with the problems of how to decide which inferences are valid for a particular mapping, or series of mappings. We also pointed to the need for decision criteria about the unit of metaphor, both between discourse units as well as within them (cf. Crisp et al. 2002; Steen 2005b). The phenomenon of embedded metaphor also drew our attention but could not be further addressed in this place. It has connections with other well-known topics, such as mixed metaphor, which are all on the agenda for future research (cf. Goatly 1997). For now we wish to end on a more positive note: the procedure has proved to be helpful in ordering and tackling many of these phenomena, which are all crucial for the analysis of metaphor in poetry.

Author's note

This research was performed as part of Vici program "Metaphor in discourse: Linguistic forms, conceptual structures, conceptual representations", sponsored by the Netherlands Organization for Scientific Research, NWO, 277–30–001.

I am grateful to the editors and two anonymous reviewers, who offered helpful comments on a previous version.

References

Black, Max
  1962   *Models and Metaphors.* Ithaca, NY: Cornell University Press.
Bovair, Susan and David Kieras
  1985   A guide to propositional analysis for research on technical prose. In:
          Bruce K. Britton and John B. Black (eds.), *Understanding Expository
          Text*, 315–362. Hillsdale, NJ: Lawrence Erlbaum.
Cameron, Lynn
  2003   *Metaphor in Educational Discourse.* London/New York: Continuum.
Charteris-Black, Jonathan
  2004   *Corpus Approaches to Critical Metaphor Analysis.* London: Palgrave
          MacMillan.
Crisp, Peter
  2005   Allegory, blending, and possible situations. *Metaphor and Symbol*
          20(2): 115–332.
Crisp, Peter, John Heywood and Gerard J. Steen
  2002   Identification and analysis, classification and quantification. *Language
          and Literature* 11(1): 55–69.
Dirven, René and Ralf Pörings (eds.)
  2002   *Metaphor and Metonymy in Comparison and Contrast.* Berlin: Mouton
          de Gruyter.
Fauconnier, Gilles
  1997   *Mappings in Thought and Language.* Cambridge: Cambridge Univer-
          sity Press.
Fauconnier, Gilles and Mark Turner
  1998   Conceptual integration networks. *Cognitive Science* 22(2): 133–187.
Fauconnier, Gilles and Mark Turner
  2002   *The Way We Think: Conceptual Blending and the Mind's Hidden Com-
          plexities.* New York: Basic Books.
Freeman, Donald C.
  1993   'According to my bond': *King Lear* and re-cognition. *Language and Lit-
          erature* 2(1): 1–18.
Freeman, Donald C.
  1995   'Catch[ing] the nearest way': *Macbeth* and cognitive metaphor. *Journal
          of Pragmatics* 24: 689–708.
Freeman, Donald C.
  1999   'The rack dislimns': Schema and metaphorical pattern in *Anthony and
          Cleopatra. Poetics Today* 20(3): 443–460.
Freeman, Margaret H.
  1995   Metaphor making meaning: Dickinson's conceptual universe. *Journal
          of Pragmatics* 24: 643–666.
Freeman, Margaret H.
  2000   Poetry and the scope of metaphor: Toward a cognitive theory of litera-
          ture. In: Antonio Barcelona (ed.), *Metaphor and Metonymy at the
          Crossroads*, 253–282. Berlin/New York: Mouton de Gruyter.

Freeman, Margaret H.
2002   Cognitive mapping in literary analysis. *Style* 36(3): 466–483.
Gardner, Helen (ed.)
1972   *The New Oxford Book of English Verse.* Oxford: Oxford University Press.
Gentner, Dedre and Arthur B. Markman
1993   Analogy--Watershed or Waterloo? Structural alignment and the development of connectionist models of analogy. In: Stephen J. Hanson, Jack D. Cowan and C. Lee Giles (eds.), *Advances in Neural Information Processing Systems,* 855–862. San Mateo, CA: Morgan Kaufman Publishers.
Gentner, Dedre and Arthur B. Markman
1997   Structure mapping in analogy and similarity. *American Psychologist* 52: 45–56.
Gibbs, Raymond W. jr.
1993   Process and products in making sense of tropes. In Andrew Ortony (ed.), *Metaphor and Thought* (second ed.), 252–276. Cambridge: Cambridge University Press.
Gibbs, Raymond W. jr.
1994   *The Poetics of Mind: Figurative Thought, Language, and Understanding.* Cambridge: Cambridge University Press.
Giora, Rachel
2003   *On our Mind: Salience, Context, and Figurative Language.* New York: Oxford University Press.
Goatly, Andrew
1997   *The Language of Metaphors.* London: Routledge.
Hoey, Michael
2001   *Textual Interaction: An Introduction to Written Discourse Analysis.* London: Routledge.
Kintsch, Walter
1998   *Comprehension: A Paradigm for Cognition.* Cambridge: Cambridge University Press.
Kittay, Eva F.
1987   *Metaphor: Its Cognitive Force and Linguistic Structure.* Oxford/New York: Oxford University Press.
Kövecses, Zoltan
2002   *Metaphor: A Practical Introduction.* Oxford: Oxford University Press.
Lakoff, George
1986   The meanings of literal. *Metaphor and Symbolic Activity* 1(4): 291–296.
Lakoff, George
1993   The contemporary theory of metaphor. In: Andrew Ortony (ed.), *Metaphor and Thought* (second ed.), 202–251. Cambridge: Cambridge University Press.
Lakoff, George and Mark Johnson
1980   *Metaphors We Live by.* Chicago: Chicago University Press.

Lakoff, George and Mark Johnson
1999   *Philosophy in the Flesh: The Embodied Mind and Its Challenge to Western Thought*. New York: Basic Books.
Miller, George A.
[1979] 1993 Images and models, similes and metaphors. In: Andrew Ortony (ed.), *Metaphor and Thought* (second ed.), 357–400. Cambridge: Cambridge University Press.
Perfetti, Charles
1999   Comprehending written language: A blueprint of the reader. In: Colin Brown and Peter Hagoort (eds.), *The Neurocognition of Language*, 167–208. Oxford: Oxford University Press.
PragglejazGroup
In press A practical and flexible method for identifying metaphorically used words in discourse. *Metaphor and Symbol* 22(3).
Reinhart, Tanya
1976   On understanding poetic metaphor. *Poetics* 5: 383–402
Richards, I.A.
1936   *The Philosophy of Rhetoric*. New York: Oxford University Press.
Semino, Elena, Jonathan Heywood and Mick H. Short
2004   Methodological problems in the analysis of metaphors in a corpus of conversations about cancer. *Journal of Pragmatics* 36(7): 1271–1294.
Steen, Gerard J.
1994   *Understanding Metaphor in Literature: An Empirical Approach*. London: Longman.
Steen, Gerard J.
1999a   Analyzing metaphor in literature: with examples from William Wordsworth's "I wandered lonely as a cloud". *Poetics Today* 20(3): 499–522.
Steen, Gerard J.
1999b   From linguistic to conceptual metaphor in five steps. In: Raymond W. Gibbs, jr. and Gerard J. Steen (eds.), *Metaphor in Cognitive Linguistics*, 57–77. Amsterdam: John Benjamins.
Steen, Gerard J.
2002a   Metaphor identification: A cognitive approach. *Style* 36(3): 386–407.
Steen, Gerard J.
2002b   Towards a procedure for metaphor identification. *Language and Literature* 11(1): 17–33.
Steen, Gerard J.
2005a   What counts as a metaphorically used word? The Pragglejaz experience. In: Seana Coulson and Barbara Lewandowska-Tomaszczyk (eds.), *The Literal-Nonliteral Distinction*, 299–322. Frankfurt am Main: Peter Lang.
Steen, Gerard J.
2005b   Basic discourse acts: Towards a psychological theory of discourse segmentation. In Francisco J. Ruiz de Mendoza Ibanez and Sandra M. Peña Cervel (eds.), *Cognitive Linguistics: Internal Dynamics and Interdisciplinary Interaction*, 283–312. Berlin/New York: Mouton de Gruyter.

Steen, Gerard J.
   2007   *Finding Metaphor in Grammar and Usage: A Methodological Analysis of Theory and Research.* Amsterdam: John Benjamins.
Steen, Gerard J. and Raymond W. Gibbs, jr.
   2004   Questions about metaphor in literature. *European Journal of English Studies* 8(3): 337–354.
Sternberg, Robert R. and Georgia Nigro
   1983   Interaction and analogy in the comprehension and appreciation of metaphors. *Quarterly Journal of Experimental Psychology* 35A(1): 17–38.
Van Dijk, Teun A. and Walter Kintsch
   1983   *Strategies of Discourse Comprehension.* New York: Academic Press.
Weaver, Charles A. III, Suzanne Mannes and Charles A. Fletcher (eds.)
   1995   *Discourse Comprehension: Essays in Honor of Walter Kintsch.* Hillsdale, NJ: Lawrence Erlbaum.

Common foundations of metaphor and iconicity

Ming-Yu Tseng

When we deal with "metaphor" or "iconicity", it is important to bear in mind that "creative metaphors" and "poetic iconicity" are still symbolic – still signifiers – and therefore that they have the same semiotic foundation as everyday language in terms of what constitutes a sign. That is, whether we are carrying on a casual conversation or reading a poem, semiotic concepts such as signifier, signified, the relationship between them (i.e. signification) are all at play. Therefore, I believe studies of language, including the language of literature, may well be enriched and consolidated in an inclusive, integral or integrationist view of language in which "literary" and "non-literary" language need not be treated as mutually exclusive. Instead, literary and non-literary texts share a wide range of linguistic resources available in language, and they exemplify language uses in contexts, involving not only language but also speaker/writer, listener/reader, communicative purpose, situation of context, etc. (Fowler 1981: 80–85; cf. Toolan 1996: 140–180). Adopting this "inclusivist" approach, we may then find that links between the various types of signification, e.g. between metaphor and iconicity, are really worth exploring because they contribute to meaning in many speech genres.

Neither metaphor nor iconicity is exclusively the property of literature. Lakoff and Johnson (1980) have demonstrated that metaphors are a part of everyday language and that they affect how we think and perceive rather than being mere poetic embellishments. The inseparability of metaphor from thought applies to all metaphors, literary or non-literary, although literary metaphors tend to be creative in expression and are thus more "risky" in that the reader may not grasp the message, if there is one single message to grasp (Bhaya Nair, Carter, and Toolan 1988: 27). Similarly, when talking about "poetic iconicity", we need to be aware that it does not necessarily have a marked difference from the iconicity found in non-literary genres. Like metaphor, iconicity is part and parcel of the process of representation and communication.

[...] [S]ymbols without iconic and indexical dimensions are inert; icons and indices without symbolic form are less than genuine signs. [...] they [i.e. icons and
indices] are an integrated part of the whole human interaction. The very existence of explicitly engendered symbols is dependent upon icons and indices at
implicit (corporeal, felt) levels of tacit knowability. But icons and indices cannot emerge into the arena of explicitly articulated knowledge without their
proper symbolic attire. (Merrell 2001: 101)

Meaning, though mediated through signs and symbols, is based on our
shared human experience such as bodily sensations, images, bodily orientation and kinesis, and relations of proximity and of causality, which are
in turn connected with iconicity and indexicality. The existence of an
enormously wide range of human experience engenders the production of
signs and symbols, while signs and symbols in their turn give form and
substance to as-yet-inarticulate human experiences. This integral or holistic view of signs partly explains the pervasiveness of iconicity.

Based on Langer's (1953, 1967) theory of art that emphasizes "the semblance of felt life", Freeman's article on poetic iconicity contends that one
of the main tasks for cognitive poetics is to disentangle the intricate relationship between form and feeling, or structure and affect. This shift of
emphasis towards the question of form-feeling corrects the imbalance
found in most iconicity studies, which tend to address only the form-meaning resemblance or correspondence. Or rather, the emphasis redirects attention to the affective function of iconicity. However, "the semblance of
felt life" is not captured only in fictional art; it can also be exemplified in
non-literary genres, for example, a moving true story, an emotional fun-
draising appeal, etc. Generally speaking, iconicity is inevitably part of any
representation of experience (cf. Downes 2000; McGreevy 2005). The
matter is complicated, though not necessarily obscured, by the fact that
one does not always feel what one is "supposed" to feel either as a result of
reading or of directly experiencing a person or event. For example, after
reading the line "Withered flowers today blossomed yesterday", Freeman
comments that "it makes us feel the effects of decay". However, not everyone would feel the effects of decay; instead, some may feel the effects of
bloom because the contrast between withered flowers and blooming ones
could make us want to cherish flowers" peak moments all the more. Or
some may feel the effect of process from bloom to decay rather than just
decay – the result of the process.

Drawing on insights from neuroscience and evolutionary biology
amongst others, Deacon's (1997) view of iconicity reinforces the inevitable relationship between iconicity and representation. He sees icons, in-

dices, and symbols as forming a hierarchical relationship, with iconicity as the most basic means of representation (Deacon 1997: 69–79): "To spell it out, the competence to interpret something symbolically depends upon already having the competence to interpret many other subordinate relationships indexically" (Deacon 1997: 74). Thus, the competence to interpret something indexically depends upon the competence to interpret something iconically: "Iconic relationships are the most basic means by which things can be re-presented. It is the base on which all other forms of representation are built" (Deacon 1997: 77). This semiotic chain underlying signs and symbols (or symbolic signs) helps to explain the permeation of iconic mappings in discourse and text.

Freeman's analysis of Emily Dickinson's "malaria" poem evinces the permeation of iconicity. She explains that, on the iconic level, the words, structure, and layout of Dickinson's poem are diagrammatically and imagistically linked to its affective meaning. Freeman's analysis shows that various linguistic forms and structural arrangements are used in pairs to "link writer to disease, words to infection, and readers to victims": two transitive verbs (e.g. "stimulate" and "inhale"); two intransitive verbs (e.g. "lie" and "breeds"); two past participles (e.g. "dropped" and "folded"); and syntactic arrangement (e.g. each stanza divided into syntactic units). Her stylistic/linguistic analysis is couched in a cognitive-semiotic integration network proposed by Brandt and Brandt (2005). I would like to further elaborate on two points arising from her analysis: firstly, linguistic devices in manifesting iconicity; secondly, the reception of iconicity.

Underpinning Freeman's analysis of iconicity is a set of linguistic devices that exhibit iconicity. A more explicit and systematic model showing how iconicity can be verbally realized would strengthen the theoretical foundations of iconicity in literary and in non-literary texts. Haiman (1999) suggests that traces of iconicity exist in the process from "ritualization" (i.e. conventionalization of actions) to verbalization: physical action gives rise, mediated by linguistic styles (i.e. a particular manner of speaking) and speech acts, to specific, articulated propositions. Along this path of what he calls the "sublimation trajectory", the degree of iconicity decreases. For example, there exist some subtle differences between doing a prostration or kneeling down and a "small voice" that accompanies the churchgoer's action; between talking like a fool and actually saying "I am a fool". From ritualization to verbalization, the degree of iconicity is reduced as the first-hand corporeal experience is replaced by words – corporeal experiences such as performing an action, seeing the action per-

Realities	+← Linguistic Style	+← Speech Acts	+← Propositional Language
Physical actions	Suprasegmental features	Performative verbs	Onomatopoetic words
Temporal/Spatial	Narrative tone	Illocutionary forces	Morphemes
	Typographical layout		Words evoking auditory, visual senses
	Punctuation showing emotion		Repetition
	Deviant spelling		Parallelism & symmetry
	Consistent choice of words showing connotative meanings		Word order Syntactic structure Sentence length

Figure 1. The dramatization trajectory (Tseng 2004a: 351)

formed, uttering one's thought or emotion with an attitude, hearing utterances. The concept of the sublimation trajectory is formed obviously from the viewpoint of textual *production*. I have expanded and modified Haiman's model by adding a list of linguistic features associated with iconicity and by seeing iconicity not only from the perspective of production but also from that of reception (Tseng 2004a). I call the process of tracing iconicity the "dramatization trajectory" (see figure 1) because identifying iconicity animates language just as the language of drama animates players and audience and creates vivid impressions – apparent realities – by its performance.

Because of the limitation of space, I can only briefly explain figure 1 and its implications. Propositional language refers to "the propositional content of what is said", including words, morphemes, and grammar. This is also the locutionary level of language. The concept of "speech act" is predicated on the view of language as utterances and draws our attention to the illocutionary force of language. Through performative verbs (e.g. "I *order* you to step forward") and the illocutionary force of an utterance, whether it is a sentence or a text, language is used to perform acts. This is a more dynamic form of iconicity than propositional language. The category "linguistic style" is also based on the view of seeing language as utterances. It refers to manners of speaking, i.e. the voice that conveys emotions and attitudes. In speech, one's voice is accompanied by suprasegmental features like stress and pitch, which can have a special vocal effect. In writing, punctuations (e.g. "??????" or "!!!!!!") and deviant spelling (e.g. "Peeeeerhaps") and a consistent choice of words can express tones of voice. Linguistic style is a more accentuated form of iconicity than speech act and can be subtly distinguished from speech act. For example, there is a difference between uttering something in a domineering voice and giving an order: the latter can be done in a non-domineering voice. Similarly, one can utter a threat in a non-threatening voice, or one can state "I am happy" in a voice that does not sound happy. Physical actions and bodily movements are vividly visible; therefore, they embody a higher degree of iconicity than speech.

Figure 1 has several implications. First of all, iconicity evinces the dynamism of language, transmitting verbal force that fuses words and world (see also Tseng 2004b). "The process of identifying iconicity amounts to seeing a series of transitions from a more static, arbitrary and symbolic mode of signification to a more dynamic, motivated, iconic mode of signification" (Tseng 2004a: 351). The arrow ← in figure 1 indicates the direction of the track from linguistic descriptions to realities depicted. The plus symbol + suggests the verbal force transmitted by iconicity in order to mirror reality. That is, by tracing iconicity, the reader sees language gradually charged with verbal force that affects the reader through not only propositional language but also speech acts and manners of speaking. Secondly, iconicity finds expression in various linguistic devices. Thirdly, iconicity is best seen as "accumulative homology", a mish-mash, a cocktail, a peppering of linguistic devices interacting and contributing to the overall effect.

Freeman's chapter on iconicity shows her awareness that metaphor and iconicity can co-occur. As she writes, the Malaria poem has an effect on readers "not simply by blending the ideas of writing and disease to create the metaphor of a word as infection, but by making this metaphor iconically represent ourselves as readers reading Dickinson's text and as a result inhaling the semblance of 'Despair.'" However, her analysis does not quite develop how metaphor and iconicity can be entwined perhaps because it is not the main concern of her article. Hiraga's (2005: 57–90) account of links between metaphor-iconicity is the most detailed treatment of the subject, but the main theoretical model that Freeman uses comes from Brandt and Brandt's (2005) cognitive-semiotic model of metaphor, which is not a model originally intended to deal with metaphor-iconicity links. Brandt and Brandt's model of metaphor still needs further clarification and development since the project of synthesizing blending theory and semiotics is too large in scale to be sufficiently treated in a paper. A few issues arising from this model remain underdeveloped. For example, where does the mind or the inter-subjective agent that processes and interprets discourse exist in Brandt and Brandt's model? On what principle is the "relevance space" derived? Is it a strength or drawback to separate the semiotic space from representation and reference as suggested in Brandt and Brandt model?

Steen's chapter on metaphor has attempted to make steps of metaphor identification as explicit as possible and, therefore, offers pedagogical potential for teaching how to locate metaphor in literature. Significantly, he spells out the mechanisms involved from linguistic cues through propositions and analogical structures to conceptual structures of metaphorical mappings. Nevertheless, it is equally important to ask whether metaphor identification whilst reading literature is really always a neat, clear-cut process of isolating the metaphorical from the literal. Literal and metaphorical meanings can be seen as on a continuum that involves a set of clines: between conventionality and unconventionality, approximate similarity and distant similarity, speaker's responsibility and addressee's responsibility, force aimed at stabilized meaning and force stretching meaning potential (Tseng 2006: 34–39).

Although Steen's chapter is only concerned with metaphor, his discussion of the metaphors in Lord Alfred Tennyson's "Now Sleeps the Crimson Petal" could have been enriched and reinforced by attending to the iconicity in the poem. According to Peirce (1960: 2.276–277), metaphor is a type of icon. It comes as no surprise that the metaphors that Steen has analyzed in the poem contain traces of iconicity. Take for example his analyzing the flower ("petal" and "lily") and the animal ("milk white peacock") as metaphors for a human – possibly the persona's beloved. He suggests that the mappings between the domain of nature and the human domain indicate the qualities of being inactive and tired. However, this metaphorical understanding is strengthened by the poem's consistent choice of verbs that suggest inertness and passiveness, e.g. "sleep", "droop", "lie", etc. The similarity shared by these verbs is a type of intralingual iconicity (Johansen 1996: 48–50). Moreover, the similarity within the language system is extended to something beyond language, and this type of intersemiotic similarity is also a type of iconicity (Johansen 1996: 49). Seeing the intralingual iconicity of these verbs and connecting it with the metaphorical mappings from nature to human – the persona's dearest – we almost automatically link the separate metaphors, thus heightening their coherence and intention. In addition, aware of how the language iconically and metaphorically represents the persona's beloved being in a state of inertness and passivity, we can better understand why the poem ends with the imperative: "So fold thyself, my dearest, thou, and slip/ Into my bosom and be lost in me". The metaphorical-iconic representation of someone being in a passive state paves the way for her being ordered to do what she is told. Another iconic quality manifested in the poem is the recurrent syntactic structure of adverb-verb-subject: "Now sleeps the crimson petal" (line 1); "Now droops the milk white peacock" (line 5); "Now lies the Earth all Danaë to the stars" (line 7); "Now slides the silent meteor on" (line 9); "Now folds the lily all her sweetness up" (line 11). This device of inverting the normal subject-verb order brings the temporal adverb and the action to the forefront and thus highlights the "now-action" theme of these lines. This syntactic pattern is foregrounded because it is used throughout the poem. Arguably, the theme of the syntactic pattern iconically mirrors the persona's perceptual world: time and action are more prominent than the agent or doer. The repeated uses of the word "now" point the reader to the present time and generate a feeling of being in an ever-present time-frame. The series of highlighted actions culminate with the fronting of the verb in the imperative: "So fold thyself, my dearest, thou [...]". These subtle iconic qualities are entwined with the metaphors in the poem. Therefore, they may well be considered with metaphor, especially in the context of expounding poetics. Indeed, I have argued elsewhere that iconicity functions to manifest the interplay between the literal and the metaphorical (Tseng 2006). Because it emerges partly from imagery evoked by the source domain or input space(s), iconicity can be said to contain traces of the literal. It is part of the literal narration since it contributes to the mimesis of a reality depicted by the text. Nevertheless, it is not just the literal since it conveys meanings more than the literal does. Besides, it coexists with metaphor in meaning creation.

Steen is clearly aware of some of the problems and limitations in his framework of identifying metaphor in five steps. For example, he mentions that certain issues are not fully addressed – such as mixed metaphor (i.e. using two metaphors in obvious conflict; e.g. "That wet blanket is a loose cannon") and embedded metaphor (i.e. using a verb or a noun in a non-literal fashion, e.g. "The white peacock *glimmers* on to me"). Other relevant issues that he has not mentioned include, for instance, whether two-domain mappings are always appropriate for identifying metaphor or many-space mappings are sometimes more appropriate (e.g. using

"The surgeon is a butcher" to mean "The surgeon is incompetent"; see Grady, Oakley and Coulson 1999: 103–104); whether the difficulty in making inferences in step 5 (Steen), i.e. cross-domain mappings, derives from innovative thinking that underlies some metaphors or whether the difficulty can be alleviated by recourse to conceptual metaphors; to what extent metaphors in literature rely on or challenge conceptual metaphors.

Reading the two chapters makes me ponder what insight cognitive linguistics has offered to poetics – a new methodology for analysis of literary discourse, a new perspective from which to see into textual production or reception, or/and a stimulus to make textual signification and interpretation explicit? From my reading of the two chapters, I believe at least it contributes to a better understanding of not just *what* literary texts mean but also *how* they mean. While Steen's and Freeman's chapters have their respective focus, reading them together would bring us deeper into the process of meaning-making and shed more light on the depth of cognitive poetics than if we read them separately.

References

Bhaya Nair, Rukmini, Ronald Carter and Michael Toolan
  1988   Clines of metaphoricity, and creative metaphors as situated risk-taking. *Journal of Literary Semantics* 17(1): 20–40.
Brandt, Line and Per Aage Brandt
  2005   Making sense of a blend: A cognitive-semiotic approach to metaphor. *Annual Review of Cognitive Linguistics* 3: 216–249.
Deacon, Terrence W.
  1997   *The Symbolic Species: The Co-Evolution of Language and the Brain.* New York: W. W. Norton.
Downes, William
  2000   The language of felt experience: emotional, evaluative and intuitive. *Language and Literature* 9(2): 99–121.
Fowler, Roger
  1981   *Literature as Social Discourse: The Practice of Linguistic Criticism.* London: Batsford Academic and Educational.
Grady, Joseph E., Todd Oakley and Seana Coulson
  1999   Blending and metaphor. In: Gerard J. Steen and Raymond W. Gibbs (eds.), *Metaphor in Cognitive Linguistics*, 101–124. Amsterdam/Philadelphia: John Benjamins.
Haiman, John
  1999   Action, speech, and grammar: the sublimation trajectory. In: Max Nänny and Olga Fischer (eds.), *Form Miming Meaning: Iconicity in Language and Literature*, 37–57. Amsterdam: John Benjamins.

Hiraga, Masako K.
  2005   *Metaphor and Iconicity: A Cognitive Approach to Analyzing Texts.* Basingstoke: Palgrave Macmillan.
Johansen, Jorgen Dines
  1996   Iconicity in literature. *Semiotica* 110(1–2): 37–55.
Lakoff, George and Mark Johnson
  1980   *Metaphors We Live By.* Chicago: Chicago University Press.
Langer, Suzanne K.
  1953   *Feeling and Form: A Theory of Art.* New York: Charles Scribner's.
Langer, Suzanne K.
  1967   *Mind: An Essay on Human Feeling.* Baltimore: Johns Hopkins Press.
McGreevy, Michael Wallace
  2005   Approaching experiential discourse iconicity from the field. *Text* 25(1): 67–105.
Merrell, Floyd
  2001   Properly minding the sign. *Journal of Literary Semantics* 30(2): 95–109.
Peirce, Charles Sanders
  1960   *Collected Papers,* 8 vols. Charles Hartshorne, Paul Weiss and Arthur W. Burks (eds.). Cambridge, Mass.: Harvard University Press.
Toolan, Michael
  1996   *Total Speech: An Integrational Linguistic Approach to Language.* Durham: Duke University Press.
Tseng, Ming-Yu
  2004a   A framework for tracing iconicity. *Semiotica* 149(1–4): 343–360.
Tseng, Ming-Yu
  2004b   Iconicity as power: examples from Wordsworth and Zen discourse. *Journal of Literary Semantics* 33(1): 1–23.
Tseng, Ming-Yu
  2006   Iconicity in the interplay of the literal and the metaphorical: An example from William Blake's *Jerusalem. Journal of Literary Semantics* 35(1): 31–57.

Metaphor and figure-ground relationship: comparisons from poetry, music, and the visual arts

Reuven Tsur

There was an old joke in Soviet Russia about a guard at the factory gate who at the end of every day saw a worker walking out with a wheelbarrow full of straw.[1] Every day he thoroughly searched the contents of the wheelbarrow, but never found anything but straw. One day he asked the worker: "What do you gain by taking home all that straw?" "The wheelbarrows". This paper is about the straw and the wheelbarrow, about shifting attention from figure to ground or, rather, about turning into figure what is usually perceived as ground. We are used to think of the load as "figure"; the wheelbarrow is only "ground", merely an instrument. Our default interest is in the act, not in the instrument.

1. Basic gestalt rules of figure-ground

One of Anton Ehrenzweig's central claims in his seminal book *The Psychoanalysis of Artistic Vision and Hearing* ([1953] 1965) is that the contents of works of art is best approached in terms of psychoanalytic theory, while artistic form is best approached in terms of gestalt theory. He has most illuminating things to say on these issues, both with reference to music and the visual arts. While I am not always convinced by his application of psychoanalysis to works of art, I find his discussions of gestalts and what he calls "gestalt-free" elements (discussed at the end of section 2) most compelling and illuminating.

Further, gestalt theory has been systematically applied to the visual arts by Rudolf Arnheim (1957), and to emotion and meaning in music by Leonard B. Meyer (1956). Cooper and Meyer (1960) applied it to the rhythmic structure of music. One of the earliest and perhaps the most im-

---

1. The sound files for this article are available online at
   http://www.tau.ac.il/~tsurxx/FigureGround/Figure-ground+mp3New.html

portant application of gestalt theory to literature is Barbara Herrnstein-Smith's mind-expanding book *Poetic Closure* (1968).

During the past two and a half decades I myself devoted much research to poetic prosody; I have found that many of the aesthetically most interesting issues regarding poetic rhythm, rhyme patterns and stanza form can be understood only through having recourse to gestalt theory (e.g., Tsur 1977, 1992: 111–179, 1998b, 2006: 115–141; Tsur et al. 1990, 1991). In the present paper, I will discuss the prosodic and syntactic elements in relation to only one excerpt, by Shakespeare (section 6); otherwise I will mostly explore figure-ground relationships in the projected, extralinguistic world.

What gestalt theorists call "figure-ground relationship" is one of the most interesting issues in gestalt theory, both from the perceptual and the artistic point of view. The *Fontana Dictionary of Modern Thought* provides the following definition:

> **figure-ground phenomenon.** The characteristic organization of perception into a figure that "stands out" against an undifferentiated background, e.g. a printed word against a background page. What is figural at any one moment depends on patterns of sensory stimulation and on the momentary interests of the perceiver. See also GESTALT.

Look, for instance, at figures 1a and b. In figure 1a the pattern of sensory stimulation allows to see either a goblet or two faces; the perceiver may alternate between seeing the black area as figure and the white area as ground, or vice versa. In the droodle presented in figure 1b, obviously, the four triangular shapes with the pairs of elliptical dots in them are the shapes; the white space between them is the ground. This configuration is reinforced by the caption. However, when one shifts attention to the white space in the middle, one will discover that it has the shape of a distinct "formée" cross, which has now become the figure, and relegates the triangular shapes to the background (see also Tsur 1994).

In this respect gestalt theorists discovered that some of the common-sense perceptual phenomena are not at all to be taken for granted as it would appear to the man in the street. They not only brought to attention a most interesting phenomenon, but also laid down rigorous rules of the perceptual organization processes that create figure-ground relationships. The better the shape, the more it tends to stand out as a figure and, less tautologically, there are rigorous principles that account for what makes a shape "better" or "worse". Indeed, we always try to experience things in "as good a gestalt way as possible".

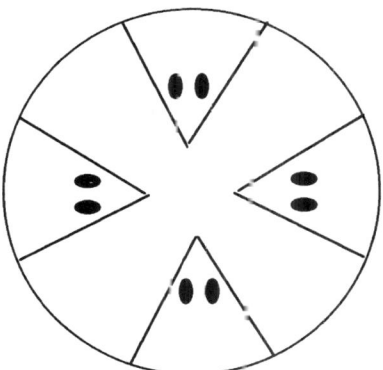

Figure 1a. You can either see a figure of a black goblet standing in front of a white ground, or you can see two white faces, looking at each other, in front of a black ground

Figure 1b. Four Ku Klux Klansmen looking down a well

Let us just hint briefly at the most important Gestalt laws by which the mind organizes perception into Figure and Ground. Hochberg (1964: 86) names the following: (A) **Area**. The smaller a closed region, the more it tends to be seen as figure. Thus, as the area of the white cross decreases in figure 2 from *a* to *b,* its tendency to be seen as figure increases. In figure 1a it is easier to see a black goblet against a continuous white ground than two faces against a black ground. (B) **Proximity**. Dots or objects that are close together tend to be grouped together into one figure. In figure 3 the more or less evenly distributed dots constitute the ground; the figure, the enlarged print of an eye, is generated by similar dots packed more closely together. This is, also, how TV and computer screens and printers as well as photo reproductions work. (C) **Closedness**. Areas with closed contours tend to be seen as figure more than do those with open contours. (D) **Symmetry**. The more symmetrical a closed region, the more it tends to be seen as figure. I have not specifically illustrated (C) and (D), but most of our examples in this paper illustrate them.

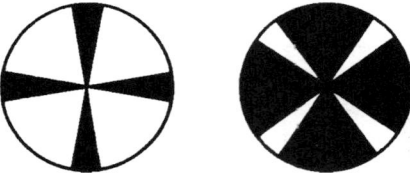

Figure 2. The 'Area' Gestalt law

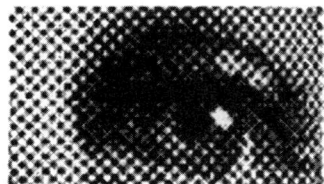

Figure 3. The 'Proximity' Gestalt law

(E) **Good continuation.** Importantly, perceptual preference is given to the figure-ground arrangements that will make the fewest changes or interruptions in straight or smoothly curving lines or contours. All three drawings in figure 4 contain the digit 4, but one can discern it only in *b* and *c.* In *c* the ground consists of lines curving as smoothly as possible, setting off the straight lines and segregating the shape of the digit 4. In *a* and *b* the straight lines of the digit are part of the same smoothly curving contour. However, figure *a* conceals the *4* in a larger and closed gestalt, whose entire contour consists of a single solid continuous line, whereas *b* sets off the straight solid lines of the digit from the dotted line in the rest of the figure.

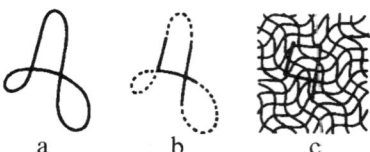

a   b   c

Figure 4. The 'Good continuation' Gestalt law

2. Figure and ground in the visual arts

For the study of art, one insight should be added to our basic set of rules.[2] "Shape may [...] be regarded as a kind of stylistic "mean" lying between the extremes of chaotic overdifferentiation and primordial homogeneity" (Meyer 1956: 161), where "primordial homogeneity" is a sort of "no-thingness", and "chaotic overdifferentiation" a kind of "too muchness". "Chaotic overdifferentiation" constitutes perceptual overload on the cognitive system, which alleviates this overload by dumping it into the background as an undifferentiated mass. Thus, good shapes tend to stand out as figures, whereas both "primordial homogeneity" and "chaotic overdifferentiation" tend to be relegated to ground. The minute curves with their changing directions in figure 4c may serve as a rudimentary example of overdifferentiation.

In figure 1b the "triangles" are well-differentiated closed shapes symmetrically distributed in the area; the pairs of dots further differentiate them. The caption reinforces our "interest" in them. The triangular areas are much smaller than the white space separating them. This space in the middle, however, yields a sufficiently symmetrical and closed shape to become figure when shifting attention to it. Once you discover this white cross, you find it difficult to suppress it. One key term for the perceptual distinction between figure and ground is, then, "relative differentiation". Both in music and the visual arts partially overlapping good shapes may blur each other so as to form an overdifferentiated (hence, lowly differentiated) background. Irregularly distributed lines and dots suggest chaotic overdifferentiation and make a rather poor shape; but, as we shall see soon, when they occur within the closed area of a shape, they render the shape more differentiated relative to other similar shapes and tend to shift it in the *figure* direction.

Such artists as M.C. Escher deliberately experiment with the figure-ground phenomenon in visual perception. Escher himself described the organizing principle of figure 6 (and similar drawings) as follows:

---

2. Other specific insights relevant for visual arts concern e.g. colour interaction in figure and ground: "The incisiveness of form, such as the comparative sharpness of its outline, or its pregnant shape, or the conflict or parallelism between superimposed or juxtaposed forms and so on, can be summed up as qualities of a "good" gestalt. We can summarize therefore that colour interaction between figure and ground stands in inverse proportion to the good gestalt of the figure" (Ehrenzweig 1970: 172).

In each case there are three stages to be distinguished. The first stage is the reverse of the final stage – that is, a white object on a black background as against a black object on a white background. The second stage is intermediary between the two, and is the true, complete division of the plane, in which the opposing elements are equal (Escher 1992: 164).

Three points in Escher's experiments are relevant to our problem. First, though according to gestalt theory the better the shape the more it is likely to be perceived as figure, sometimes the same shapes may serve as figure or as ground. Thus, additional differentiating devices seem to be at work. Second, the dots and lines on some shapes seem to serve as such "differentiating devices" that may turn them into figure (some of the fish have lines on one fin, and no lines on the other, which turns them half figure, half ground, emerging, as it were, "from nowhere"). In one instance in figure 5, one single dot within the area (indicating, as it were, the eye of the "bird") slightly shifts the shape in the direction of figure. Third, with very little conscious effort we can almost freely switch from one organization to another, sending figure shapes to the ground and vice versa. At the right end of figure 6, for instance, the eye oscillates between seeing the white patches as schematic fish or a continuous shapeless background to the black fish; at the left end, conversely, the black patches can be seen as schematic fish or a continuous background to differentiated white fish.

Intimately related to figure-ground perception are Anton Ehrenzweig's (1965) terms "thing-free", "gestalt-free", and "thing destruction". Ehrenzweig explores the various relationships between well-defined shapes ("prägnant gestalts") and gestalt-free, inarticulate "mannerisms" in painting and music. Taking a close look at a good wallpaper, says Ehrenzweig, we may see a series of similar, well-designed shapes, one beside the other. Looking at it from a distance, we will find the wallpaper gestalt-free, ambiguous (his Chapter II); we may project on it any shape. A good wallpaper passes unnoticed; nevertheless, it makes all the difference whether it is there or not. Similarly, in a painting, or even an etching, while we direct attention to the shapes of the picture, we subliminally perceive such gestalt-free elements as *chiaroschuro* effects, shades and lights, irregular brush strokes and scribblings. It is these elements that give the picture its particular depth, its plastic quality. It is not impossible to imitate the shapes drawn by a great master – but imitating them will only prove that what gives them their peculiar character are precisely the barely noticed irregular strokes so difficult to imitate.

Figure 5. Escher: Liberation

Gestalt-free elements are frequently created by the superimposition of well-defined shapes, which sometimes "blend" so successfully that it takes a great conscious effort to tell them apart and contemplate them in isolation. When the artist dissects "the thing shapes around him [...] into arbitrary fragments and rejoins them into irrational form fantasies" (143), Ehrenzweig speaks of "thing-destruction" and "thing-free qualities". Both in music and painting the combination of gestalts and gestalt-free qualities typically underlie the figure-ground phenomenon. In music the tones and melodies are the things and gestalts. The *quality* of the tone is created by subliminally perceived irregular sounds, or repressed overtones. Both in painting and music, an increase of "depth", "thickness", "plastic quality", reinforcements of gestalts can be noticed with the increase of the gestalt-free elements, with the increase of their irregularity – up to a certain point of greatest "saturation"; this passed, the gestalt-free elements begin to draw conscious attention and give way to completely different qualities.

According to Ehrenzweig, and anticipating our next section on music, what distinguishes great masters of the violin is precisely this large, unnoticeable amount of irregular vibratos and glissandos. With salon musicians and second-rate singers the glissandos and vibratos become consciously audible – which is why some people feel them so "cheap", sentimental. In true polyphony, the superimposition of various melodies creates sustained passages of inarticulate (gestalt-free) structures. Thus, polyphony as thing-free hearing is comparable with the painter's thing-free vision (Chapter V).

Another quality of the tone, its colour, is determined by its *overtones*:

> [W]e usually hear a single tone, the fundamental. The others are "repressed" and replaced by the experience of tone colour which is projected onto the audible fundamental [...]. Without tone colour fusion we would have to analyse the complex and often confusingly similar composition of overtone chords, in order to infer the substance of sounding things and identify them. Hence, a conscious overtone perception would be biologically less serviceable (p. 154).

Harmonious fusion of tones consists in the mingling of the overtones of various tones, thus creating a *thing-free quality*, that is, a "mixture" of overtones to which no tone corresponds. Ehrenzweig quotes Arnold Schönberg, who contends in his book on harmony that many composers are in a continuous chase after the still unheard overtone.

In poetry, as we shall see, thing-free and gestalt-free qualities are typically generated by the connotations of words, or when abstract nouns are associated with space perception, or when attributes are transformed into abstract nouns and manipulated into the referring position: "*Brightness* falls from the air", "The *gentleness* of heaven broods o'r the sea" or "This city now doth like a garment wear / The *beauty* of the morning".

3. Form in other senses

Although figure-ground organization is not restricted to visual perception, its application in other domains is not always straightforward. As to the nature of the ground, for instance, there seems to be a crucial difference between the visual and the other modes of perception. Meyer writes: "It is difficult, if not impossible, even to imagine a visual figure without also imagining the more continuous, homogeneous ground against which it appears. But in "aural space", in music, there is no given ground; there is no necessary, continuous stimulation, against which all figures must be perceived" (1956: 186).

> Due to the absence of a necessary, given ground in aural experience, the mind of the listener is able to organize the data presented to it by the senses in several different ways. The musical field can be perceived as containing (1) a single figure without any ground at all, as, for instance, in a piece for solo flute; (2) several figures without any ground, as in a polyphonic composition in which the several parts are clearly segregated and are equally, or almost equally, well shaped; (3) one or sometimes more than one figure accompanied by a ground, as in a typical homophonic texture of the eighteenth or nineteenth centuries; (4) a ground alone, as in the introduction to a musical work – a song, for instance – where the melody or figure is obviously still to come; or (5) a super-imposition of small motives which are similar but not exactly alike and which have little real independence of motion, as in so-called heterophonic textures (Meyer 1956: 186).[3]

In a series of brilliant experiments Al Bregman demonstrated the principles of gestalt grouping in the auditory mode. In his first example he demonstrated the principles of "Proximity" and "Area'. The sequence used consists of three high and three low tones, alternating high and low tones. When the cycle is played slowly, one can clearly hear the alternation of high and low tones. When it is played fast, one experiences two streams of sound, one formed of high tones, the other of low ones, each with its own melody, as if two instruments, a high and a low one, were playing along together. When the sequence is played fast, the Law of Proximity works in two ways: the tones are "nearer" together in time than in the slow version; and the higher tones are "nearer" to each other in pitch than

---

3. Meyer's use of the term "ground" refers to gestalt theory. It should be noted that in music theory this term has a technically defined, somewhat different sense. This difference of senses may be one source of the disagreement reported below between Harai Golomb and myself.

to the lower ones. Consequently, they organize themselves into two segregated but concurrent figures, each in its own register.

Listen online to the demo experiment on the author's website:

Al Bregman's Demo CD	Explanation of Example	Go straight to Sound file 01	Sound file 01 amplified

In his works for unaccompanied cello and violin Bach experimented with exploiting the gestalt rules of perception and figure-ground relationships thus generating polyphonic music on a single string instrument. When we say that two melodic lines occur *at the same time,* much depends on how long is *the same time,* that is, much depends on the duration of what we construct as the "immediate present". How does Bach fool the listener into thinking that he hears more than one line at a time? In respect of poetic prosody I have argued that the span of "the same time" is determined by the span of short-term memory. That might apply to Bach's music too.

Music Excerpt 1
Listen online to an excerpt from Menuet I from Bach's Unaccompanied Violin Partita No. 3 in E major.

Music Excerpt 2
Listen online to an excerpt from Fuga alla breve from Bach's Unaccompanied Violin Sonata No. 3 in C major.

Music Excerpt 3
Listen online to an excerpt from Menuett from Bach's Unaccompanied Cello Suite No. 2 in D minor.

To impute unity on his different melodic lines, Bach relies on the gestalt principles of **proximity** (generating harmony and counterpoint by way of restricting each melody to its own discrete register) and **good continuation** within each register (or pitch range). He suggests simultaneity of the separate melodic lines by sounding successive fragments of each melody in alternation with the other, within the constraints of short-term memory and the gestalt rules of grouping. In this way he generates in Excerpts 1 and 3 a melodic line plus a background texture. In Excerpt 2 he accomplishes the feat of a fugue on a single string instrument, in which the melodic line in the second voice appropriately begins in the middle of the melody in the first voice. Technically, this works as follows. The melody of the fugue sounds something like **taa–TAM–tataRAMpampam**; and so forth. The two long notes **taa–TAM–** are simple enough to be played simultaneously with a more complex, faster melody (**tataRAMpampam**) in the other register. At the same time, it is grouped into a single figure with the ensuing **tataRAMpampam** section in its own register, which, in turn, coincides – according to the rules of the fugue – with the two long notes in the other register.[4]

4. Figures in narrative

In narrative the figure-ground phenomenon is not at all easy to track; and sometimes, as in music, the absence of a ground implies the absence of the whole phenomenon. Nonetheless, credit is due to the sociolinguist William Labov (1972) for his ingenious attempt to put this notion to use with reference to narratives. He pointed out that certain grammatical forms tend to relegate descriptions to a static ground, while some other grammatical forms tend to "foreground" the action of the narrative, which is the perceptual figure. One of the sad results of Labov's technique – for which he certainly cannot be blamed – is that quite a few linguists and literary critics who ignore the gestaltist origin of these notions "diagnose" figure and ground in a text by applying Labov's grammatical categories quite mechanically. Labov's own practice is far from "labelling"; it is, indeed, highly functional, using linguistic categories to trace the transformation of experience into story grammar showing how language can organize experience-in-time as figures and ground. Very much in harmony with common sense and intuition, he pointed out (in the stories he collected in Harlem on a "memorable fight") that certain grammatical forms tend to foreground information as figure, and some tend to relegate

----

4. More generally, Ehrenzweig writes: "To the extent to which a musical note is fitted into a clean melodic "line" it is prevented from fusing into harmonic tone "colour"; conversely a strong chord will temporarily fuse the loose strands of polyphony into solid tone colour so that the separate melodic lines disappear altogether. I have mentioned that the ear constantly oscillates between the harmonic fusion and polyphonic separation of the melodic lines; this conflict between "form" and "colour" belongs to the very life of music. A harmonically too luscious piece will soon lose its impact if it is not poised against a tough polyphonic structure" (1970: 173).

Figure 6. Escher: Woodcut II, strip 3

it into the ground.[5] But this is a relative matter, and poets may turn the distinctions backside forward. At any rate, labelling objects as "agents" or "instruments" in isolation has nothing to do with the issue. The Cognitive Linguist Ronald Langacker, by contrast, explicitly acknowledges the gestaltist origins of the figure-ground notion. As will be seen, his conceptions are very similar to the ones expounded in the present article (Langacker 1987: 120, 1990: 75) although, again, when they were applied to poetics by others, something went astray.

I have elsewhere discussed at considerable length the figure-ground relationship in a passage by Milton resulting from an interplay between prosodic and syntactic gestalts and gestalt-free elements in the "world stratum" of the work, in an attempt to account for what Ants Oras (1957) described as perceptual "depth" (Tsur 1977: 180–189, 1992: 85–92). In prosodic and syntactic structures too, good gestalts, strong shapes, tend to yield figures; where strong shapes blur each other or interact with gestalt-free qualities, they tend to blend in a ground.

5.   Figure and ground (?) in poetry: Emily Dickinson

In her 2000 paper, "Poetry and the scope of metaphor: Toward a cognitive theory of literature", Margaret H. Freeman discusses several poems by Emily Dickinson. In relation to one of them she discusses the nature of Time in language and poetry.

---

5. It would be worth one's effort to investigate, in a separate study, how the resulting mental images do or do not preserve the gestalt rules for visual perception.

How do we understand time? It is commonly understood in two ways, depending on figure-ground orientation. That is, we can perceive time as a figure with respect to some ground, as when we say "Time flies when we're having fun", where time is seen as passing quickly across some given funfilled space. Or we can perceive time as the ground for the figure, as when we say "The train arrived on time". Both these ways of looking at time come from a very general metaphor in our thought processes: the EVENT STRUCTURE metaphor. [...] (Freeman 2000: 266)

This is not quite accurate. While one can make out a reasonable case for detecting a figure-ground relationship in "Time flies when we're having fun", in "The train arrived on time" the arrival of the train does not occur against a ground of which "time" is a part. There is an essential discrepancy between the structure of language and the world's structure. One complex unitary event must be described by many juxtaposed words. The number of words or even the number of nouns in a clause does not reflect the number of entities referred to. If we say "The train arrived", we refer to a single event. Likewise, "The train arrived on time" refers to a single event without ground: "on time" merely specifies one aspect of the arrival. We could say, as well, "The train's arrival was marked by exact adherence to an appointed time", or "The train arrived punctually", or "The train was punctual". As we have seen in the case of the straw and the wheelbarrow, the factory guard (and the typical audience of the joke) may perceive, in certain circumstances, the instrument with which the action is performed as ground. But if we say, for instance, "He cut the tree with an axe", we are faced with a unitary event; "with an axe" merely provides more information on the one action. To such sentences, I would say, the figure-ground distinction is not applicable. But if we *must* use a figure-ground language, the appropriate notion will be: "the train's arrival on time", or "cutting the tree with an axe" is figure without ground just as, according to Leonard B. Meyer, sometimes the case may be in music too.

Freeman (2000: 267) goes on with her exposition:

For example, a very common metaphor for time is TIME IS A HEALER. This metaphor for time depends on the EVENT STRUCTURE metaphor which entails EVENTS ARE ACTIONS, which in turn entails TIME IS AN OBJECT. The EVENT STRUCTURE metaphor is shaped by the notion of causality, in which an agent is understood to bring about an event. Thus we say "Time heals all wounds". But Dickinson rejects this metaphor:

They say that "Time
assuages" –
Time never did assuage –
An actual suffering
strengthens
As sinews do – with Age –

Time is a Test of
Trouble –
But not a Remedy –
If such it prove, it
prove too
There was no Malady –

Fascicle 38, H 163, 942 (J 686)

Let us confine our attention to the following aspect of Freeman's discussion of time as an "EVENT STRUCTURE metaphor": "we can perceive time as a figure with respect to some ground [...] or we can perceive time as the ground for the figure". In harmony with our foregoing observations we might add that we can also perceive time as a figure with no ground at all.

Just like jokes or Escher's drawings, poetry produces forceful aesthetic effects by figure-ground reversal. But Freeman's illustration of this process is not unproblematic. She writes: "She [=Dickinson] rejects the idea of time as an agentive figure working against the ground of suffering and replaces it by reversing figure and ground. In the second part of the poem, it is suffering or "trouble" that is perceived as the figure against the ground of time". According to the present conception, however, suffering is not ground for time as an "agentive figure", but figure (without ground) in its own right: "An actual suffering strengthens with Age". Likewise, "Time is a Test of Trouble" is not ground, but figure without ground. "Time" is not presented against a ground that is a "Test of Trouble", but it is presented as "Time-as-a-Test-of-Trouble" – the many words describe several aspects of one referent. Thus, figure-ground reversal can hardly be attributed to Dickinson's poem.[6]

---

6. What is the difference between "Time is a Test of Trouble" and "Time-as-a-Test-of- Trouble"? In the former case it is asserted as true that being a Test of Trouble is attributed to Time; in the latter, the unitary entity is merely presented to contemplation, not asserted as something that has actually happened. In either case, being Time and being a Test of Trouble are not attributed to separate entities, but to one unitary referent.

Freeman founds her argument (personal communication of August 18th, 1998) upon the following assumption: "Time is a healer of wounds identifies Time as an agent; Time is a test of trouble identifies it [=time] as an instrument". According to the conception outlined above, there is no reason at all why an instrument should not be granted the status of a figure. The question is not whether Time is identified as an agent or an instrument, but what kind of attention it attracts. Consider, for instance, the following four sentences: "Time is a healer", "Time assuages", "Time is a Test of Trouble", and "Time is a Remedy". In all four cases Time is in the focus of our attention, while the various predicates attribute to it some kind (or degree) of activity.

What is more, in this poem a distinction between agent and instrument cannot be taken for granted either. Consider "Time is a healer" and "Time is a Remedy". Both sentences attribute to Time the same kind of activity: it heals; but "healer" is said to be an agent, whereas "Remedy" is an instrument. In fact, dictionaries define "healer" as "one who or that which heals" – that is, one can hardly tell whether the word suggests an agent or an instrument. "Time heals" expresses by a straightforward verb an activity that is expressed by nouns in the other two sentences; one cannot tell, however, whether it is an agent or an instrument; that is, whether it heals as a physician or as a remedy. What is more, "Time assuages" (which is after all the phrase used in the poem), may be perceived as "comforting, soothing, lessening pain" more as an ointment than as a person. Only one thing is certain: that in all these sentences, and especially where we have their cumulative effect in the poem, "Time" stands out as a figure; and I doubt that there is a ground there at all.

One of the most fruitful insights of Christine Brooke-Rose in her *A Grammar of Metaphor* is that noun metaphors are much more effective in conveying figurative activities than verb metaphors. "Whereas the noun is a complex of attributes, an action or attribute cannot be decomposed. Its full meaning depends on the noun with which it is used, and it can only be decomposed into species of itself, according to the noun with which it is associated: an elephant runs = runs heavily, a dancer runs = runs lightly" (Brooke-Rose 1958: 209). "All Genitive relationships are activity relationships", she says (149); "with *of* in other relationships, I have constantly stressed its verbal element" (Brooke-Rose 1958: 155). Applying her distinction to our poem, "Time is a Test of Trouble" suggests that it *tests* troubles, *i.e.* the clause attributes a straightforward activity to Time. Brooke-Rose gives additional examples from her (huge) corpus.

As I have suggested above, in the sentences "Time is a healer", "Time assuages", "Time is a Test of Trouble", and "Time is a Remedy" the verb predicate and the various kinds of noun predicates alike attribute some straightforward activity to Time, and present it as figure in the focus of attention. We cannot know from the text in what way Time tests troubles: whether it actively puts troubles to a test, or merely turns blue in bases and red in acids as the litmus paper. Nor can we know whether troubles are static as alkaline solutions and acids to be tested by some "litmus paper", or are more active. One thing seems to be quite certain however: that the testing Time is the figure, and troubles are part of the unitary testing process. Our attention is focused on Time. In Emily Dickinson's poem, "reified" Time is perceived as a figure, whether as an agent or an instrument. Most likely, I suggested, the figure-ground distinction is irrelevant here, because such clauses are experienced as a "single gestalt" (to use a pet phrase of Langacker's), and no labelling of isolated parts (Time as figure, Remedy as ground, or vice versa) can illuminate them in any way.

6.   Figure and ground (?) in Shakespeare

Peter Stockwell's book on Cognitive Poetics includes a chapter "Figures and Grounds" (Stockwell 2002: 13ff.). In what follows, I will reconsider one of his examples, said to be an application of Cognitive Linguistics. In order to proceed in Stockwell's own terms, I have extracted from his chapter four criteria for perceiving some part of the perceptual field as "figure":

1. A literary text uses stylistic patterns to focus attention on a particular feature, within the textual space. [...] In textual terms, [...] "newness" is the key to attention (18).
2. The most obvious correspondence of the phenomenon of figure and ground is in the literary critical notion of foregrounding. [...] Foregrounding within the text can be achieved by a variety of devices, such as repetition, unusual naming, innovative descriptions, creative syntactic ordering, puns, rhyme, alliteration, metrical emphasis, the use of creative metaphor, and so on. All of these can be seen as deviations from the expected or ordinary use of language that draw attention to an element, foregrounding it against the relief of the rest of the features of the text (14).

3. In other words, attention is paid to objects which are presented in topic position (first) in sentences, or have focus, emphasis, focalisation or viewpoint attached to them (19).

4. Locative expressions [...] are expressed with prepositions that can be understood as image schemas. [...] The image schemas underlying these prepositions all involve a dynamic movement, or at least a final resting position resulting from a movement [...]. For example, the title of Kesey's novel has a moving figure ("One") which can be pictured as moving from a position to the left of the ground ("the Cuckoo's Nest"), to a position above it, to end up at a position to the right of it. In this OVER image schema, the moving figure can be seen to follow a path above the ground. Within the image schema, though, the element that is the figure is called the trajector and the element it has a grounded relationship with is called the landmark (16).

Now consider the following passage.

Puck: How now, spirit! whither wander you?
Fairy: Over hill, over dale,
    Thorough bush, thorough briar,
    Over park, over pale,
    Thorough flood, thorough fire,
    I do wander everywhere
    Swifter than the moone's sphere ...
(*A Midsummer Night's Dream*, William Shakespeare)

Figure or not, intuitively the Fairy's first four lines are exceptionally foregrounded. If we look at the first three criteria for perceiving some part of the perceptual field as figure, it will be evident why. According to the second criterion, foregrounding within the text can be achieved, among other things, by repetition, rhyme, alliteration, or metrical emphasis. Consider the anaphora in this passage. Such a repetition can certainly be seen as a deviation from the expected or ordinary use of language. It consists of the repetition of two prepositions, *over* and *thorough*, used four times each. This repetition certainly affects foregrounding. Moreover, since the pairs of prepositional phrases introduced by "over" alternate with those introduced by "thorough", one perceives a higher-level repetition pattern too. Semantically, the nouns governed by the prepositions are also perceived as repetitions, on a higher level of abstraction: all of them denote some space in nature, and suggest some opposition and difficulty to get through. In each line there are two roughly equal prepositional phrases, lending to the line a symmetrical organization. This symmetry is reinforced by another repetitive scheme, alliteration. In the first line, the two nouns end with the same speech sound: *hill–dale*. In the rest of the lines, each pair of nouns begins with the same speech sound: *bush–briar, park–pale; flood–fire*. Thanks to the nouns' place in the line, the alliterations reinforce symmetry and parallelism.

In harmony with criterion 3, the eight adverbials of place are topicalized – they are dislocated from after the verb to the beginning of the sentence; they are brought into focus. This device is closely related to the one mentioned in criterion 1. The question "How now, spirit! whither wander you" mentions the agent ("trajector") and the fact that she is moving in space, but the adverb *whither* focuses attention on the scene or destination of the motion, which will be the new information in the answer.

I have suggested that these four lines are perceived as exceptionally prominent, are forced on the reader's or listener's attention; and that such perception can be accounted for by the first three of those criteria. Stockwell, by contrast, quotes the first five lines of the fairy's answer as a good example of the fourth criterion, and suggests that the moving person is the figure and the places enumerated are the ground: "Trajector (I, the speaker Puck [*sic*]) takes a path flying above the landmark (hill, dale, park, pale)" (17).

In view of my foregoing discussion, this is a rather mechanical application of two notions: that scenery is typically perceived as ground; and that image schemas underlying some prepositions all involve a dynamic movement which, in turn, is perceived as figure. Suppose that instead of writing a poetic drama, Shakespeare made a silent movie. In this case, quite plausibly, the flying shape of the fairy would be perceived as figure, the hills and dales etc. as ground. But, as Stockwell writes, "a literary text uses stylistic patterns to focus attention on a particular feature, within the textual space". In the passage under discussion the stylistic patterns focus attention on the adverbials of place in the first four lines, not on the agent. Stockwell seems to have rechristened the well-worn terms "foregrounding" and "deviations from the expected or ordinary use of language" as "figure-ground relationship", to make them conform with cognitive theory. In his text analysis, however, "foregrounding" applies, while a "figure-ground relationship" is not necessarily to be found. In fact, I strongly suspect that there is no ground to be found here, even though there are differences of relative emphasis. Indeed, what Stockwell rules as "ground" happens to be the most emphatic part of the fragment under analysis.

As said, Stockwell does not mention prosodic organization, which further flaws his analysis, since the gestalt laws of perception noticeably affect the fragment and significantly contribute to poetic effects. The first four lines have an alternating pattern of rhymes; the next two lines form a couplet. Both patterns yield strong, symmetrical gestalts. But according to the gestalt law of Proximity, the latter yields a stronger gestalt than the former, capturing the reader's or listener's attention (which is a typical figure-making feature of the text). The focusing effect of the transition from quatrain to couplet ought to be reinforced by the fact that the first four lines describe landscapes (which are prone to be perceived as ground), whereas the ensuing lines describe actions (frequently perceived as figures). And nevertheless, when examining the transition from the quatrain to the sequence of couplets, one must notice a most unexpected experience, a transition from a more focused kind of attention to a more relaxed kind, rather than vice versa.

One reason for this is, certainly, that the stylistic devices we have discerned in the quatrain are absent from the sequence of couplets. Moreover, the devices mentioned interact with some prosodic devices. The iambic and trochaic tetrameters have a very compelling, symmetrical shape. Let me spell out this prosodic structure:

Óver hill, Ø / óver dále,
s w   s   w s w s

Thorough búsh, Ø / thorough bríar,
  s   w   s   w   s   w   s w

Óver párk, Ø / óver pále,
s   w   s   w s w s

Thorough flóod, Ø / thorough fíre,
  s   w   s   w   s   w   sw

I do wánder / éverywhere
s w s   w   s   w   s

Swífter than the / móone's sphére ...
  s   w   s   w   s   w   s

In this example linguistic patterns and versification patterns are marked independently and then mapped on each other. The alternating s and w letters under the verse lines mark the regularly alternating metric strong and weak positions. The character Ø in the middle of the first four lines marks an unoccupied weak position. The accents on certain vowels mark lexical stress. In this verse instance, lexical stress occurs only in strong positions, but not in all strong positions. In the first four lines a lexical stress occurs in every third and seventh (strong) position, emphatically confirming the versification pattern. "Trochaic tetrameter" is a verse line in which an sw unit occurs four times (as in lines 2 and 4). The last w position may be dropped (as in lines 1, 3, 5–6). The trochaic tetrameter is divided into two symmetrical halves by a caesura exactly after the fourth (weak) position (marked by a slash). Caesura may be "confirmed" by a word ending or phrase ending; when it occurs in mid-word (or less critically in mid-phrase), it is "overridden", generating tension, or blurring the versification pattern. In the present instance, an unoccupied (weak) position at the caesura confirms it even more emphatically.

To let us feel the effect of the verse lines with unoccupied weak positions, I will corrupt for a moment Shakespeare's verse, so as to make it conform with the pattern from which the genuine lines deviate (occasional nonsense is inevitable):

Óver móuntain, óver dále,
s w   s   w   s w   s

Thorough bórder, thorough bríar,
  s w   s w   s w   sw

Óver párking, óver pále,
s w   s w   s w   s

Thorough flúid, thorough fíre,
  s w   sw   s w   sw

I do wánder éverywhere
s w s   w s w   s

Swífter than the móone's sphére ...
s w   s   w   s w   s

The symmetrical structure imputes an exceptionally obtrusive caesura after the fourth metrical position. The verbal structure may confirm this caesura, or may override it, generating tension or blurring the division. In the present instance, two parallel prepositional phrases occupy both sides of the caesura, reinforcing the symmetrical division. This symmetrical and well-articulated arrangement is reinforced, as we have seen, by alliteration. Both the symmetry of the segments and the articulation of the caesura are further enhanced by an unoccupied weak position, after the third position. Consequently, the line is segmented into two exceptionally well-articulated short segments. In the ensuing couplets, by contrast, no unoccupied position occurs. Syntactically, the linguistic units at the two sides of the caesura do not parallel, but complement each other, yielding a relatively long perceptual unit. What is more, in the line "Swifter than the / moone's sphere" the caesura occurs in mid-phrase, after the article "the", considerably blurring the symmetrical structure. According to the gestalt laws of organization presented at the beginning of this article, "the smaller a closed region, the more it tends to be seen as figure", *pace* Stockwell's assertion that one of the features that will, most likely, cause some part of a visual field or textual field to be seen as the figure is that "it will be [...] larger than the rest of the field that is then the ground" (15).[7] This may explain why the continuous lines of the couplets, as opposed to the symmetrically divided lines of the quatrain, are felt to relax rather than strengthen the focus of attention.

This passage has, nevertheless, one aspect of which Stockwell could make out a very convincing case, but he does not. The emphatically enumerated places might serve as the ground against which the fairy's flight would be perceived as "swift". The less penetrable the terrain, the more wondrous is the fairy's swiftness. The shorter the phrases, the swifter is their alternation. However, he stops short of even quoting the line that indicates speed (he ends his quotation with the word "everywhere"). Apparently, his task is to label everything before OVER "trajector"; everything after it – "landmark".

One might accuse me of being unfair to Stockwell, because he did not intend to exhaust the Shakespearean passage, merely illustrate the image schema. Furthermore, there may be many additional aspects that influence our final impression from the text, but the core meaning of the image schema is appropriately illustrated by this example. In a textbook the author must be brief. However, all the examples in Stockwell's section "Figure and Ground" illustrate only this image schema; moreover, a look at the other examples of this section suggests that even those that can be discussed very briefly distort the focus of perception in a like fashion. The

---

7. Cf. Langacker: "Figure/ground organization is not in general automatically determined for a given scene; it is normally possible to structure the same scene with alternate choices of figure. However, various factors do contribute to the naturalness and likelihood of a particular choice. A relatively compact region that contrasts sharply with its surroundings shows a strong tendency to be selected as the figure. Therefore, given a white dot in an otherwise black field, the dot is almost invariably chosen as the figure; only with difficulty can one interpret the scene as a black figure (with a hole in it) viewed against a white background" (1987: 120 and ensuing discussion).

image schema OVER cannot be used as a diagnostic tool of figure-ground relationship.

In Stockwell's "cognitive poetic analysis" of a wide range of works figure-ground relationships boil down, eventually, to labelling expressions as "trajector" and "landmark". I said above that he applies the terms figure-ground mechanically. What moves "over" is automatically ruled "trajector", what is under the wheels – automatically "landmark". These labels are not verified against some sort of human response. The noun governed by "over" is "landmark", therefore "ground", and there's an end on it. In the following quote, however, if one may judge from the title and syntactic structure, it is the dog who is in focus.

> it gets run over by a van
>
> ("Your Dog Dies", Raymond Carver)

"The trajector (van) crushes the landmark (your dog)", says Stockwell (2002: 17). However, the fact that he became flat and motionless relative to the moving car and is under its wheels does not change the fact that the dog is in focus. Grammatically, too, it does not say "a van ran over your dog", but chooses the passive voice, which manipulates the patient (your dog) into focus.[8]

A sympathetic reader made the following critical point concerning my analysis of "it gets run over by a van":

> The discussion of Trajector-Landmark configurations apart (i.e. Stockwell's vs. Langacker's options), in functional linguistics the principle of end-weight, or end-focus, is a well-established one. As such, "by a van" receives maximal attention in terms of new information and emphasis. It (the dog/trajector) remains as given information. In the active voice ("a van ran over your dog") it is the dog which is in focus, not the van. The van remains as backgrounded, given information.

---

8. Langacker (1990: 75) uses the terms "trajector" and "landmark" quite differently from Stockwell, much more in harmony with the conception propounded here: "The choice of trajector is not mechanically determined by a predication's content, but is rather one dimension of conventional imagery. Indeed, the asymmetry is observable even for expressions that designate a symmetrical relationship. Thus X resembles Y and Y resembles X are not semantically equivalent; in the former, Y (the landmark) is taken as a standard of reference for evaluating X (the trajector); in the latter these roles are reversed". Compare this to "A van ran over your dog" and "Your dog gets run over by a van".

This comment forced me to refine my argument, with reference to M.A.K. Halliday's (1970: 163) following distinction:

> Given and new thus differ from theme and rheme, though both are textual functions, in that "given" means "here is a point of contact with what you know" (and thus is not tied to elements in clause structure), whereas "theme" means "here is the heading to what I am saying".

Halliday calls the latter "psychological subject". In our description, then, "it (your dog)" is the "psychological subject", the "theme" (as opposed to "rheme"), the "heading to what the speaker is saying". If the figure-ground distinction is relevant at all to this line, then "figure" must be identified with the "psychological subject", the "theme", "the heading to what the speaker is saying" rather than with either the "given" or "new" information. In other words, in "it gets run over by a van" the all-important fact conveyed is that my dog is killed. The passive voice serves to highlight this all-important fact by manipulating it into the theme and relegating the instrument into the rheme. The new information, "by a van", fills in a hitherto unknown, relatively unimportant detail.

Or consider the following quote from Shelley:

> Thine azure sister of the spring shall blow
> Her clarion o'er the dreaming earth
> ("Ode to the West Wind", Percy Bysshe Shelley)

Again, "[t]rajector (from clarion blast) covers and pierces the landmark (earth)" – says Stockwell (2002). However, the spring shall blow her clarion not merely "o'er the earth" as suggested by Stockwell, but "o'er the dreaming earth". Earth is not merely the place over which the clarion will be blown, but an agent in its own right, who is to be woken up by its sound. After having rechristened figure-ground as "trajector" and "landmark", Stockwell goes on to talk about his examples in the latter terms, forgetting that he is supposed to talk about figure-ground relationship more generally. His terms, as we have seen, do not necessarily account for our perceptions of figure and ground in a poetic text. Moreover, revealing an "image schema" of dynamic movement in such prepositions as *over* is tautological in most instances. In most of the examples provided they are governed by such motion or action verbs as *wander, ran over, blow*. The dynamic movement exposed in the preposition is already expressed by the verb. This is very different from Christine Brooke-Rose's handling of the genitive link between two nouns.

To conclude, image schemata do not work wonders by themselves. One must, rather, adopt L.C. Knights' (1964: 229) position in a slightly different context: one must "admit that all the work remains to be done in each particular case". But Stockwell, in his analyses, "applies rules" rather than respond to individual poetic qualities. Thus, when Leonard B. Meyer says that unlike in visual perception, in music one may have figure without ground, I strongly suspect that this is the case in poetry too. In other words, I suspect that figure without ground contributes to a poetic quality which is not captured by Stockwell's conceptual apparatus. Stockwell's "cognitive poetic analysis" of Ted Hughes' poem shows similar problems, but space prevents me from demonstrating this.

7.   Figure-ground reversal in music: "Moonlight" Sonata

This section is devoted to the problematic (or flexible) relationship of figure and ground in music. I referred above to Ehrenzweig, according to whom taking a close look at a good wallpaper we may see a series of similar, well-designed shapes, one beside the other. Looking at it from a distance, we will find the wallpaper gestalt-free, ambiguous. The same applies, *mutatis mutandis*, to a series of similar, well-designed shapes, one after the other. All through the opening movement of Beethoven's "Moonlight" Sonata there is a series of obsessive rising sequences of three notes, as in music excerpt 4. In this section I will consider one such series which in one masterpiece serves as ground, in another as figure. We will also note that the performer may manipulate the listener's perception of figure-ground relationships.

In the course of writing this paper I compared a wide range of performances of Beethoven's Sonata. Eventually I decided to quote here two of them, of unequal fame, by Alfred Brendel and Dubravka Tomashevich, a student of Rubinstein's, because they illustrate most clearly the contrast which I want to bring out: that the performer has considerable control over presenting the triplets as ground or as figure.

Music Excerpt 4
Listen online to Alfred Brendel's performance of excerpt 4 (a), and Dubravka Tomashevich' performance (b).

Andante

Figure 7. The first two bars of the triplets in the Don Giovanni trio

Marcia Green drew my attention to a remarkable similarity between this passage and a passage in *Don Giovanni:* in the short trio of the three basses, Don Giovanni, Leporello and the dying Commandatore ("Ah, soccorso! son tradito!"), the orchestra plays exactly the same kind of repeated rising series of three notes. Here, however, it is deeply buried in the "ground", and even after repeated listenings I could only vaguely discern a dim um-pa-pa in the background, as in Music Excerpt 5.

Figure 8. The first four bars of the triplets in the Moonlight Sonata

Music Excerpt 5.
Listen online to the Don Giovanni trio in Klemperer's recording (a). Listen to the triplets at the beginning of the same when the midrange is overemphasized (b). Listen to a piano extract of the triplets alone, played by Mira Gal (c).

Green's suggestion (with which I disagree) is that this similarity indicates a personal relationship of the oedipal kind between Beethoven and Mozart. For me the most important part of the comparison is that Beethoven took a piece of ground music, that has a typical ground texture, and placed it in the focus of the sonata movement dominating for no less than six minutes the musical space. I had a long dialogue on this issue with Harai Golomb, professor of literary theory, theatre studies and musicology, who is certainly much more competent on music theory than me, and I could not reach the ensuing conclusions without his insightful help.

We agree that Beethoven did not "imitate" the triplets from Mozart, and that this similarity does not indicate any significant relationship between them, either as composers or as persons (as Green would have us think). So, what is the point in pointing out the similarity besides the sheer piquancy of the comparison? The juxtaposition of the two works foregrounds the different character of the two applications of the same technique. The similarity of Beethoven's triplets to Mozart's – which in the Mondschein Sonata, in contrast to Don Giovanni, are in the focus of the listener's attention – foregrounds the difference between them. Golomb agrees that there is in the sonata a distinct, monotonous, repeatedly rising ta-ta-ta sequence. This sequence is exceptionally boring from the rhythmical point of view, resembling the typical "ground" texture in the Don Giovanni excerpt, and many other works. At the same time, the magic of the movement is due, he says, to tensions and resolutions in the harmonic structure of the whole, both in the sequence of triplets and the interplay of the various simultaneous melodic threads. There are three simultaneous threads in this movement, in, roughly speaking, the high range, the midrange and the low range. The aforesaid triplets constitute the middle thread in this complex. There are the lower harmonic chords which, we both agree, generate a ground of tensions and resolutions, making a major contribution to the affective impact of the movement; and there is a higher sequence of longish notes which add up to a mildly rising and falling *melody,* which is the real figure of the movement. This melody, he says, though considerably diffuse, is more differentiated than the obstinately repeated ta-ta-ta series (as in Excerpt 6). In my opinion, both the middle and the high threads are figure, although there is, from time to time, a "dialogue" between the highest and the lowest thread, skipping, as it were, the middle thread. Now one thing appears to be certain. That this dialogue does not turn the lowest thread into figure; it remains ground relative to the other two threads.

Music Excerpt 6
Listen online to Alfred Brendel's performance of excerpt 6 (a), and Dubravka Tomashevich's performance (b).

In harmony with my argument in the present paper, I assume here, too, that figure-ground relationships are not determined once for all in all circumstances. As we have seen, "what is figural at any one moment depends on patterns of sensory stimulation and on the momentary interests of the perceiver". My point is that in the case of a musical performance, "the momentary interests of the perceiver" can be manipulated to a considerable extent by the performer, by rather evasive cues: in different performances different threads of the "patterns of sensory stimulation" may be foregrounded, by mild shifts of attention to and fro, as e.g , in the visual arts, in Escher's drawings. My own view of the passage may have been influenced to a considerable extent by Alfred Brendel's performance on Philips 438 730–2. In this performance, the middle thread is somewhat louder relative to the other threads than in some other performances. As a result, the higher thread (as well as its dialogue with the lower thread, when perceived) is perceived as an *intrusion* into the "figure", the middle thread. This intrusion, in turn, will increase the sequence's tendency to reassert its integrity – according to the gestalt assumption that a perceptual unit tends "to preserve its integrity by resisting interruptions". In this instance, the perception of figure-ground relationships can be further manipulated by the treatment of the longish notes of the highest thread. If their differentiation and connectedness into a melody is emphasized in the performance, they will attract attention as figure; if they are presented as more discrete notes, they will be perceived more as events intruding upon the rising sequences of three notes. My purpose here is not to offer a systematic comparative research of performances. What I want to emphasize is this: in Brendel's performance (more than in Tomashevich's), the high thread is perceived more as a series of irruptions than as a melodic line. This is due to two features of the performance. First, in 6a the second thread is louder relative to the other two threads than in 6b; and secondly, Brendel performs the higher thread in a peculiar way. Compare Excerpt 6a to 6b. In the higher thread, we hear twice a group of tam-ta-tam on the same note, followed by a slightly higher one. Owing to amplitude dynamics and Brendel's "pianists' touch", this higher note is perceived as exerting a greater effort to intrude rather than as contributing to a continuous melodic line. The result is monotonous and exceptionally dramatic at the same time.

It is illuminating to consider the amplitude dynamics of the two performances in this excerpt. Figures 9–10 show the plot of amplitude envelope of the first tam-ta-tam group in the two performances. The three notes are of equal pitch. But, in Brendel's performance, each one of them begins with a distinct obtrusion of the amplitude envelope. In Tomashevich's performance, by contrast, the first two notes slightly fluctuate at a low level, and are followed by a third note of disproportionately great amplitude. Add to this that though both performances are "overdotted", the

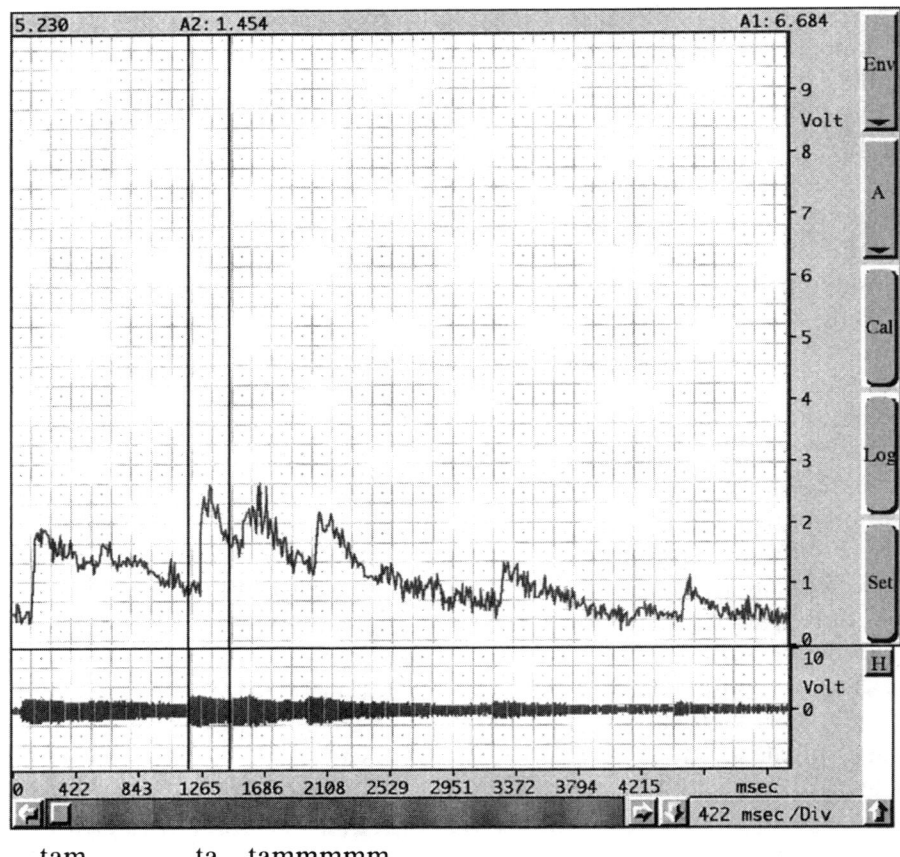

tam   ta   tammmmm

Figure 9. The envelope plot of music excerpt 6 in Brendel's performance

duration of the middle note in Tomashevich's performance is shorter: 273 msec, as opposed to Brendel's 296 msec. As a result, in Tomashevich's performance the first two notes are subordinated to the third one; the middle note is perceived more as a "passing note", leading forward to the third note. This tends to merge the three notes into one melodic line. In Brendel's performance, by contrast, the three notes are perceived as more discrete, have relatively greater perceptual separateness. The middle note is perceived not only as a note in its own right, but also as more grouped with the preceding one. Translating Lerdahl and Jackendoff's transformational terminology (1983) into plain English, backward grouping generates tension, forward grouping – relaxation.

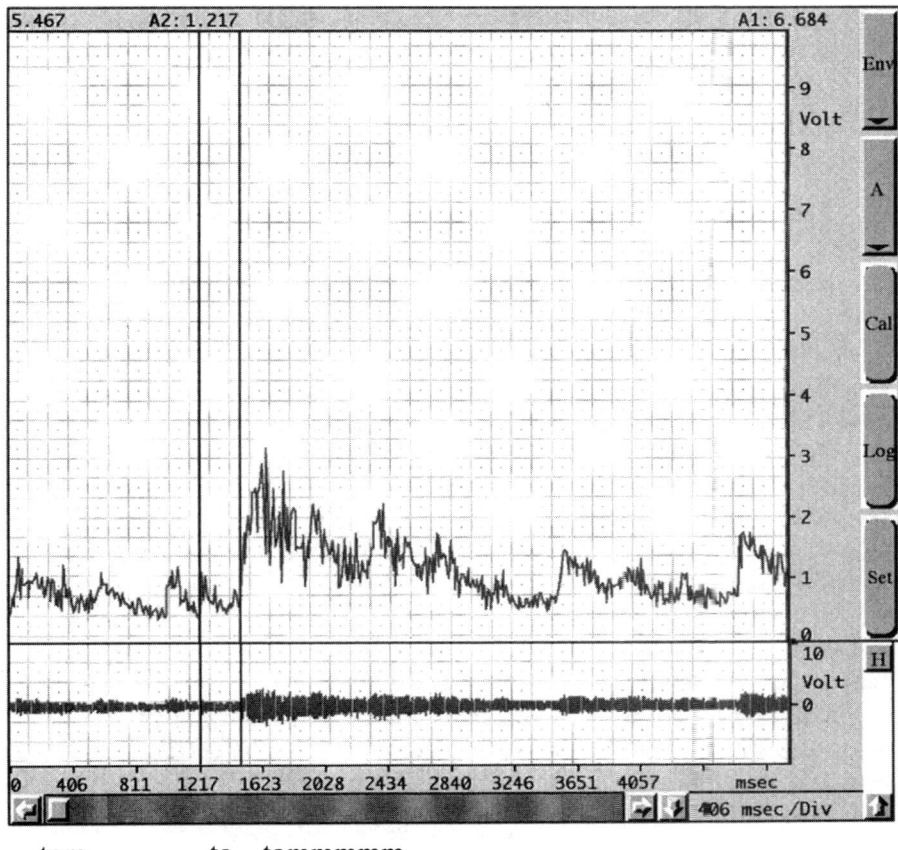

tam   ta tammmmm

Figure 10. The envelope plot of music excerpt 6 in Tomashevich's performance

    Julian Haylock, who wrote the music notes for the sonatas on Alfred Brendel's CD, suggested, quite impressionistically, what is the perceived effect of all this: "The opening *Adagio Sostenuto* [...] is quite unlike anything previously composed for the keyboard", and he speaks of "its dream-like texturing" which is in this case, certainly, the artistic purpose of promoting a typical background texture to the status of a figure or, at least, of causing it to dominate a full-length sonata movement. According to Meyer, as we have seen, "the musical field can be perceived as containing a ground alone, as in the introduction to a musical work – a song, for instance – where the melody or figure is obviously still to come" (1956: 186). It is the typical background texture pushed into the foreground throughout a full movement that is "quite unlike anything previously composed for the keyboard"; and this is also the basis for "its dream-like texturing" – reinforced by its interplay with the other two threads, as discussed above.

8.   Literature: figure-ground reversals of the extralinguistic

We have seen in Escher's drawings that they grant the perceiver considerable freedom to foreground certain shapes as figure or relegate them to an undifferentiated background. Such an "aspect switching" requires only minimal mental effort. Escher discusses at some length what kinds of shapes allow such flexibility of perception. He does not discuss the means by which he tilts the perceiver's inclination in one direction or the other. I have suggested that when the same closed area is repeated, lines or dots on it tend to bestow on it differentiation and induce us to perceive it as a figure; their absence, as ground. I have also suggested that the perceptual apparatus can easily overcome these "directive" means, by some conscious effort.

Likewise, in Beethoven's sonata the performer may manipulate the listener's perception of figure-ground relationships by connecting the notes of the higher thread into a perceptible melody, or leaving them as discontinuous, solitary events. Here the listener is more at the performer's mercy, and "aspect switching" requires greater mental effort.

In what follows, I will consider four literary texts that exploit this readiness of human perceivers to switch back and forth between figure and ground. All four texts achieve their effect by inducing readers to reverse figure-ground relationships relative to their habitual modes of thought or perception. As I insisted above, my examples, except the Shakespeare excerpt, do not concern figure-ground relationships generated by prosodic and syntactic structures (as I have done elsewhere)[9] but perceptions of, or attitudes toward, processes in extralinguistic reality. Consider the following poem by Shelley:

---

9. For instance: "An infringing stress obtrudes upon the integrity of the line which, in turn, strives to establish its shape in the reader's perception. In run-on lines, deviant stresses may exert themselves more freely, may interact with other Gestalt-free elements, blend into a Gestalt-free ground, or even soften those features that would, otherwise, count toward strong shape" (Tsur 1991: 245).

A Song

A widow bird sate mourning for her love
   Upon a wintry bough;
The frozen wind crept on above,
   The freezing stream below.

There was no leaf upon the forest bare,
   No flower upon the ground,
And little motion in the air
   Except the mill-wheel's sound.

In auditory perception, irregular noises (which constitute an overload on the cognitive system and most effectively violate the "Law of Good Continuation") are usually dumped into the background. But when Shelley ends his "Song" with these two lines, he turns into figure a percept that most commonly is dumped into the ground. And this is enormously effective here. I have elsewhere discussed this poem at some length. Here I will reproduce only part of my discussion of the last two lines. They have a rather complex function within the whole. *Little* as a part of the sequence "There is no ... No... And little..." suggests "none at all"; in this sense, "And little motion in the air" is one more item in the list of analogous items suggesting *deprivation.* In this sense, it seems to herald an unqualified statement that generates a psychological atmosphere of great certainty. In her book *Poetic Closure*, Herrnstein-Smith indeed claims that unqualified statements generate a psychological atmosphere of certainty, of conclusiveness. Consequently, they are particularly appropriate to serve as "poetic closure", to arouse a feeling that the poem is ended, not merely ceases to be.

The subsequent preposition *except,* however, makes a substantial qualification to this statement, substituting the "a very small amount" for total exclusion; that is, there is an exclusion from the total exclusion, an exception to nothingness: a mill-wheel's sound. The relation of the mill-wheel to its sound is like the relation of a thing to a thing-free quality. In the description, attention is directed away from the stable thing itself (the mill-wheel) to the thing-free sound. This perturbation of the air becomes another item in the list of items with reduced activity; by the same token, it foregrounds the presence of the air, a thing-free entity *par excellence* pervading the scene. The shift of "little" from the meaning "none at all" to "only a small amount", i.e. this qualification of the unqualified statement, performs a "poetic sabotage" against the determined, purposeful quality of the poetic closure, replacing the psychological atmosphere of great certainty with a psychological atmosphere of *un*certainty, contributing to the emotional quality of the poem. This emotional atmosphere has been generated by the abstraction of certain qualities from parallel concrete items in the description. Both the emotional quality and the poetic sabotage of closure are reinforced by another aspect of the mill-wheel's sound, which I wish to point out through an idea borrowed from Joseph Glicksohn. The mill-wheel's sound, being continuous noise (irregular both in rhythm and pitch), displays "chaotic overdifferentiation", and is typically dumped in the auditory ground. By forcing to the reader's attention a percept that typically serves as ground, the poem increases the emotional quality of the perception, and emphasizes that *there is no* figure to be contemplated, reinforcing the quality of deprivation. Thus, the poem ends with "a ground alone, as in the introduction to a musical work [...] where the melody or figure is obviously still to come" (Meyer 1956: 186). When it occurs at the end of a work, its lack of progress does not prepare for something to come as in the introduction to a musical work, but suggests some disintegration: the poem does not *end,* it passes out of existence, fades away.

The next two examples can be regarded as displaying different degrees of one kind: reversals concerning time. Consider the following Sonnet by Sir Philip Sidney:

Leave me, O love which reachest but to dust;
And thou, my mind, aspire to higher things;
Grow rich in that which never taketh rust,
Whatever fades but fading pleasure brings.
Draw in thy beams, and humble all thy might
To that sweet yoke where lasting freedoms be;
Which breaks the clouds and opens forth the light,
That doth both shine and give us sight to see.
O take fast hold; let that light be thy guide
In this small course which birth draws out to death,
And think how evil becometh him to slide,
Who seeketh heaven, and comes of heavenly breath.
    Then farewell, world; thy uttermost I see;
    Eternal Love, maintain thy life in me.

I have elsewhere discussed the light imagery of this sonnet at considerable length (Tsur 1998b, 2003: 320–328). Now I will devote attention to the third quatrain.

Let us work out the internal logic of this image, in terms of mental habits and their manipulation by literary means. I will argue that the central device of this passage is a reversal of figure-ground relationship. But before discussing that, I wish to examine this passage in light of what Kenneth Burke calls "Scene-Act Ratio" and "Scene-Agent Ratio". In these Ratios "Scene" typically serves as ground to "Act" and "Agent", which are typically the figure. Burke proposed to analyse human motives and actions in terms of the "dramatic pentad": Act, Scene, Agency, Agent, Purpose.

> Using "scene" in the sense of setting, or background, and "act" in the sense of action, one could say that "the scene contains the act". And using "agents" in the sense of actors, or acters, one could say that "the scene contains the agents".
>
> And whereas comic and grotesque works may deliberately set these elements at odds with one another, audiences make allowance for such liberty, which reaffirms the same principle of consistency in its very violation. [. .] In any case, examining first the relation between scene and act, all we need note here is the principle whereby the scene is a fit "container" for the act, expressing in fixed properties the same quality that the action expresses in terms of development. (Burke 1962: 3)

In the case of Sidney's poem, the scene and the act define the nature of the agent as well as his purpose: the Soul *comes from* heavenly breath and *goes to* (seeketh) heaven; according to Burke, this is a way to say in spatial and temporal terms that the Soul is (in the present) of a heavenly essence ("temporization of the essence"). George Lakoff and his followers would speak here of the event structure metaphor PURPOSEFUL ACTION IS A JOURNEY; the purpose of the action is expressed, very much in Burke's spirit, by the place to which the journey leads. A more specific instantiation of this metaphor is LIFE IS A JOURNEY.[10]

In this poem, the purpose of the journey is presented by two different *ends:* "Who seeketh heaven, and comes of heavenly breath", and "In this small course which birth draws out to death". These two destinations have opposite implications. One presents "Life as full of meaning"; the other presents "Life as totally meaningless". There is all the difference if "this small course" leads to the grave or to heaven.

---

10. It is quite characteristical of the present critical vogue that referees of my papers frequently suggest that in some place or other I might mention Lakoff's work; but so far they have never suggested Burke.

Particular occasions of birth and death in everyday life are perceived as figures, and life only as ground, at best. But when we speak of Human Life, *Life* becomes the figure, only marked at its extremes by birth and death, which thus become ground. In Christian religious traditions Life is only a transient episode for the soul which "seeketh heaven, and comes of heavenly breath". Religious rhetoric frequently attempts to bring man to an *insight* into this truth by using paradoxical epigrammatic phrasings (such as "Whosoever will save his life shall lose it" – Mark 8.35). Religious poetry may attempt to do this by a sudden shift of attention from the habitual *figure* to its *ground,* the markers of its extremes: Sidney gently manipulates attention from "this small course" to "birth" and "death", which are only meant to mark the extremes of life.[11]

Now notice that purpose is not absent from the image; it is only translated into a different visual terminology.

> let that light be thy guide
> In this small course which birth draws out to death,

In my paper on the cognitive structure of light imagery in religious poetry I discussed this poem at great length. I pointed out a wide range of meaning potentials in the light image, many of which are exploited in this poem. *One* of them is related to Lakoff's conceptual metaphor KNOWING IS SEEING: Light gives instructions, shows the way. Another one is derived from the fact that the Light comes from an invisible and inaccessible source in the sky. Thus, these two lines do not express life's purpose by a place that serves as the destination of the journey; but this purpose is re-

---

11. The changing relationship between shapes and their edges as figure-ground relationship is well brought out by the following two locutions concerning geographic configurations: with reference to the US, the phrases Western Coast and Eastern Coast foreground the dry land between them as figure, the water being part of the ground; with reference to the Middle East, the phrases Eastern Bank and Western Bank foreground the water between them as figure, the dry land being part of the ground. For political reasons, the dry land of "The Western Bank" has now become figure in its own right.
   This also follows from the gestalt principle of Area mentioned above: the smaller a region, the more it tends to be seen as figure. Indeed, the river Jordan between the two banks is a mere "thin line", between two areas of vast land beyond the banks. In America, by contrast, the vast lang between the coasts is a relativeley small area as compared to the two Oceans beyond them.

introduced by another conventional metaphor: light as knowing, understanding, or proper guidance.

My second illustration, a quotation from Beckett's *Waiting for Godot*, brings this same figure-ground reversal to an absurd extreme:

> Astride of a grave and a difficult birth. Down in the hole, lingeringly, the gravedigger puts on the forceps.

The tramp Vladimir sharpens Sidney's inverted image to absurdity: Man passes straight from the womb to the tomb, assisted by the gravedigger's forceps. In a world in which "God is dead", there is nothing beyond, and what is in between is meaningless and negligible. The emotional disorientation aroused by this understanding is reinforced by the grotesque image, the typical effect of the grotesque being, as pointed out by Thomson (1972), "emotional disorientation". In our everyday perception, birth is the beginning of life; death its cessation. What matters is life itself. Both in Sidney's and Beckett's image the two extremes, birth and death, or the womb and the grave become the figure; what is between them (life!) serves only to connect them. And the shorter the connection, the more meaningless life becomes.

A similar and most interesting instance of figure-ground reversal is provided by the great Hebrew poet, Nathan Alterman, in his poem "I will yet come to your threshold with extinguished lips". In this poem the speaker expresses his hope that he will yet reach his beloved, in a state of exhaustion, though. The poem ends with the only thing he can still offer her:

> The silence in the heart between two beats –
> This silence
> Is yours.

This is a variation on the age-old poetic convention "My true love has my heart and I have his", in which "heart" stands for AFFECTION, LOVE. It is also a metonymy for LIFE. Love, life, affection dwell in the heart; the heart, in turn, is enclosed in the body. Heartbeats are minute, barely perceptible events; whereas the silence between the beats is even less perceptible. We are faced with the *innermost* emotional experiences. Consider the Scene-Act ratio *innermost–intimate*. They are intimately related the latter is derived from Latin *intimus* =innermost, superlative of (assumed) Old Latin *interus*. The Microsoft Word Thesaurus gives, among others, the following partial synonyms for *intimate*: "dear, inner, deep". Alterman's metaphor suggests something that is most minute and insignificant, but, at the same time, involves the innermost, most precious, deepest, most intimate feelings of the heart.

We are not aware that our heartbeats occur against a ground of silence; that we could not perceive beats if there were no periods of silence between them. The figure-ground reversal of Alterman's metaphor, relegating the beats to the ground, brings this to awareness. This generates conflicting emotional tendencies: a *witty* reversal foregrounding a *desperate* gesture. The reversal exposes the perceiving consciousness to an absence, a thing-free quality, instead of positive focused events to which the imagination can hold on. Typically, such lack of hold inspires the perceiver with awe and uncertainty; here this is overridden by the psychological atmosphere of certainty generated by the "ultimate" connotations characterized above as "innermost, most precious, deepest, most intimate", generating both an intense emotional quality and a powerful closure.

9.   Summary and wider perspectives

Figure-ground relationship is an important notion of gestalt theory. Theorists of the psychology of music and the visual arts made most significant use of it. In course of this paper we have encountered serious problems with the application of these notions in poetry criticism. The most important attempt to import this distinction to linguistics and literary theory is William Labov's. Unfortunately, some linguists and literary critics regard Labov's work as a model for technical exercises rather than a source of insights into some significant part-whole relationship. This paper made the point that such grammatical terms as "agent" or "instrument" are not foolproof diagnostic tools. Rather, figure-ground relationship is an important element of the way we organize reality in our awareness, including works of art. In my dealing with poetry I have focused attention on figure-ground relationships in extralinguistic reality rather than in the interaction between prosodic and syntactic structures, as I had done in my earlier work. I argued that poets may rely on our habitual figure-ground organizations in extralinguistic reality, and exploit our flexibility in shifting attention from one aspect to another so as to achieve certain poetic effects by inducing us to reverse the habitual figure-ground relationships. This flexibility has precedent in music and the visual arts. I have examined four examples from four literary masterpieces. An important concomitant of these readings was to demonstrate that in most instances one may not only identify these reversals in the text, but may also suggest their effects. In Sidney's poem and the excerpt from Beckett the resulting "message" could be paraphrased in a straightforward conceptual language. But this is quite misleading. What is important here is not so much the "message" conveyed, but the insight resulting from the shift of mental sets. In Shelley's poem, the conceptual "message" diminishes to a minimum, and the main effect of the reversal is an intense perceptual quality that can only be approximated by such descriptive terms as "uncertainty, purposelessness, dissolution, wasting away".

This may lead us to some wider stylistic perspectives. According to Ehrenzweig (1965), the irregular or endlessly-repeated "scribblings" that typically constitute ground both in visual and auditory perception are perceived subliminally, but render the figure fuller, more plastic. A good wallpaper in a room, he says, goes unnoticed; but it makes all the difference. Labov treats ground as a means for evaluating experience in storytelling. In the "Moonlight" Sonata it is the ground that gives the enormous dramatic accentuation to the endlessly-repeated rising triplets and the higher sequences of three notes of equal pitch. The present paper has been devoted to instances of auditory, visual and verbal art in which the normal figure-ground relationship is defamiliarized or even reversed.

In Western art and poetry there is a "witty" as well as a "high-serious", emotional tradition. Figure-ground manipulation, too, may have an emotional or witty effect. The examples from Escher, Sidney and Beckett may be considered as artistic devices generating a witty quality of some degree or other. In extreme cases the witty turn may cause a shock experienced as emotional disorientation. In Romantic poetry and music, by contrast, when exposed to ground texture usurping the place of figures, readers and listeners may detect some structural resemblance between such texture and emotional processes, experiencing it as an emotional quality.[12] This is

---

12. Ehrenzweig claims that students of the great masters of painting or the violin can imitate the visual or melodic figures they produce; it is their irregular, gestalt-free, subliminally perceived brush strokes or vibrati and glissandi "sandwiched" between the tones that they find hard to imitate. It is these irregular "scribblings", he says, that convey the unconscious contents of art. Ehrenzweig, however, does not tell us how these scribblings convey uncon-

what happens, I suggest, at the end of Shelley's "Song", and more force-fully, in the first movement of Beethoven's "Moonlight" Sonata. In Alter-man's poem, I suggested, both a witty and an emotional quality may be perceived; the reader may, perhaps, perceive these two aspects simulta-neously, or even switch between them at will.

One of the major functions of poetry is to yield heightened awareness. It may be the heightening of the awareness of the reality perceived, or of the cognitive mechanisms that enable us to perceive reality. The self-examination of cognitive mechanisms is still an investigation of reality; the investigation has merely lost its directness (cf. Pears 1971: 31). Escher's experimentation with figure and ground, for instance, yields a heightened awareness of our perceptual mechanisms.

Instances of figure-ground reversal, especially those that arouse emo-tional disorientation, may have an effect similar to mystic paradoxes. So, Steven T. Katz' words on mystic paradoxes may apply to some instances of figure-ground reversal too:

> Such linguistic ploys exist in many places throughout the world, usually con-nected with the conscious construction of paradoxes whose necessary violation of the laws of logic are intended to shock, even shatter, the standard epistemic security of "disciples", thereby allowing them to move to new and higher forms of insight/ knowledge. That is […], [the mystics] intend, among other things, to force the hearers of such propositions to consider who they are – to locate them-selves vis-a-vis normal versus transcendental "reality". (Katz 1992: 7–8, cf. Tsur 2003: 207–208)

This is the conspicuous purpose of the figure-ground reversal in Sidney's poem, though considerably mitigated by its conventionality. The same device in Beckett's play is intended to shock, even shatter, the standard epistemic security of the audience so as, by contrast, to make it painfully aware of the meaninglessness of the *Condition Humaine*. In the religious poem, disorientation is followed by reorientation; in the theatre of the ab-surd, by contrast, the basic assumption is that "God is dead", and there is no "transcendental 'reality'".

---

scious contents. So, I prefer to fall back on his notions of gestalt-free and thing-free qualities in which, I suggest, viewers and listeners may detect some structural resemblance to emotions.

References

Arnheim, Rudolf
1957   *Art and Visual Perception.* London: Faber & Faber.
Brooke-Rose, Christine
1958   *A Grammar of Metaphor.* London: Secker & Warburg.
Burke, Kenneth
1962   *A Grammar of Motives* and *A Rhetoric of Motives* (in one volume). Cleveland/New York: Meridian Books.
Cooper, Grosvenor W. and Leonard B. Meyer
1960   *The Rhythmic Structure of Music.* Chicago: Chicago University Press.
Ehrenzweig, Anton
[1953] 1965 *The Psychoanalysis of Artistic Vision and Hearing.* New York: Braziller.
Ehrenzweig, Anton
1970   *The Hidden Order of Art.* London: Paladin.
Escher, M.C.
1992   The Regular Division of the Plain. In: J.L. Locher (ed.), *M.C. Escher – His Life and Complete Graphic Work,* 155–172. New York: Harry N. Abrams Inc. Publishers.
Freeman, Margaret H.
2000   Poetry and the scope of metaphor: Toward a cognitive theory of literature. In: Antonio Barcelona (ed.), *Metaphor and Metonymy at the Crossroads,* 253–281. Berlin/New York: Mouton de Gruyter.
Halliday, M.A.K.
1970   Language Structure and Language Function. In: John Lyons (ed.), *New Horizons in Linguistics,* 140–165. Harmondsworth: Penguin Books.
Herrnstein-Smith, Barbara
1968   *Poetic Closure.* Chicago: Chicago University Press.
Hochberg, Julian E.
1964   *Perception.* Englewood Cliffs, N. J.: Prentice-Hall, Inc.
Katz, Steven T.
1992   Mystical Speech and Mystical Meaning. In: Steven T. Katz (ed.), *Mysticism and Language,* 3–41. New York: Oxford University Press.
Knights, L.C.
[1928] 1964 Notes on Comedy. In: E. Bentley (ed.), *The Importance of Scrutiny,* 227–237. New York: New York University Press.
Labov, William
1972   *Language in the Inner City: Studies in the Black English Vernacular.* Philadelphia: University of Pennsylvania Press.
Lakoff, George
1993   The Contemporary Theory of Metaphor. In: Andrew Ortony (ed.,) *Thought and Metaphor,* 202–251. Cambridge: Cambridge University Press.

Langacker, Ronald W.
  1987   *Foundations of Cognitive Grammar.* Stanford, Ca.: Stanford University Press.

Langacker, Ronald W.
  1990   *Concept, Image and Symbol.* Berlin/New York: Mouton de Gruyter.

Lerdahl, Fred and Ray Jackendoff
  1983   *A Generative Theory of Tonal Music.* Cambridge Mass.: MIT Press.

Meyer, Leonard B.
  1956   *Emotion and Meaning in Music.* Chicago: Chicago University Press.

Oras, Ants
  1957   Spenser and Milton: Some Parallels and Contrasts in the Handling of Sound. In: Northrop Frye (ed.), *Sound and Poetry,* 109–133. New York: English Institute Essays.

Pears, David
  1971   *Wittgenstein.* London: Fontana.

Stockwell, Peter
  2002   *Cognitive Poetics. An Introduction.* London/New York: Routledge.

Thomson, Philip
  1972   *The Grotesque.* London: Methuen.

Tsur, Reuven
  1977   *A Perception-Oriented Theory of Metre.* Tel Aviv: The Porter Institute for Poetics and Semiotics.

Tsur, Reuven
  1992   *Toward a Theory of Cognitive Poetics.* Amsterdam: Elsevier (North Holland) Science Publishers.

Tsur, Reuven
  1994   Droodles and Cognitive Poetics – Contribution to an Aesthetics of Disorientation. *Humor* 7: 55–70.

Tsur, Reuven
  1998a   Light, Fire, Prison: A Cognitive Analysis of Religious Imagery in Poetry. *PSYART: A Hyperlink Journal for the Psychological Study of the Arts,* article 980715. Available HTTP: http//www.clas.ufl.edu/ipsa/journal/articles/tsur02.htm.

Tsur, Reuven
  1998b   *Poetic Rhythm: Structure and Performance – An Empirical Study in Cognitive Poetics.* Bern: Peter Lang.

Tsur, Reuven
  2003   *On The Shore of Nothingness: Space, Rhythm, and Semantic Structure in Religious Poetry and its Mystic-Secular Counterpart – A Study in Cognitive Poetics.* Exeter: Imprint Academic.

Tsur, Reuven
  2006   *"Kubla Khan" – Poetic Structure, Hypnotic Quality and Cognitive Style: A Study in Mental, Vocal, and Critical Performance.* Amsterdam: John Benjamins.

Tsur, Reuven, Joseph Glicksohn and Chanita Goodblatt
 1990   Perceptual Organization, Absorption and Aesthetic Qualities of
         Poetry. In: László Halász (ed.), *Proceedings of the 11th International
         Congress on Empirical Aesthetics*, 301–304. Budapest: Institute for Psy-
         chology of the Hungarian Academy of Sciences.
Tsur, Reuven, Joseph Glicksohn and Chanita Goodblatt
 1991   Gestalt Qualities in Poetry and the Reader's Absorption Style. *Journal
         of Pragmatics* 16(5): 487–504.

Hiding in plain sight: figure-ground reversals in humour

Tony Veale

1. Introduction

The abstract to Reuven Tsur's paper promises a wide-ranging analysis of figure-ground organization in language and art by way of the great historical exponents of the phenomenon, and for the most part, this is precisely what Tsur delivers. By drawing on a wealth of examples, from Bach to Beckett, Tsur reminds us how deeply ingrained is the distinction between figure and ground in everything from wallpaper to Shakespearean sonnets. But Tsur's paper is more than a catalogue of pyrotechnical examples or an excuse for historical name-dropping, since he also surveys the underlying cognitive mechanisms to which the figure-ground distinction can apply itself, such as the system of embodied conceptual metaphors that cognitive linguists claim is central to human thought. Along the way, Tsur additionally reminds us, via Ehrenzweig, that to understand the figure-ground phenomenon in terms of psychological gestalts, one must also consider the role of "gestalt-free" elements that lend complex compositions their peculiar character. By evoking Ehrenzweig's notion of "thing-destruction", Tsur nicely captures the often wrenching effect of figure-ground reversal, in which one is forced to do psychological violence to a cognitive representation to achieve a creative effect. This disturbing effect is perhaps nowhere better experienced than in the comprehension of a good joke, since jokes often forego the subtlety of art in favour of an altogether more visceral and aggressive language-delivered blow.

In fact, Tsur begins his erudite tour of the figure-ground landscape with a joke. The tale is a classic one, amply demonstrating the use of figure-ground reversal as a production strategy in humour: a sly worker nightly pushes a wheelbarrow of straw past the watchful eye of a suspicious sentry, who believes the straw to be a convenient hiding place in which valuable products might be smuggled from his factory Of course, it is the wheelbarrow itself that is smuggled through the factory gates; our refusal to focus on this artefact, and bring it into the conceptual foreground where it might be logically scrutinized, means that we readily assume the same wheelbarrow is in use, night after night. In the terminology of Fauconnier and Turner (2002), we "integrate" the successive events of the joke so that the wheelbarrows of different nights become one and the same, and we fail to see the cumulative value of the worker's hoard. Because we, like the sentry, only recognize the failure of our assumptions at the very end, the joke deftly makes the sentry our representative in the narrative (for this reason, I have always preferred the version in which the wheelbarrow is full of fresh cow manure, as this heightens the visceral punch delivered by the joke: the sentry is not just fooled, but physically degraded by his suspicions). Whenever we comprehend a narrative, our critical faculties constantly play the role of such a sentry, applying intuitions about what is salient and important and what is not. Sometimes, as in humour, these intuitions are subverted by a wily jokester, prompting us to comb through worthless straw for a pay-off that lies elsewhere.

Tsur's article does an excellent job of surveying the poetic and artistic usages of the figure-ground relationship, showing how the focal point of a structure is sometimes just a distraction from its intended meaning. But with the exception of the opening joke, which establishes the background for his exploration in cognitive poetics, Tsur chooses not to foreground the humorous role of figure-ground structuring. This is a shame, because with humour our end-point is not a mild aesthetic frisson, but an altogether more obvious and well-timed cognitive punch. Since one can more easily tell when this punch is lacking, humour is the ideal laboratory in which to study the subtle workings of mechanisms like figure-ground reversal (henceforth, FGR). So if I might be allowed to perform an FGR of my own, this topic will form the main substance of my response to Tsur's article.

2.   Figure-ground reversal and humour

The most obvious uses of figure-ground reversal in humour, such as the wheelbarrow joke cited by Tsur, can give the impression that FGR is just one of many possible tactical ploys that can be used to generate humour, by allowing a jokester to turn the tables on the hapless reader and his in-narrative correspondent (e.g. the sentry). For instance, Attardo, Hempelmann, and Di Maio (2002) see FGR as just one of many (27 and counting) possible logical mechanisms that can be used to contrive a clash of interpretations. These logical mechanisms plug into a larger framework, called the GTVH (the General Theory of Verbal Humour), which serves as the vehicle through which each logical mechanism (or LM) is activated and textually deployed. To use the notions of wheelbarrow and straw from Tsur's Russian joke, Attardo Hempelmann, and Di Maio view the GTVH as the "cognitive wheelbarrow" in which humour is delivered from the initiator to the reader, and in which FGR becomes just one more kind of "logical straw" among many others. For example, another kind of logical straw for the GTVH wheelbarrow is the LM of false-analogy, as evident in the joke: "my brother always dreamed of being a tree-surgeon, but it wasn't to be; he would always faint at the sight of sap '. Humorous examples of false-analogy all start from a reasonable analogy (such as tree-surgeon = medical-surgeon, tree = patient) but stretch this analogy to draw unfounded conclusions (such as the idea that tree sap is as unsettling a sight as human blood). Resorting to an FGR on my own, one that I hope is not also a false-analogy, I will argue here that FGR is not the straw but the wheelbarrow itself. In other words, reorganization of the figure-ground profile of a narrative (or *re*-profiling) to alter its social dynamic is the general means whereby humorous effects are created.

Of course, the figure-ground distinction is everywhere in language. Whenever one topicalizes a sentence, as in "with the gun she shot him down", or uses the passive voice, as in "the apple was eaten by Snowwhite", one is subtly altering the figure-ground landscape to give more prominence to one idea over another. So at this point I must disagree with Tsur's assertion that "to such sentences [describing unitary events], I would say, the 'figure-ground' distinction is not applicable". The notion of figure and ground is inextricably bound into the linguistic notion of obliqueness, and one cannot linearize a set of ideas into a string of words without giving more precedence to some ideas over others Since precedence is a relative notion, I simply cannot buy into Tsur's notion of a "figure without a ground". To my ear, this is much like claiming the existence of a hypotenuse without a triangle.

Nonetheless, in the context of a joke, trivial considerations such as obliqueness rarely make an appreciable difference. To be funny, FGR must be used to deliver the appropriate cognitive punch to our sense of social order. Consider, for instance, the following exchange between the boxer, Muhammad Ali at his pugilistic and linguistic prime, and a female flight attendant. Though physically mismatched, she easily proves his verbal equal:

Flight attendant: Buckle your seat-belt, Mr. Ali, we're about to take off.
Muhammad Ali: Superman don't need no seat-belt!
Flight attendant: Superman don't need no airplane neither.

This exchange is an example of a humour-producing strategy that I and my colleagues Kurt Feyaerts and Geert Brône call humorous "trumping" (e.g., see Veale, Feyaerts and Brône 2006). Note how the stewardess does not actually disagree with Ali, but takes his assertion at face value and appears to accept it as true (as signalled by the dialectical use of "neither"). In doing so, she does not simply rebut Ali's assertion, but uses a corollary of his own argument to demonstrate the inherent stupidity underlying his egotistical posturing. The effect of the FGR is intensified by the mastery of its delivery, as demonstrated by the speed ("quick-wittedness") with which it is executed. By responding to a request concerning his seat-belt with an observation about Superman, Ali's conversational goal is clear: we are to understand Ali and Superman as being the same entity. This understanding is helped in large part by the reader's knowledge of Ali's public persona, and of his oft-trumpeted (though light-hearted) belief in his own superhuman prowess. The stewardess subverts this identification of Ali with Superman by taking the broader view, in effect saying "If you can fly like superman, why are you on my plane?". In other words, her understanding of the entity that Ali introduces into the dialogue (Superman), coupled with her understanding of the immediate context (airplanes and assisted flight) allows her to demonstrate what Feyaerts, Brône and myself (2006) call "hyper-understanding" in humour. Hyper-understanding trumps plain understanding every time, just as knowledge trumps opinion and insight trumps assertion.

3.   Hiding in plain sight

The FGR in the previous exchange is very subtle indeed, and occurs when the stewardess shifts the focus of the dialogue from the seat-belt (of the airplane) to the airplane itself. Indeed, this shift would hardly be noticeable if not for the dramatic social and inter-personal effect that it creates. This supports my earlier contention that humour is the ideal laboratory in which to study figure-ground distinctions, since, in a joke (as opposed to a poem, or a piece of music), such tiny movements can yield disproportionately large and obvious effects.

However, it is important to note what does not happen in the previous exchange: The stewardess' reply does not create an incongruity that must be resolved. Not only is her observation a logical extension of Ali's assertion, she overtly agrees with what he says (though not with the implication of what he says, namely, that he is superman). Her reply does not hinge on a misinterpretation of what has already been said; if anything, it represents a hyper-understanding, of both the Superman mythos and the context of being in an airplane. Neither does her reply require the listener to back-track and re-interpret an earlier utterance. Her reply does not introduce a new script, or conceptual frame, through which the preceding utterances must be re-interpreted. In fact, the stewardess does not introduce any new concepts with her response. The concept Superman is already an established referent in the dialogue, while the concept Airplane forms the very obvious (if unspoken) setting of the dialogue. Insofar as her response forms the "punch-line" of the humorous exchange, it is not markedly informative with respect to the previous utterances.

To summarize then, this exchange does not conform either to the incongruity-resolution view of humour (e.g., see Ritchie 1999 for a review), the forced-reinterpretation view (Suls 1972), the script-switching (Attardo, Hempelmann, and Di Maio 2002) or frame-shifting views (Coulson 2000) or even the marked-informativeness view (Gicra 1991). The stewardess simply re-uses what is plainly available in the narrative context to subvert the opposing goals of her interlocutor. Both have conflicting goals in a zero-sum game (to buckle or not to buckle a seat-belt), so her verbal victory is also a tangible victory insofar as she achieves her goal but her opponent does not achieve his.

Frame-shifting and script-switching occur whenever a narrative is viewed through a different conceptual prism, to yield a very different interpretation, such as when seduction is viewed as assault (or vice versa), rescue is viewed as unwanted interference, or drowning is viewed as a pleasure swim (as in the joke in which an Irishman falls into, and drowns in, a vat of Guinness beer, yet gets out twice before dying to use the toilet). No change of script or frame is discernible in the Ali dialogue: we never leave the frame of assisted-flight or shift to a different meaning of the term "Superman". Nonetheless, some *re-profiling* of the internal structure of the assisted-flight frame does take place, to temporally give more emphasis to the big picture ("airplane") than to the little details ("seatbelts"). In addition, a simple reformulation of known facts concerning Superman also takes place, but this reformulation also amounts to a simple FGR-based re-profiling of the Superman mythos rather than a jump to an alternate concept. The consensus fact that "Superman is capable of unassisted flight" is reformulated as "Superman does not need an airplane to fly". The latter is an obvious element of the Superman mythos, though one that is rarely foregrounded. But in doing so, we obtain one further reformulation, "Someone who needs assisted flight cannot be Superman". Of course, the stewardess states neither of these facts explicitly. To do so would be as unfunny as to say "but you're not superman". Rather, because these facts are hiding in plain sight, much like the clues in a whodunit story, we are left to work out the conclusion – that Ali is no Superman – for ourselves.

4.   The social dimension of FGR

Tsur concludes his discussion by noting that "what is important here is not the 'message' that is conveyed, but the insight resulting from the shift of mental sets". He thus takes the sensible position of (implicitly) dividing figure-ground-reversals into those that yield cognitively interesting insights, and those that do not. In Tsur's wheelbarrow joke, for example, the message concerns the actions of a specific sentry, but the insight is a more general one, namely "things are not always as they seem". One can argue, as I have in Veale (2004), that readers seek out insights in what they read, actively and opportunistically seeking to make their readings yield the most interesting results. For instance, in the Ali dialogue one can interpret the stewardess's reply as a simple message about Superman and leave it at that. Because Superman does not "need" to fly in an airplane, it does not necessarily follow that Superman should not "want" to fly in an airplane. Nonetheless, we gain a deeper insight if we push the interpretation further and opportunistically assume her reply to contain an implicit challenge to Ali's egotistical identification of himself as superhuman. Ali could rebut this challenge with the rejoinder "But I love to go first-class", further reinforcing the heroic identification of himself by using "I" to respond to a claim about "Superman" (as noted in Veale, Feyaerts and Brône 2006, trumping can always invite counter-trumping). But he does not, and the challenge holds. The resulting insight of the joke might thus be summarized: "people are more likely to believe in an inconsistent state of affairs if it flatters their ego to do so".

    In poetic, artistic and musical uses of FGR, there are good aesthetic reasons to assume the purposeful use of FGR, and Tsur's paper provides an interesting tour of this aesthetic landscape. In humour, furthermore, there is a strong social dimension to why certain uses of FGR yield a cognitive punch and others do not. The wheelbarrow joke uses FGR to execute a triumph of common-sense (the workman) over authoritarianism (the sentry), while the Ali exchange demonstrates how simple common-sense can puncture the pomposity of a self-aggrandising protagonist. Ali, a world-champion heavyweight boxer, is convincingly counter-punched and KO'ed by a woman! Note how the joke has more social resonance if we imagine, as I have here, that the flight attendant is female. In each case, the FGR itself is insufficient to generate humour, rather, it is the social resonance that the FGR is used to generate that makes the end-result appear witty. This shouldn't be surprising, of course. One could not imagine a cognitive theory of gossip, say, that did not attempt to model the social dimension of the information that gossip trades upon, and the same should be true of humour. Without this social dimension, which plays on our entrenched beliefs about status, ego and acceptable behaviour, FGR is just an empty "cognitive wheelbarrow".

Nonetheless, by recognizing that FGR is a general purpose vehicle for carrying meaning and generating insights, some aesthetic and some humorous, we have made an excellent start. But it is important that we do not make the same mistake as the sentry in Tsur's joke, and over-value what are often the most foregrounded aspects of humour – such as incongruity, forced-reinterpretation, script-switching and frame-shifting – at the expense of what lies beneath. FGR is not just one of many possible strategies for creative thought, but may well be the master principle at work in each. If we allow ourselves to become enamoured of the most foregrounded aspects of creative thinking, a truly productive account may well escape through the front gate, all the while hiding in plain sight.

References

Attardo, Salvatore, Christian F. Hempelmann and Sara Di Maio
   2002   Script oppositions and logical mechanisms Modeling incongruities and their resolutions. *Humor: International Journal of Humor Research* 15(1): 3–46.
Coulson, Seana
   2000   *Semantic Leaps: Frame-shifting and Conceptual Blending in Meaning Construction.* New York/Cambridge: Cambridge University Press.
Ehrenzweig, Anton
   1965   *The Psychoanalysis of Artistic Vision and Hearing.* New York: Braziller.

Fauconnier, Gilles and Mark Turner
  2002   *The Way We Think. Conceptual Blending and the Mind's Hidden Com-
          plexities.* New York: Basic Books.
Giora, Rachel
  1991   On the cognitive aspects of the joke. *Journal of Pragmatics* 16(5):
          465–485.
Ritchie, Graeme
  1999   Developing the incongruity-resolution theory. In: K. Binsted and
          Graeme Ritchie (eds.), *Proceedings of the AISB Symposium on Creative
          Language: Stories and Humour*, 78–85. Edinburgh: Society for the
          Study of Artificial Intelligence and the Simulation of Behaviour.
Suls, Jerry M.
  1972   A two-stage model for the appreciation of jokes and cartoons: An in-
          formation-processing analysis. In: Jeffrey H. Goldstein and Paul E.
          McGhee (eds.), *The Psychology of Humor*, 81–100. New York: Aca-
          demic Press.
Veale, Tony
  2004   Incongruity in humor: root-cause or epiphenomenon? *Humor: The In-
          ternational Journal of Humor Research* 17(4): 410–428.
Veale, Tony, Kurt Feyaerts and Geert Brône
  2006   The cognitive mechanisms of adversarial humor. *Humor: International
          Journal of Humor Research* 19(3): 305–338.

Part III: Stance

Deconstructing verbal humour with Construction Grammar*

Eleni Antonopoulou and Kiki Nikiforidou

1. Introduction

As can be easily attested in the literature on cognitive stylistics (Semino and Culpeper 2002) and cognitive poetics (Stockwell 2002) the main insights of Cognitive Linguistics exploited for the analysis of literary texts are the ones bearing on conceptual metaphor and blending. Similarly, in cognitive linguistic approaches to humour, "marked construals" (as candidates for humorous effect) are accounted for in terms of well established construal mechanisms, such as metaphor, metonymy and conceptual blending (Brône and Feyaerts 2004). Use made of other trends within the cognitive paradigm, such as frame semantics, is restricted to early versions of Fillmore's theory (up to Fillmore 1985). In Humour Studies, scripts/frames have been (independently) used in both Raskin's (1985) SSTH (Semantic Script Theory of Humor) and its offshoot, the GTVH (General Theory of Verbal Humor) (Attardo 2001).[1] The current development of frame semantics into a fully blown linguistic theory, i.e. Construction Grammar (henceforth CxG), has not been applied either to humour or to literary texts yet. This paper is the first attempt to apply CxG to the analysis of verbal literary humour.

The focus on "verbal" requires an explanation, since the term has been used to imply both "verbal" as opposed to "referential" and "language based" as opposed to "visually triggered" humour. The former distinction refers to the manipulation of the *signifiant* rather than the *signifié* and has a long history (dating from Aristotle and Cicero) as does the

* We would like to thank Anna Despotopoulou, Sophia Marmaridou and Villy Tsakona for their input, as well as the two reviewers for comments and suggestions. Errors and omissions are entirely our own. Research for this paper was partly supported by grants no 70/4/5754 and 70/4/5531 of the Special Research Fund of the University of Athens.

1. For an overview of scripts, frames, scenes etc. and their use in AI, see Emmott (1999: 23–41).

paraphrasability test used to distinguish between the two types (see Attardo et al. 1994: 32; Hempelmann 2004: 389). The typical case of verbal humour is punning resting on lexical homonymy or polysemy and therefore defying paraphrase, unlike referential humour. We actually envisage a verbal-referential continuum, where typical wordplay (exploiting lexical ambiguity) occupies the leftmost end, while pragmatically or discoursally based language play (exploiting pragmatic or textual ambiguity) occupies points to the right of punning, that we suggest are still more "verbal" than referential. Straightforward punning will not be addressed here, mainly because it characterises text types other than literary ones, such as jokes and advertising. Although the exploitation of discoursal or textual ambiguity has been discussed within different frameworks (see Simpson 2003: 20–35), we will address it here as well (section 4) with the aim of embedding it in a cognitively-based approach which allows for a uniform treatment of discoursal ambiguity and constructional phenomena exploited in humour.

Indeed, what does not seem to have been even identified, so far, as verbal humour is the manipulation of the formal, morphosyntactic properties of whole grammatical units or "constructions". In section 3, we will argue that, by focusing on the conventional semantic, pragmatic, discoursal, or textual properties attached to units longer than single words, with fixed formal properties, CxG is uniquely equipped to provide a principled description of different types of verbal humour. More precisely, CxG is centrally concerned with phenomena discussed as *coercion*. Coercion refers to the clash between the syntactic and/or semantic properties of a word with those of the construction in which the word is embedded and the principles that guide coherent, consistent interpretations in such cases of conflict. In the following sections, we shall discuss examples of coercion in some detail making explicit all the mechanisms involved and their contribution to humorous interpretation. Our claim is then that the manipulation of such properties presupposes metalinguistic awareness; the reader in such cases is expected to be aware of the fact that part or all of the humorous clash lies in knowledge about language itself (see also Attardo 1994: 146–47). Hence all the instances discussed here involve such awareness as the trigger of possible humorous exploitation.

For a cognitive account of *literary* humour, perhaps the most crucial questions among those raised in humour theory are (a) whether humour is different from the rest of language, and (b) whether literary humour is different from non-literary humour. From a cognitive linguistic perspective, the possibility that cognitive mechanisms tailor-made for humorous discourse could exist is ruled out (cf. Brône and Feyaerts 2004; Brône et al 2006; Veale et al 2006 but also Attardo 2006: 356–7 on the non-specificity of logical mechanisms for humour). Without bearing directly on this issue, our data raise however a different type of problem that, as we show, is not treated adequately within the GTVH. In particular, we are interested in a principled, fine-grained analysis of the relation between "normal" language use and "marked" discourse (which may be humorously interpreted). If such analysis is cognitively based, it should directly reflect the construals leading to "deviance". In that sense, our answer to the second question is also a qualified "No".

Literary texts as written (and often well-planned) texts, may sustain a certain device, or a specific schema more systematically than spontaneous oral discourse. But anyone who has studied long, humorous oral narratives cannot fail to see the similarities, rather than the differences, between literary and spontaneous oral humour as art. Therefore, although we are sympathetic to views like Triezenberg (2004) and Jackson (2005), who emphasize the uniqueness and creativity of literary discourse, and we agree with the inherent indeterminacy of interpretation, we would like to attract attention to the fact that we work on a level *before* literary interpretation, i.e. we do not deal with the possibly multiple, socio-culturally and/or historically grounded interpretations a literary critic may engage in. For us, investigating literary humour implies focusing on text chunks drawn from literary discourse, identifying instances of incongruity and offering a principled account of what it is exactly in the wording that renders those instances incongruous. Our objective is to show the relative advantage of applying to the investigation of literary humour a cognitively based linguistic theory, which can account in a uniform manner for form-meaning relationships. In that sense we will be engaged in a linguist's "close-reading" which does not aim at replacing literary analysis, but substantiating and supporting common sense judgements, while at the same time restricting ad hocness.

2.   Grammatical theory and humour theory: background and prerequisites

In the following sections, we analyze literary humour drawing on the principles and methodological tools of CxG. Since CxG is a theory of grammar, it follows that our analysis will center on the contribution of language to humorous discourse and effects, and more precisely on the contribution of grammatical constructions of any type and degree of specificity. However, any analysis should be also couched in and/or contrasted with existing theories geared specifically to the analysis of humour. Prevalent among these is the GTVH (Attardo and Raskin 1991; Attardo 2001) which is not only the most influential theory of humour in contemporary research, but also the only fully developed (linguistic) theory available today for the analysis of literary humour.

In this section, we present some background on CxG and GTVH without aiming for exhaustive coverage. Instead we focus selectively on those aspects of either theory that will figure centrally in the ensuing discussion, aiming to show how a CxG based analysis may complement a general theory of humour. Our claim eventually is that the insights and results in CxG-based research may successfully highlight important sources of incongruity, the latter being an essential component of humour analysis in many theories, including GTVH.

2.1. The GTVH made easy

The GTVH inherits from its predecessor (SSTH) the assumption that for a text to be humorous, it must be compatible (either fully or partially) with two scripts which are opposed to each other, while at the same time retaining a partial overlap. The first script (activated on the basis of lexical information available at the point of processing) is at a subsequent point "opposed" by information provided in the second script activated at the punch line of a joke. Hence the two scripts, responsible for the incongruity inherent in any humorous text, are the negation of each other, in a special, technical sense (Raskin 1985: 108). In the GTVH this notion is further elaborated with emphasis attached to the context forcing specific elements of a script to become foregrounded or more salient (Attardo 2001: 18–19).

All the specifications of the script oppositions (SO) are expressed in binary opposition terms, e.g. in (1)

(1) Algernon:
    The amount of women in London who flirt with their own husbands is perfectly scandalous.
    (Oscar Wilde *The Importance of Being Earnest*: 285)

the opposed scripts are "it is scandalous to flirt with someone else's vs. one's own husband".[2]

A significant contribution of the GTVH is the identification of "strands" (Attardo 2001: 83–88). The analysis of a humorous text results in a consideration of thematic or formal relations between jab (and punch) lines appearing along the text's linear representation. Three or more lines related on the basis of any common Knowledge Resources (KRs – see note 2) form a strand, which may then be relatable to other ones, thus forming "stacks". In an obvious sense, strands and stacks contribute to the humorous coherence of a text and while Attardo (2001, 2002) illustrates their application to a short story (also Tsakona 2004), they are equally applicable to other text types such as drama and film-scripts (Antonopoulou 2004).

Strands based mainly on formal similarities (number of common KRs) are perhaps traumatically reminiscent of structuralism, but thematic similarity is also mentioned in the theory. Antonopoulou (2004) suggests that thematic similarity seems to lie lower than the first level of oppositions (normal/abnormal and the like) but higher than very specific script content, like an "arch-script" or a "schema". In this sense, thematic similarity is directly related to construal and allows also for the inclusion of discoursal and socio-cultural properties of scripts (we in fact take this approach in the texts analysed in sections 3 and 4).

What we see as the main problem with the GTVH and a main motivation for a more language-based (and, in this paper, construction-based) approach to humour is the language KR. Attardo (2001: 22) claims explicitly that "as any sentence can be recast in a different wording (using synonyms, other syntactic constructions, etc.) any joke can be worded in a (very large) number of ways without changes in its semantic content". This implies that almost all humour is approached as referential.[3] Hence,

---

2. The method of analysis, therefore, requires first the identification of the humorous instances in a literary text, as sources of incongruity. Each instance is treated as the punch line of a joke, but termed a "jab line" if it is non-final. Besides the SO, five additional parameters are then supplied. All these are called "knowledge resources" (KRs) and are considered to inform jointly the jab/punch line (see also Attardo 2002). The KRs identified by the theory are presented in detail in Attardo (1994: 222ff, 2001: 22ff) and summed up in Brône and Feyaerts (2003: 5).

3. Attardo (1994: 22–29, 95, 230–53) and Attardo et al (1994: 27–28) do discuss the verbal-referential distinction at length, yet it is practically only punning triggered by lexical ambiguity which appears under the Language KR in the GTVH, as attested in the analyses offered in Attardo 2001.

the language KR standardly receives the value "irrelevant" even when the text analysed is literary (see Attardo 2001: 163- 201).[4]

The downgrading of the language factor is not a problem restricted to literary texts as Emmott (1999: 42) and Triezenberg (2004: 413) suggest. Indeed, for Cognitive Linguistics any difference in wording amounts to a difference in construal, and this applies to all texts, literary or not, humorous or *bona fide*. Differences in the discoursal properties of texts, such as register, for instance, imply the activation of different scripts. Despite the fact that the GTVH recognizes such properties, in the analysis of literary humorous texts actually offered (Attardo 2001), no attempt is made at a principled, detailed account of the relation between the syntactic-semantic properties of the linguistic sign (whether a word or a larger unit) and the relevant part of the script it activates. This is precisely the gap filled by CxG by integrating the insights of frame semantics with the principles of syntactic/grammatical theory and relating the specifics of any linguistic encoding with the specifics of the construal that has given rise to it.

2.2. Construction Grammar made brief

That meaning is identified with conceptualization (our ability to construe a situation in alternate ways) is an uncontested tenet in Cognitive Linguistics (cf. Langacker 2000, 2002), which allows for subtle and fine-grained analyses in linguistic semantics. Less obvious perhaps is the observation that it is not only lexical units which evoke distinct conceptualizations, but also grammatic-syntactic, morphological, or even phonological triggers. Hence sentences which differ slightly, or not at all, at the lexical level may still convey different meanings if they involve different syntactic, morphological, etc. patterns: Every distinct form is matched with distinct semantic-pragmatic, discoursal, and/or textual features.

This is precisely the insight exploited in Construction Grammar. In this framework, constructions are grammatical patterns representing conventional pairings of meaning and form, analogous to words, and grammar is viewed as a structured inventory of such pairings (Goldberg 1995; Fill-

---

4. The reason behind this downgrading is probably the fact that both Raskin's (1985) SSTH and Attardo and Raskin's (1991) GTVH were originally modelled on jokes (as a text type) and "referential" rather than "verbal" (i.e. punning) jokes, in particular. It is fairly obvious that, for the humorous effect of a referential joke, the Language KR, i.e. the actual wording of the text, is of little importance.

more and Kay 1995; Kay and Fillmore 1999; Michaelis 2005). No strict division between syntax and the lexicon is assumed; while lexical constructions (i.e. words) differ from syntactic ones in internal complexity and in the extent to which phonological form is specified, both lexical and syntactic constructions represent the same type of meaning and form pairs. The semantic pole of any construction (lexical or syntactic) is in turn defined in terms of frames; in this sense, CxG subsumes frame semantics and incorporates valuable insights from frame semantic theory, none the least the rejection of a strict dichotomy between semantics and pragmatics. Crucially for present purposes, information about topicality, focus, register, genre etc. is therefore represented in constructions alongside purely semantic information (Goldberg 1995: 7).

Also crucial is that the semantic specification of any construction may involve basic, experientially grounded and conceptually elaborate scenes such as transfer or causation, readily describable in frame semantic terms. While such scenes may be *part* of the meaning of individual lexical items, they may exhaustively represent the meaning of entire constructional patterns. Consider example (2), an instance of the "ditransitive construction" (Goldberg 1992, 1995):

(2)   She knit him a sweater for his birthday.

The verb *knit*, as a verb of creation, normally licenses two thematic roles, an agent and a theme, or more precisely a "knitter" and a "knitted". In this case, as Goldberg (1995: 120–32) argues, we may claim that the recipient role is licensed by the ditransitive construction itself Because of the event type it designates, the ditransitive construction, represented by the form *NP V NP NP*, licenses *three* thematic roles, an agent, a theme and a recipient. In this account, the valence of the verb *knit* "is augmented up to that of a verb of transfer because the (ditransitive) construction in which it is embedded designates an event of transfer" (Michaelis 2005: 10).[5]

---

5. Notice that the only possible interpretation for example 2 is that of "intended transfer". In other words, the sentence cannot mean that she knit him a sweater so that he wouldn't have to do it himself or that she knit him a sweater for the purpose of demonstrating knitting. This observation argues in favour of the recipient role being associated directly with the construction rather than with the frame of the verb knit, which would need to have a special sense like "X intends to cause Y to receive Z by knitting" (Goldberg 1995: 141).

Valence augmentation can be therefore handled elegantly in a constructional framework; in fact, as argued in Michaelis 2005, this particular kind of *coercion* (see also Michaelis and Ruppenhofer 2001; Goldberg and Jackendoff 2004) is a predictable side effect of semantic composition in constructional frameworks which posit two sources of thematic structure, the verb *and* the construction. As we show in section 3, this type of coercion, which relies on the simultaneous recognition of constructional and lexical meaning and the possibility of discrepancy between them, offers insights as to the rise of humorous effects and the source of incongruity. In addition, the merging of lexical and constructional meaning provides for a "compactness" effect which is irreplaceable in humorous discourse (cf. Antonopoulou 2002, 2004; Attardo 1997: 407).

In the ensuing analysis of literary humour we refer also to another kind of coercion, of the semantic variety (De Swart 1998; Michaelis 2004, 2005, Fillmore et al. 2003). Semantic type shifting or coercion is not marked by any syntactic or morphological changes in the word involved, and in this sense it is a truly invisible kind of reinterpretation triggered by the need to resolve semantic conflicts. Michaelis (2005) identifies two types of semantic coercion, endocentric and exocentric. *Endocentric coercion* stems from the violation of the normal semantic properties of a word, as in (3):

(3)   It wasn't that big an office, but the walls dripped modern art...
      (Ian Rankin, *Set in Darkness*, 2000)

In (3) *modern art* is construed as something liquid or "drippable" under the influence of the meaning of the verb, conveying the implication that the decoration was excessive and overdone.[6] *Exocentric coercion* occurs when a particular construction imposes a construal on the elements that appear in it. Consider for instance (4) (from Michaelis 2005), an instance of the "determination construction":

(4)   Give me some blanket.

---

6. It is of course possible, as suggested by one reviewer, to say instead that the complement "modern art" triggers a metaphorical interpretation of the verb drip. The question that arises, however, is whether this meaning can be described in a general, context-independent way, sanctioning a polysemy status for this lexical item. Furthermore, in CxG (as in most grammatical theories) it is the verb which determines the syntactic and semantic specifications of its complements.

In (4), the count noun *blanket* is interpreted as a mass noun in the presence of unstressed *some*. Both endocentric and exocentric effects are systematically exploited in humorous texts, since the inherently implicit nature of coercion renders it particularly suitable for humour: a paraphrase making this meaning (and the resulting incongruity) explicit would destroy the humorous effect.

From the preceding discussion, it becomes obvious that in CxG meaning is attributed directly to schematic constructions such as the ditransitive or the determination ones. Such patterns are characterized as "schematic" (Langacker 1987) or "formal" (Fillmore, Kay, and O'Connor 1988) because the slots provided by the construction can be filled by any word which is semantically and syntactically appropriate for a given slot. Schematic constructions, in other words, contribute meaning to the sentence containing them irrespective of the actual words that fill them, as opposed to substantive (or lexically filled) constructions in which all elements are fixed (e.g. *It takes one to know one*). It is precisely the existence of schematic constructions (which cannot be listed in the lexicon) that has motivated the proposal for a construction-based grammar because parts of their semantics-pragmatics and/or syntax cannot be predicted from their components by general combinatorial syntactic and semantic rules. Hence the notion of the construction, where syntactic, semantic, pragmatic or even discoursal properties can be directly associated conventionally with a particular pattern. Grammar can now be seen as an inventory of constructions ranging from the fully substantive to the fully schematic (e.g. the subject-predicate construction). In this light, it makes sense to characterize a particular construction as semi-schematic or semi-substantive, acknowledging that it may contain simultaneously idiosyncratic and derivable properties.[7]

We conclude this brief introduction to CxG in the same way we started it, i.e. by reference to the syntax-lexicon or schematic-substantive continuum. Humorous discourse, as we show in the following sections, exploits this continuum to the full; first by relying frequently on the meaning(s), often implicit, that can only be attributed to a construction as a whole and secondly, by playing on the continuum as such, that is by treating substantive constructions as schematic. In either case, the relevant in-

---

7. So, the ditransitive construction, for instance, is strictly speaking semi-schematic. While it exhibits a fair amount of productivity, it is also constrained by allowing only certain classes of verbs (cf. She knitted him a sweater vs. *She chose him a sweater).

congruity can only be assessed if we recognize constructional meaning of various degrees of schematicity.

3.   (Semi-)schematic constructions as the loci of incongruity

3.1. Argument-structure constructions: incongruity as coercion

Early attempts to apply CxG to an understanding of humorous discourse, and in particular scalar humour, include Bergen and Binsted (2004) and Antonopoulou (2002). In this section, we look at constructions exemplifying coercion, i.e. discrepancy between constructional and lexical meaning. It is important to emphasize right from the start that we see co-ercion as a cognitive (certainly not humour specific) phenomenon, naturally couched in more general phenomena such as the prototype and deviations from it or foregrounding vs. backgrounding. Coercion is by definition some sort of marked linguistic use (in the sense that it crucially involves some clash in the specifications of the word vis-à-vis the construction) which, however, relies on the simultaneous recognition of the unmarked (prototypical) case (see Brône and Feyaerts 2004 for a similar argument). As a marked (and in this sense creative) instance of language use, it can also be seen as serving the purpose of foregrounding (cf. Stockwell 2002: 14); indeed, as we shall be arguing, what is foregrounded in such cases is the linguistic discrepancy between the word and its context, illuminating the essence of verbal humour as such.

The CxG treatment of coercion effects relies, as noted, on the possibility of assigning particular thematic roles and their syntactic realization to a construction as a whole, rather than to a particular verb (see 2.2). In this sense, the type shifting undergone by the verb is only licensed constructionally, in the context of a particular argument structure associated conventionally with the construction. This is humorously exploited in (5)–(7):

(5)   *Keith* squats forward and *fights his mother's thigh up into the car,* while Frank leans sideways...
       (Martin Amis, *Dead Babies*: 163)
(6)   And indeed as *each toothpaste Whitehead squeezes into the Morris,* the chassis drops two inches...
       (Martin Amis, *Dead Babies*: 163)
(7)   *He* sat up and by degrees *worked his feet to the floor.*
       (Kingsley Amis, *Lucky Jim*: 64)

Examples (5) and (7) illustrate the "caused-motion" construction (Goldberg 1995), while (6) instantiates the "intransitive motion" construction related to the caused-motion one through a subpart inheritance relationship (Goldberg 1995: 78). The caused-motion construction licenses three thematic roles, namely cause, theme and goal, realized respectively as the subject, the object and the oblique complement. The intransitive motion construction licenses only two arguments, a theme and a goal, realized as the subject and the oblique complement. The semantics associated with the argument structure of the caused-motion construction is that the causer argument directly causes the theme argument to move along a path designated by the directional phrase (Goldberg 1995: 152), while for the intransitive-motion construction, the theme argument simply moves along the directional path.

In this light, consider the use of *fights* in example (5), which appears in a scene describing the efforts of an unusually fat family (the Whiteheads) to fit into their car. It is clear that while both a causal and a motion reading are associated with this example (Keith causes his mother's thigh to move), this is not the case with (transitive) *fight* outside the constructional context (e.g. *He fought the enemy*). Related to this is the fact that while *fight* can, as we have just seen, independently sustain an object (though not a directional complement – cf. *He fought the enemy* but **He fought into the office*), it does not bear the same semantic relationship to its object in the construction as in a simple transitive sentence. So (8a), for example, does not entail (8b):

(8) a. Keith fights his mother's thigh up into the car.
     b. Keith fights his mother's thigh.

Example (8a) instantiates a situation in which the agent role associated lexically with the verb *fight* is fused (see section 2.2) with the cause role licensed by the caused-motion construction. The theme role associated with the verb may be also said to fuse with the theme role of the construction, although not as a "theme-opponent", i.e. the role it has in (8b). Finally, the oblique argument is contributed directly by the construction. The result is a merging of lexical with constructional meaning where the original semantics of *fight* (acting against an opponent) retains only part of its background frame, the one presupposing difficulty and/or effort and possibly evoking circumstances of war. Everything else is cancelled out by the construction which imposes a "moving object" interpretation on the theme argument, in the direction specified by the prepositional phrase.

It is precisely the meaning which is contributed constructionally (and which, as we have just argued, cannot be attributed to the word *fight* and its associated frame) that gives rise to incongruity and the associated humorous effect. Casting the opposition in humour theory terms, the relevant scripts may be said to contain a binary opposition between "getting one's leg in a car on one's own" and "getting one's leg in a car as a result of an external causal force", the latter arising only in the constructional context. As we show in the following section, the construal of the "thigh" as an object moved by an external force distinct from its owner (i.e. the mother) is embedded in the humorous coherence of the text, organized around the systematic construal of the Whiteheads as an undifferentiated indiscrete mass. While this coherence may be served by explicit metaphors, it may be also served by implicit constructional meaning, which is precisely the point we forward in this study. In this light, consider also example (6), which both lexically *(toothpaste, squeeze)* and constructionally contributes to the same coherence. The constructional meaning involved in this case is the one associated with the intransitive motion construction, depicting movement of the theme argument in the direction of the goal. And it is the presence of *squeeze*, which in this context expresses the means of motion, that maintains the humorous strand (see section 2.1) of "undifferentiated mass of flesh". In other words, coercion, by definition, foregrounds the linguistic incongruity per se, which may in turn be exploited in the creation of a superordinate, text-global opposition (in this case, discrete – indiscrete).[8]

Example (7) from *Lucky Jim* is given a similar analysis, in which the caused-motion interpretation cannot be attributed to the lexical semantics of *work* but to the pattern as a whole. To appreciate the humour of this example one needs to know the previous context, since the reason the character referred to by "he" has such difficulty getting out of bed is given in the elaborately detailed preceding text on how he had been too drunk the previous night to even notice that he had burnt with his cigarette the bedclothes of his host who is also his boss (see section 4.2). Once again, the relevant incongruity resides in the semantics of the construc-

---

8. "By definition" because coercion refers to clashing or marked uses of words in specific constructional contexts, and foregrounding is precisely served by markedness. The suggestion we forward here is that such markedness is recognised and resolved (in the sense of arriving at a coherent interpretation) in much the same way that it is recognised and resolved in everyday, fully conventional occurrences of coercion.

tion, imposing an external-cause interpretation to a normally self-propelled, trivially easy action. The semantic effect of the construction is further evident in the construal of *feet* as an object completely separate from their owner despite the co-reference of the subject pronoun with the possessive (*his*). This, we suggest, is due precisely to the constraint associated with the caused-motion construction (Goldberg 1995: 166–67) to the effect that no cognitive decision can mediate between the causing event and the entailed motion.[9] It is for this reason that *feet* cannot trigger the otherwise well entrenched metonymy PART for WHOLE (Lakoff 1987: 273–274) which applies productively to body-parts (e.g. *We need more hands around here*, etc.), and is construed only as an object moving under a force.

3.2. Mass-count reversal constructions: coherence in coercion

Coercion effects are manifested productively in jab lines involving totally schematic constructions, e.g. (9):

(9)   Anna Halsey was about two hundred and forty pounds of middle-aged putty faced woman in a black tailor-made suit.
       (R. Chandler, *Trouble is My Business* [1939] 1950: 2)

Here, the count noun *woman* is construed as a mass noun and therefore the humorously resolved incongruity is not lexically but constructionally derivable. Evidently, no paraphrase of (9) which does not involve the coerced construction would have the same humorous import. At the very least, what is here *implicit* (and residing in the construction) should have to be explicitly stated, therefore destroying the humorous effect of the line (cf. Dolitsky 1992: 33).

In Cognitive Linguistics, the distinction between mass and count nouns is considered to rely on four independent properties: *bounding, homogeneity, contractability* and *replicability* (Langacker 1987: 18–19). The count noun *lake*, for example, designates "a limited body of water whose boundaries are specifically included in the scope of predication' (i.e. they are inherent to the conception of a lake). The mass noun *water*, on the contrary, is not intrinsically bounded in this domain and it portrays its profiled

---

9. As all other constraints associated with the construction, this constraint also follows, according to Goldberg, from the fact that the caused-motion construction expresses "direct" (or single-event) causation.

region as homogeneous. Besides, a mass noun displays contractability: "any subpart of an instance is itself a valid instance of the category" (Langacker 1987: 18–19). Therefore, a fragment of *a brick* (count) is not itself a brick, but both the fragment and the brick as a whole instantiate the substance *brick* (mass). When an instance of a count noun category is added to another, the result is two separate instances (replicability), while when two instances of the mass category are combined, the result is a single, expanded instance (Langacker 1987: 18–19).

In the light of the above, consider the first part of *XL Whitehead* from *Dead Babies*, which illustrates nicely the contribution of the relevant constructions to coherence and the creation of humorous strands. In the passage, the employment of a clash between the two conceptualizations is resolved in the direction of the mass portrayal winning over the count one. Typical exocentric coercion is humorously exploited, targeting obesity in the scene with the Whiteheads already mentioned in 3.1:

(10) How am I expected to drive with arse all over the gear-lever?
(11) There's still a bit of arm hanging out
(12) Some of my leg is still out there

In (10) the count noun *arse* appears in violation of the "determination construction" constraints requiring a definite or indefinite article in front of a count noun. In this sense, the determiner (article), indeed its absence, forces a construal of the count noun as mass. In CxG terms, a lexical feature is in conflict with a constructional feature with the result that the ontological index of the noun shifts from an individual to a cumulative entity, i.e. a type involving only masses and groups (see 2.2 above, Michaelis 2005: 20). The shift characterises the prepositional phrase *with arse all over the gear-lever* as a whole and is non-attributable to the individual words composing it. In this sense, bounding is suspended.

The same effect is achieved in (11) by the presence of the count noun *arm* in the noun phrase *a bit of arm*. *Arm* is construed as some kind of "stuff", not a part of a specific individual, but rather a type of flesh. What points to that kind of construal is partly the semantics of *bit* (meaning a small amount of something, e.g. *a bit of sunshine*) and partly the type of noun phrase it (consequently) requires as a complement. Its typical complements are not construed as having discrete parts but rather as being homogeneous. This is further foregrounded by the absence of a determiner in front of the count noun *arm*. In the resulting script (activated by the whole sentence), heterogeneity is cancelled.

In (12), the whole (of which "leg" is a part) is encoded through the possessive pronoun *my*, hence the determiner requirement is satisfied, and strictly speaking, since *some* is stressed in this environment, it is not immediately obvious that it corresponds to the unstressed *some* accompanying mass nouns (as in *have some soup*). Still, the singular noun required after both stressed and unstressed *some* followed by a prepositional phrase headed by *of* must be construable in terms of a quantity. Hence standard grammars of English provide a unified description of "assertive" *some* in both determiner and nominal function as "taking the *of* construction" and as requiring plural count or mass nouns" (see Quirk et al. 1972: 222–223). In CxG terms, different aspects of the mass (as opposed to count) semantic features are evoked in (12) drastically changing the lexical frames that would be activated if the nouns appeared within different patterns. Contractability and replicability are cancelled because of the actual constructions used. As a consequence, the incongruity resides in the construal of the Whiteheads as an indiscrete mass of flesh of uniform composition.

This is signalled right at the beginning of the scene with the Whiteheads and their car through different means. The first exchanges between them foreground the homogeneity by explicitly showing their inability to attribute specific body parts to specific individuals:

(13) 'Whose horrible great leg is this?' – 'Is this your bum, Keith, or Aggie's?' – 'I don't care whose guts these are, they've got to be moved' – 'That' s not Dad's arm…it's my leg!'

These are followed by even more explicit reference to a cumulative/mass type entity, i.e. toothpaste:

(14) And indeed, as each toothpaste Whitehead squeezes into the Morris, the chassis drops two inches…

At that point Mrs Whitehead is asked by her husband to close the door. She responds to the request by producing (12) (*I can't, Frank. Some of my leg is still out there*). The son, Keith, is therefore asked to *give [his] mother a hand with her leg*. Here's the follow up:

(15) Keith squats forward and <u>fights his mother's thigh up into the car,</u> while Frank leans sideways and tugs at the far door-strap with one hand and <u>a fistful of Mrs Whitehead's top</u> with the other. Aggie,

Keith's sister, sits crying with shame in the back seat; she sees her family conflate into one pulsing balloon of flesh.
'Come on – nearly home.'
'No!' shrieks Flora. 'There's still a bit of arm hanging out!'
'Got it' pants Keith.
The door closes noiselessly and to ironic cheers from the crowd the four grumpy pigs chug out into the street.
'Get your arse off the gear-lever woman' Frank demands as they pull up at the lights, 'How'm I expected to drive with arse all over the gear-lever?'
(Martin Amis, *Dead Babies*: 163–164)

It is the undifferentiated mass interpretation of the whole which allows Keith to tug *a fistful of Mrs. Whitehead's top* and Aggie to encode the situation as a conflation of the whole family *into one pulsing balloon of flesh*. The Whiteheads as a whole are only bounded by the car (and rather unsuccessfully at that). Adding them up does not amount to four entities but to a "single expanded instance" in Langacker's sense. At the same time, replicability is explicitly cancelled in the balloon metaphor.

Interestingly, the most explicit of these encodings is in fact the metaphor. The most implicit ones are those couching the constructional semantics of (10) – (12) above. The humorous *coherence* of the text lies, we suggest, in the sustained mass-feature-values superimposed on count-feature values, with one or more of the relevant semantic properties being foregrounded at each step. As we have shown, such properties may be derived from the clash of the word with its constructional context, the lexical semantics of the words involved (including metaphorical extensions), or from the suspension of real-world knowledge. Unless the process of coercion is identified and its effects captured, the similarities of the various scripts opposed in this extract are intuitively accounted for, rather than based on a principled, informed recognition of the incongruity trigger.[10] In other words, constructing individuals as a mass of flesh (which is the dominant image in this extract) while targeting obesity is constructionally determined and achieved through a reversal of the discreet/non discreet opposition. This image is also supported by lexical (*arse*) and discoursal (terms of address) choices marked for low register and evoking vulgarity.

---

10. In principle, the GTVH could identify the relevant strand here provided that it allows the Language parameter to feed directly the opposition inside the scripts.

A linguistic analysis cannot account for the reasons why these options are made by the author. It can however produce results which are independently consistent with a literary account of the humour of the novel as "black", cynical and "flaunting a moral deficiency" (Stevenson 2004: 458). The interpretation of the actual construals depends obviously on the literary researcher's agenda and methods of analysis (Emmott 1999: 69).

## 4.	(Semi)-substantive constructions as the loci of incongruity

4.1. A cognitive approach to the recycling of fixed expressions

A central claim in the present work is that language play can be effected at *any* point along the schematic-substantive continuum, exploiting *any* aspect of the formal (phonological-morphological-syntactic) or conventional semantic features of a linguistic expression of *any* length and complexity. Therefore, ambiguity (the source of typical wordplay/punning) can also be detected in the pragmatic-discoursal-textual meaning of a language chunk. In section 3, we have already shown that CxG can account nicely for the conventional semantic-pragmatic properties of semi-schematic constructions, which have in general gone unnoticed. In this section, we show that it can also account for the humorous exploitation of semi-substantive constructions, i.e. the (more or less) lexically filled idiomatic expressions (Fillmore, Kay, and O'Connor 1988; Nunberg, Sag, and Wasow 1994). These have been the topic of much work in Cognitive Linguistics (see selectively Gibbs 1994; Langlotz 2006) and have been analysed in the humour literature as well (see Simpson 2003: 20–29). While we agree with Simpson's identification of the actual level on which incongruity arises in such cases, i.e. the discoursal, we certainly disagree with the accompanying implication in his work to the effect that discoursal units are not cognitive units as well (Langacker 2001: 143; Emmott 1999: 270–1). Besides, a CxG approach allows for a uniform analysis of schematic and substantive constructions and for a principled description of the humorous effects as relying on treating the latter as instances of the former. In other words, incongruities at the discoursal and/or socio-cultural levels are treated as a side effect of yet another type of constructional property, i.e. the discoursal or socio-cultural properties of a given schematic or substantive construction.

Literary texts do not rely on straightforward punning alone to create verbal humour, but exploit the relative compositionality and transparency of linguistic expressions which may be more or less fixed for the ordinary language user, but allow inventive decomposition of their fixedness (Cacciari and Tabossi 1993; Gibbs 1994; Croft and Cruse 2004: 231).[11] We will call such manipulations "recycling" after Redfern (1997) and "recontextualisation". Very inventive language play can perform manipulations all along the schematic-substantive continuum. Consider J. Joyce's *Ulysses* where language play ranges from morphological creations (*anythingarian*) to neologistic compounding of two words into one (*charlatan* and *Lacan > charlacan*) to encoding idioms (*bread-and-butter > bread-and-butterfly*) to sequences of semi-fixed expressions: *Lord Tennyson* and *gentleman farmer > Lawn Tennyson gentleman poet*. The effectiveness of the final sequence depends evidently on the possibility for the decoder to recall the source of verbal play which rests, in its turn, not only on paronymy (*lord – lawn*) but also, crucially, on the retention of the conventional meaning of the whole sequence as an identification one (e.g. Noam Chomsky Professor of Linguistics). Similarly, in the much quoted "Come forth Lazarus. And he came fifth and lost the job" from *Ulysses*, the intertextuality and the biblical register of the first sentence are as much part of its conventional semantics as its literal meaning.

In literary humorous discourse, fixed expressions are often used by authors for implicit metalinguistic comments which, unlike straightforward punning characterizing other text types, can sustain coherence and contribute to style. In such cases, the unit is broken up and language is looking at/inside itself. This self-reflexive humorous device can be brought to a principled analysis using CxG. In the next section, we attempt an analysis of an extract from *Lucky Jim* along these lines.

4.2. Coercion and discoursal incongruity

The protagonist in *Lucky Jim*, Jim Dixon, has just woken up in the house of his Head of Department (Prof. Welch) suffering from a dreadful hangover. He is slowly discovering the disaster he has caused the previous night in his host's guest room: His cigarette has *burnt itself out on the blankets, the rug and part of the bedside table.* He then exhausts himself cutting round the edges of the burnt areas of the bedclothes and shaving the burnt part of the rug with a razor blade.

---

11. But cf. Veale et al 2006 for arguments to the effect that ordinary language users are also capable of manipulating and exploiting fixed idioms.

(16) Dixon heeled over sideways and came to rest with his hot face on the pillow.
This, of course, would give him time to collect his thoughts, and that, of course, was just what he didn't want to do with his thoughts (J1); the longer he could keep them apart from one another, especially the ones about Margaret, the better (J2). He sat up and by degrees worked his feet to the floor" (J3).

One of the alternatives he considers in order to avoid confronting his hosts is

(17) clearing out at once without a word to anybody. "That wouldn't really do, though, unless he cleared out as far as London (J4) ... He sighed; he might as well be thinking of Monte Carlo or Chinese; ... He clung to the mantelpiece... crumpling like a shot film-gunman. Had Chinese its Margarets and Welches? (J5)

He then goes into the bathroom, writes obscenities against Welch in the mirror, rubs them off and looks at himself:

(18) His hair, however, despite energetic brushing helped out by the use of a water-soaked nail brush, was already springing away from his scalp. He considered using soap as a pomatum, but decided against it, having in the past several times converted the short hairs at the sides and back of its head into the semblance of duck plumage by this expedient... As always, though, he looked healthy and, he hoped, honest and kindly. He'd have to be content with that.
He was all ready to slink down to the phone, when returning to the bedroom he again surveyed the mutilated bedclothes.[12] They looked in some way unsatisfactory.
(Kingsley Amis, *Lucky Jim*: 63–65)

J3 is already discussed in a previous section as an instance of exocentric coercion. J1 and J2 are instances of recycling the same idiom "collect one's thoughts", in the pun-like tradition of reanalysing a "dead" metaphor. The feature of metaphoricity is part of the idiom's conventional meaning. That it can be recycled through ellipsis in J1 and a literal rein-

---

12. Note that the phrase *mutilated bedclothes* is an instance of endocentric coercion (see 2.2).

terpretation in J2 points to the idiom's relative compositionality and transparency. Evidently, however, unless the conventional, idiomatic meaning had already evoked the first (expected) script, no incongruity would have been present in either J1 or J2. And in fact, unless the mechanism at work is identified, J1 at least can be easily missed.

In J4 the linguistically marked incongruity rests entirely on shifting the frame of *clear out* which does not allow a determination of the goal of motion (as evidenced in a search of the BNC). It is therefore another instance of exocentric coercion (already discussed in section 3) as is also the case with J5 where the plural marking of the proper names (*Margarets and Welches*) seems to turn the (otherwise referential or even non-incongruous) scripts to verbally based ones. Consider the difference with a near paraphrase: "Did Chinese also have people like Margaret and Welch?" Coercion results here in proper names being treated semantically as common nouns, so the supposition of unique reference, prototypically carried by proper names, is cancelled. The plural morphology signals a cumulative (group) construal and at the same time an isolation of a specific, contextually determinable, set of characteristics evoked by the specific proper names. This is a metonymic construal of proper names, marking in this context the pretensions Dixon is faced with. Hence the incongruity relies on a metalinguistic awareness which feeds the overarching schema of humorous coherence in the text: clownish behaviour vs. linguistic sophistication.

Discoursal incongruity emerges as a characteristic of the humorous effect in the novel as a whole, and is highlighted here explicitly by the repeated use of *of course* marking conversational discourse and clashing with the third-person narrative. In other words, free indirect discourse itself produces an incongruity deriving from discourse markers evoking conversation scripts (*of course*), embedded within an interior monologue frame, and manipulated by the narrator (third-person narrative). The metalinguistic awareness present in the recycling of idioms evidences sophistication, if not analytical thinking. The same applies to the use of high register expressions (*expedient, survey the mutilated bedclothes*), which clashes with the slapstick comedy of the situations described.

Literary accounts of the novel's humour (Lodge 1966) considered its main source to be the contrast between Dixon's inner and outer world, linked through his picking up "a cliché – his own or another person's – and mentally subjecting it to verbal scrutiny" (Lodge 1966: 253).We are also highlighting the humorous exploitation throughout the novel of metalinguistic awareness. Amis's "ludic" writing and "fascination with puns" is also contrasted to his "anti-modernist prejudices" and "vernacular style" (Lodge 2002: 190). To such considerations a linguistic analysis cannot be expected to contribute.

5. Conclusion

In the foregoing analysis of literary humour with CxG, we have considered our goal to be an interdisciplinary one; the cognitive approach taken has been specifically identified as a supplement to, and not a substitute of, literary analysis. An interdisciplinary approach, further, requires mutual understanding of the goals of the disciplines involved. To this end, we set out to show why CxG can bridge the gap between the wording of the message and its possible interpretations, while sharing with all cognitivist models an understanding of the linguistic system as encompassing cognitive processing, and therefore the potential of different construals, of world knowledge. It is essentially this understanding of language, which is absent from non-cognitive models, that renders them alien to the purposes of literary analysis.

We have argued that the preoccupation of CxG with "marked" encodings and their treatment as cases of coercion may prove to be a valuable methodological tool for text analysis to the extent that such cases are exploited in creative or neologistic literary discourse. CxG allows for a principled description of the possible interpretations by providing an "X ray" of the relationship between unmarked and marked encodings and between a marked encoding and its underlying construals. Equally illuminating and usable in the analysis of literary texts is the realization that such markedness need not be restricted to the word and its unexpected use in a particular context, but can actually involve whole constructional patterns to which CxG attributes directly semantic, pragmatic and/or discoursal properties. Indeed, we have suggested that the identification of such semi-productive – semi-idiomatic constructions and the detailed description of their properties is the main contribution of CxG to literary analysis, since the potential of such cases for creative exploitation, unlike that of lexical items, has not been recognized so far in the relevant literature. In addition, linking such patterns directly with discoursal properties and socially-determined conditions answers any criticism to the effect that cognitive approaches in general tend to ignore social or discoursal parameters. If language is grounded in discourse and social interaction (Langacker 2001: 143), then context, shared knowledge, and constant

updating of the information (Brône, Feyaerts and Veale 2006) are necessarily taken care of.

The reference to a "principled description" above may sound deterministic to literary scholars (see Stockwell 2002: 8; Jackson 2005: 524) or suspicious of "linguistic imperialism" (Raskin 2004: 432–3); this, however,
may be due to different perceptions of interdisciplinarity. Ours, as stated
repeatedly, sees the kind of study undertaken here as a step before literary
interpretation as such, feeding however directly into the possible readings
a literary scholar may provide by grounding the text firmly into its socio-
cultural context (Jackson 2005: 532). In the Amises texts we have in fact
attempted to show how the results of a CxG-based analysis bear not only
on the humorous coherence of the relevant passages but also on the major
themes of the narrative, in line with and in support of plausible literary
readings of those texts. The two texts illustrate what the Amises shared,
i.e. satiric metalinguistic awareness, as well as their divergent stance towards cliché: The father's subjecting it to scrutiny, the son's regarding it as
the key to bad art (Childs 2005: 35). If the linguistic endeavour still seems
to the literary minded to be "revealing the obvious" (Jackson 2005: 526),
we certainly welcome the endorsement of our findings through different
routes, in the true spirit of interdisciplinarity.

Since the present work focused on humorous texts, any results are also
relevant to humour theory and the issues therein. A significant contribution of a CxG approach to humour is that it fills in a noticeable gap in the
GTVH and in any theory which focuses on content rather than form,
thereby underrating the role of language. We have specifically shown how
the incongruity whose resolution gives rise to humour may often reside in
the coerced interpretation as such, i.e. in the marked, clashing, or unexpected occurrence of an element in a given construction and the principles
which guide the interpretation in such cases. In this sense, our approach
tallies with other cognitive linguistic approaches to humour, which also
highlight the relationship between the marked and the unmarked, the
prototypical (normal or salient) and the non-prototypical. Importantly,
however, the present work ventures also into the nature of verbal humour,
suggesting that incongruities exploiting the semantic, pragmatic or discoursal properties of conventional constructions should be treated as instances of verbal rather than referential humour. As noted in Emmott
(1999: 42), "in literary text, in particular, the wording is often an important part of the text...[and recent studies] indicate that readers pay greater
attention to the surface form of literary material than to the surface form
of other genres [...]". It seems therefore plausible that a minimal require-

ment for the analysis of literary humour is due consideration and principled treatment of the language factor.

References

Amis, Kingsley
  [1954] 1961 *Lucky Jim*. London: Penguin.
Amis, Martin
  1975 *Dead Babies*. London: Jonathan Cape.
Antonopoulou, Eleni
  2002 A cognitive approach to literary humour devices: Translating Raymond Chandler. *The Translator* 8(2): 235–257.
Antonopoulou, Eleni
  2004 *Humour in Interlingual Transference* (Parousia Monograph Series no. 57). Athens: University of Athens.
Attardo, Salvatore
  1994 *Linguistic Theories of Humor*. Berlin/New York: Mouton de Gruyter.
Attardo, Salvatore
  1997 The semantic foundations of cognitive theories of humor. *Humor: International Journal of Humor Research* 10(4): 395–420.
Attardo, Salvatore
  2001 *Humorous Texts: A Semantic and Pragmatic Analysis*. Berlin/New York: Mouton de Gruyter.
Attardo, Salvatore
  2002 Cognitive stylistics of humorous texts. In: Elena Semino and Jonathan Culpeper (eds.), *Cognitive Stylistics: Language and Cognition in Text Analysis*, 231–250. Amsterdam/Philadelphia: John Benjamins.
Attardo, Salvatore
  2006 Cognitive Linguistics and humor. *Humor: International Journal of Humor Research* 19(3): 341–62.
Attardo, Salvatore, Donalee Hughes Attardo, Paul Baltes and Marnie J. Petray
  1994 The linear organization of jokes: Statistical analysis of two thousand texts. *Humor: International Journal of Humor Research* 7(1): 27–54.
Attardo, Salvatore and Victor Raskin
  1991 Script theory revis(it)ed: Joke similarity and joke representation model. *Humor: International Journal of Humor Research* 4(3/4): 293–347.
Bergen, Benjamin and Kim Binsted
  2004 The cognitive linguistics of scalar humor. In: Michel Achard and Susanne Kemmer (eds.), *Language, Culture and Mind*, 79–92. Stanford: CSLI.
Bradbury, Malcolm
  1987 *No, Not Bloomsbury*. London: André Deutsch.

Brône, Geert and Kurt Feyaerts
  2003   The cognitive linguistics of incongruity resolution: Marked reference point structures in humor. (Preprint no.205). University of Leuven: Department of Linguistics.
Brône, Geert and Kurt Feyaerts
  2004   Assessing the SSTH and GTVH: A view from cognitive linguistics. *Humor: International Journal of Humor Research* 17(4): 361–372.
Brône, Geert, Kurt Feyaerts and Tony Veale
  2006   Humor research and cognitive linguistics: Common grounds and new perspectives (Introduction: Cognitive Linguistic Approaches to Humor). *Humor: International Journal of Humor Research* 19(3): 203–228.
Cacciari, Cristina and Patrizia Tabossi (eds.)
  1993   *Idioms: Processing, Structure, and Interpretation.* Hillsdale NJ; London: Lawrence Erlbaum Associates.
Chandler, Raymond
  [1939] 1950 *Trouble is my Business.* Harmondsworth: Penguin.
Childs, Peter
  2005   *Contemporary Novelists: British Fiction since 1970.* Houndmills, Basingstoke, Hampshire: Palgrave Macmillan.
Croft, William and Alan D. Cruse
  2004   *Cognitive Linguistics.* Cambridge: Cambridge University Press.
De Swart, Henriette
  1998   Aspect shift and coercion. *Natural Language and Linguistic Theory* 16: 347–385.
Dolitsky, Marlene
  1992   Aspects of the unsaid in humor. *Humor: International Journal of Humor Research* 5(1/2): 33–43.
Emmott, Catherine
  1999   *Narrative Comprehension: A Discourse Perspective.* Oxford: Oxford University Press.
Fillmore, Charles
  1985   Frames and the semantics of understanding. *Quaderni di Semantica* 6(2): 222–254.
Fillmore, Charles, Paul Kay and Catherine O'Connor
  1988   Regularity and idiomaticity in grammatical constructions: The case of *let alone. Language* 64: 501–538.
Fillmore, Charles and Paul Kay
  1995   *Construction Grammar Coursebook.* Manuscript, University of Berkeley, Department of Linguistics.
Gibbs, Raymond W.
  1994   *The Poetics of Mind: Figurative Thought, Language, and Understanding.* Cambridge: Cambridge University Press.
Goldberg, Adele
  1992   The inherent semantics of argument structure: The case of the English ditransitive construction. *Cognitive Linguistics* 3(1): 37–74.

Goldberg, Adele
   1995   *Constructions: A Construction Grammar Approach to Argument Structure*. Chicago/London: The University of Chicago Press.
Goldberg, Adele and Ray Jackendoff
   2004   The English resultative as a family of constructions. *Language* 80: 532–568.
Hempelmann, Christian F.
   2004   Script opposition and logical mechanism in punning. *Humor: International Journal of Humor Research* 17(4): 381–392.
Jackson, Tony E.
   2005   Explanation, interpretation, and close reading: The progress of cognitive poetics. *Poetics Today* 26(3): 519–533.
Kay, Paul and Charles Fillmore
   1999   Grammatical constructions and linguistic generalizations: The *What's X doing Y* construction. *Language* 75: 1–33.
Lakoff, George
   1987   *Women, Fire, and Dangerous Things: What Categories Reveal about the Mind*. Chicago: University of Chicago Press.
Langacker, Ronald W.
   1987   *Foundations of Cognitive Grammar, Vol. I: Theoretical Prerequisites*. Stanford, CA: Stanford University Press.
Langacker, Ronald W.
   2000   *Grammar and Conceptualization*. (Cognitive Linguistics Research 14). Berlin/New York: Mouton de Gruyter.
Langacker, Ronald W.
   2001   Discourse in Cognitive Grammar. *Cognitive Linguistics* 12(2): 143–188.
Langacker, Ronald W.
   2002   Deixis and subjectivity. In: Frank Brisard (ed.), *Grounding: The epistemic footing of deixis and reference* (Cognitive Linguistics Research 21), 1–28. Berlin/New York: Mouton de Gruyter.
Langlotz, Andreas
   2006   *Idiomatic Creativity: A Cognitive-Semantic Model of Idiom-Representation and Idiom-Variation in English*. Amsterdam/Philadelphia: John Benjamins.
Lodge, David
   1966   *Language of Fiction: Essays in Criticism and Verbal Analysis of the English Novel*. London: Routledge and Kegan.
Lodge, David
   2002   *Consciousness and the Novel: Connected Essays*. London: Secker and Warburg.
Michaelis, Laura
   2004   Entity and event coercion in a symbolic theory of syntax. In: Jan-Ola Östman and Mirjam Fried (eds.), *Construction Grammars: Cognitive Grounding and Theoretical Extensions*, 45–88. Amsterdam/Philadelphia: John Benjamins.

Michaelis, Laura
    2005   Construction Grammar. URL: http://spot.colorado.edu/~michaeli/
            Michaelis_ELL_C G.pdf
Michaelis, Laura and Josef Ruppenhofer
    2001   *Beyond Alternations: A Constructional Model of the German Appli-
            cative Pattern.* Stanford, CA: CSLI.
Nunberg, Geoffrey, Ivan A. Sag and Thomas Wasow
    1994   Idioms. *Language* 70: 491–538.
Quirk, Randolf, Sidney Greenbaum, Geoffrey Leech and Jan Svartvik
    1972   *A Grammar of Contemporary English.* London: Longman.
Rankin, Ian
    2000   *Set in Darkness.* London: Orion.
Raskin, Victor
    1985   *Semantic Mechanisms of Humor.* Dordrecht: Reidel.
Redfern, Walter
    1997   Traduction, puns, clichés, plagiat. In: Dirk Delabastita (ed.), *Traduc-
            tio: Essays on Punning and Translation,* 261–269. Manchester and
            Namur: St. Jerome and Université de Namur.
Semino, Elena and Jonathan Culpeper (eds.)
    2002   *Cognitive Stylistics: Language and Cognition in Text Analysis.* Amster-
            dam/Philadelphia: John Benjamins.
Simpson, Paul
    2003   *On the Discourse of Satire.* Amsterdam/Philadelphia: John Benjamins.
Stevenson, Randall (ed.)
    2004   *The Last of England?* Vol. 13, *The Oxford English Literary History,* Jon-
            athan Bate (general editor), 2002–2004. Oxford: Oxford University
            Press.
Stockwell, Peter
    2002   *Cognitive Poetics: An Introduction.* London: Routledge.
Triezenberg, Katrina
    2004   Humor enhancers in the study of humorous literature. *Humor: Inter-
            national Journal of Humor Research* 17(4): 411–418.
Tsakona, Villy
    2004   Humour in written narratives: A linguistic approach. Unpublished
            Ph.D. Dissertation. University of Athens.
Veale, Tony, Kurt Feyaerts and Geert Brône
    2006   The cognitive mechanisms of adversarial humor. *Humor* 19(3):
            305–339.
Wilde, Oscar
    [1895] n.d. *The Importance of Being Earnest.* In *The Works of Oscar Wilde.* Lon-
            don and Glasgow: Collins.

A commentary on Antonopoulou and Nikiforidou

Salvatore Attardo

Antonopoulou and Nikiforidou have written an excellent contribution to the linguistic study of humor. It highlights and analyzes a set of phenomena that has received little or no previous attention and provides scholars with the analytical tools to analyze further texts which function on the same basis. I think that the significance of their effort is primarily in that it broadens the definition of "verbal humor" significantly, by including coercion, and therefore may lead to more interesting work. So far, the traditional definition of verbal humor (i.e., humor involving the signifier) had been mostly limited to puns. I had argued that logically one should extend it to alliterative humor, to stylistic humor, and to some forms of irony in which no clear "punch line" was identifiable (in which, for example, the dissonance between form and content gave us the incongruity of humor). Coercion works using different mechanisms but is clearly in the same "family".

Furthermore, Antonopoulou and Nikiforidou's contribution brings together cognitive linguistics and the General Theory of Verbal Humor (GTVH)[1] in a constructive way, which is an excellent idea, which I applaud. I would nonetheless like to address two issues, in this respect.

1) My first remark concerns the relationship between Antonopoulou and Nikiforidou's analysis and the GTVH. The authors rightly say that the GTVH (but this is true of any other humor theory) has had very little to say about these phenomena. However, this is not because, as the authors claim, the GTVH treats all humor as referential. The GTVH clearly accounts for the fact that verbal humor functions differently, in part, from referential humor.[2] Within the GTVH framework, analyses of alliterative humor, stylistic humor, and, more generally, of diffuse disjunctors come very close to the type of analysis presented by Antonopoulou and Niki-

---

1. I assume that the reader is familiar with the GTVH, if not otherwise, at least from the authors' discussion of it in the paper.
2. Only in part, of course: the semantic basis of humor remains in place even in verbal humor. To put it differently, there is no humor without meaning.

foridou. Indeed, the authors point out, in note 10, that the GTVH is compatible with their data, since it allows in verbal humor to "short circuit" the hierarchy of knowledge resources and select script oppositions (i.e., the incongruity of humor) directly from the language level.[3] In a sense, what the authors have done is take an aspect of the Language knowledge resource and develop it. In conclusion, the authors have filled a significant gap in the GTVH-based analyses of humor and show nicely that their analyses fit in with and complement the GTVH. For example, the "humorous coherence" of the text is none other than our old GTVH friend, the strand.

So, if not because the GTVH is referential-humor-centric, why had it neglected this specific phenomenon? The answer is simply that the types of texts analyzed were different. For example, Wilde includes relatively little play on language of the type that Martin Amis, a renowned postmodern stylist, uses. It stands to reason that, as we apply the GTVH and other approaches to increasingly diverse texts, we will be confronted with a variety of mechanisms and phenomena.

2) My biggest concern with the analysis presented by Antonopoulou and Nikiforidou is the fact that the authors repeatedly qualify the phenomena as "marked" (and once even as "deviant", presumably a slip up). I do understand this choice, since e.g. type coercion seems to behave qualitatively differently than "regular" semantic amalgamation. Yet, I think we should resist the temptation.

As I have stressed elsewhere, the mechanisms at play in humor are not humor-specific. To see humor as "marked" comes dangerously close to postulating humor-specific mechanisms. Humor is one of the many cognitive effects that can be achieved by linguistic means. Just like emphasis on a zero-degree literal meaning which would pre-exist all non-literal interpretations appears to be psychologically un-real, I suspect that emphasis of a serious mode which would pre-exist logically all non-serious modes will turn out to be a pedagogical fiction, in the best case scenario. I have discussed elsewhere (Attardo 1999, 2000, 2003; Eisterhold et al. 2006.) what a model that does not privilege a serious (cooperative) mode would look like, so I will not pursue this further.

---

3. See Attardo 1994 for examples of these analyses.

Finally, I have a disagreement with the authors: they are obviously concerned of sounding "deterministic" or "imperialistic" to literary scholars, i.e., they feel that literary scholars are "nervous" about the deterministic or imperialistic linguists. Antonopoulou and Nikiforidou go to some length to appease them.

I think that the free market should reign in the marketplace of ideas (how's that, for a metaphor?). If (cognitive) linguistics has something interesting to say about literary texts, then it should say it, whether it ruffles the feathers of literary scholars or not. Similarly, if a literary scholar has something to say about a text that a linguist is working on, he/she should say it. Ideas should be welcomed and freely exchanged whatever their provenience: whether they come from (cognitive) linguistics or literary theory. In the end, all that matters is how useful they are.

References

Attardo, Salvatore
 1994   *Linguistic Theories of Humor.* Berlin/New York: Mouton de Gruyter.
Attardo, Salvatore
 1999   The place of cooperation in cognition. European Conference of Cognitive Science (ECCS'99) Siena: 459–464.
Attardo, Salvatore
 2000   Irony as relevant inappropriateness. *Journal of Pragmatics* 32: 793–826.
Attardo, Salvatore
 2003   On the nature of rationality in (neo-Gricean) pragmatics. *International Journal of Pragmatics* 14: 3–20.
Eisterhold, Jodi, Diana Boxer and Salvatore Attardo
 2006   Reactions to irony in discourse: Evidence for the Least Disruption Principle. *Journal of Pragmatics* 38(8): 1239–1256.

Judging distances: mental spaces, distance, and viewpoint in literary discourse

Barbara Dancygier and Lieven Vandelanotte

Much of the recent research in cognitive linguistics relies on explaining how spatial concepts influence our understanding of linguistically relevant conceptual constructs on higher levels. Many of the mappings now known as "conceptual metaphors" (see Lakoff and Johnson 1980, 1999) have been talked about in terms of their image-schematic structure and spatial aspects of their source (and target) domains. For example, one of the most common metaphorical mappings, LIFE IS A JOURNEY, uses readily available image-schemas such as "path" or "location", while also building on a metaphorical understanding of goals, difficulties, or progress in terms of "destinations", "obstacles" and "motion along a path", evoked via the EVENT STRUCTURE METAPHOR. The same correlations also underlie mappings such as PURPOSEFUL ACTIVITIES ARE JOURNEYS, which finally leads to the possibility of talking about life in terms of a journey. As these and many other examples suggest, basic spatial configurations are a very rich source of new linguistic usage, reaching broadly across different conceptual domains.

It has been said repeatedly that conceptual metaphors are readily used beyond lexical forms, to structure grammar and discourse. Numerous studies have also shown how metaphorical mappings are extended and elaborated in literary discourse. However, most of the studies we are familiar with focus on how a lexical metaphorical usage is extended into the interpretation of a specific semantic domain or a literary text. In this paper, we want to investigate the entire path a single spatial concept travels from its primary spatial meaning, through various levels of linguistic usage. In order to fully reveal the meaning-constructing power of such a concept, we will consider data from the grammar of conditional sentences, through a specific form of represented speech and thought in narrative discourse, to poetic works by different authors.

The concept we will focus on is that of *distance*. It has already been used quite broadly in cognitive and functional linguistic accounts of different grammatical phenomena, but the senses vary considerably.

We will review some of these uses below, in an attempt to also propose a coherent understanding of the concept across various language domains.

1.   Space and time

The primary sense of "distance" is a spatial configuration profiling two spatial locations, separated by additional space, possibly linked by a physical or visual path going from one to the other. The concept is very salient in our culture, and has prompted an emergence of further concepts and tools used in measuring distance – such as various measuring units (feet, meters), objects (rulers or measuring tapes), and methods of representing distance (maps, travel itineraries, etc.).

It has also been observed early on that spatial landscape, involving distance as one of its conceptual primitives, is a source domain for most of our understanding of time (for other conceptualizations of time see Evans 2004). The temporal understanding of distance emerges from two conceptual metaphors, first discussed by Lakoff and Johnson (1980, 1999). Both mappings involve projecting the spatial concepts of landscape, orientation, landmarks and spatial perspective onto our conceptualization of time. The two models differ in how motion through the temporal landscape is related to the observer: while expressions such as *I am approaching the deadline* profile the "ego" as moving through the landscape in the direction of the landmark, other expressions, such as *The deadline is approaching*, present the "ego" as stationary, and temporal landmarks (events) moving in the direction of the observer. In both models orientation plays an important role, so that the observer is facing the future (*The deadline is a long time ahead*), while the past events are located in the landscape already experienced (*The deadline is already behind us*). The basic nature of these mappings has crucial influence over our understanding of motion as metaphorically making events and people closer or more distant, which is then used in important mappings which define our understanding of events (EVENT STRUCTURE METAPHOR) or relationships.

The metaphor is reflected not only in verbs like *approach*, *come*, or *go*, in many prepositions, and in adjectives like *close* or *remote*. It is quite naturally extended over our understanding of tense and aspect forms (assuming that past events are more distant from the conceptualizer than the present situation), or expressions such as *be going to*, and is also reflected in commonly used gestures.[1] Not surprisingly, the metaphor is also interestingly extended in poetry. The beginning of Philip Larkin's poem "Going" is a good example of how the metaphor is reflected in poetic discourse:

(1)   There is an evening coming in
       Across the fields, one never seen before,
       That lights no lamps.

Critics agree that the poem can be read as a poem about death, or perhaps more accurately, about an experience of death (its original title was, not surprisingly, "Dying day"). The word *evening* is often used to refer to the conclusion of life, along with other expressions suggesting the LIFETIME IS A DAY metaphor, and here the meaning is reinforced with the suggestion of darkness (DEATH IS NIGHT / DARKNESS). What is most interesting is the contrast between two deictic verbs used – *going* appears in the title, and *coming* in the first line. *Go* typically marks motion away from the speaker's deictic centre,[2] while *come* represents moving in the opposite direction – towards the speaker's deictic centre. Death is often talked about in terms of leaving the speaker's experiential domain (*She's gone, She's no longer with us, She passed away*), so the title of the poem can naturally be read to suggest the death of the poem's ego, while the coming of the evening can be interpreted as the arrival of death. Both expressions are thus metaphorically using the conceptualization of time to talk about the event of death, and apply it to the experiential sphere of the ego, but they also underscore the tension between the ego's experience of "going" and the event of death, which is outside the ego's sphere of control.

The understanding of time as space can be further extended into the domain beyond time. Fleischman's seminal concept of temporal distance metaphor (1989, 1990) captures the observation that a speaker may choose the expressions which primarily indicate distance in time, such as past tense of main verbs and modals, to signal social distance or politeness. When a request is phrased with expressions like *I was wondering if you could help* the use of the past tense forms *was* and *could* signals the

---

1. The work by Nuñez and Sweetser (2006) on Aymara, a language which conceptualizes the future behind the ego, not ahead, was actually started with the observation of the gestures accompanying the stories they tell.
2. For a further discussion of the deictic aspects of *go* and the contribution they make to the interpretation of the poem, see Burke (2005).

speaker's intention to avoid impositions – not to put the act requested "in the hearer's face" – to use another expression indicating distance.

Outside of the tense usage, the understanding of social relations in terms of distance is also easy to find. In the travel narrative *Passage to Juneau*, the author, Jonathan Raban, describes the experience of driving on the highway and noting road signs warning against driving too close to the car ahead.

> (2) At intervals of every mile or so, giant placards stood on the verge of the carriageway, saying KEEP YOUR DISTANCE! They might as well have been addressing the coupled carriages in an express railway train [...] Keeping one's distance on this overcrowded island had always been a thorny problem. Within my own living memory, the vast and labyrinthine intricacies of the class-system had helped to compensate for England's chronic absence of breathing space. [...] The country house, at the end of its rhododendron-guarded drive, lay *at an immense remove, in language and manners*, from the village that provided its postal address. (2000: 250–251, italics ours)

The transition the text makes from understanding distance spatially and extending it over the British class divisions and language usage illustrates the salience of the lexical realizations of distance metaphors, but also suggests another sphere into which the concept of distance can be metaphorically extended – the metalinguistic domain. However, as we will suggest below, metalinguistic distance is a category which can be applied to grammatical phenomena as well.

The correlation between the use of tense forms and the concept of distance is also related to the category of epistemic stance, as introduced by Fillmore (1990). Fillmore observes that the choice of verb morphology in conditionals and temporals correlates with the marking of the speaker's epistemic stance, positive, neutral or negative. Among the grammatical distinctions that the concepts help to make is the contrast between *If you come, we'll talk about it*, where the speaker is not committed to the hearer's visit becoming a fact (neutral stance), and *If you came/had come, we would talk/have talked about it*, where the speaker does not expect the hearer to visit (negative stance). The negative commitment of the latter example was further elaborated in Dancygier (1993, 1998), under the rubric of hypothetical distance, and in Dancygier and Sweetser (2005), where the term used was epistemic distance. The concept of distance in all these terms is used in the epistemic sense – the speaker's current knowledge indicates a low likelihood or impossibility of a future development under consideration. In this sense, the concept of distance describes the speaker's perception of a gap between the hypothetical possibility of the event described being or becoming a fact, and the speaker's own belief in the matter.

The cases described above thus resemble Fleischman's idea of distance in that the verb forms are the primary (though not unique) means of expressing it. However, the distancing devices may be different. There are negative stance verbs, like *wish*, which always require that distance is marked in the following clause (*I wish I had more time* refers to the future, while *I wish I had had more time* to the past). But there are also expressions of uncertainty such as verbs (*seem* or *appear*), epistemic modals (as in *He may have finished*), or hedging devices such as *I think* or conditional clauses (as in *If I remember correctly, the deadline is tomorrow*). All such expressions, and there are numerous examples of different kinds of forms playing a similar role, have the function of presenting the utterance as different from an ordinary assertion or prediction. When the situation warrants it, the speaker may express an unhedged assertion or prediction by saying *He didn't come and so we didn't get to talk, I'll talk to him soon* or *The deadline is tomorrow*. Consequently, the use of grammatical devices such as past tense, the conjunction *if*, or embedding in a higher sentence with a verb of knowing or thinking has a distancing effect, such that the speaker's utterance is presented with less conviction or force. In what follows, we will focus on two types of distancing usage in English, using the mental spaces theory as our framework. We will then show how one of the types of distance contributes in a specific way to understanding poetic texts.

2.   Unassertability

Conditional constructions were commonly discussed examples of linguistic expressions in which states of affairs and events may be described as non-factual. The observation led to an exhaustive account of counterfactuality in conditionals, and in similar constructions. However, conditionals are understood counterfactually (or hypothetically) when specific verb forms are present, while in the remaining cases they may be claimed to have a factual interpretation. The contrast is represented by sentences like (3) and (4):

(3)   If she was hired, she doesn't need our help any more.
(4)   If she had been hired, she wouldn't need our help any more.

Both sentences start with a protasis referring to the past, and continue to describe its consequences in the present, but (3) suggests that the hire may be a fact, while (4) makes it clear that it did not happen. The interpretation of the protasis in sentences like (3) has been described as "factual" or as "given", to reflect the understanding that the speaker has acquired the knowledge of p (she was hired) from the hearer (*If, as you say, she was hired...*), that the speaker accepts it to be true, and continues the reasoning on its basis. Such an interpretation of conditionals like (3) resembles the descriptions of the evidential (or "hearsay") constructions in other languages.

However, the factuality of p in conditionals like (3) has been seriously questioned in recent literature. Dancygier (1998) builds a strong argument against postulating a factual interpretation for any conditional protasis. In short, the argument is that the conjunction *if* prevents the clause in its scope from becoming factual, because it is a marker of some degree or level of unassertability. Sentences like (3) rely heavily on the discourse grounding of p, and the content of p, even if earlier asserted by the hearer or derived from contextually available knowledge, is not asserted by the speaker. Dancygier points out that describing the protasis in (3) as factual is not helpful, since the status of p in the real world is not the issue in such conditionals. What the hearer considers to be a fact (she was hired), may in fact be wrong, and, while the speaker of (3) may believe the hearer's assertion, she is not asserting p herself.

In Dancygier (1998) the cases of sentences like (3), where the speaker is tentatively presenting an assumption which she herself is not asserting, were described as examples of epistemic distance. At the same time, later work on conditionals uses the same term in the sense roughly equivalent to Fillmore's negative epistemic stance – in this sense, the term applies to examples like (4), where the speaker's knowledge suggests that p is not the case. The senses share important features, such as the speaker's hesitation to present a clause as an assertion for reasons related to what the speaker actually knows or expects to be true, which justifies the use of the term "epistemic". But it is also the case that there are important differences between the two uses, even though both are most saliently present in conditionals.[3]

The main difference is the role of what the speaker knows, as opposed to what the speaker learns (consider Akatsuka's [1985] distinction be-

---

3. There are in fact many linguistically valid differences, but any further discussion would go beyond the scope of the present paper. See Dancygier and Sweetser (2005) for more discussion.

tween knowledge and information). In (4), the speaker marks her knowl-edge that the hire did not happen, and imagines a hypothetical situation where it did. In (3), she has no prior knowledge about the hire, receives in-formation from the hearer (or another source), and tentatively assumes its validity, at least for the purposes of current discourse. This does not indi-cate lack of trust in the hearer's words, but lack of genuine current knowl-edge of the state of affairs. The difference between these two epistemic sources of low assertability is important enough in English (and other languages) that it is in fact marked through verb forms. In (4), the whole set of forms, which Dancygier and Sweetser call *distanced*, marks the speaker's negative stance, while (3), which has neutral, rather than posi-tive stance, uses unmarked forms, appropriate to the straightforward de-scription of the situations discussed. Both sentences are thus marked with epistemic distance, but of a different kind: one is roughly equivalent to Fillmore's negative stance ([4]), the other ([3]) to neutral stance.

3. Distance as a mental space set-up

The above review of numerous existing uses of the concept of distance shows that the term, though intuitively appropriate in all cases, has been used in application to different domains – space and time, knowledge, or politeness. The range of cognitive domains thus evoked resembles Sweetser's description of content, epistemic and speech act domains (Sweetser 1990). This seems to further confirm our suggestion that the concept of distance is naturally extended to various domains of meaning. The choice of the domains is thus not entirely determined by the specific structure of the domains as such (as is the case for most metaphorical mappings), but it fits into a broad understanding of cognitive realms where a number of linguistic forms behave similarly. This correlation further confirms the need to propose a uniform description of the under-lying concept.

   We will attempt to define the concept of distance, as it applies to the dif-ferent spatial, temporal, and epistemic uses described above, in terms of the theory of mental spaces – the theory which views a variety of linguistic expressions as prompts for the construction of small cognitive packets which are set up, activated, or manipulated as discourse progresses (Fau-connier [1985] 1994, 1997). Mental spaces allow language users to operate mentally in situations that are removed from the speaker's here and now – the future, the past, different locations and spatial orientations, imagined situations, fictional worlds, other people's lives, etc. Even this cursory description makes it clear that all of the ways of understanding distance that we mentioned above lend themselves to the mental space analysis. In fact, we want to suggest that the basic spatial understanding of distance provides a mental space set-up which is then projected into other domains – time, social relations, or epistemic structures.

The basic sense of distance assumes (at least) two spatial locations which are separated from each other with additional space, and an observer who can view both locations and perceive the space between them. That "space in-between" is what is referred to as distance. The degree of distance may be described loosely (*far apart* versus *close up*), or measured according to the appropriate conventions (e.g. the metric system). The ability to measure assumes that the conceptualizer can trace the extent of the "space in-between", by mentally scanning it or applying a measuring tool, such as a ruler. When this happens, the conceptualizer (the speaker) has to add directionality to the concept – you can measure the distance from A to B, or from B to A. The conceptualization is the same whether we are performing the mental scan or whether the ruler is used, so that the lowest value of distance coincides with one point and the actual measured value coincides with the other. If one of the points is then chosen as the speaker's deictic centre, so that the speaker's location coincides with it, the set-up assumes that one of the two locations is a point from which the other one can be viewed. The speaker's deictic location thus becomes a locus of the speaker's viewpoint, so that distance from the other location can now be talked about as "distance as perceived by the speaker".

The kind of set-up discussed can naturally be described in terms of mental spaces. We are capable of conceptualizing two spaces at the same time, and the simplest case is when the two spaces represent two spatial locations. Language users are capable of mentally shifting the viewpoint from "here" to "there", and of perceiving the distance separating them. All the metaphors of distance described above follow the same mental space configuration, whether the spaces are temporal ("now" and "then"), social, or epistemic (states of knowledge determined by different viewpoints).

We want to argue that all the "distance" phenomena discussed in this paper rely on this basic mental space set-up – with two separated spaces, and the speaker's deictic alignment with one of them. In order for a mental space to be set up, there has to be a prompt that triggers the space's construction. The prompt may be lexical, grammatical, gestural, visual, etc., but it typically initializes the space as "located" in space (*in London*), time (*yesterday*), or epistemic base (*he thinks*). The structure of the space thus set up has to contain the parameter prompted for, but it is not limited to it, so that discourse context or the conversational record may decide on further elements (discourse history, participants, encyclopaedic knowledge, etc.). Furthermore, the structure of the space can be further enriched by inferences, frames, inheritance from other spaces, etc. (a more detailed discussion would exceed the limits of the present paper).

In the cases of distance set-ups, then, there are also inferences to be derived: that the "distant" space is less accessible to the speaker, that the speaker is less affected by it, that the speaker's interaction with it is limited, etc. (this inference is particularly useful in social distance). But one can also infer that the speaker is able to mentally locate herself in the distant space, regardless of its nature, and reason about it. Mental access to distanced spaces is necessary for the conceptualizer to adopt different viewpoints – a very basic and indispensable cognitive ability.

We can explain now how the two kinds of epistemic distance represented in (3) and (4) differ in terms of their mental space and deictic centre configurations. The case of negative epistemic stance represented in (4) requires that the speaker, located in her base space with its temporal and epistemic set-up, imagines a new mental space occupying the temporal location of a space known to be factual. The factual space (*she wasn't hired*) thus inhabits a past temporal location, but, by virtue of being factual, is not distanced epistemically. The counterfactual protasis (*if she had been hired*), on the other hand, inhabits an imagined space, which is attached to the same temporal location as the known factual one. Both spaces are thus distant from the speaker's present location, but the counterfactual one is double-distanced, temporally, and epistemically. However, both rely on the speaker's current deictic centre; that is, both are perceived as distant from the same viewpoint – the speaker's "present moment" and the speaker's "present knowledge". The difference is that one is only distant in time, while the other is additionally distant in that it represents a knowledge base which is different from the speaker's current base. However, for the purposes of current discourse, the speaker assumes the non-factual knowledge base as the space from which she will reason further. Consequently, two scenarios are available at the same time. They allow the speaker to reason about an imagined course of events, while using a different epistemic viewpoint. But both epistemic viewpoints (the real one and the imagined one) are anchored to the speaker's deictic centre and profile the speaker as the only discourse participant.

Sentences like (3) use distance in a different way. There are two speakers, or, in less clear-cut cases, two independent epistemic spaces – the space A deictically aligned with the speaker uttering (3), with no prior knowledge of p (whether she was hired or not), and the space B, suggesting that p (*she was hired*). Space B is the discourse source of the utterance "she was hired", which is then incorporated into (3), so in effect it is co-opted into the reasoning in space A, without losing its independent "Space B" status. Thus, when Speaker A says *If she was hired, …*, Speaker B's utterance becomes a part of Speaker A's discourse, though not necessarily of her knowledge base. A sentence like (3) thus represents one deictic centre of Speaker A, but maintains two discourse contexts – A and B, with their independent knowledge bases.

The way in which one utterance, subordinated to one speaker's deictic centre, may represent the two discourse stances and two speakers is best explained through blending – an operation on mental spaces which treats some selected spaces as sources of structure, or inputs (Fauconnier and Turner 1996, 1998a,b, 2002). The selective projection from the inputs leads to a blended space which contains new structure, not available in either one of the inputs alone. The process is one of the basic mechanisms of emergence of new meanings and operates on many levels of linguistic structure. In the simplest case, a new compound, such as *a cash cow*, creates a new meaning construction which uses some features from the domain represented by *cow* (a provider of desirable food, meekly allowing us to take as much of it as we need and not asking for anything in return), and some from the domain of *cash* (another desirable commodity, usually requiring plenty of effort to acquire). The emergent meaning describes an easy, undemanding, and unlimited source of money.

Instances like (3) represent a network of spaces which profiles two speakers or two sources of knowledge contributing jointly to one of the speakers' utterance. Initially, the set-up has two input spaces. In Input A, there is speaker A, considering a friend's career, not knowing what the current situation is. In Input B, there is a speaker B, who has reasons to believe that the hire took place. The utterance of (3) continues the conversation from the point of view of A, while using an assumption originating in B. The speaker in A is not subscribing to the news about the hire or presenting the hire as a fact, but is blending it into her discourse thread. It will remain clear, though, thanks to the non-assertive force of *if*, that the utterance represents only the viewpoint of A, while employing a thought from B. Let us add that many different spaces can serve as Input B: speaker A could be evoking an earlier conversation, possibly with different participants, a written source, or even something A herself had said on another occasion or joked about. The important thing is that the resulting utterance blends selected aspects of form and meaning from A and B to satisfy the needs of speaker A's viewpoint and the discourse context.

It should be clear from the remarks above that mental spaces can be distinguished by different kinds of information, depending on what aspect of the utterance functions as a space-builder. The same situation can thus be located spatially (*In Canada, hockey is popular*), temporally (*During Stanley Cup play-offs hockey is popular*), or epistemically (*I think hockey is popular, Hockey seems to be popular*), but it can also require accessing a different discourse context, or at least may be marked as not belonging to the discourse context aligned with the speaker's deictic centre. This is the type of distance we are postulating for (3). In the next section, we will explain the discourse features of the set-up that makes it possible.

4. Distanced discourse

Recent work in cognitive grammar, and especially in mental spaces theory, incorporates discourse parameters in different ways and to a different degree. Langacker (2001) introduces the concepts of the "current discourse space" and the "ground" to refer to the aspects of on-going discourse which are shared by the interlocutors and used in the subsequent conceptualizations. A somewhat similar understanding is proposed by Coulson and Oakley (2005), through their concept of "discourse grounding", which makes various interpretations of specific blends possible (e.g., the blend underlying the expression *a cash cow* could have positive connotations for the recipient of the cash, and negative ones for the person who is unknowingly being "milked", and the speaker or the hearer may be profiled in one of those roles). In a broader linguistic context, Verhagen (2005) discusses a variety of linguistic phenomena which suggest that the construals performed by speakers are typically not just subjective, but *intersubjective*, since the mental space which is the locus of conceptualization incorporates other viewpoints as well, for instance that of the hearer, or of another participant who is profiled in the discourse context. For example, the speaker saying *Mary is not happy. On the contrary, she is really depressed* is not merely negating Mary's happiness, but formulating the thought in opposition (*on the contrary*) to a suggestion present in the "ground" (or "current discourse space") that Mary is happy. The construal of the object of conceptualization (Mary's feelings) is thus first filtered through the mental space which Verhagen calls Subject of Conceptualization, or Ground, profiling at least two participants (one of them being the speaker) who may view the object of conceptualization differently.

Verhagen's proposal is important to our discussion since it accounts for all the discourse situations where the speaker is not the only source of subjectivity and the hearer's, or another participant's viewpoint is evoked. The range of phenomena discussed by Verhagen covers constructions such as the *let alone*-construction, some cases of negation, clausal complements and some discourse connectives. However, the examples which this paper focuses on go further, in that they mark the possible discrepancy between the speaker's conceptualizations and that of the "other" in the very choice of words. The echoic nature of the examples which use the discourse of the "other" in this way can also be captured in terms of the framework of "fictive interaction", as introduced by Pascual (2002). Pascual distinguishes several types of mental spaces in an on-going interaction, but the concept most pertinent to our examples here is that of a "verbal performance" space, which contains the information on "the use of communicative devices, both verbal and non-verbal, and which frames the relationship between the utterers and *their messages*". (italics ours, Pascual 2002: 83). In Pascual's description, the verbal performance space describes discourse types involving irony, sarcasm, and those additionally marked by devices such as quotation marks in writing, or gestural imitation of quotes in face-to-face interaction. The verbal performance space participates crucially in the blend representing the multifaceted character of discourse.

In Pascual's framework the concept of "fictive interaction" covers a number of types of linguistic expressions, including fictive commands such as *Call me crazy* or expressions of the type *Don't you dare poor-thing me!*. All these utterances resemble our examples in that they call up a discourse space outside of the speaker's subjective ground (but not necessarily outside of the current discourse space), and incorporate it into the present flow of discourse. Furthermore, they often mark, as the examples we will discuss do, a certain degree of distance between the speaker's and the hearer's subjectivities, while consistently maintaining the speaker's viewpoint in the utterance in question. However, there are important differences as well. First, the "interaction" aspect of Pascual's cases is more salient than in our examples. Fictive interaction snippets evoke more than one assumption communicated in a different discourse context, so that a different exchange is evoked with it, representing a "type", rather than "token". Also, the degree of incorporation into current discourse is, at least in some instances, of a much looser kind than in the cases we are considering below, where the "seams" do not show. Furthermore, the examples we will be analysing are often marked with other types of distance as well. While acknowledging important similarities between Pascual's and Verhagen's concepts on the one hand, and our examples on the other, we will propose to describe the cases analysed in this paper as instances of *distanced discourse*.

To return to our original example, we believe that sentences like (3) are blends which occur within the current discourse space, but use a verbal performance space to create an expression which smoothly incorporates utterances originating in different discourse spaces and/or different subjectivities into the flow of the current discourse space. Although the features of the verbal performance in each case may be different, they do maintain the blended flow of discourse, while clearly marking the epistemic distance between the speaker's and hearer's (or other participant's) subjectivities. This specific kind of distance needs to be distinguished from the types we discussed earlier, although it is perfectly possible for the discourse distance (as we will call it) to arise as a result of epistemic, social, or temporal distance. Given that the kind of distance we are distinguishing here involves the evocation of not just the thought, but also the discourse context, we will use the term *distanced discourse* to cover all of these cases.

We will also try to give specific descriptions of the grammatical forms used in distanced discourse. The tense forms used to mark temporal distance are co-opted to mark polite distance and are also used to mark the epistemic distance in (4). Consequently, the lack of adjustment of verb forms in (3) suggests that discourse distance is most salient in this case. There are similarities between (3) and (4) (each set-up represents one deictic centre, that of the actual speaker, and two epistemic stances). The crucial difference is that (4) remains within the current discourse space – the speaker is the "author" of both the truthful and the imaginary version of events, while (3) uses two discourse spaces – the one where the knowledge about the hire originates, and the current discourse space. The discourse space B – the source of the protasis – could be aligned with another discourse participant, a written or visual source of information, or even the speaker "posing" as someone else (in the "devil's advocate" kind of argument). But the set-up maintains two discourse spaces, while subordinating them to one deictic centre. Throughout the remainder of this paper we will explore other instances of the type of distancing illustrated by (3) and further apply the concept of distanced discourse to narrative and poetic texts.

We remarked above that discourse distance may be combined with other kinds of distance. While distanced spaces may be set up as spatial or temporal (based on the space builders used), they will also, as we said above, maintain some of the structure inherited from higher spaces in the network and obtain some through access and inferences. But not all spaces have to enrich the discourse aspects of the set-up. If the speaker sets up a temporal distanced space with the use of *yesterday*, she may still retain her own viewpoint, knowledge base, or status of conceptualizer. Only a set-up wherein other speakers (with viewpoints, knowledge bases, etc,) are profiled is subject to discourse distance interpretation. In (4) the speaker remains the only discourse participant, though she chooses to alter her knowledge base for the purposes of the reasoning, and embeds the new line of thought in her discourse. In (3), the speaker is mentally accessing another discourse space where a participant, from the point of view of her own knowledge base, says something the speaker is now co-opting into her reasoning, without changing her knowledge base. The distance thus emerges from evocation of another discourse context and another knowledge base.

Such an understanding of distance coincides with two types of relationships among spaces which have been postulated so far. The mechanism of *mental space embedding* represents one space as a sub-space of another, and is typically marked by the projection of stance-marking verb forms from the higher space to the lower one. For example, the apodosis of (4) is embedded in its protasis and is thus marked with the same distanced forms. The competing mechanism of *mental space evocation* consists in a kind of "echoing", or re-introduction, of a space set up elsewhere in the shared discourse context, where the evoked space retains its form and stance, but is incorporated into the current discourse. We can thus treat distanced discourse as a specific case of mental space evocation.[4]

Interestingly enough, conditionals are also a source of examples where discourse distance appears in correlation with a different kind of epistemic distance. It is widely accepted that futurate conditionals do not use *will* in protases, and use present tense instead, as in *If he comes to dinner, we'll have some wine*. There are, however, instances where *will* is possible, as in *If he will come to dinner, we'll have some wine*. Dancygier (1998) discusses *will*-protases as instances of hearer's perspective, but it should be clear from the discussion above that those "cited" predictions (where the

---

4. For a further discussion of space evocation see Dancygier and Sweetser's (2000) discussion of *since*, and Dancygier's (2004, 2005) work on the narrative.

speaker relies on another speaker's prediction of "his" arrival to justify the decision to have wine) are also instances of discourse distance, where the prediction uttered is not in fact the speaker's, and is thus epistemically distanced too.

As the preceding discussion suggests, conditionals are by no means the only construction where distanced discourse in the sense just defined appears, though they are a very clear case. More specifically, we are suggesting that the same description can be given to what has become known as "metalinguistic negation" (Horn 1985, 1989). Sentence (5) illustrates the point:

(5)   The paper wasn't good, it was brilliant!

The description using the adjective *good* clearly does not originate in the speaker's discourse. There must be another space where *good* was used or suggested, and the speaker of (5) uses the negation to reject the wording from the other discourse space, and to propose her own description – *brilliant*. Verhagen's discussion of the uses of negation would probably include the metalinguistic cases, but his focus is on the intersubjective nature of the meaning constructed, and not on the choice of wording. The cases of distanced discourse we will be discussing vary in the degree of emphasis put on the linguistic forms used, and on the consequences of the choices, but they clearly preserve the echoed wording to a high degree.

The correlation between metalinguistic uses and distanced discourse can also be seen in another category of conditionals, called metatextual (Dancygier 1998) or metalinguistic (Dancygier and Sweetser 2005). Consider (6):

(6)   It was good, if not outright brilliant.

The speaker's intention to self-correct, which is clear in sentences like (6), sets up two discourse spaces, in which the same speaker is portrayed as describing the same situation in two different ways. In a sense, the hearer of (6) is left with the impression that the speaker is either "thinking on her feet", or hesitating as to the best choice of wording. Furthermore, there are examples of metalinguistic conditionals where other discourse standards are explicitly invoked, as in (7):

(7)   I've just met John's significant other, if that's the expression to use these days.

The protasis of (7) sets up a different verbal performance space, where the current standards of appropriateness are established; the speaker's current discourse space also has a standard to guide her choices, but she is acknowledging the fact that the standards in the two spaces may be different.

While all of the metalinguistic uses described rely on distanced discourse in a crucial way, they also display characteristics specific to metalinguistic use. While in other cases discussed above the actual meaning or illocutionary force is an important reason for evoking the discourse fragment in question, in metalinguistic cases the language forms themselves and their appropriateness or acceptability are in focus. We will thus continue to distinguish metalinguistic uses as an independent subcategory.

In the following section we will use the concept of distanced discourse to look at constructions commonly occurring in narrative discourse which explicitly evoke another discourse space – various categories of speech and thought representation (STR). We will argue, among other things, that the concept of distanced discourse helps distinguish a category of STR which has not been fully recognized so far.

5.   Distanced discourse and represented speech and thought[5]

The examples of distanced discourse discussed so far involve grammatical constructions, such as conditionals and negation, in which the involvement of distinct discourse spaces has not been generally recognized in the literature until recently. In this section we turn to a discussion of speech and thought representation, for which the involvement of different discourses is more widely accepted, irrespective of the specific framework adopted. The whole point of speech and thought representation is, after all, to say something about what others say or think, or what the speaker

---

5. The terms "represented speech and thought" and "speech and thought representation" (STR) are used instead of "reported speech" or "speech and thought presentation" because the phenomenon involves representing something as speech or thought; not merely "reporting" or "presenting" actual speech or thoughts. As is well known, there is not always a real "prior" utterance which is subsequently "reported" or "presented" (von Roncador 1980 1988; Fludernik 1993). Note also that we use the terms as referring to all types of speech and thought representation, whereas Banfield (1982) used the term "represented speech and thought" to refer specifically to what is usually called "free indirect discourse".

herself at some other time or place has said or thought. There is thus always at least one participant, the one responsible for conjuring up another's discourse, and another participant whose discourse is being represented. If we need to make the technical distinction explicit, we will refer to the former as the "current" speaker and to the latter as the "represented" speaker. More often than not, in fact, even more information is available about the speech situations involved. For instance, the identity of the current speaker's addressee as well as that of the represented speaker's will affect the form and function of the representation. In narrative texts in particular, there is usually a rich spatio-temporal context, with a wide variety of well-profiled participants who can fill the roles of current and represented speakers. What is more, as we will see, the whole question of who is addressing who in the current and in the represented speech situation can find expression in deictic categories such as person and tense, as well as in the choice between different referring expressions (pronouns vs. proper names for example).

For these reasons, it may be more immediately obvious that speech and thought representation involves distinct mental spaces, and may in a sense be grammatically more informative about their grounding than, say, metalinguistic negation or conditionals. The point we want to make, however, is that there exists among the types of speech and thought representation a rather specific counterpart of the distanced constructions discussed so far. It seems fair to say that to represent an utterance as someone else's (or indeed one's own former or potential) speech or thought always involves some degree of disassociation with the content of that utterance: "framing" an utterance in this way allows one to *say* it without *asserting* it or showing any kind of commitment towards it (Davies 1979; McGregor 1997). In this general sense, any instance of speech or thought representation is always "at a remove" from straightforward, non-reportative discourse, regardless of the specific subtype (direct, indirect, etc.).

However, one subtype has recently been described which instantiates the particular pattern discussed so far under the rubric of "distanced discourse" (Vandelanotte 2004a, 2004b), viz. that in which a distinct discourse space, blended with the speaker's current discourse space, is merely evoked without a shift of viewpoint. What is particularly significant about this in the context of STR constructions, where many formal features mark partial or total shifts of deictic centre, is that the category we introduce here represents another participant's speech or thought *without* a shift of deictic centre. To illustrate this point, consider example (8), in which parts from a transcribed telephone conversation are reproduced.

The speaker in these short extracts is Joyce, who is talking over the phone to Lesley about a third party who was making inquiries about Lesley:

(8) *She said um::n e::m did I know if you were teaching [...] She said did I know if you were teaching* I said (.) well I know she has been [...]
(attested data qtd. Holt 1996: 228, also qtd. partly Holt 2000: 433–434; italics ours; original transcription simplified)

While Holt (1996, 2000) in her analysis adopted a reading as direct speech for the three sentences in (8), closer inspection reveals that such a reading can only be maintained for the last sentence, *I said well I know she has been*. In order to see why, it is important to bear in mind that all the while Lesley, the person referred to not only as *she* in *she has been* but also as *you* in *if you were teaching*, is being addressed over the phone. In the first two sentences, then, there is no shift in the deictic centre from which the reported clause *did I know if you were teaching* is plotted. In a rendering as direct speech, we would expect to see *do you know if she (Lesley) is teaching?*, with a shift from the deictic centre of Joyce to that of the third party inquiring about Lesley. It is only in the last sentence in (8) that Lesley (Joyce's current interlocutor) is not referred to as a second person but as a third, reflecting her status as "someone being talked about" in the earlier conversation *about* rather than *with* Lesley. This is why we can tell that *I said well I know she has been* is direct speech: a shift has taken place from Joyce's current deictic centre to her past deictic centre at the time of this earlier conversation.

Where does this leave the first two sentences of (8)? In our view, these instantiate a distinct type of speech and thought representation, referred to as "distancing indirect speech or thought" (DIST), in which the speaker's deictic centre is held constant but a distinct discourse space is evoked. This type differs from all three types traditionally distinguished: direct, indirect and free indirect speech or thought. Without going into too much detail, let us briefly point out some essential differences. One characteristic that sets indirect speech or thought (IST) apart from the other types is its different syntactic structure: it allows and (following verbs of asking and wondering) sometimes requires a complementizer, and it disallows non-declarative finite clause structure in its reported clause (e.g. *I asked him if he'd care to join us* vs. *'Would you care to join us?', I asked him*). A defining characteristic of what we call DIST is its deictic singularity – all manner of deictic expressions are referred to the deictic centre of the speaker – whereas the other types display different degrees of "deictic shift" (cf. von Roncador 1988). In direct speech or thought (which we will refer to as DST), this deictic shift from the current speaker's deictic centre to that of the represented speaker is complete: a new axis from which deictic relations are plotted is assumed in the reported clause. This means, among other things, that first person pronouns in the reporting and the reported clause refer to the current and the represented speaker respectively:

(9)   Then he said to *me*, "*I'*m a veteran. *I* fought in the South." (CB, npr; italics ours)

In terms of mental space structure, the mental space of the reported clause in DST comes to be adopted temporarily as a new base space (Sanders and Redeker 1996: 296).

   While the deictic shift in DST is full, that in free indirect speech or thought (FIST) is only partial. In FIST, as is well known, grammatical person of pronouns is not determined by the represented speaker's viewpoint, but by that of the current speaker, while other deictics such as spatiotemporal adverbials are construed from the former's viewpoint. This has been noted particularly in connection with the co-occurrence of past verb morphology and present time adverbial deictics, producing what has been called a "NOW in the PAST" (Banfield 1982) or a "WAS-NOW paradox" (Adamson 1995), exemplified in (10). It is less generally recognized that indirect speech or thought in fact allows very similar phenomena, rather than being entirely and exclusively a current speaker's "paraphrase", as can be seen from example (11).

(10)   Where *was* he *this morning*, for instance? Some committee, she never asked what. (Woolf, *Mrs Dalloway*, p. 10 qtd. Banfield 1982: 93; italics ours)
(11)   Cross looked at Eva. Though she had stopped sobbing, Cross could see that she didn't quite follow what was being said. Cross felt that *now was* the time to co-operate with the Party, to demonstrate class consciousness, to cast his solidarity with the revolution. (CB, usbooks, italics ours)

With this in mind, the question that still needs to be considered briefly is why the italicized sentences in (8) are not amenable to an analysis as FIST, traditionally regarded as *the* type that bridges the gap between direct and indirect speech. After all, in keeping with what was said above about FIST, the grammatical person of pronouns in these sentences can be said to be referred to the current speaker Joyce, and not to the represented speaker Lesley. In a nutshell, the reason for this, we believe, lies with the fact that the *raison d'être* of free indirect discourse is the coherent but oblique (non-direct) representation of a character's consciousness. The expressivity represented in the reported clause of free indirect discourse is thus exclusively that of this character or "self" (Banfield 1982), as is equally the case in direct speech or thought. The deictic peculiarities of free indirect discourse ensure, however, that the "loudness" of DST (van der Voort 1986) is avoided: the represented utterance or thought in free indirect discourse is non-exchange directed or non-response soliciting. More concretely, no one is directly addressed in it, whereas direct speech or thought allows the direct address of the represented addressee, and DIST that of the current addressee (as with *you* in [8]).[6]

Instead of offering a "closed off" oblique representation of a represented speaker's consciousness, the reported clause of DIST as in the italicized sentences in (8) *appropriates* and *echoes* their (real or imagined) utterance or thought. Unlike in DST, where the *she* persona's mental space would be represented as a new base space (*do you know if she is teaching?*), in DIST this space is evoked from the deictic centre of the current speaker Joyce as *did I know if you were teaching*. Similar examples can be found in attested (12) as well as in fictional (13) dialogue. Note that the direct speech equivalents of the italicized utterances are *would you* (or maybe *will you*) *start tomorrow* and *when are you going* respectively.

(12) [the speaker is offered a job] this was a Wednesday ((was it right)) so *would I start the next day – and perhaps put in for that Friday as well* – m and that that would be my first week's pay (Survey of English Usage S. 2.12.91 qtd. in Fludernik 1993: 84; italics adapted)

(13) 'What time does your train go?'
'Heavens, what a question.' She glanced laughingly at John, sharing the joke. 'You don't come to meet me, and the first thing you ask is, *when am I going?* Half-past six, if you must know. What would you like to eat?' she added, as one of the ladies in print overalls came and stood by them. (Philip Larkin, *Jill*; [1946] 2005: 73; italics ours)

---

6. Full treatment of the complex nature of free indirect discourse is beyond the scope of this paper, but see Vandelanotte (in press) for a detailed exposition of the "non-addressivity" of free indirect discourse, and of the consequences of separating out free from distancing indirect speech or thought for the pragmatics of free indirect discourse.

In poetry as well, dialogue can be represented in direct speech or in DIST, or in a combination of the two. In (14) we quote from Michael Dennis Browne's poem "Philip Larkin", in which the I-persona, like the author a university lecturer in literature, suddenly finds himself in the elevator with a poetically revived Philip Larkin, who turns out now to be part of the maintenance crew at his university. The parts of the ensuing dialogue represented in direct speech are clearly marked by means of quotation marks; those for which we propose a reading as DIST have been italicized.

(14) [...] He's wearing a dark blue
        uniform; the logo over the left pocket, just under
        the name PHIL, looks like a scarab. Larkin sees me
        staring. "Scarabaeus", he says, "tough little shiteater.
        Gets the job done."

        I'm going to third. Where's he going? "Basement",
        he says. *He'll wait while I go up, then he'll go down.*
        [...]
        We talk. *Since death, he's been traveling, working
        on and off (anything but libraries), seeing the world
        at last. He's loosened up. He's still into jazz, the
        old kind. Right now, he's working late shift in this
        building*, the one I've been working in all these
        years – teaching, among other things, him.

        (Michael Dennis Browne, "Philip Larkin"; 1999: 3)

In the two instances of DST in this extract, there are in fact no deictic indications that force a reading as direct speech: it is merely the author's use of typographic conventions that betrays his intention for this to be read as a shift to a new base space, that of Larkin. In the remainder of the poem, not reproduced here, the direct speech status of the parts enclosed in quotation marks is also deictically signalled. For instance, the use of *your* in the I-persona's utterance "I was at your grave last year with Anthony Storey" can be contrasted with the form *his* which would be used in a DIST rendering. Similarly, in a stretch of direct speech attributed to Larkin at the end of the poem, "They can stick this on it, if you want" a DIST rendering would have had *if I want*.

In order to see this, it is important to bear in mind the situation of utterance (Lyons 1977; Davies 1979) of the poem. In (8), we witnessed the direct telephone conversation between Joyce and Lesley (with Lesley being currently an addressee) *about* another conversation (viz. between

Joyce and someone else about Lesley, who was thus only a third party talked about in this prior conversation). The poem in (14), on the other hand, is essentially a narrative told in the historic present and taking place between the I-persona and the reader, in which the prior dialogue between Larkin and the lecturer is represented (in direct speech) or evoked (in DIST). It is only by carefully keeping track of the speech participants at different times that we can see why the pronoun *you* referring to Lesley in (8) signals DIST, whereas in a case like "I was at your grave last year" in the context of (14), *your* referring to Larkin signals DST.

With this situation of utterance in mind, it should be clear why the italicized parts of (14) are not amenable to an analysis as direct speech but represent instead "distanced" discourse. A direct rendering, with a deictic shift resulting in a new base space, would naturally involve the lecturer and Larkin referring to one another as *you*, and to oneself as *I*: *where are you going* instead of *where's he going*, *I'll wait while you go up* instead of *he'll wait while I go up*, and *I've been travelling* instead of *he's been travelling*. Rather than yielding the floor extensively to the represented speaker each time, in the italicized sentences in (14) the poet has chosen to evoke the represented speaker's discourse space from his own deictic centre, perhaps for the purpose of pithiness, or to give to these passages a less "dramatic" and, one might say, more "narrative" flavour: instead of allowing the character to take centre stage by using direct speech, in the passages of DIST the narrator remains tangibly present in the representation of another's utterances or thoughts. While "distance" is almost self-evidently construed in the use of such a clearly signalled device as direct speech ("this is not me speaking"), it is thus arguably more subtle and unexpected (and therefore perhaps more "informative") in what we call DIST and in distanced discourse more generally: in them, a distinct, quite independent (rather than embedded, as in [4]) mental space is evoked despite the fact that the deictic centre is held constant. The fact that we have or can obtain such specific knowledge about the situation of utterance in examples like (14) presents a marked difference with the examples of conditionals and metalinguistic negation discussed previously, in which, as we have seen, the source of the mental space evoked in the distanced discourse may be quite vague and difficult to pin down.

The examples so far have focused exclusively on cases in which the protagonists were referred to by means of pronouns. Besides this type of example, there is another type in which DIST can be contrasted fruitfully with both DST and FIST, viz. that in which represented speakers and/or represented addressees are referred to by means of proper names or descriptive noun phrase. An example of this from literary discourse involving proper names is given in (15); one from spoken language involving a descriptive noun phrase in (16).

(15) A conversation then ensued, not on unfamiliar lines. *Miss Bartlett was, after all, a wee bit tired, and thought they had better spend the morning settling in; unless Lucy would rather like to go out? Lucy would rather like to go out, as it was her first day in Florence, but, of course, she could go alone. Miss Bartlett could not allow this. Of course she would accompany Lucy everywhere. Oh, certainly not; Lucy would stop with her cousin. Oh no! that would never do! Oh yes!* (*A Room with a View*; Forster, p. 20 qtd. in Banfield 1982: 207; italics ours)

(16) The draft will be abolished then? *Well, that far the minister wouldn't go. Clarity will only come in the priorities memorandum, in a few months.* (*de Volkskrant* 11 November 1992 qtd. in Redeker 1996: 226; translation hers)[7]

While the problem of proper names appearing in passages that might easily be mistaken for free indirect discourse has been noted (e.g. Dillon and Kirchhoff 1976; Banfield 1982; Fludernik 1993), no fully satisfactory account seems to have gained wide acceptance.[8] In our view, this type of example illustrates once more the phenomenon of distanced discourse, in which distinct mental spaces are evoked (for instance those of Lucy and Miss Bartlett in 15) from one and the same deictic centre, that of the current speaker. Let us discuss briefly why this should be so.

The angle from which we would like to approach this is that of accessibility theory (Ariel 1990) and its application to pronominal anaphora (e.g. Reinhart 1975; Van Hoek 1997). According to the theory, different noun phrase types mark different degrees of accessibility, that is to say, different degrees to which a referent is signalled to be mentally "activated" in the hearer's mind. What is of interest for our present purposes is this: pronouns signal high accessibility (they signal to the hearer, essentially, that they already know the referent being talked about) whereas full noun phrases (descriptive noun phrases but also proper names) signal low accessibility, and can thus be used to introduce or, for instance after paragraph breaks in longer texts, re-introduce referents. Now in any speech

---

7. The Dutch original reads as follows: "De dienstplicht wordt dus afgeschaft? Nou, zo ver wilde de bewindsman niet gaan. Duidelijkheid komt er pas in de prioriteitennota, over enkele maanden".
8. For a detailed discussion of the main attempts to deal with this issue, and particularly for a critique of Banfield's (1982) proposed category of sentences representing "nonreflective consciousness", see Vandelanotte (2005: 189–201).

event, the roles of speaker and addressee are inherently highly accessible: in any conversation between two people, for example, while you might use a vocative as a form of address, the subject of any statement or request will normally be a pronoun, and not a proper name (e.g. in talking to Ruth one would normally say *Did you get my e-mail?* rather than *Did Ruth get my e-mail?*). Likewise, in talking about oneself one does not normally use one's proper name but rather the pronoun *I* (except in special contexts, such as solemn oaths, or, surprisingly, interaction with small children).

This fairly basic observation helps to understand the difference between DIST and both direct and free indirect discourse. In the latter two forms, the "accessibility organization" (essentially, the choice of noun phrase type: pronoun or full NP) is that of the represented speaker, who is thus construed as a point of view in the reported clause. This implies that proper names or descriptive noun phrases are not normally used in direct and free indirect discourse to refer to represented speakers nor to represented addressees. In (15), *Miss Bartlett* and *Lucy* are precisely this: mostly alternating represented speakers, but also, in the case of *Lucy*, represented addressees (in *unless Lucy would rather like to go out?* and in *Of course she would accompany Lucy everywhere*). Similarly in (16), *the minister* is the represented speaker. The difference between direct and free indirect discourse in this regard thus lies not with "accessibility organization", for this is determined by the represented speaker in either case, but only with grammatical person (first, second, third), which remains tied to the current speaker in free indirect discourse.

Turning to DIST, then, it is there that *both* accessibility organization *and* grammatical person remain the current speaker's prerogative. If, in the linear development of a text, the current speaker judges it necessary to introduce or re-introduce referents, she can freely do so in DIST. In an example like (15), it seems clear that disambiguation forms an important motivation for the repeated use of proper names – using pronouns would probably lead to unintelligibility, since both characters are female (who is responsible for which statements?). This in its turn suggests that using free indirect discourse in representing a dialogue such as (15) obliquely would be rather cumbersome, as it too would result in a succession of sentences with pronominal subjects (*She was, after all, a wee bit tired...She would rather like to go out... She could not allow this...*). As well, a series of closed-off representations of different characters' consciousness, which is essentially what a sequence of sentences of free indirect discourse with alternating represented speakers would be, would result in the loss of the "feel" of dialogue.

DIST is thus an interesting case of distanced discourse in that it has the means to evoke more than one represented speaker. The cases we looked at earlier in this paper all involve the incorporation of distanced discourse into the syntactic structure of the actual speaker's discourse. In DIST, with its potentially dialogic structure, the complexity of discourse to be represented is higher, but the linguistic signals of the distancing are becoming more robust as a result. We assume, then, that the specific use of referring expressions in DIST is not just a peculiarity of this STR form, but that it emerges out of the basic characteristics of distanced discourse. Another effect that may be noted in connection with (15) and similar examples is the subtle irony on the part of the current speaker (or "narrator"), who in echoing the almost melodramatic exchanges about a rather mundane decision – will Lucy go out on her own or not – seems to be gently mocking the petty concerns of the characters. This, again, is something that in our view is not compatible with free indirect speech or thought, in which the current speaker's attitudes do not intervene.[9] In DIST, on the other hand, the appropriation and echoing of another utterance allows all manner of current speaker's attitudes to be expressed, whether they be more associative or dissociative (for an overview, see Vandelanotte 2004b and in press).[10] One type of fairly frequent conversational example is that in which people ironically echo negative comments made by others about themselves (e.g. *I was nothing but a poor excuse for a teacher*).

The ironic, or more generally "attitudinal", tone of distanced discourse is thus an effect we can find across the examples considered so far. Metalinguistic negation, as originally described by Horn (1985, 1989), was clearly used with that effect (hence the temptation to treat it simply as an instance of echoic mention, which puts it in line with a common understanding of irony). Conditionals relying on distanced discourse for irony

---

9. This departs from the traditional view in which free indirect speech tends to be correlated with irony, and free indirect thought with empathy (see e.g. Leech and Short 1981). Once the existence of DIST alongside free indirect discourse is recognized, this allows one to avoid this apportioning of two rather divergent pragmatic functions (current speaker's irony vs. empathy in the readers) to two sides of the same linguistic coin (free indirect discourse).
10. This use of the notion of echo in itself echoes the relevance-theoretical definition of the term as involving at once metarepresentation (offering a representation of a representation, as in speech and thought representation) and attitude (a speaker's more associative or more dissociative attitude towards the metarepresented utterance or thought). See for instance Iwata (2003) and Noh (2000).

have also been noted earlier – consider the so-called "indicative counter-factuals", such as *If he passes the exam, then I'm Mickey Mouse*, where the distanced protasis is presented as leading to absurd conclusions, and thus reveals the actual speaker's attitude as well. The examples of poetic discourse which we discuss below also rely on distanced discourse to achieve their attitudinal effects. The DIST narrative mode is perhaps the most salient example of what distanced discourse accomplishes. It is at the same time the category of distanced discourse which has most visibly developed its own formal indicators, which mark it as distinct from other narrative modes. As we suggested above, the narrative form naturally involves discourses contributed by different speakers, but other STR styles give different weight to the specific role of the current speaker and the current speaker's point of view, which accounts for the peculiarity of DIST. However, as we have been arguing throughout the paper, distanced discourse is found in a variety of discourse types and constructions. In our next section, we will show that it also has a role to play in poetic discourse. Our specific examples will come from a variety of poems by Philip Larkin and the Nobel prize winning Polish poet Wisława Szymborska.

6. Distanced discourse in poetry

In this section, we will show how the use of different types of speech and thought representation – direct discourse and DIST – in Philip Larkin's poetry contributes in different ways to the "intersubjectivity" of his poems. We include examples of direct discourse here alongside DIST to show how ostensibly direct discourse snippets can be seen as instances of distanced discourse when they are extracted out of imagined discourse contexts and used in the construction of attitudinal rather than representational meanings. Their evocative (rather than strictly dialogic) role in poetic texts thus parallels the effects achieved in other distanced cases we have presented. While we can discuss only a limited number of examples within the scope of this paper, our observations are based on a reading of the "1946–1983" section of Anthony Thwaite's original (1988) edition of the *Collected Poems*.[11] As we will show, direct discourse in Larkin's poetry

---

11. More recently a new edition has appeared in which the poems are presented in the way they were published by Larkin, rather than chronologically according to (estimated or established) time of writing.

serves to illustrate a point by quoting usually hypothetical or "anonymous" speakers. Because these quotes are signalled not to have been uttered or thought by an identifiable conceptualizer at an identifiable time,
they introduce a measure of distancing. The distancing attitudes carried
by DIST in Larkin's discourse will be shown to include metalinguistic incredulity vis-à-vis utterances present in the discourse context, and irony
vis-à-vis commonly held opinions.

Turning to direct discourse first, the typical scenario is one in which
there is an explicit reporting clause and/or the reported clause is printed
in italics, as in (17),[12] in which there is both an overt reporting clause
I could say and an italicized complement:

(17)   No, I have never found
       The place where I could say
       This is my proper ground,
       Here I shall stay
       (from "Places, Loved Ones")

This example illustrates another common feature of direct discourse in
Larkin as well, viz. the fact that more often than not, the reported utterance was not actually said at all, or was not said by one specific person on
one specific occasion. That there is not always a "real" prior utterance
underlying occurrences of direct speech was noted before, for instance
by von Roncador (1980, 1988), who spoke of "non-literal" direct speech
(*nichtwortliche direkte Rede*), Tannen (1986), who spoke of "constructed"
dialogue, and Fludernik (1993), who stressed the point that mimetic representation in represented discourse is ultimately an illusion. In (17), both
the negation (*I have never found*) and the modal *could* indicate that the report is "hypothetical" rather than "real". Similar cases are cited in (18), in
which a "real" reported question is followed by a possible answer that was
not, in fact, uttered (*I wanted to retort* – but didn't), and in (19), in which
the I-persona is wondering now whether anyone thought the italicized
part about him forty years back:

(18)   'Was that,' my friend smiled, 'where you "have your roots"?'
       No, only where my childhood was unspent,
       I wanted to retort
       (from "I Remember, I Remember")

---

12. All examples in this section are quoted from Larkin (1997).

(19) [...] I wonder if
     Anyone looked at me, forty years back,
     And thought, *That'll be the life;*
     No God any more, or sweating in the dark

     About hell and that, or having to hide
     What you think of the priest. He
     And his lot will all go down the long slide
     Like free bloody birds. [...]
     (from "High Windows")

In the examples above the current speaker is evoking possible discourses which do not or did not actualize. A slightly different but related use of "non-actual" direct discourse is that in which there is no immediate "local" indication of its not representing actual speech, such as a modal or a negated form, but where it is nonetheless clear that only one possible or typical utterance is evoked because it is characteristic of a given interactional frame or script. To see what we mean by this, consider the following excerpt from "Poetry of Departures":

(20) Sometimes you hear, fifth-hand,
     As epitaph:
     He chucked up everything
     And just cleared off
     [...]
     So to hear it said

     He walked out on the whole crowd
     Leaves me flushed and stirred,
     Like *then she undid her dress*
     Or *Take that you bastard;*
     Surely I can, if he did?
     (from "Poetry of Departures")

The quotes in (20) are perhaps less "unreal" than "typified": they give representative examples of the type of thing one hears whenever someone just packs up and leaves (*He chucked up everything and just cleared off; He walked out on the whole crowd*). The I-persona seems to meet this kind of behaviour with a mixture of envy and incomprehension. Interestingly, a set of different quotes, reminiscent of erotic or violent scenes in movies or novels, is used to convey his uneasy reaction (*then she undid her dress; Take that you bastard*). In the remainder of the poem, the conflict of emotions aroused in the I-persona is resolved: he would do exactly the same right now, if only it "weren't so artificial, / Such a deliberate step backwards". Poems with similar typified quotes include "Self's the Man" and "Sympathy in White Major", both in their own way reflections on the tug between self and society (cf. Vandelanotte 2002: 412–418).

These are, then, the main uses to which direct discourse is put in Larkin's poetry: to indicate what could have been said but (perhaps) wasn't, or to give representative examples of the type of thing usually said in a given scenario or frame (e.g. when people walk out on their lives, in a marriage, at a funeral). In either case, we would argue that direct discourse, with the shift to a new mental "base" space it involves, is used in a general sense to "illustrate a point". Similar functions were ascribed to direct speech or thought by Mayes (1990) and Holt (1996), who apart from its dramatizing function (adding to the "liveliness" of the discourse) discussed the use of direct discourse to provide evidence in a clear and economical way: rather than explaining laboriously what a speaker's claim, opinion or state of mind is, one can immediately conjure this up by quoting her.

Compared with DIST, to which we will turn below, the attitudinal effect in these cases of "evoked" direct discourse is less immediate, in the sense that the unspoken or typical utterances conjured up in it are not as such criticized or debunked, but illustrate the poem's persona's point. The current speaker's appropriation of another's discourse in DIST, on the other hand, always simultaneously involves the former's often critical attitude towards the represented utterance, for instance of incredulity or irony. This is not to say, of course, that within the discourse context the views of the poem's persona may not contradict those represented in direct discourse. In "The Life With a Hole in it", for example, the I-persona's disagreement with the direct quote attributed to ' People (women mostly)" is even rendered explicitly and vocally:

(21)   When I throw back my head and howl
       People (women mostly) say
       But you've always done what you want,
       You always get your own way
       – A perfectly vile and foul
       Inversion of all that's been.
       What the old ratbags mean
       Is I've never done what I don't.
       (from "The Life with a Hole in it")

One final point to be made in connection with the "illustrative" function of direct discourse is that the illustrations given in it need not be "truthful" or "reliable". This is not just because the represented discourse may not actually have occurred, as we have seen, but also, more fundamentally, because the current speaker or persona of the poem may be, in narratological terms, "unreliable" (cf. Booth 1961: 158–159). The case in point here is Larkin's well-known poem "Vers de Société", which evolves from outright refusal to join the "forks and faces" at a party to accepting the invitation for fear of worse (viz. thoughts of "failure and remorse"). The italicized parts in the opening stanza (22) are represented in what seems to be direct speech, as shown by the reference of the first person pronouns (*I* refers to Warlock-Williams in the first quote but to the poem's persona in the second; in DIST, all occurrences of the first person pronoun would refer to the latter). However, it is clearly not the case that Warlock-Williams phrased his invitation in the way he is here portrayed to have done ("crowd of craps", "waste their time and ours"):

(22)   *My wife and I have asked a crowd of craps*
        To come and waste their time and ours: perhaps
        You'd care to join us? In a pig's arse, friend.
        Day comes to an end.
        The gas fire breathes, the trees are darkly swayed.
        And so *Dear Warlock-Williams: I'm afraid –*
        (from "Vers de Société")

In a sense, this peculiar use of direct discourse presents a mirror image of DIST: while in DIST someone else's words are put into the mouth of the current speaker, in (22) it is the latter who puts his own words into the mouth of the represented speaker, Warlock-Williams. Attitudinal distancing vis-à-vis the party invitation does not happen through an echoic, ironic evocation of the inviter's discourse in that of the invitee, but through a distortion of the inviter's mental space. As in DIST, this involves a blend of the mental spaces of the current speaker and of the represented speaker, but the deictic centre from which this blend is construed is different: it is that of the current speaker in DIST, but of the represented speaker in cases like (22).

In the creative usage exemplified in (22) we end up with a kind of speech and thought representation which defies neat categorization in terms of the four types discussed in section 5 (direct, indirect, free indirect, and DIST): deictically it is not amenable to an analysis as DIST, but in terms of the stance expressed it cannot be read as direct discourse either. The specific blend exemplified in (22) *can* however be analysed as distanced discourse. Only here it is the case that the discourse associated with the overall utterer of (22) – the poem's persona – is evoked in the "secondary" discourse, aligned with this so-called "Warlock-Williams", rather than the other way around (as in DIST). In all our other examples, it was each time the secondary discourse that was evoked in that of the utterer or "current speaker".

Let us turn, now, to DIST in Larkin's poetry. In our view, it is possible to distinguish two (related) types in the data, with the difference hinging on whether or not the DIST clearly echoes something explicit or implicit in the preceding interactive context. Cases in which this is indeed so resemble the examples from dialogue discussed in section 5; the other cases call to mind Pascual's (2002) notion of fictive interaction discussed in section 4. As a first example of "real" interaction represented in DIST, consider (23), taken from "Dockery and Son". In this poem, the I-persona visits his old college and talks to the Dean, whose directly represented question "And do you keep in touch with –" is quickly abandoned to give way to the questions the I-persona asks himself:

(23) [...] 'And do
      You keep in touch with –' Or remember how
      Black-gowned, unbreakfasted, and still half-tight
      We used to stand before that desk, to give
      'Our version' of 'these incidents last night'?
      (from "Dockery and Son")

Conceivably the partial quotes "our version" and "these incidents last night" represent what the Dean said to the students rather than the other way around, and so the use of the first person "our" betrays (partial) DIST rather than a direct representation (which would have "your version").[13] By appropriating and echoing the Dean's original words, the I-persona can gently mock the weightiness of his words ("version", "incidents") which invite comparison with a serious police interrogation.

Two more examples in which something in the context is echoed are (24), about the effects a self-proclaimed faith healer has on his audience, and (25), a poem about the I-persona's biographer Jake Balokowsky who is discussing his subject with someone else. In both cases, the echoic evocation of the literal (in 24) or inferred (in 25) preceding utterance serves to express the I-persona's attitude of incredulity or exasperation ("how can you ask what's wrong; isn't it obvious?", "what do you mean, 'what's he like,' didn't I just tell you?").

---

13. The second partial quote, on the other hand, does seem to be direct considering the deictics ("these", "last night").

(24) [...] *Now, dear child,*
What's wrong, the deep American voice demands.
[...]
What's wrong! Moustached in flowered frocks they shake:
By now, all's wrong. [...]
(from "Faith Healing")

(25) [...] They both rise,
Make for the Coke dispenser. 'What's he like?
Christ, I just told you. Oh, you know the thing,
That crummy textbook stuff from Freshman Psych,
Not out of kicks or something happening –
One of those old-type *natural* fouled-up guys.'
(from "Posterity")

The metalinguistic flavour of this type of example seems clear: the prior utterances are evoked not to serve straightforwardly as questions or exclamations, but rather to question the very appropriateness of saying them in the first place.[14]

What can also be noted with regard to the examples just discussed is that they bear fewer traces of their reportative nature than the direct discourse examples discussed previously: neither italics nor reporting clauses tend to be used. In the preceding examples this may not matter so much, since there is still a clearly "interactive" set-up in which a prior utterance is echoed. In the examples to which we now turn, and which represent the second subtype of DIST we propose to distinguish in Larkin's poems, this (near-)absence of clear markers of speech or thought representation is more important. If both a clear dialogic, interactive context (of the kind you do find in 23–25) and a reporting clause are absent, and usually also italics, it becomes very difficult indeed to even ask the question who the original speaker of the echoed utterance is. In such cases, other discourse is evoked without any indication of the speech event (speaker-hearer, time, place) in which this other discourse supposedly originates. We would like to suggest that this is essentially because the identity of the original speaker(s) is immaterial: the point of these "submerged" evocations is merely to respond to them. More specifically, in the examples we will discuss what is evoked is usually public opinion or a view commonly held, to which the

---

14. Cases like (24–25) have been dealt with in the pragmatic literature under the rubric of "echo questions" (e.g. Banfield 1982; McCawley 1987; Yamaguchi 1994; Noh 2000; Iwata 2003). The categories of DIST and of echo questions are not coextensive, but to explain why would lead us too far (see Vandelanotte 2005: 307–312 for discussion).

poem's persona reacts dismissively or ironically. Consider (26), for instance, taken from the poem "Reasons for Attendance" in which the I-persona considers the question why he is standing outside while his peers are dancing "solemnly on the beat of happiness" inside:

(26) [...] Why be out here?
      But then, why be in there? Sex, yes, but
      what is sex? Surely, to think the lion's share
      Of happiness is found by couples – sheer

      Inaccuracy, as far as I'm concerned.
      (from "Reasons for Attendance")

In response to his self-musings, the I-persona considers the possible answer "sex", concedes that it may seem a reasonably good answer ("yes"), but goes on to deny its importance, albeit in a brilliantly half-hearted manner ("sheer / inaccuracy", where one would expect a far stronger collocate of "sheer" such as "nonsense"). While in a single lexical word like "sex" there are of course no deictic or other indications that prove that distanced discourse, specifically DIST, is involved, we believe this is the interpretation that does justice to its functioning as an echo of received wisdoms on the question why young people go out to dance. No actual or even imagined direct communication with some identifiable speaker who might have uttered the word "sex" is suggested to take place; the "interaction" is entirely fictive and takes place within the I-persona's private thoughts, between himself and, one might say, society at large.

A lengthier example that shows similar features is (27), from a poem in which loneliness is valued positively, "Best Society" (the title referring to oneself as one's own best company). Here again, even though the difference between direct discourse and DIST is formally neutralized in the absence of clear deictic markers, the absence of any interactive set-up of interlocutors in terms of which direct discourse could be made sense of, as well as the ironic attitude expressed towards the opinions on our virtues, suggest that an echoic evocation of public opinion is involved:

(27) [...] for what
      You are alone has, to achieve
      The rank of fact, to be expressed
      In terms of others, or it's just
      A compensating make-believe.

> Much better stay in company!
> To love you must have someone else,
> Giving requires a legatee,
> Good neighbours need whole parishfuls
> Of folk to do it on – in short,
> Our virtues are all social; if,
> Deprived of solitude, you chafe,
> It's clear you're not the virtuous sort.
> (from "Best Society")

One can already sense in these lines that the I-persona does not in fact agree with the position that "our virtues are all social"; in the wider context of the poem this becomes abundantly clear. The next line, for instance, is "Viciously, then, I lock my door", and the poem ends with an image suggesting that it is only in "uncontradicting solitude" that one's true self can unfold and emerge. The clearest hint of distancing in the excerpt cited above is probably the choice of rather deprecatory words in "whole parishfuls / Of folk to do it on". This calls to mind the blend in the extract from "Vers de Société" (22), but there, as we saw, the deictic centre adopted was that of the represented speaker in a special kind of "distanced" direct discourse. Here there is no identifiable represented speaker, but the I-persona's echo of traditional views on virtue and society in (27) turns out to be as unreliable as the distorted quote in (22).

Other clear examples of poems which dissociatively evoke opinions outside any interactive set-up of conceptualizers include "Essential Beauty", a poem about advertisements, and "Homage to a Government", about the withdrawal of British soldiers. In the former, what advertisements want people to believe is echoed ironically:

(28)   Well-balanced families, in fine
         Midsummer weather, owe their smiles, their cars,
         Even their youth, to that small cube each hand
         Stretches towards.

Likewise, the poem "Homage to a Government" bespeaks disagreement with the policy to bring the soldiers home by repeating as a kind of refrain the phrase "it/this is all right" (e.g. *Next year we are to bring the soldiers home / For lack of money, and it is all right*). The repetition of this ironic echo also puts into relief the poem's title, which in the final analysis can only be understood as being highly ironic.

At the end of this exploration,[15] we hope to have shown that in Larkin's poetry there are different types of "intersubjectivity", i.e. different ways in which other viewpoints are incorporated into the "main" viewpoint, that of the poem's speaking subject. When, in direct discourse, the perspective shifts temporarily to a distinct base space, the floor is yielded to an often hypothetical or "typical" speaker to illustrate a point. On the other hand, when the main space is blended with a distinct space but the viewpoint adopted continues to be that of the poem's speaking subject, DIST is used. In cases with a clear interactive set-up, in which some prior utterance is echoed, the attitude expressed is usually something like mockery or incredulity. In cases where no one in particular is echoed but a more or less "anonymous" received opinion is evoked, the attitude expressed is one of disagreement. Finally, in one case (that of "Vers de Société"), it was argued that a blend occurs between the speaking subject's space and that of Warlock-Williams, but the deictic centre adopted is the latter's rather than the former's (as would be the case in DIST).

What has also emerged in this discussion is that poetry may use speech and thought representation rather differently than narrative texts. In stories and novels it is relatively rare to come across stretches of represented utterances or thoughts which cannot be attributed to one of the characters. Admittedly it may often require some effort on the part of the reader to identify who says or thinks what, but usually this is part of the deal: to know whose consciousness is being conjured up tends to matter in narrative. In poetry, it seems to us that this may sometimes *not* matter. Much poetry lacks the intricate interactive structure which narratives, with their different characters, have, and because of this the identity of represented speakers may be unimportant. A case in point here is formed by the "anonymous" echoes of public opinion discussed above, which we analysed as DIST on account of the absence of reporting clauses in addition to the lack of any interactive set-up of different "characters" as one finds this in a narrative.

We have found an extreme case of such disregard of individual speakers' identities in the poem *Funeral* by Wisława Szymborska.[16] The poem

---

15. Cases in which the poem's speaking subject puts his own discourse into relief by using clauses such as *or so I feel* have not been included in this discussion because, as suggested in Vandelanotte (2002), they involve "subjectified" rather than "representational" DIST (on this distinction, see Vandelanotte 2004b, in press: Ch. 8).

16. We are using the translation by Stanisław Barańczak and Clare Cavanagh, published in the volume *Nothing Twice: Selected Poems*, Wydawnictwo Literackie, Kraków (1997).

consists entirely of bits and pieces quoted from conversations at a funeral, a point which only becomes clear in the poem's title, as there is absolutely no "scene setting" nor any introduction of the "speakers" in the poem. There might be two or more, perhaps they are close friends of the deceased but maybe not, they may be being overheard by the poet's persona – there's no way of telling; apparently the identities of the different speakers are so unimportant that they can be dispensed with altogether. While some of the turns of dialogue represented seem not out of place at a funeral, since they are comments about the deceased, many others consist essentially of the everyday small talk that forms an important lubricant for social interaction. Finally, the closing lines suggest that the ceremony is over and all the participants are leaving. Here are some examples, cited from different parts of the poem:

(29)   "so suddenly, who could have seen it coming"
        "stress and smoking, I kept telling him"
        "not bad, thanks, and you"
        "these flowers need to be unwrapped"
        "his brother's heart gave out, too, it runs in the family"
        [...]
        "two egg yolks and a tablespoon of sugar"
        "none of his business, what was in it for him"
        "only in blue and just small sizes"
        [...]
        "give me a call"
        "which bus goes downtown"
        "I'm going this way"
        "we're not"

Out of context, many of these utterances would call up a context of casual conversation at, say, a supermarket, or in a bar. Because the poet's persona stubbornly refuses to intervene visibly in any way,[17] it is only the title that forces one to integrate all these snatches of conversation with the context of a funeral. At one level, this may be perceived as bitterly ironic: instead of joining in heart-felt mourning, people see fit to discuss recipes, clothes, and bus lines. At another level, however, the irony may be mild rather than bitter: the very fact that commonplace concerns command our attention even at a funeral can serve as a sign of life as it were beating

---

17. Needless to say, there is of course a lot of "construction" going on on the part of the poet's persona in the way in which quotes are represented and arranged.

death. As Packalén (2004) observes in her discussion of this poem, "as death grips life, life also intervenes in death".

Formally, there are just a few features which prompt an interpretation of the separate lines in (29) as DST: the quotation marks (though these are unreliable, as they are sometimes used with FIST or DIST as well) and the first person pronouns, which we assume refer to different speakers in different lines, and not to the poet's persona (or "current speaker"). On the other hand, there is at least one crucial feature that is missing to make this into convincing DST: we have no clue as to who the represented speakers and addressees are in what precise situation of utterance. Along the lines explored for the "anonymous" echoes in Larkin, we would like to suggest that this adds a distancing effect: the snippets of conversation are merely evoked for the poetic purposes of the poet's persona rather than given a real, quasi-independent existence of their own as would be the case in full-fledged DST.

The distancing effect is also due to the very contrast between the solemn occasion and the casualness of the conversations. While not profiled as a conversational participant in any way, the poem's persona frames the discourse snippets in such a way that they form a coherent sequence – from greetings, through chat, to leave-taking. The conversational "event" represented, with its sequence and its level of casualness suggesting an encounter among friends,[18] is at a socially structured remove from the ritual closure to a person's life. The two discourse spaces represented in the text are socially distanced, and the distance between them is the very point of the poem. The dialogue fragments are not representative of particular speakers, topics, or conversational events – they are only representative of the discourse genre one would expect at a different kind of event. The poem's ironic tone thus relies on social distance.

In our discussion of poetic texts thus far we have relied mainly on their discourse features, and the contrasts among different distancing effects of particular types of representations of discourse. We will now return to our general characterization of the concept of distance and its different mental space realizations, to show how the shared conceptual underpinnings of many instantiations of distance can prompt a level of poetic coherence which would otherwise be difficult to explain. To show various kinds of

---

18. The casualness appropriate among old friends or distant family members is much clearer in the language of the original. (This remark is not intended as a criticism of the translation, which is excellent, but as a comment on the difference between levels of casualness available in English and in Polish).

distance at work in a single poem, we now turn to a discussion of the text from which our paper took its title, "Judging Distances".

7.   The poetry of distance

In this section we will propose a more detailed analysis of Henry Reed's poem, "Judging distances", which illustrates most of the theoretical concepts we introduced and exemplified so far. The poem was published in 1943, as the second one in a series titled "Lessons of War" (the other two, "Naming of Parts" and "Movement of Bodies", share the context of military training and some of the poetic features characterizing the series, but are beyond the scope of this paper). In "Judging Distances", Reed uses the discourse frame of military instruction, on the related tasks of reporting on a landscape and judging a distance, both of which have to be performed according to specific rules and using specific expressions.

(30)   Judging Distances

1	Not only how far away, but the way you say it
2	Is very important. Perhaps you may never get
3	The knack of judging a distance, but at least you know
4	How to report on a landscape: the central sector,
5	The right of the arc and that, which we had last Tuesday.
6	And at least you know
7	That maps are of time, not place, so far as the army
8	Happens to be concerned – the reason being,
9	Is one which need not delay us. Again, you know
10	There are three kinds of tree, three only, the fir and the poplar,
11	And those which have bushy tops to; and lastly
12	That things only seem to be things.
13	A barn is not called a barn, to put it more plainly,
14	Or a field in the distance, where sheep may be safely grazing.
15	You must never be over-sure. You must say, when reporting:
16	At five o'clock in the central sector is a dozen
17	Of what appear to be animals; whatever you do,
18	Don't call the bleeders sheep.
19	I'm sure that's quite clear; and suppose, for the sake of example,
20	The one at the end, asleep, endeavors to tell us
21	What he sees over there to the west, and how far away,

22   After first having come to attention. There to the west,
23   Of the fields of summer the sun and the shadows bestow
24   Vestments of purple and gold.

25   The white dwellings are like a mirage in the heat,
26   And under the swaying elms a man and a woman
27   Lie gently together. Which is, perhaps, only to say
28   That there is a row of houses to the left of the arc,
29   And that under some poplars a pair of what appear to be humans
30   Appear to be loving.

31   Well that, for an answer, is what we rightly call
32   Moderately satisfactory only, the reason being,
33   Is that two things have been omitted, and those are very important.
34   The human beings, now: in what direction are they,
35   And how far away, would you say? And do not forget
36   There may be dead ground in between.

37   There may be dead ground in between; and I may not have got
38   The knack of judging a distance; I will only venture
39   A guess that perhaps between me and the apparent lovers,
40   (Who, incidentally, appear by now to have finished,)
41   At seven o'clock from the houses, is roughly a distance
42   Of about one year and a half.

The first three stanzas can be naturally interpreted as tokens of what the sergeant-teacher might be saying to the young soldiers in the course of instruction. This part of the text is thus readily interpretable along the lines of our discussion of DST in Larkin's texts, but the interactive context is more specific, with the speaker (in this part) addressing the young soldiers being instructed, and with the poem's persona being one of the addressees. However, we should also note that the "lecture" relies on the concept of distance in many ways.

It starts with the most basic spatial use of distance, as appropriate to the topic of instruction (*far away*, 1.1), to shift to the metalinguistic concept of distance in the same line (*the way you say it*).[19] In fact, one could

---

19. In the discussion to follow we are deliberately not addressing the convention of imposing the image of the face of a clock onto a map, or other one-dimensional representations of an area. The usage, though undoubtedly indicative of an interesting blend of methods of representing time and space, is in fact highly conventionalized and also used here as an element of the broad distance metaphor, but is not a central example of the mappings we are attempting to unravel.

read the discourse through the first three stanzas as a metalinguistic attempt to establish norms of describing reality through vocabulary options which tone down any attention to specificity or detail. *A barn is not called a barn* (1.13), *sheep* have to be called *animals* (1.17), any tree in sight has to be assigned to one of three categories – all of these strategies, while useful from the military point of view, deprive what is seen of much of its content. The simplicity of the description allows one to avoid ambiguity and confusion, but it also has an effect on the speaker, who is now required not to notice anything that could bring about a personal or emotional response. The function of the army lingo becomes clear – metalinguistic distance helps to create emotional distance.

The first 18 lines also contain a number of expressions of epistemic distance: *things only seem to be things* (1.12), *appear to be animals* (1.17), etc. The general rule is: *never be over-sure* (1.15). These expressions represent epistemic distance in its most straightforward sense – marking lack of certainty. But the usage departs from natural discourse in one important way – in attested cases, speakers adjust their epistemic stance to the situation at hand, so that in effect some utterances will be marked by distance, while others will not. The instruction encourages the students to do something different – mark epistemic distance throughout their report. Certainly, it would be unusual not to say you are seeing sheep when you are actually seeing sheep, but this is exactly what the army requires. It might seem that the approach is reasonable, since it is less risky in a military context to economize on descriptive detail than to make a mistake in identifying an object. But the "side-effect" of this is reducing the world around the soldier to a blur of superordinate level categories, such as humans or animals, and forcing unnatural conceptualizations which avoid basic level categories. Given that basic level categories are the natural linguistic choice (also for children, who'd prefer *a car* to *a vehicle*), thanks to daily interaction with their representatives, the all-encompassing epistemic distance has the effect of depriving the description of anything related to the speaker's direct experience, and, consequently, creating emotional distance.

The fact that conceptualizations include emotional stance is becoming widely acknowledged. Some constructions, better known for their epistemic stance features, have recently been described as marking positive emotional stance (consider Dancygier and Sweetser's [2005] discussion of *I wish* and *if only*). Also the concept of grounding, as discussed in Coulson and Oakley (2005) (see above), represents a very general mechanism whereby emotional attitudes can be included in the conceptualization. Furthermore, Slingerland (2005) proposes more specific ways of representing emotional aspects of blending, arguing that they are present even if not explicitly expressed. Any further discussion would go beyond the scope of the present paper, but the point we are making (with Reed) is that linguistic expressions can be chosen to specifically exclude (rather than naturally include) emotional involvement and the speaker's choice of words may reduce the emotional response by increasing distance.

In fact, some related usage has been captured in the metaphor INTIMACY IS CLOSENESS (Lakoff and Johnson 1980, 1999), which is widely present in expressions such as *a close friend* or *she seemed so distant*. The mapping has been postulated as projecting from the physical domain of bodily proximity into the emotional domain of intimacy, with an added explanation that being physically close to someone coincides, in common human experience, with the sense of an emotional relationship – for example, you are not expected to hug an enemy, but it is natural to accept bodily closeness in the company of a lover. Given the kinds of lexical expressions claimed to represent the metaphor, usually varieties on the use of the adjectives *close* and *distant*, we can argue that the mapping captures one of the uses of the concepts of distance as such and gives it an emotional dimension. It is also natural to extend the emotional understanding of distance from the domain of relationships among people to the relationship between people and situations. One can give a positive evaluation of a person or an idea using very similar expressions, as in *My aunt is very close to me* and *The idea of helping people is very close to me*. In fact, both of these expressions resemble the kinds of data we are analyzing in this paper and could be explained via a mental space set-up of the kind we have argued for.[20]

In the second part of the poem the frame of instructional interaction is taken further, to explicitly bring in the kind of discourse which contrasts with the prescribed military lingo. In the fourth stanza the sergeant asks a soldier to report on what he sees to the west, to practise the material just taught. He addresses *the one at the end, asleep*, and the response comes immediately (1.22–24), but does not describe any objects at first. Instead, the answer starts with a rich and full colour description of the sunlit landscape. Before we go on to the next stanza, let us consider the question of

---

20. It should be clear from our discussion so far that the concept of distance applies to different domains, and it is natural to use the same vocabulary of distance to different domains. We believe a thorough vocabulary study could provide a still deeper explanation of the varied senses of distance, but it is beyond the scope of this paper.

the participant to whom this piece of discourse should be attributed. The addressee of the question, the sleeping soldier, is a candidate, but he is not likely to engage in a poetic vision of the summer sun. It is more plausible to suggest that the answer is the inner, not articulated response of the poem's persona, whose viewpoint, and the choice of poetic discourse, seems the closest to Reed's own. If this interpretation is chosen, then the rest of the poem is an example of distanced discourse – an imaginary exchange between the poet-soldier and the sergeant. The exchange could not have occurred in the military discourse context evoked, but the conversational scenario is playing itself out in the soldier's mind as a dialogue. The poet-soldier is the one among the listeners to be struck by the dehumanizing effect of the army discourse, and it makes sense for him to mentally "rehearse" a natural, sensitive response to the view in the distance and immediately confront it with the response it would inevitably bring from the sergeant.

Lines 25–27 describe two lovers, in tender terms, while lines 27–30 "correct" the description, turning it into a proper military report on a landscape. *Dwellings* become *houses*, *elms* are changed into *poplars*, *a man and a woman* are now *what appear to be humans*. Then the response from the sergeant points out the gaps in the report. In the last stanza, however, the pretence of a dialogue disappears. Although the words are ostensibly attempting to answer the question about *how far away* the lovers are (echoing the one from line 1), and all the required expressions of epistemic distance are used, the stanza shifts away from the pretend-dialogue pattern. The pronoun *I* is here representing the poem's persona, rather than the soldier-trainee, and the function of what is said is reflexive, rather than interactive. It is the poem's closure, which brings everything together.

The crucial expression in the last stanza is *between me and the apparent lovers* [...] *is roughly a distance of about one year and a half.* The spatial distance initially to be measured becomes temporal distance, but the expression of temporal distance does not, as one could expect, separate the speaker's "now" from the scene with the same lovers a year and a half earlier. It separates two temporal spaces, though. The present one, with the poem's persona (a young soldier-poet) in the army, and the past one (a memory, perhaps, of the pre-war times), with the same young man loving a woman in an idyllic setting. The two spaces are not only separated by time, but they are also different emotionally, as the emotional distance imposed by the army training is absent from the scene with the lovers. They *lie gently together*, and they do not *appear to be loving* – they do love.

The interpretation which puts the poem's persona, emotionally and mentally, in the pre-war warmth and beauty, while allowing him to physically remain in a "lesson of war", attests to the meaning potential of the concept of distance, as we tried to describe it here. In fact it puts into question the interpretation of all the descriptive fragments starting in line 22 (*There to the west ...*) as referring, at least at face value, to a landscape seen from the training site. It might be argued (in fact, we believe it *should* be argued) that the sergeant's question prompts a memory of a pre-war scene right from the start. Under this interpretation, the next two stanzas represent three discourse voices in two discourse spaces: the poem's persona's description of his happy memory evoked by the sergeant's question (lines 22–27), his "rehearsed" answer to the question (lines 27–30), and the sergeant's expected answer (lines 31–36). They can all be understood as metalinguistically distanced, since they contrast different ways of talking about the same past event: first as the poem's persona might describe it, then as he would have to phrase it when answering the question in class, and finally, as the army discourse would want it to be phrased. However, the issue here is not just different standards of appropriateness, which all metalinguistic uses share, but the emotionally crippling consequences of the metalinguistic distance of military discourse. The discourse contrasts the poem relies on are thus an example of how the attitudinal aspects of distanced discourse may structure the understanding of the text as a whole, and constitute a poetic device in its own right.

The painful and reluctant attempt to look at one's happy past as a "military landscape" is the main thought of the poem – after all, any landscape a soldier looks at was at some point a scene of someone's happiness. The emotional distance the army so insistently tries to instill in the soldier's language and thought will never work – Reed says – because you cannot fully distance yourself from your own experience and its emotional value. In as much as a child cannot talk about a cuddly teddy bear as *a stuffed toy*, we cannot talk or think about lovers as distant human beings or objects *at seven o'clock from the houses*. The basic level categories we tend to use naturally carry an experiential and emotional load we cannot easily distance ourselves from. In a sense, Reed's poem brings all kinds of distance together, only to tell us that we cannot detach ourselves away from our emotional selves.

8. Conclusion

The concept of "distance", while basically spatial, turns out to yield a surprisingly broad spectrum of meanings – from temporal through epistemic,
metalinguistic, and social, all the way to discourse bound. It is also present,
whether lexically or semantically, in an imposing range of phenomena – descriptions of space, tense and aspectual forms, constructions such as conditionals and metalinguistic negation, unusual modes of representing interaction (such as Pascual's [2002] "fictive trialogues"), and various modes of
narrative discourse. Finally, as we tried to show, it may structure poetic discourse in ways which are difficult to coherently explain through other means.
The consistency and clarity of the message we read in Reed's poem is not
only prompted by his use of the specific meaning of distance, but through
a multi-faceted use of the concept as such. While the poem lacks straightforward expressions of emotional distress, it does convey these feelings
through its reliance on various interconnected understandings of distance.
   There is clearly some difficulty involved in attributing the emergence of
a variety of divergent meanings to just one type of projection of conceptual structure. It is hard to trace form-meaning correlations when there
is no one concrete form to look for, but rather something as abstract as
a specific mental space configuration. We hope to have shown, however,
that mental space evocation can (and should) be understood as a partial
projection – in other words, a linguistic form may evoke a frame, but not
all of the frame has to be used in constructing the meaning. At the same
time, the more salient and schematic the concept, the more likely it is that
it will help structure more complex concepts – the role of image schemas
in metaphorical projections is a case in point. In the discussion above, we
suggested that "distance" is such a salient and schematic concept.
   Whereas the early attempts to treat distance as a metaphorical concept
did successfully explain the data at hand, the broader usage reviewed above
suggests a more complex set-up, involving two mental spaces (with different
topologies) and, quite crucially, the conceptualizer's alignment with the
viewpoint of one of those spaces. It may seem painfully obvious now to say
that a huge area of linguistic usage requires the speaker's perception of two
different mental spaces and her ability to use either the one deictically
aligned with her or the other one as a viewpoint space. But the range of
meanings relying on the set-up calls for a non-obvious explanation, and we
have tried to suggest some of the mechanisms involved. The evocation potential of the concept of "distance" reminds us of the wonderful plasticity
of other simple spatial concepts, such as the vertical axis structuring numer-

ous domains of thought in terms of the up/down opposition.[21] It is possible that some further investigation of the extensions yielded by simple spatial configurations will lead us to a more holistic understanding of a variety of language forms, including the language of literary discourse.

The analysis we propose also poses important questions regarding the specificity or non-specificity of poetic discourse. The cases of Larkin's poems and Reed's "Judging Distances" convince us that there is no straightforward answer to the dilemma, but they do offer a glimpse into how the question may be approached. While all the types of distance expressed can be traced back to colloquial use of language and to its narrative discourse instantiations, the context of a poetic text seems to allow for some elements to be missing. The difference is best seen in the examples involving distanced discourse, where poems fail to profile a specific speaker or blend the poem's persona's discourse with that of the other. This in itself is not a distinguishing feature, as discourse snippets which could not be clearly attached to any particular conceptualizer were present in many of our colloquial examples and in the examples of fictive interaction given by Pascual. The important difference, though, is the fluid boundary between DST and DIST, especially when the poem's persona is involved. In colloquial discourse the "unclaimed" pieces of distanced discourse are still aligned with the current speaker's deictic centre and discourse goals. In some poetic texts, however, the poem's persona (the closest equivalent to the "speaker") may hide behind the discourse and, for some part of the text, remain on-stage only as the presenting participant – similarly to Booth's "implied author" in the narrative. At the same time, the discourse schema itself may still remain very much "on-stage", structuring the interpretation of the text.

The question of how widespread the strategy is in contemporary poetry requires further research, but the examples we have looked at so far suggest that poetic discourse may rely more heavily than other forms of discourse on mental space evocation. In our brief discussion of Szymborska's "Funeral" we noted that the bits of dialogue evoke a discourse type which re-

---

21. Many of the mappings traditionally seen as a part of the EVENT STRUCTURE METAPHOR seem to be good candidates. For example, we were repeatedly worried about researchers using the framework of conceptual metaphor and labelling diverse areas of usage under the rubric of LIFE IS A JOURNEY mapping, when all that was really involved was the schema of "motion forward". It seems that a thorough investigation of such concepts in terms of mental spaces and viewpoint ("moving from space 1 to space 2") might be fruitful.

mains in contrast with the general framing of the social event profiled. This seems similar to the analysis of Sylvia Plath's poem "The Applicant" proposed by Semino (1997), where the apparent incoherence of the discourse comes from the mixture of tokens of different schemas. A similar comment could be made with regard to Larkin's "Vers de Société" and Reed's "Judging Distances" (and other poems not discussed here). The *evocation of discourse schemas*, rather than actual discourse, seems an appropriate choice for a poetic text, as significantly more meaning can be read from the broad frame of "an interview", "a funeral", or "army training" than from any individual's contribution to the realization of the frame.

The evocation of spaces which have not been clearly set up earlier and the fact that they may be evoked very partially is what might explain the openness of poetic texts to different interpretations – a feature which remains prototypical according to many poetry analysts and which also prompts literary critics to be cautious about accepting the results of a stylistic or cognitive analysis as relevant. The opinions expressed in some responses to the research in cognitive poetics (e.g. the recent review by Jackson 2005) suggest that literary critics see the cognitive poetics and stylistics attempts to contribute to the discussion as restricting the freedom of interpretation and favouring one (often considered obvious) understanding. We see the results of our research as suggesting a different conclusion, though. The evocative nature of much of contemporary poetic discourse is precisely what might explain the variety of interpretations and contribute to the non-triviality of cognitively-based analyses. To give just one example, it is perfectly possible to read Reed's poem as representing the actual conversation in the training context, with the poem's persona aligned with the soldier *at the end*, and to understand the description of the landscape as that of the real landscape, the one in which the training is happening. We opted for a different interpretation in this paper, but if the other one were proposed, it would rely on another understanding of the mental spaces set up, which could be argued to be prompted by the text. The open-endedness of a poetic text as a discourse event (the indeterminacy of speakers, settings, temporal and spatial parameters, etc.) is what makes many interpretations possible.[22] But it does not follow that these in-

---

22. A recent book by Hiraga (2005) develops the idea of a variety of relationships between the form of a poetic text and its meaning. We have no space to engage in a broader discussion here, but we are clearly not alone in believing that the specificity of a poetic text relies on its ability to use one form to prompt for different interpretations.

terpretations cannot be arrived at via a cognitively informed reading. On the contrary, we believe that the tools we are developing will lead to a better appreciation of the richness of meaning a single poem can represent.

References

Adamson, Sylvia
   1995   From empathetic deixis to empathetic narrative: Stylisation and (de-) subjectivisation as processes of language change. In: Dieter Stein and Susan Wright (eds.), *Subjectivity and Subjectivisation: Linguistic Perspectives* 195–224. Cambridge: Cambridge University Press.
Akatsuka, Noriko
   1985   Conditionals and epistemic scale. *Language* 61: 625–639.
Ariel, Mira
   1990   *Accessing Noun Phrase Antecedents*. London: Routledge.
Banfield, Ann
   1982   *Unspeakable Sentences: Narration and Representation in the Language of Fiction*. Boston: Routledge and Kegan Paul.
Booth, Wayne C.
   1961   *The Rhetoric of Fiction* (Phoenix books 267). Chicago: University of Chicago Press.
Browne, Michael Dennis and Anne Jenkins
   1999   Five poems. *American Poetry Review* 28(1): 3. Accessed via EBSCO-host on February 10, 2000.
Burke, Michael
   2005   How cognition can augment stylistic analysis. *European Journal of English Studies* 9(2): 185–195.
COBUILD
   s.d.   *The Bank of English* corpus [http://www.cobuild.collins.co.uk]. London: Collins Publishers.
Coulson, Seana and Todd Oakley
   2005   Blending and coded meaning: literal and figurative meaning in cognitive semantics. *Journal of Pragmatics* 37: 1510–1536.
Dancygier, Barbara
   1993   Interpreting conditionals: time, knowledge and causation. *Journal of Pragmatics* 19: 403–434.
Dancygier, Barbara
   1998   *Conditionals and Prediction: Time, Knowledge and Causation in Conditional Constructions* (Cambridge studies in linguistics 87). Cambridge: Cambridge University Press.
Dancygier, Barbara
   2004   Visual viewpoint, narrative viewpoint, and mental spaces in narrative

discourse. In: A. Soares da Silva, A. Torres and M. Goncalves (eds.), *Linguagem, Cultura e Cognicao: Estudos de Linguistica Cognitiva* vol. 1/2, 347–362. Coimbra: Livraria Almedina.

2005   Blending and narrative viewpoint: Jonathan Raban's travels through mental spaces. *Language and Literature* 14(2): 99–127.

Dancygier, Barbara and Eve Sweetser
2000   Constructions with *if, since* and *because*: Causality, epistemic stance, and clause order. In: Elizabeth Couper-Kuhlen and Bernd Kortmann (eds.), *Cause – Condition – Concession – Contrast*, 111–142. Berlin: Mouton de Gruyter.

Dancygier, Barbara and Eve Sweetser
2005   *Mental Spaces in Grammar: Conditional Constructions* (Cambridge studies in linguistics 108). Cambridge: Cambridge University Press.

Davies, Eirian C.
1979   *On the Semantics of Syntax: Mood and Condition in English.* London: Croom Helm.

Evans, Vyvyan
2004   *The Structure of Time: Language, Meaning and Temporal Cognition* (Human Cognitive Processing 12). Amsterdam: John Benjamins.

Fauconnier, Gilles
1985   *Mental Spaces: Aspects of Meaning Construction in Natural Language.* Cambridge (Mass.): MIT Press.

Fauconnier, Gilles
1997   *Mappings in Thought and Language.* Cambridge: Cambridge University Press.

Fauconnier, Gilles and Mark Turner
1996   Blending as a central process of grammar. In: Adele Goldberg (ed.), *Conceptual Structure, Discourse, and Language*, 113–130. Stanford: Center for the Study of Language and Information.

Fauconnier, Gilles and Mark Turner
1998a   Conceptual integration networks. *Cognitive Science* 22(2), 133–187.

Fauconnier, Gilles and Mark Turner
1998b   Principles of conceptual integration. In: Jean-Pierre Koenig (ed.), *Discourse and Cognition: Bridging the Gap*, 269–283. Stanford: Center for the Study of Language and Information.

Fauconnier, Gilles and Mark Turner
2002   *The Way We Think: Conceptual Blending and the Mind's Hidden Complexities.* New York: Basic Books.

Fillmore, Charles J.
1990   Epistemic stance and grammatical form in English conditional sentences. *CLS* 26: 137–162.

Fleischman, Suzanne
1989   Temporal distance: a basic linguistic metaphor. *Studies in Language* 13(1): 1–50.

Fleischman, Suzanne
  1990   *Tense and Narrativity: From Medieval Performance to Modern Fiction*
          (Croom Helm Romance Linguistics Series). London: Routledge.
Fludernik, Monika
  1993   *The Fictions of Language and the Languages of Fiction: The Lin-
          guistic Representation of Speech and Consciousness.* London: Rout-
          ledge.
Hiraga, Masako
  2005   *Metaphor and Iconicity.* New York: Palgrave Macmillan.
Holt, Elizabeth
  1996   Reporting on talk: The use of direct reported speech in conversation.
          Research on Language and Social Interaction 29(3): 219–245.
Holt, Elizabeth
  2000   Reporting and reacting: Concurrent responses to reported speech. *Re-
          search on Language and Social Interaction* 33(4): 425–454.
Horn, Laurence
  1985   Metalinguistic negation and pragmatic ambiguity. *Language* 61:
          121–174.
Horn, Laurence
  1989   *A Natural History of Negation.* Chicago: University of Chicago
          Press.
Iwata, Seizi
  2003   Echo questions are interrogatives? Another version of a metarepresen-
          tational analysis. *Linguistics and Philosophy* 26: 185–254.
Jackson, Tony E.
  2005   Explanation, interpretation, and close reading: The progress of cogni-
          tive poetics. *Poetics Today* 26(3): 519–533.
Lakoff, George and Mark Johnson
  1980   *Metaphors We Live By.* Chicago: Chicago University Press.
Lakoff, George and Mark Johnson
  1999   *Philosophy in the Flesh: The Embodied Mind and Its Challenge to West-
          ern Thought.* New York: Basic Books.
Langacker, Ronald W.
  2001   Discourse in Cognitive Grammar. *Cognitive Linguistics* 12: 143–188.
Larkin, Philip
  1997   Reprint. *Collected Poems.* Ed. Anthony Thwaite. New York: Noonday
          Press. Original edition, London: Faber and Faber, 1988.
Larkin, Philip
  2005   Reprint. *Jill.* London: Faber and Faber. Original edition, London:
          Faber and Faber, 1946.
Leech, Geoffrey N. and Michael H. Short
  1981   *Style in Fiction: A Linguistic Introduction to English Fictional Prose*
          (English Language Series 13). London: Longman.
Lyons, John
  1977   *Semantics.* Cambridge: Cambridge University Press.

Mayes, Patricia
   1990   Quotation in spoken English. *Studies in Language* 14(2): 325–363.
McCawley, James D.
   1987   The syntax of English echoes. *CLS* 23: 246–258.
McGregor, William B.
   1997   *Semiotic Grammar*. Oxford: Clarendon Press.
Noh, Eun-Ju
   2000   *Metarepresentation: A Relevance-Theory Approach*. (Pragmatics and Beyond New Series 69). Amsterdam: Benjamins.
Nuñez, Raphael E. and Eve Sweetser
   2006   With the future behind them: Convergent evidence from Aymara language and gesture in the crosslinguistic comparison of spatial construals of time. *Cognitive Science* 30: 401–450.
Packalén, Małgorzata Anna
   2004   A domestication of death: The poetic universe of Wisława Szymborska. Online publication at Nobelprize.org [http://nobelprize.org/nobel_prizes/literature/articles/packalen/]. Accessed 26 July 2006.
Partee, Barbara H.
   1973   The syntax and semantics of quotation. In: Stephen R. Anderson and Paul Kiparsky (eds.), *A Festschrift for Morris Halle*, 410–418. New York: Holt.
Pascual, Esther
   2002   *Imaginary Trialogues: Conceptual Blending and Fictive Interaction in Criminal Courts*. Utrecht: LOT.
Raban, Jonathan
   2000   Reprint. *Passage to Juneau*. New York: Vintage Books. Original edition, New York: Vintage Books, 1999.
Redeker, Gisela
   1996   Free indirect discourse in newspaper reports. In: Crit Cremers and Marcel den Dikken (eds.), *Linguistics in the Netherlands 1996*, 221–232. Amsterdam: Benjamins.
Reinhart, Tanya
   1975   Whose main clause? (Point of view in sentences with parentheticals). In: Susumu Kuno (ed.), *Harvard Studies of Syntax and Semantics* 1, 127–171. Cambridge (Mass.): Dept. of Linguistics, Harvard University.
Sanders, José and Gisela Redeker
   1996   Perspective and the representation of speech and thought in narrative discourse. In: Gilles Fauconnier and Eve Sweetser (eds.), *Spaces, Worlds, and Grammar*, 290–317. Chicago: University of Chicago Press.
Semino, Elena
   1997   *Language and World Creation in Poems and Other Texts*. New York: Addison Wesley Longman.
Slingerland, Edward
   2005   Conceptual blending, somatic marking, and normativity: a case example from ancient Chinese. *Cognitive Linguistics* 16(3): 557–584.

Tannen, Deborah
   1986   Introducing constructed dialogue in Greek and American conversa-
          tional and literary narrative. In: Florian Coulmas (ed.) *Direct and In-
          direct Speech*, 311–332. (Trends in Linguistics 31.) Berlin: Mouton de
          Gruyter.
Vandelanotte, Lieven
   2002   *But forced to qualify*: Distancing speech and thought representation as
          a symptom of uninformedness in Larkin. *Leuvense Bijdragen (Leuven
          Contributions in Linguistics and Philology)* 91(3–4): 383–426.
Vandelanotte, Lieven
   2004a Deixis and grounding in speech and thought representation. *Journal of
          Pragmatics* 36(3): 489–520.
Vandelanotte, Lieven
   2004b From representational to scopal "distancing indirect speech or
          thought": A cline of subjectification. *Text* 24(4): 547–585.
Vandelanotte, Lieven
   2005   Types of speech and thought representation in English: Syntagmatic
          structure, deixis and expressivity, semantics. PhD dissertation, Univer-
          sity of Leuven.
Vandelanotte, Lieven
in press *Speech and Thought Representation in English: A Cognitive-Functional
          Approach* (Topics in English Linguistics 65). Berlin: Mouton de
          Gruyter.
van der Voort, Cok
   1986   Hoe vrij is de vrije indirecte rede? *Forum der Letteren* 4: 241–255.
Van Hoek, Karen
   1997   *Anaphora and Conceptual Structure*. Chicago: University of Chicago
          Press.
Verhagen, Arie
   2005   *Constructions of Intersubjectivity: Discourse, Syntax, and Cognition*.
          Oxford: Oxford University Press.
von Roncador, Manfred
   1980   Gibt die Redewiedergabe Rede wieder? *L.A.U.T.*, Series A, Paper no.
          71. Trier.
von Roncador, Manfred
   1988   *Zwischen direkter und indirekter Rede: Nichtwörtliche direkte Rede, er-
          lebte Rede, logophorische Konstruktionen und Verwandtes* (Linguis-
          tische Arbeiten 192). Tübingen: Niemeyer.
Yamaguchi, Haruhiko
   1994   Echo utterances. In: Ronald E. Asher (ed.), *Encyclopedia of Language
          and Linguistics*, 1084–1085. Oxford: Pergamon Press.

The event that built a distanced space

Jeroen Vandaele

If we may believe that cross-disciplinary thinking produces benefits for all disciplines involved, then two questions seem to concern us here: (1) what does Poetics stand to gain from Dancygier and Vandelanotte's article on distanced discourse, and (2) why might their cognitive linguistic analyses of such discourse profit from dialogue with the field of Poetics? First I will try to summarize and defend Dancygier and Vandelanotte's answer to the first question. Next, I will reluctantly assume the role of a traditional poetician in an attempt to further promote dialogue between the authors and Poetics. In fact, the following should merely clarify in which direction I will be pulling the various brands of "distancing discourse" that I have just put to use (*if we may believe*; *seem to concern us*; *stand to gain*; *might*; *reluctantly assume the role*). But perhaps the general tone of the previous stretch of discourse will not have been all that distancing. The next stretch will hopefully tell, for that is what the genre of academic writing (unlike literature) is about.

Poetics tries to describe and explain the sense-making mechanisms of literature and is interested in speech genres in general, since literature can embed any real-life genre. Thus, when Dancygier and Vandelanotte survey some *langue*-based distancing mechanisms in terms of Mental Space Theory (MST), they offer a toolbox for fine-grained analyses of literary language as well. Their examples (3) and (4) could easily have been part of a novel, as my adaptations (1) and (2) show:

(1) "If she was hired, she doesn't need our help any more", Peter replied to Susan.
(2) Mark was slightly irritated. If she had been hired, she wouldn't need our help any more.

Dancygier and Vandelanotte point out that the difference between the *if*-clauses of (1) and (2) is not merely one between *potentialis* ("if she was hired") and *irrealis* ("if she had been hired"). Also, the similarity between both *if*-clauses is not limited to their expressing conditionality. On the level of *parole*, or discourse, conditionality should be interpreted as "un-assertability", that is, as the current conceptualizer's (Peter's and Mark's) unwillingness to verbally or mentally assert that she was hired. More importantly, their mental space analysis shows that the *potentialis* in (1) is a *potentialis*-for-the-speaker and at the same time a fact for (and from) the hearer, while Mark's *irrealis* thought in (2) contrasts with an "actual" mental space ("she was *not* hired") which also belongs to Mark and not necessarily to somebody else. Whereas Peter replies to a *de dicto* mental space originated in Susan, Mark is involved in thinking beyond his own *de re* mental space.

Since the macro-genre of (more or less realistic) fiction tends to import real-life schemes into its own fictional logic, such analyses may also be useful if we want to understand novelistic characters, how they interact and how the narrator presents them. The epistemic distance expressed via *if*-clauses and past tenses may contribute to the internal dynamics of story worlds: Which propositional content has which cognitive status for which characters and (how) do characters use and negotiate these contents and their status? Sentence (1) may hint at a hidden antagonism between Peter and Susan. Sentence (2) seems to spell out Mark's solitary frustrations. A principled linguistic account may thus serve poetic analysis. What Mental Space Theory offers is not merely a notational variant of what can also be grasped in common language – which it can – since MST connects these findings with a global theory of how the mind works. In order to think beyond their here-and-now, people (characters) think and interact through "mental spaces", small cognitive packets which blend in often unprecedented but always describable ways to form new "emergent" meanings. Peter e.g. transforms the contents of Susan's asserted knowledge space into a distanced space for his own use. Students of narrative theory may find such views on the mind attractive enough to incorporate them in their research on fiction.

Dancygier and Vandelanotte have more to offer to Poetics. In fact, their analysis aims to cut across discourse levels by means of a "transversal" concept that is both global and specific: distance in/of mental spaces. In its global sense "distance" includes or refers to such categories as "doubt", "thought experiment", "counterfactuals", "report", "irony", "fiction", etc. Simultaneously, the notion of distance remains unified in its various senses and is perhaps more palpable than other concepts on which it sheds light: "tone", "mode of representation", "modality", "speech and thought representation", "possible world", or even "mental space". Using the concept of distance, Dancygier and Vandelanotte argue that the *langue* of "space-builders" – forms that prompt a mental space other than the "base space" of the current speaker – includes a particular linguistic configuration that allows speakers/writers of English to use "distanced discourse" in Speech and Thought Representation. This is their second contribution to Poetics.

Indeed, given that Speech and Thought Representation (STR) is part of the core business of literary and "natural" narrators (to use Fludernik's [1996] term), the study of STR occupies a central position in the poetics of narrative as well – although poetic and linguistic accounts of STR tend to take each other's ends for means (see e.g. McHale 1978 for an authoritative poetician's view on linguistic accounts). Twentieth-century linguistic taxonomies present three basic categories of STR: direct "discourse" (or "speech and thought", DST), indirect discourse (IST), and free indirect discourse (FIST). Dancygier and Vandelanotte call for a fourth type, "distancing indirect speech or thought" (DIST), "in which a distinct discourse space, subordinate to or blended with the speaker's current discourse space, is merely evoked *without* a shift of deictic center": "both accessibility organization *and* grammatical person remain the current speaker's prerogative". In the field of pronominal anaphora, "accessibility organization" concerns the identification of the entities to which nouns and pronouns refer. In STR, "accessibility organization" basically refers to the current speaker's (i.e. the narrator's) choice between a pronoun or full noun phrase to refer to a represented speaker or conceptualizer: the choice for a noun-headed NP or a pronoun is seen as a (linguistic) sign of the viewpoint taken. Since FIST and DST refer to quotees by means of pronouns, their first-level narrator (their current speaker) "suggests" that the accessibility of referents is supposedly high. Since the accessibility of represented conceptualizers is hypothetically higher for participants *within* the represented level (i.e. for quotees) than it is for participants on the first discursive level (i.e. for current speaker and listener), FIST and DST may be perceived as types of discourse that adopt the represented conceptualizer's viewpoint. In DIST, Dancygier and Vandelanotte's fourth category, the current speaker often opts for noun-headed NPs and thereby implies lower accessibility of referents and, hence, suggests a current speaker's viewpoint (i.e. his/her own viewpoint on the embedded discourse). This is what happens in the Lucy and Miss Bartlett dialogue, where the embedded interlocutors are subordinated to the current narrator's viewpoint. In DIST, full noun phrases are not obligatory but always possible to refer to embedded-discourse participants. In any event, DIST's current speaker always remains in charge.

Now, how does the traditional poetician in me value DIST? I do agree that the linguistic configuration seems to warrant an interesting category of STR in which the current speaker (quoter) holds complete control over the represented speaker or conceptualizer (quotee) – s/he remains the deictic center of the dialogues s/he represents so that s/he may call his/her current addressee "you" (instead of "s/he") even in quoted dialogue: "She said uhm did I know if you were teaching?" instead of "She said uhm: "Do you know if she is teaching?"" (DST) or "Did I know if she was teaching?" (FIST). However, I disagree with the name of the category: "DIST". Even though the accessibility argument makes sense, even though nouns and pronouns may be important devices for building "distance" or "proximity" in/of spaces, I do not believe that deictic and grammatical control is sufficient or even necessary for the creation of distance in *any* type of STR. Instead, as Sternberg (1982: 119) has forcefully argued, "[g]iven the appropriate conditions in the frame [=embedding discourse] – and only these shape the inset [=embedded discourse] – any form [...] may be made to go with any representational affect":

> The supreme control lies with the frame. [...] In each case, therefore, the linguistic patterns, indicating what may be rather than what is to be done, have the least to say in the matter. They do whatever they are allowed or made to do [...]. (Sternberg 1982: 125)

This is what Sternberg calls the Proteus Principle, namely that "in different contexts [...] the same form may fulfill different functions and different forms the same function" (1982: 148). Sternberg concedes that direct quotation exhibits "the widest and most flexible variability in that it bestrides the whole scale of response, from identification to caricature and condemnation", but all forms of indirect quotation may also give rise to empathy and distance (see also Fludernik 1993). At most, then, "DIST" would seem to be an acronym for "dialogic indirect speech and thought", ironic at times (as in the Lucy-Bartlett example), playful and sympathetic at other times (as when Brown's persona meets Larkin in the elevator). Whereas FIST serves us fine for the communicative situation of narrator-narratee in narrative fiction and poetry, DIST would be a useful alternative when the narratee – a best friend or worst enemy – happens to stand right in front of the current narrator.

Non-formalist poeticians argue that some notion of "context" is fundamental in any account of meaning production in literary genres and the real-life genres they imitate or embed. Functionalist poeticians, like

Sternberg, McHale or Fludernik, attend to the functions of form, study how forms can be made to function. In such models of explanation, specific event-related discourse purposes take pride of place. Dancygier and Vandelanotte criticize the traditional linguistic taxonomy of STR yet they also seem to propose a "non-functional" taxonomy of forms – even a non-cognitive categorization, if we take cognition to be a function of a person's functioning-in-the-world. Contrary to Cognitive Linguistics' recent discovery of discourse (Langacker 2001; Pascual 2002; Coulson and Oakley 2005), Poetics has a tradition of analyzing *parole* as an event that either replicates and solidifies structures or takes (momentary or partial) distance from them, or even attempts to restructure what is pre-given. As the pioneer of "dialogic imagination" and literary "polyphony" has it:

> Dialogue, in the narrow sense of the word, is of course only one of the forms – a very important form, to be sure – of verbal interaction. But dialogue can also be understood in a broader sense, meaning not only direct, face-to-face, vocalised verbal communication between persons, but also verbal communication of any type whatsoever. A book, *i.e.* a verbal performance in print, is also an element of verbal communication. [It] inevitably orients itself with respect to previous performances in the same sphere. [...] Thus the printed verbal performance engages, as it were, in ideological colloquy of a large scale: t responds to something, affirms something, anticipates possible responses and objections, seeks support, and so on. (Vološinov/Bakhtin 1973: 95)

This idea is not restricted to purely positive dialogue, as the irony and parody specialist Linda Hutcheon explains. In order to understand parody, "[w]e must take into account the entire enunciative act: the text and the 'subject positions' of encoder and decoder, but also the various contexts (historical, social, ideological) that mediate that communicative act" (2000: 108).

Dancygier and Vandelanotte are entirely free to interpret these criticisms as total distance. And even if I objected strongly to such an interpretation (which I would), I would have to accept the Derridean or Foucauldian rule which says that a writer's discourse (*in casu* mine) can always be recontextualized beyond the control of that writer. So, in a vain attempt to maintain control, I insist that their article has reminded me of how important fine-grained linguistic analysis is for the poetic enterprise. But I myself also plead guilty, for "to quote is to recontextualize a discourse" (Sternberg's "universal of quotation", 1982: 130). Thus, the article has also reminded me that such linguistic detail deserves to be "grounded" by poetic principles of meaning-making. Instead of paying lipservice to discourse parameters, the article to which I respond could perhaps have stressed how participants in discourse situations may choose any of the one-to-many and many-to-one relations that exist between the forms and functions of STR – according to what they want to achieve. "My wife and I have asked a crowd of craps" is an instance of the direct-and-ironic possibility; most direct discourse is "illustrative" *in Larkin's poetry*; the *raison d'être* of FID (FIST) is *not* the "coherent but oblique" representation of a character's consciousness (instead, it is one possible function of this form; see also McHale 1978); *any* form of STR can "appropriate and echo" the embedded discourse; even academic commentaries do so.

References

Coulson, Seana and Todd Oakley
    2005   Blending and coded meaning: Literal and figurative meaning in cognitive semantics. *Journal of Pragmatics* 37: 1510–1536.
Deppermann, Arnulf
    2002   Von der Kognition zur verbalen Interaktion: Bedeutungskonstitution im Kontext aus Sicht der Kognitionswissenschaften und der Gesprächsforschung. In: Deppermann, Arnulf/Spranz-Fogasy, Thomas (eds.), *Be-deuten: Wie Bedeutung im Gespräch entsteht*, 11–33. Tübingen: Stauffenburg, 2002.
Fludernik, Monika
    1993   *The Fictions of Language and the Languages of Fiction. The Linguistic Representation of Speech and Consciousness*. London/New York: Routledge.
Fludernik, Monika
    1996   *Towards a 'Natural' Narratology*. London/New York: Routledge.
Hutcheon, Linda
    [1985] 2000 *A Theory of Parody: The Teachings of Twentieth-Century Art Forms*. New York: Methuen.
Langacker, Ronald W.
    2001   Discourse in Cognitive Grammar. *Cognitive Linguistics* 12: 143–188.
McHale, Brian
    [1978] 2004 Free indirect discourse. A survey of recent accounts *PTL: A Journal for Descriptive Poetics and Theory of Literature* 3, 249–287. [Reprinted in: Mieke Bal (ed.), *Narrative Theory. Critical Concepts in Literary and Cultural Studies*. Volume 1. *Major Issues in Narrative Theory*, 187–222. London/New York: Routledge.]
Pascual, Esther
    2002   *Imaginary Trialogues: Conceptual Blending and Fictive Interaction in Criminal Courts*. Utrecht: LOT.

Sternberg, Meir
  1982   Proteus in quotation-land. Mimesis and forms of reported discourse
           Poetics Today 3(2), 107–156.
Vološinov, Valentin N. (and Bakhtin, Michail)
  1973   *Marxism and the philosophy of language.* New York (N Y): Seminar
           press.

Discourse, context, and cognition

Barbara Dancygier and Lieven Vandelanotte

The views expressed in the rejoinder leave us with mixed feelings. On the one hand, we are pleased to see that our work is appreciated by a "traditional poetician", but, on the other hand, we are worried about the appreciation being expressed from a point of view which seems to be diametrically opposed to ours. We will thus use the space given to us to try and clarify some assumptions we have relied on.

In our understanding of poetics we follow Culler's belief that "poetics starts with attested meanings or effects and seeks to understand what structures or devices make them possible" (2002: vii). While various approaches to poetics rely on linguistic expressions in different ways, the shared assumption is that these "structures and devices" relate to meaning. It also follows that a search for form-meaning correlations is as crucial to poetics as it is to cognitive linguistics, which views the correlations as cognitively motivated patterns, not as strictly formal one-to-one correspondences, thus leaving enough room for the originality and creativity of poetic and narrative forms. The context obviously has a role to play in arriving at the meaning of an expression, but even the most refined analysis of the context will not substitute an analysis of the "structures and devices". We thus beg to disagree with the suggestion voiced in the rejoinder that anything can be said to mean anything and the discourse situation is all that matters.

Our disagreement with the rejoinder also comes from a different understanding of the 'cognitive' part of cognitive poetics. While cognitive constructs emerge out of embodied experience, it does not follow that talking about cognition requires talking about that experience. On the contrary, the concepts which cognitive approaches to language rely on are claimed to emerge out of experience, but they are shared across contexts (rather than in a context) and characterize the human mind rather than "a person's" mind or "functioning-in-the-world". Contrary to what the rejoinder's ironic tone suggests, the connection between higher-level mental constructs and specific discourse situations is far from obvious (though it is obvious that relying on the concept of *parole* will not suffice as an explanation).

In its rhetorical zeal, the rejoinder seems to miss the main points of our paper. We tried to contrast the forms which evoke a specific spatial view-point configuration with other forms which may be felt as "distanced" in some sense, but not in the specific sense we discuss. The term "distanced discourse", which we applied to constructions such as DIST or the so-called past indicative conditionals, evokes a mental space set-up which relies on a mental "standpoint" of the speaker as the conceptual view-point from which other mental spaces are viewed (be they spatial, temporal, social, or discursive). We thus object to the implicit equation of our narrowly defined notion of "distanced discourse" with the "global sense" of distance Vandelae refers to.

In addition, we are puzzled by the suggestion voiced in the rejoinder that, for example, DIST and FIST have not been clearly distinguished. True, they may both be loosely described as expressing the speaker's distance, but, again, not in the sense of distanced discourse we propose. We have also not tried to suggest that the use of proper names or full NPs in itself distinguishes DIST from other STR types. We refer the reader to Vandelanotte's earlier work, which makes it clear that DIST is distinguished primarily by its treatment of deictic information. In fact, it is the deictic set-up which makes DIST a good example of distanced discourse, while the more likely use of proper names is a result of this set-up, and not its source. Of course, the taxonomy we proposed remains open to improvements, but we cannot agree that there is no need to look afresh at the earlier taxonomies because all taxonomies will in the end fall prey to the all-powerful context. Moreover, replacing the "distancing" in "DIST" by "dialogic" effectively denies a possibility of any taxonomy, as in the Bakhtinian tradition invoked by Vandaele all STR is inherently dialogic "speech about speech". The logical consequence would be to also give up on FIST or DST as useful categories – or is it better to keep them, but make sure that they remain comfortably vague?

Finally, we are surprised at the rejoinder's preoccupation with our discussion of narrative discourse. Our argument cuts across several areas of grammar and usage, to lead us to the role of distanced discourse in poetry. The connection between the choice of verb forms in conditionals and discursive forms of poetic expression may seem tenuous, but it is our contention that a cognitive approach to language and poetics reveals such unexpected correlations by uncovering cognitive and linguistic sources of poetic forms. Indeed, we believe that the reliance on cognitive linguistic concepts and a recognition of the ways in which literary discourse uses and/or modifies them may help us hammer out a methodology which reaches across more levels of meaning construction – an approach which poetics scholars might then find worth considering.

Reference

Culler, Jonathan
    2002   *Structuralist Poetics: Structuralism, Linguistics and the Study of Literature*. 2nd ed. with a new preface by the author. London and New York: Routledge. First edition, London: Routledge and Kegan Paul, 1975.

Does an "ironic situation" favor an ironic interpretation?

Rachel Giora, Ofer Fein, Ronie Kaufman, Dana Eisenberg, and Shani Erez

What environment would promote irony interpretation? What contextual information would trigger or invite an ironic utterance? Is there a proto-typical environment that would render irony interpretation preferable (see Utsumi 2000, 2004)? According to Gibbs (2002: 462), it is a context that sets up an "ironic situation" through contrast between what is expected and the reality that frustrates it that would facilitate irony interpretation:

> The reason why people might find the ironic remark *This sure is an exciting life* as easy to process as when this same sentence was seen in a literal context (e.g., where the speaker said something truthful about the exciting life he was lead-ing) is because the context itself sets up an "ironic situation" through the contrast between what Gus expected when he joined the Navy and the reality of it being rather boring. Because people conceive of many situations ironically (Gibbs 1994; Lucariello 1994), they can subsequently understand someone's ironic, or sarcastic, comment without having to engage in the additional com-putation that may be required when ironic remarks are seen in situations that are inherently less ironic.

Inspired by Gibbs' (2002) view that a context featuring an "ironic situation" should facilitate ironic interpretation, we set out to investigate the nature of such contextual information.[1] The aim of this study is twofold. We first test the assumption that contexts that feature some contrast between what is expected and the reality that frustrates it would favor an ironic description of that situation compared to contexts in which no contrast is established between what is expected and the reality in which this expectation is realized (Experiment 1). To do that, we presented par-ticipants with two types of context. In one, the protagonist, say Gus, ex-pects to experience adventures in the Navy but eventually has to deal with

---

1. Note that "ironic situation" and "situational irony" are two unrelated notions. For information on "situational irony", see Gibbs (1994); Littman and Mey (1991); Shelley (2001).

uninspiring daily routines; in another, Gus anticipates mundane routines in the Navy and indeed has to deal with tedious chores. Having read these contexts, participants were presented two possible endings for each of these contexts. One in which the description of the situation is ironic – *This sure is an exciting life!* – and another in which its description is literal – *This sure is a boring life!*. If people prefer an ironic description following an "ironic situation" more often than following a nonironic situation, this will support the view that an "ironic situation" invites an ironic ending.

In Experiment 2 we test the assumption that a context featuring an "ironic situation" – a situation that centers on some frustrated expectation – will facilitate irony interpretation compared to a situation that does not but instead centers on an expectation that comes true. To do that, we measured reading times of statements (*This sure is an exciting life!*) following contexts featuring a frustrated expectation, a realized expectation, and no-expectation, in which this statement is literal. In fact, even if the different (frustrated vs. no-expectation) contexts affect similar reading times for literal and ironic descriptions of such situations, such results will be consistent with the view that, given an "ironic situation", ironies should not be more difficult to understand than literals (Gibbs 1986, 2002).

Experiment 1

In this study, we compared contexts featuring frustrated expectation vs. realized expectation in an attempt to find out whether they might differ in how they affect readers' choice of an ironic statement that describes the situation. Specifically, we presented participants with contexts in which an expectation was either realized or frustrated and asked them to choose between an ironic and a literal statement that describes that situation.

Method

Participants. Thirty-two participants including students of Tel Aviv University and friends and colleagues of the experimenters (19 women and 13 men) between the ages of 19 and 63 volunteered to participate in the experiment.

Materials. Materials consisted of 16 pairs of Hebrew contexts, and 16 filler contexts. All the contexts contained a short story, 6–9 sentences long, involving one or more characters, a negative event, and the protagonist's expectation related to that event. In half of the experimental items the expectation was frustrated (1) and in half it came true (2). Other than this difference between a frustrated and a realized expectation, the experimental contexts were very much alike. The filler items included an expectation only occasionally. All the contexts were followed by 2 target sentences. The experimental contexts were each followed by (a) an ironic depiction of how the expectation turned out (see 1a, 2a); (b) a literal description of that situation (see 1b, 2b). Both were uttered by the protagonist who earlier expressed the expectation. The filler items were each followed by a literal and a metaphoric target.

(1) Frustrated expectation

>   Shirley is a feminist activist. Two weeks ago, she organized a demonstration
>   against the closure of a shelter for victimized women, and invited the press.
>   She hoped that due to her immense efforts many people will show up at the
>   demonstration, and that the media will cover it widely. On the day of the
>   demonstration, 20 activists arrived, and no journalist showed up. In re-
>   sponse to the poor turnout, Shirley muttered:
>   a. This demonstration is a remarkable success. (Ironic)
>   b. This demonstration is a remarkable failure. (Literal)

(2) Realized expectation

>   Shirley is a feminist activist. Two weeks ago, she organized a demonstration
>   against the closure of a shelter for victimized women, and invited the press.
>   As always, she prepared herself for the idea that despite the hard work, only
>   a few people will show up at the demonstration and the media will ignore it
>   entirely. On the day of the demonstration, 20 activists arrived, and no jour-
>   nalist showed up. In response to the poor turnout, Shirley muttered:
>   a. This demonstration is a remarkable success. (Ironic)
>   b. This demonstration is a remarkable failure. (Literal)

The paired items were divided into two booklets, each containing 16 experimental and 16 filler contexts plus 2 targets following each context. All the materials, including the target sentences, were randomly presented. Of the 16 experimental contexts, half contained a realized expectation and half a frustrated expectation. One booklet contained 7 contexts featuring an expectation that was realized and 9 in which the expectation was frustrated. The other booklet contained 9 contexts featuring an expectation that was realized and 7 in which the expectation was frustrated. The subjects were not exposed to the same context twice.

Procedure. Subjects were asked to read the stories and select the most suitable ending, either (a) or (b).

Results and discussion

Results showed no preference for ironic over literal interpretations, nor did they show equal distribution of literal and ironic interpretations. Instead, it was the literal utterance that was the most preferable choice (selected in about 70% of the cases). Importantly, this was the case not just when expectation was realized but also when expectation was frustrated.

In addition, results showed no preference for an ironic target as a function of the kind of expectation made manifest. This was borne out by both subject ($t_1(31)=.27$, $p=.27$) and item ($t_2(15)=.66$, $p=.26$) analyses. Specifically, subjects chose ironic targets following a context manifesting a frustrated expectation in 30.36% of the cases (SD=27.92). Similarly, subjects chose ironic targets following a context manifesting a realized expectation in 31.60% of the cases (SD=24.84).

It is not the case, then, that a context that sets up an "ironic situation" invites an ironic reference to that situation more often than a context not manifesting such "ironic situation". It is not even the case that an "ironic situation" would equally invite ironic and literal descriptions of the situation. Rather, it is the literal description that is favored, regardless of type of expectation (for similar results, see also Ivanko and Pexman 2003, where situations involving frustrated expectations invited a literal rather than an ironic reference to that situation).

While our findings showed no preference for ironic over literal statements as a function of frustrated vs. realized expectations, they might be examined in terms of an alternative explanation. Would the size of the gap between what is said and the situation described account for speakers' preference of an ironic over a literal utterance? According to the view of irony as indirect negation (Giora 1995), the larger the gap between what is said and the situation described the more often speakers will select an ironic rather than a literal description of the situation, regardless of whether the situation features a failed or a fulfilled expectation.[2] Accord-

---

2. For examples, in the context of 1, which reports of the small number of activists showing up for the demonstration, to say that (a) *This demonstration is a remarkable success* is to state something that is distinctly removed from the actual state of affairs. Such a statement fleshes out the gap between what is said and the situation described by what is said. However, to say that (b) *This dem-*

ing to the indirect negation view, however, should such a preference emerge, this does not predict ease of processing. Anticipation of an ironic utterance need not have initial facilitative effects. Although under such circumstances, irony interpretation might be speedier than under less favorable conditions, this boosting of the ironic interpretation need not obviate or bypass initial access of inappropriate but more accessible interpretations (see Giora et al. 2007).

To test the hypothesis that the size of the gap between what is said and the situation referred to can account for a possible preference of ironic descriptions of these situations, we presented 10 irony experts (students of irony classes) with all the contexts, which, this time, were followed by the ironic targets only. We asked these experts to rate, on a 7 point scale, the size of the gap between what is said and the situation described by the ironic statement. We then looked at the gap ratings of the third (11) of the items that had received the greatest amount of ironic endings compared to the third (11) of the items that had received the smallest amount of ironic endings. Results showed that readers' choice of an ironic target was a function of the size of the gap: The third most popular ironic endings received higher gap ratings (5.91, SD=0.51) than the third least popular ironic endings (5.55, SD=0.57), t(20)=1.57, *p*=.06.

Similarly, comparing the third (11) of the ironic items rated highest in terms of gap size to the third (11) of the items rated lowest in terms of gap size reveals that the upper third was more often selected as an ironic ending (36.4%, SD=19.3%) compared to the lower third (24.4%, SD=17.1%), t(20)=1.53, *p*=.07.

In all, these findings indicate that the preference for an ironic statement is not sensitive to the type of expectation induced by context. Instead, it is guided by the size of the gap between what is said and the situation described. (For more evidence supporting the view that irony hinges on the gap between what is said and what is referred to, see Colston and O'Brien 2000; Giora 1995; Giora et al. 2005a,b).

---

onstration is a remarkable failure is to state something that more closely reflects the actual state of affairs and thus hardly maintains any gap between what is said and the situation described. While the former is usually interpreted ironically, the latter is taken to be literal. Indeed, when the gap is somehow narrowed down by a hedge such as *not* as in (c) *This demonstration is not a remarkable success*, readers still interpret it ironically, but to a lesser extent than when it is not hedged and the gap is more distinct (see Giora, Federman, Kehat, Fein, and Sabah 2005a; Giora, Fein, Ganzi, and Aikeslassy Levi 2005b).

Results of Experiment 1, then, do not favor a context exhibiting a frustrated expectation over a context exhibiting a realized expectation in terms of how they prefer an ironic statement over a literal one. Further, contrary to Gibbs' (2002) assumption, situations featuring a frustrated expectation are not perceived as inviting an ironic statement more often than or as often as a literal statement.

It now remains to test Gibbs' second assumption that situations that feature a frustrated expectation will facilitate irony comprehension compared to those that do not. To this end, Experiment 2 was designed.

Experiment 2

In this study we test the view proposed by Gibbs (2002) that an ironic reading of a target might be facilitated by a context that sets up an "ironic situation" through contrast between what is expected and the reality that frustrates it. To do that we measure reading times of targets embedded in different contexts – a context featuring a frustrated expectation, a context featuring a realized expectation, and a context featuring no-expectation. We aim to find out whether targets' processing times will differ as a function of the nature of the contextual expectation – frustrated vs. realized vs. no-expectation. While contexts featuring expectations bias the target statements toward the ironic interpretation, the contexts featuring no-expectation bias their reading toward the literal interpretation. If reading times of targets following contexts that feature a frustrated expectation are faster than those following contexts that feature a fulfilled expectation, this will argue in favor of the view that an "ironic situation" indeed facilitates irony interpretation. Even if reading times of targets following such contexts are faster than those following a neutral context, this will support the view that an "ironic situation" promotes ironic interpretation. However, if there is no difference between reading times of targets following contexts featuring an expectation whether frustrated or not, but, in addition, such targets take longer to read than following a neutral context, this will argue against the view proposed by Gibbs (2002) that contextual information featuring an "ironic situation" facilitates irony interpretation.

Method

Participants. Sixty students of the Academic College of Tel Aviv Yaffo (41 women, 19 men), aged 20–26, participated in this experiment for a course credit. They were all native speakers of Hebrew.

Materials. Materials included 15 triplet experimental items, 5 filler items and 2 practice items, all followed by a Yes/No comprehension question. The fillers and practice items were all literally biased. The experimental items were divided into 3 types of context, 5 of each type, each followed by the same target sentence and the same final sentence. One type was ironically biased and featured frustrated expectation (3), another was also ironically biased and featured a realized expectation (4), and another was literally biased and featured no expectation (5). The 3 types of contexts, although not identical, were rather similar. The materials were selected on the basis of 2 pretests that established which items were rated as most ironic (pretest 1) and which stood out, as indicated by the number of responses to questions, as satisfying the requirement for featuring the 3 types of expectations mentioned above (pretest 2).

Thus, the aim of the first pretest was to establish that the two types of ironically biased contexts (3–4) indeed had similarly ironic targets, but such that would be distinctly more ironic than the assumed literal target, which should be rated as lowest on the irony scale. To do that we engaged 24 participants (14 women, and 10 men), aged 21–36 years old, high-tech employees, all native speakers of Hebrew, who volunteered to participate in the pretest. They were presented 23 items as in (3–5) and were asked to read them and rate the targets (which were highlighted) on a 7 point irony scale.

The second pretest aimed to ensure that our contexts featured a frustrated expectation (3), a realized expectation (4), and no-expectation (5). Materials were the 23 items used in pretest 1. Twenty-four Tel Aviv University students (17 women, 7 men) aged 22–66, all native speakers of Hebrew, volunteered to participate in the pretest. They were asked to read the contexts and the target sentence and to answer the following Yes/No questions:

a. Did the protagonist of the text (whose name was indicated) have an expectation?
b. If so, was the expectation fulfilled?

For the experiment we selected 15 triplet items, so that the frustrated and realized expectations would be similar in their expectancy scores (replies to question (a) of the 2nd pretest). However, there was still a difference between them. The mean expectancy score for the frustrated expectation was 89% (SD=21%), for the realized expectation – 77% (SD=18), and for the no-expectation – 32% (SD=21%). Those expectancy scores all differed from each other significantly (all p's<.0001), suggesting that a frustrated expectation is easier to identify as an expectation compared to the realized expectation, and that no expectation is also relatively easy to identify as such. Regarding the fulfillment of the expectation (question (b) of the 2nd pretest), the frustrated expectations were found to be indeed unfulfilled (M=2%, SD=4%), while the realized expectations got a high fulfillment score (M=81%, SD=21%). The difference between the two was significant, t(14)=15.34, p<.0001). Lastly, based on the first pretest, while the two types of ironies did not differ in ironiness – 5.97, SD=0.35, for the frustrated expectations; 5.90, SD=.45, for the realized expectation, t<1, n.s. –, they differed significantly from the literal targets which scored only 2.27 (SD=0.78) on the ironiness scale, t(14)=15.00, p<.0001, t(14)=16.99, p<.001. We have thus ensured that even though contexts featuring a frustrated expectation were more easily recognized as featuring an expectation compared to contexts featuring a fulfilled expectation, they were both evaluated as featuring expectation compared to contexts exhibiting no expectation. We further ensured that the contexts containing an expectation were similarly biased ironically while the contexts exhibiting no expectation were different, scoring low on the ironiness scale.

(3)   Frustrated expectation

Context:
Yair and Anat moved to Paris. A friend of theirs recommended a real estate agent she knew, who indeed immediately sent them photos of amazing apartments in romantic attics in the center of Paris. They were really excited. When they arrived at the apartment they found out that the photos distorted the reality. The apartment they chose was actually a 25m² without even enough space for the luggage. Frustrated, Anat said to Yair:

Ironic target sentence:
"We are having a great start here in Paris, ha?"
Final sentence:
Yair looked quite shocked.
Comprehension question:
Are Yair and Anat happy with the apartment?

(4)   Realized expectation

Context:
Yair and Anat moved to Paris. They went to a real estate agent who sent them photos of optional apartments. This way of selecting an apartment looked quite problematic. How can one pick an apartment just from looking at photos? One should visit the apartment before deciding he is going to live there. When they got to the apartment they found out that the photos distorted the reality. The apartment they chose was actually 25m^2 without even enough space for the luggage. Frustrated, Anat said to Yair:

Ironic target sentence:
"We are having a great start here in Paris, ha?"
Final sentence:
Yair looked quite shocked.
Comprehension question:
Are Yair and Anat happy with the apartment?

(5)   No expectation

Context:
Yair and Anat moved to Paris. They heard about an available apartment from a friend and decided to first move there and then, after having moved there, to make up their mind as to whether to stay there or shop for another one. When they arrived in Paris, they found that the apartment was just amazing, located in the center and designed in a way that met their standards exactly. Anat said to Yair:

Literal target sentence:
"We are having a great start here in Paris, ha?"
Final sentence:
Yair looked quite shocked.
Comprehension question:
Are Yair and Anat happy with the apartment?

Procedure. Participants were tested individually. They were seated in front of a computer screen in a quiet and well lit room and were asked to read the context paragraph. When they have read the paragraph they had to press the space bar and were presented with the target sentence. Having read this sentence they pressed the space bar and were presented with the final sentence. A Yes/No question followed when they had pressed the space bar indicating they have read the final sentence. They had to respond to this question by pressing the Yes or No designated key. Reading times of targets were recorded by the computer.

Results and discussion

Two participants were excluded from the analyses after making more than 25% errors in responding to the Yes/No comprehension questions. To ensure a perfectly counterbalanced design, two participants were randomly excluded from each of the two other conditions. The final analyses are thus based on 54 participants (18 in each condition).

Reading times of targets, for which the participants failed to answer the Yes/No comprehension questions correctly, were excluded from the analyses (overall, 35 out of 810 RTs, about 4.3%). Since the data were skewed and contained many outliers, the raw data was logarithmically transformed, before the analyses were run. However, for simplicity, the means and SDs are reported here before the transformation. Both subject (t_1) and item (t_2) t-tests were performed. Findings show that "ironic situations" did not facilitate irony comprehension. They demonstrate that there was no difference in the mean reading time of ironic targets following either a context featuring a frustrated expectation (1927 msec, SD=421) or a context featuring a realized expectation (1906 msec, SD=453), $t_1(53)<1$, n.s., $t_2(14)<1$, n.s. However, they were both significantly longer than the reading time of literal targets following contexts featuring no expectation (1819 msec, SD=506). Thus, reading times of ironic targets following a context featuring a frustrated expectation compared to the reading times of literal targets were significantly slower, $t_1(53)=1.99$, $p<.05$, $t_2(14)=1.37$, $p=.10$. Reading times of ironic targets following a context featuring a realized expectation compared to the reading times of literal targets were significantly slower, $t_1(53)=2.09$, $p<.05$, $t_2(14)=1.23$, $p=.12$ (but less so for the item analysis probably because of the small number of items). When the same t-tests were performed on the raw data (not subjected to the logarithmic transformation), the results were the same, just less significant.

These findings then argue against the view that a context featuring an "ironic situation" – a situation that sets up a contrast between what is expected and the reality that frustrates it – should facilitate irony interpretation to the extent that it may be tapped directly and be as if not easier easy to understand as a literal alterative (Gibbs 1986, 2002). Instead, they replicate previous results showing that, regardless of context strength, interpreting irony takes longer to process than equivalent salience-based (e.g., literal) utterances (Giora 1995; Giora et al. 2007; Pexman, Ferretti, and Katz 2000; Schwoebel, Dews, Winner, and Srinivas 2000, among others).

General discussion

In this article we set out to test the hypothesis that irony interpretation should be (i) promoted as well as (ii) facilitated by a context that involves an "ironic situation" – a situation that sets up a contrast between what is expected and the reality that frustrates it (Gibbs 2002). To do that, we first examined the possibility that an "ironic situation" indeed favors an ironic description of that situation (Experiment 1). We then turned to test the assumption that an "ironic situation" would facilitate irony interpretation (Experiment 2).

In Experiment 1 we compared contexts exhibiting an "ironic situation" which involves a frustrated expectation with contexts not exhibiting such a situation but instead involving an expectation that comes true. Our findings show that literal endings were preferred over ironic ones, and that both types of contexts invited the same amount of ironic endings, suggesting that there is nothing unique about any of these contexts that might invite an ironic description of the situation described. However, a reanalysis of the results in terms of an alternative theory was attempted. According to the indirect negation view of irony (Giora 1995; Giora et al. 2005), it is the gap between what is said and the situation described by what is said that accounts for ironiness. Indeed an inspection of the results along these lines reveals that, having been presented with both alternatives, subjects opted for an ironic ending more often than for a literal ending when the gap between what is said and the situation referred to was large, regardless of type of expectation (frustrated/realized).

In Experiment 2 we showed that while the ironic interpretations always took longer to read than the literal ones, they took equally long to read regardless of whether they followed an "ironic situation" or not. An "ironic situation", then, did not facilitate ironic interpretation.

Based on these studies, it seems safe to conclude that a context that sets up an "ironic situation" through contrast between what is expected and the reality that frustrates it neither invites an ironic statement nor facilitates its interpretation. The claim, then, that rich and supportive contextual information can facilitate irony interpretation (Gibbs 1986, 2002) has not gained support here. *Au contraire.* These results support an alternative view that, regardless of how supportive a context is of an ironic interpretation, it does not allow appropriate interpretations to circumvent inappropriate but salient meanings and interpretations based on these meanings (which here coincided with literal interpretations). As a result, salience-based interpretations were faster to derive (as also shown by Giora et al. 2007).

Still, it is also possible to claim that, since it was not established here that a context featuring an "ironic situation" invites an ironic utterance (Experiment 1), the contexts used in our experiments do not, in fact, constitute strong contextual information. Would a context that induces an expectation for an ironic utterance eventually facilitate such an utterance? In Giora et al. (2007) we examined such contexts. On the assumption that expectancy may be built-up by preceding stimulus sequences (Jentzsch and Sommer 2002; Kirby 1976; Laming 1968, 1969; Soetens, Boer, and Hueting 1985), we proliferated use of ironic utterances in contexts preceding ironic and literal targets. Such contexts indeed induced an expectation for an oncoming ironic utterance. Notwithstanding, even these highly predictive contexts did not facilitate ironic utterances compared to salience-based (literal) interpretations, which were always activated initially. So far, then, most of the evidence adduced argues against the claim that a rich and supportive context facilitates ironic interpretation.

Acknowledgments

The studies reported here were supported by a grant to the first author by the Israel Science Foundation (grant No. 652/07), Adams Super Center for Brain Tel Aviv University, and by Tel Aviv University Basic Research Fund. We also thank two anonymous reviewers for very helpful comments.

Correspondence concerning this article should be addressed to Rachel Giora, Department of Linguistics, Tel Aviv University, Tel Aviv 69978, Israel. E-mail: giorarhpost.tau.ac.il

References

Colston, Herbert L. and Jennifer O'Brien
  2000   Contrast and pragmatics in figurative language: Anything understate-
          ment can do, irony can do better. *Journal of Pragmatics* 22: 1557–1583.
Gibbs, Raymond W. Jr.
  1986   On the psycholinguistics of sarcasm. *Journal of Experimental Psychol-
          ogy: General* 115: 3–15.
Gibbs, Raymond W. Jr.
  1994   *The poetics of mind.* Cambridge: Cambridge University Press.
Gibbs, Raymond W. Jr.
  2002   A new look at literal meaning in understanding what is said and impli-
          cated. *Journal of Pragmatics* 34: 457–486.
Giora, Rachel
  1995   On irony and negation. *Discourse Processes* 19: 239–264.
Giora, Rachel, Shani Federman, Arnon Kehat, Ofer Fein and Hadas Sabah
  2005a   Irony aptness. *Humor. International Journal of Humor Research* 18: 23–39.
Giora, Rachel, Ofer Fein, Jonathan Ganzi and Natalie Alkeslassy Levi
  2005b   On negation as mitigation: The case of irony. *Discourse* Processes 39:
          81–100.
Giora, Rachel, Ofer, Fein, Dafna Laadan, Joe Wolfson, Michal Zeituny, Ran Kidron, Ronie Kaufman and Ronit Shaham
  2007   Irony processing: Expectation versus salience-based inferences. *Meta-
          phor and Symbol* 22: 119–146.
Ivanko, L. Stacey and Penny M. Pexman
  2003   Context incongruity and irony processing. *Discourse Processes* 35:
          241–279.
Jentzsch, Ines and Werner Sommer
  2002   The effect of intentional expectancy on mental processing a chronop-
          sychological investigation. *Acta Psychologica* 111: 265- 282.
Kirby, Neil H.
  1976   Sequential effects in two-choice reaction time: Automatic facilitation
          or subjective expectancy? *Journal of Experimental Psychology: Human
          Perception and Performance* 2: 567–577.
Laming, D. R. J.
  1968   *Information theory of choice-reaction times.* London Academic Press.
Laming, D. R. J.
  1969   Subjective probability in choice-reaction experiments. *Journal of Math-
          ematical Psychology* 6: 81–120.
Littman, David and Jacob L. Mey
  1991   The nature of irony: Towards a computational model of irony. *Journal
          of Pragmatics* 15: 131–151.
Lucariello, Joan
  1994   Situational irony: A concept of events gone awry. *Journal of Experi-
          mental Psychology* 123: 129–145.

Pexman, Penny M., Todd Ferretti and Albert Katz
  2000   Discourse factors that influence irony detection during on-line reading. *Discourse Processes* 29: 201–222.
Schwoebel, John, Shelly Dews, Ellen Winner and Kavitha Srinivas
  2000   Obligatory Processing of the Literal Meaning of Ironic Utterances: Further Evidence. *Metaphor and Symbol* 15: 47–61.
Shelley, Cameron
  2001   The bicoherence theory of situational irony. *Cognitive Science* 25: 775–818.
Soetens, E., Boer, L. C. and Hueting, J. E.
  1985   Expectancy or automatic facilitation? Separating sequential effects in two-choice reaction time. *Journal of Experimental Psychology: Human Perception and Performance* 11: 598–616.
Utsumi, Akira
  2000   Verbal irony as implicit display of ironic environment: Distinguishing ironic utterances from nonirony. *Journal of Pragmatics* 32: 1777–1807.
Utsumi, Akira
  2004   Stylistic and contextual effects in irony processing. In: Kenneth Forbus, Dedre Gentner and Terry Regier (eds.), *Proceedings of the Twenty-Sixth Annual Conference of the Cognitive Science Society*, 1369–1374. Mahwah, NJ: Lawrence Erlbaum Associates Inc.

Appendix

Sample items
Experiment 1

(1a) Frustrated expectation

Dina was preparing to go out on a date with a guy she had met on the internet. According to the description he had put on the website, and the chats they had had, she was expecting to meet a handsome and witty man. Upon arrival at the place where the two had set to meet, she saw an ugly creature, which later on turned out to be humorless as well. When she got back home, she told her friend Miri about her date:

a.   I had a cool date (Ironic)
b.   I had a bummer date (Literal)

(1b) Realized expectation

Dina was preparing to go out on a date with a guy she had met on the internet. In order to avoid disappointment, she prepared herself for a meeting with a guy whom she would not like. Upon arrival at the place where the two had set to meet, she saw an ugly creature, which later on turned out to be humorless as well. When she got back home, she told her friend Miri about her date:

a.   I had a cool date (Ironic)
b.   I had a bummer date (Literal)

(2a) Frustrated expectation

Danit was about to join the army. She had wanted to be assigned a challenging position, and applied for an aviation course. When she arrived at the induction center, an appointing officer informed her she will be appointed a secretarial position near home in Tel Aviv. Danit said:

a.   My military service is going to be terrific. (Ironic)
b.   My military service is going to be a drag. (Literal)

(2b) Realized expectation

Danit was about to join the army. Since she knew that the army does not promote women, she assumed she'd be assigned an insignificant job. When she arrived at the induction center, an appointing officer informed her she will be appointed a secretarial position near home, in Tel Aviv. Danit said:

a.   My military service is going to be terrific. (Ironic)
b.   My military service is going to be a drag. (Literal)

Experiment 2

(1a) Frustrated expectation

Context:
Sagee went on a ski vacation abroad. He really likes vacations that include sport activities. A relaxed vacation in a quiet ski-resort place looked like the right thing for him. Before leaving, he made sure he had all the equipment and even took training classes on a ski simulator. But already at the beginning of the second day he lost balance, fell, and broke his shoulder. He spent the rest of the time in a local hospital ward feeling bored and missing home. When he got back home, his shoulder still in cast, he said to his fellow workers:

Ironic target sentence:
"Ski vacation is recommended for your health"
Final sentence:
Everyone smiled.

Comprehension question:
Do you think Sagee will go for a ski vacation again?

(1b) Realized expectation

Context:
Sagee went on a ski vacation abroad. He doesn't even like skiing. It looks danger-ous to him and staying in such a cold place doesn't feel like a vacation at all. But his girlfriend wanted to go and asked him to join her. Already at the beginning of the second day he lost balance, fell, and broke his shoulder. He spent the rest of the time in a local hospital ward feeling bored and missing home. When he got back home, his shoulder still in cast, he said to his fellow workers:

Ironic target sentence:
"Ski vacation is recommended for your health"
Final sentence:
Everyone smiled.
Comprehension question:
Do you think Sagee will go for a ski vacation again?

(1c) No-expectation

Context:
Sagee went on a ski vacation abroad. He has never practiced ski so it was his first time. He wasn't sure whether he would be able to learn to ski and whether he will handle the weather. The minute he got there he understood it was a great thing for him. He learned how to ski in no time and enjoyed it a lot. Besides, the weather was nice and the atmosphere relaxed. When he got back home, he said to his fel-low workers:

Literal target sentence:
"Ski vacation is recommended for your health"
Final sentence:
Everyone smiled.
Comprehension question:
Do you think Sagee will go for a ski vacation again?

(2a) Frustrated expectation

Context:

After several times in which Meital moved apartments with the help of friends, she decided to order movers for the job. She wanted other people to carry everything for her, take the stuff down from the current apartment and take it up to the new one, all in one ride and without a need to beg and apologize to her friends. But on the moving day the movers were 2 hours late, didn't behave nicely, and also dropped the box with all the fragile stuff, and everything was broken. When the movers asked for their payment she told them:

Ironic target sentence:
"You are really worth the money."
Final sentence:
The owner of the moving company didn't respond.
Comprehension question:
Is Meital happy with the moving company?

(2b) Realized expectation

Context:
Meital was moving to a new place. After she didn't manage to find a pickup truck, she decided to order movers. She already knew that this deal was not worthwhile: the movers are always late and are not really responsible. But she didn't have a choice. Indeed, on the moving day, the movers were 2 hours late, didn't behave nicely, and even dropped the box with all the fragile stuff, and everything was broken. When the movers asked for their payment she told them:

Ironic target sentence:
"You are really worth the money."
Final sentence:
The owner of the moving company didn't respond.
Comprehension question:
Is Meital happy with the moving company?

(2c) No-expectation

Context:
After several times in which Meital moved her apartment with the help of friends, she decided to order movers for the job. She found a company in the yellow pages and hired them. On the moving day everything worked smoothly the movers came on time, took everything very fast and treated the fragile things properly. When the movers asked for their payment, she told them:

Literal target sentence:
"You are really worth the money."
Final sentence:
The owner of the moving company didn't respond.
Comprehension question:
Is Meital happy with the moving company?

Commentary on 'Does an ironic situation favor an ironic interpretation?'

Albert Katz

Even within an ironic context, there is an inherent interpretive ambiguity in the comprehension of a statement. The irony on hearing someone utter: "You are my best friend" only exists if the comment as uttered is understood as insincere. Otherwise it would be understood as sincere, an assertion or description of some (literal) event. The ambiguity is tacitly understood by interlocutors and it is for this reason that conversational ironists provide hints as to their ironic intent, such as use of a specific tone of voice, use of explicit referential markers, use of hyper-formality, use of hyperbole, and so on. It is usually taken that none of these "hints" by themselves are necessary or sufficient to produce a sense of irony in the comprehender. Although the target statement might by itself drive an ironic interpretation, it is usually held that the main factor is the incompatibility between the nature of the statement and the ecology in which it is produced.

Giora et al. ask a fundamental question: what is there about a context or ecology that invites an ironic interpretation? They start from the premise suggested by Raymond Gibbs, Akira Utsumi and others that there is an ironic situation or ironic environment that facilitates the generation and comprehension of a statement as irony. The specific version of an "ironic situation" tested by Giora et al. is attributed to Gibbs (2002) and is based on the argument that there is a contrast between a given expectation and the "reality" of the situation in which this expectation is realized. The position of Utsumi (2000) is very similar but he adds that there has to be also "a negative emotional attitude (e.g., disappointment, anger, reproach, envy) toward the incongruity between what is expected and what actually is the case". He goes further by asserting the ironic statement must display the contrast or incongruity.

The studies by Giora et al. are an important first step in deconstructing aspects of a situation that makes it an "ironic" situation. The logic of the two studies reported are to see whether participants produce an ironic completion (study 1) or comprehend the ironic statement more rapidly (study 2) when the critical statement is presented in a context that meets the criteria for an ironic situation compared to a context that does not meet those criteria. In both studies, there were no reliable differences between the two conditions of importance. Unfortunately the logic of inferential statistics is such that a failure to find a significant difference is not obviously interpretable because the lack of difference might be due to any one of a host of reasons. As such, one must be especially cautious in accepting the authors claim that those ironic situations neither invite ironic usage nor facilitate irony comprehension.

In study 1, participants are presented short passages (textoids) that have the following characteristics: the reader is told that a character in the textoid has a given expectation, and through the unfolding of the textoid realizes that this expectation is either met or not met. In each case, participants are then given two possible comments that the character might say in that textoid, one of which is consistent with the reality (a literal commentary) whereas the other is inconsistent with the reality but consistent with the original expectation (an irony). The prediction was that if ironic situations invite an ironic use then participants would complete the textoid with the irony when an expectation was not realized. Instead what they found was that in about 70% of the time the comment chosen was the literal alternative, regardless of expectation status.

The "literal" choice might just reflect the use by the participants of Gricean principles, such as attempting to be relevant. And, as noted earlier, the failure to find differences might be due to many factors not controlled in the study. Some such sources of "noise" include: (a) failure to ensure that the so-called ironic option was in fact perceived as ironic by the participant (b) failure to ensure that the context itself was seen as one that invites an irony, (c) failure to confirm that the textoid indicated a clear negative emotional attitude, as suggested by Utsumi and (d) failure to ensure that the statement was a prototypic example of what an ironist would actually say if s/he were placed in that context in real life.

Post hoc analyses attempted to correct for some of these shortcomings. For instance, an analogue of the ironicity of the context and verbal comment was determined using "gap" ratings, finding, in general that a preference for the ironic alternative was observed when there was a high degree of incongruity between what was said and the situation described. The authors indicate this shows that "gap" (and not failed expectation) is the important factor. One could conclude however, that what these data might show is that only 1/3 or so of the experimental stimuli were in fact good displays of an ironic environment. Based on Toplak and Katz' (2000) analysis of materials used in psychological studies of irony, there is a more generalized problem found in most experimental studies of irony (including, alas, some that I have published): most materials are neither situationally real nor employ instances of verbal irony that reflect how a person would actually speak in the situations reflected in experimental textoids. These materials may show a similar problem.

Study 2 examined the comprehension side of the ironic situation hypothesis in an experiment consisting of three basic conditions: the failed/frustrated condition and the realized expectation conditions analogous to those observed in the first study and, most appropriately, a comparison, no-expectation condition. In this study a different dependent measure is employed: time to read the critical statement. Unlike study 1, the authors now employed materials that confirmed the comments were appropriately ironic and the expectations were appropriately generated by the content of the textoids. It would be interesting to use these same materials and replicate the methodology of study 1. Regardless, the results of study 2 indicated that reading time was longer for the ironic statements than for the literal usage, and that it did not matter whether or not the irony followed a failed or realized expectation. The greater reading time for the ironic conditions (compared to the literal, no-expectation condition) is comparable to other findings in the literature. The failure to find a difference between the two irony conditions is novel though, as noted earlier. a failure to find a difference is much more difficult to interpret than actually finding a difference. The much better control of the materials employed here however strengthens the possibility that there are no real processing differences in comprehending ironies based on failed expectations and those that do not.

So what is there about context that promotes irony?

Despite the methodological concerns expressed above, there is very important positive message one should take from the study by Giora et al., a message that should not be under-valued. They demonstrate that comments on failed expectations alone are not a *necessary* condition for inviting irony use or in facilitating comprehension, though failed expectation might ultimately be shown to be a sufficient condition for creating an ironic environment. The studies reported by Giora et al. do not answer what may in fact create the contrast that produces a sense of irony. I would argue that for a comprehensive examination of that question one has to consider a set of issues.

First, based on a corpus of experimental findings, it is known that with textoids similar to those used here, a sense of irony is produced rapidly, during the act of reading the ironic comment (see Katz, Blasko, and Kazmerski 2004; Pexman, Ferretti, and Katz 2000). So any psychological processes that one may wish to propose must be those that work online and be understood in terms of the type of mechanisms, both psychologically and neurologically, that work rapidly. This would implicate mechanisms that work interactively and probably in parallel. Second, it may prove more helpful in the long run not to look for a set of defining features intrinsic to the ironic context. Rather, I would propose that experimenters should examine carefully how people interact with their environment, and try to understand the attendant conceptual structures involved in that interaction. As such, context would not be limited, as was done here (and in virtually all of the literature), to verbal materials or to discourse contexts. Context involves not only information provided in the discourse but to knowledge of the world and to individual differences that people bring to their interactions with other people (see Katz 2005; Blasko and Kazmerski 2006). Widening the definition of "irony" or "ironic situation" would permit more meaningful examination of the irony as displayed in photographs, film, and other examples of artistic expression, in addition to those studied as depicted in novels (or experimental textoids). Finally, it might prove useful to conceptualize ironic situation in the following way: an ironic ecology is one that is rich in the number and strength of "hints" or "constraints" that invite irony. This definition would remove the definition as being based on a small set of necessary and sufficient conditions. Identifying "hints" that come from various sources (referential markers, pragmatic knowledge, interpersonal preferences, cultural expectations, etc.) and studying how these hints are evaluated, weighted and combined, would motive theorists to consider the type of neural and psychological mechanisms that can exploit this range of knowledge to produce a sense of irony.

References.

Blasko, Dawn G. and Victoria A. Kazmerski
    2006   ERP Correlates of Individual Differences in the Comprehension of Nonliteral Language. *Metaphor and Symbol* 21: 267–284.
Gibbs, Raymond W.
    2002   A new look at literal meaning in understanding what is said and implicated. *Journal of Pragmatics* 34: 457–486.

Katz, Albert
  2005   Discourse and social-cultural factors in understanding ronliteral lan-
          guage. In: Herbert Colston and Albert Katz (eds.), *Figurative Language
          Comprehension: Social and Cultural Influences*, 183–207. Hillsdale (N.J.):
          Erlbaum and Associates.
Katz, Albert, Dawn G. Blasko and Victoria A. Kazmerski
  2004   Saying what you don't mean: Social influences on sarcastic language
          processing. *Current Directions in Psychological Science* 13: 186–189.
Pexman, Penny, Todd Ferretti and Albert Katz
  2000   Discourse factors that influence online reading of metaphor and irony.
          Discourse Processes 29: 201–222
Toplak, Maggie and Albert Katz
  2000   On the uses of sarcastic irony. *Journal of Pragmatics* 32: 1467–1488
Utsumi, Akira
  2000   Verbal irony as implicit display of ironic environment: Distinguishing
          ironic utterances from nonirony. *Journal of Pragmatics* 32: 1777–1806.

A reply to Albert Katz's commentary

Rachel Giora, Ofer Fein, Ronie Kaufman,
Dana Eisenberg, and Shani Erez

A prevailing view within nonliteral language research assumes that a sufficiently rich and supportive context facilitates processing very early on by
allowing comprehenders to select the contextually appropriate (nonliteral)
interpretation of an utterance without having to go through its inappropriate (literal) interpretation first ("The direct access view", Gibbs 1994). To
examine this view, our study focused on irony interpretation. It was designed to test a specific type of a rich context termed "ironic situation" –
a situation featuring a **frustrated** expectation (Gibbs 2002). According to
Gibbs (2002), an "ironic situation" (i) prompts comprehenders to antici-
pate an ironic remark, and as a result, (ii) prompts them to activate this
remark's ironic interpretation directly and exclusively, while bypassing its
inappropriate (literal) interpretation. An "ironic situation" should thus facilitate irony interpretation.

We test these predictions in two experiments. In Experiment 1 we examine whether an "ironic situation" indeed favors an ironic remark. We therefore compared it to a minimal-pair context, which featured a **fulfilled** expectation. The results of this experiment do not support the view that an
"ironic situation" encourages comprehenders to opt for an ironic remark.
Au contraire. Participants clearly opted for a literal interpretation. This on
its own defies the assumption that an "ironic situation" prompts readers to
expect an ironic remark.

Indeed, in this respect, an "ironic situation" did not differ from the control context. Although we agree with Albert Katz that the logic of inferential statistics "is such that a failure to find a significant difference is not
obviously interpretable", this can only be relevant to the lack of difference
between the two types of context, but not to the differences found within
each of them.

Notwithstanding, what these null results do show is that our study failed
to come up with an alternative "ironic situation". Clearly, here we did not
aim to propose such an alternative (but see Giora et al. 2007 for contexts
raising an expectation for an ironic remark and their null effect on irony interpretation).

In Experiment 2 we test the second prediction of the direct access view, according to which, following an "ironic situation", ironic interpretation should be facilitated. The results of Experiment 2, which also controlled for the fact that such items were perceived as ironic compared to items perceived as literal, do not support this view either.

We agree with Katz that it might be insufficient for an "ironic situation" to be defined on only one feature and that for a context to raise an expectation for an ironic remark it might require a cluster of features. But proposing and testing these features was not among the aims of our paper. Our suggestion of an alternative analysis, which rests on the view that it is the "gap" between what is said and what is described (Giora 1995) that might account for the ironiness ratings, was not intended to remedy for the poverty of the features defining an "ironic situation". The notion of a "gap" is not a feature of contexts but a relation between contextual information and the way it is described or referred to. Indeed, Katz, Pexman and their colleagues made several attempts at testing contexts that might affect irony interpretation immediately (Ivanko and Pexman 2003; Ivanko, Pexman, and Olineck 2004; Katz and Pexman 1997; Pexman, Ferretti, and Katz 2000).

References

Gibbs, Raymond W. Jr.
  1994   *The Poetics of Mind*. Cambridge: Cambridge University Press.
Gibbs, Raymond W. Jr.
  2002   A new look at literal meaning in understanding what is said and implicated. *Journal of Pragmatics* 34: 457–486.
Giora, Rachel
  1995   On irony and negation. *Discourse Processes* 19: 239–264.
Giora, Rachel, Ofer Fein, Dafna Laadan, Joe Wolfson, Michal Zeituny, Ran Kidron, Ronie Kaufman and Ronit Shaham.
  2007   Irony processing: Expectation versus salience-based inferences. *Metaphor and Symbol* 22: 119–146.
Katz, Albert N. and Penny M. Pexman
  1997   Interpreting figurative statements: Speaker occupation can change metaphor into irony. *Metaphor and Symbolic Activity* 12: 19–41.
Ivanko, L. Stacey and Penny M. Pexman
  2003   Context incongruity and irony processing. *Discourse Processes* 35: 241–279.
Ivanko, L. Stacey, Penny M. Pexman and Kara M. Olineck
  2004   How sarcastic are you? Individual differences and verbal irony. *Journal of Language and Social Psychology* 23: 244–271.

Pexman, Penny M., Todd Ferretti and Albert N. Katz
    2000   Discourse factors that influence irony detection during on-line reading.
            Discourse Processes 29: 201–222.

Commentary on Giora et al. – from a philosophical viewpoint

Edmond Wright

Intriguing though the experiments of Rachel Giora and her associates have been, I, as a philosopher – and appreciator of irony wherever discerned have felt uneasy at the claimed universality of the conclusions. However secure they were for the limited circumstances of the experiments, I do not feel that they sustain the extension to actual examples more characteristic of its occurrence, whether in life or literature.

Let us begin by examining the following letter that appeared in the correspondence columns of the English newspaper *The Independent* on Friday, December 22nd, 2006, under the heading "Buying Britain' :

> Sir: I am rather worried about Bruce Paley's suggestion that we may as well sell off the country to the highest bidder (Letters, 18 December). This would mean Johnny Foreigner owning our Premiership football teams, our water companies, our power industry and God knows what else besides.
> – KEVIN MURPHY, Southampton

It is often said by newspaper editors that irony is not advisable either in letters or in the news columns because there are so many naïve readers about that the ironic message is all too likely to be taken as gospel truth. For some the very appearance of words in a newspaper becomes probable evidence of their truth, it being for them a "paper" about "news". The contextual clues to the presence of irony are, because of the very nature of the slyness of the writer's ambiguity, deliberately kept almost at the subliminal level.

Let us, for example, tease out the indications in the letter itself that all is not what it seems. The initial phrase "I am rather worried" gives the first faint clue. As an expression it is both informal and lacking in emotional insistence, belonging to a context in which someone is only mildly concerned about what is to follow, and in which he or she is expressing that minor concern verbally in some everyday situation to a present hearer in active dialogue. Since the letter is on the possibly disturbing topic of Britain's wealth being leaked abroad and it is one addressed to a wide public in a national communication medium (both strong contextual clues in themselves), there is a disguised inconsistency in this shift from an expected seriousness of rhetorical style. The informality neatly matches that of the description of what the problem is, namely, the "selling off the country to the highest bidder", which presents the disappearance of Britain's wealth abroad as the outcome of an auction, and in this case, the informality and the crude commercial allusion become a sign of the purported writer's astonishment, the equivalent of his or her gasp of disbelief. One has to say "purported writer" because the whole letter emerges as a dramatic act, one in which a strictly false – nay, fictive – identity is being adopted.

The next contextual clue lies in the use of the insulting nickname "Johnny Foreigner". This nickname, with the mocking rhythm of its glaring double assonance (in International Phonetic Alphabet: [ɔ... i, ɔ... i]) and alliteration ([n]), and its use of the name-diminutive "Johnny" (not uncommonly used by adult males in England as a would-be stand-in for a name when addressing a boy to emphasize the boy's inferior status – it was frequently used by the headmaster at my school even though he knew the boy's real name perfectly well), convey a distinct impoliteness that sharpens the insult.

The next clue is the list of possessions that our purported writer believes might pass into foreign hands if the present policy is not checked: to appreciate the irony one has to know that all the properties he mentions (Premiership football teams, water companies, the power industry) are in fact *already* in foreign hands.

The next clue, which acts as a climax to the irony, is the exclamation "God knows what else", which is used when a speaker fears the worst. It implies that our fictive speaker is far from knowing that the ownership of those properties he has mentioned has vanished abroad; furthermore, he mentioned them only to emphasize the danger that might lie ahead were they to be "sold to the highest bidder", which is the worst outcome he could fear – one, of course, that has already occurred.

The last we can mention are the clues available to anyone who had read Bruce Paley's statement in some earlier edition of the paper (I had not), or was aware from some other source that this topic was a current one.

So one may say that the contextual clues were multiple and powerful in spite of their ostensible concealment. Nevertheless, what the editors fear no doubt happened when some people read through that letter, in that they took it literally, for, as you can see, some of the clues are near-subliminal. Because of this, there is cast at least an initial doubt on the generality of Giora et al.'s conclusions, particularly that it is definitely not the case that "rich and supportive contextual information" does not "facilitate ironic interpretation", because, not only is there no discussion of the variation in degrees of appreciation of irony from person to person, but no recognition of the fact that mere number of persons responding or not responding is no reliable guide to its presence of such "rich" evidence. An irony might be justified by a single observer whose judgement he or she is ultimately able to argue for with subtle and persuasive rhetoric, an argument that might sway the judgement of all the rest of the group.

Detection of contextual clues is obviously not a simple matter. Jane Austen wrote a whole novel, *Emma*, about a character who was unable to detect even the most obvious clues, and, further, dismiss them when they were pointed out to her by more perspicuous persons, or, better, persons not blindly prejudiced as she was. She even perversely interpreted them to favour her own wishes. For example, Emma is approached by Mr. John Knightley, taken privately aside, and warned that Mr. Elton, the vicar, was paying undue attention to her and she appeared to be encouraging him. She was under the illusion that she, acting as secret matchmaker, was leading Mr. Elton towards a proposal of marriage to Harriet Smith, an attractive but propertyless girl of illegitimate origin, whereas the truth was that Elton was setting his sights on Emma and was taking advantage of the frequency of the invitations to her side. Her conviction of the rightness of her judgement shows in her reflections upon this encounter with John Knightley:

> [...] she walked on, amusing herself in the consideration of the blunders which often arise from a partial knowledge of circumstances, of the mistakes which people of high pretensions to judgement are forever falling into [...]
>
> (Jane Austen, *Emma*, Ch. XIII)

Relevant here to note that Emma, in being "amused", was enjoying an irony, in that she was crediting herself with knowledge superior to that of John Knightley, a nice illustration of the fact that contextual clues are dependent upon individual judgement. We readers, prompted with a better view of the "circumstances", can ironize her irony – just as we can with Austen's own ironies in her novels. A percipient critic can here and there undermine some of Austen's most secure judgements as reflected in those ironies, making significantly new interpretations to which no one else had attained.

In contrast, there are many people who try to read Austen and find her boring, the reason being that they lack the percipience of those critics. It is clear that they are unable to pick out the contextual clues that are present in abundance in every chapter. For the practised reader, on the other hand, it is easy to detect the clues that escape Emma, but one can fairly ask the question "What of clues that are never detected?" Sherlock Holmes may have the alert curiosity that draws his attention to a broken edge on a bridge coping-stone, but it never came to the notice of Dr. Watson even though he saw as much of the bridge as Holmes, yet that minor damage was the evidence that showed that a woman had deliberately committed suicide in an attempt to make her death look like murder in order to implicate someone else.

The philosopher Edmund Husserl relates of the case in perception when one realises that one has been sensing something for a while without attending to "it". He cites the case of the barking of a dog which one suddenly, not only becomes aware of, but also aware of the fact that the dog has been barking for some minutes prior to that moment of realisation. During that time in which it was only being sensed, one cannot fairly describe the barking as "it", since for the hearer it was not selected out as "some*thing*". One can add that, if the dog stopped barking before the person became aware of the sound, the (non-)hearer might perhaps truthfully say afterwards that they heard no*thing*. For some detached observer that barking might have constituted a contextual clue to some ironic situation, but "its" presence could not produce any irony for the (non-)hearer. Contextual clues have to be noticed, attended to; they do not exist apart from the relevant human situation, and relevance is always a matter of *motivation*. There is a danger in science and elsewhere of making Emma's mistake of, not only of objectifying too soon, but allowing the currently familiar and habitual acceptation of things to provide unquestioned premises. One is reminded of John Dewey's frequent assertion that advance in philosophy came about when philosophers ceased to concern themselves with the "customary" problems and asked new questions altogether (Dewey [1911] 1998: 109–10).

Human judgement, always motivated by fear and desire, even though hidden in their milder, indirect forms of intention, is therefore always involved in the perception of irony, as it is in all perception. We all, in the Gricean manner as Albert Katz says above, have to act on the hypothesis that our words fit the world "literally", as we say, that is, we have to act *as if* it were the case that *la langue*, the "letter" (*litera*), defines all around us and in us its ideal fixity: otherwise we should never be able to get our actually *differing* understandings in any kind of the rough overlap that is required if we are to try to correct another's concepts and percepts (Grice

1975). Here is an example from the conversation of two birdwatchers engaged in a bird count:

A: You know that bird you just counted on the tree.
B: Yes, what about it?
A: It was two-and-a-bit leaves.

A and B had to behave *as if* there were a purely single referent before them (here referred to by A as "that bird", and by B as "it") in order that the "literal" could be updated. One might say that A provides a "contextual clue" that transforms the reference for B. A's "referent" was different from B's. It is vital that we do take an objective world for granted, that is, that our referents are all the same, but that is just so that we can facilitate the updating of them. We have to be ideal objectivists in order to allow for *la parole* to shift *la langue* about the world. As the linguist Sir Alan Gardiner argued, each actual application of a word to the real involves a shift of reference and thus of meaning, however infinitesimal (Gardiner 1944: 109). One can therefore say with some confidence that all words in actual practice are operating with disguised ambiguity, where the "disguise" is one we *have to* adopt in order to achieve the partial co-ordination of our differing referents. Strictly speaking, the "literal" is an illusion, but one we cannot do without.[1]

We can here carry forward Katz's advice that, in considering the relation of irony to the contextual clues that may or may not be noticed, that one cannot confine the investigation only to verbal clues. We would then make the same mistake of those who read linguistic investigations of humour (e.g. Raskin 1985) and imagine that taking linguistic examples alone will provide a full explanation of the nature of humour.

One can go further. As we have just seen, when one person updates another about the world, as Holmes does for Watson, and A does for B, the speaker had become aware (like Husserl's person hearing the dog for the first time) of something that had not even been teased out from the continuum of experience as a separate thing. It was not already present for the participants in the situation until the speaker attended to that portion of his or her experience and (hopefully) saw its relevance to their mutual concern. The aim of the speaker in dialogue, is after all to bring to the notice of someone who is taking the world *literally*, that is, according to the currently established, familiar, and habitual taking-for-granted of the

---

1. For a full philosophical account of this theory, see Wright 2005.

world, and transform their understanding of it, – thus, we might say, "ironize" it. Contextual clues are not lying about already labelled with their relevance, so it is no surprise that the "naïve" miss them, as we saw with the letter in *The Independent*.

Katz mentions also the danger of the subjects of the experiments applying Grice's principles too slavishly. One thinks of Milgram's subjects, who, under the regime of the laboratory were led into a blind obedience to the point where they were applying what they believed to be exceedingly painful stimuli to their "victims" (Milgram [1974] 1997). Under the regime of the laboratory it is very likely that subjects will behave obediently, unquestioningly, and so in the case of the experiments we are considering, favour the "literal" over the "ironic" or the "figurative". They are only doing what we all have to do *initially* in dialogue, behave as if our own personal referent is precisely the same as that of the other, particularly where our trust in the other is immediate.

References

Dewey, John
    [1911] 1998 The problem of truth. In: Larry A. Hickman and Thomas Alexander (eds.), *The Essential Dewey* (2 vols.), 101–129. Bloomington/Indianapolis: Indiana University Press.
Gardiner, Sir Alan
    1944   De Saussure's analysis of the *"signe linguistique"*. *Acta Linguistica* 4: 696–719.
Grice, Herbert Paul
    1975   Logic and conversation. In: Donald Davidson and Gilbert Harman (eds.), *Logic and Grammar*, 64–75. Encino (Ca.): Dickenson Pub. Co.
Milgram, Stanley
    [1974] 1997 *Obedience and Authority: An Experimental View*. London: Pinter and Martin.
Raskin, Victor
    1985   *Semantic Mechanisms of Humor*. Dordrecht: D. Reidel.
Wright, Edmond
    2005   *Narrative, Perception, Language, and Faith*. Basingstoke: Palgrave Macmillan.

A reply to Edmond Wright's commentary

Rachel Giora, Ofer Fein, Ronie Kaufman,
Dana Eisenberg, and Shani Erez

Edmond Wright's main contention is that, unlike the artificial conditions with which participants are presented in laboratory experimentations, real life situations are much richer in contextual cues and therefore guarantee irony interpretation. We definitely agree, as would anyone, that irony interpretation relies on contextual information for its derivation. In fact, there is no disagreement within psycholinguistics that context plays a crucial role in utterances' interpretation. There are, however, disagreements as to *when* and *how* context affects these interpretive processes. Based on the graded salience hypothesis (Giora 1997, 1999, 2002, 2003), in this paper we take issues with a theory that spells out the kind of context that is assumed to facilitate irony interpretation *initially* (if not exclusively) before a salience-based interpretation is derived (Gibbs 1986, 2002). We show that, regardless of such contextual information, participants took longer to understand ironic items than to understand their salience-based (often literal) interpretation. Such results argue against the view that rich contextual information (as specified by Gibbs) can facilitate irony *immediately*. Instead, they support our view that salience-based interpretations are primary and cannot be by-passed even when (the specific) rich context (tested) is biased in favour of an ironic interpretation.

Note that we are not claiming that our results suggest that the items we tested are not ironic (in fact we showed that they are), nor that readers were not able to interpret them ironically (after all most of them replied in a way that shows they understood the irony). We only provided evidence consistent with the view that making sense of irony is slowed down by a salience-based albeit contextually inappropriate interpretation.

Could there be factors other than those suggested by Gibbs that enrich contextual information to the extent that it allows comprehenders to tap ironic interpretations **directly** and exclusively? Katz and his colleagues came up with a few suggestions, but when tested, these factors were not shown to facilitate irony interpretation immediately (for a review, see Giora et al. 2007).

The analysis of Wright's examples is yet another case in point. For instance, Wright's reading of his first example highlights many clues that could, in theory, safely lead readers down the ironic path. Nonetheless, the ironic interpretation of the relevant utterances, embedded in this richly predictive context, was lost on many readers who did not get the irony but instead opted for its salience-based (literal) interpretation (as was initially done by most of our participants). And needless to say that if it takes an argument "fortified with subtle and persuasive rhetoric" to sway such judgments or interpretations, as suggested by Wright, this on its own is evidence that it is difficult to arrive at an ironic interpretation.

Although we have tested only one theory, most of the evidence in the literature supports our view. And even when demonstrating that some contexts are indeed predictive of an ironic interpretation, these contexts nonetheless failed to effect *initial* facilitation for irony compared to salience-based interpretation. This was true even under conditions in which comprehenders were exclusively exposed to ironies (in their contexts) (Giora et al. 2007).

One of the environments assumed by many to encourage ironic turns is that shared by friends. However, studies, looking into how irony is responded to in conversations among friends, attest to the high accessibility of irony's contextually inappropriate but salience-based (literal) interpretation: Most of the responses to ironic turns addressed its literal interpretation (Eisterhold et al. 2006; Giora and Gur 2003; Kotthoff 2003).

Wright is right in that some people might fare better than others on irony. Indeed, in Ivanko et al. (2004), (self-reported) ironists, as opposed to nonironists, interpreted irony swiftly. Still, if it takes an expert on irony to fare well on irony, doesn't this tell us something about the complex nature of irony?

References

Eisterhold, Jodi, Attardo, Salvatore and Diana Boxer
    2006   Reactions to irony in discourse: evidence for the least disruption principle. *Journal of Pragmatics* 38: 1239–1256.
Gibbs, Raymond W. Jr.
    1986   On the psycholinguistics of sarcasm. *Journal of Experimental Psychology: General* 115: 3–15.
Gibbs, Raymond W. Jr.
    2002   A new look at literal meaning in understanding what is said and implicated. *Journal of Pragmatics* 34: 457–486.

Giora, Rachel
   1997   Understanding figurative and literal language: The graded salience hypothesis. *Cognitive Linguistics* 7: 183–206.
Giora, Rachel
   1999   On the priority of salient meanings: Studies of literal and figurative language. *Journal of Pragmatics* 31: 919–929.
Giora, Rachel
   2002   Literal vs. figurative language: Different or equal? *Journal of Pragmatics* 34: 487–506.
Giora, Rachel
   2003   *On our mind: Salience, context and figurative language.* New York: Oxford University Press.
Giora, Rachel, Ofer, Fein, Dafna Laadan, Joe Wolfson, Michal Zeituny, Ran Kidron, Ronie Kaufman and Ronit Shaham
   2007   Irony processing: Expectation versus salience-based inferences. *Metaphor and Symbol* 22: 119–146.
Giora, Rachel and Inbar Gur
   2003   Irony in conversation: salience and context effects. In: Brigitte Nerlich, Zazie Todd, Vimala Herman and David D. Clarke (eds.), *Polysemy: Flexible Patterns of Meanings in Language and Mind,* 297–316. Berlin: Mouton de Gruyter.
Ivanko, L. Stacey, Penny M. Pexman, and Kara M. Olineck
   2004   How sarcastic are you? Individual differences and verbal irony. *Journal of language and social psychology* 23: 244–271.
Kotthoff, Helga
   2003   Responding to irony in different contexts: cognition and conversation. *Journal of Pragmatics* 35: 1387–1411.

Part IV: Critique

How cognitive is cognitive poetics?
The interaction between symbolic and embodied cognition

Max Louwerse and Willie Van Peer

1. Introduction

The field of literary studies has long suffered from a methodological identity crisis. For decades strongly motivated researchers have been fighting an uphill battle to make the study of literature empirical to get the field out of this crisis. Societies like the International Society for Empirical Studies of Literature and Media (IGEL), the Poetics and Linguistics Association (PALA), and the International Association for Empirical Studies of the Arts (IAEA) have played an important role in this process. It is somewhat surprising that a methodological identity crisis had to be diagnosed and treated, since few other scientific disciplines have been questioning fundamental methodological issues. Difficult to imagine is that a discipline like Physics would doubt the value of empirical research. Equally difficult to imagine is that a discipline like Psychology would have any hesitations with empirical research. To most literary scholars, however, the empirical study of literature was (and still largely is) considered questionable at best. To a small elite group of researchers investigating literature empirically is not only self-evident but also unavoidable. How else could one get answers to questions like what writers do when they write, what readers do when they read, what the literary culture does when it reacts to new developments, and what the characteristics are of a literary text. Instead, unobservable magic was supposed to be part of the "scholarly" process.

It could be countered that the kind of objects studied in literary studies, or the kind of mental activities involved in processing them demand a degree of subjectivity on the part of the scholar that is not easily amenable to empirical methods of study. It is then argued that what readers engage in when they encounter literary texts are processes very much tied to individual and social norms and values, to identification or to the interrogation of social practices or the ideological bases upon which they rest. And indeed this kind of interminable self-reflexivity is the daily practice one can observe in most programs of literary studies. Many people would argue that under such conditions it is not easy to employ empirical methodology, because the processes going on are invisible to the eye, they are subjective in nature, and depending on value orientations. We do not deny such characteristics of these phenomena, but we do disagree that they in any way prohibit the use of empirical methods. To begin with, traditional literary scholars often confound difficulty with impossibility. True, it is not always easy to come up with strict operationalizations of such mental activities that go on during reading. But neither is it easy to measure the speed of light, or to reconstruct the history of the earth. "Not easy" is not the same as "not possible". It seems to us that most literary scholars have given up the idea of empirical research *even before* they have given it a try. In that way, they are involved in a self-fulfilling prophecy: because scholars declare the task to be nigh impossible, it is never tried, and this is subsequently used as evidence against any future effort to do so.

Fortunately, literary studies does, however, sometimes show signs that it wishes to liberate itself from its methodological identity crisis. Cognitive poetics has played an important role in this process, either as a facilitator or as the end product. Volumes like Semino and Culpeper (2002), Steen and Gavins (2003), and Stockwell (2002), as well as the current volume serve as (empirical) evidence that "cognitive" is the way to go in literary matters. As becomes clear in these volumes, cognitive poetics applies the principles of cognitive science to the interpretation of literary texts. Cognitive science, which is the scientific study of mind and intelligence, is a highly interdisciplinary enterprise, as it incorporates the fields of psychology, linguistics, anthropology, education, neuroscience, and computer science. It may be obvious to the reader of this volume what cognitive poetics entails, what cognitive science entails, and how these can go together. But as we will show, there are some basic issues in serious need of further discussion.

Gavins and Steen (2003: 2) describe cognitive poetics as follows:

[Cognitive poetics] suggests that readings may be explained with reference to general human principles of linguistic and cognitive processing, which ties the study of literature in with linguistics, psychology, and cognitive science in general. Indeed, one of the most exciting results of the rise of cognitive poetics is an increased awareness in the social sciences of the special and specific nature of literature as a form of cognition and communication. What is noted at the same time, however, is that this special position of literature is grounded in some of the most fundamental and general structures and processes of human cognition and experience, enabling us to interact in these special and artistic ways in the first place.

It could be debated (although the issue is not central to our argument) that the social sciences have become increasingly aware of the special and specific nature of literature as a form of cognition and communication, thanks to cognitive poetics. For instance, literary discourse and figurative language have repeatedly shown up in handbooks on cognitive psychology such as, for instance, Gernsbacher (1994), Graesser, Gernsbacher, and Goldman (2003), Traxler and Gernsbacher (2006), Van Dijk and Kintsch (1983), Louwerse and Van Peer (2002) and Wilson and Keil (1999). This may suggest then that cognitive poetics has not changed the social sciences, but that cognitive poetics borrows theories and principles from the cognitive sciences. That would mean that the unidirectional relation is opposite to what is stated in the description quoted above. This is an important observation, because of the second and more pertinent issue we would like to raise, that of what is *not* said in the above description. Cognitive poetics does not just apply principles found in the cognitive sciences. It has, on the contrary, a built-in bias because it carefully selects what to borrow (and what not). For instance, it tends to not borrow principles from computer science and computational linguistics, despite the appropriateness of these principles for the study of literary text and discourse. Instead, cognitive poetics relies for its concepts and methods heavily (if not almost exclusively) on cognitive linguistics. Clearly, a field cannot borrow from each and every area of an interdisciplinary conglomerate like cognitive science. But by not choosing computational linguistics and by emphasizing cognitive linguistics, it has made an essential decision with regards to cognition and language (and their interaction). It has come to assume that language comprehension is strictly embodied, as is held in cognitive linguistics. Understanding the words in a literary text has to involve activation of embodied experiences we have with these words. Against this view we argue that this embodiment bias does neither justice to the topic of investigation (literature) nor to the field from which cognitive poetics borrows (cognitive science).

To gain understanding of the embodiment bias, we need to discuss some recent developments in the cognitive sciences with regards to the nature of language comprehension, which show language comprehension as both symbolic and embodied. This is followed by computational analyses of examples from cognitive poetics that were considered embodied. More specifically, examples will be taken from chapters in Stockwell (2002) to show that symbolic approaches can also capture aspects of meaning.

2.   Symbolic and embodied aspects of language comprehension

The cognitive revolution in the 1950s, a response to behaviorism that ruled psychology since the early 20th century, started the cognitive sciences. Whereas behaviorism emphasized the study of observable behavioral processes and dismissed the study of inward mental processess, the cognitive sciences emphasized the importance of human mental processes. The invention of the computer undoubtedly played a crucial role in understanding these processes and provided researchers with a tool to model them. These days marked the start of artificial intelligence and computer science. These fields consider human thinking being not much different than computational thinking. Indeed, computational models allowed researchers to test hypotheses even without human experiments.

Probably as a reaction against these symbolic approaches to language comprehension, researchers in the 1980s started to conjecture that symbolic processes alone could not explain language comprehension, because symbols are not grounded in bodily experiences. Thought experiments related to this symbol grounding problem illustrated the limitations of symbolic processes (Harnad 1990; Searle 1980). For instance, imagine attempting to read a literary text in an unknown language. Somebody hands you a dictionary that allows you to translate the words on the page into that of another foreign language. A dictionary of that foreign language translating the words into yet another language will not help much either. The reason is that the symbols remain ungrounded. This thought experiment shows that symbols remain meaningless, like the symbols in a computer, until the symbols get grounded or embodied into the physical world. A word like "spoon" means an eating or cooking utensil with a shallow bowl attached to a relatively long handle only because we have physical experiences with spoons in our world. That is, we can pick up spoons, we can throw them, can bend them, can use them as a miniature mirror and can even use them to eat cereal or soup. This embodied approach to the meaning of "spoon" is different from a symbolic approach. In the latter approach the meaning of spoon comes about through the interrelations of the word "spoon" with other words. For instance, we know what a spoon is because the linguistic context of the word with the words "fork" and "knife", or with a word like "eating".

Two competing approaches to language comprehension can be distinguished in the 1990s: a symbolic approach emphasizing the computational nature of symbols and an embodied approach emphasizing the grounding of symbols in the physical world. The symbolic approach gained impetus with computational models like Latent Semantic Analysis (LSA; Landauer and Dumais 1997) and Hyperspace Analogue to Language (HAL; Lund and Burgess 1997). Take LSA (http://lsa.colorado.edu), for instance. Meaning is captured by mapping initially meaningless words into a continuous high dimensional semantic space, which more or less simulates cognition (Landauer 2002). More specifically, a first-order process associates stimuli (words) and the contexts they occur in (documents). Based on their contiguity or co-occurrence, stimuli are paired. These local associations are next transformed by means of Singular Value Decomposition (SVD) into a small number of dimensions (typically 300) yielding more unified knowledge representations by removing noise. Like language comprehension, memory for the initial local associations (surface structure) becomes memory for more global representations (the central meaning). LSA can thereby be seen as a theory of knowledge representation, induction and language acquisition (Landauer and Dumais 1997; Landauer 2002; Louwerse and Ventura, 2005). Let's illustrate this with the following three sentences.

(1)   The dog barked against a tree in the park.
(2)   The cat climbed into a tree in the park.
(3)   The squirrel jumped from branch to branch.

Based on first-level co-occurrences, "dog" and "cat" in the first two examples are semantically associated, because their contexts share the lexical items "tree" and "park". However, the semantic relatedness in LSA is not (only) determined by the relation between words, but also by the words that accompany a word. This means that a semantic association can be found between "cat" and "squirrel" even though they do not share any context. The fact that "branch" and "tree" may share a context in another document, however, or even the fact that the semantic neighbors of "branch" and "tree" share a semantic context (or the neighbors of the neighbors of the neighbors of the neighbors of "branch" and "tree"), allows for a semantic association. This means that words may never occur in the same document for LSA to still compute a semantic association.

The method of statistically representing knowledge has proven to be useful in a variety of studies. It has been used as an automated essay grader, comparing student essays with ideal essays (Landauer, Foltz, and Laham 1998) and performs as well as students on the TOEFL (Test of English as a Foreign Language) tests (Landauer and Dumais 1997). More recently, LSA has also been used for several other applications. First, it plays an important role in Coh-Metrix (Graesser, McNamara, Louwerse, and Cai, 2004; Louwerse, McCarthy, McNamara, and Graesser 2004), a web-based tool that analyzes texts on over 50 types of cohesion relations and over 200 measures of language, text, and readability. LSA measures the semantic relatedness between sentences, paragraphs and texts. LSA has also been used in intelligent tutoring systems like AutoTutor and iST-ART. AutoTutor engages the student in a conversation on a particular topic like conceptual physics or computer literacy. AutoTutor uses LSA for its world knowledge and determines the semantic association between a student answer, and ideal good and bad answers (Graesser et al. 2004). iSTART uses LSA in its teaching of reading strategies to students by providing appropriate feedback to students' self-explanations (McNamara, Levinstein, and Boonthu 2004).

Obviously, LSA is not synonymous to a symbolic approach to language understanding. At the same time, it can be seen as a model (both theoretical and applied) of language comprehension. Moreover, it has been considered by many as the example model of symbolic language comprehension (Glenberg and Robertson 2000; Landauer and Dumais 1997). Whereas other corpus-based models of word meaning may provide similar results as LSA (Louwerse, Lewis and Wu 2008), LSA is insensitive to sparsity problems that are present in many other corpus linguistic approaches.

But many psychologists and cognitive scientists have argued that corpus-based models of word meaning can simply not be the whole story. For instance, embodied theorists (Barsalou 1999; Glenberg and Robertson 2000) claim that word meaning can never be fully identified by associative models using only amodal symbols. Without grounding the words to bodily actions in the environment we can never get past defining a symbol with another symbol. Indeed, a wealth of information shows language comprehension is fundamentally embodied. For instance, comprehenders' motor movements match those described in the linguistic input. Klatzky, Pellegrino, McCloskey, and Doherty (1989) showed comprehension of verbally described actions (e.g. the phrase "picking up a grape") to be facilitated by preceding primes that specified the motor movement (e.g. grasp). Glenberg and Kaschak (2002) found similar evidence measuring how much the sensibility of a sentence is modified by physical actions. When subjects read sentences like "Mark gave you a pen" and used a congruent action (press a button close to the body of the subject), reaction times were lower than when an incongruent action (press button away from the body of the subject) was applied. Zwaan, Stanfield, and Yaxley

(2002) measured response times for pictures matching the content of sentences and pictures that did not. For instance, they used sentences about a nail being pounded either into the wall or into the floor. Response times for pictures matching the sentence (e.g. vertically oriented nail for sentence in which nail pounding into the floor) were faster than for mismatching pictures, leading to the conclusion that subjects simulated the scenes described in the sentence. Similarly, Zwaan, and Yaxley (2003) showed that spatial iconicity affects semantic judgments (the word "attic" presented above the word "basement" resulted in faster judgments than the reverse iconic relationship), suggesting that visual representations are activated during language comprehension.

3. Symbolic interdependency

With evidence concurrently supporting the symbolic approach and the embodied approach, how can language comprehension be explained? We have argued elsewhere that language comprehension is both embodied and symbolic (Louwerse 2007; Louwerse 2008; Louwerse and Jeuniaux 2008; Louwerse, Cai, Hu, Ventura, and Jeuniaux 2006). We proposed a Symbol Interdependency Hypothesis based on Deacon's (1997) hierarchy of signs, which is in turn based on Peirce's (1923) theories. Peirce identifies three types of signs: icons, indices and symbols. In icons a direct relation between the sign and what the sign represents can be observed. For instance, a picture of one of the editors of this book represents the editor of this book. There are physical similarities between picture and person. In indices that relation is not as direct. Instead, indexical relations are situated in space and time. An example is the fingerprint of one of the editors. The fingerprint itself does not represent the editor, but represents the presence of that editor at some point in time at some particular place. When time goes by, the interpretative link between presence of editor and his footprint tends to weaken. Finally, there are symbols. In symbols the relationship between the sign and what the sign represents is determined by convention. The wedding ring of the editor represents that he is married. But different cultures could have a different symbol for marriage, as long as the cultural community agrees on the symbol. Language is also an example of symbols. Deacon (1997), based on Peirce (1923), argues that icons, indices, and symbols have a hierarchical relationship with each other, whereby indices are built from combinations of icons, and symbols are built from combinations of indices. Moreover, relations between these signs can operate at one level (symbols being related to other symbols) and at different levels (symbols being related to indices and icons). Deacon claims that this hierarchy of different levels of signs can help us explain why humans have language, but other species do not. Humans are symbolic species – they can make links between symbols and between symbols and indices and icons – whereas other species cannot build the bridge between indices and symbols (although higher species like chimps can get very close).

According to the symbol interdependency hypothesis, language comprehension can be symbolic through interdependencies of symbols, but it can also be embodied through the dependencies of symbols on indices and icons. It thereby makes two important predictions. First, language comprehension is typically symbolic, although there are conditions under which embodied representations are activated, as is the case in deep processing or when comprehenders are cued to activate other modalities. This does not mean language comprehension is solely symbolic, because comprehenders can always activate embodied representations (indices and icons). It merely means comprehenders can often rely on the symbols in language to bootstrap meaning. Second, because language has evolved to become a communicative short-cut, language structures now represent relations in the physical world: language has encoded embodied relations. As examples of these encoded structures, Louwerse (2007) lists examples like subjects always preceding objects (Greenberg 1963), and categories being determined by the way we perceive the structure of the world (Rosch 1978).

What does this exposé on language comprehension mean for cognitive poetics? Considering the reliance of cognitive poetics on theories in cognitive science and thereby on theories of language comprehension, one would expect the evidence found in favor of the symbol interdependency hypothesis to be extended to cognitive poetics. That is, the examples which cognitive poetics uses to show that the understanding of literary language is embodied, can also be applied in a computational approach and be given alternative explanations. In the remainder of this chapter we will follow Stockwell's (2002) *Cognitive Poetics. An Introduction* and take examples from the first chapters of this book, "Figures and grounds", "Prototypes and reading", "Cognitive deixis" and "Conceptual metaphors". We will apply a symbolic approach to complement his embodied analyses.

4.   Figure and ground

Figure and ground are central concepts in cognitive poetics (Stockwell 2002) taken from early 20th century Gestalt Psychology. Similar elements are grouped together (figure) and contrasted with dissimilar elements (ground) in order to perceive an image coherently. For instance, supporters distinguish soccer teams on the basis of the colors of their shirt, grouping the same color shirts and contrasting them with different-color shirts. In literary studies figure and ground are used in the notion of foregrounding, the process by which something is given prominence by the reader of a text (Van Peer 1986). Foregrounding allows the author to defamiliarize the reader by foregrounding certain aspects of the text. Foregrounded stylistic traits in the text give prominence to the figure, differentiating it from the ground (e.g. the prominence of the main character Hamlet in the title of the play). Stockwell argues that readers activate image schemas, i.e. mental pictures that readers use as basic templates to understand common situations. These image schemas are supposed to be embodied and consist of a trajector (figure) that has a grounded relationship with a landmark (ground) through a path. Note that this may be seen as an improvement over traditional methods of text analysis, as it allows a clearer formulation of hypotheses. As an example, Stockwell uses the following lines from Shakespeare's *Midsummer Night's Dream*:

Over hill, over dale,
through bush, through briar,
Over park, over pale,
through flood, through fire,
I do wander everywhere.

Stockwell argues that readers interpret these lines by outlining the "I" in this fragment as the trajector/figure who takes a path flying above the landmark/ground (hill, dale, park, pale). Two questions arise, however. First, what is the evidence that readers activate these image schemas in examples like the one above? Secondly, the claim is that these image schemas are embodied. What is the cognitive evidence for this claim? Moreover, does the claim entail that non-embodied approaches will not be able to grasp the gist of the passage? Does the linking of the last line (trajector/figure) to the remainder of the passage (landmark/ground) help to form the backdrop of this summary? Does this really require an embodied representation?

Table 1. LSA cosine matrix of Shakespeare lines

	1.	2.	3.	4.	5.
1. over hill, over dale	1	0.2	0.87	0.12	0.19
2. through bush, through briar	0.2	1	0.24	0.66	0.2
3. over park, over pale	0.87	0.24	1	0.16	0.2
4. through flood, through fire	0.12	0.66	0.16	1	0.13
5. I do wander everywhere	0.19	0.2	0.2	0.13	1

To answer these questions, we entered the five lines of the Shakespeare text in an LSA matrix comparison using the literature-with-idioms LSA space (528 factors). This space consists of English and American Literature from the 18th and 19th century from the Project Gutenberg page. The space is composed of 104,852 word types, 57,092,140 word tokens and 942,425 paragraphs, with 338 dimensions. Cosine values were computed between each of the five lines, resulting in a 5x5 matrix, presented in table 1.

Following the method used in Louwerse et al. (2006) and Louwerse (2007) the LSA matrix of cosine values was next supplied to an ALSCAL algorithm to derive a Multidimensional Scaling (MDS) representation of the stimuli (Kruskal and Wish 1978). That is, the matrix of LSA cosine values was transformed into a matrix of Euclidean distances and these distances were scaled multidimensionally by comparing them with arbitrary coordinates in an n-dimensional space (low cosine values correlate with large distances, high values with short distances). The coordinates were iteratively adjusted such that Kruskal's stress is minimized and the degree of correspondence maximized. The fitting of the data was good (Kruskal's stress =.067, R^2 = .993) with a two-dimensional scaling. The graphical representation of the two-dimensional output is presented in figure 1. What becomes apparent in this figure is how the line considered to be the trajector/figure ("I do wander everywhere") is differentiated from the other lines, considered to be the landmark/ground.

Thus, the results Stockwell obtained from his analysis using an embodied approach is much the same as those obtained from an analysis using a symbolic approach. The fact that 18th and 19th century texts were used for the LSA space will not affect the results. First, the strength of LSA lies in the higher-order dependencies, whereby results are not dependent on individual words but on higher-order relations between the co-occur-

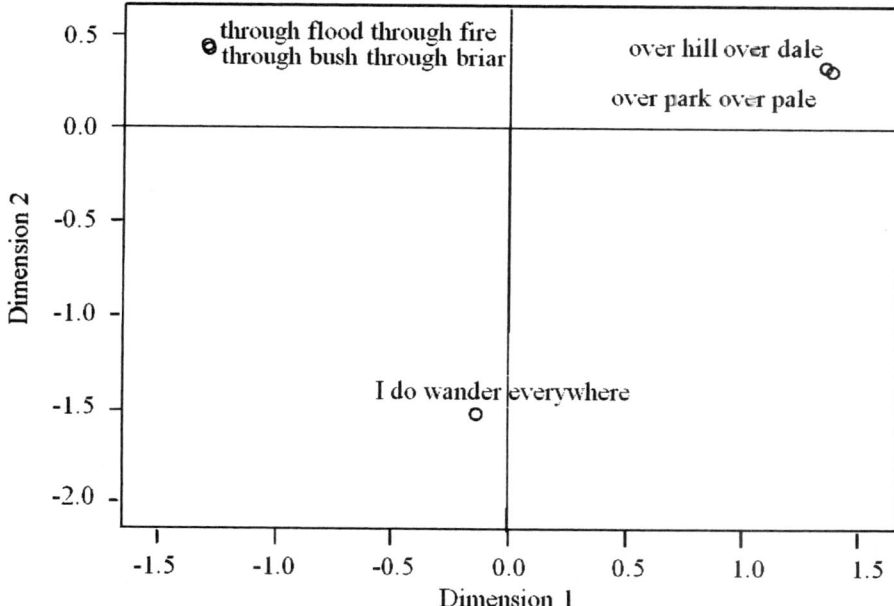

Figure 1. MDS representation of LSA cosine matrix of Shakespeare lines

rences (of the co-occurrences, etc.) of words. Secondly, the comparison presented here is between Shakespeare texts only. Even with a less than ideal LSA space, the comparison between a non-manipulated Shakespeare text and a manipulated Shakespeare text stays.

Admittedly, the text sample is short, and may have been more convincing (still) if we had used a longer extract from the play. However, let's continue this foregrounding example by butchering the Shakespearean lines into something that looks less aesthetically appealing like the following lines.

I wander over hill and dale
and through bush and briar
I wander over park and pale
and through flood and fire
I wander over grass and trees

The last line does not seem to represent the trajector/figure anymore. When the same method is used and the LSA cosine matrix (Table 2) is applied to an MDS ALSCAL algorithm, a representation emerges that is

Table 2. LSA cosine matrix of butchered Shakespeare lines

	1.	2.	3.	4.	5.
1. I wander over hill and dale	1	0.11	0.87	0.05	0.7
2. and through bush and briar	0.11	1	0.14	0.65	0.16
3. I wander over park and pale	0.87	0.14	1	0.09	0.75
4. and through flood and fire	0.05	0.65	0.09	1	0.06
5. I wander over grass and trees	0.7	0.16	0.75	0.06	1

presented in figure 2. The prominence of the trajector/figure that is missing from the butchered passage does not show up in the MDS analysis.

We do not argue that foregrounding can be explained simply by dumping lines of text in a computer. We do claim, however, that it is wise not to put all one's eggs in the embodiment basket, and instead also consider alternative approaches, particularly if these approaches are complementary.

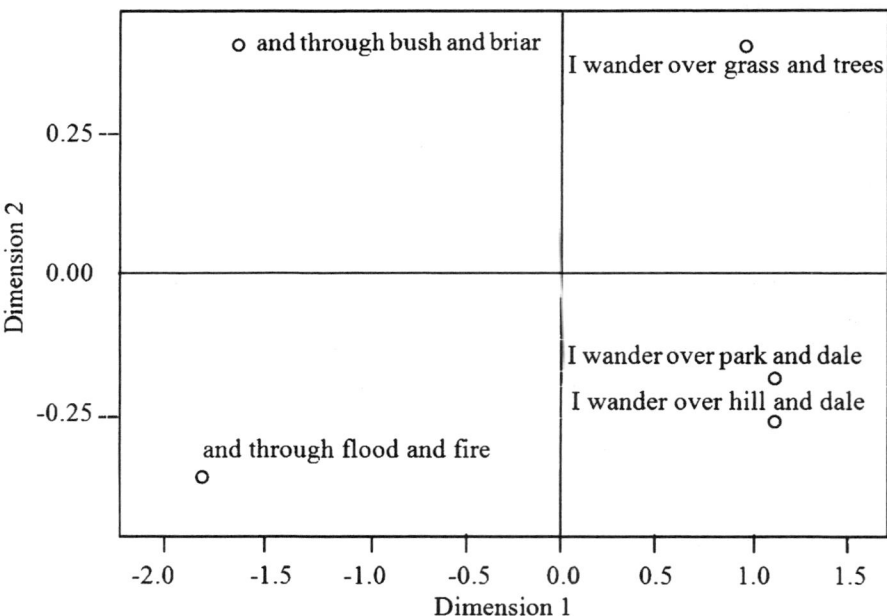

Figure 2. MDS representation of LSA cosine matrix of butchered Shakespeare lines

5.   Categorization and prototypes

In the following chapter Stockwell (2002) shows how categorization and prototypes, key concepts in cognitive science, are important in literary language. How do we know that an "eagle" is a good member of the family "bird", but "ostrich" and "penguin" are not? Stockwell argues that we know this because of our interaction with the environment, our embodied experiences. The question is whether a symbolic approach would yield similar results.

Louwerse et al. (2006) conducted a number of studies whereby they used LSA to categorize concepts. They found that LSA was able to represent words used by Collins and Quillian (1969) into a hierarchical framework, clustering words like "wings", "feathers" and "fly" with the word "bird", but "fin", "gills" and "swim" with the word "fish". The clustering analysis also showed how "animals" "eat", have "skin", "move", "bite", are "dangerous" and "edible". Similarly, Louwerse et al. (2006) conducted a number of studies investigating category membership using Rosch's (1973) data. In Rosch's study participants rated the typicality of members of a category on a scale, showing that participants were consistent in their ratings (e.g. "robin" is a more typical member of the category "bird" than "chicken" is). Furthermore, participants were faster in judging whether a picture belonged to a certain category when the picture showed a typical member than when it was a non-typical member (Rosch 1975). Eight categories (fruit, science, sport, bird, vehicle, crime, disease and vegetable) with six members in each category were taken from Rosch (1973) (see also Akmajian, Demers, Farmer, and Harnish 2001). LSA results showed a significant correlation between experimentally obtained rank of category and LSA cosine value. This correlation per category showed that five out of the eight categories (bird, crime, fruit, sport, vegetable) had significant correlations. The remaining three categories (disease, science, vegetable) did have the expected pattern, though these did not search the significance level, most likely due to the small number of cases (6 per category).

The categorization found in results from human experiments can also be found in the results from computational analyses, showing that categorization is not solely based on embodied factors, as Stockwell argues. In addition to referring to Rosch's studies on categorization, Stockwell argues that categorization also applies to literature, for instance in the way we categorize genres. We can take this a step further and determine how literary authors can be classified. Take for example "Dante", "Dickens",

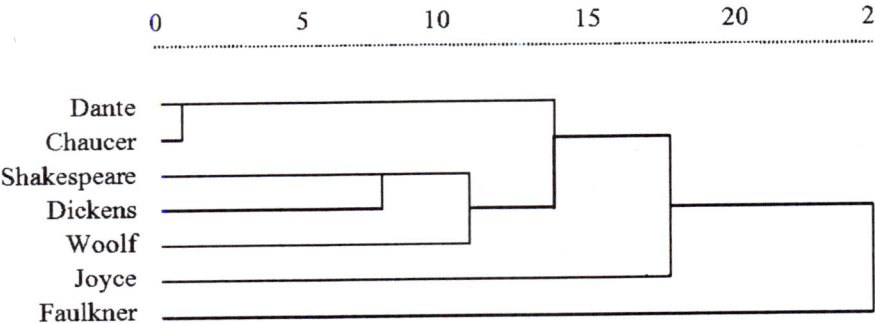

Figure 3. Hierarchical cluster analysis of LSA cosine matrix of literary authors

"Faulkner", "Joyce", "Shakespeare", and "Woolf". These words were entered in an LSA analysis using the Touchstone Applied Science Associates (TASA) semantic space. The TASA corpus consists of approximately 10 million words of unmarked high-school level English texts on Language Arts, Health, Home Economics, Industrial Arts, Science, Social Studies, and Business. This corpus is divided into 37,600 paragraphs, (averaging 166 words per paragraph) and is considered one of the benchmark corpora in computational linguistics, because it approximates the language familiarity of a college level student (Kintsch 1998; Landauer and Dumais 1997). We did not use the literature space from the previous study, because we are not interested here in literature per se, but in texts about literature. The LSA cosine matrix was next supplied to a hierarchical cluster analysis, resulting in the clustering presented in figure 3.

A simple semantic analysis of these words results in a cluster suggesting a close relation between Dante and Chaucer, as well as Shakespeare and Dickens. Woolf is closest to these latter two, and Joyce and Faulkner, particularly the latter, is furthest away from the other groupings. The higher-order relationships alone between these words can inform us how they can be clustered.

Again, the argument we are trying to make is not that any classification of literary authors can simply be done by computers. Leaving the question aside how literary authors could be grouped through an embodied approach, the argument we do want to make is that alternative approaches other than embodiment should be considered.

6.   Cognitive deixis

In the next chapter, Stockwell discusses cognitive deixis, the language feature anchoring meaning to a context. Examples of deictic terms are personal pronouns like "I", "you" and "we", and adverbials like "here" and "there" for which the meaning crucially depends on the point of view of the speaker; and on the concrete spatial and temporal context and situation in which these words are used. For instance, "I" has a different referent for me than for you (let alone the referents of the other personal pronouns expressed in this sentence). Stockwell argues deixis as being central to embodiment. To some extent it is true that deixis is problematic for a symbolic approach, because it is difficult to capture the meaning of deictic items that are by definition pointing to referents in the physical world. The question, of course, is whether this is a weakness of the symbolic approach per se or if this is due to the limited information LSA is given access to. To determine whether LSA is able to capture meaning in deictic items, the best we can do is compute whether it is able to group these deictic items on the basis of their textual information alone. We use personal pronouns ("I", "you", "we"), possessive pronouns ("mine", "yours", "ours") and possessive adjectives ("my", "your", "our") to test this. Our prediction is that LSA is able to cluster singular items separately from plural items (e.g. "I" vs. "we"), thereby clustering person (e.g. "I", "my", "mine" vs. "we", "our",).

Two things are worth mentioning. First, based on the way LSA works, we have no reason to believe it will be able to cluster these items, since the higher-order relationships for words co-occurring for one (e.g. "I") are likely to be identical to the contexts of the other (e.g. "you"). Secondly, and more importantly, if a symbolic approach is unable to cluster deictic items, embodiment processes must always be active in language processing or at least in processing deixis. On the other hand, if a symbolic approach is able to cluster these items based on their textual occurrence, the argument made by the Symbol Interdependency Hypothesis can be extended: some of the meanings can be derived from the text, but ultimately we can ground language to referents in the physical world. As before, an LSA matrix was computed, this time using the 18 personal pronouns, possessive pronouns and possessive adjectives, and applied to an MDS ALSCAL algorithm. Results are presented in figure 4.

It is obvious from this Figure that singular items are clustered separately from plural items. The pronoun "it" and the possessive adjectives form an exception, possibly because of the ambiguous status of the word

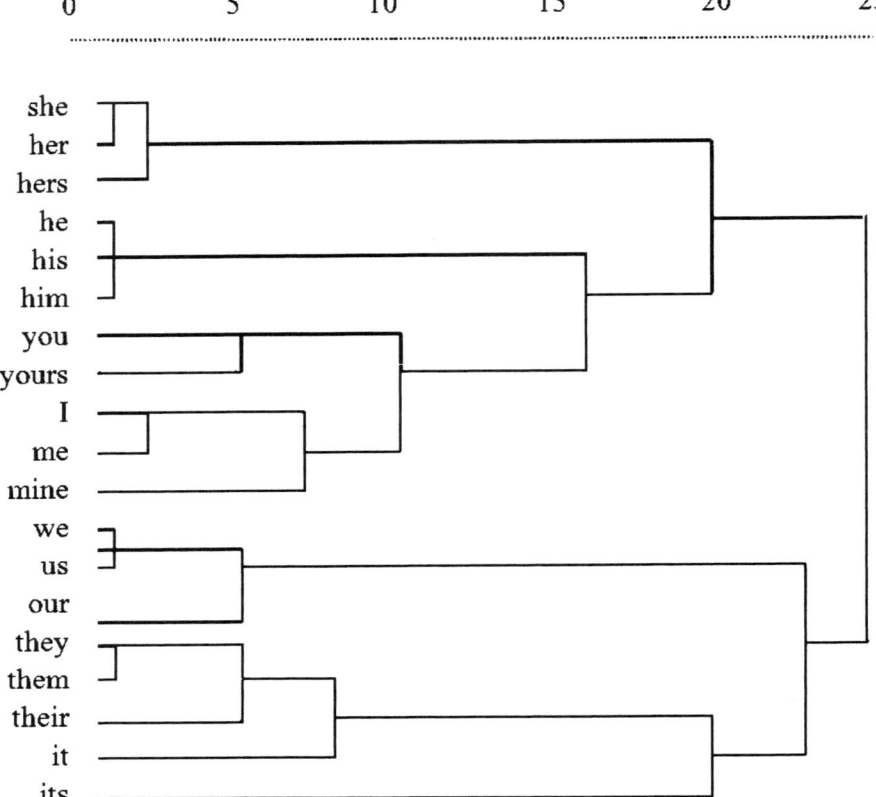

Figure 4. Hierarchical cluster analysis of LSA cosine matrix of personal and possessive pronouns and possessive adjectives.

"it" in its referring, anticipatory, cleft, and prop uses. For the singular
cases, third-person items are clustered and first- and second-person items
are clustered.

The analysis here does not demonstrate that deictic words are not embodied. It merely aims to show how deictic items cluster in intuitively accurate ways. Cognitive deixis can therefore be explained from an embodiment but also from a symbolic point of view.

7. Conceptual metaphor

This paper cannot be ended without addressing conceptual metaphors, since they form a central topic of interest in cognitive linguistics (Lakoff, 1987; Lakoff & Johnson 1980, 1999). Conceptual metaphors are formed by the blending of two conceptual domains, a source domain and a target domain. The source domain is the conceptual domain from which metaphorical expressions are drawn, whereas the target domain is the domain we try to understand. Take, for instance, the metaphor "my lawyer is a shark." My lawyer is the "vehicle" or "target", the new element to be described and "shark" is the "tenor" or "source" of the familiar element. Central to the cognitive linguistic approach to conceptual metaphors is that metaphors are not a matter of language but a matter of thought (Lakoff & Johnson 1980, 1999). Moreover, researchers in cognitive linguistics, as well as those in cognitive poetics, argue that conceptual metaphors are embodied. According to them, understanding conceptual metaphors requires linking target and source, the latter more than the former, to embodied experiences. For instance, up-and-down serves as a source domain for a variety of targets, as in "his spirits rose / his spirits sank". If conceptual metaphors are strictly embodied, there is little hope for a symbolic approach explaining metaphors.

Kintsch (2000), however, proposed a predication model that extends LSA and can approximate the meaning of metaphors by constraining the meaning of words that are compared. Consider, for instance, the sentence "that man is a shark". Using Kintsch's proposal, semantic associates are computed such as "fish", "jaws", "dangerous" and "fin". These words are then compared to "man" whereby only those words associated with "man" are kept (in the above example the semantic associate "dangerous"). The elegance of the predication model is that it can distinguish between "that man is a shark" and "that shark is a man".

For illustrative purposes here, we ignore this order effect and take the first three metaphors presented in Stockwell's (2002) conceptual metaphor chapter and compute those words that form the nearest semantic neighbors of these metaphors. That is, we are asking LSA to pick up the word that is semantically closest to the target word. Since we are looking for adjectives (e.g. that man is a shark – that man is dangerous), we are selecting the first adjective that is returned by LSA. Results of the metaphor and their nearest neighbor are presented in table 3. However, the argument can of course be made that these adjectives are simply the closest words to either one of the two words (target or source). To rule out this

Table 3. Metaphors/target/source and their nearest semantic neighbors with the cosine value

Metaphor, target and source	Nearest adjective neighbor	Cosine value
the man is a shark	dangerous	.56
man	honest	.41
shark	amphibious	.41
that man is a wolf	dangerous	.58
man	honest	.41
wolf	brute	.46
Juliet is the sun	glorious	.54
Juliet	artistic	.48
sun	golden	.51

explanation, Table 3 also lists the nearest neighbor for target and source separately, showing that the semantic nearest neighbor for the metaphor (target *and* source) is different than that for either target or source.

These simple examples show the use of LSA as a tool to approximate the meaning of conceptual metaphors, and that it is not only an embodiment approach that can do this. Even more recent developments (e.g. Fauconnier and Turner 2002) do not annul the results obtained through our LSA showing that a symbolic approach can account for the data just as well. We do not argue that LSA can explain all metaphors. Nor do we propose that one just needs to enter metaphors in it and out comes the meaning. Instead, we claim that symbolic and embodied approaches are complementary. Apparently, cognitive poetics has not made a careful analysis of symbolic approaches, but simply latched on to the (embodied) assumptions of cognitive linguistics, ignoring complementary approaches.

8.   Conclusion

We started this chapter by welcoming the empirical approach in cognitive poetics, but observing a certain fundamental bias based on theories of language comprehension in support of strict embodiment. We countered this bias by showing how language comprehension is both symbolic and embodied: embodied representations do not always have to be activated, and language has encoded many embodied relations. To show how a symbolic approach can be applied in a field like cognitive poetics, we took examples from Stockwell (2002) and analyzed them, using LSA. It needs to be emphasized here that we chose Stockwell's text with respect, as it is considered a milestone in the field, as one of us has stated in writing. We selected four chapters (figure and ground, prototypes, cognitive deixis, conceptual metaphor) and illustrated how LSA analyses can shed light on the processes of meaning construction just as well as embodiment theory does. We thereby believe we have shown that a symbolic approach is at least worth considering in interpreting language and literature. Adding a symbolic approach augments the theoretical and methodological validity of cognitive poetics.

Acknowledgments

This research was supported by grant NSF-IIS-0416128 Any opinions, findings, and conclusions or recommendations expressed in this material are those of the authors and do not necessarily reflect the views of the funding institution. Correspondence concerning this article should be addressed to Max M. Louwerse, Institute for Intelligent Systems / Department of Psychology, University of Memphis, 202 Psychology Building, Memphis, Tennessee 38152–3230.

References

Akmajian, Adrian, Richard A. Demers, Ann K. Farmer and Robert M. Harnish
    1990   *Linguistics. An Introduction to Language and Communication.* Cambridge, MA: MIT Press.
Barsalou, Lawrence W.
    1999   Perceptual symbol systems. *Behavior and Brain Sciences* 22: 577–660.
Collins, Allan and Ross M. Quillian, M.
    1969   Retrieval time from semantic memory. *Journal of Verbal Learning and Verbal Behavior* 8: 240–248.
Deacon, Terrence
    1997   *The Symbolic Species: The Co-evolution of Language and the Human Brain.* London: Allen Lane.
Gavins, Joanna and Gerard Steen (eds.)
    2003   *Cognitive Poetics in Practice.* London: Routledge.
Fauconnier, Gilles and Mark Turner
    2002   *The Way we Think: Conceptual Blending and the Mind's Hidden Complexities.* New York: Basic Books.

Gernsbacher, Morton Ann
    1994   *Handbook of Psycholinguistics.* San Diego, CA: Academic Press.
Glenberg, Arthur M.
    1997   What memory is for. *Behavioral and Brain Sciences* 20: 1–55
Glenberg, Arthur M. and Michael Kaschak
    2002   Grounding language in action. *Psychonomic Bulletin & Review* 9: 558–565.
Glenberg, Arthur M. and David A. Robertson
    2000   Symbol grounding and meaning: A comparison of high-dimensional and embodied theories of meaning. *Journal of Memory and Language* 43: 379–401.
Graesser, Arthur C., Morton Ann Gernsbacher and Susan J. Goldman (eds.)
    2002   *Handbook of Discourse Processes.* Mahwah, NJ: Erlbaum.
Graesser, Arthur C., Shulan Lu, George T. Jackson, Heather Hite Mitchell, Mathew Ventura, Andrew Olney and Max M. Louwerse
    2004   AutoTutor: A tutor with dialogue in natural language. *Behavioral Research Methods, Instruments, and Computers* 36: 180–193.
Graesser, Arthur C., Danielle S. McNamara, Max M. Louwerse and Zhiqiang Cai
    2004   Coh-Metrix: Analysis of text on cohesion and language. *Behavior Research Methods, Instruments, and Computers* 36: 193–202.
Greenberg, Joseph H.
    1963   Some universals of grammar with particular reference to the order of meaningful elements. In: Joseph H. Greenberg (ed.), *Universals of Language*, 73–113. Cambridge, MA: MIT Press.
Harnad, Stevan
    1990   The symbol grounding problem. *Physica* D 42: 335–346.
Kintsch, Walter
    1998   *Comprehension: A Paradigm for Cognition.* New York: Cambridge University Press.
Kintsch, Walter
    2000   Metaphor comprehension: A computational theory. *Psychonomic Bulletin and Review* 7: 257–266.
Klatzky, Roberta L., James Pellegrino, Brian P. McCloskey and Sally Doherty
    1989   Can you squeeze a tomato? The role of motor representations in semantic sensibility judgments. *Journal of Memory and Language* 28: 56–77.
Kruskal, Joseph B. and Myron Wish
    1978   *Multidimensional Scaling.* Beverly Hills, CA: Sage University Series.
Lakoff, George
    1987   *Women, Fire, and Dangerous Things: What Categories Reveal about the Mind.* Chicago: University of Chicago Press.
Lakoff, George and Mark Johnson
    1980   *Metaphors We Live By.* Chicago: University of Chicago Press.
Lakoff, George and Mark Johnson
    1999   *Philosophy in the Flesh: The Embodied Mind and its Challenge to Western Thought.* New York: Basic Books.

Landauer, Thomas K.
  2002   On the computational basis of learning and cognition Arguments
          from LSA. In: Brian H. Ross (ed.), *The Psychology of Learning and
          Motivation* 41: 43–84. Amsterdam: Elsevier.
Landauer, Thomas K. and Susan T. Dumais
  1997   A solution to Plato's problem: The latent semantic analysis theory of
          acquisition, induction, and representation of knowledge. *Psychological
          Review* 104: 211–240.
Landauer, Thomas K., Peter W. Foltz and Darrell Laham
  1998   An introduction to latent semantic analysis. *Discourse Processes* 25:
          259–284.
Louwerse, Max M.
  2007   Iconicity in amodal symbolic representations. In: Thomas Landauer,
          Danielle McNamara, Simon Dennis and Walter Kintsch (eds.), *Hand-
          book of Latent Semantic Analysis*, 107–120. Mahwah, NJ: Erlbaum.
Louwerse, Max M.
  2008   Embodied representations are encoded in language. *Psychonomic Bull-
          etin and Review* 15: 838–844.
Louwerse, Max M., Zhiqiang Cai, Z., Xiangen Hu, Mathew Ventura and Patrick
  Jeuniaux
  2006   Cognitively inspired natural-language based knowledge represen-
          tations: Further explorations of Latent Semantic Analysis. *Inter-
          national Journal of Artificial Intelligence Tools* 15: 1021–1039.
Louwerse, Max M. and Patrick Jeuniaux
  2008   Language comprehension is both embodied *and* symbolic. In: Manuel
          de Vega, Arthur Glenberg, and Arthur C. Graesser (eds.), *Symbols and
          Embodiment. Debates on Meaning an Cognition,* 309–326. Oxford: Ox-
          ford University Press.
Louwerse, Max M., Gwyneth Lewis, and Jie Wu
  2008   Unigrams, bigrams and LSA. Corpus linguistic explorations of genres
          in Shakespeare's plays. In: Willie Van Peer and Jan Auracher (eds.),
          New Beginnings in Literary Studies, 108–129. Newcastle: Cambridge
          Scholars Publishing.
Louwerse, Max M. and Willie Van Peer (eds.)
  2002   *Thematics: Interdisciplinary Studies.* Amsterdam/Philadelphia: John
          Benjamins.
Louwerse, Max M. and Mathew Ventura
  2005   How children learn the meaning of words and how LSA does it (too).
          Journal of Learning Sciences 14: 301–209.
Louwerse, Max M., Philip M. McCarthy, Danielle S. McNamara and Arthur C.
Graesser
  2004   Variation in language and cohesion across written and spoken reg-
          isters. In: Kenneth Forbus, Dedre Gentner & Terry Regier (eds.), *Pro-
          ceedings of theTwenty-Sixth Annual Conference of the Cognitive Science
          Society,* 843–848. Mahwah, NJ: Erlbaum.

Lund, Kevin and Curt Burgess
  1996   Producing high-dimensional semantic spaces from lexical co-occur-
          rence. *Behavior Research Methods, Instrumentation, and Computers* 28:
          203–208.
McNamara, Danielle S., Irwin B. Levinstein and Chutima Boonthum
  2004   iSTART: Interactive strategy trainer for active reading and thinking.
          Behavioral Research Methods, Instruments, and Computers 36: 222–233.
Peirce, Charles S.
  1923   *The Collected Papers of Charles Sanders Peirce* (C. Hartshorne, P. Weiss,
          & A. Burks, eds.). Cambridge: Harvard University Press.
Rosch, Eleanor
  1973   Cognitive representation of semantic categories. *Journal of Experimen-
          tal Psychology: General* 104: 192–233.
Rosch, Eleanor
  1978   Principles of categorization. In: Eleanor Rosch and Barbara B. Lloyd
          (eds.), *Cognition and categorization*, 27–48. Hillsdale New York: Law-
          rence Erlbaum.
Searle, John R.
  1980   Minds, brains, and programs. *Behavioral and Brain Sciences* 3: 417–57.
Semino, Elana and Jonathan Culpeper (eds.)
  2002   *Cognitive Stylistics: Language and Cognition in Text Analysis.* Amster-
          dam/Philadelphia: John Benjamins.
Stockwell, Peter
  2002   *Cognitive Poetics: An Introduction.* London: Routledge.
Traxler, Matthew J. and Morton Ann Gernsbacher (eds.).
  2006   *Handbook of Psycholinguistics.* San Diego, CA: Elsevier.
Van Dijk, Teun A. and Walter Kintsch
  1983   *Strategies of Discourse Comprehension.* New York: Academic Press.
Van Peer, Willie
  1986   *Stylistics and Psychology; Investigations of Foregrounding.* London:
          Croom Helm.
Wilson, Robert A. and Keil, Frank C. (eds.)
  1999   *The MIT Encyclopedia of Cognitive Sciences.* Cambridge, MA: MIT
          Press.
Zwaan, Rolf A. and Richard H. Yaxley, R.H.
  2003   Spatial iconicity affects semantic-relatedness judgments. *Psychonomic
          Bulletin & Review* 10: 954–958.
Zwaan, Rolf A., Robert A. Stanfield, and Richard H. Yaxley
  2002   Language comprehenders mentally represent the shapes of objects.
          Psychological Science 13: 168–171.

Incorporated but not embodied?

Dirk Geeraerts

The paper by Louwerse and Van Peer made me realize something quite remarkable: it is possible to value the actual research people do, but to disagree to no small extent with the way in which they situate their own research within a wider context. On the one hand, I endorse the corpus-based analysis of literary texts that Louwerse and Van Peer illustrate with a number of case studies, and I cannot agree more with their suggestion that such a methodology should be applied more extensively. I have argued as much on a number of occasions: see Tummers, Heylen, and Geeraerts (2005), Geeraerts (2006), so I could hardly disagree here. On the other hand, I find their overall argumentation against an 'embodied" form of cognitive poetics to be rather misleading. By pitching a "symbolical", corpus-based form of analysis that is allegedly not based on embodiment against "embodied" cognitive poetics, they basically seem to be fighting a straw man. Let me try to explain why.

Louwerse and Van Peer's framing of their own research activities consists of a combination of a methodological and a theoretical approach. Methodologically, they advocate a corpus-based methodology that uses Latent Semantic Analysis (LSA) to analyze the co-occurrence behavior of words (or larger chunks of language use) in a large number of different texts; statistically reliable differences in the contextual distribution of those linguistic expressions reveal differences in their semantics.

Theoretically speaking, their methodological emphasis on the analysis of co-occurrence behavior is motivated by a Peircean hierarchy of linguistic signs, in which natural language is supposed to consist largely of symbolic (rather than iconic or indexical) signs. Knowledge can be transmitted, it is argued, through the "interdependence" of symbols; if we interpret that interdependence in terms of co-occurrence in actual discourse, the choice for an LSA-type distributional analysis of co-occurrence patterns turns out to be theoretically motivated.

Both aspects of their approach are contrasted with an "embodied" approach. Taking Stockwell (2002) as a reference point, they present case studies showing that everything Stockwell reveals by his "embodied" approach can also be detected by using a "symbolic" approach. Such a symbolic approach is argued to be superior because of its empirical nature.

Given the opposition drawn up by Louwerse and Van Peer, this is the main difficulty I have with their position: they equate a theoretical opposition between a "symbolical" and an "embodied" framework with a methodological contrast between an empirical and an intuitive approach, but such an equation is unmotivated.

As a first step, let us note that there is no necessary relationship between the "symbolical" position and the corpus method put into practice by Louwerse and Van Peer. In both directions, in fact, the relationship is a loose one. On one hand, their own case studies establish that you can do corpus studies of "embodiment" phenomena, that is to say, using a corpus methodology does not predispose for a symbolic theory along Peircean lines. In a larger context, needless to say, the booming business of corpus linguistics shows quite clearly that a corpus methodology can be applied in a multitude of theoretical contexts: corpus linguistics is not theoretically specific.

On the other hand, it would seem that a symbolic view of language along Peircean lines does not lead exclusively towards a corpus methodology: Louwerse and Van Peer would not want to discard experimental research as a valid empirical approach, would they?

On a general level, such a loose relationship between a method and a theory (looser than what Louwerse and Van Peer suggest) is exactly as it should be: methods are supposed to be neutral with regard to theories, or more precisely, methods are supposed to decide between theories. (Admittedly, there are some Kuhnian complications here, but let us not try to solve them here.) As such, it is strange to see a particular method being advocated on the grounds of its relationship with a specific theory. Louwerse and Van Peer mention that the reluctance to adopt empirical methods that is sometimes found in literary theory is unthinkable in the exact sciences, but by and large, their own blending of a theory and a method would be just as unthinkable.

We can now take a second step, and have a look at the way in which Louwerse and Van Peer represent the "embodiment" position; again, we may distinguish between theoretical and methodological aspects. Theoretically speaking, they equate the embodied approach with a focus on the iconic and indexical aspects of language: "Language comprehension can be symbolic through interdependencies of symbols, but it can also be embodied through the dependencies of symbols on indices and icons". It's unlikely, however, that this type of theoretical framework is what Cognitive Linguists talking about embodiment have in mind. Admittedly, it is not always clear what exactly they mean, and the notion "embodiment" is very often used in Cognitive Linguistics as a hyped signal of group coherence rather than as an actual analytical concept. Even so, a minimal interpretation of "embodiment" in Cognitive Linguistics would not be that linguistic meaning is predominantly iconic or indexical, but rather that it is "embodied" because it evokes the full range of experience that comes with a concept: linguistic meaning, in other words, is encyclopedic rather than just structural.

We may illustrate this with the example of a symbolic sign mentioned by Louwerse and Van Peer: "In symbols, the relationship between the sign and what the sign represents is determined by convention. The wedding ring of the editor represents that he is married. But different cultures could have a different symbol for marriage, as long as the cultural community agrees on the symbol". But different cultures do not only have different symbols for marriage, they also have different institutions of marriage and different cultural models that come along with the symbol. An "embodied", experientialist, encyclopedic conception of meaning implies that it may be necessary to grasp this broad background to get a good idea of how the sign functions.

Consider the following example. A few years back, the Dutch author and actor John Lanting wrote and produced a successful comedy entitled *Een trouwring mag niet knellen*, "A wedding ring should not pinch". In order to understand that title, the reader has to know, first, that the relevant cultural model of marriage comes with a vow of sexual exclusivity, and hence, a restriction on one's personal freedom of behavior. Second, the reader has to be aware that the ring is usually worn on the finger (and is not, for instance, worn on a rope along the neck or stored in a shrine) and may therefore hurt when it is too tight. And third, the reader has to appreciate the humorous contrast between the common-sensical plausibility of the literal interpretation of the title, and the culturally transgressive nature of the plea for sexual freedom implied by the figurative interpretation.

While the third feature may just require a general poetic sensitivity, the other two involve "embodied", experiential, encyclopedic knowledge – knowledge of the world rather than just knowledge of the language, even if it is knowledge as trivial as that wedding rings are worn on the finger. Crucially, however, there is nothing specifically indexical or iconic about knowing that in the cultural environment of Lanting's comedy, marriage evokes the cultural model of fidelity, etc. If this broad experiential grounding is indeed what Cognitive Linguists approximate with a term like "embodiment", Louwerse and Van Peer are wrong by identifying embodied meanings with indexical or iconic meanings. A fortiori, they are wrong in contrasting embodied meaning with symbolical meaning: knowledge of the broad experiential background is simply part of the conventional symbolic meaning of a term like *wedding ring*.

Further, if we now turn to the methodological side of the embodied approach, we should note that Louwerse and Van Peer neglect to specify it. Given the dual nature of their own "symbolic" position, one would expect to see a description of what they argue against in terms of *both* theory ánd method. And yes, the embodiment position is described in theoretical terms, but what is methodologically specific about it is not made explicit, nor is it argued that a specific method would logically follow from the embodied position as it is theoretically (but questionably) defined by Louwerse and Van Peer. The implicit contrast with their own corpus-based method, however, suggests that they are thinking of a purely interpretative approach – an approach, that is, that takes the literary text as an object amenable to immediate subjective interpretation. This is further supported by their insistence on the necessity of an empirical turn in literary studies – an approach, that is, that maximalizes the search for objective textual correlates of the proferred interpretations, and that treats those interpretations as testable hypotheses, as one would do in the exact sciences.

And indeed, most of the work presented in cognitive poetics takes this methodological form. Given that this type of methodology is still the standard one in literary studies (as Louwerse and Van Peer make explicit in their introductory passage), the innovation brought by cognitive poetics lies in the interpretative framework it provides, not in the methodological way it tries to put that framework to the test – which is traditionally interpretative and non-empirical in the sense advocated by Louwerse and Van Peer.

Taking this into account, and given that the theoretical framing of Louwerse and Van Peer's opposition to the practice of cognitive poetics is questionable, as we have seen, I am led to conclude that the real substance of their disagreement resides in the methodological contrast between an empirical (a fortiori corpus-based) approach and a traditionally interpretative one. The argumentation by Louwerse and Van Peer, in other words, has to be deconstructed (*sit venia verbo*): what is framed as a theoretical opposition with methodological consequences basically boils down to *just* a methodological opposition.

To avoid any misunderstanding: if this is indeed a correct interpretation, I side unreservedly with Louwerse and Van Peer on the necessity of more empirical work. Two further remarks need to be made, though. First, it would be incorrect to equate an empirical methodology with just LSA, as Louwerse and Van Peer may seem to do. Within the field of automated, corpus-based analyses of meaning, LSA is but one of a number of techniques (see Agirre and Edmonds 2006 for an overview). In addition, there is a rich tradition of stylometry that employs a variety of statistical, corpus-based methods next to meaning determination algorithms, and that has been applied intensively to literary texts (e.g. in the context of authorship identification debates). Pushing cognitive poetics further on the empirical path would certainly have to imply that the empirical methodology is not restricted to LSA, but that a broad repertoire of empirical techniques is developed, and that the specific value of each technique is minutely investigated.

Second, it would be incorrect to equate Cognitive Linguistics with just the intuitive, non-empirical methodology that is dominant in cognitive poetics. The trend towards the use of empirical methods in Cognitive Linguistics is growing (see Geeraerts 2006 for an overview), and with due cause: if Cognitive Linguistics is to live up to its ambition to contribute to Cognitive Science, it will have to talk the empirical language of Cognitive Science. Louwerse and Van Peer's article is a stimulating demonstration that (even) cognitive poetics can come along with the methodological drift of Cognitive Linguistics towards empirical research.

References

Agirre, Eneko and Philip Edmonds
    2006   *Word Sense Disambiguation*. Berlin: Springer Verlag.
Geeraerts, Dirk
    2006   Methodology in Cognitive Linguistics. In: Gitte Kristiansen, Michel Achard, René Dirven and Francisco J. Ruiz de Mendoza Ibáñez (eds.), *Cognitive Linguistics. Current Applications and Future Perspectives*, 3–31. Berlin: Mouton de Gruyter.
Stockwell, Peter
    2002   *Cognitive Poetics: An Introduction*. London: Routledge.
Tummers, José, Kris Heylen and Dirk Geeraerts
    2005   Usage-based approaches in Cognitive Linguistics: A technical state of the art. *Corpus Linguistics and Linguistic Theory* 1: 225–261.

Incorporated means symbolic *and* embodied

Max Louwerse and Willie Van Peer

In a response to our contribution, Geeraerts, who we would like to thank for his provocative insights, argues that we confuse theoretical and methodological contrasts: We "equate a theoretical opposition between a 'symbolical' and an 'embodied' framework with a methodological contrast between an empirical and an intuitive approach, but [he argues] such an equation is unmotivated".

Let us first get rid of one misconception. By no means do we equate an embodied framework with an intuitive approach. We explicitly refer to the work by Barsalou (1999), Glenberg and Robertson (2000), Klatzky, Pellegrino, McCloskey, and Doherty (1989), Glenberg and Kaschak (2002), Zwaan, Stanfield, and Yaxley (2002), and Zwaan and Yaxley (2003). It is undoubtedly true that we have not given a complete overview of all the experimental psychological and neuroscientific evidence for an embodied account of language comprehension, simply because this would fill an edited volume in itself (see Pecher and Zwaan, 2005 for an overview). However, nothing is further beyond the truth than that we argued that an embodiment account is intuitive.

So if we do not equate a theoretical opposition between a "symbolical" and an "embodied" framework with a methodological contrast between an empirical and an intuitive approach, do we equate anything at all? In fact, we equate a theoretical opposition between a "symbolical" and an "embodied" framework with a methodological contrast between an empirical and an *experimental psychology* approach (and we can only hope that *experimental psychology* is *not* what Geeraerts meant by "intuitive"). Such an observation is in fact very much motivated. There is far more computational linguistic than experimental work available that can be identified as symbolic, and there is far more experimental than computational work available that can be identified as embodied. Exceptions are available for the embodiment approach (see Louwerse, Cai, Hu, Jeuniaux, and Ventura, 2006 for an overview). There is no valid reason why methodology has followed the theoretical distinction (other than that computers are simply more symbolic than embodied), but it has.

Do we argue that a symbolic approach is superior to an embodiment approach, as Geeraerts argues? Absolutely not! But neither do we argue that an embodiment approach is superior to a symbolic approach. In our contribution we do, however, observe such a bias for the latter in cognitive poetics. Instead, we explicitly argue that in language comprehension *both* symbolic and embodied approaches play an essential role. We do emphasize two points: One is that we consider empirical approaches to be superior to non-empirical approaches, the other that cognitive poetics neglects to select computational linguistic methodologies.

Do we then at least equate an empirical approach with LSA, as Geeraerts suggests? Not at all! In our work we have applied eye tracking methodologies, connectionist models, corpus linguistic techniques, reaction time techniques, survey methodologies, even the development and testing of *embodied* animated conversational agents. All of which we very much consider empirical methodologies. We have simply used LSA because it is a powerful, yet relatively simple, technique to construct associative meaning. And we know it works well to replicate findings obtained in embodiment experiments (Louwerse 2007; Louwerse et al. 2006). To our knowledge, techniques used in stylometry and word sense disambiguation, to which Geeraerts refers, have not (yet) been employed in dealing with embodiment findings, let alone have they been applied in cognitive poetics, though we would very much welcome such an effort.

We "basically seem to be fighting a straw man", according to Geeraerts. If that straw man embodies a cognitive poetics which carefully selects an embodiment approach to investigate language understanding and which ignores empirical methodologies in these investigations, then we wholeheartedly agree.

References

Barsalou, Lawrence W.
  1999   Perceptual symbol systems. *Behavior and Brain Sciences* 22: 577–660.
Glenberg, Arthur M. and Michael Kaschak
  2002   Grounding language in action. *Psychonomic Bulletin & Review* 9: 558–565.
Glenberg, Arthur M. and David A. Robertson
  2000   Symbol grounding and meaning: A comparison of high-dimensional and embodied theories of meaning. *Journal of Memory and Language* 43: 379–401.

Klatzky, Roberta L., James Pellegrino, Brian P. McCloskey and Sally Doherty
   1989   Can you squeeze a tomato? The role of motor representations n sem-
          antic sensibility judgments. *Journal of Memory and Language* 28:
          56–77.
Louwerse, Max M.
   2007   Iconicity in amodal symbolic representations. In: Thomas Landauer,
          Danielle McNamara, Simon Dennis and Walter Kintsch (eds.), *Hand-
          book of Latent Semantic Analysis*, 106–120. Mahwah, NJ: Erlbaum.
Louwerse, Max M., Zhiqiang Cai, Z., Xiangen Hu, Mathew Ventura and Patrick
          Jeuniaux
   2006   Cognitively inspired natural-language based knowledge represen-
          tations: Further explorations of Latent Semantic Analysis. *Inter-
          national Journal of Artificial Intelligence Tools*, 15: 102 –1039
Pecher, Diane and Rolf A. Zwaan (eds.),
   2004   *Grounding Cognition: The Role of Perception and Action in Memory,
          Language, and Thinking*. Cambridge, UK: Cambridge University Press.
Zwaan, Rolf A. and Richard H. Yaxley, R.H.
   2003   Spatial iconicity affects semantic-relatedness judgments. *Psychonomic
          Bulletin & Review* 10: 954–958.
Zwaan, Rolf A., Robert A. Stanfield, and Richard H. Yaxley
   2002   Language comprehenders mentally represent the shapes of objects.
          Psychological Science 13: 168–171.

Epilogue.
How (not) to advance toward the narrative mind

Meir Sternberg

1. Question time

Knowledge begins with questions, develops and regenerates by hard self-questioning, and tests itself against alternative inquiries. For what happens otherwise, look at the record of discourse cognitivism to date, particularly on its main front, story analysis. How come a project that began with such dreams and fanfare, then invested such efforts over the years (in a number of sub- or inter-disciplinary thrusts), exhibits such an unhealthy balance sheet? Will the revolution promised, and still latent in the shift of emphasis to the workings of the discursive or, specifically, narrative mind, ever materialize there? Nothing has so impeded the advance "toward a cognitive narratology" as the uncritical (if anything, self-congratulatory) attitude prevalent among both practitioners within cognitivism and promoters abroad, especially regarding fundamentals.[1]

They tend to ignore, at best to underplay and localize, the multiple weaknesses that cognitivist story analysis has betrayed since its rise in the 1970's: limitations, speculations, provincialisms, underequipment, infightings, false starts, dead ends, half-baked restarts, inconsistencies between programme and performance. Still less is the result acknowledged, if perceived at all. After thirty effortful years, nothing like a comprehensive theory of narrative based on the turn inward – oriented to the mind on the move along the discourse sequence – has ensued from the cognitivist project; nor has a steady advance toward it; nor has even an inquiry into what has gone wrong and how to reconceive the enterprise. All these are conspicuous for their absence, and a cause for disappointment, in the eyes of an informed outsider with a parallel mentalist orientation: one who, like my-

---

1. The original version of this commentary was written in response to the paper on narrative by David Herman. At the invitation of the editors, I then incorporated shorter references to other chapters in this volume. The focus on narrative as paradigm case, including its connection to language and amenability to linguistics, particularly cognitive linguistics, remains unchanged.

self, has concurrently sought to theorize narrative as a unique discourse-length processual activity and experience. Within the field, instead, the claim of a revolutionary turn is apparently taken for the deed; the "science" of cognition, actually hole-ridden and in its infancy, for the highway to (storied) text-processing, beyond the ken or reach of humanistic "impressionists"; the trade name "cognitive", even among its humanistic (e.g., literary) bearers and users, for a sufficient marker cum guarantee of novelty; the self-image, for a practice that justifies itself regardless of difficulties, empirical, theoretical, methodological, let alone from an exterior viewpoint. So much so that this tendency and its sad effects need to loom large in any overview, as a key to the domain's problems and prospects alike.

Overdue, question time has recently come at last. Witness the challenges now presented and debated in the otherwise friendly arena of *Poetics Today*, like the special issue in 24:2 (2003) on "The Cognitive Turn?", with follow-ups there and elsewhere[2]. So, not even the plea of unawareness remains to excuse the ongoing ostrich-likeness all too often exhibited still by the discipline – much less by its overzealous importers into poetics, stylistics, narratology, cinematology. But whether cognitivists are unable or unwilling to meet the (inter)discipline's difficulties on the storytelling front, the penalties incurred come to the same thing. Unhappily, David Herman's "Cognitive Approaches to Narrative Analysis", driving "toward a cognitive narratology", offers an example of this persistent obliviousness, rather than yet another exception to it, as you would expect of an up-to-date survey by a narratologist. Its oddities as such only accumulate all along, compounding one's sense of a missed opportunity to assess the state of the art, in the interests of a genuine advance toward self-knowledge and therefrom to the pursuit of mind-centred discourse (here, narrative) knowledge, whether labeled "cognitive" or otherwise. Even specifying the miss, within the limits of a commentary on that survey and kindred matters in this volume, therefore promises, if not to redress the balance, then to give a truer idea of what has happened, or not, or not yet, in the relevant encounters with the genre, and to serve those urgent common ends better. Selected references to work done by myself and others on the topics concerned will help to fill out the argument.

---

2. E.g., the multi-disciplinary exchange, coordinated by Els Andringa and David Miall (2004), in response to Sternberg (2003a, 2003b), Sopory (2005), Jackson (2005), Abbott (2006), Boyd (2006), Spolsky (2007), and in this volume, Vandaele and Brône, Wright, and Vandaele. Indeed, this volume's whole article/commentary format embodies the wanted spirit of critical cooperation.

2.   What enters into a cognitive narratology?

2.1. Action models: achievements, shortfalls, correctives

"Study of the cognitive dimensions of stories and storytelling has become an important subdomain within the field of narrative analysis". Herman's opening claim is disputable on various grounds, and his ensuing account of the "important subdomain" hardly bears it out. If anything, alas, this sequel so multiplies the grounds for objection and skepticism as to render the claim even shakier than usual: more vulnerable to attack by opponents, more dubious to seekers of an alternative paradigm or new directions, less credible to the impartial observer and the interested reader. All to the disappointment of well-wishers who know better, some looking in vain here for the notable cognitivist drives, branches, alliances, investments, achievements, some for the reconsiderations and correctives and developments urgently needed, some for the overall balance. Where partisanship blinds and boomerangs, a hard-headed stocktaking is likely to pay off sooner or later: this rationale has guided my own overview, "Universals of Narrative and Their Cognitivist Fortunes" (Sternberg 2003a, 2003b, also 2004). Herman mentions it in passing, as a caveat, yet to no visible effect. Readers will therefore do well to compare the two accounts.

Clear, detailed, and knowledgeable, Herman's survey is informative as far as it goes, but it doesn't go nearly far enough or deep enough. The limits of coverage meet the eye at once. The three issues singled out as "focal concerns" – "role/character", "emotion discourse", and "perspective" – encompass only a fraction of the field, and its corners rather than long-time cruxes at that. Cognitivist story analysis, instead, has always focused on action models, "plot" in a large sense, if you will. This mainstream ranges from story grammarians to schema builders to situation modelers, of all kinds, from psychologists to AI story-generating and -reading programmers, even to some linguists, from adjusters of Vladimir Propp's *Morphology* to reinventors of the wheel, from disciplinary isolationists to consumers or producers of "literary" narratology (including Herman himself elsewhere) as well as some cinematic equivalents. Here accordingly mass together the goals and efforts, the pioneers and programmes and practices, the junctures and splits, the attainments and shortfalls, the measures and lessons of the field as a whole over the decades. Whether auspicious or otherwise or mixed, all this record of action patterning ("processing") deserves better than silent replacement by a random trio of secondary concerns.

The extent of the omission is as hard to believe, or to describe and repair in a nutshell, as to explain. Here are a few typical salient absentees, detailed in my overview (Sternberg 2003a,b). Within the cognitivist mainstream, they include the field's single most important *and* most double-edged contribution to narrative theory: Schank and Abelson's *Scripts, Plans, Goals, and Understanding* (1977), with its diverse, multidisciplinary followings and follow-ups to this day.[3] Not for nothing has its influence outreached its immediate focus on how the computer simulates the human mind in reading and generating stories, with the usual AI priorities or pressures. Justly famous for the "script" – the routinized event-line that escaped notice before – the book has yet larger claims to the story analyst's attention. These claims even exceed the rest of the aids it offers to understanding the event-line (e.g., the titular "Plans, Goals", and later also Themes, Memory Organization Packets, Explanation Patterns). The project represented by it is an exemplar of two, indeed often twinned, major cognitivist thrusts: the engagement with action logic, parallel to the literary critical work on it since Aristotle, and with our storied memory, another issue broached by Aristotle, but sorrily neglected in the poetic tradition (Sternberg 1990a: 61–65). More is the pity that the neglect still persists in literary cognitivism, for both thrusts are equally relevant to the plot-minded narratologist.

Nor does their relevance end there. In this volume, for example, both memory and action logic are passed over in Semino's useful overview of recent approaches to (story)world construction, down to Fauconnier and Turner (2002). The surveyor and the surveyed alike don't even seem aware of the role played by these two forces in world-making, as in discourse processing generally. From a discourse-wide or, inversely, a typology-minded viewpoint, that role even outreaches the horizons of mainstream cognitivism itself. Thus, described and narrated worlds polarize by the logic that governs their construction: that of space within a framework immobile in time, as against that of time, or chrono-logic, whose dynamism can mobilize even spatial coexistents. (E.g., landscapes change, things as well as agents relocate, the world's furniture enters into causal enchainment.) The implications for the constructive process and the ultimate product are evidently far-reaching. The more so because descriptive and narrative objects (e.g., static vs. dynamic characters) or segments

---

3. Even listing a selection of them would take too long. But sequels by the original collaborators themselves include Schank (1984, 1990, 1999), Schank and Abelson (1995a, 1995b).

(e.g., the opening vs. the action of *Père Goriot*) often meet in one text.[4] Similarly with the difference in recall between short and long texts: just think of how it affects the fullness, the connectivity, the consistency, the revisability of the world progressively built up in our mind. Also, the two forces variously cross. Owing to its action logic, a narrative is thus easier to retain than a description, whether in short- or long-term memory, with further significant consequences, processual and poetic. (See already Aristotle – in the above reference – or Lessing's *Laocoon.*)

As noted, such viewpoints and workings go beyond the concerns of Schank et al. But the glaring holes typically left in Semino[5] where they have made a promising (re)start not only attest to the ongoing isolationism within cognitivism but also warn against taking at face value the now popular story of cognitivism as a steadily developing enterprise.

On the other hand, even regarding these two cruxes, as well as the "script" itself and other, bigger, more flexible event-schemas, the Schank and Abelson inquiry betrays an array of central disciplinary weaknesses. Disciplinary, I emphasize, because they have yet to be outgrown in (and, we'll find, beyond) the mainstream approaches to the narrative genre. Again, contrary to what Herman's silence on early cognitivism implies, and others declare outright, the later isn't necessarily the better "wave", or "generation", certainly not relative to this pioneering work with its typical flaws:

(1) Story and storyhood are left undefined, at best ill-defined, whether as or vis-à-vis narrative/narrativity. (Cognitivism sometimes distinguishes this pair.) The inquiry having thus failed both to delimit the (sub)generic object and to pinpoint the generic hallmarks, the dangers of confusing story/narrative with other discourse types and of mistaking its own essentials for variables, or the reverse, join liabilities. Given the ends, forms, processes that the genre shares with all messages – a fortiori, with all (e.g.,

---

4. For how such meeting affects storyworld construction, see already Sternberg (1978) passim or Sternberg (1983d) on the James Bond saga or, inversely, 1981 on narrativity as an aid to descriptivity. Either way, the balance of power hinges on the emergent contextual teleologic.

5. For example, her survey begins by introducing possible-worlds theory via two descriptive sentences (section 3). Next, however, she couples one of them with a novel, gives narrative-centred references to the theory's import into the study of "fiction", and herself illustrates from two short tales. Both genre and size thus lose their differential force, as concerns mobility and memory, respectively.

descriptive) representations, let alone temporal (e.g., linguistic, hence linearized) representations – what keeps it *sui generis*?

(2) Of narrative's two definitional and infinitely twinnable sequences – the told vs. the telling, what happened vs. how the what's unfold before us, the reconstructed chronology vs. the given temporal order – the former alone officially enters into the theory. "Action" is all, its discourse presentation out of sight and mind. Worse, the two often get conflated. This makes it impossible to capture the reader's gradual, equivocal processing of the narrated action by trial and error. (After all, even a script-bound event-line takes time to unfold, or reconstruct, and can always twist out of the expected order in the process.) The single-track analysis therefore misses the rich interplay between the genre's two constitutive linearities, with all the effects produced throughout (e.g., an intriguing mystery resolved, a character surprisingly disclosed, a false impression planted, then uprooted with a vengeance).

(3) Moreover, these interlinear effects alone account for how the telling selects and combines the told. What else would explain why the discourse launches, sustains, orders, terminates the narrative process as we encounter and experience it from moment to moment? In the absence of these effects, therefore, how's remain without why's, forms without functions: even goal-directed acts and agents remain without goal-directed tales about them at a higher level, which freely invents and shapes the action for its own ends. In brief, the cognitivist approach to date – like the Structuralist, and like any narratology that intermixes them, Ryan (1991) or Herman style – has no strategic explanatory power, no global operative sense-making rationale. To gain such power, a theory must orient itself to the driving forces behind the storyworld-and-storytelling twofold as a reference point. This overdue reorientation alone can (and, I hope, will at last) supply mentalist narratology with a firm basis in our experience of narrative, uniquely driven between the sequences peculiar to the genre: indeed, *between the lines*, in the fullest sense. As befits a master principle, it will run throughout my argument.

(4) The single-track analysis of the narrative twofold also compounds loss with fallacy. It erases the difference (even in terms of action logic proper) between real-life and represented events, immediate and discourse-mediated processing, the everyday mind operating on a first-order reality in flux and the literary mind engaged with a stretch of opaque referential lan-

guage. This erasure is often even declared an article of cognitive faith: all "mental representations" of, say, doings or agents supposedly work alike. It's like reducing a portrait to the portraitee, however stylized or fictionalized the given image we encounter on the wall. A fundamental category mistake, down to confusing things with the words about them.

(5) The favoured sequence itself is only brought to bear on rudimentary mini-stories, admitted by Schank et al. to be a far cry from "the novel", and comparable to the textoids fabricated by the experimentalists in the discipline's psychological branch. Inversely, when applied to "natural" or artistic discourse, by other cognitivists, this weak sequential machinery usually generates the obvious in heavy jargon or misses the point or breaks down.[6] The new insights yielded, if any, trace less to it than to the analyst's native wit and skill. Further reasons for such inadequacy include:

(6) A static, because material-bound and reified, preconception of story interest (the narratologist's "tellability"). Schank himself typically pre-loads with "absolute interest" a fraction of the representable objects, namely, "death, danger, power, sex, and large quantities of money". Others add or substitute risk, trouble, conflict, unusualness ... Whatever the chosen few, such a priorism runs not only against the infinite variability of interest (according to factors ranging from socioartistic hierarchy to novelty value to individual liking) but also against the empirical evidence of irreducible variety in the elements that readers have found appealing, poignant, tellable. Further, it exhibits afresh the single-track analysis of the genre's twofold sequence, because those absolute interests supposedly attach to the action: to the narrated matter rather than the narrative manner, let alone their contact, least of all their context. (A narratological cognitivist like Ryan 1991 goes so far as to preach this divide.) Even within the action itself, the reifying of certain isolated materials betrays an overemphasis on externals (counter to the inward turn of modernism, for instance, as well as of cognitivism itself) along with an atomistic approach. Most generally, its pseudo-universals would arrest into an immutable scale what culture, including history and art, relativize without end: the dynamism of interest value is alone eternal. In short, this material-boundness stands opposed to the mind's boundless flexibility. (For details, see Sternberg 2003b: 572ff.)

---

6. For some recent examples, see Jackson (2005), Spolsky (2007).

(7) The mind gets reduced to cognitive-conceptual workings, exclusive of emotivity, to suit the unfeeling computer – or, elsewhere, the meaning-based schema and grammar, storied or linguistic. So "cognition" flattens into knowledge representation devoid of affection and evaluation; "processing", already impoverished by (2)-(6), into understanding the action without reaction. (Contrast the "poetics of impact" below.) Not that any other of the field's subdisciplines has undertaken or managed to cover, let alone distinguish, the emotions generated by the narrative process, but that artificially simulating the mind rules out this half of our human experience altogether.

(8) Nor, within the forced-and-favoured mental half, is the computer as reader equal to narrative's ubiquitous (because constitutive, interlinear) play of ambiguity about the world-in-action: gaps, forking hypotheses, unresolved open-endedness. Such gaps, which we humans negotiate in every reading, with pleasure and profit, would expose the machine to an explosion of inferences. Similarly, if to a lesser degree, with action modeling outside AI: e.g., story grammars, comprehending procedures, the linguist's event "construals", or the psychologist's test routines. Compared with the AI programmer's schematism, their rage for lucidity, as well as for meaning, is even more doctrinal, because less forced, if at all, by logistic pressures. Either way, ambiguity accordingly counts here as a cognitive evil to be eliminated from the process at any cost, rather than as a generic universal, let alone a processual and aesthetic value.

"Understanding" itself thus reduces in turn to stable, determinate, ideally effortless comprehension of what happened. Historically, this marks a throwback to the Aristotelian ideal of closed and lucid ("whole") form: a neoclassicism that mirror-images postmodernism's rage for indeterminacy. Nor is postmodernism the only overreaching antipole. Voices within "second-wave" cognitivism have recently poured scorn on the very computational approach taken by the discipline founders. Such categorical negation overlooks the decisive role played by inferential processes (not least the readerly face of action logic) in narrative sense-making, whole-building, and response generally. Call it what you will, we must compute our way through the uncertainties of discourse as best we can. There, human life and life-imaging being what they are, probable closure must indeed satisfy us. Yet stricter, deductive reasoning may help locally – how else would you infer entailments? – provided it's kept in its place, rather than elevated into an ideal, algorithmic in goal as in method. The trouble is not with human computation, privileged or simulated, but with its formalizing into a drive toward meaning and lucidity alone, so as to target a univocal understanding that befits a machine.[7]

(9) Among other corollaries, the role of language diminishes to the vanishing point. No wonder Schank et al. bitterly opposed Chomskyan linguistics. His computerized Script Understander, for example, operates on a language-free translation: its input derives from a conceptual system whereby more or less equivalent forms (words, sentences) on the discourse surface (e.g., go, walk, run...) mechanically reduce to a uniform semantic representation. An obvious reductionism, but widely paralleled among grammars, schemas, situation models, possible-worlds logics, and indeed beyond them. Who, in any field, has assimilated language (as distinct from loosely and selectively adding it) to a theory of narrative, even of verbal narrative in its narrativity? No better is the reversal of priorities attempted in Structuralism and linguistic cognitivism – as though genre were grammar (or metaphor) and a story were a long sentence.[8] What competent narratologist today would found or focus or model narrative theory on language, given that narrativity doesn't reside there, any more than in other semiotic codes? The medium certainly defeats either extreme cognitivist approach, leaving its precise role to be determined by some holistic yet flexible alternative. (On which more below.)

Like the strengths of this ground-breaking AI inquiry, then, the weaknesses are principled and paradigmatic: all, or most, also typify cognitivist action-directedness elsewhere and its literary offspring. They haven't been repaired by latter-day cognitivism, either, certainly not as a set or in this central arena, failing the necessary strategic shift indicated here. Some partisans may wish to imagine otherwise, but witness the dozens of variants, older and recent, cited in my overview (Sternberg 2003a,b) or added as we proceed. For now, observe how often there recur below comments on the failure to mark off real-life from represented world, or (as in

---

7. For parallel mechanical, virtually mind-less approaches to inference in linguistics, pragmatics, the philosophy of language, and of law, with their unworkable formalisms opposed to a functional alternative, see Sternberg (2001b, 2003b: 545–46, 2008). Possible-worlds theory is vulnerable to much the same objections.
8. Even so, there is a remarkable family likeness to Schank et al. in the priority of "conceptualization", hence preverbal meaning: see section 5 below.

Semino) the narrative from the descriptive genre – always incurring some further minus(es) among those just listed as typical of the discipline.

Still, the set of minuses outlined have their own claim to high narratological relevance, if only in warning against roads not to be taken or against disciplinary (sometimes, crossdisciplinary) lacunae and imbalances to be addressed. So have the few exceptions to one or more of the nine negative rules just generalized: e.g., Brewer and Lichtenstein (1982) or Bruner (1986, 1990, or recently 2002) or Gerrig (1993) in psychology, Turner (1996) as a literary-minded adherent of cognitive linguistics, Ryan (1991) and Fludernik (1996) in narratology, or, much nearer to home, Bordwell (1985, followed by, e.g., Tan 1996) on film, among others noted in my overview. Whatever difficulties with action processing may remain there, and whether or not they outweigh the correctives, a partial improvement on the disciplinary paradigm (if only in this or that single regard) is an improvement still.[9] For better or worse, therefore, here lies the main tradition that cognitivism bequeathes to its practitioners and importers, to its resumers as to would-be reformers on the narrative front.

2.2 Poetics of Mind and Card-Carrying Cognitivism

Outside this mainstream, Herman's survey blanks out further projects and lines associated with the discipline, even where their special concerns apply or actually extend to narrative. One case in point is evolution-minded cognitivism, as represented in the collections edited by Abbott (2001), Richardson and Steen (2002), Richardson and Spolsky (2004). Among their claims to notice are the bearings on literary evolution, narrative diachrony included. However tentative, or speculative, these attempts at least revisit in cognitive terms a vital discourse axis neglected, indeed unapproachable, elsewhere in the field. They may complement poetic and sociopoetic approaches to the stories of history, stories in history. The models initiated by the Russian Formalist Viktor Shklovsky (1929), and famously illustrated from Sterne's *Tristram Shandy* within the tradition of the novel, have a particular relevance to any cognitive evolutionism. For the effect of making the artwork strange to the receiver is cast there as the mainspring of development. (See the special double issue "Estrangement Revisited" in *Poetics Today* 26:4/27:1).

---

9. This also holds for Herman (2002), titularly focused on logic, with an actional frame of reference to suit.

Thus far, Shklovsky's notion of defamiliarizing has been applied in synchronic cognitivist analyses, as in van Peer (1986), Cook (1994) and Miall and Kuiken (e.g., 1994). But Herman never refers to these, either. More's the pity because, from an interdisciplinary view, this famous idea offers an attractive meeting ground. Likewise markedly absent from this "cognitive narratology" are the event schemas behind figuration, according to Lakoff et al.; or the approaches to world-making outlined by Semino here; or the mental imaging of time and/or space (from Piaget to Levinson 2003); or, apropos "talk", Sperber and Wilson ([1986] 1995) on relevance in communication; or, apropos both "character" and "perspective", how the overall images of mind (subjectivity, consciousness) theorized in the field compare with those underlying stories or assumed and debated by narrative analysts. The silenced majority grows.

Most conspicuously and typically absent, however, is the mass of mind-related, even mind-centred work done over the ages by professionals in literature and narrative itself, under banners other than cognitivism. Russian Formalism, just noted, re-enters here on a much wider scale: for better or worse, it has correlated the *fabula/sjuzhet* opposition (the basis of modern narratology) with automatized/deautomatizing perception, turning on whether the narrative follows or ruptures the narrated, chrono-logical, hence psychologically imperceptible event-line. Disordering supposedly equals defamiliarizing. Here is a major movement's foundational thesis about narrative as perceived in or against time, complete with a rationale, a basic double polarity, a large following in poetics – and so with an invitation to joint, psychonarrative reanalysis and testing. From this entire ongoing movement, Herman singles out instead the anti-psychological branch, now virtually defunct at that: Vladimir Propp, the would-be objective morphologist, and his heirs in Structuralism, are invidiously juxtaposed with their alleged cognitivist betters.

There abound further examples, earlier and later, of programmes in literary study that, as will appear, might directly, often decisively benefit the advance "toward a cognitive narratology", but never surface here. What I call the poetics of impact ("affect") suggests itself, because it would help to repair the chronic neglect of storied emotivity. Launched by Aristotle (with pleasure, pity-and-fear, the unexpected as master affects), such poetics ranges all the way to Lessing's *Laocoon* and the illusionist/anti-illusionist tradition (Sternberg 1999) to the neo-Aristotelian Chicago School (Crane 1952) to Barthesian hedonism; the Chicago School also doubles, in this affective capacity, as the modern adapter of the rhetorical approach to narrative, via Booth (1961) and its lineage.[10] Again, genre theory includes affect-driven accounts of tragedy, comedy, melodrama, the detective story, the cinema. Or, geared to meaning, rather than affect,[11] the various reader-response lines arisen since the New Criticism. Or, needless to repeat, the theory of the narrative mind at work developed on a wide front by myself and others in the Tel-Aviv school, with associates elsewhere: it will serve as the main counterpoint throughout the argument below. And still further omissions will emerge in the sequel.[12]

Exactly because an overview must be selective, the selection exercised here by Herman grows increasingly puzzling with the magnitude of the blanks, now carried to the limit of totality. Why this wholesale exclusion of convergent precedents and parallels and pathways to "a cognitive narratology"? Doesn't it even run against the declared intention to heal the rift between the arts and the sciences, "the two cultures"? The wonder might lessen if the survey nevertheless restricted itself to hard-line cognitivist research – grounded in experimental mind sciences – or what passes for such. But the research actually surveyed here would then itself fail to qualify, either, as would the surveyor. One looks in vain for empirical evidence, even of the kind current in poetics, never mind the laboratory. Rather, with all aspirations to scientific rigour jettisoned, and no substitute qualifying agenda or measure visible, the name "cognitive" is the thing. Herman's insistence on the label per se as dividing line extends further the sad tradition of cognitivism's own cliquishness, whereby the self-isolations from otherwise mentalist outsiders and other-minded insiders and mere followers in-between have joined negative forces.[13] As the

---

10. Uri Margolin observes a similar omission in Culpeper here: "the rhetorical approaches" to narrative "link textual features with cognitive and emotional effects", so that "they constitute cognitive stylistics par excellence."

11. One leading practitioner, Stanley Fish (1980), nevertheless refers to his method as "affective stylistics."

12. As already briefly indicated apropos Semino and Culpeper – again with further glances below – Herman's narrow frame of reference is paralleled elsewhere in the volume; but it's never equaled, any more than the scale of the topic.

13. Among importers and promoters of the field, this restriction of reference to (some) card-carrying fellow cognitivists is typical enough: even inquiries recognized and adopted by experts as "cognitive", though originating elsewhere, often don't qualify. Thus, literary followers of Lakoff's and/or Turner's approach to metaphor ignore its poetic antecedents over the last centuries (Adler and Gross 2002, Goodblatt and Glicksohn 2003); Turner (1996:

chain of exclusion lengthens and courts studied ignorance in return, the chances of fruitful exchange between the "cultures", name-bearers, cliques progressively diminish, along with the grounds for it. One wonders therefore whom this survey addresses, and with what persuasiveness.

The more so because the three issues singled out by Herman as "focal" hardly compare with cognitivism's action-mindedness, such as it is. They are much less wide-ranging, representative, established: off-centre, in brief, relative to the field's priorities and performance, hierarchy and history. Nor do they come first by the narrative genre's own rationale, as a discourse sequentially unfolding a world-in-time, or on the list of the holes to be repaired in its variform cognitivist modelling, as diagnosed above. Yet even for secondary issues by all these criteria, the three are far narrower and poorer than may appear or than their discussion suggests, and without any visible line of growth toward centrality on their own, at that. Just as a statement being true isn't yet a reason for making it, so their being genuine issues – and they certainly are – doesn't yet justify foregrounding them exclusively in an interdisciplinary survey devoted to a chosen few. Whether they should have received wider cognitivist attention and along which lines, or what the neglect implies and how to overcome it, are different matters. In putting the record straight, though, we'll touch upon such matters as well.

3.   Role/character in narrative

Across its usages here, "role/character" encompasses nothing like the genre's characterological range and repertoire, themselves divisible into subdomains: ideas of characterhood; models, types, aspects, functions of character; and arts of characterization. (To leave aside their distribution among the genre's kinds or their changing, often "estranged" fortunes

---

120ff.) also disregards all that has intervened in point-of-view theory since Booth (1961), not least the growing emphasis on (re)construction; Stockwell (2002) has been charged with "misrepresentation" in ignoring "a decade of careful, related work" on discourse and ideology "by Spolsky, Crane, Zunshine" and other fellow workers outside his circle (Hart 2006: 232); yet Zunshine herself (2006: 77ff.) postdates the turn toward inferring the unreliable narrator to recent literary cognitivist work, which, for a change, openly refers the shift back to Tamar Yacobi in poetics (e.g., 1981, 1987a, 1987b). Circles within circles.

along cultural or literary history.) The whole domain now shrinks, instead, to how narrative existents fulfil actional "roles" (e.g., Hero) under the guise of particular "characters" (e.g., Tom Jones). This question alone interested the movement that has notoriously least invested and succeeded in the study of character, namely, Structuralism from Propp to Greimas; and regarding it, we now hear, cognitivism has done better. For the narrowness as well as the apparent continuity of the newer approach, just observe the terms applied to the figures: "actant", "actor" or, later, Emmott's "enactor".

However, if the tag recurs and the claims escalate – Emmott's book flaunts the title "Narrative Comprehension", no less – the object of study itself has both narrowed further and migrated elsewhere. While hailed by Herman as a cognitivist advance over Structuralism, Emmott (1997) actually piles reduction on reduction in minimizing the scope of role/character: it comes down to the decoding of referring expressions – especially how to match *he/she/it* pronouns with the narrative participants. The shrinkage in focus thus runs all the way from storied personages to the manifest terms indicating them to person-deictic terms to a subset thereof (the one deemed least central, subjective, problematic at that, in both linguistic and literary analysis, relative to the "I" or the "I/you" correlation).

The shrinkage also goes with a threefold shift of focus. Instead of actional roles in the narrative deep structure (e.g., Propp's Hero, Villain, Helper...) enacted by particular characters (e.g., Hamlet, Claudius, Horatio...) across media, we now have to do with the verbal reflexes of certain discourse-roles, with who's who in third-person deixis on the surface of language. Moreover, once subtextual "roles" change into referents, or even referring terms, and textualized "characters" into pronouns, or anaphoras, the shift in focus doubles as one in level. With Herman's translation of the Structuralist binarism to Emmott, these binaries in effect lose their depth/surface, underlying/overlying relation to assume a correlative superficiality. What entity plays the role of *it* here?, for example, now means, To what does "it" point (or, as an anaphora, point back)? The sea change in "role" vis-à-vis Structuralism, then, entails a double switch in range: from the all-semiotic yet generic – because distinctively narrative – to the linguistic, indeed anaphoric, regardless of genre, as when I refer to Herman by "he". Shorn of the big words in and about "this cognitively oriented approach to roles as elements of contextual frames", it amounts to a useful note on pronominal disambiguation blown up into monograph length.

Herman himself unwittingly exposes its smallness and superficiality when he replaces pronominal by visual (e.g., colour, shape) indicators of who's-who in "applying" Emmott to his comics example from *The Incredible Hulk*. What easily lends itself to substitution is nothing like integral, of course, and "characters" proper would resist it. But equally replaceable is the narrative genre itself, which has no monopoly on such indicators, verbal *or* visual. He might as well illustrate them from the reference to existents made by a sheer descriptive passage or portrait. How, then, can a few dispensable micro-linguistic pointers generate a new approach to storied roles, let alone "a theory of narrative comprehension" on the largest scale? In fact, when Emmott (2003, also 1997 passim) ventures beyond the micro-scale into global emplotment, narratologists can only shrug their shoulders.

The focus on linguistic pointers, though, highlights a generic fuzziness that elsewhere reveals itself on other levels and scales as well. Such bracketing of narrative with descriptive character or role (in any sense) is unfortunately all too widespread among literary, psychological, sociological, and literary-cognitivist approaches to the topic. In this volume, take Culpeper's "approach to characterization", which overtly defocuses language to foreground broader cognitive aspects. His chosen emphasis in effect neutralizes the operative semiotic differences built into media, so that verbal and visual characterization would again intersubstitute, at a high price, too multiple and compounded to enumerate here. We need only observe that, of the two codes, language alone enables direct, summary (e.g., epithetic) portraiture, explicit judgment, and inside views through mind-quotation; or observe how unevenly arbitrary, iconic, and indexical signifying (in particular, character-building) modes are distributed between the two; or the relative dominance in them of temporal vs. spatial existence, extension, manipulation. Even if the code's defocusing is just a matter of ad hoc priority within a language-specific approach, how to discount, let alone ignore those differences with impunity? And much the same question arises – as already with Emmott – concerning analyses specifically oriented to characters/roles born of words in literary or everyday discourse.

Worse, and still more common, there follows a declared bid for generality, one in keeping with Culpeper's generically (as well as semiotically) unspecific title. He undertakes to theorize and illustrate "characterization" across "various genres", because "the cognitive fundamentals are the same". But are they, across (say) the generically immobile and the freely mobile existent – as between description's static and narrative's freely changeable figure? In a nutshell, the latter, storied discourse enjoys the unique power of unfolding character by the logic of its own (suspenseful) development, as well as that of the temporal portraitist's (intriguing and/or surprising) disclosure: if static character/characterization is the common property of all mimesis, and dynamic characterization of static character is an extra resource peculiar to temporal [sequenced, hence emergent, e.g., verbal] mimesis, then dynamic character is reserved for narrative mimesis, along with every other component of the world-in-motion. (Sternberg 1992: 530; for details and examples see also Sternberg 1978: 56–235, 1985: esp. 186ff., 1990a, 1999, 2001a, and note 17 below.)

Culpeper typically overlooks this scalar network of differences, with its fundamental generic implications for any represented existent's cognition and semiosis and aesthetics, for the ends and means and processes available, for synchrony and diachrony and typology – all culminating in the double time-line of narrative. Once informed by this network, his entire analysis might therefore rise to quite another order of inclusiveness and discrimination joined together.[14] (Nor does Margolin's commentary repair the holes.) Instead, such is his obliviousness to this network of differences, that he even misreads E.M. Forster's celebrated flat/round polarity, in confusing the relevant dimensions and the generic options with them.

Forster opposes the "flat", single-trait character to the "round" one, endowed with multiple traits and accordingly capable of surprising us. As defined, the two polarize in complexity; and so, though Forster's own business is the novel, both character types remain open to all discourse types (or even sign types, including visual art). For simple/complex, like thin/thick and monolithic/disharmonious, entails a distinction in make-up, regardless of variables in presentational or existential mode, and accordingly crossgeneric. Not the least of these free variables is the (im)mobility that separates descriptive from narrative life, a self-contained portrait by Theophrastus or Holbein from one (e.g., Hamlet's, Elizabeth Bennet's) assimilated to a developing action and subjected to its pressures for change. Still, this variable opposes descriptivity to narrativity – and with it the respective options for changeless vs. changing existents – not flatness to roundness. Therefore, "character/characterization" of either type, flat or round, "is the common property of all mimesis".

---

14. The more so if further differences between the genres are taken into account, like that in the respective magnitudes. We touched on it apropos Semino's world-construction, a larger framework that not simply parallels but includes character.

But Culpeper gets the Forsterian typology wrong, taking its variable feature of (in)mobility for the differential constant. Oddly, the "flat" character then turns from single-trait into nondevelopmental and the "round" from many-sided into "relatively dynamic", hence also limited to narrative by silent implication. A mistake, this, in generic range as well as in typological cutting edge, and in practice as well as in principle. Consider the abrupt change often undergone by the "flat" villain in comedy or melodrama. Inversely, consider how an intricate ("round") personality is fixed (immobilized, described) in a Holbein or, like Homer's Odysseus, emerges as increasingly and surprisingly complex along the telling/reading, though again, Holbein-like, always short of development in the happening (Sternberg 1978: 56–128, 138 ff.).

Apart from its intrinsic significance, this wider outlook brings out a liability recurrent across otherwise diverse approaches to character. Emmott's generic indiscriminateness between the narrative and the descriptive (compounded by Herman with semiotic replaceability) is, then, anything but untypical. Only, what other element or means bearing on character/role is so widely shared among language's discourse kinds as the he/she/it micro-pointers to be disambiguated? Her focus on them accordingly underscores the usual oversight of genres and the difference it makes to the communicator, the processor, the analyst in face of represented existents.

Regarding disambiguation itself, such micro-features, verbal or visual, pale beside the ambiguities about the storyworld notorious among modern literary analysts (and abhorred among mainstream cognitivists). Those trouble spots least compare with the inherent discontinuities, hence uncertainties, between the times of happening and reading: the gapping-to-gapfilling movements that, on my theory, drive the whole narrative process, constitute the genre's universals, and tell apart particular generic instances by variables like the dominant processing interest. (e.g., Sternberg 1978, 1985, 1992, 2001a, 2003a,b, 2004, 2008, all with further references and all directly bearing on character/characterization, among other storied constructs; see also note 17 below.) Given narrative's ranking of word vs. world, therefore, the difference between a pronominal and a plot mystery, a third-person's elusiveness and a person's or persona's, goes beyond scope. It corresponds to that between surface form and underlying force, means and end. To integrate with the dynamics of the storied whole, further, words themselves (like all other components) will play or shuttle between equivocation and univocality, sometimes forever, unresolvably. Besides forked deictic who's-who, examples would be the enigmas posed – or thickened – by language in a detective story, a Jamesian dialogue, a monologue in Joyce or Beckett; or by troping, punning, allusion, free indirect style. All possibly keep meanings uncertain to the end, with some goal in view. The overemphasis laid here on *dis*ambiguation, instead, or its visual equivalents for that matter, again exhibits negative rule (8) above.

But even the efforts ill-spent in mainstream cognitivism on reducing ambiguity, via oversimplified action models, shine by comparison to Emmott et al. For they struggle with genuine exigencies at the heart of narrative, so that their very failures point a vital lesson about going against the multigap discourse grain. Inversely, Herman's claims for her study cut both ways: their overstatement reflects on any word-based theorizing of a world-based genre, via deixis or grammar or metaphor. This problem will resurge below, especially in the final section, apropos linguistic cognitivism.

The second allegedly alternative approach to Structuralist roles, via "the idea of position", originates in sociology or "discursive psychology". Such "positioning" concerns, not third-person referential identity, but "polarities of character" (good/bad, high/low, strong/weak) in whose terms one casts the self and/or the other during a speech encounter. But it only reveals a shrinkage cum shift along other lines, without corresponding gains in analytic depth or finesse relative to existing work on interpersonal contact. While Emmott's pronoun decoding may at least punctuate an entire text – as Structuralism's role/character pairing runs through the action's macrosequence – "positioning" is limited to the dialogue scene, to talk among characters. More exactly, and restrictively, the approach bears on talk (as autonomous interchange between speakers) rather than dialogue (as a frame-bound quotation of such interchange by a higher speaker, e.g., the overall narrator). Not that the line separating real-life talk from its re-presented, dialogic image (in literature or the cinema or TV) is drawn by Herman or his sources, any more than is its counterpart above, regarding the actional vs. the narrational sequence. Here as there, first-order and mediated reality get conflated, with substantive implications for the repertoire as well as the rationale of "positioning".

Again, a mixture typical of cognitivism, and often doctrinal at that, though now against the literary critical grain. It has already appeared as negative rule (4) above – generalized from the extensive evidence in Sternberg (2003a,b) – and will recur on every front below. Apropos character, the misequation of the represented image with the real thing, as drawn in

Gerrig (1993), for example, still persists in force, even among "literary" cognitivists, who should know better. Thus Bortolussi and Dixon: "literary characters are processed *as if* they were real people", and vice versa (2003: 140). Culpeper, in this volume, follows suit, including the import of models, schemas, roles from sociology and psychology. The opposite extreme of literary separatism doubtless cries out for a corrective, yet well short of overbalance.

Both extremes, the univalent and the separatist, tend to miss the very point at issue. It lies not in whether our knowledge of real people stretches to figural representations – it willy-nilly does, of course – but in the latter's extra mediateness as discourse images, hence their free (re)coding, adjustability, part/whole integration, especially under artistic licence. The very knowledge brought to them is always newly contingent on the overall communicative framework. Thus, the distance between encountering a fellow human in reality and a character at second hand, via a text, is no less principled, nor less maneuverable, than that between a thing and a sign of it, or between seeing/hearing and hearsay. Art only turns the built-in disparity to the richest account.

Evidently, interlocutors in ordinary talk lack many of the resources open to a dialogue, especially one framed within a narrative, a fictional one, above all. Limiting one's range to such real-life exchanges, or worse, taking them for paradigmatic, with Herman, would therefore severely hinder (if not mislead) a narratology, "cognitive" as otherwise. This focus on talk excludes each dialogic party's own interior and self-communing speech, the narrator's whole framing discourse, even the genre's macrosequential backbone: characters represented in silent, wordless exterior (inter)action, generally driven in turn by silent (e.g., planning, motivating) thought as cause to the effect.[15]

Dire poverty ensues, of course. Characters in a novel, for example, would thereby lose their hallmarks and (self-)characterizing uses as

(1) quoted speakers, their utterance always recontextualized and freely re-textualized (via interference) in the dialogue's mediation by the narrator;

(2) fictional (hence given to omniscient mind-reading, i.e., to directly, indirectly, free indirectly, and otherwise quoted inside-views, or to unrealistic integration, or to "literary" sense-making);

---

15. Contrast even cognitivism's rarefied action models, which do touch on the secret life, if only in the form of agentive goal.

(3) dramatized communicators at a higher level than dialogue, when themselves narrating to us;

(4) dynamically engaged with each other even outside their verbal interchanges;

(5) developing and/or disclosed between times, through(out) the interdynamics of the represented and the communicative process (e.g., the surprise turn whereby Pip in Dickens's *Great Expectations* outgrows his earlier self, once faced by his real benefactor).

With these absentees, most of the lesser, "position"-directed repertoire itself vanishes from sight; and irretrievably so within an approach geared to talk exchange.

Nevertheless, the overall impoverishment might yet possibly find some compensation on the local, face-to-face scale. We know so little about the dynamics of interpersonal encounter that added clues from whatever quarter are most welcome. Any literary dialogue, however, will bear witness that the "positioning" equipment offered here is unsophisticated and the output unremarkable, for all Herman's advocacy of them. Nor, what with their simplified "polarities of character", do they reflect the jockeying for position audible between the sides, and the lines, in natural talk. As early as Bakhtin's dialogism, poetics suggests more fruitful beginnings. So do latter-day narratology (e.g., Abbott 2002 on the law's narrative contestation), pragmatics (e.g., the Gricean maxims and "conversational implicature", or Sperber and Wilson's "relevance" in a self-styled "cognitive" inquiry), and Goffman's interactional analyses (especially the sociolinguistic 1981).

Not much "sociology" of character, then, still less "psychology", least of all, again, genre-specific. The very line between people and personages, between real-life (immediate) and represented (a fortiori, artistic) "discourse", newly blurs, as in cognitivism's action models, or often in its "processing" of other elements, language included – always with the predictable unhappy results.

The loss of both coverage and narrative dynamism goes yet further. Those very exchanges, as surveyed, have little traceable impact on the developing action (against the logic of speech *acts*) and Herman's gestures toward their involvement in "constructing storylines" never amount to much: see the Cheney example. This example also leaves you wondering whether and how, "redescribed as a position" – in effect, denarrativized by Structuralist criteria – "a role" essentially varies from the age-old dealings with characterization, except in its narrow characterological, as well as discoursive, scope.[16] Either narrowness also compounds the other, minimizing the coverage of talk itself, let alone dialogue. Such dialogic images attributed to humans by humans are by nature fallible, at best partial, and so always in need of validation, correction, gap-filling from the rest: from interior portrayal, self-imaging, and self-betrayal, from overt narratorial and implicit authorial lights on the dramatis personae, from the ultimate test of action, especially at the crossroads. Moreover, as "positioning" is contextual and ephemeral by definition, it also needs to be checked against the positioned figure's antecedents, including his or her characteristic "roles" in the theory's exact sense. Of this vital image-testing and -building repertoire, nothing is proposed here to the future "cognitive narratology". Stripped of the overstated language, again, it all comes down to how speakers at talk unreliably characterize ("position") self and/vs. other in the roughest terms, "as powerful or powerless, admirable or blameworthy."[17]

16. Thus "redescribed", in fact, the very term "role" is here a conceptual misnomer, with cognitive implications. Beginning with Rom Harré, theorists of "positioning" emphatically dissociate it from "role", which they take as a static idea belonging to a rival approach. Herman's association of positioning with longer "sequences" or with "stereotypes" further underemphasizes its distinctive, relatively novel ephemerality: the position assigned to you by me changes at will during our exchange.

17. Apropos character, some restarts in the field itself are more informed and promising: e.g., Bruner (1986, 1990), Gerrig and Allbritton (1990), Gerrig (1993) in psychological cognitivism, or the "psychonarrative" Bortolussi and Dixon (2003: 133–65), or the "stylistic-cognitive" Culpeper (2003, this volume). Regardless of their labels – which don't signify much – they share basic assumptions that might be profitably reviewed along the lines indicated above. Extensive literary studies range from the classic Forster ([1927] 1962) to Harvey (1965), Barthes (1974), Price (1983), Docherty (1983), Margolin (1983, 1998), or Hochman (1985); more corpus-based work keeps multiplying. For how character meshes with narrative dynamics at large, via temporal strategies of impression-formation, primacy/recency effects, for example, see Sternberg (1978: esp. 93ff., 1985: 186ff., 1992, and the 2003 overview, passim), Bordwell (1985: 38–40 and passim), Jahn (1997: esp. 457–61). In regard to "positioning" itself – as well as its narrative emplotment – compare Sternberg (1985, passim, 1991b, 1998, passim), on the intricate, often agonistic dynamics of dialogue staged throughout the Bible.

4.   Wanted: a discourse emotionology, literary and otherwise

Likewise with the next "focal concern", another import from discursive psychology, i.e., "emotion discourse". Focal? As already indicated, rather, emotivity (above all, storied emotivity) has been traditionally neglected, even avoided, in favour of cognition-as-comprehension, thus disabling any genuine mentalism. (Hence also one ground for my reservations about the label "cognitive" when applied to my work or assumed by fellow workers). But this cognitivist neglect is a sign of the times. It varies from related disciplines only in its nominal flaunting where one would expect a holistic mental enterprise, under a banner to suit. Otherwise, the rage for meaning equally typifies linguistics, pragmatics, the philosophy of language, discourse analysis, and even the literary critical mainstream since the New Criticism – as against the earlier affect-oriented tradition, going back to antiquity's "poetics of impact".

Herman still reflects this multi-disciplinary imbalance in defining "cognitive narratology" as "concerned both with how people *understand* narratives and with narrative itself as a mode of *understanding*" (my emphasis). Though unexpected, his reference to the missing emotive half is therefore welcome, and would be doubly so if it did not again prove strangely minimal; also unrepresentative of the available cognitivist exceptions,[18], such as they are, let alone the poetic tradition. The range shrinks here along two lines at once: from emotion, most of it unverbalized (or unverbalized *as* emotion) in discourse, if at all verbalizable, to emotive language; and from the reader's mobile and many-sided emotive process, as co-experiencing, inferring, opposing, subsuming that of the various characters, to the characters' manifest emotive lexicon and sound. Not, mind you, the characters' composite process of feeling, or their deepest and

---

18. Discussed in Sternberg (2003a: esp. 377 ff.) (including so-called "affective" versions of my generic universals, the suspense-curiosity-surprise trio) and recently enlarged by the currency of "the embodied mind." For a newer suggestive departure, see Margaret Freeman (this volume) on "Minding" as "Feeling, Form, and Meaning" in poetry: to be continued, one hopes. True, even where concerned with narrative, such exceptions do not generally identify or centralize the feelings and feeling dynamics and feeling/meaning traffic peculiar to the narrative experience; but nor does (still less, if anything) the "emotion discourse" chosen for mention here. The story illustrating it in Herman might well get replaced by a text discoursing on a state of mind. Yet another promised advance "toward a cognitive narratology" along non-narrative lines.

truest feeling, hidden in (e.g., Molly Bloom's) interior emotive discourse, or even their whole feeling-related talk, or their talk as a whole – emotion being as inherent to it as cognition – but certain local forms they use in talk to express or dispute feeling.

Thus Mary in the real-life example from *UFO or the Devil*. In telling about her ghastly encounter with the glowing Big Ball, she voices her fear through self-attributed adjectives, through expletives, changes in rhythm, intonation, loudness, and otherwise "expressive phonology". The tip of the iceberg, you might call it, except that the depths we know from life and literature are often more like a volcano.

Even so, limited to the vocalized part of the experience of characters, such "emotion discourse" is necessarily reported discourse about that experience (e.g., Mary's) as felt then or re-felt now: an image and index, not an instance, of original feeling. As such, the experience self-narrated in retrospect may be selective, overdramatized, indeed fancied altogether, the way Mary's own listener characterizes it. For Herman, "this speech production dismisses as so much nonsense" that listeners attempt "to other-position Mary as an hysterical imaginer of nonfactual events". But how do we know – with the original event and emotion inaccessible, without so much as a privileged inside-view and reliable guidance for a substitute? Treating the second-hand as if it were the genuine article, therefore, newly betrays the usual single-track flattening: just like the approach to the characters' action (minus its communication) and portraiture (minus its textual remove from actual beings) and expression (minus its dialogic quoting frame). In short, another represented object taken as an unmediated, first-order entity; another happening, another utterance act, divorced from the reading and the crucial interplay between the two; another thing/image category mistake.

Even relative to isolating the action line, however, the trouble spreads further yet, in various yet similarly precedented ways. This "emotion discourse" also compounds further limitations: those of the micro-scale, now down to vowel units; of its fellow import and exterior-talk correlative, "positioning"; and of their shared indifference to narrative specificity, all encountered above. As the family likeness should need no detailed rehearsal by now – a careful reading of Herman's section 3 will help – let me just briefly exemplify these cumulative shortfalls in turn, with hints at countermeasures or viable substitutes where possible.

Given the micro-scale, the claim that "literary narratives ... spy thrillers and romance novels are recognizable as such" by appeal to the interlocutors' emotive markers per se sounds like a very tall order, comparable to subdividing these kinds by their pronoun (dis)ambiguation. The next two shortfalls help to explain why. As a matter of fact, "emotion discourse" about self and/vs. other is no less partial, gapful, unreliable, and accordingly in need of correlation with all the relevant complements and correctives (interior, framing, metonymic, actional, gestural, body-languaged, even verbal *and* figural yet obliquely emotive) than the rest of "positioning" speech. By the same token, given the magnitude of this overall emotion-imaging repertoire and the variable interplay among the techniques chosen, "emotion discourse" by itself is as hopeless a guide as the rest to a discourse typology.

Actually, that discourse factor is among the least sufficient and necessary in either respect, weight or cutting edge. Thus, the emotive self-reporter and other-mind reader at talk are notorious for their blindness, groping, clichés, designs, ulterior motives, sheer inventions. Or witness literature's strategy of outer/inner counterpointing, traceable from the Bible to the Icelandic saga to Hammett and Hemingway: the turbulence within the characters (revealed to us by the omniscient teller, by violent action, by inference) polarizes with their dispassionate self-expression, sweet talk and pregnant silence included. The narrative poem "Anger in the Works", by Muriel Spark (2004: 47), miniatures this strategy of inner/vocal counterpoint, dead against "emotion discourse": "Anger filled her body and mind, it // permeated her insides, her throat // and heart throbbed with anger. ('Beware // the ire of the calm.') There was // anger in her teeth, nails and hair. // It drummed in her ears. // 'How lovely to see you,' she said, // 'Do sit down.'"

Hence, theoretically, these emotive markers are not only limited and unreliable but also dispensable and replaceable. Replaceable, moreover, even by diverse verbal indirections, among other substitutes out of their range. Just as Emmott's third-person deixis can give place to names and referring phrases, so can a subject exchange the lexically emotive "I got angry" for the actional objective correlative "I wanted to kill him". Who needs the adjective to make emotional sense of the act, wishful or performed? Herman in effect acknowledges it toward the end of the section, when he leaps from "emotion discourse" (e.g., "scared") to "emotionology" as governing and interpreting "behaviors" (e.g., "running away from a threatening agent or event"). Why, then, so dwell on the former? Nor would we need the latter in turn, if it applies to such familiar, transparent behaviour. Indeed, the claims made for "new emotionological paths and linkages" as measures of "generic innovation" are no more demonstrated (nor apparently demonstrable in this framework) than those concerning the recognition of "spy thrillers and romance novels" by their emotive vocabulary. "Wanted: A Discourse Emotionology, Literary and Otherwise" would make a truer bottom line.[19]

A fortiori, a generic emotionology, peculiar to narrative in its narrativity. As it is, Herman illustrates and generalizes from a story, but the analysis mixes storied ("took off running") and non-storied ("scared") features: narration with self- and other-description, dynamics with statics. Further, the latter component may elsewhere so predominate as to cross beyond narrative altogether. For, unlike actions, there is nothing generic about adjectives, emotives, language in general. So Herman's drive toward a better narratology once more starts on the wrong foot: with common rather than distinctive properties, with surface forms rather than the underlying forces that mobilize and specialize them. The very linguistic forms used by a speaker to tell and by another to question what he felt (or, in Herman's example, she) are as available to describing what one feels (or not) at the moment or even habitually. E.g., "I got scared" vs. 'I am (or, am always) scared": same emotive-discourse word, polar discourse genres. It is again the word's interaction with the appropriate world, in or out of action, that makes, or breaks, the difference.

Therefore, once reoriented toward how this mobile world affects us as such in the (dis)orderly telling – via the inherent, discourse-length mechanisms of suspense, curiosity, surprise between times – narrative study comes to enjoy a rare advantage. It then least depends on the advent of a general emotionology, any more than on an all-embracing comprehension theory ("cognitionology"), to formulate the universals of experience specific to its genre and to assimilate to them whatever the characters may happen (or be likely) to feel, and we about the characters, all along. Therefore, it is exactly on those universals of experience as mobilized by narrative suspense, curiosity, and surprise – our prospective, retrospective,

---

19. The quest may well begin by drawing together the numerous heterogeneous insights into "emotionology" found in the annals of various disciplines – poetics, aesthetics, psychology, philosophy, neuroscience – so as to sort out, assess, and if possible, integrate the available knowledge. (A recent step in this direction is Robinson (2005), whose references include "discursive psychology.") Further, an interdisciplinary restart promises the wanted advance in theorizing interlevel traffic among emotive factors and forces, as outlined in the commentary above. The same holds for interlevel "cognitive" traffic: e.g., the dovetailing of language-based with overall "inferology" in my analysis of Jane Austen's poetics (Sternberg 1978: 129–58) or the presupposition/factivity/epistemology juncture (Sternberg 2001b) or the law's If-Plot (Sternberg 2008).

and recognitive movements between the telling and the told – that I based
the genre's dynamics of emotion and its emotion/cognition interdynamics
(For an outline, with references that flesh it out, see Sternberg 2003a:
esp. 379–85.) On such a basis, the approach even transcends the chronic
emotive/cognitive divide: it subsumes and correlates both halves of the
mind under the same three kinetic forces. Another strong argument for
this mentalist, processual narratology, with a considerable body of work
to support it in analytic practice.

5.   Perspective between narrativity and language: an interdisciplinary test case

The third issue surveyed, "perspective",[20] is demonstrably as *non*focal in
the cognitivism of the last thirty years, and a late arrival, too. A strange
thing, really, because cognition, in or out of discourse, amounts (at least
adheres) by nature to perspectivity in the wide sense; and stranger yet, because this fundamental (near-)equivalence has been narrowed, as will
emerge, even by the cognitivist latecomers. But a fact nonetheless. On the
other hand, perspective looms large in narratology – including recent
work by literary and cinematic cognitivists – certainly much larger than
role/character, let alone emotion vis-à-vis meaning. Over the last century,
it has even received greater and finer attention than suggested by Herman's targeting of two problematic Structuralist lines (Genette, Stanzel).
Were it not for this targeting, his claim of cognitivist superiority (by appeal to linguistic cognitivism at that) would appear still less reasonable
than it does. How can the juxtaposition of such unequal disciplinary
bodies of work reflect credit on the newcomer? The odds against it would,
if anything, play into the hands of the opposite, anti-cognitivist agenda.
(Which is why my own overview [Sternberg 2003a,b, 2004] has refrained
from juxtaposing the two on this ground, except in passing.)

---

20. Scare quotes, because the usage here is other than mine. Since Sternberg
(1978: 260ff., 1982a), I have assigned "perspective" to what marks any discourse subject (author, narrator, quoter, quotee, perceiver, thinker, receiver)
and "point of view" to the interplay, or "montage", of "perspectives" in the
discourse as a whole or any segment of it. But this conceptual difference from
all the approaches cited by Herman would complicate terminologies. As a
lesser evil, therefore, my argument here, including its key reference to "montage", is generally cast in terms of the standard label, "perspective."

Even so, at a deeper, programmatic level, Herman's confrontation of these particular disciplines on this particular front is arguably more, not less, justified and suggestive than his earlier bids for advance. After all, narratology has traditionally, often definitionally addressed itself to literary or otherwise linguistic narrative; the issue of perspective has been its main battleground, as with the two Structuralisms cited, yet also before and since; the ongoing disputes include the very question whether its central concepts (e.g., narrator, time-indexing) apply outside the specific medium (e.g., to unvoiced and tenseless film). So, perhaps, a fresh start made, or inspired, by experts in language could indeed help to resolve the quarrels and generally reorient inquiry into perspective? From this quarter, such initiatives have already been launched, only to end in deadlock or marginality.[21] But then, Herman turns to a school boasting a new mental foundation, an unorthodox realignment of language with language use, and a declared interest in "perspective". So it may conceivably promise a route to a better narratology, this time.

What Herman picks in either field for coverage and comparison apropos viewpoint has grown too specialized for me to go into its detailed reanalysis here. By now, though, a more general review should be enough, or even the better way, to indicate how major problems, lessons, and prospects that we have already brought out newly extend to this domain. In disciplinary terms, they will also foreground how cognitive linguistics stands to the analysis of discourse, especially storytelling, verbal or otherwise.

Stands in reason, I mean – as one enterprise to its neighbour, one set of competences to their complements – not just in existing individual, uneven practice, such as that of Talmy and/or Langacker (Herman's authorities) vis-à-vis their narratological opposite numbers. In turn, understanding this relation or, one hopes, interrelation will highlight some fundamental difficulties in the programme and performance of the cognitivism at issue – now also relative both to traditional linguistics and to other cognitivisms, including the action-modeling branch. Inversely, coming to terms with these relations, however unflattering, has its positive face: it suggests how correlated knowledge may best serve the interests of either

---

21. The most notorious case, oriented to Chomskyan linguistics, is Banfield (1982): on which see, for example, McHale (1983), Sternberg (1982a, 1982b, 1991a), Fludernik (1993: esp. 360 ff., with further references). It's worth observing that, though long considered idiosyncratic in narratology, this formalist approach newly circulates in Duchan et al. (1995), which represents another branch of linguistic cognitivism.

discipline, and a future interdiscipline, particularly in our state of ignorance about the mind.

All along, finally, "perspective" will prove a testing ground par excellence. Not only do the two disciplinary enterprises for once meet there, but their juncture turns out to be larger than appears and they themselves turn out to involve partial analytic viewpoints on the subject matter, especially uniform among the linguists. Their ideological perspective on canonical ("grammatical") perspective compounds the difficulties vis-à-vis the narrative mind and the differences from narratology. Below cognitivism's science-like descriptiveness, for example, there lurk regular value-laden imbalances, in favour of a certain making, goal, side, norm, priority, in brief, that supposedly typifies the language we use. Despite the necessary shortcuts taken by the argument, I hope it will gradually establish these claims and draw them together, in programmatic outline at least.

First, observe the recurrence of a hole left at the heart of inquiries into storied world-construction, memory, role, character, positioning, feeling, medium. With each of these components, we have found the question of generic difference out of sight and mind, in need of raising as well as resolving. All being staples, even universals of representation in any text or form or code, and accordingly nonspecific – shared by description, inter alia – what is it that singles out their narrative variants?

Similarly with omnipresent, all-purpose mechanisms, such as the figure/ground relations centralized by Reuven Tsur and Tony Veale here. Tsur begins by illustrating figure/ground reversal from a funny story ("an old joke in Soviet Russia about a guard who …") and Veale associates this reversal throughout, as a matter of course, with jokes and humour at large of the storied kind. To sharpen the point, at least for the benefit of readers unfamiliar or unhappy with the figure/ground terminology, I would add that, in terms of impact, their reversal involves a shock of estrangement: the stories amusingly twist round our assumptions about their narrated world and/or narrative surface, with a view to perceptual renewal ("making strange"). So far, so good. But jokes, a fortiori humour, needn't operate in story form. Inter alia, the descriptive "Why is X like Y? Because…" format equally qualifies, since the accepted comparative portraiture of X vs. Y is as reversible by the answer into an unexpected figure/ground juxtaposition, with estranging impact to match. (Tsur even offers nonrepresentational equivalents, e.g., sound patterns.) How, then, does the all-purpose, crossgeneric, crosslevel mechanism work to special effect in, or on, narrative? This special impact would necessarily involve the genre's peculiar double temporality, not least its breaches and reversals of event-order with an eye to unexpected twists. If so, how does the shock of estrangement (as a crossdiscourse device) join forces with narrative surprise proper (as a gap in the narrated world abruptly opened for belated recognition)?[22] And the counterparts to figure/ground reversal in the next exchange, on "verbal humour", exemplified from novels, leave much the same dark hole between the general and the generic.

With "perspective", this hole now extends to yet another major component (arguably, *the* component) of textuality. Persistently absent throughout the approaches – narratological *or* cognitivist – is the issue's generic distinctiveness: here, the relation of narrative viewpoint to narrativity. As usual, the question itself never arises, though a prerequisite to genre-specific analysis vis-à-vis non-narrative and a measure of comparison among analyses. For "perspective" (as viewpoint on reality, or, wider, subject/object relation) cuts across every line of discourse, semiotics, art, and their most divergent practices. For example, an ancient Egyptian picture stands to one in "central perspective" as omniscient (or Genette's "non-focalized") does to restricted ("internally focalized") telling. A notorious staple and battleground of painting since the Renaissance, perspective equally attaches to all description as well as storytelling, in all media, or intermedia, to all argumentation, to all expression and reception and mentation. You simply can't represent anything, anyhow, from an absolute zero-point. So, as I've often asked before, What is narrative about so-called "narrative perspective"? How else, unless we first pinpoint its distinctiveness from other discourse types, can we trace its workings in narrative (or a particular narrative) *as such* and assimilate them to the rest of the genre's features? Within narrative itself, how else to establish the unity in variety, or explore the variety in unity, among generic manifestations of perspective in different components, works, authors, subgenres, media? (E.g., speech vs. thought, the *Odyssey* vs. *Ulysses*, Austen vs. Dickens, oral vs. written, verbal vs. visual or cinematic, respectively.)

Second, the answer to this key question – what is narrative about narrative perspective? – must lie in the genre's differentia specifica, its narrativity. Further, the answer must be sought there regardless of how narrativity is conceived: whether located in the happening itself (the objectivist

---

22. On this juncture, within a wider framework, see Sternberg (2006), in the special double issue on "Estrangement Revisited' already mentioned. Also, recall that the modern promoter of the concept, Viktor Shklovsky, highlighted examples from humour and parody.

Aristotle-old way, which still dominates both narratology and cognitivist story analysis) or in the interplay between the happening and the telling/reading sequences, on my functionalist/processual theory. For narrativity, in short, does perspective just bear on events rather than on states or existents (the only answer, I would argue, open to the entire Aristotelian line) or does it also constitute a (discourse) event in its own right and its own spacetime, mobile by nature? Mobile, because every such perspectivizing event (of telling, viewing, quoting, hearing, remembering) intersects, as well as co-extends, with the events perspectivized, so that they can always dynamize each other.[23] The latter reconception has the advantage of meeting and integrating a basic fact: that, once narrativized, perspective uniquely happens, evolves, twists, darkens, reads in time, between times – just like the action itself, with which it interacts – and so gets constructed as part of the overall generic processing. We never know who-will-tell-what-how beforehand, nor, having encountered and tentatively made it out, can we predict its deployment or forking or growth in the next stage, nor can we feel certain about our reading of these, in turn, until the very end, if ever. On either conception, though, narrativity lies in a world dynamics – whether taken by itself or also as mentally (re)dynamized along the given sequence – with direct implications for narrative perspective.

Herman's appeal to cognitive linguistics for a theory of perspective, and a superior one, is therefore a nonstarter, because misconceived. Viewpoints on the world, like the world viewed through them, cannot possibly reduce or even assimilate to the logic of words, any more than to other semiotic codes. (Less so, if anything, considering the disparity in signification between the arbitrariness of language and the reality-likeness of iconic or, especially, indexical systems. A portrait mirrors the portraitee, smoke betokens fire.[24]) And among such viewpoints, as well as among the worlds viewed, the dynamic, a fortiori, narrative's twice-dynamized kind, is uniquely complex, hence least reducible or assimilable to the word.

---

23. Even in life itself, once a new discovery or development changes our viewpoint – possibly in middiscourse – we henceforth see, tell, and act otherwise.
24. This disparity has recently been challenged anew (as detailed in Freeman here on language iconicity) and to productive effect, yet with a tendency to overreaching. For some discussion, especially apropos the classic champion of iconicity in art, Lessing, see Sternberg (1981, 1990a, 1999). For further counterbalance, note the reanalysis there of the third, indexical sign-type as a universal of representation: it generates all linkage by time, space, causality, metonymic shift and inference, in brief.

Third, that a word-based approach would fail outside language accordingly goes without saying. So does the corollary of failure: no unified, medium-free theory of narrativity, perspectivity, narrative perspectivity, nor a route to a differential, medium-sensitive analysis of their countless manifestations in narrative land. This only reinforces our earlier findings (e.g., apropos Emmott's person-deixis). This also reveals afresh the inconsistence in Herman's very citation of the comics example, with its strong visual component, and, impossibly, as an equivalent to the language-only egocentric repertoire of deixis, too. Likewise with the example of Cheyney's multimedia "positioning" on TV. Once committed to linguistics and/or language, especially in its untranslatable I/here/now subjectivity, you can't have it both ways.

What's more, the word-bound approach fails in turn within its ostensible proper domain, whose manifold ensemble outreaches it. The semiotic (verbal/visual), hence perspectival, compositeness of the above examples actually stretches to the linguist's own paradigm: oral, face-to-face (i.e., eye-to-eye) communication, including narration. It involves throughout a two-sided visual monitoring, inference, response – all with effects on the words and outlooks exchanged between the sides – though this encounter-length component usually goes unnoticed and untheorized, perhaps because out of the linguist's reach per se. Thus the wholesale absence of visual cues in Herman's "full transcript" and discussion of Mary's oral story, *UFO or the Devil*, as in the treatment of "emotion discourse" at large. Typical of corpus-based research, this minus reflects on the linguistics applied there.[25]

Nor do poeticians reckon with this fact of the discourser's eye. Though generally oblivious to ordinary interactive storytelling, even as imitated by oral literature (the singer of tales in sight) or by literary dialogue, they are equally oriented to the word, now on the page. It has even become fashionable to deplore the misleadingness of visual terminology. Focalization theorists would thus replace "Who sees?", deemed all too material and metaphorical, with "Who perceives?" The latter includes the strictly nonperceptual, epistemic "Who knows?" at that, for good measure, while continuing to ignore the perceiver's narratee as monitored percept, the way "Who sees?" did. The fact remains that in interpersonal contact, everyday or quoted or fictive, "*view*point" (or perspectivity) bears a literal, embodied, ocular as well as a generalized, figurative meaning.

---

25. So does a notable exception like the move toward audiovisual recording of testimony given by Holocaust survivors (see the special issue on "Humanities of Testimony" in *Poetics Today* 27:2 [2006]): common sense knows better.

Only, everyday "talk" again varies from represented "dialogue": the one has the advantage of immediacy; the other, of the intervening, talk-quoting narrator's versatility. The ocular contact that is built into the ordinary face-to-face encounter needs to be supplied in its mimesis elsewhere, in artistic and otherwise reported interchange. A linguistic report can thus directly quote no more than interlocutors' words; but a dialogue-rich novelistic art like Dickens's or Henry James's will extend the report to their paralinguistic activity. The quoter will then insert viewpoint-adjusting asides to us – stage directions, as it were – about the glances thrown, stolen or exchanged between the quoted dialogists, often pregnant with inference from whose-when-how to why. In the theatre and the cinema, such directions in the script are also physically embodied (even multiplied at will) in the actors' visible, expressive, lifelike eye movements. Across all differences in immediacy or semiosis, again, the represented eye has multiple percepts. This visual field, or target, actually ranges from one's partner to the here-and-now speech arena to the space around it, all of them information-laden externals that humanly elude the full (in)sight desired.[26]

If anything, the term "viewpoint" privileges one of the interlocutor's senses to the detriment of another, which equally provides us with extra-verbal clues to mind-reading, hence to viewpoint in the broader usage. The eye monitoring facial expression or body language has a paralinguistic equivalent and complement in the ear's alertness to intonation, which can always override what the uttered words tell. Far from negligible, therefore, both these nonverbal aids to mind-reading signal, reveal, weigh no less (often, actually, more) than the verbal encoding that belongs to linguistics proper. Not to mention how these senses process the written/voiced words themselves (e.g., the hearer's inner ear in Sternberg [1986]) or extralinguistic reality (e.g., the traditional concern with the be-

---

26. Or, if you like, they elude the desired God's eye view (to use a phrase that linguistic cognitivism itself [e.g., Lakoff (1987), echoed in Langacker (1995)] has borrowed from Hilary Putnam in a related connection, that of the fight against objectivist semantics, cognition, epistemology as "metaphysical realism"). Suggestively, Biblical narrative shows God transcending this ocular limit, in dialogue and elsewhere, to polarize with human constraint. "Man sees what meets the eye and God sees into the heart" (I Samuel 16:7, and discussion in Sternberg [1985: 84ff.]) In essentials, though, such ideoliterary perspectival license – "metaphysical realism" dramatized in action, counter to Lakoff et al.'s uniform world-mind-language picture – is exemplary rather than exceptional: more on this below.

holder's eye in narrative analysis since Henry James, and much earlier, of course, in pictorial theory).[27] Along with the substantive implications for the approach to viewpoint, those for the pooling of the best available disciplinary tools accordingly mount.

But then, the perspectival range of discourse – as against its surface encoding – only begins with the senses. Even beyond eye-to-eye contact, as on the telephone or the internet or the novelistic page, there always remain nonverbal, possibly never verbalized features and axes of viewpoint: knowledge horizons, perceptual factors, ontic distances, emotive attitudes, cultural markers or lenses, value schemes, self-awareness, communicativeness, intentionalities, ideologies, abilities, liabilities, and so forth. Bundling such features and axes into the mixed bag of "context", as is widely done in effect, not only blurs their distinctness and diversity. It also occludes the perspectivity of "context" itself, which is nothing but a flexible multiplex of enclosing viewpoints, (re)constructed and orchestrated afresh on each discursive occasion.[28]

Moreover, these various and variously codable axes of perspective diversify among the narrative participants, from the author downward, with tell-tale cross references (e.g., the knowing opposed to the ignorant, the right-thinking to the villain, the speaker to the soliloquist). They also grow doubly complex whenever mediating a higher-level perspective, again from the implicit authorial vantage point downward – as always in fiction and otherwise quoting transmission.

This ensues from the rule that to interpose a voice/view (i.e., a mediator between oneself and one's addressee) is to quote it; and to quote is to frame within another discourse, with other ends *in* view, which must rank above and can run against the original's. The quoted *inset*, which re-presents the original, stands to the quoting *frame* as part to whole: discourse incorporated within discourse is thereby subordinated to a higher authority in

---

27. As a syncretic art, the cinema inherits and enlarges this multifold repertoire. So, less famously, do other intermedia, especially word/image composites devised by literature and verbal narrative proper, as in the "ekphrastic" representation of visual art. There, the interart twofold (discourse about other-coded discourse) compounds perception and perspectivity generally, all within a linguistic frame: see the multiplexes and processes analyzed in Yacobi (2000, 2002, 2004).

28. So conceptualized, this familiar pretheoretical umbrella term will appear below as a shorthand, alongside the theoretical "frame", in my sense, namely: the highest operative viewpoint on the (discourse) world and the other, inset viewpoints on it.

meaning, function, and viewpoint at large. In turn, there ensue further consequences for the status of the verbal relative to the nonverbal. The frame needn't be linguistically manifest at all (as with "John would go tomorrow": the reader can grasp the sentence as a free indirect quote of "John will go tomorrow", one that is equivalent in context to the manifestly framed "John, she said to me, would go tomorrow"). But that wordless frame controls the inset even so: its absence leaves the givens, notably the verbal givens, odd or ambiguous, while its inference (i.e., a reportive-I tacitly framing "her" past speech to "me" about John into a certain free, half-backshifted inset) makes sense of them. Again, like the process of sense-making and its product and their purpose, the inset words given may be other than hers altogether; so may the propositional content and everything else.

On the way from original utterance to inset quote, then, the above rule-governed backshifting from "will" to "would" is a selective divergence (in tense, but minus time adverb) extendible in principle without end and constraint, always ad hoc. Any lower, inset perspective is not just necessarily affected (refracted, distanced, subordinated) by its framing. It is also open to interference on all its axes and their original subjective bearing: open to mixture (e.g., of the narrator's idiom, sight, insight with the quoted character's), to re- or dis-proportioning (e.g., thick, even verbatim report here, summary there), to re- or dis-ordering (e.g., the quote's gradual, untimely, gapped deployment), to the limit of plain misrepresentation by some unreliable quoter. What we have noted apropos "positioning" (in dialogue vs. talk) and "emotion discourse" (as self- or other-report) finds here its universal principle, as does, inversely, the fallacy of bracketing any source with its second-hand, inset version.

Even if the resulting complex ("montage") of viewpoints appears in verbal form, then, its disentangling by us crucially involves extraverbal ambiguities on various axes, such as, Whose (mis)information? Whose (mis)judgment? Whose feeling? Whose interest? Whose summary? Whose (dis)orderly retrospect? To these puzzles, indeed, the quote's concurrent verbal enigmas themselves (e.g., Whose phonology, lexicon, grammar, dialect?) may serve as clues: the jarring misjudgment here, and with it the unreliability, is probably the quotee's rather than the quoter's – we then infer – because cast in what sounds like his idiolect. Or the other way round, if the quoter's self-expression fits better. A means to discursive problem-solving, along with the larger goals underlying the text, the verbal component also suggests the hierarchy between the respective disciplines involved. As language to the discourse as a whole, so linguistics to making sense of the discourse.

Far from local or special, as may appear in atomistic eyes, this problem-solving operation (priorities included) could hardly be more principled and widespread, or more relevant to our concerns. The inferential process of disambiguating the montage into its component views/voices isn't limited in scope – either in form or in extent, any more than in the perspectival axes brought into play. It inheres in quotation as discourse about discourse, discourse within discourse, about the world. And once you think through this fact, the reach of the process entailed strikingly widens. It characterizes the narrative mind (itself a paradigm of the discourser's mind generally) at work on the front of perspective, in concert with its operations on plot.[29]

As a universal of quotation, the need for multilevel disentanglement runs through all quoting schemata, direct, indirect, free indirect, or variously telescoped (a one-word inside view, say). Of course, we meet the need according to our lights, often with divergent or simplistic results (witness the myriad interpretive quarrels about who quotes what in which form, or the examples below of free indirectness missed, and so degrammaticalized, in cognitive linguistics). But that doesn't affect the imperative's universality, except to stretch it further, to the limit of discourse-wide power. Not just taking quotation the wrong way, but even a reader's mistaking it for self-expression, or vice versa, is determining its perspectivity still. (Compare our daily (mis)adventures between irony and plain speech.)

The protean shapes assumed by quotation do not affect their uniquely shared perspectival montage, either, but rather confirm and diversify it. In form, as just hinted, they extend much beyond the three quoting varieties – direct, indirect, free indirect – whose supposed formal definiteness as such has led to their privileging by theory. There equally qualify constructions whose surface exhibits nothing of the criterial, let alone convention-bound, discoursing about discourse, discoursing within discourse: no *manifest* re-presenting, hence re(con)textualizing and re-perspectivizing, in short. Examples of covert quoting range from second-hand "telescoped" voice ("She agreed") or inside view ("I repented") or both ("He misheard our plea") to implicit allusion (i.e., silent intertextuality) to irony (as discordant speech, best reversible into a disapproving quote) to factive ad-

---

29. For details and applications, see Sternberg (1982a, 1982b, 1983b: esp. 172–88, 1983c, 1986, 1991a, 2001b, 2005), and the sequel here. Among the follow-ups, the references to interart quotation, given in note 27 above, especially broaden the semiotic range of the theory – as do and would others to film, painting, even music.

verbs ("Unknowingly, ...") to negation as counterspeaking or even counterquoting (Sternberg 2001b: 226–37).

The range broadens yet further when we note that in some of these quoting formations (e.g., telescoping, negating) the perspectival montage is inherent, if elliptic or latent, while in others it remains contingent: mappable onto the givens but also missable or deniable, all in the reader's eye. Thus irony, polarized between given expression and guessable intention; or the unframed variant of the free indirect style, exemplified by "John would go tomorrow" above; or, most generally, any stretch of discourse whatever that, parallel to its sense-making as quotation, can somehow be understood as the discourser's own, in propria persona, unmediated and unmediating. Such open-endedness means that no linguistic form precludes quotational framing and reading. It also means that, even having been identified as quotation, it does not yet escape ambiguity among quoting schemata (notably including the direct and the indirect, or the indirect and the free indirect, as shown in Sternberg [1991a, 2001b]). Instead, the question is always which of the sense-making possibilities suits best; and, if that of reportive montage, what or whose viewpoints compose it and how to disentangle them. Still less does any form of language rule out the quoting of any discourse act within any other act, as between speech and thought, counter to Banfield's (1982) imagined "unspeakable sentences".

In these regards, the paper by Dancygier and Vandelanotte leaves much to be desired (and Vandaele's commentary rightly opposes it to the Proteus Principle). Thus their repeated insistence that this wording is "only" conceivable as, say, direct speech, and that wording is "not amenable to" free indirectness, goes even against their own bid for an unknown reportive construction, as well as for literary imaginativeness. A world of difference separates "only" from "likeliest", "not amenable" from "least easily, or habitually or functionally, adjustable". Such insistence on Do's and Don'ts gives away in miniature that formalism dies hard everywhere: the liberation promised by the cognitivist (here cognitive linguistic) turn has yet to realize itself on the ground, beginning with the discourse analyst's mind-set.

As with form, so with size: the common denominator persists regardless, amid growing variety and against traditional myopia, born of the tendency to approach reported discourse as a language (or linguistics) unit and monopoly. Instead, fiction entails the quoting of all mediators along the line of transmission. Throughout, the world-making author, himself silent, communicates with us, his discourse partners, by re-presenting the words and thoughts, voices and views, supposed to have arisen within and about the imagined world. The entire intermediate chain of transmission there is actually a chain of quotation. The authorial fiction-ist having quoted the fictive teller, the teller proceeds to quote the char-acters at speech/thought, then the characters quote one another, all the way to the inmost quote, the last inset. A descending order of quotational scope, control, awareness; an ascending order of mediateness, subordi-nacy, irony. And fact-bound (everyday, historiographic) discourse, where the author doubles as teller, only starts that chain one link after, with the quoting of the first speaking/thinking agent, the teller's own experienc-ing-I included. This further protean modularity once appreciated, our idea of narrative, as well as of quotation, will undergo a sea change accord-ingly.[30]

In magnitude, then, the direct form, especially, can extend from quoting a single-phrase utterance or thought, to a tale-within-a-tale (Schehera-zade's, the governess's in *The Turn of the Screw*, the interior monologists' in *Ulysses*), to a novel-length dramatized ("first-person") narrative, such as *Tristram Shandy*. So can free indirectness, though less extended and continuous as a rule, like that along *Emma, Madame Bovary, Mrs. Dallo-way*.[31] All are equally framed in transmission, hence equally multiperspec-tival, on each of their multiple axes, hence equally subject to overall un-packing for intelligibility in reception. Whose lapse or licence of sight, insight, judgment, coherence, grammar, and the rest, are enigmas that face us on the macro- as on the micro-scale.

All, that is, entail gaps in the discourse about discourse about the world, which parallel and cross the gaps in the world discoursed about, so that the respective closures run together, interdependently. In sense-mak-ing, the narrative mind willy-nilly seeks to dovetail representation with communication, the told with the telling, plot with perspective, on pain of incoherence, from local to global. And the more troublesome (elusive, restless, intricate, piecemeal) the fit between them, the more salient this generic universal of joint disambiguation, which elsewhere we often im-plement in our stride. The difference is not in the language per se but in the smoothness or otherwise of its mapping onto an object/subject com-posite or network of relations. E.g., to determine whether Henry James's *The Turn of the Screw* represents ghosts, we must determine whether the governess telling of them reliably voices *or* fallibly, subjectively counter-

---

30. The same holds for equivalents in intermedia relations (e.g., a story evoking a statue, which may itself allude to an earlier artwork) or outside language altogether (e.g., one picture framing another).
31. For a comprehensive and language-sensitive monograph, see Fludernik (1993).

points the underlying, enclosing Jamesian ontology, and vice versa. Does she just mediate an abnormal event-sequence, or does she project her own ghosts onto a normal one? Yet the twofold puzzle, rich in verbal clues, defies any univocal resolution all along, to leave us with an irreducibly double plot/perspective, impossible in any possible world. (Likewise, only minus the controlling authorial frame, with real-life storytelling, as in *UFO and the Devil*: was the glowing orange Big Ball actually seen by the teller, Mary, or just fantasized?) This extreme accordingly brings to the fore the narrative rule, as well as James's modernist poetics. The action transmitted always shuttles between darkness and light in accordance with the transmission.

Yet on either of these gap-to-closure fronts – both mobile in narrative – the word comes second to the world, represented and/or discursive, perspectivized and/or perspectivizing more than one way. Evidently, like the perspectival axes themselves, the quoting mediator's operations on them, and inversely our own reading of what belongs to whom in the given mediate composite, argue for a versatile approach: protean, semiotic, culture-wide, aesthetics included.

An inescapable matter of principle, therefore, the rule of perspective's irreducibility/unassimilability to the verbal code extends in turn to all linguistic storytelling – vocal ("natural") or written, without as within literary art. And it often applies there several times over. Referring the storied viewpoint to the story's words (just like referring the story and/in its storiness to them) is attaching the whole to one of its parts: the subjectivizing function to a surface form that neither governs nor covers or monopolizes nor even distinguishes it *as* narrative. Quite the reverse. This formal part is only a means to the operative perspectival strategy, a subject-bound dimension among others (e.g., the ontic, the epistemic, the ideological, the artful) and, even as such, the common property of all linguistic discourse.

To clinch the point yet another way, examine the perspectival parameters that Herman would import from cognitive linguistics to "cognitive narratology" (indeed, to every advanced "postclassical" narratology) in the light of our key question. The outcome is clear-cut. Far from distinguishing the viewpoint specific to verbal narrative in its narrativity, *all* these imported parameters conflate it with the antipole of descriptive writing. As far as the grammar's tool-box goes, the two representational extremes – one bearing on the world in flux, the other on the world at rest – do not polarize but meet here. Thus Langacker's trio: "selection", "perspective" (e.g., figure/ground, subjectivity/objectivity, vantage point, deixis), and "abstraction" (amount of detail or granularity). Thus also Talmy's quartet: the viewpoint's "location", "distance" from the viewed object, "mode" (e.g., synoptic vs. sequential), and "direction". At best, the two imports from linguistics are geared to some filtering or orientational devices that cut across the miscellany of linguistic representations.[32] So, as with earlier common properties like world, character, role, emotivity, humour, what is narrative about narrative perspective? Blind to genre, even verbal genre, either of these perspectival sets fails narratology's leading test (or the description analyst's, for that matter). Nor does either excel by other criteria, from novelty to range to finesse.

Unsurprisingly so, and on disciplinary grounds too. Cognitive linguistics as such does not involve or bestow, nor do its practitioners often acquire besides, any special competence outside the language system: not even in language-as-discoursed, far less in narrative or otherwise generic discourse, any more than do psychologists or AI researchers or neuroscientists or noncognitive linguists. Or, in professional terms, the language/discourse juncture necessarily makes an *inter*discipline, one of the vastest and trickiest, hence requiring dovetailed analytic competences to suit. They have to suit, that is, the immense range and diversity, not of verbal functions and types and corpora alone, but also of the users (groups, individuals, speakers, hearers, writers, readers, "cognizers" at large) and the skills (knowledge, know-how, "experience") internalized by them. That immensity of both subject matters and subjective minds (viewpoints, in other words) is obviously irreducible to a grammar, nor, operationally, mastered or often so much as appreciated by grammarians. As linguistic does not subsume literary competence – almost the reverse, if anything – so with the respective meta-competences: they form an ascending order of specialized training. And literature only exemplifies one of many language/discourse junctures, along with a myriad semiotic games beyond them, narrative, above all.

---

32. No better is Fauconnier's all-purpose "mental space", which compounds sheer figurative indefiniteness with indicriminateness. Worse, "space" skews it toward the descriptive extreme, or more generally, toward patterning of, by, into coexistence. Inversely, this makes it the wrong figure for all the time-related, let alone time-dominated, objects, aspects, imperatives, resources, processes, constructs that attach to linguistic as linear discourse and culminate in narrative as a genre living between temporalities. Inter alia, Dancygier and Vandelanotte here could therefore profitably dispense with this unhelpful blanket figure.

An obvious truth, it still needs to be re-stressed. For this is where the promise of cognitive linguistics goes with a basic problem, one that, regrettably, passes for revolutionary strength. Also typically so, in line with the field's disinclination to self-scrutiny regarding fundamentals – here underlined by the critique of earlier or rival schools. And, again, most relevantly so to our business with "perspective". In the two influential linguistic enterprises hailed by Herman, viewpoint ranges even further than declared, or than may seem, being inseparable from (if not tantamount to) the language-wide umbrellas of "conceptualization/construal" plus encoding. Together, these encompass, roughly, the subjective imaging of things as it gets expressed (or mirrored) in words, and so the pairing of meaning with form undertaken by cognitive linguistics. Nowhere among cognitivism's subdisciplines do mindwork and perspective so intermesh in theory, more or less explicitly.

The counterargument that I'll outline on this wide front is accordingly best specified in direct relation to our narratological focus of interest. For now, just a few comments on the fundamental problem. To a poetician, it will ring a bell, as a cognitivist reversion to the Structuralist imperialism preached by Roman Jakobson (1960). On his platform, linguistics ranges over all verbal behaviour, all uses of language, hence subsumes all the dealings with them, including those of poetics with "verbal art". In effect, across sea changes in the approach to language, this takeover bid resurges here. Cognitive linguists may not say so, nor perhaps think so – or not with Jakobson's language-is-language consequentiality, which at least avoids half-and-half inconsistence – but it follows from the programme and increasingly translates into extramural practice, with special reference to literature again.

Briefly, then, cognitive linguistics aspires to break with the disciplinary tradition in (newly) rejecting the line drawn between system and speech-use since de Saussure (Jakobson's own antagonist). Officially gone here is the divorce of *langue* from *parole*, of competence from performance, of code from message, or coding, and so of linguistic from pragmatic (or specifically poetic) analysis.[33] This in the name of meaning, elevated to top priority and declared indivisible from the rest of our experience with the

---

33. Not that traditionalists, or so-called micro-linguists, have overlooked the problematics of the distinction, resolvable only through an idealized language system. (For a lucid account, see Lyons [1977: esp. chapter 14]). The question concerns, instead, the relative merits of idealizing, as against nullifying, the divide.

world and the communicative world alike. As the former experience ties linguistic meaning to encyclopedic knowledge, so does the latter to similarly inclusive knowledge of how *parole* works, to discourse at large. Long spurned by the mainstream of linguistics as too unruly for the system-builder's notice – and in immediate reaction to the otherwise cognitive but formalist generative linguistics – discourse becomes here a cornerstone, under whatever label.

Like the arts, sciences elude any rigorous delimitation and can gain from stretching their boundaries, however defiantly or untidily. As the record shows, this is the case here, including well-known extensions to literature (its figurative aspect, above all) and appeal to literary practitioners. Herman's statement regarding the importance that cognitive inquiry has assumed "within the field of narrative analysis" would apply with more justice to this different subfield, as to the Jakobsonian poetics of poetry at the time. Its interests and influence keep ramifying, as our volume attests. And yet, the cognitive linguistic programme doesn't seem to have been thought through, with traceable effects on the practice.

Carried to its logical conclusion, such erasure of the *langue/parole* boundary would mean that cognitive linguistics undertakes to encompass all the language games played in all kinds, corpora, eras, worlds of discourse, because it must ground itself in our communicative experience as a whole. With discourse knowledge, you can't pick and choose among usages – high or low, dated or current, artistic or professional or colloquial – any more than you can, as all-or-nothing experientialist, halve the encyclopedia. This makes an unreasonable, because self-defeating, undertaking for *codifiers* of a grammar across usages, and humanly unfeasible as well. Too much of a good thing. Yet the logical choice is between this multiple absurdity of precommitment to all things linguistic and some mentalized variant of the disciplinary code-before-use hierarchy: between wild overreaching, born of revolutionary overreaction, and newly adapted traditionalism.

This inescapable dilemma and its forced resolution would appear to have escaped notice among cognitive linguistic practitioners. So would the twin dilemma regarding encyclopedic knowledge. For worlds, factual, fancied, fictive, vary as much in their furniture and structure (existential "lexicon" and "syntax") as usages; let alone the free correlations between the two, or subjective differences in the experience of either or both. With the fundamental problem compounded, you would expect its hopelessness to be faced at least, if not to force some accommodation, duly interiorized, with the Saussurean paradigm. Even postulating a determinate language system and experiencer (out of the numerous candidates) as reference point, hence as methodological viewpoint on mental viewpoint, would help to rationalize this cognitive programme and enable judicious extension to some alternative frames of reference: only the universalist aspirations would need to wait for a breakthrough in the harder mind sciences.

Instead, the subdiscipline practises in effect a middle way, or rather, an assortment of middle ways, all necessarily arbitrary and ill-defined. The field of study gets delimited by cognitive linguists according to how each individual practitioner chooses or chances to push the line beyond *langue* – inclusively here, exclusively there – or to push it for now, subject to its redrawing elsewhere on the next occasion. But no matter where one draws the line, there remain too many diverse and discordant language uses to codify under any single system of rules. Hence the constant recourse to devices whereby some uses may nevertheless be judged superior in encoding to others: grammatical, canonical, prototypical, and the like. Call this fallback squaring the circle, or eating one's cake and having it too, or the mainstream orthodoxy under a heterodox guise; but the thing can't be practised in reason. The very judgments on so-called linguistic grammaticality etc. are usage-dependent, indeed biased for or against, and so invertible with the change of subcode, context, discourse type, reference point. Likewise, of course, with the encyclopedia, a fortiori with the twofold mental whole. If one frame's unacceptable is another's standard, or passable, if one's world knowledge is another's ignorance, if one's centre is another's periphery, then the grammar gets in theory caught between them, for it can adjudicate (or rank) only by going against *some* "experience". But it keeps adjudicating nevertheless, or else it would be out of grammatical business. (The illogic will be exemplified below from perspective and the cognitive linguistic perspective on it.)

Further, overambition goes with underequipment. Even supposing an omni-linguistics both possible and pursued in its true spirit, the armature of analytic tools needed for the job couldn't possibly be forged within linguistics alone (nor within the language-oriented pragmatics that it aspires to displace). Take Herman's authorities, second to none in the field. What qualifies a one-disciplinary Talmy or Langacker to handle phenomena outside the language code, or the sentence boundary, as they would do? Incredibly, Talmy reinvents narrative theory from scratch, generalizing over all the genre's media, "whether conversational, written, theatrical, filmic, or pictorial", in "all existent and potential forms" (2000: II, 417). A note (which I cite from the article version, since it was mostly deleted in the 2000 book) even underlines the wholesale reinvention as such, post factum. "After this chapter was almost complete, I became aware of the work of Genette (1980) and other structural narratologists and of the considerable overlap between their approaches and mine" (1995: 423, n.2): sorry, but too late for a restart on this basis or for undue worry. After all, "the cognitive perspective" will make the difference anyway, as it were, via an introspection-based approach. One can imagine what he would say were a narratologist to "embark on a project" of language theorizing "without having first consulted the relevant literature in a neighboring field". The work of an amateur, and the results show as deep as the theory's mixtures of narrativity with sequentiality, of narration with quotation, of storied with real world-imaging, of fictional (hence e.g., omniscient) with nonfictional epistemology, of latent (e.g., pictorial) with manifest or mandatory yet flexible (e.g., linguistic, cinematic) ordering in time, or of poesis with genesis. Some of the blurs will be familiar by now, along with that between the narrative and the descriptive genre regarding so-called "perspective" itself.

Similarly with Talmy's and Langacker's unguided ventures into related long-time discourse cruxes. Examples include the notions of event, speech event, speech act, participant, indirect report, or, again, viewpoint itself, where all these meet in effect. Throughout, a little knowledge indeed proves a dangerous thing, visibly and explicably so; and nowhere more so than for an inquiry committed to a grounding in experience as a whole, and with inquirers who apparently don't even know what one needs to know for the purpose. "I cannot claim any serious expertise in regard to discourse, nor any extensive familiarity with the vast literature in this area [...]. My concern is rather to articulate how Cognitive Grammar and discourse might be brought together, as a matter of principle" (Langacker 2001: 144). The two sentences read like a contradiction in terms, especially when it comes to articulating an interdisciplinary principle, and from this particular disciplinary standpoint of a discourse-based Grammar at that.

The required expert knowledge beyond the linguist's ken as such concerns not only the manifold parts and heterocosms and, specifically, perspectives (eye, ear, value, feeling, interest, existence, epistemology, artistry, self-consciousness...) in discourse, but also the ever-shifting teleology of part/whole relations there. Ever-shifting, against both the linguist's vested interest, as codifier, in pairing form with function (here, meaning) and, among the diversity of functions, in privileging the representational, information-bound one, "communicative' in this narrow sense.[34] Instead, in face of the variations open to and practised by language use, the teleology needs to be set free in principle and laboriously studied in all its empirical workings on record, among actual (or possible) experiencers. One must learn how discourse forces (beliefs, conventions, inventions, hierarchies, exigencies, licences, norms, types, poetics) govern (choose, map, pattern, adjust, recast, override at will) the forms of language to suit whatever ends operate in context: to specialize (re-systematize, perspectivize, if you will) language *into* narrative, event-oriented, as against descriptive discourse, for example. This even when the former genre dispenses with any coded event-markers, or exhibits the same verbs as would the latter. For every representation, directed perforce toward spacetime, both narrates and describes, manifestly or latently; only the balance of these forces (one oriented to time, the other to space) can therefore determine the verbal forms in play. Or, inversely, the forms can only signal, not separate or scale, the polar forces that inform them.[35] Amid comparable surface likeness, discourse forces also oppose an act of promise to a threat, an indirect to a direct and free indirect report, a speech to a thought event in any reportive form, self-expression to quotation's perspectival complex. No typology without teleology, no sense-making (top-down or bottom-up) without a sense of purpose, no viewpoint without an operative reference point, whereby alone differences assume, forfeit, modify their differential weight. Here exactly lives what I call the Proteus Principle; and to its boundless force/form interplay linguists can bring at most the systemic verbalized component of it – unless they turn toward a genuine interdisciplinarity.

As cognitivists, again, theirs would have to be for the purpose a threefold, language/discourse/mentation equipment. For the same must of extraverbal competence applies (and here, undisputably) to their theories of mind. "We must recognize that linguistic semantics is not an autonomous enterprise, and that a complete analysis of meaning is tantamount to a complete account of developmental cognition" (Langacker 1990: 3). With the difference that, unlike the considerable knowledge available to insiders about (narrative) discourse, these grand accounts of cognition re-

---

34. E.g., Langacker (1991: 1–2); or the editorial statement made in the first issue of on language as "an instrument for organizing, processing, and conveying information." This at a time when other linguistic scholars were beginning to realize what poetics (including Jakobson's) has always known: the multiple roles of language, even in its "semantic" component.

35. More, with some references, below.

main speculative and controversial even among the experts, voguish "embodiment" included. For the linguist, as for the rest of us, therefore, acquiring cognitive expertise would only bring home the meagreness and limits of existing hard knowledge, the distance between scientism and science. The larger the claims about the mind, alas, the weaker the evidence for what really, let alone universally happens in it, how, where, when, why. Beyond the fragmentary, low-level experimental findings available to psychology or psycholinguistics or neuroscience, it's all guesswork in the dark, however glorified, and likely to remain so for the visible future. The riddle of emotivity is only more often acknowledged than the unknown quantities of the embodied, categorizing, understanding, troping, blending, remembering, imagining, evolving mind. The Langacker-et-Talmy internals now directly relevant to us – the mind "conceptualizing", or "construing", and its linguistic factotum, the "coding" mind – belong to the same order of improvised grand theorizing: if anything, on the grandest scale of all, mental or disciplinary. And they are typically, cognitive-linguistically, problematic even as such, we'll discover at second glance below.

This shaky mental foundation would accordingly compromise rather than validate any inquiry built on it, whether into social action or language or literature or aesthetics or culture as a whole. One might as well turn to the armchair philosophers, or emulate them, and some do. Others, like Talmy (2000, 1: 4–6), opt for introspection as the leading "methodology" whereby to discover "scientifically" our "cognitive systems": not of language alone but also of narrative, visual perception, attention, memory, affect, reasoning, culture, and of what binds them all together (Talmy 2000, 1: 15–17; 2: 417–20). *Mirabile dictu.*

Of course, those who nevertheless prefer a speculative cognitivism to any traditional or trendy line probably have the future on their side; yet it would appear unwise to invest too much in the unknown, even so. Nor do we students of language use, literary art, narrative or semiotic behaviour need to know, for our purposes, everything that the neuroscientist (say) dreams of establishing: the thresholds of relevance markedly vary. In our state of ignorance, we'd better settle for less than the magic key to the black box: for patterns of readerly experience, above all, as the discourse analyst's baseline and guideline rolled into one.

Consider again the anchorage I suggest, to this end, in the universals of processing (prospective, retrospective, recognitive) forced on the mind along the sequence and, narratively, when caught between sequences. Caught on the move between past and future, between knowledge and incomprehension of the events told, how can the reader help wondering about the opaque developments ahead, or wanting to settle mysteries left behind, or bumping against unexpected disclosures?[36] For our purposes, descriptive and explanatory, we may well do then without a key to the enigma that lies below the enigma about the narrative mind thus solvable in functional terms; that is, do without a key to what makes humans so respond, with suspense/curiosity/surprise, to a gapped gestalt in time, to a deformed event-line, to perceptibly missing and dechronologized information, to a state (a fortiori, a process) of epistemic uncertainty and disequilibrium, or without a key to what neurally, rather than operationally, narratively, subdivides the three responses in turn. The deeper secrets, which I for one would like to know, can wait.

The more so because the dynamics built into reading a story of an action, or characters-in-action, also subsumes ("narrativizes") all the axes on which we respond to the unfolding storied world. As I've argued elsewhere (e.g., Sternberg 1978, 1985: esp. 321 ff., 1992, 2001a, 2003a: esp. 353 ff.), those universals cover and energize and integrate our whole experience of the generic discourse: what and how the reader comprehends, perceives, evaluates, feels, structures, generalizes, aestheticizes, and the rest. That the nonnarrative itself assimilates to narrativity, in the twofold generic process of disclosure cum development, has indeed emerged with each of the crossgeneric elements, means, goals, patterns, responses discussed thus far, from character onward. Evidently, the workings of suspenseful prospection, curiosity-driven retrospection, and surprising recognition must govern them all. That is why we needn't wait for a scientific, or cross-discoursive, "emotionology" or "cognitionology" or "inferology", either. For understanding what drives the genre as such, or us in experiencing it, these global narrative mechanisms are quite enough.

Nor do we really need the answers at the hidden level in order to advance still further. Further, I mean, than articulating, grouping, and, amid their family likeness, specifying the experiencer's basic mental responses to narrative – as entailing a (definite) troublesome sense of absence, ambiguity, instability, which presses for an (equally definite) attempt at

---

36. No wonder this suspense-curiosity-surprise trio has been empirically verified by cognitive psychologists – beginning with Brewer and Lichtenstein 1981, 1982 –though somewhat flattened in the process. Likewise verified, as predictably, is the reconstructive activity shared by these three experiences of time in time, namely: the ordering, and where necessary, reordering of the given into a chrono-logical sequence.

closure. In addition, we can progress from felt master effect to operative formal cause. Guided by those experienced universals, as I've often shown, we can identify, motivate, and interlink what triggers them: match the three forces with the assorted (con)textual forms (in narrative, the deformations of the event-line, which open and/or settle gaps) appropriate to their respective teleologies, always on the Proteus Principle. We thus map suspense (i.e., our felt uncertainty about the narrated future) onto an impending conflict, or the narrator's wink ahead, or the hero's fear, or a proleptic epithet, or a traditional happy/unhappy closure in doubt, for example; we map curiosity about antecedents onto an ambiguous back-reference, or a motive perceptibly absent, or a related outcome-before-cause disordering; and we map surprise onto any gap in our knowledge of the action concealed thus far and sprung on us after the event that we now belatedly re-cognize.

Inter alia, as I already noted and exemplified, perspectivity falls in turn under the suspense/curiosity/surprise workings, complete with the law of assimilating (de)formations to operative discourse roles and role-players as best one can at the time. Here, we trace verbal or epistemic or evaluative oddities, say, to their likeliest sources among the voices/views possibly responsible for them. How to unpack the disharmonious perspectival montage encountered at this juncture, always in line with the overall emplotment and subject to retrospective adjustment, more or less surprisingly? What reads best as a frame, what as an inset? Whose and wherefore the ill-formedness, the mis- or dis-information, the wrong judgment? Are they temporary or permanent? In or out of character? Betrayed, or ironically contrived and fronted, by the speaker? For example, an apparent gap in the omniscient narrator's knowledge, with the suspense, curiosity and surprise evoked, often finds its rationale in the inference of the narrator's (e.g., Austen's) self-limitation to a humanly limited viewer (e.g., Emma): the epistemic dissonance implies a perspectival montage of high with low knower; the privileged narration turns into privileged thought-quotation; the objective surface hides an exposure of subjectivity, laughable and/or sharable by us fellow humans, yet always changeable under the pressure of further disclosure or development (Sternberg 1978: 129–58, 277–305; 2007). Concerning viewpoint, as elsewhere, the restless form/function interplay endemic to discourse thus gains unequalled dynamism along this genre's twofold sequence. The narrative mind at work paradigmatically entails the still broader Protean mind.

Narrative is unmatched for the universality, the distinctiveness, and so the explanatory power of its workings. Still, also contrastable with the all-

or-nothing aspirations within cognitivism are Viktor Shklovsky's grounding of art in estrangement; or Aristotle's referral of tragedy to its pitiful-and-fearful impact on us; or an inner viewpoint explained as empathetic; or interpreting a given tale or poem by reference to what it does to us in the reading; or your daily processing of what you hear by what the utterer would probably have you believe or execute; and the like, always from mental (or mentalized) why's to manifest how's. Anchored there, in attested effects, we can advance on the discourse front, without undue conjecture, while waiting for the scientists to establish a proper grand mental architecture. In the interim, less is more.

The two Herman imports on viewpoint, then, neither observe nor repair any of these disciplinary limits. Instead, they endorse in transfer the linguist's occupational bias, as if language were the core and model of (narrative) discourse, rather than its subordinate and manifestation – and not the only one in either capacity, at that, not even within linguistic performance. Speaking of "role/character", and following Hendricks 1967, Herman rightly brands as a "category mistake" Structuralism's abortive approaches to story as a text-length sentence. (An even more ambitious precedent is Roman Jakobson's "Linguistics and Poetics", which would annex the latter, as "verbal art", to the former. Suggestively, narrative art, with its "referential" orientation, resists this takeover on the word-centred poetic model itself, to the embarrassment of the would-be annexor.) Yet much the same error now recurs in Herman's own proposal to rescale "operations at the clause and sentence level", identified by "cognitive grammarians", into "discourse-level structures in narrative".

Actually, the grammarians themselves already mix these levels in annexing to language, or to cognitive linguistics, a host of extralinguistic entities. Taken over, inter alia, are narrative, event, speech event, speech act, indirect report, participant, setting, troping – all the business of poetics, pragmatics, discourse analysis – as well as viewpoint. Not to mention the encyclopedic knowledge of first-order reality at large, which complements the school's desired grounding of linguistics in overall experience, at the cost of fundamental difficulty. Besides, as often in this volume, the school's literary followers and co-workers eagerly (re)apply the mixed theory to various discoursive topics. Still, the call for patterning discourse on language (in effect, sanctioning and widening the conflation) for the benefit of narratology, and in face of admonitory Structuralist precedent, is another matter. When it comes to narrative, recall, Talmy himself emphasizes its transmedial "cognitive system", across "conversational, written, theatrical, filmic, or pictorial" variations, before appropriating it nonetheless.

Further, Herman's jump between levels, and disciplines, goes (again, not alone) with an unquestioning adoption of the pictures of the mind at work invented by the grammarians. Or reinvented, because actually long precedented, too, in assorted noncognitive or otherwise cognitive guises, some viable, some often found wanting. "Conceptualization and construal" vs. "coding" variously echoes, or overlaps, such old binarisms as content/form, depth/surface, world/image, object/subject, type/token, intention/execution, language/style. The narratologist will even recall an analogue closer to home, the pivotal *fabula/sjuzhet* opposition.[37] Its one/many variability entails choices among alternative media and signs and perspectives as well as temporal (dis)orderings, all mentalized at that, on my account of narrative processing (e.g., Sternberg 1978: 8ff., 1992, 2003a,b; cf. Bordwell 1985: esp. 49–73; Walsh 2001). Thereby, one *fabula* can serve as the basis for infinitely many *sjuzhets*, via assorted lines of embodiment, deployment, transmission. (And also the other way round: from every *sjuzhet* encountered, we can construct, or reconstruct, infinitely many underlying *fabulas*.) So compare the alleged novelty: "One and the same situation or event can be linguistically encoded in different ways, by means of locutions that are truth-conditionally equivalent".

Transferring the "one/different" relation to the mind here only shifts, or reshifts, inward the familiar polarities, and mars the better ones by attaching the string of truth-conditionality, so as to exclude the whole gamut of equivalence relations other than propositional. For instance, why limit the "one/different" to "world/word" relations? Can't the former, one/different relation polarize, instead, between the unity in viewpoint among thoughts (experiences, "construals"), even utterances, and their divergence in other regards, as in the Jamesian novelistic model? (Single perceiver, changing perceptual objects, levels, factors.) Or, why can't the oneness reside in shared expressiveness or prosody or grammar (the way formal equivalences set up Jakobson's poetic function) and the difference in world-imaging or truth conditions? And can't both terms, the equivalence *and* the difference, reside in both of these domains, the word's *and* the world's? (This is how we produce a pun, a poem, a parody, an *Alice in Wonderland*.) Indeed, apropos truth value itself, why can't the given encoded telling ambiguate, hence multiply, the reconstructible "situation or event", or the

---

37. Most often translated as "story/discourse" and often divergently understood by theorists, but without much affecting the point at issue here.

reconstruction falsify the telling, so as to signal the teller's ontic deviance and associate it with his narrative goals or epistemic constraints? Wouldn't the "one/different" relation have much the same effect of unity-in-variety, variety-in-unity, perspectival as otherwise? The concept-first ("semantic", informational) model and hierarchy is evidently false to the changing priorities of communication at large, even from the producer's side.

Nor does "conceptualizing/construing" recommend itself on its own narrow premises. Turned inward, this old-new umbrella is left undemonstrated in cognitive terms, even questionable, we'll soon find; its modus operandi unexplained; its scope ill-defined (e.g., given the mind's definitional, all-inclusive subjectivity, why is "perspective" an "aspect" of construal, rather than co-referent or even superordinate?). Moreover, the admissions of ignorance about the black box scattered in the work of practitioners add up to a king-size caveat. Langacker himself frankly admits a hole at the heart of the matter. "Obviously, we cannot yet characterize the actual cognitive processing responsible for coding", namely, how "a conceptualization one wishes to express" relates to "the linguistic structures activated for that purpose" (1991: 294–95). Thinking before, or apart from, verbalizing? Meaning (like the old "content") prior to any form? Subjective intent ("wishes to express ... purpose") always fully and exactly realized, hence also unequivocally mirrored for the decoder, by "the linguistic structures activated"? And do we always "express" (or even conceptualize before it) for the same, information-sharing "purpose"? The statement thus encapsulates at least a quartet of dubious premises (on which more below) taken as foundational. Even so, this conceptualizing/coding key relation is admittedly, "obviously", speculative and with it, of course, either relatum and the theory's basis as a whole. If an internal reality at all, this machinery wouldn't appear very workable.

In these regards, there's little to choose between Talmy's and Langacker's familial umbrellas, as imported together by Herman into narrative and "cognitive narratology". Strategically missing there (as already hinted in "purpose"/"express" above) is the idea of many-to-many interplay: functional difference among equivalent-looking forms and functional equivalence among different-looking forms – the Proteus Principle, in brief. We all willy-nilly implement it – if only unreflectively, except in face of novelty or opacity or ambiguity, and according to our own lights – or else we would never make sense, least of all communicative sense. (Nor would the sense *makers* at the transmitting end, with the inverse proviso.) The analyst, though, needs the sharpest awareness of its radical, omnipresent workings. The Proteus Principle indeed applies already to formal units encoded in the weakly, potentially functional (because generalized) system of language: recall Saussure on differential value. Yet the Principle always newly applies, even possibly reverses its bearing, vis-à-vis any of those units' discourse instantiations: on the way from unframed, infinitely frameable sentence to multiply frame-bound (e.g., genre-relative) utterance. And once frame-bound, it gets (re)perspectivized in terms of some discourse context, with all the orientational axes entailed, accommodated, specifiable thereby.

Observe how every piece of language, complete with its viewpoint, gets *trans*formed within a reality and discourse reality such as the Bible's, dominated by an all-privileged God. When you read words uttered or inspired by him, a command ("Let there be light") may turn into a creative act *ex nihilo*, a humanly fallible into an omniscient inside view, observational whereabouts into nullity, the past or future into present-like transparency, a question into a disguise for supernatural knowledge rather than a demand for information: earth-bound into "metaphysical realism", *pace* Lakoff (1987).[38] This apparent exception is a defamiliarizing principled exemplar, because *every* case is a special case – unless and until we make it otherwise by appeal to some higher operative referent point(s) suitable and, as necessary, adjustable, to its features. The simplest sentence we encounter anywhere thus lends itself in principle to an open-ended range of perspectivizings – as between social address and hidden thought, self-expression and quotation, narrativity and descriptivity, otherworldliness and realism, factuality and fictionality, innocence and irony, figurative and literal intent... The "betweenness" may even stay ambiguous to the last, dramatizing (in art, celebrating) the victory of multiple perspectivity over unitary objectivity. Recall the narrated world's suspension between normality and abnormality, in inverse ratio to the narrating Jamesian governess's (or to Mary's). Elsewhere, in cases at the opposite extreme, the forking possibilities may escape notice altogether, because the "right" choice on every axis so leaps to our mind's ear or eye; yet some alternative(s) remains latent there nevertheless, always eligible for actualization by a less automatic receiver or an estranging context, by newly acquired knowledge or the rise of perceptible uncertainty or a surprise twist, which forces a repatterning of what has gone before. (The nar-

---

38. The opposite extreme, no less eye-opening, would be a subnormal discourser in the human condition, like the idiot Benjy in Faulkner's *The Sound and the Fury*; or, conceivably, a human existing in the company of superhumans.

rative gap-to-closure movement plays here its usual energizing role.). As with the discoursed sentence, of course, so with the forms in play within and beyond it: their reading will differ, viewpoint and all, according to the frame we infer or imagine or shift in sequence.

This iron law of protean discourse-making, therefore, governs every unit and every structure and every instance adduced by the linguists, complete with the respective prototypes and exemplary cases. They themselves always, all too often tacitly, assume some world and discourse world out of the many possible ones – the more possible in the absence of anything like a given frame around the phrase or sentence involved. Only, they reify their automatic or favoured choices: those enclosing, orienting possibles get ruled out of open-ended plurality into a uniformity that is judged as normative, because supposedly, "obviously", empirical, "ordinary", "natural", "central", "representative", "prototypical". All taken, if not for granted, self-evident, as it were, then for expert, reasoned descriptions of linguistic fact. Such predetermined framing thus freezes the form/function dynamics by arbitrary fiat – one charged with ideology, because value-laden, hence itself a matter of viewpoint – clean against the protean spirit that animates the discursive mind in life as in literature.

Here, far from revolutionary, cognitive linguistics follows the mainstream linguistic traditions, as well as those of pragmatics and discourse analysis, which it aspires to incorporate under a new banner. Like them, the ideology behind this cognitivism restricts it not only to a particular, earth-bound metaphysics (epistemology, perception, conception, ontology, even physics) but also to particular earth-bound variants selected or adapted from the irreducible diversity of what people have actually, "experientially", lived and perceived and interacted by: the ever-changing repertoires (usages, encyclopedias, lexicons, linkages) of science, philosophy, common sense, faith, art, themselves often crossed or alternated in practice. Instead, low realism takes all regardless. Favoured, even universalized, by partial judgments of the kind mentioned, these specific worldviews get imposed on language and, worse, verbal behaviour, in the name of grammar – at least as stable default values, hence viewpoints. So the analyst's perspective, on anything from coordinates to matrixes to units, substitutes for the system's and the subject's, instead of (re)constructing them. Self-projection, ultimately.

By comparison, the story grammars and action schemata developed in neighbouring cognitivisms are more inclusive: they often indeed exemplify from the stylized and unrealistic folktale, after Propp. Existential bias accordingly ranks much lower on the list of their problems with natural and literary storytelling. (Which is why I omitted mention of it at the time, among the big nine shortfalls.) The difference perhaps reflects one in focus: between world-making as an immediate concern and as an implicit coordinate of language.

Small wonder, at any rate, that Langacker translates "metaphysical realism" (Lakoff's borrowing from Hilary Putnam) into perspectival cognitive law. As a matter of theory, he judges our principled exemplar above, God's discourse, to be a mere "possible exception" to the rule of human conceptualizing, construal, "viewing" (1995: 154; cf. Fludernik [1996: 75–76]). For him, it only serves to prove and elucidate the diametric extreme of the normal viewer, "ineluctably constrained" by biology, history, spacetime, observational field. Just a contrastive abnormal background, in short, nothing like a viable option that a newly all-embracing grammar needs to accommodate, among others.

What such an accommodation of God's or God-like language use would involve – from conceptualizing to coding – has already been suggested. Recall the effects of an omnipotent's command and an omniscient's question on speech acts, for example. But the changes forced thereby would extend to Langacker's perspectival parameters themselves (e.g., "vantage point"), along with Talmy's ("location … distance … direction"). An order of viewing and voicing ensues that is different in kind from the putative rule's; and doubly so if you reckon with the disparity in that high-powered cognizer's reception (e.g., insight) as well.

Langacker doesn't even seem aware what a wide assortment of language universes and forces get ruled out of the grammar together with this "possible exception". The grammar's adequacy decreases to match. His low-realistic universal would thus leave uncovered fiction as a whole. A mirror-image of sorts to his earthbound norm, this vast discourse-type postulates instead the fictionist's God-like omniscience, creativity, and control, all exertable on otherwise realistic no less than fantastic worlds and all delegable to the narrator and the rest of the created voices/views. Langacker's restrictive unipolarity would also exclude all divinely "inspired" history telling like the Bible's, or Homer's, on which this fictional premise is modeled; all fiction-like "Suppose" games, our daydreaming and wishful thinking included; all religious and mythical language, complete with the forms and figures patterned on it in turn; even a range of established "ordinary" usages, such as the nonrealistic epistemologies behind judicial storytelling or factive statements of another's knowledge (to illustrate from two domains with a close bearing on factual truth). Not to speak of eras or codes outside modern English, and equally part of the "experience" that we bring to language or that language can activate. But then, like the original heavenly "exception", these outlaws by grammatical fiat only re-establish on an extensive scale the counterrule that, to the discoursive mind, narrative as otherwise, every case is in principle a special case: open-framed, unless and until we (fore)close it, and the sense of its units with it, by appeal to some larger network of relations, some orientational standpoint.

Reconsider the six sentences whereby Herman illustrates how one object (a raccoon family staring at goldfish) is "conceptualized/construed" in different ways. But whose mind originated, and whose agency worded, these sentences? On what occasion? To what purpose? Infinitely frameable, they destabilize Herman's analysis of their commonalities and variants alike, of their set-ups and forms and meanings and affectivities: of everything projected there, fixed rather than found, by his tacit appeal to a "self-evident" unitary (e.g., earthly, factual, literal, vocal, other-directed) reference point. Try alternative framings on those stretches of language, the way you would if they were as abruptly encountered in everyday or artistic communication, and you'll see.

Or perform much the same exercise on Langacker's own example, "Floyd broke the glass", whereby he describes the relation between an event conceptualized and a coding sentence. He himself opens the door to the exercise, only to slam it shut under the usual excuse of typicality, from the wrong end of communication and, ironically, by God-like privilege at that:

> Now there are innumerable kinds of situations for which this utterance would be appropriate: Floyd may have been dropped from a helicopter and fallen through a skylight; he may have just sounded a fire alarm; he may have inadvertently hit a drinking glass with his elbow and knocked it to the floor; he may have shattered it by singing a very high note; he may have hit a baseball through a picture window; and so on. But let us put the issue aside and assume that the utterance straightforwardly describes a particular event known in full detail – specifically, Floyd picked up a hammer, swung it at a drinking glass, made solid contact, and thereby smashed the glass to bits. Our interest lies in the options available to the speaker in the coding process. Given his intention to report the event, what construal and coding decisions does he make in arriving at the specific sentence *Floyd broke the glass*? (Langacker 1991: 295)

"And so on", indeed. Floyd may also have been an animal, a missile, a hurricane, a bridegroom in a Jewish wedding, and what not; the breakage and the glass in turn open a similar gamut of conceptualized entities to compound the numberless possible routes to coding. There is nothing "straightforward", then, about the agent/act/object permutation singled out from the rest as the "particular event" with its particular "situational" matrix cum (low-realist) metaphysics. It just happens to be postulated ("let us ... assume") by the exemplifier as the one that *has* been conceptualized by "the speaker" and now, "known in full detail", coded into the sentential example. Even so, faced with this coding on a specific occasion, how do *we* hearers/readers "know" which of the myriad possible ("conceptualizable") situated events it actually codes?[39] The linguist plays omniscient mind-reader cum normative ideologist vis-à-vis his speaker, *ex hypothesi*; but the audience at discourse decoding (unless themselves God-like) need to manage as best as they humanly can vis-à-vis the open-ended speech from an opaque mind, via some inferential framing. It all goes back to an asymmetry in perspective: knowing, because self-knowing, speaker vs. groping addressee, I-insider vs. you-outsider. Though built into earthly communication, the asymmetry is ignored by the grammar – at the cost of further mental as well as operational unrealism on its one-sided way from private thought to public language. Indeed, this being actually a producer's grammar, it needs to be complemented by at least one other grammar, anchored in the receiver and most conspicuous for its absence where linguists aim at experiential wholeness. As the very idea of a code entails mediation between the parties that appeal to it, "coding" without decoding makes at best a half of "face-to-face" linguistic reality.

This is why Herman's modelling of "discourse-level structures" on "clause and sentence" and his adoption of a questionable processing mechanism, both typical enough, aggravate each other. Of the two proposed advances from cognitive linguistics "toward a cognitive narratology", however, the jump in "level" is the more basically unacceptable. The trouble with it should be evident to one who, unlike the linguists cited, recognizes those levels as somehow distinct in the first place.

Suppose the alleged new key to perspective, the "conceptualization" umbrella, were a well-defined and well-established mental reality, instead of a slippery phantom. Even then, describing how a "conceptualized" world-item ("situation or event") gets verbalized into grammatical form would be

---

39. Possibly including figurative events, analogized, even related to idiomatic usages like "broke the ice / the heart / a rule / a spell / silence / wind"; or, supposing the tool itself evoked, possibly comparable to Virginia Woolf's "Tansley raised a hammer; swung it high in air ..." ([1927] 1969: 105), which dematerializes into a metaphor for a crushing repartee.

encoding the range of its expressibility and expressivity by the grammar of the language system involved. No more; perforce less on the way from unit to sentence: the open-ended choices multiply, and here also the difficulties, of mapping inner archetype onto expressional prototype. Similarly, only in reverse and via inference, with the decoding. But once translated to (narrative) discourse – (con)textualized, functionalized, synthesized, mobilized, re-grammaticalized at choice – that world-item will necessarily be encoded/decoded afresh, hence also newly "conceptualized", in a larger, manifold, autonomous key, to a different, possibly opposite effect. Value, interest, attitude, knowledge, worldview, reliability, and so forth: all the orientational axes already mentioned come into play now, together with the underlying sense of purpose that frames, interprets, explains, and structures their actual manifestations as how's appropriate to it. A rationale apart, therefore, from that of the language code, which it needn't select at all but subsumes and subordinates, inter alia, when it does.

Further, such incorporation ranges from unremarkably implementing the language to trans-forming it into another special agent for the operative ends: narrativizing it, for example, even against the code's grain. Thus a proleptic epithet as a generator of foreknowledge and suspense, or a (pro)noun series translated from spatial, descriptive coexistence into a storied chrono-logic (Sternberg 1981, 1983a, 1985: 321 ff., 1992 passim) – against the ready-made, here prototyped, divide between adjective or nominal and verb – or the sequences of pronominal (dis)ambiguation that miniature and reinforce the twisting event-line. But then, unobtrusive, apparently rule-governed usages do not just instantiate the code, either. Like everything (occurrence, character, arena, emotion ...) processed between the two dynamics unique to narrative, the encoded formal units must undergo change throughout the reading, under the twofold generic pressure of the narrated world's development and disclosure in time. Between them, with their constant frame-shifting, the plainest words lead eventful semantic lives as we go along.

How do these two rationales of language vs. language use interact when joined? With endless variations, of course, to which specific types and texts may set bounds, via ad hoc norms, contracts, aesthetics, frequencies, bottom-up guides, which regularize and so channel to some extent the workings of the Proteus Principle. To some extent only, because we always regularize those protean workings short of absolute certitude – of form/ function univocal matching, of failsafe foreclosure as distinct from best-possible closure pro tem – and on debatable grounds at that: witness the shifts and quarrels among literary scholars, especially interpreters, whose daily bread lies in effect there, in frame-(re)construction. The exact how's-and-why's of this tense language/discourse interplay within various corpora (genres, authors, works) is a, indeed the, major question for the empirical discourse analyst; but not the principled hierarchy of power between the rationales amid their otherness. Therefore, extrapolating from one system to another of a different order altogether, let alone to a generic subsystem – where the imagined paradigm of "grammar" actually comes to form a nondistinctive part within an otherwise discriminate (e.g., storied) whole that *in*forms it – remains as hopeless and misguided as ever. Another, Jakobson-like bid for disciplinary imperialism, in lieu of the wanted interdisciplinarity, two- or three-fold. The very best linguistics (and the cognitivist kind has much to recommend it, after all, with a still greater potential in a joint enterprise) not only has its limits but would know them and proceed accordingly, as would its followers elsewhere.

Failing a systemic reference to all the higher, extragrammatical coordinates – of discourse within language itself, of narrativity within discourse, of perspectivity within narrative – the balance of loss and gain incurred by Herman's modelling of the genre on "grammar" is prohibitive. No wonder, as with earlier wholesale transfers between these systems. Let me therefore just touch on a few unhappy yet revealing consequences for the study of perspective, with special reference to his chosen disciplinary exemplars.

I would be the last to advocate the Structuralist narratologies of Genette and Stanzel. But their invidious comparison with Talmy and Langacker – or with an approach modelling narrative on either or both – defeats itself across the board. (In Genette's case, ironically, part of the original difficulty already traces to earlier false verbal analogies, so that it's like putting out fire with fire.) How such modelling would fare vis-à-vis better narrative theories than Structuralism's will only emerge in passing or at most in outline, but is easy enough to deduce or elaborate by now. So is, I trust, the constructive force of those negatives, where the point of my entire re-comparison ultimately lies. Here as before, our question is double-edged: How (not) to advance toward the narrative mind? Only, here the "mind" at issue not only includes that of the narrating or narrated characters, as in earlier sections, but co-equalizes and often foregrounds it. Author, narrator, reader, agent: all the viewpoints involved in the genre define themselves more sharply when examined as possible "conceptualizers" or "construers".

Thus, the claim that the Genettian and Stanzelian weaknesses concerning narrative transmission may be repaired via these imports, or their discords reconciled, makes little sense. Take the view/voice polarity that is central to either Structuralist: seeing or "focalizing"/speaking, reflector/ teller, experiencing-/narrating-I. To translate this dichotomy between modalities into the grammarian's "conceptualization" would be to push it out of existence, not simply equating the dichotomized terms but eliminating them altogether. "Voice" (i.e., all narrating, from the global to the dialogic, along with all nonnarrative speaking) would then inevitably vanish, because the alleged "conceptualizing" umbrella is pre-coded, i.e., prelinguistic, *a fortiori* pre-discursive: a sheer mental ("voiceless") outlook on the world.[40] And "view" would have to disappear in turn, for the same reason. The "focalizing" or "reflecting" Emma Woodhouse expresses her viewpoint in private self-discourse (accessible to us privileged eavesdroppers alone, via direct, indirect, free indirect, telescoped quoting) no less than the Jane Austen teller does her own viewpoint, in the public, written discourse addressed to us. Either of them speaks her mind, as it were, whether in monologue or in the market-place, rather than just entertaining a mental conceptualization.[41] To this extent, the apartness of the respective disciplinary concerns would follow from the two Structuralist narratologies themselves.

However, this dividing line (and with it the threatened losses) vis-à-vis the cognitive linguistic blanket term persists, indeed sharpens, in face of refinements or crosses of the voice/view binaries that elude standard typologizing. Let me quickly exemplify. Even self-communion, though still distinctively private and discernibly opposed to public communication, is sometimes vocalized – as with Tom Jones's monologues or your daily mumbling to yourself. The two axes cut across each other to yield a third expressional variant. And hearing, i.e., private thought about another's public speech, generally preparatory to response, offers a fourth (Sternberg 1982b: 104–8, 1986, 1998: 317–24, 405–11).

But whatever the variant – voice, view, voiced view, viewed voice – it would remain distinct from the wordlessness of conceptualization. Amid

---

40. The occasional interchange in Dancygier and Vandelanotte between "conceptualizer" and "speaker" – as between "mental space" and "discourse" – is therefore a category mistake, because the former remains voiceless as such.

41. More precisely, speaks what we readers take to be her mind, and with possible variations. None of us humans (except for self-privileged grammarians, e.g., Langacker on Floyd) enjoy direct access to that conceptualizing arena and intent behind the given words, so that we must infer, or decode, our way toward it. But then, Genette and Stanzel are themselves hardly concerned with the receiver's inference-making.

this shared fourfold expressiveness, I would further add, the private/public contrast between discoursers makes a significant difference to the very norms (e.g., intelligibility) and forms (e.g., grammaticality) of the respective languages used. The communicator must, while the self-communer needn't, reckon with outside proprieties (e.g., Grice's maxims, well-formation). The difference, traditionally moderate, leaps to the eye in the stream of consciousness novel.

So, how to correlate the two narratologies via this supposed grammatical novelty divergent from both, let alone how to co-apply the respective disciplinary metalanguages without inconsistency? Evidently, neither Genette's binary nor Stanzel's gradualist approach to voice/view would survive translation into the pre-expressive, prelanguage, prediscourse "conceptualizing" that is alleged to amend and harmonize them. Nor would their revisions since, or their substitutes, or newly cognitivized departures like "experientiality" in Fludernik (1996). Another reductionism with a vengeance, this borrowing of "ideas from cognitive grammar" to "circumvent impasses created by classical narratological theories" of perspective. It erases both a genuine view/voice resemblance underplayed by Structuralists and a genuine disparity over- or mis-drawn by them, instead of proposing how to draw the likeness and the line better.[42] So the loss extends from the unity to the discriminateness to the flexible coupling of voice and view as perspectival resources. A setback instead of an advance.

Still, don't both resources (along with the crosses I finessed) entail, at a deeper level, a mind looking out on the world in its own way, and so worth generalizing across expressive variations? For Herman, this might be the point, the novel groundwork offered by the linguist. He calls it "treating construal as the common root of voice and vision – as the common denominator shared by modes of narrative mediation". But this supposed gain hardly offsets the losses. Quite the reverse, if anything:

---

42. For such an alternative proposal, by reference to narrative transmission as a whole, see Sternberg (1978: 254ff., 2005, 2007), Yacobi (1981, 1987b, 2000), Bordwell (1985: 57ff.), Panek (2006), on "self-conscious" (other-directed, audience-minded) vs. "unself-conscious" (ego-centred) transmitters. Observe especially the differential power wielded there by the neglected feature of "(un)self-consciousness", and just applied to the public/private mediators above. In such light, "the impasse" within the Structuralist narratologies at issue is breakable on a local scale and, more important, obviated due to the shift of ground.

(1) That outlooking mind, however silent or "unself-conscious", does not equal the construing/conceptualizing mind, which is definitionally prior to any linguistic/narrative/voiced/viewed surfacing from the wordless deep. Whether the latter's preverbal (or otherwise presemiotic) mentation exists at all (and if yes, where) remains in dispute among the scientific experts on the topic; also among cultures and literary practices of mindscaping since antiquity. They have assumed – in fiction, even invented – the widest range of psychologies, complete with psycholinguistics (see Cohn 1978, with earlier references).

Take just one diametric opposite to the cognitivist premise. The classical idea of mentation, as early as Homer or Plato and tremendously influential, patterns it on conversation. Thought is the discourse that the soul holds with itself. So, whether a Homeric character voices or silences what he thinks, the wording is already there, and any digging below it anachronistic as well as fruitless.

Further, recall my argument against the exclusive linkage of the one/many relation to (preverbal) conceptualizing/(verbal) coding. Among the disproofs is the fact that the genetic process leading to the coded unit may begin anywhere, not excluding a linguistic feature or structure as trigger. Thus the generation of a parody may begin with the parodied text or style, that of a poem with a metrical scheme, that of a quote with the original utterance, that of an antithesis with a familiar thesis, that of a negation or question, a fortiori echo-question, with the statement to be negated or queried, and so forth. The process that results in a linguistic coding (specifically, in a discourse-evoking message, a linguistic intertext) has thus been launched by a linguistic trigger. Even if the alleged disciplinary "conceptualization" intervenes – still a genuine if – it cannot be all preverbal, nor *the* one deep ground for all the correlated expressible surfaces, any more than being the starting point.

Much the same ontic doubt, and variability in practice, affects the conceptual or image-schematic basis attributed to metaphor since Lakoff and Johnson (1980). Doesn't language condition these underseas at all? Again, even if science were to resolve the doubt in the cognitive linguist's favour – yes to preverbal mindwork – it still wouldn't and couldn't rule out an antecedent linguistic trigger to troping, with all the implications just outlined on a more general scale. All discourse-evoking (allusive, intertextual) figurative discourse paradigmatically entails such an antecedent force. Shakespeare's "My mistress's eyes are nothing like the sun..." would thus have found its impetus in the traditional hyperbolic similes, or simile-mongering, that it overtly negates. Likewise with our reconstruction of the process as sense-makers, only in reverse, from the given allusive negation to the rage for artificial hyperbole that it estranges. Either way, the producer's or the interpreter's, there unfolds another surface-to-surface generative trajectory, with the conceptual depth at best mediating (who knows how) between the languaged extremes.[43]

The general rule outlined applies further to this top-rank specific crux, as it did to its perspectival mate. Indeed, this further application also brings out that tropes, like everything else in discourse, are a matter, or a manner, of perspective. Even if science were to establish prelinguistic mindwork, we would still need to approach the cultural and literary mindscapings on their own diverse premises. In the psycho-fictions analyzed by Cohn (1978: 21–59), for example, metaphors do not reside in or surface from the deepest level of the mind, but are contrived by the literary narrator, as omniscient mind-reader, with a view to an evocative paraphrase of the character's inchoate mentation ("thought") at that level. Here, in effect, psycho-figuration dovetails with the God's eye (inside)view, against the respective sweeping cognitivist universalisms: a compounded metaphysical bias. Theory and practice, then, join forces against any absolutism like sheer-conception-first. Instead of a common ground, or a bedrock mental reality, we have a scientific unknown, a discourse variable, and, often, a nonexistent in either realm. The silence of outlooking (or trope-making) is not yet the wordlessness imposed by fiat on the conceptualizer's/construer's perspective.

Nor does the fiat's jurisdiction end here, with the broad ranges of perspective and/as figuration. It extends to other domains or aspects of language, such as syntax or reference, and even to other-minded, otherwise focused (e.g., action-directed) cognitivist research programmes. This surfacing-from-the-deep premise makes cognitive linguistics strangely reminiscent of the ostensible polar extreme in Artificial Intelligence, where (as noted apropos Schank et al.) the computerized Script Understander operates on a language-free translation. Its input derives from a conceptual system whereby the equivalent surface forms (lexical, grammatical) in the narrative reduce to a uniform semantic representation. Likewise with higher-level action schemata and with story-generating programmes, i.e., the transmitter's end. That Gibbs (2003) associates prototypes with

---

43. In this volume, contrast Gerard Steen's five-step descent "from linguistic form to conceptual structure" in metaphor: his reconstructive procedure, complete with its automatic thought-first premise, fails the test of intertextual, language-to-language metaphoric genesis.

scripts is therefore less unexpected than may appear. Nor is it surprising that real-life story generation may also demonstrably open with a verbal trigger: Dickens's with a title, for example, Joseph Heller's with a sentence coming to him out of the blue, and either's linguistic antecedent somehow inspiring the rest of the novel. You can presumably think of equivalents from your own storytelling experience (e.g., the way one joke triggers another).

That the analogy in conceptualizing-first shows across such assorted programmes goes to reinforce my argument that this bias (the ninth on the list there) typifies the discipline. The more so, considering that the priority isn't even forced on the cognitive linguist by mechanical exigencies; here we encounter it, instead, as a sheer article of faith, declared foundational and revolutionary, because inherent to the mind's workings.

(2) So much for "the common root" or "denominator", with further implications for cognitive linguistic theorizing itself. But even in cases where this variable of basic wordless perspectivizing happens to apply, always ad hoc, as when a reliable fictive narrator stipulates it, what enlightenment do we gain? The claim of "one event or situation/alternate construals" amounts to this: that the world of objects (or, if discoursed, its mimesis in the narrative *fabula*) lends itself to numberless imagings and every subject privately registers his own image. An old truism, only with a shift of umbrellas from "subjectivity" and the like to the grammarian's novel-sounding catch-all. Nor would this shift of terms preserve the hard-earned distinctions (e.g., voice/view, verbal/nonverbal thought, vocal/silent private speech) or extensions (e.g., to the *fabula*, with its manifold and multilevel subjects), let alone allow for their refinement where necessary.

What's more, the shift to "conceptualizing" would come at a price that we've only begun to appreciate:

(3) The exclusionary fiat involved stretches wider yet. By a rule strange for cognitivists yet typical of linguists, mental language as a whole remains here out of sight, out of mind – and not at this deepest level alone. Similarly excluded by the disciplinary privileging of face-to-face encounter, hence talk, and at best talk-like, communicative writing as well, are all the surface forms of interior, private speech, monologic or inner-dialogic. This private ("unself-conscious") discourse actually runs through our secret life, in complex interplay with social address; there we often refer to it, by way of inference from the you's externals (e.g., visual paralanguage) and of self- or other-quotation from within. Literature indeed richly ex-

ploits the poetic licence of mind-reading to foreground the double linguistic existence that humans lead, and so the need for a joint, twofold, relational grammar to suit.

Wanted, therefore, as ever, are no fewer than three grammars – each with its own perspectival rationale – to complement the standard transmitter-based one; and, of all schools, you would expect cognitivism to pursue them. Let me quickly name this wanted trio in an ascending order of exteriority and reciprocity, as against purely subjective egocentricity. First, the grammar of self-communion, at issue now. Second, the grammar of reception, the need for which has arisen throughout my argument, in the references to hearing, decoding, processing, and the inherent asymmetry of communication behind them. Third, the interactive grammar of communication as a whole, designed to minimize and, ideally, to neutralize the asymmetry between the parties. All three wanted grammars, of course, would be subject to language's protean discourse re-grammaticalizing and overall re-systematizing.

As it is, poetics knows much more about these domains than linguistics: from the first, especially owing to the inward turn of modernism; through the second, whether along the lines of premodern hermeneutics or of latter-day interpretation and reading; to the third, the age-old business of rhetoric, for example. (That the knowledge accumulated in the library still awaits consolidation is another matter, an index of both the plenitude and the carelessness endemic to the discipline.) In such light, construal/coding, among other cognitivist premises, would demand further strategic rethinking. Here, the grammarian's set toward the information-giving, "communicative" function (e.g., Langacker 1991: 1–2) doesn't just prove narrow – as vis-à-vis the functional richness of actual and artistic discourse – but turns incongruous with self-discourse, whose linguistic forms *dis*count communicativeness to match. At work here is a (teleo)logic of viewpoint unto itself, protean as ever, yet egocentric to the limit (because unmindful of others) and accordingly coded. Why, then, would a narratology apply those half or quarter grammars, and to (literary) perspective, of all domains, just where we most require the missing half?

(4) The wonder grows with the blind spots. In discourse, all "viewing" (focalizing, reflecting, whether languaged or otherwise), all its voicing, however exteriorized in whatever code or coding, and much else reported in vocal expression, are essentially out of the grammar's bounds, as well as out of the grammarian's competence per se. Other obstacles apart, even if immediate discourse (what I say to you in my own name, from my own

viewpoint) could be modelled upon the sentence – one mind per language unit – mediated discourse couldn't; and all the above viewings/voicings are necessarily mediated, hence bi-mental at least, twice perspectivized. The voicer (Jane Austen, the narrating self, I at mind-quoting to you) mediates the viewer (Emma, the experiencing self, the mind quoted by me); the reporter mediates the vocal reportee.

In scope, as just re-exemplified, either kind of inset thus mediated (quoted, framed) can run from phrase-length to novel-length. In make-up, as also demonstrated already, every such mediation entails some perspectival montage, irreducible to any rule – least of all linguistic – and at best unpackable via inference. Faced with discourse, we can't even tell in advance *whether* it immediately represents the official speaker's perspective or mediately re-presents within its frame, possibly misrepresents, another's view and/or voice. Which discourse is which? And if the latter, what in the second-hand discourse is whose? Whose "(re)conceptualizing" do the words imply here, whose "(re)coding" there? So we must always work for the best fit in context, armed with the Proteus Principle as supreme director of operations on the ground: top-down, bottom-up, or correlative.

Failing to recognize this principled out-of-boundness, to save the grammar from its own systemic blind spots, comes dear. Typically, when Langacker ventures into quotation-land (1991: 253ff. and, in effect, 435–63 passim), he loses his way. The reproductive, direct-speech fallacy, the indirect reporter virtually monopolizing, or uniperspectivizing, the reported language, the obliviousness to free indirect quoting: such missteps there are all symptomatic of how the unwarranted analysis inevitably falls between the stools. It approaches reporting as a discourse ("speech") event, yet goes against the protean grain of discourse in an attempt to formalize the unformalizable assortment of reporting performances into grammatical regularity and rule-governedness.

There as elsewhere, moreover, the attempt boomerangs on the proper concerns of the grammar itself as such, encoded rules and all. For, once the grammar annexes discourse, nothing is or remains ungrammatical any longer: every asterisked or questioned example of ill-formedness, brought by the linguist as rule-generalizer, then invites sense-making in context, by appeal to one of the numberless frames imaginable. Such appeal can't even be shrugged off as idiosyncratic, exceptional and the like, since a frame entails a regularity, just like the grammarian's, only discoursive, hence possibly counter- or otherwise-grammatical. In these mental resources and the constructs they yield, the apparent ill-formation will also find what the quest that it has triggered seeks: a way to re- or trans-

formation into coherence within some larger whole, hence into "acceptability". The question is only *which* of the diverse mechanisms available for
the purpose fits best.[44]

Of these, predictably, the shift from the apparently immediate to quoted
discourse often suggests itself: as a multi-perspectival composite, quotation enables us sense-makers to shift all or some of the responsibility for
the ill-discoursed (the ill-expressed on any axis) to another's voice/view,
the quotee's.[45] Among quotational schemata, in turn, free indirect discourse predictably ranks high, given its option for uneven backshifting
and/or awkward ordering and/or unverbalized framing to be puzzled out
in the reading. Thus the free-indirect sense you can make of declared un-
acceptables like "*The picture of *himself* that hangs in *Lincoln's* study is
quite dignified looking" (Langacker 1995: 199) or "*Here came another
outburst!" (Lakoff 1987: 532), to illustrate from two random examples
out of the legion on grammarian record.[46] The linguist's dead-end of un-
grammaticality proves to be a trigger for discoursive inference of some
hidden order, according to the Law of Reciprocity: whatever is expressed,
or expressible, is explicable. Disciplinary overreaching, like underexten-

---

44. For a programmatic overview of them, see especially Sternberg (1983b,
    2001b: 139ff.), and observe how the Proteus Principle meets the Law of Reci-
    procity there. See also the next note.
45. Hence, inter alia, the centrality and distinctiveness of "the unreliable narrator"
    among integrating mechanisms: for this redefinition of (un)reliability, see the
    work on it by Tamar Yacobi in References, now widely followed and often de-
    scribed as a "cognitive" turn. Examples would be Fludernik (1999), Nünning
    (1999), Cohn (1999), Ferenz (2005). By a related logic, as hinted above, the
    mechanism of irony shifts its ground from a "verbal" device to a well-defined
    quoting strategy: a tense, bipolar perspectival montage, inferable across all
    codes, forms, lengths, or polarities in the ill-twinned viewpoints.
46. This record also includes Dancygier and Vandelanotte's "not amenable
    to ...", mentioned above. And some negative records are more tell-tale than
    others, because longer or more systematic, even systemic, or more hindering.
    For a case in point, see Sternberg (2001b) on the oversight of quotation
    (167ff.) and especially free indirectness (203ff.) in presupposition theory
    since the 1950's. Also, with the factive verb "know" as paradigm case, the ar-
    gument there further exemplifies the miscanonizing of humanly restricted as
    opposed to omniscient or quasi-omniscient epistemology, down to sentence-
    length units and everyday usage. Elsewhere, and as directly connected to our
    theme, observe the unawareness of another resource for making sense of the
    ill-formed givens, namely: their framing as interior discourse, with its
    licensed grammar and lifelike stammer.

sion or underequipment, therefore carries penalties, in inverse ratio to the benefits of interdisciplinary traffic. Why a narratologist today would have us bracket the sentence with the discourse level regardless, God knows.

(5) To top off this mystery, and the principled argument, recall the extra-linguistic, a fortiori extraverbal, axes of viewpoint. For instance, consider the transmitter's mode of existence (reinvented in Talmy 2000: II, 431, by the way). How would the grammars bear, let alone improve, on the distinction among narrators by their (human, or human-like) insidership or (transcendent) outsidership: what Genette calls "homo/heterodiegesis" and Stanzel "identity vs. non-identity" to the storyworld? *Lord Jim's* opening, "He was an inch, perhaps two, under six feet", might come from anywhere; and the implication of the narrating-I's coexistence with "him", readable into the "perhaps", turns out misleading. For the sequel rather suggests (i.e., fits) a narrator out of Jim's world. Ostensibly a give-away of shared humanity, the modal qualifier points the wrong way, and (if only in retrospect) needs some different existential-cum-functional motivation. Invoking the grammar to decide where the narrator exists would achieve less than nothing here, only complicate matters, in the absence of any reasoned division or "synergy" of labour concerning the ontology of perspective. Instead, this existential axis, with its familiar and problematic correlates in (e.g.) the existent's knowledge, must then go the way of voice/view: it would apparently vanish into some limbo between the disciplines – conveyable or conveyed through the language system, yet eluding its grasp to favour a discourse habitation, analysis, name. Into that limbo must then also fall Stanzel's "narrative situation", and with it his entire theory. For he clusters together the respective axes – voice/view with "identity/nonidentity", even adding a third one, "internal/external" – while Genette disjoins them. In short, far from finding its repair in any linguistics, or its reconciliation with its competitor, either of the theories would get into deeper trouble.

Good riddance to both? Perhaps, but that wouldn't suit Herman's claim, nor would it resolve, but merely relocate, the substantive issue be-tween the disciplines. The same fate would befall the array of extraverbal dimensions on which these Structuralists agree or quarrel or just fail to overlap with other narratologies: author/teller, complete/limited knowl-edge, omniscience/ omnicommunication, (un)reliability, (un)self-con-sciousness, word/world mimesis, text/paratext/intertext, how perspective stands to linear deployment or to the discourse as a whole... Throughout, if an either/or choice were forced, and it luckily isn't, the putative cognitivist remedy would be strategically worse than the existing question marks.

A one-sided remedy, further, Herman's scenario lacks a give-and-take, as usual among importers from cognitivism. (They tend to undervalue their home discipline regardless of the facts, including the occasional cross reference the other way: even Talmy's belated acknowledgement of parallels in Structuralist narratology. Or both ways, as in Turner's collaboration with Lakoff and Fauconnier.). His cognitive linguist has nothing to gain, nothing to learn in exchange. One might as well call outright for narratological eclecticism, unmindful of the larger picture within and between the fields. Indeed, along with that of Herman's "focal" trio, the miscellany of terms used by him for the proposed advance via cognitive linguistics (supplementing, overcoming limitations, circumventing impasses, synergizing, affording a more unified systematic treatment, shifting from taxonomy to a functionalist [?] account) points this way.

On the strategic level, again, I've outlined a more reasoned and reciprocal interdisciplinary alternative, whereby either side will find its complement – from aids to tests to challenges – in what the other is professionally best equipped to offer. (Challenges, because even the arguments against the tenet of conceptualization, or against a transmitter-based quarter grammar, may lead to fruitful second thoughts, as may arguments against the anti-psychological heritage of Structuralist narratology.) Nowhere can the parties join forces so well at the language/discourse boundary, and regardless of its precise drawing, as on a mentalist common ground. Ideally, of course, the two sides will also meet in the analyst's joint analytic competences, as already in the better revisits of literary metaphor.

On the front at issue, linguistics will then concentrate its efforts where its strength resides: on articulating the perspectivity encoded in microunits of different kinds, orders, structures, valences, latencies, latitudes. Easier said than done, of course; and the less easy to systematize, the wider the range of language use encompassed and the more observed the asymmetry in viewpoint between the parties that appeal to the code, the encoding vs. the decoding mind. But findings worth sharing with narratology are ready to hand. Thus the space/time/motion indicators conventionalized in miniature forms like prepositions, particles, nouns, verbs, adverbs, phrases, figures, or clauses (already focused in the groundbreaking Miller and Johnson-Laird 1976, and often taken up since, notably by Talmy 2000). Discourse having a richer repertoire and maneuverability, such analysis will generally endow the discourse theorist, not so much with fresh perspectival categories, as with fresh pinpoint arenas, and ultimately insights, born of the interplay between the two systems. A time-relation is a time-relation, a space-feature is a space-feature, an epistemic modalizing is an epistemic modalizing, a commitment is a commitment, however manifested, and even if never traceable or quite entrustable to any verbal form; but it pays to know their systemic encoding in the operative language – rules, blanks, options, and all. The inverse will accrue to the linguist in contact with narrative theory, as progressively outlined along my argument. Given the respective states of knowledge about perspectivity, it promises to be the larger payoff, if only in analytic and extra-linguistic and functional horizons.[47]

Regarding the categories of viewpoint that Herman would import on his agenda, though, the question now comes down to local eclectic practicalities, on an item-by-item basis. Leaving aside the dubious grand foundation, what's new or useful to narratology about Talmy's and Langacker's perspectival "parameters", or vice versa? Reconsider the former's quartet – the viewpoint's "location", "distance" from the viewed object, "mode", and "direction" – along with the latter's trio: "selection", "perspective" (e.g., figure/ground, subjectivity/objectivity, vantage point, deixis), and "abstraction" (amount of detail or "granularity"). Never mind that the two sets often transcend language and also genre, as Talmy's own bid for theorizing narrative (2000: II, 417ff.) shows. Never mind their metaphysical premises, either. Never mind even the holes in coverage or coherence left by the sets, partly because the linguists would appear unaware that

---

47. On the interdisciplinarity envisaged, I cannot go here beyond generalities, pro and con, with selected bare examples. Fuller demonstrations may speak louder, especially if involving notorious cruxes and showing the difference made by their reanalysis along such lines. For exactly this two-way traffic in action, see again my case study (Sternberg 2001b) of the commitment uniformly and uniquely built, yet multiply readable, into the language of presupposition. Its title also indicates a direct bearing on the respective perspectivities correlated there. See also next note. Finally, it would help to contrast Antonopoulou and Nikiforidou's (this volume) idea of interdisciplinarity as an approach to texts in a fixed order of descending "principledness" and ascending particularity: first "grammatical" study of form/meaning relations, then "literary" interpretation. For all its welcome spirit, their proposal newly mixes the two systems – language vs. discourse – in which the respective fields specialize and on whose boundary either can offer the other systematic aid. That some linguists happen to be astute, even "literary" readers, or vice versa, only enables them, and them alone, to cross both ways.

everything in language is perspective-laden in some respect: a corollary, this all-ladenness, of the "conceptualizing"-to-"coding" movement itself, in effect. Instead, they mainly reserve "perspective" for literal vision.[48] But let's take the parameters as given.

To a narratologist, most of them, at least, will recall what has long been known under other names: mimesis/diegesis, scene/summary, dramatic/panoramic, primacy/recency effect, chronology/anachrony, prospection/retrospection, hierarchical/subjective ordering, shot/reverse shot, time/tense, first/second/third person, observer's position, camera eye, situational context, here-and-now included, and so forth, all with refinements. (Even the conceptual and terminological variations there have parallels in the cognitivist late arrivals, which must settle their own differences before coming to the rescue.) A far cry from what mainstream cognitivism offers to the plot analyst: an internalized action logic, a foregrounding of memory, and particular schemas, like the script, where the two generic rudiments cooperate. Still, the familiarity of the viewpoint (sub-)parameters does not entail that of their encoded linguistic reflexes and *their* mates, which are equally perspectival, though treated otherwise under conceptualization/construal: in them, as always, the narratologist would find a storehouse of micro-complements, regardless.

By another practical criterion, the results yielded by Herman's application of this "rich framework" to the four Joyce examples are unremarkable, to say the least. (Compare negative rule (5) in section 2.1.) Nor do they gain much from the sporadic intermixture of the linguists' categories with the Structuralists' view/voice and further narratological analytic terms. "The exclamation marks suggest sentiments or thoughts that have forcibly struck Gabriel, and that are therefore linked to his subjectivity rather than the neutral, non-exclamatory discourse of the narrator": hardly news to students of reported speech and thought. Or, "The past-tense indicative verbs indicate that the scene is sighted from a temporal viewpoint located later on the time-line than the point occupied by the represented events": the age-old definition of the past tense reappears as a notable innovation. Another truism will surprise inquirers into visual perception, graphic perspective, cinematic close-up/long-shot, and the beholder's eye in literature. "As you get farther away from something, you see more of the context that surrounds it but with less overall detail"

---

48. Herman endorses the linguists' artificial divide of "perspective or viewpoint" from "temporal, spatial, affective, and other factors associated with embodied human experience", as at the end of 4.1 and the start of 4.2.1.

repeats itself here as a newly disclosed "systematic co-variation" among "the factors of distance, scope, and granularity", which we owe to linguistic cognitivism. In novelty value, these compare with "Mary uses an explicit emotion term (*scared*) to attribute the emotion of fear to Renee and herself", on an earlier topic (section 3). Big words, small returns – and no critical distance, any more than an incentive to narratological interdisciplinarity.

At most, this or that sub-parameter, like "direction", offers a nicety addable to narratology's existing perspectival repertoire. The other way, however, there abound candidates for import, fine-grained as large-scale; so many that one hardly knows where to begin, or wherefrom to draw further examples. Even the two Structuralist narratologies invidiously compared with the grammars, both focusing on (literary) narrative in language, provide tools and data that may benefit a grammarian. (E.g., Genette on order/duration/frequency, or Stanzel on the shuttling of person-deixis.) But experts in narrative theory will know the field's embarrassment of riches; while aspirants to interdisciplinarity, from either side, will do well to work out for themselves the balance sheets, regarding perspectival export/import, as well as the lines of potential exchange sketched earlier.

References

Abbott, H. Porter (ed.)
  2001   Special issue on "The Origin of fictions: interdisciplinary perspectives." *SubStance* 94/95.
Abbott, H. Porter
  2002   *The Cambridge Introduction to Narrative.* Cambridge: Cambridge University Press.
Abbott, H. Porter
  2006   Cognitive literary studies: the "Second Generation". *Poetics Today* 27: 711–722.
Adler, Hans and Sabine Gross
  2002   Adjusting the frame: comments on cognitivism and literature. *Poetics Today* 23: 195–220.
Andringa, Els and David S. Miall (eds.)
  2004   Perspectives on three decades of cognitivist effects. URL: *http://www.arts.ualberta.ca/igel/igel2004/debate/index.htm*
Banfield, Ann
  1982   *Unspeakable Sentences: Narration and Representation in the Language of Fiction.* Boston: Routledge and Kegan Paul.

Barthes, Roland
1974   *S/Z*, trans. Richard Miller. New York: Hill and Wang.
Booth, Wayne C.
1961   *The Rhetoric of Fiction*. Chicago: University of Chicago Press.
Bordwell, David
1985   *Narration in the Fiction Film*. Madison: Wisconsin University Press.
Bortolussi, Marisa and Peter Dixon
2003   *Psychonarratology: Foundations for the Empirical Study of Literary Response*. Cambridge: Cambridge University Press.
Boyd, Brian
2006   Fiction and theory of mind. *Philosophy and Literature* 30: 590–600.
Brewer, William F. and Edward H. Lichtenstein
1981   Event schemas, story schemas, and story grammars. In: J. Long and A. Baddeley (eds.), *Attention and Performance* IX: 363–379. Hillsdale, NJ: Erlbaum.
Brewer, William F. and Edward H. Lichtenstein
1982   Stories are to entertain: a structural-affect theory of stories. *Journal of Pragmatics* 6: 473–486.
Bruner, Jerome
1986   *Actual Minds, Possible Worlds*. Cambridge, Mass: Harvard University Press.
Bruner, Jerome
1990   *Acts of Meaning*. Cambridge, Mass.: Harvard University Press.
Bruner, Jerome
2002   *Making Stories: Law, Literature, Life*. Cambridge, Mass.: Harvard University Press.
Cohn, Dorrit
1978   *Transparent Minds: Narrative Modes for Presenting Consciousness in Fiction*. Princeton, NJ: Princeton University Press.
Cohn, Dorrit
1999   *The Distinction of Fiction*. Baltimore: Johns Hopkins University Press.
Cole, Peter and Jerry L. Morgan
1975   *Syntax and Semantics: Speech Acts*. New York: Academic Press.
Cook, Guy
1994   *Discourse and Literature*. New York: Oxford University Press.
Crane, Ronald S. (ed.)
1952   *Critics and Criticism*. Chicago: University of Chicago Press.
Culpeper, Jonathan
2002   A cognitive stylistic approach to characterization. In: Elena Semino and Jonathan Culpeper (eds.), *Cognitive Stylistics. Language and Cognition in Text Analysis*, 251–277. Amsterdam/Philadelphia: John Benjamins.
Davis, Philip W.
1995   *Alternative Linguistics: Descriptive and Theoretical Modes*. Amsterdam/Philadelphia: John Benjamins.

Docherty, Thomas
  1983   *Reading (Absent) Character: Towards a Theory of Characterization in Fiction.* Oxford: Oxford University Press.
Duchan, Judith F., Gail A. Bruder and Lynne E. Hewitt (eds.)
  1995   *Deixis in Narrative: A Cognitive Science Perspective.* Hillsdale, NJ: Erlbaum.
Emmott, Catherine
  1997   *Narrative Comprehension: A Discourse Perspective.* Oxford: Oxford University Press.
Emmott, Catherine
  2003   Reading for pleasure: a cognitive poetic analysis of 'twists in the tale' and other plot reversals in narrative texts. In: Joanna Gavins and Gerard Steen (eds.), *Cognitive Poetics in Practice*, 145–159. London/New York: Routledge.
"Estrangement Revisited"
  2005–6   Special double issue, *Poetics Today*, 26: 4/27: 1.
Ferenz, Volker
  2005   Fight Clubs, American Psychos and Mementos. *New Review of Film and Television Studies* 3(2): 133–159.
Fish, Stanley
  1980   Literature in the reader: affective stylistics. In: Stanley Fish (ed.), *Is There a Text in This Class? The Authority of Interpretive Communities*, 21–67. Cambridge Mass.: Harvard University Press.
Fludernik, Monika
  1993   *The Fictions of Language and the Languages of Fiction.* London/New York: Routledge.
Fludernik, Monika
  1996   *Towards a 'Natural' Narratology.* London/New York: Routledge.
Fludernik, Monika
  1999   Defining (in)sanity: the narrator of the yellow wallpaper and the question of unreliability. In: Walter Grünzweig Walter and Andreas Solbach (eds.), *Transcending Boundaries: Narratology in Context*, 75–95. Tübingen: Narr.
Forster, E.M.
  [1927] 1962 *Aspects of the Novel.* Harmondsworth: Penguin.
Gavins, Joanna and Gerard Steen (eds.)
  2003   *Cognitive Poetics in Practice.* London/New York: Routledge.
Genette, Gérard
  1980   *Narrative Discourse*, translated by Jane E. Lewin. Ithaca: Cornell University Press.
Gerrig, Richard J.
  1993   *Experiencing Narrative Worlds: On the Psychological Activities of Reading.* New Haven/London: Yale University Press.
Gerrig, Richard J. and David W. Allbritton
  1990   The construction of literary character: A View from Cognitive Psychology. *Style* 24: 380–391.

Gibbs, Raymond W., Jr.
2003   Prototypes in dynamic meaning construal. In: Joanna Gavins and Gerard Steen (eds.), *Cognitive Poetics in Practice*, 27–40. London/New York: Routledge.
Goffman, Erving
1981   *Forms of Talk*. Philadelphia: University of Pennsylvania Press.
Goodblatt, Chanita and Joseph Glicksohn
2003   From *practical criticism* to the practice of literary criticism. *Poetics Today* 24: 207–236.
Grice, H. Paul
1975   Logic and conversation. In: Peter Cole and Jerry L. Morgan (eds.), *Syntax and Semantics: Speech Acts*, 41–58. New York: Academic Press Cole and Morgan.
Grünzweig Walter and Andreas Solbach (eds.)
1999   *Transcending Boundaries: Narratology in Context*. Tübingen: Narr.
Hart, Elizabeth F.
2006   The view of where we've been and where we'd like to go. *College Literature* 33: 225–237.
Harvey, William J.
1965   *Character and the Novel*. London: Chatto and Windus.
Hendricks, William O.
1967   On the notion 'beyond the sentence'. *Linguistics* 37: 12–51.
Herman, David
2002   *Story Logic: Problems and Possibilities of Narrative*. Lincoln: University of Nebraska Press.
Hochman, Baruch
1985   *Character in Literature*. Ithaca: Cornell University Press.
Jackson, Tony E.
2005   Explanation, interpretation, and close reading the progress of cognitive poetics; cognitive poetics in practice. *Poetics Today* 26: 519–533.
Jahn, Manfred
1997   Frames, preferences, and the reading of third-person narratives: toward a cognitive narratology. *Poetics Today* 18: 441–468.
Jakobson, Roman
1960   Linguistics and poetics. In: Thomas A. Sebeok (ed.), *Style in Language*, 350–377. New York: Wiley.
Lakoff, George
1987   *Women, Fire, and Dangerous things*. Chicago: University of Chicago Press.
Lakoff, George and Mark Johnson
1980   *Metaphors We Live By*. Chicago: University cf Chicago Press.
Langacker, Ronald W.
1990   *Concept, Image, and Symbol: The Cognitive Basis of Grammar*. Berlin and New York: Mouton de Gruyter.
Langacker, Ronald W.
1991   *Foundations of Cognitive Grammar: Descriptive Applications*. Stanford: Stanford University Press.

Langacker, Ronald W.
    1995   Viewing in cognition and grammar. In: Philip W. Davis (ed.), *Alternative Linguistics: Descriptive and Theoretical Modes*, 153–212. Amsterdam/Philadelphia: John Benjamins.
Langacker, Ronald W.
    2001   Discourse in Cognitive Grammar. *Cognitive Linguistics* 12: 143–188.
Levinson, Stephen C.
    2003   *Space in Language and Cognition*. Cambridge: Cambridge University Press.
Lyons, John
    1977   *Semantics*. Cambridge: Cambridge University Press.
Margolin, Uri
    1983   Characterization in narrative: some theoretical prolegomena. *Neophilologus* 67: 1–14.
Margolin, Uri
    1998   Characters in literary narrative: representation and signification. *Semiotica* 106: 373–392.
McHale, Brian
    1983   Unspeakable sentences, unnatural acts: linguistics and poetics revisited. *Poetics Today* 4: 17–45.
Miall, David S. and Don Kuiken
    1994   Foregrounding, defamiliarization, and affect: response to literary stories. *Poetics* 22: 389–407.
Miller, George A. and P.N. Johnson-Laird
    1976   *Language and Perception*. Cambridge, Mass.: Harvard University Press.
Nünning, Ansgar
    1999   Unreliable, compared to what? Towards a cognitive theory of unreliable narration: prolegomena and hypotheses. In: Walter Grünzweig and Andreas Solbach (eds.), *Transcending Boundaries: Narratology in Context*, 53–73. Tübingen: Narr.
Panek, Elliot
    2006   The poet and the detective: defining the psychological puzzle film. *Film Criticism* 31: 62–88.
Phelan, James and Peter Rabinowitz (ed.)
    2005   *A Companion to Narrative Theory*. Oxford: Blackwell.
Price, Martin
    1983   *Forms of Life: Character and the Moral Imagination in the Novel*. New Haven: Yale University Press.
Propp, Vladimir
    [1928] 1968 *Morphology of the Folktale*, translated by Laurence Scott. Austin: University of Texas Press.
Richardson, Alan and Ellen Spolsky (eds.)
    2004   *The Work of Fiction: Cognition, Culture, and Complexity*. Burlington, VT: Ashgate.

Robinson, Jenefer
2005   *Deeper Than Reason.* Oxford: Clarendon.
Rosenblatt, Jason P. and Joseph C. Sitterton (eds.)
1991   *"Not in Heaven": Coherence and Complexity in Biblical Narrative.*
        Bloomington: Indiana University Press.
Ryan, Marie-Laure
1991   *Possible Worlds, Artificial Intelligence, and Narrative Theory.* Bloom-
        ington: Indiana University Press.
Schank, Roger C.
1984   *The Cognitive Computer: On Language, Learning, and Artificial Intelli-
        gence.* Reading, Mass.: Addison-Wesley.
Schank, Roger C.
1990   *Tell Me a Story: A New Look at Real and Artificial Memory.* New York:
        Charles Scribner's Sons.
Schank, Roger C.
1999   *Dynamic Memory Revisited.* Cambridge: Cambridge University Press.
Schank, Roger C. and Robert P. Abelson
1977   *Scripts, Plans, Goals, and Understanding: An Inquiry into Human
        Knowledge Structure.* Hillsdale, NJ: Erlbaum.
Schank, Roger C. and Robert P. Abelson
1995a   Knowledge and memory: the real story. In: Robert S. Wyer (ed.),
        Knowledge and Memory: The Real Story, 1–85. Hillsdale, NJ.: Erlbaum.
Schank, Roger C. and Robert P. Abelson
1995b   So all knowledge isn't stories? In: Robert S. Wyer (ed.), *Knowledge and
        Memory: The Real Story*, 227–234. Hillsdale, NJ.: Erlbaum.
Sell, Roger (ed.)
1991   *Literary Pragmatics.* London: Routledge.
Semino, Elena and Jonathan Culpeper
2002 (eds.) *Cognitive Stylistics. Language and Cognition in Text Analysis.* Am-
        sterdam: John Benjamins.
Shklovsky, Viktor
[1929] 1990 *Theory of Prose*, trans. Benjamin Sher. Elmwood Park, IL: Dalkley
        Archive Press.
Sopory, Paradeep
2005   Metaphor and affect. *Poetics Today* 26: 433–58.
Spark, Muriel
2004   *All the Poems of Muriel Spark.* New York: New Directions.
Sperber, Dan and Deirdre Wilson
[1986] 1995 *Relevance: Communication and Cognition.* Cambridge, MA: Har-
        vard University Press.
Spolsky, Ellen
2007   Review of *The Literary Animal. Poetics Today* 28: 4.
Spolsky, Ellen (ed.)
1990   *The Uses of Adversity: Failure and Accommodation in Reader Response.*
        Lewisburg, PA: Bucknell University Press.

Sternberg, Meir
[1971] 1978 *Expositional Modes and Temporal Ordering in Fiction*. Baltimore
and London: Johns Hopkins University Press.
Sternberg, Meir
1981   Ordering the unordered: time, space, and descriptive coherence. *Yale French Studies* 61: 60–88.
Sternberg, Meir
1982a   Proteus in quotation-land: mimesis and the forms of reported discourse. *Poetics Today* 3: 107–156.
Sternberg, Meir
1982b   Point of view and the indirections of direct speech. *Language and Style* 15: 67–117.
Sternberg, Meir
1983a   Deictic sequence: world, language and convention. In: Gisa Rauh (ed.), *Essays on Deixis*, 277–316. Tübingen: Gunter Narr.
Sternberg, Meir
1983b   Mimesis and motivation: the two faces of fictional coherence. In: Joseph Strelka (ed.), *Literary Criticism and Philosophy*, 145–188. University Park: Pennsylvania State University Press.
Sternberg, Meir
1983c   Language, world, and perspective in Biblical art: free indirect discourse and modes of covert penetration. *Hasifrut* 32: 88–131.
Sternberg, Meir
1983d   Knight meets dragon in the James Bond saga: realism and reality models. *Style* 17: 142–180.
Sternberg, Meir
1985   *The Poetics of Biblical Narrative: Ideological Literature and the Drama of Reading*. Bloomington: Indiana University Press.
Sternberg, Meir
1986   The world from the addressee's viewpoint: reception as representation, dialogue as monologue. *Style* 20: 295–318.
Sternberg, Meir
1990a   Time and reader. In: Ellen Spolsky (ed.), *The Uses of Adversity: Failure and Accommodation in Reader Response*, 49–89. Lewisburg, PA: Bucknell University Press.
Sternberg, Meir
1990b   Telling in time (I): chronology and narrative theory. *Poetics Today* 11: 901–948.
Sternberg, Meir
1991a   How indirect discourse means: syntax, semantics, pragmatics, poetics. In: Roger, Sell (ed.)
1991   *Literary Pragmatics*, 62–93. London: Routledge.
Sternberg, Meir
1991b   Double cave, double talk: the indirections of Biblical dialogue. In: Jason P. Rosenblatt and Joseph C. Sitterton (eds.), *"Not in Heaven"*:

Coherence and Complexity in Biblical Narrative, 28–57. Bloomington: Indiana University Press.

Sternberg, Meir
  1992 Telling in time (II): chronology, teleology, narrativity. *Poetics Today* 13: 463–541.

Sternberg, Meir
  1998 *Hebrews between Cultures: Group Portraits and Nationa. Literature.* Bloomington: Indiana University Press.

Sternberg, Meir
  1999 The *Laokoon* today: interart relations, modern projects and projections. *Poetics Today* 20: 291–379.

Sternberg, Meir
  2001a Why narrativity makes a difference. *Narrative* 9: 115–122.

Sternberg, Meir
  2001b Factives and perspectives: making sense of presupposition as exemplary inference. *Poetics Today* 22: 129–244.

Sternberg, Meir
  2003a Universals of narrative and their cognitivist fortunes (I). *Poetics Today* 24: 297–395.

Sternberg, Meir
  2003b Universals of narrative and their cognitivist fortunes (II). *Poetics Today* 24: 517–638.

Sternberg, Meir
  2004 Narrative universals, cognitivist story analysis, and interdisciplinary pursuit of knowledge: an omnibus rejoinder. In: Els Andringa and David S. Miall (eds.), Perspectives on three decades of cognitivist effects

Sternberg, Meir
  2005 Self-consciousness as a narrative feature and force. In: James, Phelan and Peter Rabinowitz (eds.), *A Companion to Narrative Theory*, 232–252. Oxford: Blackwell.

Sternberg, Meir
  2006 Telling in time (III): chronology, estrangement, and stories of literary history. *Poetics Today* 27: 125–235.

Sternberg, Meir
  2007 Omniscience in narrative construction: Challenges Old and New. *Poetics Today* 28: 4.

Sternberg, Meir
  2008 If-plots: narrativity and the law-code. In: John Pier and José Ángel García Landa (eds.), *Theorizing Narrativity*. Berlin and New York: de Gruyter.

Stockwell, Peter
  2002 *Cognitive Poetics: An Introduction.* London and New York: Routledge.

Talmy, Leonard
  1995 Narrative structure in a cognitive framework. In: Judith F. Duchan, Gail A. Bruder and Lynne E. Hewitt (eds.), *Deixis in Narrative: A Cognitive Science Perspective*, 421–460. Hillsdale, NJ: Erlbaum.

Talmy, Leonard
    2000 *Toward a Cognitive Semantics*. Cambridge, Ma: MIT Press.
Tan, Ed. S.
    1996   *Emotion and the Structure of Narrative Film*. Mahwah, NJ: Erlbaum.
Turner, Mark
    1996   *The Literary Mind*. New York: Oxford University Press.
van Peer, Willie
    1986   *Stylistics and Psychology: Investigations of Foregrounding*. London: Croom Helm.
Walsh, Richard
    2001   Fabula and fictionality in narrative theory. *Style* 35: 592–606.
Wyer, Robert S. (ed.)
    1995 *Knowledge and Memory: The Real Story*. Hillsdale, NJ.: Erlbaum.
Woolf, Virginia[1927] 1963 *To the Lighthouse*. Harmondsworth: Penguin.
Yacobi, Tamar
    1981   Fictional reliability as a communicative problem. *Poetics Today* 2: 113–26.
Yacobi, Tamar
    1987a   Narrative and normative pattern: on interpreting fiction. *Journal of Literary Studies* 3: 18–41.
Yacobi, Tamar
    1987b   Narrative structure and fictional mediation. *Poetics Today* 8(2): 335–72.
Yacobi, Tamar
    2000   Interart narrative: (un)reliability and ekphrasis. *Poetics Today* 21: 708–47.
Yacobi, Tamar
    2001   Package-deals in fictional narrative: the case of the narrator's (un)reliability. *Narrative* 9: 223–29.
Yacobi, Tamar
    2002   Ekphrasis and perspectival structure. In: Erik Hedling and Ulla-Britta Lagerroth (eds.), *Cultural Functions of Intermedial Exploration*, 189–202. Amsterdam, Rodopi.
Yacobi, Tamar
    2004   Ekphrasis from the perspective of fictive beholders: How literature dramatizes visual art. In: Ellen Spolsky (ed.), *Iconotropism*, 69–87. Bucknell University Press.
Zunshine, Lisa
    2006   *Why We Read Fiction: Theory of Mind and the Novel*. Columbus: Ohio State University Press.

Index